Courting Freedom

1860 - 1861

The Cause Love & War Series

ELLYN M. BAKER

Past Lives Publishing

Original Title: Courting Freedom

First edition: October 2025

© 2025, Ellyn M. Baker

Printed in United States of America

PaperbackISBN: 979-8-9930686-0-2
Hardcover ISBN: 979-8-9930686-2-6
E PUB ISBN: 979-8-9930686-1-9

Cover design by Dwayne Gayle

Dedication

To the families of generations past who lived through this tumultuous Civil War your dedication and contribution to our history is not forgotten.

Prologue: Winds of Change

IT BEHOOVES EVERY MAN WHO VALUES LIBERTY OF CONSCIENCE
TO REVISIT INVASIONS OF IT WITH OTHERS, OR THEIR CASE MAY,
BY A CHANGE OF CIRCUMSTANCES, BECOME HIS OWN.

~THOMAS JEFFERSON

AUGUST 1860
RICHMOND, VIRGINIA

The relentless August heat presses in on me despite the
brisk pace I set toward Butterfield's Law Office, where
Father attends business with Uncle William. It is an event I'm
told a young lady, such as myself, has no business attending.
However, buttons, ribbons, and notions at the fabric shop can
only hold a girl's attention for so long, and if they expect me
to languish in this stifling air, thick with the stench of rotting
fish, then they thought wrong. Even the James River—usually
a reliable source of cool whispers—seems to hold its breath, its
breeze choked by the late summer languor.

Irritation gnaws at me as I press my lavender-scented
handkerchief to my nose, its fragrance a feeble shield against the
foul air. Perspiration beads on my brow, soaking the crisp edges
of this once-white cotton square, each drop a tiny reminder of
the impatience steaming within. Alas, my march up the street

ceases as I spot the rich oak door and pass through its archway into the dimly lit hallway.

Though the walls guard me from the onslaught of Richmond, Virginia's miasma, I find I cannot fully escape the sounds. Through the blinded windows, the city provides a muted backdrop of horses' hooves clopping on the cobblestone and the distant shouts of a hawker echoing off the brick facades of the buildings beyond. I work to stamp this out with each step up the stairs, and then the voice of someone far closer catches my attention from a near-closed door just beyond.

Dare I pry?

The stomping of my shoes weakens to the brushing of tipping and toeing as I near the door. The only other sounds to accompany my movement is the wind tap dancing a lonely rhythm against the blinds and the voices of the men behind the door.

I peek through the crack and am greeted first by the familiar whisper of cigar smoke, earthy and pungent. It curls through the room, showing off the various books on law lining the lawyer's shelves, while acting as a silent barrier between those in the room and the stench of reality outside. Attorney Butterfield is shuffling paper and the deep muffled voices of quiet disagreement sound from my father and Uncle William, who sit on the other side of the large oak table.

They expect me to be invisible right now, and so invisible I shall remain, unlike the fly that buzzes around Attorney Butterfield's glistening bald head. Had I not wanted to purchase these notions, buttons, and ribbons, I'd be home right now enjoying the whispering pines and savory smells of the smokehouse. This blatant abandonment tests my obedience toward the men inside who now decide what will become of my life and so many more.

"Are you ready to sign the transfer contract?" the soft-middled Attorney Butterfield inquires, his voice laced with trepidation. His clear blue eyes, head—shiny and hairless save for that abominable fly—and thin twitchy lips remind me of an old bullfrog from our pond, alert and nervous. Sweat glistens on his ruddy forehead, trickling down his hot red cheeks. He mops the rivulet with a damp handkerchief. Father and Uncle William, seated across from him, grow quiet as their heads bow to scrutinize the fine print of their respective contracts.

Unfazed by these oppressive temperatures, Father's broad, muscular shoulders, a testament to his love for the land, exude both ease and vigilance. Deep-set brown eyes carry the weight of ancestral history, a constant reminder of his duty. Sun-weathered skin and lines earned through honest work imprint his face.

In contrast to his brother, my Uncle William is a short-fused powder keg ready to explode. His face is flushed, his jaw is clenched beneath his tightly cropped beard, and his dark eyes remain narrow and on the lookout for foul play with a focus on how he can get his way—betraying the simmering tension within. I think such an expression makes him look like the snake he truly is—if snakes had arms. Uncle William's arms are aggressively folded, wrinkling the tailored suit he never shuts his mouth about. In this way, he holds his hands—uncalloused and unaccustomed to matters that rise beyond trivial—close to his chest.

As the attorney's question hangs in the air, my father, Jacob Prescott, raises his head. His gaze bores into his brother's with unspoken animosity. "Where are the provisions for the Blackwell family?"

Uncle William's lips curl into a sneer; his eyes flash with contempt. "Don't worry, Jake"—sarcasm drips from my father's nickname—"I promised to keep your niggers until next spring and release them with the five hundred dollar pay as you promised."

Father's chair rips over the floorboards as he comes to his feet, shoulders broadening as his shadow stretches over the table, stealing the light reflecting in his little brother's eyes. "Call me Jake again or disrespect the Blackwells with that sort of talk and this deal is off!" His voice thunders through the room; his finger points at my uncle to drill the promise home.

"Remember, I hold the manumission papers," Father continues, voice hard as steel. "If you don't treat them with the respect they deserve, I'll take them with me, and you'll be left to the spring planting alone."

As the words ricochet through the crack in the door, a desperate gasp is trapped between my fingers as my hand springs to my mouth. A torrent of sweat courses down my back. The verbal onslaught scalds my skin. Gooseflesh rises, an icy counterpoint to the raging wildfire of words and threats that seize my ears. In my sixteen years, I have never witnessed such a brewing cauldron of bubbling anger from my father spilling over on my uncle.

The pyre burns, ignited by blood ties and birthright, flames fanned by the dry winds of their own self-righteousness. Fueled by unvoiced resentments, the shadow of favoritism, and threatened legacies, anger kindles within both brothers.

Thankful for my invisibility, I feel like a fledgling house sparrow caught in the winds of their fiery passion. My heart is hammering, desperate for me to fly out of earshot, but I am trapped, praying for rain to extinguish the flames and too curious to abandon my post.

The air in the room hangs heavier between Uncle William and Father, their eyes locked in a silent duel.

William lets out a long, exasperated sigh. "A promise is a promise. The Blackwells will be on their way as soon as the crops are in." With a glance, he catches Father's raised eyebrow and continues, his voice cracking slightly. "With the five hundred dollars you—I mean, I—by contract promised them."

Easing into the shadows, I observe Uncle's arms uncoil, and his knuckles whiten against the worn chair arms, fingers tapping out a frustrated rhythm—a silent drumbeat beneath the escalating pressure. His vow casts a leaden weight across his face. Uncle William knows what we all know—that his words, though reluctant, ensnare him in a delicate position crafted by my father, akin to a serpent cornered in a chicken coop.

My heart hammers against my ribs, echoing the frenzied beat of Uncle's fingers. Just uttering Jim Blackwell's name is the bitterest pill for my uncle. Big Jim is the lifeblood of the family land, providing the Prescotts with indispensable guidance through his calloused hands and weathered wisdom. Without Big Jim's insights, Uncle William is a captain adrift at sea—uncertain of the currents, unable to navigate the land to its full potential. Big Jim serves as the compass to my uncle's aspirations, steering him toward the realization of dreams for profit.

A flicker of hope ignites in Uncle William's eyes, then dims. He runs his hands through his hair, his shoulders relax—an unmistakable sign he's contemplating something. Did he find a loophole to escape his forced vow?

A breath hitches in my throat, the room shrinking to the space between his lips and my straining ears. He rises from his own chair, attempting to match my father's height—his back straight and his face shifting into a mask of confidence. Just as he opens his mouth—

Attorney Butterfield's voice adds a jarring note to this pause of uncertainty. "I will draft the addendum with consideration of the Blackwells and have it to you by week's end if that is suitable for all parties involved?" His offer is displayed by his sausage finger, after flipping a page on my father's copy. "But aside from that matter, do you want to sign the agreed section today?"

Butterfield's request hangs in the air once more. The silence stretches on, punctuated only by the ticking of the grandfather clock in the corner of the room.

Uncle William and Father's eyes make no shift of recognition, still locked in battle, calculating their next move like chess players in a game of life and death.

Father breaks the deadlock.

I wonder who ended up with checkmate.

"I'll sign the document when I'm satisfied with the addendum," Father says curtly. "Not a moment sooner."

Father pivots on his heel, and I turn on the ball of one foot. Father strides out of the room, as I hurry to stand against the wall. An innocent bystander, as far as anyone is concerned, but that doesn't stop the prickle of guilt from dancing across my skin.

A hand clasps my shoulder, and I jump!

Father, the anger in his eyes dwindling to embers yet still smoldering with frustration, says, "Let's go, we're in for a storm."

A Long Way from Home

THERE IS NO SANCTUARY OF VIRTUE LIKE HOME.
~EDWARD EVERETT

SEPTEMBER 1860
PRESCOTT PLANTATION, VIRGINIA

Dipping the pen into the ink, never minding the drops splattering across the page, I hold my breath in a desperate attempt to keep the dream foremost in my mind. Letters, in less than perfect penmanship, scribble the moments down before the nighttime vision flees back into my subconscious, lost forever.

September 16, 1860

A storm is coming, first spoken of in Father's words, and now within my dreams. A storm I cannot see as thunder booms from beyond and carries trouble not unlike the waves that crash upon a rocky shore. A figure stood. He said things. Things I wish I understood. There was no time to ask. Oh, how I wish I could ask. Things I wanted to know, things I need to know. Things interrupted by the bellow of my father ...

"Emilie, we need to go!"

"One moment!" I dip the pen once more, black ink leaving a trail across my nightgown.

But the thing is, it showed me things in symbols, like a puzzle ...

"Emilie Kathryn Prescott! I will leave you here if you are not in that wagon on time!" My father's voice matches the booming fist against the vibrating oak door.

A click, a creak, the door opens, and I turn to see Lucy, my lady's maid, bustle in with a pitcher of water and an armful of towels. She sets the pitcher aside on my desk, plucking the pen from my hand, and ushers me behind the dressing screen.

"Close the door, Millie!" Lucy orders. Millie, another of the house-maids, must have followed in close behind her. She always tends to the shadows of Lucy's needs. *A creak, a click,* with a firm push the door closes, muffling my father's voice as he continues barking orders to Amos and Simon to load my bed onto the wagon.

"We ... train ... catch ... -day!" Father's voice fades away, unperturbed by the closed door as his hurried footsteps descend the stairs.

Behind the screen, Lucy hands me a warm cloth to wipe my face, an action for which I have depended on her since I was eleven. Ah, the smell of rose water. How delightful. I am ever grateful for my father's unwavering senses and his refusal to sell her after her parents died of that awful yellow fever. The mere thought of my family coming down with such an illness is enough to bring back the dread of that dream. Gooseflesh ripples down my arms as the morning breeze tickles over my skin while Lucy strips away the sticky nightgown. Up and over my head, it is replaced with a crisp, cool chemise. She continues to dress me silently. Her nimble fingers fasten my stockings, shoes, and stays with deft, quick pulls at the laces. Petticoats, skirt, and top follow in quick succession.

She hands me a thin brush, which I take, and then she presents the tooth powder before her free hand grabs the peppermint water. With a dip of the brush in the water followed by a dab into the powder, I proceed to scrub and rub my ivory whites clean. A gulp of peppermint water, a swash, a swirl, and a spit into the standing wash basin. The mint is cool, refreshing my senses and placing me firmly back into reality as the dream dissipates into a distant memory.

A *tip* and a *tap* sound at the door.

"Let them in. She's decent," Lucy says to Millie.

Slipping out from behind the screen, seating myself at the small table, I let Lucy attend to my toilette. The door creaks open. Amos and Simon enter, their eyes averted as they focus on the task of dismantling my bed. Within minutes, my room of sixteen years stands vacant—save for my carpet bag, its contents ready for the journey ahead. The subdued mood of this morning is deafening, punctuated by the echoing click of Millie's shoes as she makes her way out of the room.

The vanity mirror reflects a stranger, a porcelain doll with auburn hair framing eyes that threaten to spill tears, as the realization settles in: This is my last dressing with Lucy. I clench my jaw, squeezing back the surge of brewing emotion into a tight knot. Each brush stroke, each pull, feels like a tug on my very soul. *Poise and propriety*—they chant in my head, a mantra against the building wave. *A lady,* they whisper, *must contain her emotions, even when leaving shreds of her heart behind.*

Lucy's reflection in the vanity mirror shows her dark, flawless complexion. Her delicate features exude an air of grace, complemented by the lingering fragrance of rose that clings to her clothing. Her large dark eyes hold much sadness today. *Will she miss me?*

"Chin up, Miss Emilie." Her eyes are full of knowing sorrow. "Strength is not the absence of tears, but the grace to shed them when no one's watching, or so my mama would say." Her eyes return to her work, a faint sniff to keep her own poise in check.

Our relationship is confined to the boundaries of mistress and maid, a chasm that separates our social stations. Yet in intimate moments like this, I wonder if a friendship could blossom, bridging the gap between our worlds.

Just then, the strange banging cadence returns, bringing back the memories of the driftwood in my dream.

"What is that noise?"

"The men are loading the wagons, Miss Emilie."

"No, no, the one from my dream."

As Lucy fastens the fancy netting of my snood, securing my unruly hair with a discreet wink, she announces, "Them dreams don't know nothing about reality, Miss Emilie." Finishing my hair, she adds, "There! You're pretty as a bit of paint on a dry bit of wall."

"Thank you, Lucy."

"Oh, there ain't nothing to it, Miss Emilie, and there won't be nothing to it come tomorrow either," Lucy replies, her tone brisk but her words heavy. A simple sigh follows, sweeping aside the weight of the matter. "Martha is holding breakfast for you. Hurry on, Miss Emilie, no time to dally with the dilly today."

Lucy gathers the pitcher and towels and exits the room. Her parting words hang in the air, a poignant farewell to the familiar confines of my childhood home, a reminder of the day's relentless pace and the storm of change that may be heading my way.

Still under the spell of last night's dream, I can't resist the need to continue writing down its vivid scenes. The haunting figure that beckons to me, the love that lingers like sweet apple blossoms on my nose, the ominous rumble of a storm echoing in my mind. An escaping growl announces my stomach is ready for breakfast.

Down the stairs I tread, a waltz through the dining room, a skip out the walkway to the kitchen. My nose twitches, drawn in by the salty smoked bacon, the comforting warmth of yeasty dough, and the sugary halo of deep rich molasses. A trinity of scents paints memories on my tongue, each crumb hosts a portal of memory: stolen sips of batter, afternoons kneading beside Martha, the golden joy of the oven's embrace. The symphony of aromas stirs a warm tide of nostalgia, washing away the last fragile wisps of the dream.

Pausing at the kitchen door, I overhear a conversation between my mother and Martha.

"Next summer, we will meet you in Gettysburg." My mother, Julia Prescott, draws a shaky breath before she continues. "Jacob will be thrilled to introduce you to the freed population there." Optimism brims in her words while a hint of sorrow frays the laces of her delicate voice.

"Come now, Mistress Julia, dry those tears! We'll manage here just fine; it's only a temporary separation. No need for all this sadness," says Martha, attempting to dispel the melancholy in the room. "We will be all right here; it's only for a season."

"I know, I know. I miss you already," Mother responds, blinking away the tears forming at the corners of her eyes. "But promise me when we get to Gettysburg, we will do away with all these formalities and you'll call me Julia?"

Martha hands mother a towel-covered basket. "Here, this will keep your bellies full—got some of them gingerbread cakes Mr. Jacob likes so much." Martha's warm chuckle sparks a smile from my mother.

"Thank you. If you happen upon Emilie, will you hurry her along? She's always late."

"That girl was late to her own birth, if I remember rightly," Martha recalls. The women share a moment of intimate laughter. "I'll make sure she's on time," Martha promises with a twinkle in her eye, sealing the camaraderie between them.

"Well, I find that highly unlikely," I say as I push past the door, breezing into the warmed hearth of our soon-to-be former home.

I settle down at the rough worktable. Even its familiar splinters do not detract from how much I will miss it, or the heavy drumming of pots and pans, or Martha's warm buttermilk biscuits. My mouth waters as my eyes turn to the plate of fresh bread slathered in butter.

"Well, Little-Miss-On-Time, your breakfast is getting cold. Lucky for you, I just pulled those from the oven."

I look up to her with a smirk, and she welcomes my day with a warm smile.

The savory aroma of the bacon to my left mingles with the symphony of smells filling the kitchen—smoke from a bouquet of wood and the faint sweetness of lingering molasses.

My stomach rumbles for me to start creating a mouthful of bliss: warm biscuit, cold bacon, and a bite of heaven. Butter drips between my fingers, and the flaky morsel satisfies my senses. "Martha, I hope I can make these as good as yours."

"It's simple really, cut the lard into the flour, and don't overwork the dough like you do my patience. Turns out flaky every time." Martha's wisdom carries a legacy of shared kitchen memories, including my giggles spilling forth at this moment.

"Did you pack the receipt book we made?"

I think back to that old leather-bound book, splattered in lard, dusted in flour, recipes bursting from the binding. Its pages are a culmination of my mother's insistence on a woman's education in family traditions, and it evokes my childhood all in one glorious tome. I nod.

"That syrup glue your gums together, child? I asked you a question."

"Yes, ma'am. I put it in my travel bag last night to keep it safe."

Licking the butter from my fingers, I lean over to open my bag—

"I know you're not about to touch that bag with those nasty fingers. Here, use this towel. Lord knows I raised you better."

I pluck the towel from the air as it flies like a wayward ghost that has the texture of tough love. I wipe my fingers carefully and fold it neatly, setting it beside my plate. The feeling of Martha's eyes hammering in the back of my head dissipate. Still, I hesitate for a moment, just to make sure, before reaching into my bag. From it I pull the book, pen, and ink pot. A few minutes and a dip of the pen later, I begin to jot down scattered notes about my dream.

In the background, I hear Martha humming her usual tune as she washes dishes and pulls heavy cast iron from the fire. Focusing on my work, the blank pages and a fresh leather scent different from the stained rose water paper of my own diary catches my attention.

I look up.

A leather-bound book rests to my left.

I pick it up.

"Oh," I say. "Did you get this for me?"

"Do chickens lay eggs? Of course we got it for you. How else you going to remember all your ventures and share all your greasy-finger details with me?"

My breath catches as I open the book, leather thick and cool against my fingers, whispering of sacrifice. Deep brown, unmarred by time, it bears the delicate kiss of flowers, each petal glinting with gold leaf like smuggled sunshine. Inside, the pages lie crisp and strong, ready to hold the weight of my life—stories whispered, and secrets screamed. A brass clasp, gleaming like a fallen star, waits to thread the leather tail, securing my thoughts within.

Gratitude: heavy and warm, blossoming in my chest, tangled with the prickly vine of guilt. Father's face, etched with disapproval, flashes in my mind—the scowl he'd wear if I dared ask for such a treasure. This isn't just a book, it is a token of love that will hold my life, my future, and my dreams. My heart aches with the knowledge of its cost in several trades from handmade goods, yet I appreciate the love and sacrifice made to obtain this unique luxury.

"Thank you, but you shouldn't have."

"You're not telling me what to do, are you, Little Miss?"

"Is Seth still teaching you about words?" I ask, lowering my voice.

"I only know some," Martha says, no louder than a whisper.

"I'll teach you more when you come next spring. We'll get them from this very book," I say, tapping the top of the book only to notice greasy prints on the hard leather cover. My hand goes to reach—

"Child, I know you not about to reach for that dirty rag you just wiped your greasy fingers on. I know the good Lord gave you more sense than salt in a thimble. Dear Lord, I know—"

"Amen!" I say before she can get the holy rolling.

My eyes cross paths with Martha's just as she turns to look at me. She licks the scowl off her lips as her temper melts like butter. The words to follow are a salve to the pain that coats my heart. "I'm going to miss you, Little Miss."

"What am I going to do without your sunshine when it rains?"

"Well, that's what them words are for, ain't it? You put them out like letters. I am sure someone with your good learning can make sense of that."

Martha wipes her hands on her apron, then hastily pulls a small decorative bottle of perfume from her pocket. "And here's this, too, so you don't go around smelling like a farm girl. Ain't no husband want you then. And Lord knows we can't have you a spinster."

"I don't need a husband. Husbands and children can wait, as I have more important things to do."

Martha's smile stains the windows to my soul as she wordlessly walks over and, with the tenderness of more than a friend, gathers my belongings from the table and my hands and places them in my bag. A thumb to the tongue, she brushes the grease from my cheek, and kisses the top of my head. "I promised your mother you would get out to the wagons on time."

My arms fold around her, and I hug my world, my childhood, and my surrogate mother in one single embrace.

She hugs me back, kisses the top of my head, and puts her hands on the ruffled shoulders of my brown-checked travel dress. "Little Miss, those bony shoulders need covering, lest your father cry louder than a rooster come early morning."

I blink.

My eyes widen.

"My shawl! I almost forgot it ..."

One last look at Martha.

I rush from the kitchen.

Pause just beyond the threshold.

Turn back to yell my thanks, amble through the foyer, gallop past the dining room, and burst into the parlor—I left it, where?

Memories surge like a tide as I stand in the threshold. The hush of the stately room now bears witness to the weight of time. The heavy furniture lines the space, inviting guests to sit for a while. In the corner, the piano stands stoic, holding the whispered notes of distant memories from when I played Beethoven and Mozart for hours on end. The echoes of my grandmother's laughter and encouragement follow with the gentle sway of her rocking chair. Now only specks of dust, shimmering in the morning light, linger in the air.

And in this silent moment, a vivid memory emerges juxtaposed against the serene setting—the image of her casket surrounded by flowers, the mourners' quiet tears. They haunt me. The parlor is draped in the bittersweet fabric of my past. No shawl of the present resides here.

"Emilie!" my father's voice calls from the entryway. *Come to think of it, his voice does have a bit of a cluck.*

"Emilie!" he repeats.

His demanding crow cracks open a dam of panic within me. *Where's the shawl?* My memory of it remains stubbornly blank. Bunching my skirt in my fists, I fly up the stairs, skipping two at a time, my heart a hummingbird trapped behind my ribs.

At the top of the landing, each doorway is a silent taunt. The nursery is empty, sunlight painting stripes across the bare crib. Parents' old room, bed undisturbed, his shaving strop hangs limp near the wash basin. I fling open the doors, logic drowned by the rising wave of desperation. Just as I left it, the barren room sits stoic and pensive, curtains billowing like ghosts in the wind, birds outside chirping their oblivious melodies. One last hope, the wardrobe—I rip open the doors, its cavernous depths echoing a hollow *Not here, Emilie, hurry!*

My pulse quickens as I have pressed the limits of my tardiness. Quickening my steps to the window at the end of the hall. Peering out the stained glass, the scene below unfolds. Simon and Amos wrestle with knotted ropes securing the last of our meager belongings. Father's scowling face eyes his pocket watch; it ticks out my dwindling seconds. Uncle William, an impatient hornet buzzing, shouts orders at the lingering servants. Mother, oblivious to the mounting stress, engages in casual conversation with Miss Maisy, our gardener and one of the laundresses. One detail ignites a spark of hope—the teams remain unhitched!

"Little Miss, do you think they are waiting for the cows or waiting on you? I reckon a few more minutes the cows been home, packed up their milk, and showed up for the wagon first." She places her hands on my shoulders, drawing my attention to her. Martha's voice, soft yet firm, reminds me the time to leave is near. Her reassuring hands turn me about and nudge me toward the proper path to my family, not directly out the window.

Hands that are powerful enough to knead bread, yet equally gentle to coax newborns into the world, including my brothers and me. Hands that I will not feel again for what seems like will be forever. The reality of my leaving suddenly hits me like a wave. The finality seizes my body, causing a knot in my stomach that refuses to dissipate.

My throat tightens as tears blur and spill from my eyes. My stomach lurches and my feet won't carry me any farther. I can't turn my back and leave like this. My body shifts about, and I turn to close the distance that Martha insists stays between us.

"I wish you would come with us now." My words are muffled by the crease of her warm fabric. The smell of comfort, safety, and what must be a bucket of lard. "This doesn't have to be—you can come now. You can be free; you can help me with all my important things, and I can be the one that teaches you—"

"Hush now, Little Miss, no one's got time for that foolishness. We promised your Pa we would see your uncle through the growing season and if anything, us Blackwells keep to our word. Mr. Jacob gave Big Jim our freedom papers. Freedom we'll be tasting just as the crops be jumping. Now you go on, we'll see you next year. Go on."

As Martha turns my form around yet again, she gives me a gentle push, ushering me back toward the stairs. I don't see it, but I think I can hear it. The whisper of a bit back sob.

For once I disobey her direct orders and turn back to see her retrieve a handkerchief from her apron pocket, a wrinkled scrap from one of my old aprons. It may lack the crisp whiteness of my own, but its value is immeasurable knowing it's hers now.

Martha forces optimism like a ray of sunshine. Numbly, I nod, tears uncontrollably streaming down my cheeks.

"I love you, Martha." The break in my voice reminds me of the crack in my resolve back when a terrified three-year-old me stood lost and alone facing my first thunderstorm. Martha had scooped me out of my bed back then, but she would scoop no more in the year ahead.

With a wink and a smile that would brighten midnight, she replies, "You know I do too.

"Remember, child, life is full of twists and turns. You gots to keep your heart open for all the possibilities. Don't let me be the one to hold you back."

Thankfully, the distance between me and the front door gives me time to rein in my emotions before confronting a yard full of people. My shawl lies neatly folded on the foyer table, waiting for me. Who knew fabric could be so judgmental? Stopping at the foyer mirror, I set the fabric straight as I drape it over my shoulders, pull on my straw hat, and wrestle to tuck in the flyaway ends of my hair as I secure them into the snood and fasten it all down with two hat pins. I force a brave smile in the mirror—it reflects pretend confidence back at me.

"Emilie!"

"Coming!"

Family Ties

SEPTEMBER 1860
PRESCOTT PLANTATION, VIRGINIA

The door closes and the latch falls shut, securing the old memories behind. Emerging into the brazen sunlight, I blink at the unexpected chaos sprawling before me. The carriage path, usually a scene of sedate order, is a whirlwind of people with wagons lined up and not a single horse in sight. There is a lingering hope that I might steal away to find Seth and Big Jim for a final farewell.

Why does departure feel like a bittersweet tug of war within my soul? Beyond these pines, a foreign world beckons to me, full of risks and maybe rewards? Did Odysseus ever feel so uncertain under such tumultuous times?

A clod of earth whizzes past my ear, narrowly missing my cheek. But I am not spared a second time as another clump of soil pelts my right shoulder. Dirt tumbles down my sleeve, leaving a trail of dust on my dress. Before I can even react, another missile knocks my hat forward, despite the pins anchoring it in place.

I whirl around, my irritation bubbling over.

My second oldest brother, a mischievous grin plastered on his face, eyes me with glee.

Familiar hay clings to his clothes, a comforting scent that belies the shadows playing around his sun-tanned face. hazel eyes, both playful and enigmatic, crinkle with amusement as he leans in, a question mark carved in his brow. Henry's hands, strong and rough from handling reins and ropes alike, rest on my shoulders. Their grip grounds me while the shadow he casts before us whispers of secrets brothers keep from their sisters.

"Dammit Henry, what are you doing?" I sigh, feigning exasperation even as a smile tugs at the corners of my mouth.

"Don't let Mother hear you say that." His grin widens, a triumphant glint in his eyes. "Where you sneakin' off to?"

"One last goodbye to Big Jim and Seth." Pulling away from him, I start down the path leading to the slaves' quarters. It's dusty but worn smooth by countless footsteps.

"You won't make it," Henry calls after me, his smugness tinged with a sliver of concern. "They're in the drying barn, and if you don't hurry back, you'll be stuck here with Uncle William and Aunt Jenny, and we both know they'll have you in a convent before Friday."

He is not wrong about our aunt and uncle; their disapproval of my independent spirit is a constant thorn in my side. Still, Henry's words are an unwelcome reminder of my predicament as he always manages to burrow into my business like a tick under my skin.

Turning back, I counter, "The team isn't hitched yet. I can make it in time."

Henry's brows furrow. "No, you can't. I was just in the barn; they're coming out now. That's at least a ten-minute walk, who knows where in God's green country they are now?"

I sigh, and just as grandfather used to say, I am the unfortunate dog, unable to shake him off.

Yet, I notice his smile fades as his words leave no room for argument. My mischievous brother, the source of constant annoyance, is now a pillar of support, as he too feels our impending separation from home.

"Oh, all right." I turn back, deflated.

"You said your goodbyes yesterday. Keep saying them and they will no longer be goodbyes." Henry throws an arm around my shoulder, so Mother doesn't see the mess he's made on my once clean clothes.

"I know, it's just—"

"It's just hard to let go. I know. But Martha is strong and Big Jim is—um, well–big. They will be all right, Em." My brother's voice is softer than usual. "Besides, Father did everything to secure their freedom, except take them with us today, and it was Big Jim's idea to stay behind anyway. Though I'll never understand why."

The familiar banter and playful jabs between Henry and me are a beacon of normalcy amidst the disorientating swirl of change and remind me that not everything will be lost. As we approach the wagons, the familiar drawl of Uncle William and my eldest brother, Aaron, rise in debate, their voices locked in the familiar controversy of looming change. A wry smile flickers on my lips. Not everything will be missed.

Uncle William, red-faced and resolute, punctuates his statement. "Breckinridge best take the day in November, or there will be secession in the South!"

Ah yes, the Richmond newspapers have been all in an uproar about the upcoming election between Douglas, Breckenridge, Bell, and—most controversial according to the Richmond papers—Lincoln.

Aaron, ever the voice of reason, counters in measured tones, "It depends on how each state votes. We need a good turnout to defeat Douglas and Lincoln."

Well, there, he said it—Lincoln, painted as a radical Northerner in the Richmond papers, whose platform boasts he is firmly against slavery.

Uncle William's jaw hardens with disgust at the mere mention of Lincoln, a means of great amusement for me despite its predictability, until he speaks. "He is tying our hands, between the taxes and restricting slavery in the new territories. We are going to lose our farms; Breckenridge must win."

The debate wears on, which I tune out as I take notice of Aaron holding Starlight's reins. The mare tosses her head in reaction to each throw of my uncle's hands. *Is he trying to take flight?* Granted all his flapping will in no way deter the steady logic of my brother in this debate. Then again, if by some miracle he did manage to take to the air, Aunt Jenny, a silent but reluctant sentinel, will no doubt keep him grounded given how she clings to him and his every need. Her eyes betray boredom and annoyance with her husband's squawking, but she doesn't bother herself with interrupting them. Aunt Jenny has never concerned herself with the newspapers the way I do, and I'm smart enough to know this prattle between uncle and brother is pointless.

Uncle William announces, "If this election goes the wrong way, I will secede in a heartbeat along with the other Southern states."

Pointless until now. My mouth starts to open.

But Aaron's words cut through the tension before my own opinion can be voiced. "Let's see who wins first."

I close my mouth, remembering if I dare to reiterate what the Richmond paper stated about this subject, Uncle William will know his attempts to hide the papers from me were futile. I'm in no mood for more looks of reproach from him or my leech of an aunt.

Uncle William says, "Sitting around doesn't change men. You must persuade them, bend them, make them think as you do. Didn't they teach you that in law school?"

"They did, but if the North continues to raise prices of finished goods and demand our raw materials be given at dirt cheap prices, then I'm afraid we'll be too poor to afford any of it," says Aaron.

Uncle William is quick to add, "The reputation of Virginia tobacco is strong, best in the world even. If the North doesn't wish to reconsider how they deal with the raw materials provided by the South, then we will simply sell to England, France, and the rest of the world; federal taxes be damned."

Uncle's face flushes deeper shade of red, as his rant continues.

Aaron's hand goes to stroke Starlight's neck. "Well, you had best figure something out. The plantation's profit is the least of our worries if Lincoln gets the election. People are struggling to afford a means to live given the cost of staples, and the southern people depend on legacies such as ours to stimulate the economy. "

"Yankee bastards and their greed—they have no right to raise the price of slave cloth when we are the ones providing the raw goods to make it. If it goes up any higher, I dare say we'll have to resort to our suits being tailored from it and pray for longer summers and milder winters for the sake of our property." For all his blustering, the veins in Uncle William's temples appear to pop out again.

Just then, Aunt Jenny yawns loudly. Starlight follows, and for a moment I see a similarity in them that goes beyond action—long drawn-out faces, big front teeth. The only difference is Aunt Jenny can say something if she dares. Her barely concealed disdain for the conversation momentarily draws attention away from the heated argument. Both Aaron and Uncle notice those around them. Me standing tight lipped, the horse—I mean my aunt—and Henry using my clean shoulder as a pillow and sponge for his drool.

"Ah Emilie, we were worried we would have to leave you behind. Though it's a shame you found Henry." Aaron holds my satchel open so I can retrieve my riding gloves.

Henry raises his head in alarm, wiping the spittle from his mouth. "Hey, you can't leave me here."

"We can if you don't make yourself useful." Aaron fastens the latch of my travel bag and then shoves it at Henry. "Now go load this up with yourself on the wagons."

Henry grunts at the weight of my bag. "What did you pack in here, Em?"

"Half the plantation I imagine," says Aaron.

"You two are insufferable, not that I would dream of taking either of your rooms if I stayed here or managed to shove the contents of both into my bag. Besides, Gettysburg is full of great opportunities for me. Opportunities that could be lost if I don't have everything I need."

"Opportunities for a husband, I hope." Aunt Jenny's forced smile is her dismal attempt to make light conversation.

Willing myself not to roll my eyes at her absurdity, I say politely to appease her, "I will send you an invitation if that happens, Aunt Jenny."

"A Northern boy, no doubt. He'll not be welcome here." Uncle William's cold, vacant statement is his last attempt to upset me.

Ignoring him, I mount Starlight only to have Aunt Jenny let out a gasp. Now what? I look in her direction. Her piercing blue eyes are wide with disapproval.

"Emilie! Side-saddle is preferred for genteel ladies!" Aunt Jenny's voice is as sharp as the obsidian brooch adorning her black dress. No doubt she is still in mourning over the death of fun.

I meet her gaze unflinching, a spark of defiance dancing in my eyes. "Aunt Jenny," I begin, "I cannot afford to be genteel in this terrain. If I am to ever catch a husband, I must be alive to do so and capable of running him down."

Aaron clears his throat, shifting uncomfortably.

Henry ducks away with my travel bag to avoid a pending confrontation.

Uncle William grumbles under his breath, a low rumble that speaks volumes.

But Aunt Jenny uses the awkward silence like a weapon. "But a lady's reputation—"

"Is not dependent on the position of one's legs upon a horse," I retort, unafraid of her being aghast. "My reputation will be built on my own merits."

With that, I urge Starlight forward, leading the way ahead of the wagons. The silence behind me is broken only by the rhythmic *clip-clop* of hooves and the rustle of leaves in the autumn wind.

As I ride, the crisp air fills my lungs, carrying with it the scent of freedom and possibility. I feel a new sense of liberation, a young woman on the cusp of a new adventure, and I won't let anyone dictate my fate.

Richmond to Gettysburg

DON'T LISTEN TO WHAT THEY SAY. GO SEE.

~CHINESE PROVERB

SEPTEMBER 1860
RICHMOND, VIRGINIA

We leave the verdant embrace of the plantation pines as we turn onto Plank Road. Starlight's hooves drum a familiar rhythm on the well-worn path. Once upon a time, it led to childhood adventures of treasures found in local shops. Now, it leads to a journey of a different magnitude—one fueled by purpose and hope.

The crisp dawn air gives way to the warmth of the afternoon. The sun, though still potent, lacks the searing intensity of its summer counterpart as August heat surrenders to the gentle embrace of September. This makes our journey considerably more comfortable.

The plantation fades into the distance, and a sense of calm washes over me, dispelling some of the fear that clings to me. The wind whispers through the fields, carrying conversations I long to decipher. Starlight's chestnut ears swivel, attuned to the symphony of nature as we lead the wagons toward Richmond.

As we draw nearer to the hustle and bustle of the city, houses and buildings sprout from the landscape without preamble, causing my mare's ears to twitch nervously, alert to the discordance of the streets ahead. I give her a reassuring stroke on her neck as civilization arrives in view quite abruptly.

The world explodes around us—snorting horses, creaking wagons, and shouting vendors. Starlight dances beneath me, her nostrils flaring at the offending, unfamiliar scents of industry. My fingers on the reins feel useless as I attempt to anchor her rising anxiety. Her hooves, a frantic drumbeat against the cobblestone, mirror the rising panic in my chest. The words of my riding instructor, Limerick, echo through my mind. *Sit deep, heels down, breathe. If you're calm, she'll calm.* "Steady, girl."

However, our anxieties play off one another. Me over her. Her over everything else. Fighting her is more of a headache than I can handle, and I decide to surrender. With a pull of my inside rein, I steer her about, back to the solace of the wagons that once trailed behind. Dismounting her, I remove her bridle and hook her halter to a lead rope hanging off the caboose of our entourage. She in turn lips the sturdy oak of the cart in hopes it may gift her grain or hay and snorts her disproval when it doesn't, but her preoccupation with her stomach calms the waves of nausea within mine. Now, I can at least take in the sights and sounds around us.

The train station presents a monstrous black beast of iron and steel, bellowing a challenge from across the rail yard. Starlight whinnies, a sharp cry against the cacophony of the city. The air is thick with wood smoke and the oily reek of progress. Steel tracks stretch like iron veins, beckoning to destinations lost in a hazy distance.

We witness the sights, sounds, and mixed colors of all humanity. Melodies of foreign languages weave through the air punctuated by the staccato of hurried footsteps. The symphony of street noises, of carriage wheels thundering on cobblestone, a rhythmic undercurrent of the bassy thrum of distant rails.

Together Starlight and I stand alone, two islands of unease against the swirling world around us. Her tremors subside, replaced by a watchful stillness as our caravan draws to a halt. In that moment, with her warm shoulder against my own, I find courage in the face of these new surroundings.

Father and Aaron pass the reins of their respective teams to Mother and Henry. Meanwhile, I perch myself up front beside Henry, and together we drink in the weird elixir life has to offer our senses.

Ladies adorned in silks and brocades, their jewels glittering like constellations in the afternoon light, jostle with plain-clothed women, their headscarves vibrant against the muted tones of their attire. Children, from cherubic toddlers to mischievous brats not quite in their teens—their faces a mix of excitement and apprehension—trot alongside their parents.

Henry nudges me. "Look, a pickpocket."

I see a young boy slide past an older gentleman, patting him on the shoulder with one hand while slipping his other hand inside the man's coat. A blink later and the boy vanishes back into the crowd.

"Looks like that one is going to an opera." I use an index finger to turn his face toward an overdressed woman in lace, beads, and feathers.

Henry laughs. "No, Em, that's a prostitute."

"What? How do you know? Where is she going dressed like that?"

A burst of laughter escapes him as I gasp, red-faced, trying to shake the crass words from my mind.

"Probably to the nearest hotel to make that man's dreams come true." I feel him nudge me with his knee, his body trembling with amusement.

Two figures emerge from the station.

"There they are." I point to Aaron and Father, who holds several pieces of white paper—the bits not stowed in his grip fluttering in an unforgiving wind. They walk toward us, and upon their arrival Father greets us with a long list of instructions.

"Boys, we have two hours to feed and load the animals. Then we need to ..." Father carries on with the list as I begin to worry.

Unable to wait for him to finish, I interrupt. "What about Starlight?"

Father's gaze meets mine. "Starlight will be loaded with the rest of the team. Everything must stay together for easy transfer between trains."

My heart clenches at his words. I know he's right, but the thought of entrusting my beloved horse to a stranger makes me nervous.

"How about I load her?" I ask, adding, "I don't trust her with strangers."

Father's brow furrows.

But dismissing the silent warning, I press on. "She's more comfortable with me. It's for ease of loading. I'll get her tucked in with a double bedding of straw and plenty of hay and—"

"No Emilie, it's not safe for you. The horse will be all right with me," says Father.

His decree leaves no room for argument. With a quiet sigh, I step off the wagon, untether my beloved friend, and hand her lead to Father. My fingers linger on the worn lead rope as it slips from my grasp, and I pat her neck, reassuring both of us that our separation is temporary.

The platform hums with a strange emptiness, as the echoes of another departed train hover like ghosts in the smoky air. Mother and I sit nestled on a bench, adrift in a sea of anxiety and impatience waiting for the men to return. The residual weight of what we left behind persistently presses on me. *Are we doing the right thing?* The plantation, our home for generations, now stands poised on the precipice of change, handed over to my uncle with a handshake and a sigh of resignation.

"I worry Father's decision is the wrong one," I whisper against the evening breeze.

Mother's breath escapes in a soft sigh. "It is a choice, my darling, as bitter as chicory. Your father cannot hold onto the land while clinging to his conscience. Uncle William, for all his faults, will keep the fields green and the family legacy strong, even if it comes at a cost we cannot stomach."

"But leaving feels like a betrayal." My voice chokes, my cheeks feel as though they are in a permanent state of flush, and my eyes fill to the rim with fresh tears ready to flow.

Mother's hand rests on mine, her touch is a beacon of quiet strength calming my emotional storm. "It is why we chose to keep the land in the family and walk away. We choose a different path, one where we can do what's right in our hearts to soothe our aching souls. The whispers and shunning are proof our community no longer holds a place for us. The isolation will slowly kill us if we stay."

My fists clench beneath her steady hand. "But I can't bear turning our backs, knowing he'll buy and sell lives like cattle."

"Nor can I. That's why we're starting anew, removing ourselves from an inhumane system. No more scornful glances for treating humans with respect. Just us, building our home within a community where we can be ourselves and you can follow your dreams."

The glimmer in her eyes, a spark of independence, refuses to be extinguished.

"Do you think slavery will end soon?" I whisper, the question, a fragile butterfly against the bars of our reality.

The bittersweet smile curves her lips. "I wish I had an answer. We are women, expected to tend gardens and nurture children, not uproot mountains. But remember, even a whisper can echo across a valley, and sometimes even the smallest bloom can break through the most worn cobblestone."

We sit in silence for a while watching the world spin around us, the train tracks stretching off into the unknown. The sight makes my blood pump with fresh anxieties and possibilities.

"Are you excited, Mother?" I exchange worry for hope.

A genuine, soft laugh bubbles up from her chest. "Excited? Oh yes."

"Why? Don't you like our life?"

Mother takes my hand. "I love it, but I crave the independence of my girlhood. Doing it all myself."

"All the cleaning, cooking, managing a garden and house? Sounds exhausting."

Her voice dips into a conspiratorial whisper, and I lean closer, drawn into the secret pact we are forging. "The pride in tending a good home and raising a healthy family is worth it, Em. Besides, we'll make Martha proud."

A smile beams from my face. Just the mention of Martha being proud of us is like finding the perfect rose, priceless confirmation of all our efforts.

"You're right. We'll make her proud, manage it flawlessly. After all, if she can do it, then we can too. Oh, I can't wait to see her next year, not as servant, but as friend and sister." A smile breaks through, and with it, a peace against the uncertainties that lie beyond.

Martha spent years tending our hearth and our hearts as the silent keeper of dreams and anxieties. Now, freedom beckons them to a home of their own with a roof for their own dreams to breathe. Moving, no matter the distance, makes it worth it if it means giving them a taste of liberty.

The setting sun casts long shadows across the platform, painting the world in hues of orange and gold. In the distance, the wail of a train whistle echoes, a haunting melody of farewell and a challenge to explore the great beyond. I meet my mother's gaze, a silent pact forged by our shared grief and hope. We are leaving behind the ghosts of the past, embracing the uncertainty of our future with a quiet determination of women who know our worth, our voice, and the strength of our hands.

The men return with dust settling in the creases of their clothes, painting their faces with the grime of their tasks. Henry's brow glistens with sweat, a bead poised over his eye like a mischievous insect. Mother, calm as ever, hands us each an apple to tide us over as we are about to get on the train.

"Don't eat too fast, you never know how travel will disagree with your stomach." Mother's warning forces me to slow down and chew thoughtfully, despite my stomach wanting more.

The platform fills with a crowd of frenzied passengers. Porters, laden with mountains of luggage, weave carts through the kaleidoscope of impatient travelers. The air thickens with anticipation and the acrid tang of wood smoke billows from the engines with the promise of departure.

The crowd pulses around me, a chaotic swirl of bodies and bags. The train looms before me, a behemoth of iron and soot, its black smoke staining the twilight sky. My heart quickens in my chest as I face the impossibly high step, the gateway to my unknown adventure.

A weathered hand grasps mine, calloused fingers offering a steady grip and a smile etched in sun-bronzed skin. I turn to look at the figure.

"Safe travels, miss." The porter's voice is tinged with pipe tobacco and the distant echoes of countless journeys.

"Thank you, sir." The warmth of his hand lets go as I am presented with a narrow claustrophobic aisle, the road to my seat. My feet trip over bags and the disapproving stares of fellow passengers' glares as I make my way to the small oasis. Relief floods me as I sink into the rough worn cushioned bench and feel the cool night air seep through the open window beside me.

"Emilie, close that window." Mother's voice cuts through the noise swirling around us. "You'll be bathed in soot before we leave the station." She works to transform the two bench seats into a haven for the night.

Henry stows our belongings in the overhead hatch, his eyes yearning to join the men as they retreat to the smoking car.

Father, his hand on Mother's shoulder as she rises from her task, winks at me. "Aaron and I will be in the smoking car to listen to the latest news."

"You mean gossip," says Mother.

He squeezes her shoulder and smirks. "Our business is more important than gossip, my dear."

Mother rolls her eyes and bats his hand away, which all surmounts to rich laughter echoing down the aisle as Father takes his leave.

I watch as Henry rises to follow him, only for Aaron's large hand to block his advance.

The boys exchange glares, but Aaron's words beat our brother to the punch. "Someone has to look after the ladies, wouldn't you agree?"

A little push and Henry falls back into a seat, crestfallen as Aaron disappears into the congested aisle.

Mother's knitting needles, a rhythmic counterpoint to the train's lullaby, become a fortress of calm amidst the close confines of the rail car. Henry, still brooding, hides behind his cap, while I, armed with a journal and pen, seek refuge in the inkwell of words.

September 16, 1860

Today is a day of goodbyes and sadness. Now that I am on the train, I feel better untied from emotions back home. I can safely tuck away these memories. Train travel is so much about hurry and wait; the congestion of people, new sights, new sounds and smells, it's all overwhelming. I sit here as the darkness sets in wondering what our new place will look like. When will I get to start school? Will I make friends?

"Emilie, put your things away. You will strain your eyes writing in the dark," says Mother. Heeding her warning, I cork the ink, cover the nib, dry the page, close the book, and tuck it safe into my travel bag. Sliding the bag under my feet, I press my head on the cool glass of the window to watch the landscape whiz by.

The twilight sky fades to indigo with freckles of bright stars. The train's mournful whistle echoes through the night air. Inside, the rhythmic rattle of wheels weaves a hypnotic lullaby. Passengers, lulled by the gentle rocking, gradually succumb to sleep. Heavy eyelids flutter down, soft snores and sighs blend into a chorus of slumber. The lullaby soon works its magic on me as my eyes flutter closed.

The weight of my brothers' slumbering bodies pressing against me, I awaken not only to Aaron's bad breath as his arm cradles my head—which he uses for a pillow—but Henry's snores, a rhythmic wheeze that fills my right ear. Mother and Father whisper in hushed tones while seated across from us.

"Where are we?" I croak, my voice raw with sleep and as dry as summer cotton.

"We are in Alexandria. We stay until Baltimore. Go back to sleep," says Father.

"Why are we switching trains?" The realization suddenly dawns on me.

"Different tracks, something about gauges," my father explains, his voice ever patient. "Sleep, Em, we'll talk later." Despite my blurry vision I sense a wink, and I settle my head back in the crook of Aaron's arm, drawn back into the embrace of sleep.

The sun, a dusty intruder, pushes through the soot-streaked window, heralding a new day. We disembark, grabbing a quick breakfast and tending to our needs before rushing onto our final train to Hanover.

The last five hours of the journey stretch before me like a weary road, the train's rattle a monotonous dirge. Eliot's *The Mill on the Floss*, a tragic melody mirroring the rails' melancholic rhythm, devours my attention. Restless after a time, I begin to pace the narrow aisle before finally succumbing to a nap from boredom.

An alarm blares. "Wake up!"

A violent jolt and I jump. "Wh-what? Huh? Who?"

Oh. Aaron's face is inches away from mine.

Realizing it is a false alarm, my body relaxes back into the subtle embrace of sleep, and I do my best to shake it off with a stretch, grabbing Henry's shirt in the process.

Fingernails claw into the fabric while my half-shut eyes try to blink away the cobwebs.

"Ow! Em, I'm not a mattress!"

"Close enough," I say, smacking my lips before my nose begins to scrunch.

The familiar stench of unwashed bodies, stale tobacco, and heavy perfume assaults my senses. The train, a claustrophobic chamber, pulses with the shift of people and luggage who overflow into our compartment from the aisle.

"We are almost there," Henry announces, his tousled hair reflecting his waning enthusiasm for train travel. "Finally, off this rocking bucket of bolts."

Mother, her face etched with exhaustion, tidies her disheveled hair. "Pack your bags, don't leave anything behind."

Aaron and Father begin their swim through the sea of people. Henry gathers our bags, leaving Mother and I with our small reticules for shopping.

The train screeches to a halt. The station, a brick and stone beacon, welcomes us with its platform. The crowd, a heaving tide, surges around us—families reuniting in a flurry of waves and handkerchiefs.

However, no one awaits our arrival. The realization swells up within me, leaving me adrift in a sea of strangers. My vision tunnels, shrinking to the frantic search for Mother's familiar messy bun or her brown and green shawl. But every face I meet is foreign, their smiles mocking the panic about to crest my lips.

A light touch to the shoulder, a grasp of my hand. Mother's embrace anchors me, guiding us through the ripples of town folk and into the bustling street.

"The shops are this way," she announces, her voice a lifeline in this new world.

The town unfolds before us, a merger of roads in all directions. Shops sit on every corner. A hotel in front of me, merchant stores to the right and left of me. Their windows host an array of menswear, jewelry, and grocery provisions. We head toward the grocer; the name Boyer & Sons is scrolled in the front window.

Mother pushes open the door *jing-ah-ling-ah-ling*. My gaze floats to the top of the door, taking note of the bell. *That must get annoying.* I try to softly close the door behind me so as not to cause further assumed irritation.

"Good day, ladies." The man behind the counter casts curious eyes our way. His long mustache, red cheeks, and green hues capture my attention. "May I help you find something?"

I glance at Mother as she shows him her list, and they move off in another direction. My eyes wander to a newspaper on the counter: *The Compiler,* dated Monday, September 17, 1860. *Oh, right, it's my birthday today. I almost forgot, and from the looks of things*—I glance over to Mother—*they forgot too.*

Drawn toward the paper, I discreetly turn the pages, scanning the columns of ads, court orders, and auctions. There it is—an advertisement for the Female Institute, *Winter Session starting in October!* An audible gasp escapes me before I can press my lips together to stifle the sound. A women's school! I thought I would have to attend a public school. My finger remains on the announcement, and my excitement can't help but bubble over with my delight.

"Aren't you a little too old for schooling?" I look up to see a woman who I presume is the shopkeeper's wife. She looks similar to her husband. Except instead of green eyes, hers are a clear blue, framed by wisps of hair the tone of wood with the faintest touch of ash giving color to her wisdom.

I offer a hopeful smile and say, "Yes ma'am, I am going to be a teacher."

Her raised eyebrows add a touch of suspicion as her clearwaters drink me in from head to whatever is still visible above the counter. "Well then, you have two choices, the one your finger is on or the public school. The second is a fine institution of education, particularly for those of meager means like backwater hill folk. Have you seen their ad?"

This woman's words do not strike upon deaf ears, but they do strike me dumb.

"Would you like to purchase a paper, miss?"

I fetch the coins from my reticule. "Yes ... please, ma'am."

As I deposit the coins into her hand, she assails me with a swift succession of inquiries, taking me once again unaware.

"Just off the train? I suppose you are visiting family here?"

"Yes ma'am." I nod my head.

She grimaces.

Did I say something to offend?

"Settling for good?"

"Well, my father thought it was nice enough ...?"

"Nice, *enough?*" She draws in a sharp inhale.

"Better than where we came from?" I bite my lip. *Is there any hope of appeasing her?*

"Well, of course, though where are you from exactly?" Leaning over the counter to study me, those blue eyes like icicles penetrate mine, demanding and unforgiving no matter the answers I provide. If she were any closer, I know her breath would feel hot and wet. Her heavy breathing matches her demanding tone, like a rabid dog, but would it smell the same? My nose wrinkles.

Oh wait, she asked a question, uhm ...

"R-Richmond, ma'am." The words trip out of my mouth. "We just moved here from Virginia."

Befuddled, I struggle to understand both what is going on and why?

"Well, no wonder." She cocks her head to one side, still glaring at me with the intensity of a blizzard in January.

Then, a light, if by some miracle, flickers in her eyes.

A revelation? My salvation from this conversation?

"Southerner, huh? This paper may not suit your views, but we offer another one. It doesn't come out until tomorrow."

Pulling the paper closer, I say, "That's all right, I will take this one for now, miss ... ma'am?"

I thank her, my tongue numbed by the two little words, before I attempt to fade from the counter. Mother approaches her next with the goods, followed by the store owner. They carry on a pleasant conversation while I watch, still out of sorts from my unexpected interrogation.

When it comes time to leave the store, I wonder how it is that she feels so content and happy while I am feeling ... *How dare someone do that to a perfect stranger. I will never visit this place again! She makes me so ... so ... so angry!*

Outside the shop, the crowd thins out, leaving an occasional passerby, yet the tension lingers within and unnerves me.

"Weren't they pleasant people?" Mother casts me an inquisitive look. "What's vexing you?"

"Nice enough," I reply, but the hollowness in my tone betrays the truth. "I doubt we'll be sharing tea anytime soon."

"Emilie Kathryn, what's gotten into you?" Her tone, shifting to sharp disapproval, pulls me back to reality.

"I was courteous and amiable, but she questioned me as if I were a criminal. That woman was downright rude!" My retort carries more volume than intended. *I simply cannot fathom the audacity to interrogate me in such a manner.*

I begin to mount a defense to the judge, jury, and executioner walking beside me when I see her raise her chin and shake her head. Her knowing revelation halts me in my tracks.

But I haven't even had a chance to plead my case! Is there no justice in the world?

"Your accent must have unsettled her. Folks from small towns are wary of strangers," Mother explains, as if it should have been evident to me. Yet, her composed methodical tone irks me. Not that this stops her.

"Remember, you are a stranger here. They'll warm up to you eventually, but until this community understands your intentions, you must show them respect." Her hand gestures to wave away my frustration, but then she makes an abrupt stop.

But why?

"But," she begins, pausing for emphasis.

But what?

"Your poor attitude won't aid in that."

My jaw drops and a pout begins to scribble across my brow. Her words sting me. Never in all my days did I think she would play the role of angry bee in my bonnet! Mother always gets in the final say, and just like that, the problem is buttoned up and concluded, in her mind, at least. We walk in silence, leaving me to ponder this alleged accent.

I don't have an accent. If I did, no one ever pointed it out before. Do I try to cover it or hope they'll get used to it? This isn't going to stop me now.

I turn back toward the store. Perhaps I am overreacting. The door sign is flipped from open to closed. It feels like an ominous omen. The shade snaps shut. *Yes, it all points to the fact that this endeavor will prove more challenging than I can imagine.* A shiver runs down my spine, signaling the beginning of many unforeseen challenges and mysteries on a path I can neither recognize nor fathom.

The wagons are waiting when we arrive back at the railway station. Happy to see Starlight again, I pet her neck and whisper apologies for the train ride to her. She nuzzles me in search of some reward for all her suffering, not listening when I tell her I have nothing on hand. At least this exchange distracts her from Father as he tacks her up for me, but I can't help but feel judged when it is a bit and not a carrot pressed past her lips. Perhaps this is her reason for startling disagreement when I go to mount her? Maybe I should give her time to settle after such a trip. I dismount and remove her bridle, tying her to the back of the wagon.

"We will ride later, once you stop feeling like everything is about to kill you," I say before climbing into the wagon, and we head out toward our new home on Table Rock Road.

New Neighbors

HOME IS A PLACE NOT ONLY OF STRONG AFFECTION
BUT OF ENTIRELY UNRESERVED: IT IS LIFE'S UNDRESS
REHEARSAL, ITS BACKROOM, ITS DRESSING ROOM.

~HARRIET BEECHER STOWE

SEPTEMBER 1860
GETTYSBURG, PENNSYLVANIA

The wagon creaks and groans as we travel toward our new house. Anticipation flutters in my chest as we turn onto the drive. The trees transform into a tunnel of crimson, gold, and green, their leaves blushing with the last gasp of autumn. They rustle with whispered secrets in the wind—a welcome or a warning?

I crane my neck, peering over my parents' shoulders, steadying myself, concentrating on a wisp of smoke dancing from the chimney of the two-story house coming into view. My breath catches in my throat. *Is that it? Why is there ...*

"Are you sure this is the right place?"

My father's shoulder twitches ever so slightly under my hand.

Mother's head snaps around, and her eyes flicker with irritation. "I think your father knows which house we own, Emilie."

Her reprimand makes me think I didn't see it at all. My gaze returns to the chimney. I squint, willing the smoke to puff out of the brick top—still there.

I point to the roof as the clapboard home reveals itself to us. "Then why is there smoke coming from the chimney?"

My parents, in unison, turn their heads to each other, eyes wide. I feel Father's shoulder tense.

"I guess we will find out, though Mr. Deardorf was supposed to be moved out by now."

The wagon slows to a halt, and Father secures the brake while Aaron and Henry pull up next to us, looking around for any signs of occupancy.

So, I wasn't the only one to see it.

"Aaron, you and Henry go check the barn. We might have company."

Father's orders set my brothers searching: in the barn, around the house. They disappear into the orchard while he approaches our new home and knocks ... opens the door ... then disappears inside.

Any word?

Mother and I wait, necks craned in his direction.

I see Father's arm waving us into the house, and nudge Mother before we both scramble out of the wagon to explore our new home and admire more than just the surroundings. We step up under the small, covered porch, then over the threshold.

"There is no one here." Father lifts the cover of a pot simmering on the stove. "Mm, chicken stew."

"Then who left that?" Mother's brow furrows. "You didn't hire a servant, did you, Jacob?" Her eyes search his face for answers, her mouth turning down into a pout.

My father takes Mother's hand. "No, Julia, but I did send a

pigeon earlier to tell the chicken that if it wasn't in this pot by the time we got here, I would give it a stern clucking-to."

Mother playfully smacks his shoulder, and he pretends it actually hurts as she starts squawking, "I'm serious Jacob, you remember I can cook—right?"

"Well, I hope so, we just freed Martha. Now come, Julia. Consider it a blessing you don't have to unpack and cook our first night here," says Father, and the rest of their conversation occurs in silence. My parents have a way of communicating without words—with a look, it's like they just know what the other is saying—simple smiles and meaningful glances.

The door bursts open and we all give a jump, but it's just Henry—out of breath, leaning forward on his knees, as if he ran not just through the property but to Virginia and back as well.

"No one in the barn ... You should see it! There's a workshop ..." Henry says.

Aaron, winded and holding his chest, comes up behind Henry. "I don't think woodworking ... is the first thing ... on our minds, Henry. The farmstead ... Real swell, Father."

Did Aaron just roll his eyes? I can't help but smile as the conversation rambles on, but it doesn't take long before my mind is split and then turns in full to the view of the room. Woodstove, cupboard, large seating area. The warm, savory smells of this sacred space. I breathe deep ... comforting.

The kitchen table is different from the one at home—well, our old home. It's covered in a checkered tablecloth with a bouquet of flowers in the center. The flowers spill out of the top, and among the daisies are coneflowers, roses, and greens. Drawn to the white and yellow daisies, I move toward the table to pull the vase closer. The diamond-cut green glass feels sharp in my hands. *Lovely ... And oh! What's this?*

Tucked deep into the arrangement is a small handwritten note. Plucking it from the bouquet, I open it, clear my throat, and wait for a lull ... then begin to read it aloud.

"Welcome home. Mr. Halle will arrive later today with your chickens and to see how you are all getting on. Signed Mrs. H. Halle."

An audible sigh of relief sounds in unison with a final note to this petite overture.

"Well, that solves our dilemma. Let's get some of this un-packed. Jacob, you and the boys work on the beds. Emilie and I will unpack the kitchen."

Father claps his hands. "Right, come on boys, you heard the woman. Let's not give her bark time to become a bite."

"Horses need beds too. How about I get the stalls ready in-stead?" Henry offers. "I'll even turn the horses out to pasture when I'm done."

"But you and Starlight don't like each other," I say and cannot help but arch a brow.

"No, no, she's fine, but I'll call on you if she gives me any trou-ble." Henry's hand is on the door, and he is pushing through the archway before anyone has a chance to tell him differently.

Not that this stops Father from trying. "When you finish, Aaron and I will need your help ..."

"Yes, sir," Henry says as the door closes with a rattle behind him.

"Now why did he close the door?" asks Father.

"Because he wasn't raised in a barn," says Mother.

I bite my bottom lip to stifle my giggles as I watch the two exchange another look. Then, Mother briefly sticks out her tongue before Father gives her a wink.

"Someone ate her oats today. All right, Aaron and I will bring in some crates for you ladies to unpack."

"Shut the door on your way out!" says Mother.

"What was that? You want me to put the crates in the barn?" asks Father as he heads out the door, and Aaron, who follows, closes it so quietly a church mouse might think there is company.

Mother and I laugh and turn to the cupboards.

I open one set of doors.

"They left dishes behind." I point to the mismatched, chipped Wedgwood, and the bright pink lusterware. The glasses left behind have a fine layer of dirt coating them.

"Boil some water, wash off the dust, and we will see if we can use them." The clink and clatter that follow tell me Mother's up to her elbows in a barrel of kitchen goods and straw as the men make quick work of unloading the crates—the first of many crates, boxes, and barrels from the wagon.

Pulling the dishes out of the cupboard, stacking them near the wet sink, I turn to the stove, pick up the kettle, give it a small shake, and see water slosh out. It's full. Using this I prime the pump to start the flow, then refill the kettle, and return it to the stove.

"I'm going to check the pantry," I say as I wait for the water to heat. Tying back the old curtain, I step into the narrow closet-like room with shelves floor to ceiling. There are several jars of seeds for next spring's planting, old pots and sealed crocks, all unlabeled and waiting to be opened. *How will we know if they've gone bad? At least the membranes covering them are neatly tied off with twine.* I lean forward and reach for one.

"Oh, for the love ... Oh no ... Emilie!"

Almost ... there ... "What?"

Frozen with my hand on the jar, I turn my head to see what bee has got in Mother's bonnet. She's standing at the window near the sink, shaking her head.

"Go help your brother, Starlight is acting up."

"Starlight? I think you mean Henry," I say as I set the crock back on the shelf and head out the door, with perhaps a bit more stomp to my step than necessary, and a harder yank at the door than—No, the flair is necessary!

My eyes drink in the commotion of my brother trying to move Starlight with muscle instead of understanding. I can already feel my blood start to boil. *What does he think he's doing, pulling straight back on her lead?* Starlight sits back, digs her hooves into the earth, throws her head up, and doesn't give an inch. *A thousand pounds of muscle and Henry really thinks he'll win this tug of war? Unbelievable!*

Aaron joins me on the porch. There has never been a dog to bark louder than the two of us as we shout orders to either one: "Starlight!" ... "Henry!" ... "Let go of her!" ... "She'll rip your arm off."

If one thing is to be said from this, both man and horse are stubborn!

Starlight stops pulling and figures she can run over my brother as Henry falls back, not expecting her to give up the tension.

"You stupid nag! Damn horse is trying to kill me!" Henry scrambles to get to his feet before Starlight's four hooves become his destiny.

Stepping off the porch, I approach her from the side, so she can see me, recognize me, hear my apology, and know I will never let my big dumb brother ever—

Her eye is on me. Her ear is pricked toward me. "Whoa girl ... Settle in ... Easy ..."

"Don't baby the beast, Emilie, she is about to kill me!"

I pause and glare at Henry. "I'm trying to keep that from happening! If you had just treated her like the decent soul she is—!"

"If you'd train her—!"

"If you'd not pick a fight with her—!"

"If you—"

Starlight knocks Henry over with her shoulder just as he gets back up, and her lead rope rips through his hands as she turns and takes off. Her focus is on greener pastures. My focus is on Henry. Henry's focus is on the rope he just let go of—

Oh no! He let go of the rope!

My eyes rip away from my brother only to snag on the distant hindquarters of my mare fleeing up the driveway. *What if she ends up lost? What if she goes hungry? What if I never see her again?*

"Great! Now see what you've done!" I yell before storming off after my frightened mare. *She's lost and alone, she won't know her way home, and now, I have to find her, all because I'm related to that ... that ... Oo, I will never forgive him!* Bunching my skirts up in my fists, I begin to walk faster, kicking clods of dirt out of my way, grumbling under my breath—*When I get back, he will hear my thunder! And this wagon better get out of my way too!*

I march down the dirt path, never-minding the ambling of the dumb wagon with the ancient old man, the snot nosed brat, and Starlight—*Starlight!?*

Coming toward me is a wagon driven by an older man, and to his left walks a young boy, yes, but why is Starlight prancing beside that boy with her tail flagged? *How did he get ahold of her lead? Why is she being so calm? Did he give her treats?*

She looks up, my companion and dearest friend, ears forward, head up, and then she releases her anger with a snort. *But I wasn't the one who mishandled you, Starlight!*

The boy strokes her again, encouraging her with words I cannot hear. She lowers her head, nuzzles him. *Traitor ... Who does this boy think he is, anyway?*

He can't be more than ten or fourteen at the most. He's easy with the lead, confident in his strides, but other than that, what does he have that I can't provide?

"This one belongs to you, miss?" The middle-aged gentleman slows his team to greet me with a tilt of his head and a smile.

I blink away from my thoughts, look to the older gent and give a curt nod. "If she came running like her tail was on fire, then yes, she's mine, and has always been mine, and will always be mine," I say as my gaze wanders back over to whoever this little boy thinks he is.

"Is your father ... He's expecting ..." The man asks my name or something or other.

"Yes, yes, I'm Emilie, and who might you be?" I say, still staring at this child, this toddler, who thinks he has God's gift to tame wild creatures.

"Pleasure to meet you, miss. See you when you get back to the house," the older man says, and I hear his wagon pull forward as he drives past.

The boy, this urchin, stands with Starlight.

"Thank you," I say and put my hand out to take her lead.

The boy pulls it back. "She ain't calm enough yet miss."

What did he just say to me? My eyes go wide, and I feel quite within my right to set the story straight. "I beg your pardon, but that is my horse, and you will give her back to me."

His big brown eyes narrow as his brow furrows. He shakes his head, no. "Nah miss, you'll get hurt, and that's something Pa said I can't allow, letting a girl get hurt."

"I will not get hurt, she is my horse. By withholding her from me, you are no more than a thief!" I say and go to take the lead once more.

Again, he pulls the rope back and then eases right past me as Starlight follows with a snort. "Well, she ain't really no one's, miss, unless she gots papers. You gots papers for her, miss?"

Quickening my steps to catch up to them, I skip over all formality. "I do not need to give papers to a little rotten snot nosed boy who has taken my horse on my own property!"

"Name's Billy Halle, miss, and I'm far from a boy, being all of ten, miss."

His formality burns my pride, stinging like a slap. He not only implies I am much older, but his manners are impeccable.

"She might like you a bit more if you spoke softer, you know, but I imagine once we get to the barn, she'll be calm enough."

I do not need some brat telling me how to handle my mare.

We walk a few more steps. Billy continues talking to Starlight in that baby voice. She whickers and nuzzles him. My stomach knots. *How could she do this to me?*

"How'd you catch her? Sugar cubes, carrot?" I cross my arms, looking anywhere but at her, at him, at them. *My best friend, today of all days, abandoning me.*

"No, miss, she just slowed up at the end of the drive. Didn't know where to turn, so I got hold of the rope. Now we're best friends, which I don't mind. She's got speed and grace; you ever

43

race her by chance?"

"No. And she's not your best friend. She's my best friend!" I yell, not that I mean to. He's just a little boy, but she's my horse, she's my friend, she's, he's—I'm not sure when my arms uncross and my hands ball into fists. I just know one moment I am yelling at this kid, storming past him, and that traitor of a horse—

I pause only once when I hear him ask, "Does she always run off like that?"

"No! It's my stupid brother's doing!" I say, not even looking back at the pair of them.

I forge a trail down the path, only to see Henry up ahead.

"Hey Em, looks like the Halle boy can handle your horse."

"Much better than you, Henry."

"Yeah, they do make a good match. Heard his father asking if she's for sale. We could certainly save a bundle on the hay."

The cold hand of jealousy grips me around my throat, and I feel my own palms press against my brother, shoving him, a *thud*, a cloud of dust, a grunt, but I don't look back. I can barely *choke* back the words of hate that scald my throat. This rot, this rage—it spreads itself through me. *How dare they think they can buy her? How dare they think they can sell her? How dare she have more than one best friend! How dare Henry—*

I slam the door as I pass the threshold.

"Emilie, I need you to make biscuits. We have the whole Halle family joining us tonight."

I head to the sink, grab the soap, grip the handle, and pump, pump, pump. The water spills forth. Wash, scrub, wash, flick the water off my hands, and *where's the towel?*

"Emilie Kathryn, did you hear me?" Mother's voice interrupts my thoughts.

"Yes. Make biscuits, and I'm making them, as you asked."

There it is. Wet hands swoop in to snatch the towel off the peg. I rub my hands dry and ready myself to gather the ingredients, but Mother's set everything out. Sprawled on the tabletop waiting for me. Flour, pearlash, skip the sugar, dash of salt, lard, egg, and ...

"Milk?" I turn to my mother, who hands me a pitcher.

"Mr. Halle delivered ... compliments of ... Halle ..."

I shrug. Pour the milk into the bowl, hear the wooden spoon knock about, hear Billy's mistrust, hear Henry's taunts—

His father asked to buy her ... She's my best friend ... Does she always run off?—

The wooden spoon is useless. I roll up my sleeves, and these recollections push my fingers into the dough. I throw it on the table, slam it, punch it ... I knead out anger—*How dare he*—knead out audacity—*Who does he think he is*—knead out fear? ... *I can't lose Starlight ...*

"Emilie! You knead that dough anymore and we will be eating bricks for dinner." Mother's reprimand pulls me from my pause, and a blink or two releases tears. *She's all I have left* ... I stand over the dough gasping for air, my body overwhelmed with the onslaught of the last seventy-two hours. My hands hover above the delicate ingredients, ruined, destroyed.

"I can't do this." These words hardly sound like my own, but I know they are.

A hand embraces my shoulder. "Martha?" I turn and look, but it's Mother. She holds no judgment, just pulls me into a hug.

My dough-laden hands dare not touch her.

"What's wrong? ... What's happening? ... Do you feel home-sick?"

Gulping, sniffing, my voice cracks.

"I-I can't do this," I say—more gulps and another sob. Mother steers me over to a chair, sets me firmly in it, and hands me a towel. Then she waits for me to gather my composure.

"Boys are stupid!" I blurt, and I'm not sure if whatever comes out next makes any sense but I still say it. "Henry hates Starlight. Those Halles want to take her from me because of that boy. She's *mine*, Mother! I won't let her go ever. I already had to let go of Martha and now the biscuits are ruined ... and ...and ..." Another wave of sobs rolls through me.

"Emilie, what is it?"

Sucking in another breath, I say, "And I don't want to grow up. I don't want to give up everything. This is the worst birthday—everyone's forgotten me!"

Mother pulls me into another embrace. The comfort of her arms and the smell of her lavender perfume shut out the world around me, calming my soul, enveloping me into the sweet memories of life as a small child. The world has always been safe in her arms.

"We didn't forget your birthday, Em." Her voice brushes against my hair. "Now, how about you take a nap, hmm? Aaron and your father have already set up the beds."

The tide of sobs recedes, and I shake my head and grasp onto her sleeves even tighter.

Behind me the door latch clicks.

"Where do you want—" Henry's voice cuts through the tender moment.

I feel Mother's arm motioning to him.

"What's wrong with her? If anything, I'm the one who got pushed down in the dirt."

"Henry!" says Mother.

I hear Henry backing out of the room, announcing before he slips out, "All right, all right, just thought you'd like to know the rest of the Halles are here."

Mother unclenches me from our embrace, smooths back my messy hair, and gives a warm smile. "Breathe. No one is going to sell Starlight."

We each take a deep breath, nod at each other, and understand it is time to get back to work. She dries my tears with the corner of her apron, and I ruin her good work a moment later by dampening my face with cold water from the sink. It helps pull me back to reality and regain my frayed nerves.

Peering out the window, there is no sign of the Halles, so I figure they must be unhitching their wagon in the barn. Returning to the table, the biscuits wait for me. Thankfully, the dough isn't as ruined as I thought.

The Halle family is a delightful bunch. Mrs. Halle, with her bright smiling eyes, has the patience of a saint as her brood of six children mill about with the needs and wants that come natural to young ones: the want of a snack, the need for the outhouse, the lack of ability to tie their shoes or lace their britches. I instantly admire Jane, the eldest girl who, although a year younger than Billy, helps her mother without Mrs. Halle having to say a thing. Her shy smile and large hazel eyes make her angelic. She minds her manners, but mostly minds her younger brothers ranging in age from about a year to eight years old. If one wants a snack, Jane gives an apple slice. While her mother ties the shoelaces of one, Jane is hand in hand with the toddler to the outhouse. Together, their tasks never cease, and their complaints never arise.

As for the boys, Little Joe as they like to call him is eight and is always trying to fit in with Billy and Mr. Halle. Sam is six and considers himself VanWyck's guardian, and with good reason too—Van is always touching anything and everything. Lastly, infant Robert. What can I say? He is a baby with all the needs of a cute little bundle that somehow can stink up a whole room with the kick of a chubby leg.

We set the dinner table with a mix of old and new dishes. Dinner is a savory dance of soft delights. There are potatoes, flakes of onion, and long spears of green beans swimming past islands of round carrots. All of it floats in a golden gravy, releasing the fragrant herbs: thyme, rosemary, and a sweet hint of sage. The biscuits rise high with buttered peaks—steaming, warm, and inviting. I cannot wait to enjoy such a mouthwatering splendor.

Mr. Halle, Father, Aaron, and Henry sit at one end of the table, while Mother, Mrs. Halle, and I sit at the other end. The children are placed strategically between the adults with books stacked atop Sam and Van's chairs. The boys are gleeful to be able to see over the table's edge, reaching for things they shouldn't touch. Thankfully, Mother moves the candles just past their fingertips, while Jane and Mrs. Halle settle the younger children to eat. Mrs. Halle picks up the knives at Sam and Van's places before anyone but her can cut anything, and Jane fills their glasses with milk. Returning to her seat, Mrs. Halle sighs as she settles herself into her chair for a bite of cooled stew.

"They are good boys, most of the time," she says, helping herself to a steaming biscuit.

"So much energy," I say as I watch Sam put a green bean on the end of his spoon and launch it toward Billy to get his attention.

"Sam," says Mrs. Halle.

Her level tone and stern eye gives cause for her husband to rest his hand on Sam's shoulder as the men talk amongst themselves. A squeeze is all that is given as Mr. Halle neither breaks eye contact nor pauses his conversation with Aaron and my father. Sam shrinks back into his chair as giggles peal out of Little Van, but Billy makes a face at Sam—eliciting a missing-toothed grin back at his older brother.

Mr. Halle looks away from Aaron, clears his throat, and eyes each boy to settle them back into some semblance of proper manners.

Mother bites her lip, holding back her own giggle. "Boys will be boys. I miss mine being that little sometimes."

"Plenty of dirt and discipline is required to grow this bunch into upstanding young men." Mrs. Halle nods to the basket where a slumbering Robert lies sucking his thumb, content and undisturbed. "And we've still got one more to get through this stage."

The conversation quiets, except for giggles erupting here and there at faces made between the Halle boys. We enjoy every morsel of dinner, filling our bellies and comforting our souls.

"So, what are the views of the North in this secession debate?" Aaron asks Mr. Halle.

My ears prick up. I think it is the way Aaron commands a room that grabs my attention.

"Our view is simple: We cannot afford to separate. Our country must stay whole to compete with the rest of the world." Mr.

Halle sets down his fork to pick up his glass.

"I agree about uniting as one country, but it sure feels like the government is coming down on the Southern states for having our own opinion about these matters." Aaron mirrors Mr. Halle, his fork resting at the rim of his bowl as he picks up his glass of water.

Here he goes.

Enthralled, I pause with my glass to my lips.

"How so, Aaron?" asks Mr. Halle.

"I see it this way. The South's land is more fertile, and the climate is better suited for the production of raw materials. So, it would make sense that the Northern states focus their resources on manufacturing. However, due to the dense population of voters in the North, they have a majority in Congress, whose interests and wealth only pertain to the North's wellbeing and not the South. This has led to the allowance of manufacturers undercutting Southern sellers, and then raising the costs of finished goods that they know the South relies on and must buy."

Mr. Halle nods. "There are a significant number of families still producing their own food, but what you say about many of ours being in manufacturing is true. Still, while the manufacturers might sell a few goods at higher costs, it is only so they can make sure that items like clothing, food, and their employees' wages are met. Are you saying that plantations like the one in your family's name can't afford to spend a bit extra on the people whose lives you claim as property?" Mr. Halle asks, leaning forward with interest.

Aaron continues. "I'm saying that if Northern business owners proceed to try and squeeze blood out of a turnip, then soon they will have no turnip, as the South will buy and sell to those with deeper pockets across seas who understand fair business practices, rather than watch their economy come to a halt over the greed of their fellow countrymen. Northern businessmen undercut the South when buying our materials, and then mark up the finished goods when selling the products back. The North seems to have forgotten that the South has both resources and land, so it falls on us to provide to the whole of this country. Your fellow man claims we are uncivilized, yet it would be a pity if we set a higher price on raw materials such as necessities for our own greed, wouldn't you agree?"

My gaze shifts to our guest. *Your turn, Mr. Halle.*

"Point taken; I work hard just to provide for my family. I don't know how I would provide for more. Right, there is more to this." Mr. Halle quiets, thinking.

"You're correct," Aaron says. "What frustrates Southerners most is the government's refusal to create legislation that incorporates fair business practices into the sudden increase of industrialization. The North, who holds the seat of power in Congress, seems to think that our raw materials are beholden to their manufacturers first and foremost. However, if we were to let them have it their way, it would bankrupt the South. And because we refuse to yield and expose the soft underside of our bellies to their greed, they want to deny us a say in our own livelihoods and are trying to refuse the Southerners the rights that all states have had since the drafting of the Constitution."

So, this is how gentlemen settle an argument. Thank goodness Uncle William isn't here. There would be yelling, red faces, and fencing with dinner knives by now.

"I see. Well, be that as it may, the elephant in the room, and a matter that weighs on the mind of many good Christians, is the issue of slavery. We have faced issues regarding finances and politics, but what about the human condition? What do you have to say about that?" Mr. Halle asks.

My eyes jerk over to Aaron but are snagged by Father's interjection.

"Slavery was never a decision provided to the South. During the British colonization, they brought slavery of all kinds to our shores. It started with indentured servitude. People worked for nothing more than their right to live, either to pay off a debt or work off a prison sentence. After a time, however, indentured servants gained their freedom and blended into the established populace. However, they had no education, and their labor resulted in menial tasks assigned to what the British considered the working class of our society.

"As we all know, they were more interested in raping the colonies of their worth, rather than establishing prosperous entities with educated denizens who were not British. They didn't wish to give us, the Colonists, the rights to our livelihood, so they came up with a better idea to keep power. They brought black slaves over, people easily distinguishable from the masses, and gave them what work indentured servants and other unskilled labor could do, and filled our churches with the gospel that told us it was their God-given right to do it.

"By the time the British left, slavery was woven so deeply in our faith, culture, and economy, that to free all of them as of now would mean once again the bankruptcy of the South, which a good majority would see as God's damnation of them, rather than salvation for all."

Father continues, "As for my family's legacy, it isn't easy managing four hundred acres of tobacco, corn, wheat, and animals without hands. I don't condone slavery, but I also don't have an answer to the economic and societal struggles negroes and whites alike could face if it all were to come to an abrupt halt." Weariness surfaces on Father's features, his lips thin and taut, his eyes lacking their usual sparkle.

"I see it as money and power with a blatant disregard for human life," Mr. Halle says. "As a country, we cannot continue this institution. We have a whole freed black population here, who are making ends meet, but they deserve more, and rightfully so." Mr. Halle swallows hard, twisting his own emotions into the very napkin he holds.

Father nods. "Slavery is a system that ignores a person's basic human rights." He pinches the bridge of his nose, revealing the worry in his eyes. "Most folks who own slaves just can't see it anymore. They've convinced themselves it's the way things have to be—economics, religion, and politics, all used as excuses. Trying to change their minds is a losing battle right now."

I know exactly who troubles him most—Uncle William.

My heart pounds with the vulnerability of similar emotions. Touched by the pain, I feel my eyes blink away the tears forming. Sure, Father did say *most*, but he might as well have said *all*—a majority my beloved kin and I will forever be judged by, regardless of our personal opinions. Mother pulls the glass from my lips, breaking a dam of pent-up emotion.

"If I may interject," I hear myself say. *When did I move to stand? Perhaps it doesn't matter now that I am addressing the room.* "I love our slaves like family. They helped bring me into this world, taught me to bake the biscuits you enjoy, and are just as much a part of me as the people you break bread with today. Yes, they are still bound, and yes, I see in their eyes a longing to determine their own destiny. But I didn't enslave them, and I do not possess the right to free them. Still, I ask you men— who claim such responsibilities to our nation—who will provide them with the same liberties of freedom offered to you once they are citizens?

"We have raised generations who cannot read or write, do not possess property, or have skills beyond the work their masters have given them. Their masters cannot afford to pay them as of now, the current society doesn't consider them as equals, and laws will not suddenly change this. No, I don't condone slavery, but abandoning them in a fashion that leaves them unprepared to an even harsher fate, where they slave away for pennies to keep a roof over their head with no promise of food, medication, or education like the workers who reside under the yoke of manufacturing feels equally unjust, which is why there must be a better solution to all of this.

"So, I implore you, Mr. Halle, instead of worrying over our slaves, perhaps you should petition your fellow Northerners to improve upon the rights that free men should already have. Unless you deny the poor condition of unskilled labor applied by Northern industrialization?"

My voice fades and silence falls over the room.

I am washed with the realization that I am breaking every rule of polite society: a woman speaking in mixed company—giving her opinion. My cheeks feel the heat of a crimson glow. The world spins. Confusing, damning, nauseating, choking me.

I see Henry covering his eyes.

Aaron smiling with pride.

My father's stern look, and Mr. Halle's—showing interest and yet concern.

Then I feel Mother's hand on my arm calling me back. But we both know—it's too late for that.

"Ex-excuse me," I sputter, rushing from the room.

Over the rush in my ears, I hear Mrs. Halle say, "That girl has spirit," but that is all, as I am soon out of the room and on the porch.

The rush of heat fills my body, dizzies my mind, and sends my thoughts whirling about—*What if the Halles no longer respect our family views? I just ruined all my chances here. Wait until the rumors start now. No more teaching, just the life of a recluse spinster.*

I sit down hard on the porch swing, breathing deep, trying to calm my nerves, and waiting for cold air to extinguish the rise of my embarrassment. Holding my tongue is not something I do easily. Our family is outspoken on most issues. I've listened to Aaron's court speeches, and to Father's lectures to my brothers on how to disagree without resulting in a duel. The only thing I tend to forget is that I am no more than a lady who must uphold different standards, standards I apparently forgot about tonight.

The rhythmic swinging grounds me back into my predicament. I must save face, ask for forgiveness, and show I am responsible for my actions. Besides, no one ever died of embarrassment, but I am willing to bet many have come pretty darn close.

After another moment, I pull myself off the swing, smooth down my skirt, tilt my chin in a demure fashion, and walk back into the house to make amends with our new neighbors and my parents.

Getting to Know You

THE BETTER PART OF ONE'S LIFE CONSISTS OF HIS FRIENDSHIPS.
~ABRAHAM LINCOLN

SEPTEMBER 1860
GETTYSBURG, PENSYLVANIA

Sunlight dapples the parlor floor, casting dust motes in a whirlwind around the towering crates that squat here like unwelcome guests. Wood smoke, aged paper, and forgotten memories hang in the air, thick enough to taste. Mother and I, like weary researchers, circle the crates, each one a portal brought forth from our old life in Virginia, now resting here in uneasy exile. Reaching into the half-empty wooden box at my feet, I push aside the packing straw, fingers tingling at the discovery of a paper package nestled within the box's contents. Pulling it out, I unearth the brown paper package bound with twine. Underneath the faded wrapping lie three smooth leather books, each tied with a thin leather strap. I unlatch it and peek behind the cover of the book that rests on top. Inside, my mother's neat script dances across the page, displaying perhaps a spider web of hopes, dreams, and a life chronicled before I ever existed. Anticipation thickens the air around me as I hold some part of her fragile and precious past in my hands.

My breath hitches, but then I manage to find my voice and say, "I don't think you want these on the bookshelf."

"Why not, what did you find?" Mother looks up from her own unpacking, turning toward me, her eyes widening at the set of books I am holding.

"From the looks of the handwriting, these belong to you."

I can't help but notice the soft light that sparks her eyes, and the sweet smile that collects on her lips before she says, "Oh, those are just scribblings of a young girl. I should probably get rid of them."

"Get rid of them? But they're treasures, a map to your past I want to discover. Tell me about them, please. When did you write these?"

"Let's see, the tan one is the courtship with your father, the dark brown one is our early marriage, before Aaron was born, and the last one ... I think it ends around the time you were about two or ... three years old?"

"Why did you stop writing?"

"You asked as many questions when you were little as you do now, and answering all of them, along with having to raise a family ... Well, it leaves little time for writing."

Fingering the tan journal, I bite my lip. The love story inside nudges me to ask. *Do I dare?* Looking up, I see Mother is watching me.

A knowing smile can be traced across her angelic features. "You want to read them, don't you?"

"I—I couldn't, these are your private thoughts. But if you don't mind, if it's all right with you, I swear not to tell a soul what resides within these precious folds." I remember to breathe before bursting out. "Well, yes, of course! Oh, please! Oh, thank you! I've always wanted to hear about your love story. Is it romantic?" My face blushes pink, the subject so personal. *Would I want anyone reading my diaries? Certainly not, but surely, I am my mother's most trusted confidante.*

Her hand reaches for the books as she stifles her own giggles and instead releases a tender sigh. Delicate fingers pass the pages from side to side. She hums. She smiles. She looks back to me with starlight in her eyes.

"Did you instantly fall in love with him?"

"No, that's certainly not true, he pursued me for a good long while."

"You told him no?" Hard to believe anyone would ever turn down Father.

"Em, your father was a plantation owner's son. He had all the good things going for him. I was positive he did not want a poor farmgirl turned teacher. After all, he could have had any rich plantation owner's daughter, combined their wealth, and the rest would have been history."

Her face softens as I imagine the memories flickering through her mind, each hue echoing different moments of the courtship before my time. The corner of her mouth quirks upward, touched by the youthful naivete of her own doubts. Yet, under her laugh lines, I see the crack of vulnerability exposed; it echoes a familiar feeling of my own. Seeing her face flood with waning confidence makes me sad.

"He chose you," I remind her.

"Yes, he did, Emilie. We chose each other. I mean, I did find him quite charming, despite his family's reputation." Her thumb on her left hand goes to the gold band on her ring finger, while the palm of her right hand caresses the spine of the diary. The thumb rotates the ring, as if turning back time and rewinding through her memories ... *Mostly good by the look on her face, but still, what else is she not telling me?*

"Will you tell me about it someday?" I ask, the question caught up in my breath.

"Oh, I am sure I told you our story many times already."

"And I am sure I don't know all there is to know." I wink at her and there is no hiding my salacious grin. From my understanding, Mother had a great career with a family close to the plantation, and suddenly Father swept her off her feet and with it, her career went under the rug.

"All you need to know right now is that we were always determined to carve our own path. And while we have our battles, Em, there is never doubt in our ability to triumph. We chose each other, not for what we had, but for what we dreamed of building together."

Her gaze meets mine again, steady and clear. "So, my dear, there will be plenty of time to tell you more as you grow into your own relationship with whoever the lucky suitor may be, but for now let's clean this up. After all, you still have to drop off those cookies at the Halles' this afternoon."

Mother stands, her fingers rubbing the velvet smooth leather.

I suck in a breath, feel my teeth graze my bottom lip. "Mother?"

She turns to look up from the worn and weathered book.

"Please, don't burn them. I'd like to tuck them away for that day when I need you close, and you're—and you're not near."

She holds me in her gaze. Then looks to the books in her hands. A sigh. A smile ...

Finally, she speaks. "I will entrust these to you, but please do not read them until after you marry. It will mean more to you then. Do you promise?"

The warmth of her hands still lingers on the books as I take them from her, sealing the agreement between us.

"I promise," I say. "Oh, one more thing."

Mother's steady brow arches.

"When should I ask Father about enrolling in school this fall?"

Mother sighs. "You should discuss it with him soon. Doesn't the term start in a week or two?"

"Tonight then? After dinner, I mean."

"I am sure that will be fine. Now, the cookies, Emilie."

Starlight and I ride up to the Halle farm with the fresh baked jumbles. It's from an old recipe I pulled from my receipt book Martha ensured I brought with me. The cookies are twisted into heart shapes, smell of nutmeg and rosewater, and contain a secret spice passed down through many generations.

Settled a short distance from the road, the meandering drive of the Halle family rolls lazily between two unending fields leading to—emptiness? No children, laughing or squalling. Not even the sound of an axe chopping or a backdoor closing. Where is everyone? Ghosts appear to inhabit the porch's rocking chairs, a soft creak from a steady breeze. I dismount and tie Starlight to a leaning fence post. Pulling the jumbles out of the saddlebag, I walk to the door.

Creak. The rockers greet me as they sway. It feels silly, but I wave to their unseen occupants, and they don't seem to mind. Perhaps it is not the wind that whooshes through the outbuildings, howling in delight. Then again, perhaps my presence startles the leaves, rustling and then racing to destinations unknown, whispering goodbye before they have had the chance to say hello. The noises drown out what would otherwise be the deafening quiet of an unwelcome stillness.

"Hello?" My greeting falls into the grasp of the breeze. My knuckles echo against the weathered wood, three staccato beats followed by an aching pause. I lean back on my heels, waiting, confused, questioning. *Where could you possibly hide six children?*

"Anyone home?" I shout at the closed door staring back at me, the jumbles weighing heavier now, not that the rich dark wood cares about my aching arm.

The warm timbre of a voice, though, issues a response. "Can I help you?"

Ghosts are just flights of fancy, and doors don't talk, Emilie! So that must mean ...

My heart ricochets about my chest as I spin like a top, meeting not just eyes, with an entire cosmos in their hazel depths, but a whole person, a whole man to accompany those hues reflecting mystery. His dark hair tumbles back from his bronzed brow. He is young, like me, his sleeves rolled high to reveal muscular sinew beneath a tan hide that begs to be traced. He wipes his hands on a handkerchief, the rough linen a stark contrast to the smooth skin beneath. His hand extends.

My hand hesitates at first and then finds his.

His calloused hand engulfs mine, the warmth seeping through my delicate limbs, as if kissed by sunlight. His thumb, a slow, deliberate whisper, traces a line down the back of my grasp sending shivers dancing up my arm. I fight back a gasp.

"Name's Stephen Byrne," he declares. His voice rumbles as rich as the earth after rain. "And you are?"

Our gazes lock, his smile widening as he turns my hand over. The air crackles, charged with the unspoken promise of what comes next. He bends down, leans over, his lips touching skin, turning me scarlet as he plants a searing kiss. My breath hitches, caught in the sudden intimacy, my brain fumbling for words that won't come out.

The world tilts, my senses overloaded by the burn of his touch, yet the sweet scent of hay and horses clinging to him seems to keep me grounded in this moment shared between us.

He tilts his head, waiting, his eyes holding me captive.

"I-I'm ..." My mouth like a rusty hinge slowly opens, voice creaking out. "Emilie Prescott. N-nice to meet you."

His hazel eyes root me to the spot, hold me, suspend me. I can't look away, can't break free from the sinew he's woven around my hand, that singular smile knowing he's grasped more than my flesh but my attention as well. This stranger, summoned by the autumn breeze, steals my breath, my words, and in that moment ...

Loose strands of auburn hair rustle around my crimson cheeks.

"Pleasure to make your acquaintance, Miss Prescott. Are you here to call on Mrs. Halle?"

I blink. Open my mouth again. Close it. *Cough*. Yes, that's it! "Yes, Yes, I have these for her."

He lets go of my hand. It's now cold, clammy, gross. My mind clears as I wipe it against my skirt.

"Afraid I'll infect you?"

"No, it's just—"

He smirks. "They should be back any minute. They went to town for a few things. You are welcome to wait."

"I can sit awhile," I say and plant myself in the rocking chair, the bundle of cookies resting in my lap.

"Are those the 'these' you were referring to?" He gestures to the bundle.

"Oh, yes, those, I mean these, yes, these are jumbles. A thank you gift for the Halles. They were kind enough to help us move in the other day."

"How nice. Suppose I can extend their hospitality. Would you like a glass of cold tea? Mrs. Halle made a fresh batch this morning."

"Yes, thank you," I say, briefly meeting his eyes as the flutter—like leaves against the autumn breeze—returns to my stomach.

"I can put those on the table if you want to set them down." He stretches out his hand, bronzed and worn, a natural glove from work.

I hand him the bundle of cookies and he takes them, disappearing into the kitchen. Mr. Byrne is at ease here, like a puzzle piece slotted perfectly into place. Ease that makes me squint with suspicion. I don't remember the Halles mentioning him, a name tossed into the whirlwind of conversation among all the commotion that came with our first day here. Perhaps he is some mysterious relative emerging from the shadows?

Mr. Byrne returns a few minutes later, bearing two glasses of tea and a warm smile with the silent offer. Accepting the glass from him, I avoid touching his hand, remembering the reaction I just experienced. I'm not sure I want to be held like that again.

"Thank you," I say, returning his smile, then averting my gaze.

The creak of the rocking chair changes its tune as he sits next to me. A slurp from his sip of tea. Perhaps he is not a distant relative, but raised with the livestock in the barn.

He clears his throat. "So, you must be the daughter of the new family who moved into the Deardorff house."

I nod. "I assume so. Never personally met them, but I can say the place is beautiful."

Looking back to him, I feel stiff by comparison. Suppose it wouldn't hurt to relax. I lean back in the chair, his eyes watching me—my eyes watching him. *He looks so handsome, hazel eyes dancing with the light, that smile, his chest, those hands ...* The chair going back, back, baaa— "Whoa!" I startle and shift, looking at the tea in the glass, thankful not a drop has spilt.

Did he notice?

"I helped old man Deardorff prune his fruit trees last spring. They should produce good fruit this year."

He must be pretending not to.

I nod, pretending nothing happened as well. "They are doing just that. We will have plenty to harvest."

Stephen sits on the edge of his chair, placing the glass on the table between us. He leans in. I lean back again, but not too far back, not again.

"Where are you from?"

"Virginia," I reply. "It's different here, but I like it so far."

I dare to meet his gaze. The hazel pools have not diminished, still my insides host a whirlpool for my thoughts.

Stephen scoffs. "It's really not all that wonderful but rather a judgmental, opinionated place. You'll see once you're here a while. Everyone knows everything about everyone else." He furrows his brow, the light in his eyes dimming momentarily, like clouds covering the sun. He shifts, sitting back in his chair, opening the space between us.

"If it's terrible here, are you planning to leave someday? Where will you go? Does the western frontier tickle your fancy?" I grin at him, trying to make light of the sudden change in his mood.

Stephen folds his arms, rolls his eyes, and shakes his head.

Did I strike a tender nerve in him?

"You have no idea, do you? I bet the likes of my life never crossed that pretty little head of yours." The sarcasm drips from his lips, the clouds in his eyes darkening with the brewing storm of discontent.

"I guess it didn't." I bristle at his cold gust of words. "Why don't you fill in the details." I cast an equally icy glance his way. The conversation doesn't call for such a storm, but I'll match him with my personal blizzard any day.

"Hey now, no need to get up in arms."

The weather chides us both. A gust of wind blows his dark hair into his eyes. Irritated, he rakes his hand through his dark waves. I pay my own loose ends no mind, but I wonder, *what does his hair feel like?*

Wince. *Did I mean to bite my lip?*

He leans forward, his fingers touching the fabric of my skirt. I shift, moving away from him, his eyes still locked with mine.

"One thing you must know about me, Miss Prescott, is I am direct. You'll always know where I stand." He winks, and a mischievous smile tugs at his mouth.

"I'll remember that," I say, bringing my glass to my lips as I look away.

Stephen sighs, and his chair creaks. My eyes shift back—his presence won't let them stray far. I admire the sharp angles of his jaw, long muscular arms, his shirt tucked beneath the tapered hem of his ... and long strong legs, yes, legs! *He would certainly be a catch for someone. Not me of course, someone else. Has he ever kissed a girl?*

"Anyway, it will take a miracle for me to move out of this town. My parents made it clear; I am to carry on the family farm right here. They are most likely taking applications for my future wife too if you're interested." He gives a lighthearted laugh, yet the seriousness of the statement shines through the facade, clear as a rooster's wake-up call in the morning light.

"Sounds like a secure future for you."

"More like a jail." Stephen's gaze darts from mine. "You wouldn't understand, being a girl and all."

"I completely understand," I say. "Family legacy as one's destiny was the story of my brother's future. Until my father sold the plantation to my uncle, that is. Aaron is still next in line unless they produce a male heir of their own."

"But that's his future, not yours. You don't have to live it."

"Your future is up to you. It can be an honorable position or a prison. You decide."

Stephen swallows hard, blinking, and then he levels me a stern look while saying, "Again, I don't think you understand the gravity of this situation, which is to be expected of a woman. So, I will explain again. My parents have planned my whole life. I don't get to decide. It's that simple. Surely you understand the marriage bit. Why, I bet you are being forced into marriage as we speak."

"Actually, I won't marry for another few years." I smile sweetly, happy to shatter his expectations of me. After all, I know where I stand in the face of society's dictations.

There is pleasure in watching him fight to keep the facade of calm on his face. Cute. His eyes give it away though, no doubt wide with the shock of my audacity. Then he opens his mouth. "No, you can't wait. You'll be a spinster. Who will want you then?"

Stephen's knuckles may be tightening around the chair arms, holding him in place, but my nails are now pressing into the glass I hold in my hands.

"I can and I will, Mr. Byrne. Besides, men marry spinsters all the time, and I'll not sacrifice myself to home and family before I am good and ready—not when I can do good as a teacher come next spring." A butterfly of pride flutters in my chest.

He grunts like the beast he is and asks, "You would rather be a spinster than a happily married woman doing your duty to husband and children?"

I nod, not shying from his glare. My winning this debate depends on it.

"Well, with that attitude you will be a spinster sooner than later. What a waste of a good woman." He sits back in his chair again, as if there is no coming back from his jab.

"If I am such a good woman, as you say, why does age matter? It's just a random number society puts on women. I dare say I'll be like a fine wine, even better later."

Checkmate, Mr. Byrne!

We sit in silence.

Our gazes remain locked, not with the joyous spark of igniting embers, but with the clash of flint against granite. The thrill of our first connection? More like the bitter tang of a green apple, promising sweetness but providing unripe defiance.

It appears with the way the conversation has come and gone with the wind that we are at odds with each other.

The silence grows.

The silence lingers.

This reminds me of the game Henry and I played as kids: Whoever speaks first is the loser. This will be easy. I'm still the winner.

He knows nothing about my stubbornness.

What if he is judging my priorities?

A faint jingle emerges from the distance, rescuing me. I turn to see the Halles and their team of horses arrive with a wagon full of provisions.

The stalemate is over!

The wagon stops near the porch as the children scramble out, the older ones helping the younger.

Mrs. Halle greets me with a wave and asks, "Miss Emilie, what are you doing here?"

"Just stopped by to deliver a 'thank you' of baked goods. Mr. Byrne kept me entertained, more or less, while I waited."

Mrs. Halle smiles and gives a nod. "How nice, did you enjoy each other's company?"

"Oh yes, we had a staring contest, and I won." I flash her a grin, nudging Stephen aside as I step in front of him.

"That has yet to be determined." His voice is low enough for me to hear but not the others. His hands go to my shoulders, his firm grasp moving me aside. From his height alone he casts his eyes down to me, though I'm sure it is intentional. "Miss Prescott, I'm going to be of some actual use and go unload the wagon." As he looks away from me, he adds in greeting, "Mrs. Halle."

"Oh, you're so funny, Mr. Byrne. Ha. Ha." My voice twitters using my best southern belle accent. I look to Mrs. Halle. "Silly boys think muscles solve everything. By all means, Mrs. Halle, let me lend you a hand by taking that baby from you."

"Oh, thank you, Miss Emilie. If you could be a dear and put him down for his nap?" She motions for her eldest daughter. "Jane, show Miss Emilie Robert's crib."

Jane hops down from the wagon and pulls on my sleeve. "This way, Miss Emilie."

Jane's ringlets bounce as she leads the way in quick strides, through the door, around the kitchen table, into the parlor, and into a small room on the left. The darkened room is tightly packed with furniture. It smells of musky sleep, warm and comfortable.

I look at her, and she points to the crib, moving the blankets aside, directing me like a mother who knows her child, except this is her brother.

"Lay him here," she whispers. "He sleeps on his side."

The moment juxtaposes two generations, two sets of hands, weaving the same tapestry of love over this sleeping child. Is this how Jane will be as a mother? Molded at the age of ten?

Gazing back to the sleeping babe, I see his features shimmer in the soft light, impossibly perfect at his miniature scale. Beneath the sheltering layers of blankets, his body radiates a gentle warmth. The velvety down of his hair tickles my skin as I lean closer, entranced by the tiny curl of his fingers against his cheeks. Delicate, feathery lashes fan over his closed eyes and his perfect lips are pursed in a dreamy pout. A tide of tenderness surges through me, washing away every thought except the wonder of this miracle in my arms. The weight of responsibility, once daunting, now effortless as I cradle this darling cherub in a cloud of blankets. Who knew life could bring such awe—

"Miss Emilie!" Mother Jane's harsh whisper is insistent. She pats the crib.

"Sorry, he's adorable."

Jane rolls her eyes. "He's cute when he sleeps—not so much when he wails all night."

She smooths the blankets, a miniature reflection of her mother mirroring a future scene. We both watch him for a moment, holding our breath in anticipation. Satisfied, Jane nods toward the door, tiptoeing out, pulling the fabric of my skirt and me with her. "Come on, he'll wake soon enough."

The farewells linger in the air like the scent of spices, but as the door shuts behind me, a different mood descends. The memory of watching the baby's peaceful slumber flickers in my mind like a fragile flame, momentarily eclipsing the image of Stephen's mocking grin.

As I lead myself and Starlight home my mind goes over that insufferable, handsome, rude, and yet charming miscreant, Stephen Byrne. It's not like he's my type. I mean I would never think to marry him. Not now, not ever. Even if he looked at me under the spell of cupid's arrows and confessed his undying love to me, in that smooth rich deep voice of his ... I sigh in contempt, of course. He is too traditional and headstrong. *He would never make a good husband for me. I'll have a partner and no other, especially not a master.*

Good riddance, my day could have really done without all of this, except for the baby, he was kind of cute. I shake my head and, as if in agreement, Starlight shakes hers too.

I approach my father after dinner dishes are complete. He sits quietly on the porch, taking in the peaceful night air. The crickets serenade us as the sun disappears over the mountains. Father draws thoughtfully on the pipe stem, blowing the stream of smoke from his mouth. His features are relaxed as he stares off into the night.

"Father, can we talk?"

"Mhmm?"

He turns to me with a glint in his eyes and smiles at me as I sit across from him. The pungent, aged, smooth tobacco brings back generations of memories from my former home. The smoke dances between us, encircling us in a protective cloud.

"You wanted to talk?"

"Oh right, um, well you see, I was wanting to know, rather ask, if I can enroll in school in October as I figure it will take a few months to prepare for the teacher's exam in May, and well, you know how I desperately want to follow in Mother's footsteps. And I think we can all agree that it would be wise to start my teaching career before I devote my life to a husband and children ..."

Father nods.

His silence is unnerving. My knee bounces in a frantic beat, being the only way my nerves can escape right now as my words continue to bleat my plea. "... And I can get the details tomorrow if you'd like."

The crickets are deafening, no doubt trying to match the tempo of my foot tapping. I step on my toes to stop my knee from knocking.

Oh, why did I open my big mouth? One would think I would've learned by now not to try and fill the vastness of father's voiceless opinion with my own meaningless prattle. I suck in my bottom lip, nibbling, hoping, praying.

"... Emilie?"

"Yes?" I ask, hearing my voice squeak.

"I asked, what about marriage? Don't you think you will need to take a husband soon?"

"Oh yes, but it will only take me eight months to complete my certification, and you know I am sure I will meet plenty of eligible bachelors, and wouldn't you rather me be married off to somebody who can match the wit you blessed me with? Rather than some old farm boy who resents his family legacy and has no respect for—"

Father puts his hand up before taking his pipe from his mouth. He rubs the bridge of his nose, sighs heavily. "Farm boy aside, though I assure you there is nothing wrong with a man such as myself, what if none of these supposed eligible bachelors you speak of meet your standards or, worse yet, think you too forward and refuse to take you for a wife? Do you fully understand the fate of a spinster?"

"Well—"

"I'm not finished, that was rhetorical. And yes, this old farm boy knows a thing or two about big words and life, and you, my dear Emilie, would do well to listen."

I hear my heart hammering in my chest. I remind myself to breathe.

Father takes a brief puff from his pipe, shaking his head. A few more grey hairs have probably arrived too. "Emilie Kathryn, your mother and I know you will make an excellent teacher."

He falls silent, looking away to gather his thoughts. The wait feels like I am staring down at the raging ocean, unable to move forward or back, my heart a steady thrumming in my ears.

"I understand but—"

His eyes flash at me with annoyance once again. "You don't fully understand the consequences of being a single woman. Society will shun, ostracize, and gossip about you. Your Great-Aunt Hazel, God rest her soul, went through such torture just to be taken advantage of and have a child out of wedlock. She died in childbirth. I won't bear to see it happen to you."

Annoyance dissipates into pain, his eyes moist with Aunt Hazel's memory, or so I imagine.

Father clears his throat, speaking softer now. "Others will not understand why you are going against tradition. Your mother and I love you dearly, but we do not desire for you to waste away under our roof until our dying breath. Our hope for you is to grow to be a happy woman with the wealth of a decent husband and beautiful family. And I know it doesn't seem like it now, but this will fill you with more joy than a classroom full of children."

Blinking, he looks away. Silence and stoicism return to his features.

A strangled sob claws at my throat, trapped like a rabbit in a snare. I bite my lip, holding it. I can't show him I'm weak by crying. My breath stutters in my chest, each inhale a shallow rasp, each exhale a hiss laced with desperation. My eyes burn as the hot molten tears creep forward and melt into pools ready to cascade down burning cheeks.

No welling up. I suck in a breath and with it—a sniffle.

The deafening silence.

Tick-tock, tick-tock.

My throat tightens its grip.

Tick-tock, tick-tock.

I bite my lip again, trying to keep the hot tears from spilling from my eyes.

Father sighs, and I know he doesn't mean to make me cry. I try to keep it in, to hold it in, to—I sniffle again.

"Emilie, we realize you will never be satisfied until you follow your dreams. So, I will let you get your teaching certificate with the—"

"Oh Father, thank you, thank you, I will make you proud you won't regret—"

His hand goes up, stopping me from hugging him just yet.

"With the condition that you will not turn any suitor down, and you will marry as soon as you find a beau."

"Yes, sir!" I say, jumping up like a freed rabbit who just got another chance at life. I throw my arms around him and kiss his cheek, never minding the rough whiskers. "And I am sorry about the 'farm boy' remark."

"Mhmm, now go get ready for bed." He gives me a quick squeeze back and releases me, adding, "and tell your mother I want to speak with her when she is done with her knitting row."

The porch floorboards sing with a familiar creak as the one true mistress of his heart steps out of their abode, the echo of her soles muffled by the encroaching heavy blackness of twilight. Jacob sits on the swing; its rhythmic *moan—groan—moan—groan* seems to mock his growing frustration. His hair, usually meticulously combed, lies in windswept disarray, a whisper of the battle he just experienced with his strong-willed daughter. The pipe, his constant companion, lies abandoned on the side table, cold and forgotten.

How do we as parents set our tiny lioness loose in the jungle, roar echoing in the face of societal expectations? Emilie, their brave, brilliant child, armed with nothing but her intelligence and audacity. None of it would shield her from the cold demands, the suffocating rules, the ... cages society builds around every woman. Her vibrant life, brimming with hope, could easily be bruised, tarnished, perhaps even extinguished in a single, brutal encounter.

The creak of the porch boards announce she finished her knitting. His heart brightens with anticipation of their reunion.

She pauses before the swing. His eyes drift from the tips of her boots to her wondrous form to the sparkle of starlight carried in her gaze, which reigns from above, the unspoken questions swirling in their depths like leaves caught in an autumn wind. The crease in her brow strums the notes of concern in her expression. Does her heart thrum with ache for him too? Is he no longer the handsome capable rogue her dreams prompted her to venture off with? Is he just a farm boy with the strain of confrontation etched into his age lines as he tries to figure out women? Again?

"May I sit?" she asks, her voice caressing him. The question, a mere formality, holds a universe of unspoken emotions. He nods, his own voice caught up in the thickness of unspoken trepidation. Still, he opens his arm to her offering a silent haven waiting to embrace her.

Julia settles beside him, the warmth of her body seeping into the chill of his anxiety, her head resting in the familiar crook of his shoulder, his worn work shirt nuzzling her cheek. His kiss on the top of her head is as soft as butterfly wings, despite his sigh that follows, carrying the weight of a whole oak forest.

"That bad, hmm?" Julia reaches for his hand, her fingers intertwining with his, offering the silent strength he desperately needs.

"About as we both expected." His voice rasps, rough from the emotion of the battle. "She's determined to teach. How do we say no to that?" He stares down into pools of blue that know the tides of a woman better than he ever will. "She's no longer a baby who fits within the crook of my arm, as light as a feather, helpless with her tiny hand around my finger, that I can hold ... protect, she's"— he clears his throat—"independent, and I don't know where I went wrong but—she doesn't like farm boys."

"What?" his wife asks, clearly as confused as he is.

"She doesn't like farm boys."

Jacob feels her head shift against him, a nuzzle with each shake in what seems to him as disbelief as she suffocates a laugh before saying, "She is also young, and young women don't know what they want." Her finger pokes at his chest. "And that includes farm boys." The prod of her pointed finger turns into a gentle pat. "However, once she develops friendships here, she'll see her friends marry, have children, set up homes, and she'll want that too."

Jacob looks down at his wife, doubt in his eyes.

"I promise she's going to want that for herself, Jacob." Julia smiles at him and bites her bottom lip. He notices the mischievous glint and has half a mind to make her spill her suppressed giggles with a tickle when she says, "Farm boys, hmm?"

He doesn't bite, rather he returns the question. "Is that what happened to you, Julia?" The coolness in his earth-brown eyes searches for warmth in her sky-blue hues. Flecks of concern sit on the surface, waiting to be watered down by what he can figure as nothing more than a woman's logic. "Did you marry me because everyone else was getting married, and this lowly farm boy was all that was left?"

Julia playfully nudges him, and the giggle spills out without the prompting of tickling digits.

He arches a brow waiting for her giggles to subside.

"No, I married you because you are a great catch and easy to look at. The farm boy just meant you can handle your own."

A touch of a smile finally graces his lips, but the concern in his eyes has yet to dissolve into joy. "And did you ever regret leaving your teaching job?"

Squeezing his hand, she nuzzles deeper into his shoulder. "Honestly, Jacob, you never gave me a chance to miss anything. When I married you, sure, it took a while to adjust to plantation life, as expected, but our life became filled with children and laughter. How could I ever regret the blessings our marriage has brought to us through our love?"

Jacob feels his chest rumble with the satisfaction of a low chuckle. He kisses her forehead and pulls her closer to ward off the chill of the night air.

"What are you thinking?" Julia asks.

"I think our daughter might need help to find a husband, and I am just the farm boy to do it." Jacob relaxes as this realization calms his last taut nerve, but then Julia pushes away from him, interrupting their warm connection, raising an invisible wall of cold between them while her eyes bore into his.

"Ha, you think she is stubborn now? She'll not tolerate an arranged marriage. No, Jacob, we will do no such thing." Her pointer finger stabs at his chest with the last three words, her eyes flashing a protective glint of defiance that he knows is all her own.

At this he can't help but smile. "All right," he says, submitting to her whims, as he requests she does the same for him. Arms still enfolded around her, he pulls her back to him, back into their closeness, requesting her comfort once again.

"You underestimate me. Of course, she will think it's her idea. All we need to do is make acquaintances available. And I already have someone in mind who I believe is quite available," says Jacob.

He notices his wife arching a brow before she snuggles up against him, her delicate hand to his beating heart, right where she belongs.

"If you say so."

Branching Out

NOVEMBER 1860
GETTYSBURG PENNSYLVANIA

The low hum of a debate vibrates through the warmed kitchen at breakfast. The smell of sizzling bacon, peppery fried potatoes, and the earthiness of fresh coffee is a strange counterpoint of comfort to the discussion of discontent that looms over the Prescott table. Perhaps I should not round the corner. Perhaps I should head straight for the door, so I can breathe in the fresh air of sweet liberty out on the porch and go about my business without a care. Perhaps I should realize I do not have either of those options because as I pass the threshold to the kitchen, I cannot help but see out of the corner of my eye the newspapers spread across the table, and likewise my curiosity cannot help but pull me into the maelstrom of a fight.

The headlines, stark black print against the worn wood of the farm table, scream defiance. They are the cause of discord for the Prescott men and announce that Lincoln and Douglas have won the election.

"Well, that is going to upset Virginia and all the Southern states," Father comments with a cup of coffee in hand.

"I know what's not upsetting ..." I say. No one acknowledges me, but I'll wait.

"Upset? Father, this is going to cause secession all over the South! This is the worst outcome this country could hope for." Aaron fixes his eyes back to the tiny print.

"I am certainly hopeful that this test—" I begin again.

"Can you imagine the look on Uncle William's face this morning? Won't surprise me one bit if he doesn't have a fit of apoplexy," says Henry, stifling a chuckle. "Poor Aunt Jenny."

Covering my mouth to mask a snort, I bite my cheek to keep my composure in check before my eyes dart toward my mother. Her face is hard with disappointment. Her glare is aimed in Henry's direction. The words to follow are only natural. "Henry Arthur, what a terrible thing to say."

Several sets of hands pass the bacon around the table as I take my seat, spread jam on my toast, and enjoy my first bite.

"Henry, if you please, as I was saying"—Aaron picks up a piece of bacon and uses it as a classroom pointer, to further his case—"Lincoln is not Southern friendly; he's going to have to work to get the South to go along with his objectives."

"Well, my objective is passing this—" I begin again.

Aaron shoots a glare at me. "Em, please."

How dare he reprimand me!

Narrowing my eyes at Aaron, a knot sours the strawberry preserves on my tongue.

This family! I wonder what normal families talk about. My annoyance traverses through the punctuated beat of my tapping fingers on the tabletop.

Aaron continues, "His speeches are beautifully spoken. On one hand he speaks of a prosperous nation, strong economy, and internal improvements. Then he simultaneously speaks of containing the expansion of slavery and preserving the Union."

"How is he going to do that if the South secedes?" asks Henry, leaning forward, drawn in by Aaron's eloquent speech.

I interject with a heavy sigh. *Am I invisible here? I saw them glance at me. They won't ignore me forever.*

"Aaron," Mother says, "Mr. Lincoln knows the institution of slavery cannot go on."

"I agree, Mother, but farmers can't simply just free them. It is irresponsible—the farms will lose production, and we will have a whole population of homeless, who do not have a proper education to prosper in society."

"Speaking of education, today is the day!" I announce over the conversational buzz. "I am taking the teacher's exam!"

All eyes turn to me.

Finally!

Father sets down his cup.

Mother smiles back at me, a glint of pride in her eyes.

Aaron is still annoyed by my interruption.

Henry clears his throat, then sets down his half eaten jellied toast. "You are really going through with it? Why do you dream of teaching a classroom of unruly brats?" His eyes bore into mine; a question mark etches its way into his raised brow, and that smirk—I take a deep breath.

"It's what I've always wanted, you know that."

"Why? Why can't you find a husband and hatch your own brood to teach? Just like Ma educated us." Henry's smirk still lingers.

"I'm not a chicken, Henry! The proper term is children. You'd know that if you finished school."

"I work with my hands, it's good and honest. I don't need schooling."

"Henry!" Mother shoots another glare his way.

"I mean, I have—well, Ma taught me all I need to know to raise a family just fine."

Father clears his throat.

Henry's face flushes red.

"Well, um, they both educated me just fine." He clears his throat and carries on. "Honestly, you don't need all this learning to have a good life. But never mind me, Em, it's you who is making the mistake here." Alas, he rises from the table to take his leave, no doubt preparing to do some monotonous task like feeding the chickens.

Am I the lone hen left to protect the coop filled with my hopes and dreams from the lurking coyotes? Are they abandoning me for my determination?

My brother's traditional views aren't contested by anyone else at this table.

A flood of color stains my cheeks, my palms grow clammy, my gut twists in knots, and the only sound for my ears to contend with is my pounding heart. Deep breaths, be a—*Nope!*

"How narrow minded of you, Henry!" I fire back in anger, stamping out his dismissal. "As you can see, I have no prospects for marriage. I need to help support this family. Teaching offers me that." My fingers twitch with irritation, inching closer to the salt cellar sitting in front of my plate.

Henry pauses in his escape from the table. Our eyes not only match but meet head on. "You have no prospects for marriage because you are stubborn and opinionated. Men are afraid to

77

approach you." His blunt words seek to bludgeon my resolve, that smirk of his makes it feel like our discussion is child's play to him.

"Henry! Be kind." Mother's reprimand falls on deaf ears.

The soft *thunk* of Aaron's coffee cup is heard before he clears his own throat. "What Henry is trying to say, dear sister, is that men are short of temper with smart, strong women such as yourself. Therefore, they do not have the patience with that kind of thing, and a woman must learn her place in a relationship for the relationship to be a success—a lesson you have yet to grasp."

I flinch, trying to shake the words ricocheting in my brain. *Why? I thought they—I thought at least Aaron of all people—supported me.*

Feeling my resolve and self-worth shatter like a mirror into a million pieces, I blink back the tears creeping over the edges of my eyes.

"I—I can't believe you just said that, Aaron." Gulping back the emotion, my tongue as dry as cotton, I say, "I expect that from him, but you?"

I bite my lip and hold back the pain as I try to reach, stretch, and grasp for the purpose that threads my dreams. Then I say, "An intelligent woman is not a curse, and I will show you all what I am made of."

My chair shrieks across the floor, mocking what my vocal cords hold within. I adorn my coat, settle my heavy bag of books on my shoulder, and let the slamming of the front door break the silence. Let them have their wall of unvoiced disappointment. I do not need their wishes for luck. I do not need them telling me that what I am capable of is impossible.

I do not need them, though I yearn for their faith in me, if not my dreams—dreams that now burn brighter than their disapproval. I will teach.

Watching the schoolyard fill with children, each of them paired off into groups with like minds for them to talk, chase, and play together, I sit on my and Sarah's meeting bench, waiting for my other half to arrive. She is my beacon of light and hope from the harsh reality of my family's abandonment this morning.

The cluster of schoolteachers gather, a band, a private club with a status above my own. Their eyes survey the playground, talking amongst themselves before entering the school to prepare their classrooms for the day. One day, I will be their equal; I will hold their status. Just two more tests, and I will have access to their exclusive realm. This sight heals the wounds inflicted by my brothers' words.

"Are you ready for the exam?"

I jump and shift to see the woman who sits beside me. Sunlight catches Sarah's hair, turning it into a halo of shimmering gold, spun tight into braids and gathered up into a bun. The updo looks like a child's attempt to appear older, but I can't fault her. Her eyes, bright and clear as the sky, sparkle with eternal laughter and help eclipse the faint indentation of a pox mark on her cheek. It sits like a whisper, a tiny shadow in the sunshine of her smile, the scar of a past she has endured. No, not a child. A young woman, who, like me, seeks to stand on her own.

My best friend's words spin me out of my thoughts as she plops herself beside me on the bench and lets out a giggle at my shock. "I hope you snap out of whatever this is before we sit for the exam. Then again, studied all night I did, what if I can't stay awake?"

I watch her fight back a contagious yawn and it's my turn to laugh. It's good to see her. "If you had started studying weeks ago like me, you wouldn't have to stay up all night."

"Yes, I know, but I was busy with—do you remember that boy I told you about?"

"William?"

"No."

"Frank?"

"Emilie!"

"What? You have a new crush nearly every week," I say with a tease.

"I meant Thomas!"

"Oh yes, that one. What about him?"

"Well …" Sarah bites her bottom lip and I wait for what feels like eternity for her to spit something, anything out.

"Well?"

"Well, he said hello to me last Sunday at services." She squeals and claps a hand over her mouth, eyes darting for listeners before she carries on. "Can you believe it, he finally sees me!"

"Took him long enough. I was starting to think he was blind."

My family could learn a thing or two from me on how to support someone.

Sarah sighs. "Oh Emilie, I'm lucky. We both know I'm a ghost fading into the background. My mother says so every day. Besides, you're the pretty one with your big brown eyes, red hair, and winning personality." Her shoulders slump, and her pink mouth forms into a pout. It reminds me of my many encounters with first graders who don't get their way.

My hand reaches out and rests atop hers. "Sarah, as thankful as I am for the compliment, and ever wishing you weren't the only one to think such—didn't I tell you from the first day we met, other peoples' opinions shouldn't matter? You're a whole person, with a great personality, and smart, too, Sarah. If you weren't, I don't think we would be the best of friends. Any man who doesn't want that is a fool."

"Actually, I don't think you said that. I think I told you that the day we met just over there." Sarah points to the willow tree in the corner of the schoolyard. "If I remember correctly, you were sitting by yourself and worried you wouldn't make friends."

"And look where we are now. So, try taking your own advice, hmm?"

Her arms open and sweep me up into a hug, "Oh Emilie, we are more than study partners, both working toward the goal of teaching this brood. Aren't we?"

I laugh and hug her back, my eyes scouring the schoolyard taking note of children pulling each other's hair, eating bugs, and doing other disturbing acts that I am told stem from innocence. "Of course we are, and who knows, one day we might graduate to chasing each other with bugs, making us the purest of playground friends."

We laugh again, releasing not only each other, but the worries of what is to come with the exam. Sarah carries on, talking about Thomas, talking about teaching, talking about anything and everything. She is a bubbly bright package, decorated with colorful fabrics and matching bows, delivering her quirks and all their joy directly to my heart. Just what I need today!

One of the teachers, Mr. Warner, appears at the door. He reaches up and pulls the rope to summon the students to class.

CLING-CLANG-CLING-CLANG!

"Look at him." Sarah's eyes rest on him, and a smile warms her face.

"Mr. Warner? Looks the same as always."

"No, but he is handsome." Sarah steadies herself from a feigned swoon. "Do you think he would catch me?"

"Ah, looks like I need to pen a note. Something along the lines of, 'Well, Thomas, looks like your week is up early,'" I say, smiling over at her after throwing the lifeline to her fleeting heart.

"But ..."

"But what about Thomas?" I remind her. Sarah's head snaps back to me.

"Well, of course, I still fancy Thomas. That's not what I meant! Did I tell you ..."

"Tell me later, Sarah 'Lovelorn' Williams. We are going to be tardy for class."

At noon, Sarah and I meet in an empty classroom.

Mrs. Irwin blows in with her arms full of ruffling papers. Her black dress covers her from wrist to ankle, and the spectacles perched across her beaked nose convey her as a strict disciplinarian. However, despite her firm approach with her students, she does give way to her kind heart when she feels a softer guiding hand is necessary. This allows her to teach both remedial and teacher apprentice classes.

"Ladies, I am so happy we made it this far. Are you ready for the exam?" Mrs. Irwin smiles at both of us, a quiet reminder we are her prized students, blessed not only with sharp wit but talent.

"Yes, as ready as"—Sarah yawns before she can finish—"can be."

"Did you study last minute, Miss Williams?"

Sarah looks down, averting her eyes from our all-knowing seer.

"I will take that as a yes." Mrs. Irwin turns, setting her sights on me. "Miss Prescott, I know you are prepared."

"Well ..." I swallow hard, my mind seems to empty of everything

I so carefully tucked inside the nooks and crannies over the weeks. My mouth feels like cracked soil during a drought, while my heart thrums a chorus of beguiling *what ifs* over and over again.

"On second thought—maybe if we could—you know, go over it one more time?" I croak.

Sarah looks at me, mouth open, eyes wide. "Emilie Prescott, if you are not prepared then I'm afraid, my dear friend, we are all doomed. Not just me, but the many hopeful students to come to this classroom with the aspiring dream of becoming a beacon of—"

"Yes, Miss Williams, I dare say we and all future generations understand the detriment of your statement. Miss Prescott, take a deep breath, I'm sure you will do just fine."

I take a deep breath and exhale as Mrs. Irwin gives out the exams. *If the exam were on soliloquies, I dare say Sarah has got it.* I stare at the back of the booklet set down before me. But it doesn't have soliloquies, it has reading assessments, questions that beg in-depth answers guided by logic, and equations of various difficulties.

"All right ladies, you have three hours to complete this test."

My nerves begin jumping, and I worry my penmanship will look messy. Fingers wrap around my pencil; I feel the wood bend under my grip ...

Mrs. Irwin looks at her watch. "You may begin."

Turning the pages over, I flip through them ... grammar, arithmetic, US history, orthography, and geography. I set the pencil down, wipe my sweaty palms on my skirt, take a deep breath ...

Wait, I don't know any of these questions.

Somewhere reason answers—*maybe you should read them first.*

The mantel clock pushes me to hurry with each tick, every tock leading me to the next question.

I turn the page. I feel better breezing through the grammar section ...

Next page US History, the questions are ticked off one by one ...

Give the epochs into which US History is divided ...

Name the events connected with the following dates: 1607, 1620, 1800, and 1849 ...

Next page Arithmetic ...

Hurry, you are running out of time.

Looking to the clock, my next exhale comes in relief—*No, I have time, plenty of time.*

A wagon box is 2 feet deep, 10 feet long, and 3 feet wide. How many bushels of wheat will it hold?

Counting again ...

Six more problems like this? Why can't they give me straight numbers?

Name and define the Fundamental Rules of Arithmetic.

Flipping the page—Geography, this one is easy.

My head begins to throb as I reach the last page—Orthography.

I am ten questions from the end, the clock says I have forty-five minutes to answer ten questions ...

What is meant by the following: Alphabet, phonetic orthography, etymology, syllabication?

What is the following, and give examples of each: trigraph, subvocals, diphthong, cognate letter, lingual?

I don't know how I did it, perhaps a remarkable leap of faith, but I finish all ten questions with seven minutes to spare. Bleary-eyed, I look up to see Mrs. Irwin, biting her lip and watching the clock as the last of the time ticks by. My gaze shifts over to my neighbor, Sarah, who is still deep within the questions of her test. I then stare down once more at my own.

There is still time remaining. What if what I have isn't good enough? Maybe I should change question two on page five? But what if I don't get it changed in time?

"Time!" Mrs. Irwin announces with perhaps a bit too much excitement as her hands clap together.

I set the pencil down, and relief washes through me, leaving my body an empty vessel of exhaustion. *What do I do now?* I spent the last several months focusing on my studies, living, breathing, eating, and sleeping all of this.

"Miss Prescott." Mrs. Irwin's voice comes to me despite the doubt clouding my mind.

I look up to see she is motioning me to come to her, so being the dutiful pupil I am, I stand, walk toward her desk clutching the pages in my hand, and try to give them to her—

A tug ... A pull ...

"I can't seem to let it go, Mrs. Irwin," I say.

She smiles, picks up a book from her desk, leans over and drops it over my foot. My eyes widen and I go to catch it, letting go of my exam in the process.

"You're not the first one, Miss Prescott," Mrs. Irwin says, her fingers already sifting through the pages with a curious and yet quizzical eye from behind those spectacles. "Hmm ... Yes ... How do you think you did?"

"I, well, maybe ... I could ask the same of you, Mrs. Irwin," I say. All her hemming is making me nervous. "Perhaps I can go over my answers once more?"

"Perhaps you should have done that in those last few minutes you had to spare. Never mind, though. It won't do any good to change things now. I know you did your best."

I nod. "I did—I know I did, I just, well, I just hope it is enough."

"All right then. Go home, rest, and be proud of your accomplishments today. I know I am proud of you."

My heart warms with my teacher's vote of confidence. "Thank you, Mrs. Irwin."

But her attention is beyond me; through her spectacles, she is now looking at Sarah still trying to fill in answers while scrambling through the pages of her exam. "Miss Williams, your test?"

"Five more minutes! I'm almost done with this one!"

"Miss Williams, you've already had the five minutes it took for me to get Miss Prescott's exam." Mrs. Irwin motions to the door, sending me away.

Stepping out of the classroom, the halls are vacant of students and teachers. Everyone left an hour ago. Outside a swing moves, silent in the wind from my window view, though I suppose the chains creak for no one but God alone to hear.

I head down the stairs, each step an echo. I step out into the school yard and, sure enough, hear the swing's groan and moan. Perhaps it reflects my anxiety or my exhaustion. I cannot imagine the life of a swing, never seeing a smiling face, only the backside of people despite the joy it brings.

Turning out of the schoolyard and walking down the block and a half to the boarding stable, I'm greeted by my chestnut friend who gives a soft nicker, and nuzzles my face, my ear, my neck, that twitching fuzzy lip no doubt searching for a treat.

"I don't have anything for you yet, Starlight," I say as the groom brings out the tack.

She pushes me with her head, her silent demand wondering no doubt if "yet" means "now."

"That's my fault, Miss Prescott. You see I got some sugar mints. Mr. Perry's new recipe he wants folks to try out. I'm not big on them, but the horses love them. Get jealous if one gets them but the other doesn't. Here's a bushel for you to take, and spread the word, would you? I know Mr. Perry would be thankful."

"I see." I pull one of the treats out while he tacks Starlight up, and her ears immediately prick forward with that fuzzy upper lip of hers wiggling for the sweet I have in store for her. It doesn't take long for her to crunch down on it and ask for more, one head bump, two head bumps.

"You can have another when we get home!"

A nicker of a plea is her response.

Just before reaching the center of town, it dawns on me. I better pick up another writing tablet and some more pencils. Next week's lessons promise a challenge in English and geography. Tying Starlight to the post outside the Boyer & Sons, up two steps and through the door, the jingle of the bell announces my arrival with the same song as my first time here.

Mr. and Mrs. Boyer look to the door.

"Good day," I say. "I would like to purchase a writing tablet and two pencils, please."

Mr. Boyer chimes in, with a happy song in his deep baritone voice, deeper than the bell on the door, "Let me get those for you."

This leaves me and Mrs. Boyer looking at each other.

I shift my weight from one foot to the other.

"Have you and your family settled in all right?" Mrs. Boyer asks.

"Yes, ma'am, everything is going well. We are enjoying the hospitality of Gettysburg, new friends, and neighbors."

The room quiets, she and I looking at each other, her face unreadable. *Is she still judging me?* Stephen's warning ripples through my thoughts: *This place is judgmental and small, just you wait ...*

"I see you have a lovely selection of fabric," I say, gesturing to the bolts of cloth behind her.

"There is a sale on muslin this week," Mrs. Boyer offers, her hands clasped in front of her with an amenable enough smile for customer service. "I will be happy to show you." But her eyes, what do those overcast blues show? I cannot quite tell.

"I would love to look around, but no time today. How long is the sale?" I ask.

Mr. Boyer interrupts, "I have what you need right here. Let me add that up for you. Shall I add a paper, we just got these in."

"No, thank you. My father said he will pick one up later today."

Mr. Boyer arches an eyebrow at me. "All right then, pleasant day, miss."

"Pleasant day to both of you." I smile, turning to take my leave. At the door I turn back to see Mrs. Boyer, her voice speaking low to her husband, overcast blues eyes still watching me.

A sense of relief washes over me as I step out into the street. My first encounter with Mrs. Boyer may have been a bad day for her, but still, the looks she gives me are quite unnerving, to say the least. Securing my supplies in a small pack behind Starlight's saddle, I ready myself to go home. As I turn, I hear my name, rather urgent. I hear it again. Searching the street, filled with other wagons, riders, and walkers, in the distance, a wagon rumbles toward me. Father is waving at me. Someone is seated next to him, but who is—he? I sigh but wait for them.

"Did you pick up the newspaper?" he calls to me, slowing the wagon.

Starlight's fuzzy upper lip butts in thinking that because we have stopped—I push her away. "No sir, do you want me to go back?"

My eyes dart to the man beside him; he is about my father's height as they sit shoulder to shoulder in the seat. Each stolen glance sparks a tiny flicker of excitement—he's slim yet muscular, his arms are defined, shoulders strong. Father drones on, and my glances last a bit longer—a farm boy—his tanned hands, brim pulled down covering his eyes. Brown, hazel, evergreen hues? I surmise.

I see you—handsome man. I feel you watching me. Show me what's under that brim.

"... so, I promised Mr. Marsh a ride home today. We don't want him or us to be late for dinner."

My mind slips back to breakfast. *I am not sure I want to return to the table of damnation, though maybe they will apologize.*

"Emilie, are you listening to me?" Father's voice rumbles like a storm cloud.

"Yes, sir, I am going to pick up a paper and meet you at home, right?"

"No, wait yes, but—I want to introduce you to Mr. Marsh first." Father's big hand folds over the shoulder of the man who I presume to be Mr. Marsh.

"My apologies, it has been a long day," I say and provide a polite nod.

"Now that I have your undivided attention. Mr. Marsh, this

is my daughter Emilie. Emilie Kathryn Prescott. Emilie, this is Mr. Thaddeus Marsh. He works with me at the carriage factory."

"I see. Well, if we are using full names, I have no doubt my father has shared with you all my secrets, Mr. Marsh, but that aside, the pleasure is mine."

Did my father see the hint of a glare from me, or is this what Mother meant when she said men could be dense?

Mr. Marsh removes his hat to reveal a smile, a slow bloom ending with the accompaniment of his sapphire eyes, deep pools shimmering with the remainder of sunlight, holding me captive—*Is my mouth hanging open? I think my mouth is hanging open.* I close it, square my shoulders. *Not today.* My hands make momentary fists as I glance at my father, who's grinning as if he's already won our little argument.

"Pleasure to meet you, Miss Prescott."

My eyes draw back over to Mr. Marsh, to Thatcher? Thaniel? What was his name? Who cares? His grin makes his face light up, his wink a playful gesture of fun.

I smile back but then remember my promise to myself and tame my features to that proper young woman. "Mr. Marsh, pleasure to make your acquaintance."

"I hope to see you again soon." The deep timbre of his voice envelops me like my favorite quilt, warm, inviting, secure.

No! I refuse. I grit my teeth, take a deep breath, and smile in a fashion that is unlike a hungry predator. "Until next time, then."

Father's cough and his voice intrude before I feel the haunting anxiety of having made myself a fool. "So, I will see you at home then?"

"Agreed." I swallow hard and watch as he turns the wagon toward home, leaving me to return to the store to retrieve the newspaper, and contend with a strange emptiness within my soul.

It's hunger, or exhaustion, not him, that would be ridiculous, I chide myself.

Starlight's furry lip tickles my cheek. "Does this look like home to you, my friend?"

Her muzzle bumps against me as if to say *yes*.

"You're just as bad as Father. You'll have to wait, just like him."

After drudging back into the store I return to Starlight, sigh, and mount up again.

Back on the road, I am left to my thoughts. Random test questions flit through my mind, but it is Mr. Marsh and those sapphire eyes who invade my solitude more than anyone or anything else. *I must be mistaken, I met him for two minutes. There is no way I can be drawn to him. It is completely impractical ... but he saw me.*

Starlight shakes her head, picking up her pace to a trot, pulling me out of my thoughts as she bounces me into the present.

"Looks like you have some pent-up energy, or you're looking forward to that treat—"

Before I have time to survey the road ahead, we're off! Thankfully, the ground is smooth, straight, and vacant, and the run is safe for both of us as I rise in the saddle to meet her strides. My trainer Limerick's voice reminds me: *When you run, you run together, be one with your horse.* The echoes from long ago feel as fond and warm as the majestic animal that stretches out beneath me.

Without time to unpin my hat and secure it to the saddle, much less test my footing in the stirrups, I feel all sense of proper decorum unravel as the winds of freedom sweep over us. My copper hair matches Starlight's mane; my skirts catch within the playful breeze, and as we sail forward down the empty road, the wind causes the layers to billow around me and expose my legs.

Ah yes!

I rise within a cloud of fabric while my heartbeat races with excitement to meet Starlight's thunderous hooves. Power rests beneath me, control resides at my fingertips, and I am giddy with happiness as my worries of proper decorum are blown away. If this is what liberty feels like, I want it for the rest of my days!

A frown etches deep lines into Mr. Locher's forehead. Stephen watches the old man read the small print, the newspaper inches from his nose. It's only proper that Stephen visits with the old codger for a few minutes before heading home after a long day of fixing the aging neighbor's fences. As he waits for Mr. Locher to either finish his reading or go blind, whichever comes first, he plays with a long stalk of grass between his fingers, enjoying the last of the greenery before the snow begins to fall.

Moments crawl into minutes, and at last Stephen clears his throat. "What's the news?"

The old man grumbles to himself. Stephen ties a knot into a blade of grass and hopes Mr. Locher is capable of more.

"Bah! What is this world coming to? If those darn fools are dead set on fighting—well then, let them kill themselves." Mr. Locher crumples the paper, and finally bothers to set his eyes on Stephen, who at this point regrets saying anything at all.

"I'll tell you something, boy. If you get it in your head that war is an adventure, come chat with me awhile. I'll tell ya what it's really like." He punctuates the statement with a wag of his crooked bony finger, aged by hard work and time, but never war—not unless he came fighting out of the crib, or so Stephen wagers.

"Is that before the time you had tea with George Washington, or after the time where you threw said tea into the harbor?" asks Stephen with a smirk.

Mr. Locher glares at him. "Not that old, but I know a thing or two, now you listen here. Fight'n isn't worth nothin'. Politicians will keep on arguing and young men will lose their lives over nothin'. Don't think for one minute it is worth anythin', it's a recruiter's job to sell lies!"

Stephen's foot dangles off the edge of the porch as his back leans against the column. "Is that what you told the governor of South Carolina?"

The dirty look Stephen expects from Mr. Locher never comes, and Stephen's eyes follow the man's dusty brown gaze with his own questionable "why" furrowed into his brow.

Both now watch the road. The weather is sunny. No wind means dust devils are unlikely, yet the sound of horse's hooves beats a tiny cloud into view on the horizon.

Stephen watches and waits.

The whirlwind of dirt and fall's debris grows into a storm as the rider closes the short distance from the drive. Someone is running hard and fast.

"It must be the Halle boy racing his father's horses again," Stephen interprets the sound for the aging Mr. Locher.

"That boy has no common sense. Wait 'til I tell his Pa about his recklessness."

Stephen presses off the column, standing upright, and then takes a few steps toward the road while keeping his boots on the old porch boards. His hand is to his forehead, blocking out the late day sun. "Then again, I don't recall any of the Halle boys taking to wearing skirts."

"Skirts? Boys are now wearing skirts!"

The rider flies past, long auburn hair flowing behind her like streamers in the wind. No more than a puff of fabric surrounds the horse's middle, where pants and boots should be. Yet she rides with experience astride an animal twice her size.

Stephen smiles. *Miss Prescott, what other talents do you possess?*

"Yeah, and they got long hair with ribbons in them too. Boy, I tell you what is this world coming to? Might need to go to war to escape becoming a housewife, if it comes to that."

Stephen hears Mr. Locher stand up, though he's not sure if it is the old man or the rocking chair that groans more.

"Let me see … Boy, that ain't a man, that's a woman!"

"Try telling her that. She's the Prescott girl, from the family living in the old Deardorff place. Not sure how they do things in the South, but I reckon you won't find a woman raised around here with that kind of mouth or position on a horse."

Gooseflesh rises on Stephen's skin, followed by a wave of excitement. She haunts him in his waking thoughts and visits him in his sleeping dreams. Her charisma is enchanting, as if she casts a spell upon him. Perhaps she is more than a woman … a beguiling fairy? The thought of her floods him with ideas of how he can capture her independence and tame her to become a proper wife. His wife.

"Can't say I've met them," says Mr. Locher.

"Just wait until you do. She's rather enchanting, witty, educated—" Stephen's cheeks hurt from the smile stretching his lips. The thought of her does that to him.

"You got the grin of a fool if I ever saw one. You should know your parents would never approve of something like that." Mr.

Locher's warning is like a pebble in his shoe, annoying and painful to hear, but also easy to discard.

"But she ..." Stephen sighs as his mood slips behind a mask of masculine composure. His father's words echo in his head. *You don't know what is best for you. A young man must maintain tradition and marry a good woman to run this farm successfully. I didn't break my back to watch this place fall to shambles under your care. We have a reputation to uphold!*

However, his words are not so easy to hold back. "But what about what I want? Shouldn't being a free man in a country that stands for liberty and justice for all provide me with the right to choose my own wife?"

Mr. Locher shakes his head. "And when you are a man you will have that right. But until then, be wise and take your parents' advice."

"But by law I am a man!"

Their eyes meet. Generations of wisdom meet two decades of defiance, each wanting to let go of this painful struggle— man vs. boy, wisdom vs. whim. In one long moment of silence, they retreat and look away, each deciding the subject best be left alone for now. Stephen doesn't need another father and Mr. Locher's companionship deserves more respect than where this argument will lead them.

"Law don't make a man. Coming back next week?"

"Yes, how about Tuesday? We'll finish the back fence."

"That'll be fine. I got to get inside, the missus is waiting with the dinner." The smell of fried potatoes and ham reminds Stephen he has his own dinner waiting at home for him.

"Next Tuesday it is, Mr. Locher. See you then."

The walk home allows him time to think, to ruminate on her. *How does a man even woo a woman like her? A woman who doesn't think she needs me, a woman who is too stubborn to admit to the error of her ways. Her parents? No, surely by now if they had any control over her, they would have scrubbed her pretty little head of those silly notions, right? What kind of woman isn't interested in love? What kind of woman chooses a career over marriage? What kind of woman loses her hat to the wind in a mad dash on a stunning horse, racing as one without a care?*

Stephen picks up the hat and dusts it off. Emilie Prescott is an enigma, a riddle, a mystery, without a box. I just have to solve her, to figure her out, tame her chaotic energy, and make her see she is missing out.

New Friends

THE TIME TO MAKE FRIENDS IS BEFORE YOU NEED THEM.
~PROVERB

DECEMBER 1860
GETTYSBURG, PENNSYVANIA

What an honor! How exciting—to be included in the Teacher's Tea Party at Sallie's house today. Sarah and I accepted our invitations on Wednesday, and we haven't stopped talking about it ever since. Standing in front of the mirror, I recheck my outfit. The cold chill of the morning gives way to the warmth of flannel petticoats layered under a wool green and gray checked skirt with a matching top.

All I need now is ... searching through the wooden chest at the foot of my bed—

Nope ... How about under the bed? ... Still, no ... Tucked away in a drawer? The old, wooded dresser resists my pulls on its brass handles, and screeches open only after a harder tug. There it is—one matching gray shawl. *Perfect!*

I check my hair one more time. A loose strand of auburn falls on the back of my neck, pins stick out here and there like sticks and twigs, forcing my frizzy bits into place and becoming no more than tiny flags of surrender. It's times like this I really miss Lucy. She always made me feel beautiful. She understands my hair and how to tame it with the pins, but more than that, I just miss her.

I stare at myself in the mirror. Hands smoothing over my wool skirt. A practiced smile. A practiced curtsey? I teeter more than I totter. Perhaps not. I sigh.

Will the new teachers accept me?

How do I best impress those who have known each other since their grade school days?

My fingers have already taken to playing with the pleats as I stand there, and I stop if only to wonder how Mother's voice chides me even when she is not around.

One day I will not be the schoolgirl who plays with the pleats in her dress, but a respectable teacher, or so I hope. I dream of the days where my status will be elevated to these women I will have tea with—when we can survey the playground, chat among ourselves, and prepare classrooms, as a united front, as the leaders of generations to come.

I am getting there, but I better get to the kitchen before I am late. On my way, I pick up my knitting basket in the parlor, breeze into the kitchen, and head straight for the hooks that hold my outside cloak and bonnet.

"Good morning," I chime, sweeping past the table heading for the door. "I will meet you in the barn, Father, I don't want to be late. This is an important day, you know."

"Emilie," Father calls to me, stopping me with his brisk tone.

I pause with my hand on the doorknob and then turn both it and me toward him. Our eyes meet.

"I—in my lifetime with you, I have never seen ..." Father's lips carry a smile and a glint of teasing sparkles in his eye.

Leaning forward ... waiting ... *What is he talking about?*

He laughs.

"Seen what?" I snap, my patience shortened by my nervousness.

"You're an hour early."

My eyes widen. *Is this where Henry gets his sarcasm?* "No! No, I'm not, it's—"

"Which means, you can eat breakfast," Mother reminds me. "And then you can help me clear the table."

I sigh, release the doorknob, and join my family at the table.

"I guess I can't wait to make friends," I say, feeling defeated by the hour.

"Did you sleep well?" asks Mother.

Buttering a piece of toast, I answer. "Not really. My room is freezing, and my fire went out last night."

"I'll have to find the heavy winter curtains and make sure Henry stocks your room with firewood." She assures me by pouring me a cup of hot tea. "Here, take it with lemon and honey, I don't want you to catch your death."

Father gets up from the table and moves his dishes to the sink. "Finish up here and be ready in fifteen minutes, I have to get to work."

"I'll be out in twenty," I say, because being early is a once in a lifetime event.

A fresh blanket of snow fell last night, creating a canvas, a white backdrop—still, cold, and silent. Pushing the lap blanket aside, stepping out of the sleigh, and gathering my basket, I smooth my skirt and fidget in one spot because I'm freezing, or so I tell myself. We've arrived at Sallie's house, as if by some miracle, fashionably on time.

But what if I'm not fashionable?

"Quarter to three then?"

I blink and look at him, giving a nod.

"All right then, I will pick you up at quarter to three. Have a good time." He gives a quick smile and a nod before he calls to the team and is off. Did he repeat himself in hopes that I wouldn't forget?

I smirk. *He said three, right? I think so.*

Turning to the door, Sallie greets me. "Miss Prescott, welcome." Dark hair without a strand out of place frames her oval face, and the evergreen eyes that accompany her thin yet gentle smile promise better times, like spring and acceptance. I hope.

"Please call me Emilie. We will soon be colleagues," I say, stomping the snow off my boots, fussing with my hair, and pressing out my skirt once again.

Sallie takes my cloak and hat and hangs my things on a hook alongside a multitude of similar ones, in a variety of colors and sizes. The house welcomes me in, with the smell of old tobacco smoke and bacon grease. The rooms are quiet, no sound except for the rustling and clinking of silverware from somewhere.

"The test went well then?" Sallie is a studious proper teacher, serious in nature, plain as the day is long. Her reputation precedes her for running a strict classroom, but she appears to have a warm heart, and I recall this is an event among equals not pupils and instructors.

"Oh, I hope so. Mrs. Irwin is still working on them. Did Sarah make it today?"

A frown deepens the lines on her forehead. "I'm sorry. Sarah sent word; she won't be here." Sallie changes the subject. "I remember the test was hard. You'll learn a lot between now and then." Sallie's hesitant smile speaks volumes about the test but offers not a whisper about the faces waiting just inside the parlor. And that, perhaps, is the most unnerving of all.

"I will take all the lessons I can get, if I get a passing score in May." My nerves begin to dance, as doubts darken my optimism like a stray cloud on a sunny day.

"Come this way, we are visiting in the parlor." Sallie pushes through the doorway, revealing a rose-hued haven. Floral and striped wallpaper suffocates the room, and a fading scent of lilacs lingers in the air. Inside, chairs and sofas huddle in a circle, their plush cushions promising comfort. A stove burns low in the corner, casting long shadows across the room. Two empty dining room chairs beckon us closer.

Sallie waits for everyone to look at her ... We wait ... and wait ... I bite my lip, my fingers tracing the wicker of my basket.

Sallie finally claps her hands. "Everyone?" The room hushes, and a skeptical curiosity falls on each face looking in my direction. Even if I were blind, I could sense all their eyes of equal and different colors settle upon me. Their hands, having stopped mid-task, now settle into laps of various colors: gray, green, black, and blue, in textures of stripe, check, and plain.

"Everyone, this is Emilie Prescott. You may recognize her from the apprentice class. She recently moved here from Virginia."

My heart bangs in my ears, as a forced smile, too frightened to show itself, makes its way to my face through the twitching of my lips. My mouth dries up as if cotton balls were stuffed behind my cheeks. My hand, feeling the need to do something besides toy with my pleats, offers a small wave as the other one clings with white knuckles to my basket.

One of them, with simple brown hair and brown eyes but a dazzling red skirt, brightens up and pats the seat beside her. "Come sit, there's plenty of room."

Walking into the circle of lionesses and skirting around legs and baskets to sit down, I hold my basket in my lap. I watch all their eyes take a critical once over, which makes me wonder if I'm the next course to be served.

Sally clears her throat.

Across from me a young woman with a green skirt speaks without an introduction. "I recognize you; you and that Sarah girl are in Mrs. Irwin's class. I hear she teaches the remedial class too." Her smile is sweet enough, but her beady eyes are sour and barely noticeable over the large, beaked nose. I dare say, not even the wind could give volume to that mousy brown hair of hers. Still, I grit my teeth and bear her off-color remarks. It's too soon to make enemies, is it not?

"She also teaches the apprentices. Weren't you in her class a year ago, Beckie?" Sallie interjects. "Let's be kind"—her eyes sweep over the rest of the women—"and introduce ourselves properly."

"I'm Beckie," says the green skirt grinch with a flourish of her hand. Her beak nose is still directed toward me, and with it her eyes, or so I imagine.

The next greeter, a blonde in blue, pipes up, "I'm Liza, nice to meet you, Emilie. And this is Ginny, she's busy with wedding plans."

Ginny gives me a nod, brushing a stray wisp of coal black hair behind her ear and turning back to Liza. "Well anyway, Liza. Shall I go with two ruffles or three on my wedding dress? You see, I don't know whether I should spend it on the dress or the embossing on the invitations. We all know how important it is to put on proper airs for his relatives. They are coming from New York City, after all."

Liza chews her lower lip, as if her answer would finalize the decision.

"You know your hips are already wide enough for children, do you really need to burden your audience more with three ruffles? And who's going to appreciate Mr. Wimbleton's handiwork on those invitations? I imagine they will look simple given what can be purchased in the city." Beckie prattles on, "Why I imagine, they'll end up in a box or the fireplace within three weeks."

"Beckie!" Liza gasps.

"Ginny, I think you would look beautiful no matter the fabric or how many ruffles you choose, and your invitations will be cherished by anyone lucky enough to receive one." Sallie motions to quiet the rambunctious conversation with a well-practiced gesture.

In a lower voice, Liza comforts her friend, patting her leg. "Yes, of course, you will be beautiful. We all can't wait to see you, and I for one won't toss your invitation in the fire."

Turning to me, Liza says, "So, Emilie, how do you like Gettysburg so far?"

"More civilized than Virginia I expect." Beckie glares over her tatting project. The delicate lace she creates is light and airy in contrast to her personality.

"There's really no difference between the two. It's why I am getting on just fine." I meet Beckie's eyes, with equal intensity. Why is she so harsh?

"But didn't you have slaves? I bet that was fun." Ginny leans forward to hear the story.

"What do you mean by fun?" I ask, my nose wrinkling and a frown forming in my brow.

"Well, I mean, you don't have to do work, and you can boss people around all day." Pausing as a thought occurs to her, Ginny then adds, "Though, I bet you wouldn't know if you were at boarding school all semester."

Beckie sighs. "Honestly, Ginny, it's obvious she is too plain for boarding school. Why don't you tell us what it is really like, Emilie." A smirk she shares with no other than the devil traces her lips.

Challenge accepted. Sorry ladies.

"Well, it's nothing like you imagine. They are like family, you know." My cheeks flush warm from the memories and my smile grows from the shock and awe between the gaggle of them.

"No, not family," Liza pipes up, clarifying the subject. "She's talking about your negros, the ones you own." Liza's eyes are wondering and big. She seems to drink in her surroundings, still innocent and child-like.

"Yes, and they are like family. You heard correct. They were there since my birth, they helped raise me, teach me, guide me, and I am eternally grateful for all of them. One of the families is expected to move here after next spring's planting. Maybe I will host a tea so you all can meet them."

Their gasps ripple through the room. Feet once rooted to the carpet now shuffle as they squirm in their seats. Even Beckie's eyes are wide—I can see the flecks of green envy peering back at me. They look at me and then at each other. Everyone's speechless. The mantel clock drowns out the silence but doesn't hurry time. Liza's face drains of all color. If Henry were here, we could bet on whether she'd faint. Beckie and Ginny look at each other while Sallie checks her pocket watch, avoiding the conversation altogether.

I've often wondered why the black population keeps to themselves, even in Gettysburg. I think I'm beginning to understand, but there is time enough for change, especially while I'm here.

"So, how about the suitors, have you met anyone interesting?" The color is slowly returning to Liza's face, and the rest of them seem to snap out of their stunned silence as soon as boys are mentioned.

Henry would have won that bet. I can't wait to go home and tell him.

"I mean we all know, there aren't any good ones left like my Anthony, he is an absolute catch, and he put a ring on my finger." Ginny wiggles her finger making the diamond sparkle in the light for everyone's delight, especially her own.

"Ginny, we all know how lucky you are, but there are plenty for the rest of us. Besides, dear Anthony has flaws, every man does," Beckie says. "Like that double chin that will look like a rooster's waddle by the time he's thirty."

Ginny huffs. Liza comforts her with a pat to her leg, reassuring her once more. Then all their eyes return to me. *Great ...*

My mind races to how I am going to avoid this conversation.

"I've only made a few acquaintances, no one special."

"Do tell Emilie, maybe I can save you some heartache." Beckie looks over the row of tatting as she deftly continues, shuttle and thread dancing in her hands.

"Just because you dated every eligible bachelor in town, Beckie—" Sallie starts.

"—and in Chambersburg," Liza adds, perking up, loving the titillating news of the forthcoming gossip.

Beckie's embarrassment only lasts so long though.

The ladies look up from their work, and the circle suddenly closes into an eerie, small closeness of inquisitive eyes pinning me down. My face flushes with a warm pink glow under the heated intensity of their stares.

"Do they have names?" Ginny asks.

"Umm, well I just, it's really only an acquaintance with each of them—one time, a short time really." I shift uncomfortably in the chair beneath me. "It feels hot in here, is anyone else hot?"

The young ladies, like a choir of owls, question, "Who?"

I sigh. "Well, there's Stephen Byrne and Thaddeus Marsh. That is all, and I have no opinions of either." I lie as Stephen's warning echoes in my mind. *It's a small, judgmental, opinionated place. You'll see ... Everyone knows everything about everyone else.*

Another hush falls over the group, heads shaking, seats shifting, mouths opening before snapping shut, able to chew on nothing more than speculation.

Have I done it? Have I evaded this baneful conversation?

"Oh, not Stephen." Liza covers her mouth, holding back her dismay.

"Not Stephen—what? Why?" I ask, my voice climbing in pitch.

My eyes dart to Liza. *She knows something. Whatever it is, I will not act surprised. Am I acting surprised? Am I looking surprised?*

Liza covers her mouth, shaking her head, refusing to tell me what she knows.

"Mrs. Byrne is trying to find a wife for her son, Stephen. Liza's family was approached, and poor Liza was forced to see him, until her father—"

"Beckie, no!" Liza's eyes widen with horror. "Stay away from him, Emilie. He's no good and his family—"

"Just wait, Emilie. Once that woman smells you are new here, you'll be next," Beckie states with a smile to match a cat with a canary.

The icy cold warning reminds me of wind howling through the drafty windows during a winter storm. A chill creeps up my spine.

"Ladies, if my mother hears such gossip, we won't finish the afternoon," Sallie interrupts with a desperate plea. She turns to me. "We will tell you another day, Emilie." Her gaze is all but reassuring.

Sallie's little sister pops into the parlor, a cute little brown dress to match ringlets of brown hair. She sidles up to Sallie, whispering to her with a confidential hand to the young woman's ear. Sallie brightens before dismissing her. "Thank you, we'll be right there." The girl runs from the room with a giggle in the wake of her pitter-pattering steps.

"Looks like lunch is served. Shall we go to the dining room?"

The change of rooms brings a lighter feel to the group, and the subject changes to school. Seated around the table, we share a meal of sandwiches, tea cakes, and of course the main event, tea. I listen as they chat about everything from managing a classroom to getting your first job at the school.

"You must pass the certification test first, then it is best to start applying right away," Sallie offers, between bites of ham and cheese.

"Once you get a class, set up the rules immediately, don't spare the discipline. The superintendent looks for teachers who are strict," Beckie offers, then turns to Sallie. "Isn't that how you impressed them Sallie?"

Now this is the advice I am hoping to get here.

Sallie swallows before answering, "I guess so. I hope my skills go beyond my discipline, though. But Beckie's right, it is important."

"Well, you can have my class, Emilie. Anthony and I will be starting a family as soon as we can," Ginny says. "It's a good group, perfect for new teachers."

"Oh, how so?" I ask.

"The children are eager to learn, mostly. They are attentive so far." Ginny sets down her teacup before she adds, "though they are still too scared to misbehave."

"Just wait until next year," Beckie interjects.

"What about you, Liza, what is your advice?" I ask, wanting to hear from the much quieter girl, who seems to disappear into her chair, her eyes still wide and cautious. Liza loves to gossip but seems to add little to this conversation.

"Don't allow the boys to get away with anything," Liza offers. "Pull out your ruler and don't be afraid to use it, right Sallie?" Liza looks to Sallie, shrinking back into her chair and hiding her mouth behind her tea cake.

"Liza is a first-year teacher," Sallie says. "She is learning much this year."

"Everyone starts somewhere. We lose a lot of teachers in the first month," Beckie chimes in.

Ah yes, I can see her optimism shine all over the dining room.

"I will take all of your advice to heart. Thank you." I stand as we start to return to the parlor.

"You are going to need it," Beckie says. "The first year is brutal. By the look of you now, I'd give you two weeks if you were to start tomorrow. Let's hope the months ahead will be enough preparation, if only barely." Beckie's eyes fill with doubt as she surveys me from head to toe and then leads the way out.

My jaw flexes and I suck in a breath as I follow the devil's kin. *She will not get the best of me, not here, not now anyway.*

Ginny joins Beckie and me, saying, "Stop telling tales, Beckie. Mrs. Irwin is a great teacher. You'll be ready, Emilie, don't fret. Mind you, you have the best books possible. My father donated them last year."

How does she exist without a mirror?

"Books?" I ask.

"Yes, your teacher texts." Ginny seems irritated that I didn't know the books are indirectly linked to her family, and I'm not about to bow down and worship her after finding out.

The day ends around 2:35 p.m. as Beckie and Liza take their leave. Ginny soon follows as her new shiny sleigh glides up to the door.

"Oh, it looks like the hired help is here," Ginny announces about the next sleigh arriving as she rushes out the door.

However, it's not the help, it's my father. I smirk. "I'll just be a moment in the outhouse, best to go before the journey home."

Fifteen minutes later, Sallie opens the front door.

"Thank you for inviting me. I enjoyed the visit."

"You're very welcome. Now when you pass, don't forget to apply right away. I know I will be happy to have you come aboard as a teacher."

"I can't wait to join you all," I say, feeling included for the first time, though it's a shame it happened toward the very end of our visit. "See you on Monday."

The icy raw wind whipped up my skirt, sending my cloak wrapping around my legs. I reach back to pull my hood over my bonnet. As soon as I am safe on the walkway, I look up to see my seat in the sleigh taken by ... um ... what's his name? Oh, yes, Mr. Marsh.

"And where am I supposed to sit?"

"You'll just have to squeeze in I'm afraid. In the time it took you to gather your things, I was able to pick up Thaddeus, run some errands, grab a newspaper, smoke a cigar, untack the team, groom them, beat Thaddeus in a push up contest—"

"You're not funny!" I say, having to hold back my own grin and force a scowl.

"Neither are you. Hell had a chance to freeze over in the time it took you to step out." Father chuckles.

It's the rich warm laughter of the man who sits beside him that turns my ears a scarlet red.

How dare they laugh at me? How dare he laugh at me! How dare I enjoy the sound of it ...

Mr. Marsh steps out and offers me a hand up into the sleigh. I fill his waiting hand with my basket and climb aboard without his assistance, seating myself next to my father, as I always have in past times. The only difference here is that once I am settled, I gather my skirts, not wanting Mr. Marsh to wrinkle the folds as he settles himself next to me.

He gives me a piece of the lap blanket, and our legs can't help but touch in the close quarters. Yes, my leg to his leg. A strong, firm, thick leg. *Oh, but really, it's just a leg and our situation cannot be helped.*

We can't help but sit shoulder to shoulder either—one of those broad, well-defined, warm shoulders against mine. *But still just a shoulder. It makes no difference, does it?*

The warmth of him seeps over me. I feel something warm nudge against my foot. *Oh no, not foot to foot too. I cannot bear it, it is a Goliath by comparison to mine.* I shift a bit to look down but see only the warm pot of coal peeking out from under the fabric of skirt.

"I thought your feet might like the warmth." His eyes meet mine—the deep blue eyes like a cluster of forget-me-nots, holding a promise of strength and a hint of adventure. I feel his hands smooth the gaps of the blanket protecting me from the bite of cold air.

"Thank you, but you will need a bit of this too," I say, nudging the pot back toward him, an effort that is brought to an abrupt stop as I feel the side of him press even closer into me. *How can this be?*

"We'll share it. I am an equal warmth opportunist." Thaddeus pushes a bit more of the blanket toward me.

Father clears his throat. "Did you have a nice time?"

"More or less. Sallie is a gracious host. The others? Well, I need to get to know them better."

"Tough audience," Thaddeus says.

"More or less," I say looking at him, just to enjoy those eyes.

Silence.

Thaddeus shifts, looking ahead, and I am forced to come up for air, no longer allowed to drown in pools of blue.

I turn to Father, who appears focused on driving the team, but I see that satisfied grin on his face. *Yes, I bet he did plan this.*

Thaddeus says, "Your father tells me you are becoming a teacher."

My head whips around. "Yes, my plan, above all, is to teach."

"And find a suitor, who has the patience of a saint," Father adds.

"To withstand this family, yes, saintly patience is always a plus for a suitor," I say with a shoulder nudge in father's direction. He bumps me back and I feel myself bumping into Thaddeus. My cheeks flush. "Sorry."

"No need to apologize. If you wanted me off the sleigh, I dare say you would have tried harder." Those blue eyes hold a hint of mischief, and I giggle despite myself. He smiles back at me. *Did he just wink or blink off the fresh flurries?*

"So, Miss Prescott, when are you taking the teachers' exam?" Thaddeus asks.

"Please, our confines are so close. Call me Emilie. It seems we are destined to get to know each other."

"If you'd rather, I can—"

My hand goes to the top of the blanket covering his as our eyes meet again, smiles tugging at our mouths in unison.

"Don't be silly, Mr. Marsh. The warmth will do us good. Now back to you. I will be taking the certification in May," I say, a heat rising in my cheeks for reasons unknown to me. *If he wasn't so darned polite in such an adorable way.*

"Right, well if I am to call you Emilie, you may call me Thaddeus. Though if I may ask—I mean with all due respect and curiosity"—Thaddeus clears his throat—"may I?"

"You may," I encourage as his face flushes.

"Why—I mean, why do you want to be a teacher?" Thaddeus asks.

"Because, I feel every child must have the opportunity to learn." I stop myself from my usual rant. I don't want to bring up marriage, I like him.

"That is quite the accomplishment, congratulations."

I blink. *Did I hear him correctly?*

"Did I say something wrong?"

"No," I say, biting my lip. "That is—that's just so nice to hear. Thank you."

I feel his hand on mine, a long meaningful squeeze, as I am "forced" to lean into him as the sleigh turns into the drive of the Marsh residence.

"Excuse me," I say. "The horses are rambunctious."

"They are ready for the barn I think."

We both look away, our cheeks red from the cold or—it's the cold.

The sleigh slows to a stop. Thaddeus gets out and tucks the blanket near me. His fingertips prod at my upper thigh, but a pile of skirting and blanket still separates him from me. My cheeks burn redder at this point, and I silently beg my teeth to chatter—because of the cold.

"Thank you for the ride home, Mr. Prescott."

"Not at all Thaddeus. See you tomorrow?"

"Yes, of course." Thaddeus turns to me, in all my glorified red, and nods his head with a slight wink.

"Good evening, Miss Prescott ... I mean Emilie."

"Good evening, Mr. Thaddeus."

He turns to walk into the house, and my eyes follow him. The front door opens, and a woman greets him and beckons him into his family's sanctuary. It is only after he disappears past the doorway that I notice the home is a modest stone and clapboard farmhouse with a soft welcoming glow in the window. The smoke curls steadily out of the chimney. A cow's mournful cry from the barn breaks through the icy dusk.

Father calls to the horses as we turn for home. I wrap the blanket around my legs, fingers brushing where Thaddeus once prodded, and immediately miss the warmth of him. The coals at my feet are colder than I recall. I wiggle my toes making sure I can still feel them.

"You planned that, didn't you?" I ask Father as we turn out of the driveway.

"I don't know what you are talking about. I just gave the boy a ride home."

I lean into him, another nudge at his shoulder. Father's eyes laugh with a guilty grin on his face.

"Let's go home."

My bones ache in sympathy with the wind moaning outside, mirroring the exhaustion thrumming through every fiber of my being. All I crave right now is an escape—anywhere but here, anywhere that will allow me to quiet the echoes of this difficult day. With a sigh, I sink into the familiar embrace of Jane Eyre, seeking solace in her modern-day fictional world.

Just as Rochester whispers sweet nothings to Jane, a crisp white envelope plops onto the page, shattering my tranquil illusion and thoughts of Thaddeus's smile.

"What's this?" I ask, picking up the smooth card. It is strangely cold against my fingertips. Red wax emblazoned with the initials "M.B." seals the secrets shut within.

"A gentleman dropped it off earlier today," Mother says, as her needles resume their rhythmic clicking. "Didn't recognize him myself."

"M.B.? I don't know anyone with these initials." A chill snakes up my spine, causing the fine hairs on the back of my neck to stiffen me more than the winter wind seeping through the windows.

"Well, unless you plan to stare a hole through it, you might want to open it," Mother suggests, her voice laced with unnerving nonchalance.

With trembling fingers, I crack the seal. A card slides out, revealing elegant gold script on one side: "Mrs. Maura Byrne." On the other is what I imagine to be her penmanship:

Mrs. M. Byrne presents her compliments to Mrs. Prescott and Miss Emilie Prescott and requests the pleasure of their company at her residence on Saturday afternoon, the eighth of December, at the agreeable hour of half past two.

Pleasant indeed. The elegant script taunts me, as it spells out the promise of excitement, while twisting joy into a grotesque parody. Perhaps this is because her words mock me with civility, masking an undercurrent of something—sinister?

Beckie's warning echoes in my head, stark and chilling: *Once that woman smells you are new here, you'll be next.* Now, her words sit heavy on my chest, as Liza's big eyes mirror my growing terror and are next to play on my thoughts. *Stay away from him, Emilie. He's no good and his family ...* The ominous words leave an abyss of unspoken darkness hanging in my mind.

"Emilie Kathryn, what is it?" Mother's voice cuts through the silence, a lifeline to the brewing storm of fear. "You look pale as a ghost." Her concern is tinged with a hint of annoyance.

Forcing a smile, the effort tastes like ashes in my mouth, "It's ... it's an invitation from Mrs. Byrne. For both of us."

"How lovely!" How I wish my mother's expression didn't brighten. "When are we going to visit?" How I wish she had asked why instead of when.

"This Saturday, half past two." My voice cracks with forced excitement. *Does my pearly white smile seem too aggressive?*

"Well then, of course we'll go! It's a good time to make new acquaintances." Mother returns to her knitting, leaving me drowning in a lake of conflict.

Is she oblivious, or is this simply another social expectation I must endure?

My gaze darts around the room, seeking escape, but there is none. Trapped by societal expectations and my own fear, I can only nod silently, the invitation clutched in my clammy hand. As I try to resume my visit with Rochester and Jane, the words blur before my eyes, replaced by the chilling vision of the Byrne family and the warnings of my new acquaintances.

Are the warnings true? This is a seemingly harmless invitation ... or is it the first step into a nightmare I won't be able to escape?

The answer, like the shadows cast by the fireplace that lengthen throughout the room, remains hidden in unnerving silence.

The Calling Card

IT'S PRETTY SIMPLE, PRETTY OBVIOUS: PEOPLE'S FIRST
IMPRESSION OF PEOPLE IS REALLY A BIG MISTAKE.

~VINCENT D'ONOFRIO

DECEMBER 1860
TABLE ROCK ROAD
GETTYSBURG, PENNSYLVANIA

The scent of fresh cinnamon rolls baking in the woodstove swirls through the air, mingling with the solemn tones of the Sunday morning devotional. Mother's voice, usually filled with warm comfort, holds a forced cheer as she speaks of Advent—a season of hope amidst the shadows of our failure to feel comfortable in a congregation again. Our expulsion from our church family over a year ago stings like an open wound as they could not accept our "all men should be free" ideals. I cling to the hope of the season, trying to ignore the gnawing anxiety growling in my stomach.

Mother's words drone on and on and on. I'm happy she never thought to become a preacher, not that I think a woman can become such. Alas though, it is time to turn our famished souls away from God's grace, and our stomach toward the food that awaits.

Advent is meant to be a season of hope, yet all I feel is unease. The prospect of the visit to the Byrnes' residence looms heavy like rain laden clouds on the horizon—their whispered reputation still casts a long shadow over my thoughts. The ladies' hushed gossip about "dark secrets" and "strange happenings" cling to the Byrne name like cobwebs. My heart trips a frantic rhythm against my ribs, yearning for the comfort of my family. The house will be eerily quiet once Aaron leaves for Richmond next month, his future hanging on the rumors of war.

"What are you wearing for our visit this afternoon?" Mother's voice startles me from my reverie after breakfast as she stands in my room and combs through what little there is of my wardrobe.

Her eyes, usually sparkling, hold a glint of apprehension I cannot ignore but she evidently doesn't recognize.

My fingers wrap around the velvet bonnet she holds out to me, its soft texture a stark contrast to the gripping fear nibbling through my breakfast.

"I think the blue dress will do," I mumble so my voice doesn't betray the tremor in my limbs.

"Hmm." Mother scrutinizes me, a crease forming between her brows. "Perhaps the green one? It flatters your eyes and brightens your complexion."

"I'm not a show horse, Mother. Besides, I don't want to seem overly ..." My voice trails off, the truth hanging heavy in the air. "... Ostentatious?"

Mother's brow arches, "I hardly think—"

"You don't understand. I heard the ladies speak about Mrs. Byrne—"

Do I dare tell her what was said?

"Gossip, is it? Oh Emilie, didn't today's sermon mean anything to you? It is so un-Christian-like to judge a woman by what others say of her." The disappointment in Mother's eyes hurts and I look away.

"I'm sorry."

"You will look lovely, no matter what you wear. Just remember." Mother tilts my chin with a delicate finger, forcing me to greet her gaze once more. "A smile and kind word go a long way."

But are words enough to navigate the treacherous waters of the Byrne household? Doubt eats away at me like a relentless rodent. As I smooth the folds of the green dress Mother coaxes over my head and the rest of my body, the wool fabric feels scratchy and suffocating. It isn't just the material, it is the oppressive weight of anticipation, the unspoken secrets swirling in the air.

Picking up the bonnet again to place it on my head this time, I notice the weight of the crushed velvet mirroring the weight of the anticipated visit. The Byrnes are a mystery, a puzzle with pieces missing, and I, a curious unprepared participant. I must sift through the gossip, separating fact from fabrication.

Mrs. Byrne can't possibly be everything everyone says.

As the slippery ribbons are pulled into a bow at my chin, a whispered prayer dances off my lips, a flicker of hope, a plea that I, in the eyes of Mrs. Byrne, will not be targeted as the future Mrs. Stephen Byrne.

We pull up to the Byrne residence. A pristine neat house stands proudly in front of a backdrop of orchards—row after row of trees. Stephen is correct. He is part of a large fruit-growing family. The house speaks of explicit wealth made from hard work, gleaned from the soil, and encouraged from the earth.

Henry secures Mother's departure from the sleigh and reaches for my hand as I step down.

"Looks like a good family for you," Henry teases. "I hear they have an eligible bachelor."

"I am having tea, not getting engaged." I glare at him sharper than usual, stepping on his boot, partially by accident, yet perfectly timed.

"Testy today. Is the prospect of marriage coming too close for comfort, dear sister?" He drops my hand and offers mother his arm to escort her to the door.

Where's my arm? Not that I need it or want it—Boys!

The flower gardens in front of the house are tucked into dormancy under blankets of snow. The smooth stone walkway is cleared of the cumbersome white flurries, welcoming us into the unknown. The large black door with a brass knocker—so bright it appears to wink at us—shines from under the covered porch. Henry gives three sharp knocks.

We wait ...

The door creaks open; a gentleman stands there to greet us.

"Welcome, I am Mr. Jack Byrne. Are you here to call upon my wife?" he asks. It comes as no surprise to me that Mr. Byrne is a man who feels at home among his trees. The trunk of his body is tall and lean with his joints grafted together in awkward shaped knobs. His eyes, nose, ears, and even mouth appear to have been pruned by God and life's experiences—sharp and angular. Alas, brown hair frosted gray at the roots depicts the season of his age.

Henry is the first to speak up. "Pleasure to make your acquaintance, Mr. Byrne. I am Henry Prescott, and this is my mother, Julia Prescott, and sister, Emilie Prescott."

Who knew? My brother has manners after all.

"Come in, come in ladies. The missus will be right down."

Henry stands at the threshold and addresses Mother, "I'll return for you in an hour or so." He leaves us inside the doorway, escaping back to the sleigh with what I can only imagine as suppressed glee.

The entryway to the house is shadowed as the hallway leads

to another door out back. Light filters from the large windows in the rooms on either side of the corridor, helping it feel less cramped.

"Right this way." Mr. Byrne shows us to the second room on the right. "Please take a seat. I will let my wife know you are here." Mr. Byrne mirrors a tree and leaves.

Mother and I look at each other, smiles forming on our lips. Hers depicts excitement while mine is a matter of politeness.

My ears listen to the tick-tock of a clock on the mantel. I think back to all the times, save for this one, which I have been fashionably late and say, "At least I'm—"

"Don't say it, Little Miss. I am sure she will be right here."

My heart warms as Mother uses Martha's name for me, but I bite my tongue as I notice she also mirrors Martha's stern look.

The parlor is warmed by the afternoon sun, the furniture neatly arranged with sculptures meticulously placed on small round tables, and family likenesses line the mantel next to the incessant tick-tocking of that clock. The smell of lilac stings my eyes as I turn around to see Mrs. Maura Byrne entering the room.

"Sorry for the delay," Mrs. Byrne says without introduction. "It is a pleasure to make your acquaintance. Please sit." The rustle of the stiff emerald green and black taffeta of her afternoon gown quiets, as she sits in the well-worn ladies' chair to the left of the couch, which Mother and I plant ourselves in for the visit.

Mother takes over, saying, "Thank you for inviting us to your lovely home. Please call me Julia, and this is my daughter, Emilie."

Mrs. Byrne smiles at me. Her beady dark eyes feel like bugs creeping up my skin as she surveys me from head to toe. My legs shift and my hands brush over the pleats of my skirt, hoping to expel the creepy-crawly sensation she gives.

"It is a pleasure to make your acquaintance, Mrs. Byrne." I force a smile, sitting up straight, feeling like I'm in competition with the sculptures she already possesses.

"The pleasure is all mine, and please, call me Maura. May I be the first to welcome you to Table Rock Road? Everyone is excited to make your acquaintance." The wrinkles in her cheeks deepen as she smiles, and her lips pull back to show yellowed teeth.

"We look forward to calling on our neighbors." Mother is good at quick polite replies. I allow them to carry on as I continue to survey the room. There are large paintings of birds and nature, accented with smaller drawings of apple and pear trees. Cozy and warm in the daylight and at night, I am sure, if one enjoys gaudy spectacles. A larger portrait of an older man, serious and formal, takes its honored place above the mantel.

I feel Mother nudge my leg.

Hmm? What? I turn to look at her, and she gestures with a tilt of her head to Mrs. Byrne.

"I said, how do you like Gettysburg so far, Miss Emilie?" Mrs. Byrne repeats.

"Pardon me, I was just—" The telltale crimson races up my neck as I motion to the pictures and artwork.

"I see. Do you appreciate the art?" she asks.

"Yes, ma'am. The pictures are beautiful, and the sculpture— is that a John Rogers piece?" I say, trying to mask the embarrassment.

The tabletop sculpture shows a couple in front of a preacher with a cat and dog staring at each other—everyone appears at odds.

"Yes, that is called Coming to the Parson, one of my favorites indeed." Her eyes shift toward me, waiting for a reaction.

Parson indeed. I am sure you cannot wait. As for me, I will wait—forever if I must.

"It's most lovely," I say, careful to keep the sarcasm of my thoughts out of my tone.

Turning back to my mother, Mrs. Byrne smiles with the same giddiness of Liza at the thought of gossip. She leans forward ready to spill all her knowledge. "Julia, let me tell you about our lovely neighbors here."

"With all the farms we passed, how will I learn all of their names?" Mother says, trying to match her excitement.

"That's right, you're not from around the corner, but from— wait, I don't even know where you're from. How embarrassing, please do tell?" asks Mrs. Byrne.

"Oh, I suppose, that would be a good place to start." Mother pauses a moment. "We—I mean my husband, Jacob, and two sons, Aaron and Henry, arrived from Virginia a few months back. We are looking forward to all the possibilities Gettysburg has to offer that the South unfortunately does not."

How did Mother not mention me?

"Possibilities? You certainly haven't been out and about much have you? I mean Gettysburg is a lovely close-knit community— we know all there is to know about each other and aid each other's families any way we can—but outside of a quiet country life there are not many other possibilities to experience." Mrs. Byrne smiles.

Wait ... she forgot the judgmental, opinionated part ...

I look to Mother, whose brow flinches a bit. "Sounds lovely. I can't wait to hear about them." A kinder smile than I could ever muster appears on Mother's face, masking her disbelief in Maura's words.

"Speaking of possibilities, Miss Emilie, do you have a beau you are entertaining for marriage?" asks Mrs. Byrne. The inquiring beetles that shape her beady eyes gnaw right through me.

And it begins. I warned my mother! Stay strong—stay strong Emilie.

"No, ma'am, not yet. I am training for my teaching certificate. Afterward, I might entertain the thoughts of a potential husband," I say, matching her stare, though I hope my brown eyes are not as buggy as hers.

"Oh, independent, aren't you?" Mrs. Byrne laughs to herself. "Hopefully you're right. There is an age limit to catch the most eligible bachelors, you know, and I wouldn't want you to miss out."

I squeeze Mothers' leg in an I warned you kind of way.

"That's what we love about her. Emilie's passionate about teaching. We know there will be a husband sooner or later. Until then, she's following her dreams, and when she finally decides to have a family, she'll have the best of both worlds."

A distant stomping sound comes from the direction of the window, and my curiosity strains to see what, or rather who, it is all about—anything to free me from this prison of a parlor. Outside, I see Stephen at the back door. His wavy hair again covers his eyes as he looks down, washing his hands at the pump.

My heart skips a beat ...

The back door creaks ...

I hold my breath ...

Heavy footfalls come toward the parlor.

My heart pounds in my chest. *I know I hoped he would be too busy to bother with us today, but dear God, forgive my fickle ways, and let him come in to rescue me!*

His steps grow closer and then distant once more, and I feel my pounding heart sink to the floor.

"Stephen, is that you?" Mrs. Byrne's high-pitched shrill tweaks my ear.

"Yes, Mother," he calls back. The plodding of his boots stops. The floor creaks as he shifts his weight, his steps growing louder until he sounds like he is just behind me.

Dare I look his way?

"Come, come, introduce yourself to our guests." Mrs. Byrne claps her hands.

Stephen steps out of the doorway and into view, his work shirt and trousers smudged with the toils of the day. Those hazel hues reflecting the shift of seasons rest on his mother, though a brief glance is blown in my direction. He leans down to kiss her cheek, before turning his attention to my mother.

Not me?

"Hello, Mrs. Prescott. It is a pleasure to meet you." Stephen takes Mother's hand and kisses the back of it before letting it rest once more in her lap. I don't recall Mother wearing that much rouge when we left. Besides, she is married. What does she care what Stephen thinks or does or—

"I see where your daughter gets her beauty."

I swallow hard, feel a heat rise in my cheeks, and look away. *Issues of complexion are natural for a redhead, we blush at everything, besides it is a mite bit stuffy in here.*

Mother stifles a giggle, not even hiding her affliction!

"Pleasure to meet you, Mr. Byrne. This is my daughter."

Stephen shifts. Clears his throat.

Mother nudges me.

Fine. I turn to meet his hazel eyes—deep as the multifaceted foliage of fall. They lock onto me, holding me captive in ways I never imagined, and then his deep voice rumbles my name. "Miss Prescott, pleasure to make your acquaintance again." My hand floats up under the touch of his own, and warm soft lips press into my delicate skin.

Swallowing hard, I clear my throat. "St-Stephen, it-it's a pleasure to see you again."

The stare down between us returns as he plants all sorts of thoughts in the recesses of my dark eyes ... silence grows ... adults shift in their seats. Is this the sort of silent conversation that occurs between Mother and Father?

Stop it! My lips part.

Stop what? A smirk toys with his dimples.

The charming act! I close my mouth, letting the thinning line of my lips create a natural wall.

His eyebrows lift. *I can't help it if you fall for it every time I look at you.*

My eyes narrow. I won't fall for you ...

We'll see ... He lets my hand go, a silent dare to return it to the warmth of my lap that we both know shares the heat of my cheeks.

Mrs. Byrne clears her throat, placing a hand on his arm. "Stephen, will you be a dear and prepare the tea for us? I want to tell Mrs. Prescott about the upcoming festivities."

"Think nothing of it. I will be right back." Stephen turns to leave, then pauses to address my mother. "Mrs. Prescott, may I take Emilie for a stroll around the farm? I'd like to show her around."

"Of course, I am sure she will enjoy some fresh air," Mother says, looking at me, patting my leg.

My shoulders tighten, and I shift with a quiet sigh. Nobody in this room can deny, save for perhaps Maura, that these couch cushions feel like shards of glass—or perhaps my rump has grown so dull of the conversation that it has decided to nap without me. Either way, I suppose I did ask for this, but still—I'm not just any woman. Stephen needs to know that.

I look over my shoulder at him. "If you would like some company, Mr. Byrne, all you have to do is ask," I say.

"I'll think about it." He turns, leaving the room.

My jaw drops, closes, and flexes as lips purse.

The stunned silence is broken by Mrs. Byrne. "As I was saying Julia, the best way to get to know the neighbors is to join our festivities for the holidays."

Mrs. Byrne drones on about the visiting parties, like the barn dance on New Year's Eve. "It's a quaint get-together. We enjoy each other's company after a year of work, raising barns, planting, and harvesting together. Who knows, the young ones often start calling on each other after the magical barn dance come midnight, and we all know how that leads to courting and such."

Maura's eyes shift to me. "Mind you, there are plenty of eligible bachelors to pick from, Emilie."

I must fight back the urge to roll my eyes. *Who knew we had an official matchmaker on Table Rock Road.*

"Every girl needs a variety to choose from," I say. The forced smile returns, and I can start to feel an ache in my cheeks.

"How can we help?" Mother asks. "Emilie and I would love to lend a hand in any way we can, right?"

"Of course," I say. "I can't wait to make friends."

The clatter of dishes sliding across a silver tray announces Stephen's return. He sets the silver tray on the center table, neatly placing each cup adjacent to us, and sweeps his hand above the arrangement.

"There you are ladies." Stephen nods at my mother, as he steps toward me with his hand outstretched.

"Miss Prescott, if you would do me the honor to accompany me on a stroll?"

My hand reaches out to him and, forgetting myself, I stand to allow him the privilege of escorting me to the hall, but the niceties stop there. Outside, I turn to him. "Took you long enough to 'think about it,' and how dare you ask my mother's permission to escort me, but not consider asking for mine!"

Stephen shrugs. "You took my hand, didn't you?"

The smirk on his face manages to tease a lousy crook from the corners of my lips, a hint of a smile, I suppose. "I was being polite."

"As was I." He offers me his arm. "Would you like to go this way or continue to stand on the porch like a grump?"

This time I roll my eyes, but I also put my hand on his arm.

He laughs. I kind of like the sound of it, but only kind of.

Stephen guides me around the farm. I think for a time or two of establishing my independence from him, but am obliged to keep hold of his arm, as the snow is slippery, and my footing is treacherous. We wander from the barn to the henhouse, then walk into the orchards and up a small rise, so he can show me the rest of the trees they manage. On our way back to the house, I notice a smaller homestead down the hill.

"Who lives down there?" The quaint building is a tidy place, meticulously kept, with shuttered windows and a perfect peaked roof. It is hard to tell if anyone inhabits the place.

"Oh, that's my first home, once I marry, that is. My parents lived there before their parents passed the big house to them." Stephen turns to look at me. "Cozy, isn't it?"

"Impressive. You have a large tract of land complete with everything you need for the rest of your life, and you don't want this? What more could you possibly want?" I say, watching his expression shift from light, full, and whimsical, to sallow, plain and serious.

"Oh, I want the land. It's being told that I have no choice but to take it that bothers me. Isn't it the same with you? If you are told what to do, it sours the transaction and diminishes all desire to do just that. If you are given a choice, it is more pleasing to the palate, wouldn't you agree?"

I avoid his eyes, thinking about his words. He is strangely poetic and smart. I shiver thinking about him ... those eyes ... that irritating smirk ... his words filled with sugar and daggers all at once.

Stephen takes my hand, tucking it back into the crook of his elbow, which shelters my fingers from the blue tinge that they are starting to take on. "Come, the cold's too bitter for a blossom such as yourself. I better get you back."

We walk back to the house, longing for the warmth of the parlor and the tea. Just as we pass the large oak, I see a lone swing, long forgotten because boys turn to men and toys of the past become discarded and frivolous.

"Come on, let's have some fun," I say, pulling him out of this suffocating act of decorum and toward the swing, my actions so surprising to him that we both know he has little choice but to agree.

The rope looks weather worn, but it's still intact. The seat is an old thick barn board, but there are no cracks or wood rot.

"Looks safe enough," I say.

"Haven't been on it in years—got no idea," Stephen says, though that mischievous glint matches my own eyes.

I untie my bonnet, set it aside, and sit on the seat. *Bounce, bounce* ... The seat holds firm.

"Give me a push, would ya?"

Stephen shakes his head, but his hand goes to the small of my back and pushes me gently forward. I kick my legs to gain momentum, not a dainty young maiden, but a woman who wishes to obtain new heights. Another push from behind, and small sways turn to full swings, bringing back the joyful memories of my childhood during a once youthful spring.

"Have you ever wished to be a bird, to fly without a care in the world?" I ask, leaning back as my body dives down, eyes casting back to meet him.

"Except for predators, finding food and shelter? Sure."

"Such a realist, Stephen," I say and give a halfhearted laugh. The swing is in full extension. My skirt billows around me as excitement escapes in the jubilation of delightful squeals and a wild grin. *Creak.* This experience is bliss. *Whish.* The cold breeze thrills me. *Groan.* My eyes set to the horizon as he pushes me again. Whish. I feel a tug. A discordant note strums my conscience. *Creak.* The fibers strain. *Groan.* I swing higher, fall backward. His hand on my back propels me forward, another hitch, and a tug. *Snap.* Perhaps an icy branch? *Whish.* My eyes trail up the length of the rope. *Groan.* My stomach clenches as I spot fraying threads. *Creak.* My eyes widen, and my fingers instinctively grip the ropes tighter. *Snap.*

"Stephen, make it stop! Stop! The rope is giving way!"

Whish.

"What? I don't see anything," he says playfully.

Creak.

"The rope—"

Groan.

Do I jump, wait, or—

Creak.

Oh, God!

"I still don't see it." His tone taunts me.

Whish.

"STOP IT NOW!" The panic in my voice gets his attention.

Groan.

Stephen tries to grab my waist to stop the momentum. The next pass, his arms swoop around me—*CRACK*!

My body presses to him. His weight overcomes me. The sensation of frozen solid earth, the sturdy sinew of his arms, both unyielding—one of them slams against my back, the other smashes into my arm. A mouthful of fabric muffles my scream; it tastes of his sweat. I gag. My other arm is assaulted. With a thud, my body greets unforgiving earth once more, and at last the world stops spinning—but my head is still throbbing as fresh air is driven from my lungs.

Twigs, sticks, and acorns try to embed themselves into my flesh without consideration for the fabric of my dress as Stephen's body shelters me ... from what? Blue sky? Certainly not my fall. Or the discomfort of our tumble. Though I suppose I should be thankful for his large hands, which hold my head with those knobby Byrne fingers—and yet he does not have to think of the time it will take to untangle my now ruined hair. He just gets to look at me, with those wild hazel eyes while—grinning?

What exactly is there to smile about?

"I can't breathe," I say with a rasp.

Stephen blinks.

His body stiffens.

We both blush.

He scrambles off me, dusts off his clothes, and only then offers a hand to me.

Some gentleman. Just as I go to accept it, he pulls it back and

I give him a look, wondering if he can read my thoughts once more, that I am done with his dirty tricks!

He wipes the very hand he refused me against his trousers, and then thrusts it back out to me once more. "Sorry."

"Are you sure?" I ask, but accept his hand, and let him pull me to my feet.

My hands sweep over myself, as do his, as he tries to assist me in getting the dirt and snow off my cloak, the sticks and leaves out of my hair—and why is he brushing there? I smack his hand away.

"But you look a mess." His comment is not encouraging.

"I know, I've got it. Just stop touching me."

"Are you hurt?" He brushes debris off the back of my cloak again, his hand traversing the length ever lower. I'd slap his hand again if I could reach it, but I can't, so instead I turn away from his hands, which chase after some bits he missed. Around and around, we go ...

"Will you stop! It's nothing!" I say using both hands this time to smack his own away. "No worse than a fall from a horse. Though I must admit, I never had one fall on top of me."

Stephen pulls back his hands as though my next bit of action will be a bite, and it just might. "Fine, be a tree. I feel more at home around them than girls anyway." He inspects himself, brushing any leftover debris from the tumble. "Though I will say, my father always said, I am as strong as a horse." He grins at me.

Oh, that's right, his father—and his mother. What will his parents think of me now?

I push my crazed hair back into my bonnet, hoping no one will note the obvious, as the need to embrace social dictations comes to the forefront of my worries.

"Don't fuss, I will protect your reputation."

With what, that stupid grin of his? Does he realize the seriousness of the situation! I fix him another glower and hear the rumble of his chuckle as he offers me his arm. "It won't be that bad, though I'll admit I've never had to face your mother."

"I am more worried about yours."

Stephen gives a humph. "Why? Concerned you won't make her lineup of eligible women?"

"No, I think I ruined my chances on that already. Something about being too independent."

"That you are." His chuckle returns with that absurd grin.

We arrive at the house, and Stephen opens the door. "Your humiliation first?"

"Sure, why not. It's not like I have to live with her."

Stephen hangs my cloak and hat, while I try to tuck one of the many stray hairs back into place. Then he offers me his arm once more and escorts me back to the parlor.

Mrs. Byrne's gasp at the sight of us is heard above all else, including the rattling of her teacup. "What on earth happened to you two?"

Here we go.

At first, Mother's eyes widen at my disheveled appearance, but with an exhale she releases her shock with contempt, and allows her expression to ask only the quiet question of *What happened?*

Stephen steps in front of me, offering an explanation first. "We had a mishap with the old swing."

"Mishap! Lord! Stephen, didn't I say that swing should have been taken down ages ago? You stopped playing with it a decade back!"

Nudging Stephen aside, I announce, "I'm fine, just a bump or maybe a small bruise. I am sorry about your swing, Mrs. Byrne."

She and I stare at each other, me confident and her suspicious, but of what I'm not sure. I see Stephen flinch out of the corner of my eye. *Is he afraid of her?*

"I should say! Why were you swinging so high on that contraption? Putting my son in such a precarious position of decorum. How scandalous and unbecoming of a woman!"

Mrs. Byrne flips her fan from her pocket and begins fanning herself, disgusted at the sight of me.

"Julia, I do not know how young girls are expected to behave in the backwoods of Virginia, but here such behavior is only thought to be expected of—" Mrs. Byrne's mouth stops short as her gaze catches my mother's. I'm not sure what sort of look is given, but it's interesting to note the sudden shift in Maura's demeanor. "But I'm sure it was a mistake, Emilie. Do sit down, you must be exhausted after your ordeal."

"Thank you, ma'am," I say and sit dutifully beside Mother, who now wears the polite sweet smile I've always known her to have with company. My gaze shifts back to Stephen, who shifts impatiently from foot to foot.

"Thank you for the walk, Stephen. I had a lovely time."

"My pleasure." He bows to me and takes his leave.

I wonder what he would have said if not in mixed company ...

Good Will to All

DECEMBER 1860
TABLE ROCK ROAD
GETTYSBURG, PENNSYLVANIA

Butterflies dance in my stomach like snowflakes caught in the swirling wind, mirroring the frenzy of activity engulfing the farmhouse. The scent of pine boughs mingles with sweet vanilla sugar, each battling for dominance, a welcoming accent adding to the house that now gleams like a nervous debutante. Can we pull off a Visiting Day, worthy of Table Rock Road's seasoned hostesses or will our attempts crumble like the batch of sugar cookies I delicately place on the silver tray? The last two weeks have been a flurry of planning, volunteering, and laughter—a hopeful attempt to prove we belong.

Now, as the mantle clock ticks toward eleven, a knock on the door shatters my nerves and the silence—the social whirlwind is arriving.

"Henry, the door," Mother says.

"Got it!" Henry pulls at his neck trying to loosen the knot

Mother meticulously fastened moments ago. I must admit he looks a bit out of place dressed in a crisp white shirt, cravat, and stunning burgundy vest. However, despite Mother's efforts, his hands show the tell-tale signs of the brother I know and love. Father made him shine his shoes, and his fingers are still black, even after he scrubbed them with lye soap.

"The Weltys are here," Henry's announcement alerts us to our places.

Mr. and Mrs. Welty with their daughter Louisa enter the parlor. My eyes go to Louisa. Like Henry, I have never seen her dressed in a formal visiting gown. She appears stiff, as I believe her corset is too tight, but her figure is perfect. All beauty has a price.; I give her a warm smile, but hope my eyes reflect my condolences for the suffering she must endure today.

After presenting the family with refreshments, I join the circle of ladies consisting of my mother, Mrs. Welty, and Louisa. I address Mrs. Welty. "Thank you for coming. We are happy to have you visit today."

"We are happy to be here. You and your mother always make Louisa and me feel included at our meetings, it is nice to finally come visit you for a change." Mrs. Welty's bashful grin lights up her dark brown hollow eyes. She has fading beauty, worn down by raising three daughters and the responsibilities of hard work, dedication, and other challenges that come with maintaining a farm.

"Your generosity and the use of your parlor for our sewing circles is much appreciated by everyone," I smile, offering the plate of cookies to her.

The truth is she is not as included in the ladies committee meetings. Rumors about her scatterbrained ideas and the foul odor of her cats cause the ladies to whisper among each other when she leaves the room.

I hear the men chatting at the other side of the room as Henry offers, "Our fields will be planted in one to two days, then I will be down to help."

"Much appreciated, Henry," Mr. Welty says, turning to Father. "You bought a nice place here. It got too big for Mr. Deardorf when his children took their own homes, and his wife died. He was a good neighbor indeed."

Looking back to the circle of ladies, Mother and Mrs. Welty chat on as I spy Louisa watching my brother. Her eyes linger on his form with a sparkle, and she has an unmistakably dreamy smile. As Henry turns his head, her eyes dart away, a faint pink floods her neck and rushes up through her face.

"Are you feeling well, Louisa?" I ask, catching the big wide eyes and natural rouged cheeks as she looks back at me.

"I don't know what you mean, Emilie. I'm quite well, yes—yes indeed." Louisa swallows hard, reining in her composure and blinking away the guilt of lingering too long.

"So did you attend the barn dance last year?" I ask changing the subject. "How many eligible suitors do you think will attend?"

"I know of at least four, but I am not interested in them. I grew up with most of them and don't consider them husband material."

I watch as her gaze floats away and briefly back to Henry who is deep in conversation with the men. Then as if some bell chimes in Mrs. Welty's head, she sets down her cup, thanks mother for the visit and stands—signaling to her family it is time to depart.

Henry and I gather coats, cloaks, and bonnets, dispersing the items back to their owners, and with a brisk whoosh of icy wind, they take their leave with waves and good cheer. Before the door closes, Mother and I rush to the parlor, scoop up the plates and cups, and swish off to the kitchen. We wash, dry, and place the dishes back on the sideboard in the parlor. Ready for—

"The Halles are here," Henry announces as we hear him open the door, his greeting echoing down the hall. Mother and I scramble for the lone towel to dry our hands in a rush so we can greet our guests. On our way out, Mother grabs my arm.

"Your apron!"

I reach back to tug at the ties, releasing the garment, pulling it over my head, and dropping it over a chair as we sweep out with a swish of fabric, our hoops colliding as we bustle down the hallway.

Arriving in the parlor, I smile as my gaze captures Jane Halle, her perfect ringlets adorning her pale, porcelain face. *If she were a doll, I would want her on my shelf.* Jane is a miniature adult, primmed and dressed in the finest dress the Halles can afford.

Who is watching the boys?

"Mrs. Halle, Jane, Mr. Halle, may I offer you some refreshments?" I ask.

"Oh, no thank you, though it all smells delightful," Mr. Halle pats his stomach and turns to greet my father and Aaron, who invite him to the barn to show him something. Henry grabs up Mr. Halle's coat and the men disappear from the room.

"Jane, Mrs. Halle? Refreshments?"

After handing them their requested refreshments, I take a seat, leaning in toward Jane, whispering to her, "Who is watching the boys?"

Jane lights up with a big grin. "Billy has to watch them, and he hates changing diapers!" This elicits a giggle as Jane is enjoying her special status right now.

I can't help but laugh with her before asking, "Do you have a craft you do for fun, Jane?" I want to know the girl behind the adult persona.

She looks down. "I'm not sure it's fun, but Mother is teaching me how to knit."

"Oh, I knit too," I say. "I love making scarves."

Jane screws up her face, "I don't like it yet. I always end up with fewer stitches than I start with."

Mrs. Halle adds, "Practice, practice ... and more patience, dear."

Jane looks to me, her eyes pleading.

"Unfortunately, she is correct," I say. "It took me a long time too."

"Oh, all right," Jane says. "I'll give it another go."

Mrs. Halle addresses me, "Miss Emilie, how is school going?"

"Very well, but I'm still unsure if I will be ready in time for May."

"I am sure you will do just fine, dear," Mrs. Halle's kind words are reassuring.

"Are we ready for the festivities tomorrow night?" Mother asks.

"Yes, the ladies came this morning to decorate the barn. We chased away the mice and set the barn cats in there to finish the rest. I expect we'll have a lovely time tomorrow."

"We'll also have some fat barn cats," Jane giggles. "Emilie, I can't wait to see your dress."

"I hope it fits," I say biting my lower lip, "and if not, Mother is good at improvising, so I will be presentable." *I hope.*

The mantle clock chimes, Mrs. Halle looks at the time, sighing, "I suppose we should get back to your brothers, Jane."

"Yes, Mother, I'm worried the house will burn down if we stay too long." A pout forms on her tiny mouth. "See you tomorrow, Miss Emilie."

"I look forward to it, Jane."

Mother and I give the ladies their cloaks and hats as Mr. Halle enters through the kitchen.

"I suppose we should get back," Mr. Halle turns to his wife.

"Thank you, we had a lovely time visiting," Mrs. Halle gives Mother's hand a quick squeeze. "See you all tomorrow night."

We bid the Halle family good day at the back door, while Henry announces the Lochers, a father and son duo, are at the front door.

"Mother, I will tend to the dishes, if you delay them at the front door," I say scurrying off to clear the parlor for our next set of visitors. I overhear the men making small talk in the entryway as I try not to drop the cups and saucers.

"Welcome to the area. This is my son, John, and his wife ..."

"Thank you. Please come in. May we get you something to warm up?" Father offers.

Not until I wash these dishes.

Reaching for the kettle, I splash some hot water into the basin and begin to scrub, trying not to scald my fingers in the process. After dropping the second plate back into the water, I pump some cold water into the basin as well.

I turn to Mother just as she sweeps in. "We need two teas and two ciders," she announces.

"I feel like we are running a restaurant," I say with a giggle, pouring the sticky apple cider with a ladle into a larger cup. My fingers are starting to appear unkept like Henry's. Mother pours out some hot tea, gathers the tray, and places the milk and sugar to add balance.

"Who gets these?" I say adding the cups of cider to the tray.

"The Locher men. Be sure to offer those cookies."

The parlor is lit by the flames in the fireplace. Henry is adding new logs for warmth, while Aaron gathers the taper candles to light when the sun goes down. Father is talking to the Locher men, while the ladies sit straight back, prim and proper on the couch. They remind me of wooden statues, their serious eyes and pursed lips accompany their drab black dresses. They look like twin storm clouds hovering over a picnic.

"Gentlemen, your cider," I say, carefully handing the first cup to the father with smooth tanned hands and then the second cup to the son who has rough blackened, calloused hands.

The smooth-hand father looks at me. "Do you have a chestnut quarter horse about fifteen hands high?"

"Yes, sir. I do."

"Was it you running past my place about a month ago?" the elder Locher inquires. "You are getting a lot of attention, young lady."

The rough-handed son then says, "Lucky, we didn't have that much rain, or your gallivanting could tear up our roads. The ruts are bad enough."

"I'm sorry, gentlemen. We have not been properly introduced," I say and glance toward my father, sitting to my left.

Father recognizes his cue to rescue his damsel in distress. "This is Mr. David Locher. He is a weaver and his son, John, is a blacksmith. They live at the end of Table Rock Road. Mr. Locher and John, this is my daughter, Emilie."

"You look about her size, and since I know no other family would let their daughter ride that reckless, it must be you," the elder Locher continues. "I dare say, if I saw your ankles, I would know it was you."

A gasp and twitter sounds from the ladies' seating area, and I take note of the twins narrowing their eyes and whispering to each other.

Mother looks confused.

"Ankles? What are we talking about?" Henry lights up as he enters the room with the Byrnes following close behind.

The room stands still, and I am frozen in my mortification. The men in front of me are aghast, the ladies beside me praying for my salvation, Henry grinning—that stupid grin—and Stephen Byrne smirking, all at my expense!

And how can we forget Mrs. Byrne, who has yet another reason to give me a scowl of sheer disapproval.

I may have just been cancelled as the next Mrs. Stephen Byrne.

A heat wave of nausea hits me, weakening my knees, wobbling my ankles. I feel like I am going to faint. I am left to flee from the room, wordless and burning with humiliation. I retreat to the kitchen to splash cold water on my face and ground me back into this horrifying reality of humanity. I can't escape one day without some sort of shame coming my way. Inside the larder, I find some ginger to crush into a tea for my stomach when I hear—

"Emilie ... Em, where are you?" Henry asks in a forced whisper.

I make him wait. I can neither bear further humiliation, nor do I want to face Mr. Byrne.

"Come on, Em, I'm starving. Where are the sandwiches?"

"Look in the bread box," I answer from behind the larder curtain. I hear him open the box, while I hold the bottle of crushed ginger in my hands, waiting for him to leave. Suddenly, the curtain parts. Henry leans in, "You're a popular subject in there. You best stay hidden awhile. These are great by the way." I see a hand clutching a sandwich before he disappears altogether and the curtain ripples back into place.

I stay put, not wanting to escape the safety of this room, when I hear Stephen.

"Henry, did you find her?"

"In here. Want one?" I hear them chewing and munching, then—

"Hey, Emilie, are you coming out?"

"No," I say.

Stephen is the last person I want to face right now.

"Aw, why not? No one cares. It was just an ankle. Come on ..."

I don't even need to see that smirk to know he's still wearing it!

"Stephen, leave me alone," I say, hoping for once he will do as he's told.

His face peeks through the curtain, as he holds the ends shut, so his head looks like it's just floating. "When can I see your ankles?"

I push out of the larder, furious and embarrassed. "How about never, Mr. Byrne!"

Henry and Stephen burst out laughing, practically rolling on the floor with embarrassing, humiliating, disgusting, laughter. They then slap each other on the back and leave out the back door.

Gathering myself together, I make some ginger tea and rejoin the party in the parlor with a tray of small sandwiches and cookies. Once I am done passing those to each guest with painted pleasantries, I finally seat myself in the empty chair in the ladies' circle. The men are chatting on about farming and whatever else they speak about. Father replaced their ciders with short glasses of whiskey.

Another knock on the door sends Aaron to receive our next set of guests. Shortly thereafter, I turn to see the Marsh family enter the parlor, Mr. and Mrs. Marsh with their sons, Ian and Thaddeus—I gulp.

Thaddeus is helping his mother with her cloak. Mother excuses herself to offer the family refreshments. Before the Marshes are seated, the Lochers stand to take their leave, sending Aaron scurrying to gather their coats and cloaks. Once again I am frozen in place, and my stomach is sounding the alarm for a bit more ginger tea.

Mrs. Locher says, "Thank you for a pleasant afternoon."

Unable to tear my eyes from Thaddeus, I hear myself say, "Very welcome. Thank you all for coming."

Mrs. Locher leans in, pulling me to her. "I will pray for you, my dear. Pray for your intact reputation and that your propriety remains pure."

The other Mrs. Locher interjects, "Yes, we wouldn't want you to become a spinster. That would be a dreadful shame. You are easy to look at, my dear," I hear sweet giggles as a wave of heat washes over my cheeks. How much of that did Thaddeus hear?

"Thanks," I murmur, with another hard swallow as I offer a smile to Thaddeus and hope he doesn't believe a word of true rumors and that he stays right where he is.

My view of Thaddeus is perfect. He is listening to the men's conversations. He is dressed for visiting in a nice coat, dark blue vest, and a cravat neatly tied at his neck. He and I make quick eye contact. I blink at him, and he responds with a slight smile, looking away to the conversation.

"Where is Stephen?" Mrs. Byrne asks.

"He ran out the backdoor with Henry," I say. I feel the weight of the woman shift the tide of the couch and decide that now is the best time to see if my legs still work, "Can I get refreshments for anyone?"

Mrs. Marsh pipes up, "Julia, you told me about the patterned fabrics for the—what was it?"

"Oh yes, for the quilt I will piece together this spring. Do you want to see the fabric?"

"I would be delighted. I just love the design. And if you don't mind, may I see the house? We never visited the Deardorf family. They were very private," Mrs. Marsh confides.

"Absolutely," Mother stands inviting her to follow. "Come with me."

Mother and Mrs. Marsh leave the parlor, and I am left in the circle of Mrs. Byrne's company.

"I will have some more of those sandwiches, though perhaps I should give you my recipe instead," says Mrs. Byrne.

I pretend not to hear her and steal another look to Thaddeus. He is watching me. We watch each other smiling. I wish I could hear his thoughts like my parents seem to do on almost every occasion.

Bits and pieces of the men's conversation talked about some broken part father has in the barn. They make an agreement for them to go see it. In unison, they move to the front hall, gather their coats and head for the barn. Ian follows behind like a faithful puppy. At the slam of the door, I breathe a heavy sigh of relief.

"I asked for sandwiches, did you hear girl?" asks Mrs. Byrne.

I turn to look at Mrs. Byrne and politely say, "Of which there is a tray in the kitchen. Please make yourself at home."

Mrs. Byrne glares at me with two beady eyes, right down her pointed nose. I figure I'm already off the list of approved ladies for her son, so what could possibly make things worse?

We sit there staring at each other for a solid heartbeat before she gets up and heads down the hall. I laugh, and a chuckle joins my own.

"Miss Prescott, it's a pleasure to see you again. May I sit?" asks Thaddeus.

"It would certainly be easier to talk with you," I say, patting the cushion beside me.

"Oh, that close? Are you sure?" The glint in his deep blue eyes accent his dimples.

"It is you who needs to be wary, or haven't you heard?" I say, scowling, a pout forming at my lower lip.

Thaddeus walks over to sit next to me. "Don't believe I have. May I ask? I'd rather hear it straight from the horse's mouth."

"I'm sure you will hear it sooner than later. This town loves to gossip."

Thaddeus leans back against the couch cushion. "I have not heard this gossip. If it's about you, I am sorry, but you're just not that popular."

"Mr. Locher told everyone he saw my ankle when I raced Starlight past his home a month or so ago. Sure, my skirt may have billowed up a bit, but why would he mention it? I don't understand—"

"Well—" Thaddeus begins.

"—and now their wives are praying for my salvation, my propriety, and that I don't become a spinster! And don't even get me started on what Mrs. Byrne thinks, not that I care." I look to Thaddeus. His face is calm, and his head nods along with what I hope is empathy and not boredom. Then he goes to open his mouth—

"Worse yet, Stephen asked if he could see my ankles! Can you believe the nerve?"

Thaddeus and I look at each other. It is so easy to just look at him, but what is he waiting for? *Why is he just watching me?*

"Anything else?" he asks.

"No, why?"

"I don't want you to think I always interrupt you. And for the record, I don't want to see your ankles, unless of course you want to show them to me." His eyebrows raise slightly with a playful grin breaking out over his lips.

I giggle, place my hand on his, and pat it gently.

"Thank you. That is quite kind and respectful of you, but I believe I will decline."

"Well then, I guess I'll just have to keep a look out on Table Rock Road."

Silence ...

Fidgeting ...

Shuffling ...

"Are you looking forward to the dance tomorrow night?" Thaddeus asks.

"Yes, I haven't danced in a long time."

"If I may be forward—"

"I thought you weren't going to ask about my ankles."

"I'm not," he bites back a smile giving a soft chuckle instead, "but I did want to ask if you will save me a place, on your dance card, that is."

"Which dance?" I ask falling back into his looks, wanting to stay lost in them for the rest of my days. "Let's see, you look like an accomplished dancer. I suppose I could take you on for the first, maybe the fifth, perhaps even the last?"

Thaddeus' face turns scarlet, "Well, I—"

"How about a waltz?" I ask. Our eyes meet, the challenge is accepted.

"Would you mind if we practice first?"

"Practice...when?"

"How about now?" Thaddeus stands up and stretches his hand to me.

I stand to face him.

He places my left hand on his shoulder. I feel the strong smooth muscle through his coat. Then he takes my right hand in his. His touch is warm, his callouses smooth as his fingers wrap around my own, allowing my hand to seemingly disappear into his. Our eyes meet as we ready to step. *Have his eyes always been this deep? Our closeness is thrilling, it's hard to remember to breathe much less—*

Thaddeus clears his throat, "Who's counting?"

"I will," I whisper.

"One ... Two ... Three ..." I try not to look at his feet—it's a sign of a beginner. Tentatively we step, our toes safe from each other's—so far.

Back ... side ... close, forward ... side ... close.

"How's school?" he asks.

Back ... side ... close, forward ...

"I passed my pretest."

Side ... close, back ...

"Excellent work," he nods as he turns me again. We are lost in the rhythm of the dance, a silent tune playing just for us. With ease we continue, "I must say, Miss—"

My eyes look up to him. I miss a step, nearly trip, he pulls me closer, catches me in his arms, finger tapping the rhythm on my shoulder as he sets me back on my feet where my propriety belongs. My cheek brushes his shoulder. I smell his cologne. Is that bergamot and what else?

I should back up, but oh, what else is this scent? His scent, intoxicating as it is—from?

"Call me Emilie," I say, looking up at him.

He clears his throat, turning me to avoid the table, then twirling me. I gasp.

"Are you alright, Emilie?"

"Yes, you are more accomplished than you let on Mr—"

"Thaddeus," he interjects.

"Thaddeus," I repeat.

I hear heavy footfalls coming down the hall.

I count aloud again, "One ... Two ... Three ..."

Henry is notorious for sounding like a herd of animals when he walks. The back door slams. Thaddeus looks down at me.

"We are practicing. No harm in a dance partner, right?" I ask.

He smiles back. "Here's the finale, ready?"

I nod as he turns me twice, then dips me low suspending me inches from the ground in his strong arms, his shoulders going taut. My lips are inches from his. His warm breath caresses my cheek as my back rests secure against the sinew of his leg.

Suspended in each other's embrace ... his wink ... his smile ...

"That is a great finish," I say through giddy and yet uncontrollable giggles.

His eyes sparkle with amusement as he lifts me to my feet. A step back, his hand still a lifeline in mine. His bow meets my curtsy. Our gazes lock together like two puzzle pieces meant to be—brown eyes playfully greeting the incoming tide of his deep blue pools, a silent understanding passing between us.

"I eagerly await you signing my dance card tomorrow night," My cheeks flush from the exertion.

"Bring a sharp pencil. I will wear out a dull one."

A tremor shoots through me as his fingertips brush mine, sending a spark dancing up my arm, then a mischievous wink before he lifts my hand to his lips. The kiss, light as a feather yet charged like lightning during a summer storm, ignites a thrilling warmth, capturing my breath with it. His soft breath whispers unspoken promises, renews my lungs, and lingers in my presence just a moment too long. A whiff of cologne with a teasing scent I still cannot recall, unique to him—bergamot and lemon?

The warmth of his hand fades, replaced by a phantom tingle that makes my fingertips ache for his return. A lingering glance into his deep blue depths, and I swear I hear a silent whisper from his soul, *I will miss you.*

"Tomorrow night then," I whisper back an echo from my lips and heart. Propriety might bind me, but every fiber of my being screams to throw myself into his arms, feel his warmth, bask in his understanding of me, and inhale the masculine intoxication that is—

Slam!

The parlor door bangs open like a gunshot, jarring the laughter from our throats, I squeak with surprise, and whip my head around Thadeus's broad shoulder expecting Henry to be laughing at us with a lovelorn kissy lips mock. Instead, Henry stands framed in the doorway, his usual jovial grin replaced by a grimace. His hand, white-knuckled, gripping Stephen's arm, and pinning him down.

Stephen, his face masked in jealousy, turns to ice the moment my gaze meets his. His eyes, usually a starry cosmos of warm hazel mystery, now hard and dark like the earth just before a thaw—shards of accusation glint from within their depths.

My breath hitches in my throat, my heart hammering with

fear against my ribs. My fingers claw into my skirts, longing for Thaddeus to—

"I see you haven't learned anything today, Miss Prescott. First ankles, now pressing your body so wantonly against this man." Stephen hisses as his finger stabs in Thaddeus's direction.

"She did no such—" Thaddeus moves in front of me.

"Who made you judge and jury of my propriety sir?" I step aside and forward challenging Stephen on my own terms, his words enough to chase the fear right out of me and leaving rage nipping at the tip of my own tongue. Henry pulls harder on Stephen's arm to keep him there.

"Oh no, don't challenge her, she will rip—" Henry's warns.

Stephen ignores him saying, "Someone has to do it. You obviously don't care to save yourself."

The vein in his neck pulses, and I narrow my eyes at it, at him, wishing for nothing more than it to burst.

"If and when I need saving, Mr. Byrne, you will be the last to know because just like your mother, you fail to see past your own nose! Now, good day, Mr. Byrne, and more importantly good riddance!"

I turn back to Thaddeus and take a breath, hoping my words are not too glib by the likes of Stephen Byrne interrupting the paradise Thaddeus put me in. "Good day, Thaddeus. I look forward to dancing with you tomorrow night. Can I show you out?"

Thaddeus takes no offense, and I slip my arm around his as Thaddeus escorts me to the door.

"Are you seeing him?"

"I have no ties to Mr. Byrne, despite what you saw there. And he has no promises from me."

"If all goes well." Thaddeus begins.

"I look forward to seeing your name on my dance card, Mr. Marsh." I watch him, holding out for one more second in his gaze.

"I'll bring the pencil, Miss Prescott. Good day."

The latch sounds, the promise hanging between us warms my soul. I will have to deal with Mr. Byrne another time, but for now, it appears Henry has quite the handle on the back door.

New Years Ball

EVERY NEW BEGINNING COMES FROM SOME
OTHER BEGINNING'S END. ~SENECA

DECEMBER 1860
TABLE ROCK ROAD
GETTYSBURG, PENNSYLVANIA

The world rumbles louder today. The newsprint screams secession accusations across the national breakfast table. South Carolina, the first domino to fall, casts a long shadow of unease over our family. Worry gnaws at the edge of my excitement, a discordant note amidst the anticipation of tonight's ball.

Thaddeus.

His name alone sends the hummingbirds fluttering in my ribs, a reminder of the intoxicating laughter we shared last night. Yet, the question still lingers, unspoken amidst the celebrations, will the music tonight be enough to drown out the drums of war? A fleeting thought flickers—ask Father, ask Arron—but for now, I must answer the call of the dance. Worry can wait.

Tonight, we welcome this New Year together.

"Mother, where's my ball gown?" I say, rushing into my parents' bedroom.

"I believe it's in the trunk we put at the end of your bed, unless—" Mother pauses tapping a finger to her lips. Despite the fact moving day was three months ago, we are still trying to find where we placed items.

"Unless?" I urge her to think faster, wishing I could do it for her.

"—my wardrobe! Yes, let's try that." A smile of confidence graces her lips.

We both head to the wardrobe and open the large doors to find an array of dresses from elegant formal wear to tea dresses and ... Ah yes, the blue and yellow checked ballgown I wore to my first dance at age fifteen. Pulling it with care from the wardrobe, a flood of memories comes with the full spectacle of it.

I was a shy fifteen-year-old, wanting to dance, but the boys were also too shy to ask. I danced with my brothers and father that night and envied the sixteen- and seventeen-year-olds who already had beaus filling up their dance cards. I loved the waltzes and giggled at the broom dance. I vowed to always choose the boy over the broom. After all, it looked preposterous to dance with a silly broom. Today, the realization that I am now the seventeen-year-old waiting to have her dance card filled is—

"Are you going to stare at it or try it on?" Mother's voice brings me back to reality, "And what are you smiling at?"

"It's just my first ball, the only suitors I had to dance with were my brothers and Father."

"Oh Emilie, I'm sure this year things will be different. Why, I imagine this year they will be the ones struggling to find room on your dance card, while Stephen, and Thaddeus, and any other eligible bachelor, will be in the thick of battle for just a few minutes of your time. They're quite smitten with you, you know."

"Stephen? No, he may like me, but I have no interest in his bad manners or caddy attitude. In fact, I hope he stays home," I say, shaking my head. His icy cold stare is still stamped in my mind from last night, the gooseflesh threatens to answer with a ripple of cobbled bumps on my arms.

"Are you cold?" Mother's face pinches with concern.

"More worried this won't fit," I say.

"I should have pulled this out days ago." Mother fluffs out the skirt, looking for moth holes and other stains.

"It's a little late now, and besides, we had no time, remember?" I say as I strip down to my chemise, struggle into my corset, and wiggle into my hoop—tying it at my waist. I put my arms over my head waiting for the cloud of fabric to swallow me whole. Mother fastens the skirt that has two buttons at the back; I feel her use the outermost button. Next, I cautiously slip into the bodice, careful not to pull the ties through the eyelets. The first armhole is snug; a little tug—there. Placing my hands on the boned bodice, I hold it in place as Mother tightens the laces to close the back.

Pull ... tug ... suck in my breath.

Pull ... tug ... catch my breath.

Pull ... tug ... I grunt and Mother sighs.

"Em, we are going to need a new dress."

"What! Does it close?" Panic rises and my voice cracks.

"Shh. Let me finish," Mother sucks in her breath, while I go back to holding mine...

"There, look." Mother says as she has finally finished squeezing me in like jelly in a roll.

I turn to the mirror, eyes wide with shock. I bite my lip. "Oh God, what happened?"

"I think you became a woman."

"I should say! How am I going to cover this? ... I can't wander about with all of *this* spilling over!" The mirror reflects a bodice capturing all my bosom, smashing my ample flesh together, and pushing me over the top of the low-cut curve. Panic swells within me and threatens to spill out of my dress. I let out a long sigh.

"They already made fun of my ankles, now this?" I point to the overflowing bodice, "Can you sew a ruffle or how about a neckerchief?" I ask while looking around the room for anything to cover myself.

"We have less than an hour before we leave, and you know I can't sew a ruffle. I don't have a neckerchief either."

On the bureau, I spy a sandalwood fan. I love the delicate scent; will it be enough though to save my reputation? Reaching past her, I grab the fan and flip it open, covering the top of the bodice.

"How about this?" I say, chewing on my lower lip.

Maybe I shouldn't have wished Mr. Byrne to stay home. Maybe it should be me instead.

Mother eyes me and gives a small nod before brushing her hand over my skirt, as if petting my gown will make things better. "A fan and a shawl will have to do; we don't have time for much more."

"Is the length alright? Is it too short? Maybe I should just stay home?"

Do hearts pound this hard when they are broken like a fragile soap bubble at the idea of it all? I blink back a hot tear.

Mother fastens a lace choker at my neck with a blue stone at the center. She clips on two blue stoned earrings, and hands me a pair of lace gloves. As I don the gloves, she fetches a blue shawl that only sort of matches and something from her jewelry box.

"Nonsense, you will do no such thing, Emilie Kathryn," Mother drapes the shawl around my shoulders, fastening each end together at the center with a broach Father gifted her on her last birthday.

A gasp escapes me as I look down in wonder at it, not expecting her to entrust me with such a precious keepsake.

Mother thinks nothing of it though as she spins me around. "Now go sit. We haven't much time before your father yells up the stairs."

I plop down on the wooden bench at her vanity, and she deftly pulls out my pins, brushes out my hair, and twists it up into an updo. Her practiced fingers then comb back wisps of frazzled hair but leave the baby curls at my temple to frame my youthful visage. She then hands me a powder puff instructing me to hold my breath and puts a light dot of rouge on my cheeks. I open my eyes and must admit; it all seems magical how pretty I appear with just a few minutes of her tender loving care.

When she finishes, she instructs me to help her into her gown. Afterward I sit on the edge of her bed, while watching her transform from Mother to the maiden Father probably dreams of. The mirror seems to roll back time, turning mother into an eighteen-year-old with all the anticipation and giddiness of going to a dance. Was she remembering those early days with Father? Just as Mother places the last of the rouge on her lips—

"Ladies, we are leaving in five minutes!" Father's voice calls up the stairs.

One last look in the mirror, and Mother and I heed Father's call. Mother, first down the stairs, is greeted by Father—handsomely dressed in his Sunday best. His eyes brighten as a smile stretches across his lips at the sight of her.

I hope my husband looks at me that way.

Father holds out her cloak, as mother turns for him to wrap it around her shoulders. I descend the last two stairs to see Henry's eyes widen, but he is not looking at me eye-to-eye.

"Will it hold?" he asked.

Father checks him upside the back of his head.

"It was a compliment!" says Henry.

I suck in a breath and try to ignore my insufferable sibling, flipping open the fan to cover myself, as Aaron holds my cloak open for me.

"Thank you, Aaron," I say, buttoning the cloak closed.

"Here you will need these too. It is brisk out there," Aaron hands me a rabbit muff. My fingers slide over the satin inside, already warm and inviting. "You have certainly grown up since you wore that dress last."

"How come he doesn't get smacked upside the head?" I hear Henry ask Father as they leave for the barn.

I shake my head and look at Aaron. "Is it too revealing?"

"No," he assures me, "though I'm sure you won't need to dance with your brothers tonight."

"But I saved a dance for you," I say. "Unless you promised yourself to somebody else?"

"Not yet," Aaron nudges me to the door. "Let's go."

We make our way to the sleigh. Mother and I situate ourselves in the back, covering up with the lap blankets, as Henry pushes a pot of warmed coal between our feet.

"The basket," Henry hands us a basket full of food and dishes for dinner.

"I almost forgot. Thank you for remembering, Henry," Mother settles the basket in her lap.

Aaron and Father sit in the front seat, and Henry squeezes in next to the men up front.

"Henry, be careful not to fall out," Mother calls to him.

"Make sure to pick me up," he says.

Father calls to the team, and we are off toward the Halle farm.

The stars are bright in the night sky. There is no wind, but the air is chilled as I can see my breath puff out in white little clouds. Aaron and Father talk quietly, their conversation reminding me about the newspaper from this morning.

"Aaron, did you see the paper?" I ask. "I wanted to ask you about South Carolina."

"I read it," Aaron shifts in his seat to face me.

"Will there be more or—"

"I'm afraid the South is going to stand on this issue. I think this is the beginning of something," Aaron sucks in his breath. "I just hope that something doesn't come to war, but what choice is there?"

"There is always a choice," Father breaks in. "It is a matter of listening and compromise."

Aaron looks from Father back to me, his face furrowed in thought. "I say we worry about this another time. Tonight, let's celebrate our new neighbors and the new year ahead."

"All right but I still want to hear your opinions—later, that is."

"Emilie," mother interjects, "this is a man's problem."

"I will be happy to leave it up to the men, but we are all affected by this," I say, "and so I feel it is a woman's right to know."

Aaron chuckles, "Later Em. We will talk about it later." He turns back just as Father turns the sleigh up Halle's drive. He put me off, as I know there is more to the secession of South Carolina, but for tonight, I intend to enjoy this dance.

The frost-kissed barn, its weathered timbers shimmering like aged silver under the faint glow of lanterns, beckons me closer. Curiosity tugs at my sleeve, as I push open the creaky door, stepping into a scene straight out of a winter dream.

Warmth envelops me like a welcome hug. The air buzzes with life, a symphony of laughter and chatter mingles with scents of stews, roasts, and pies. Spices dance on my tongue, a promise of culinary delights. Overhead, paper snowflakes pirouette, their whimsical shadows flitting across the faces of my neighbors, young and old, swirling and mingling in celebration.

"Julia! Emilie!" Mrs. Halle draws us over to a table. "Here are your dance cards. The dishes go over on the buffet. You're welcome to make yourselves at home at any table."

Jane hands us our cards. "Here you go," She leans closer to me. "Miss Emilie, your dress is beautiful."

"Thank you, Jane, are you staying to dance this evening?" I ask.

Jane shyly shakes her head. "I have to watch the boys." A pout forms at her lower lip.

"I'm sorry," I say. "Soon, you'll be dancing though, soon."

"Emilie, I need to put these things down," Mother readjusts the basket weighing heavy on her arm. I wave at Jane, who smiles as we turn away.

We walk over to the buffet tables filled with delectable treats and dishes—cast iron and colored glassware, all wrapped up in tea towels. Stews, roasted meats, venison, beef, lamb, and pork. The other dishes are comprised of baked vegetables and potatoes. At the end of the table sits the cakes, cookies, and sweet delights. My stomach growls in anticipation. We drop off two dishes of baked squash and a tray of leftover cookies—*I am tired of looking at those.*

Mother leads the way to an empty table. The crowd of familiar faces swirl around as we pass by them, their laughter and good cheer charging the room with warmth and celebration.

"Emilie, stay here. Set the table. I'll find your brothers and father."

I nod as she slips back into the crowd. The basket sits like a beacon in the center of the table, but the dance card, a small booklet, is in my hand. The smooth paper beckons to me, pages of possibilities, new adventures, and thoughts of Thaddeus warm me—a smile. Paging through the dances, excitement builds as I take note of each number—waltzes, reels, polkas, and a broom dance. Why do I want his name to fill the pages?

A burst of laughter makes me look up—Stephen Byrne.

Is he flirting with Louisa Welty and...who's that? Another girl?

Stephen stands on the other side of the barn laughing, signing his name, and teasing a lady with her dance card, keeping it just out of reach as she tries to take it back. Her giggles are a high note dancing above the low rumble of the room. Just as the girl jumps up to pull her card from his hand, which hovers above her head, Stephen's eyes meet mine.

His hazel hues, playful and bright with mirth, no longer hosts a darkness that consumes everything with jealousy. His eyebrow arches as his gaze leaves my eyes to linger—

I swallow hard and pull my shawl in front of me. Stephen's mouth turns down, a frown of disappointment forming. His gaze trails back to mine. I hold his look for a moment, blink, and look away. A chill races up my spine, and the hair on the back of my neck stands up with what feels like a razor's edge. If he signs up for the broom dance with me, I will dance with the broom.

"There you are! Finding you is like trying to find one of your lost needles in Mother's parlor rug. What a great turnout," Henry slides into the chair beside me.

"I thought you were going to set the table?" Mother joins us.

"I—I am getting to it," I say, getting up to pull the basket closer. Setting down the dance card, I turn to the place settings and finish this chore.

Tinkle-tinkle-tinkle. A small bell chimes, asking for silence from the crowd.

Mr. and Mrs. Halle give a quick welcome speech as I search the room for Thaddeus. His presence will calm my nerves.

The Halles, the Weltys, and the Lochers ...

Why is it taking so long to spot him? ...

The Byrnes, a family I don't know, and another one I've never met ...

He promised ...

Father nudges me, whispering. "We are saying grace."

I sigh, but bow my head, and tune out the prayer led by Mr. Halle in favor of my own request, *Dear God, please let Thaddeus fill out my dance card and make this the most magical night I've ever experienced, but not forever experienced because if this to be the fondest night of my life, I might very well die of boredom in the many days I hope to come.* I wait for the amen. After the prayer, everyone turns their attention to what some would consider the main event, the buffet table.

Plate in hand, my shawl slips off my shoulder.

A hand puts it back, warm and comforting—*Thaddeus?*

I turn to look.

"Don't lose that," Aaron says, "You can't catch a chill before the dance."

"Thank you," I will a smile and disguise my disappointment for Aaron's sake.

156

The line slows, and the shawl slips again.

Turning to Aaron, I hand him my plate. "Hold this," I say and readjust the broach of the shawl, securing it for what I hope is one last time. Turning to Aaron, he gives back the plate.

"I don't need this falling off into the stew," I say gesturing to Mother's gift.

"Certainly not." Aaron is watching me. "So, who are you looking for? Crane your neck anymore and I fear it'll break off," he smirks.

"Why would I be looking for anyone?" I ask.

"You have a dance card to fill, don't you? Didn't Mr. Marsh promise to dance with you? I heard—"

"Yes, Aaron," I put a small piece of ham and a scoop of potatoes on my plate.

"Haven't seen them yet."

"He promised he would be here." I step away from the buffet and seat myself at my family's chosen table.

My appetite leaves despite my anticipation from earlier. My confidence is waning and this dress—

Pushing the food around my plate, I impatiently wait for the chatter to die down.

How is anyone expected to dance if they eat so much?

I push a pea around the mound of potatoes and through bits of leftover ham. Staring at the unappetizing piece of cake perched on the edge of my plate it looks like a dried out crumbled mess. The whole meal lost its appeal.

"Emilie, you are not eating," Mother's voice interrupts my thoughts. "Are you feeling all right?"

Looking up, I am met with concern in her eyes. Everyone's plate is empty. Mine is still filled with food, appearing more like a sculpture with each passing minute, barely touched. Everyone lends me a curious eye.

"I'm fine, just want to be light enough to dance," I say, adding a smile to cover the sadness they don't need to know about. The sound of chairs scraping over the floor and the rush of moving people divert their attention from me.

"Well, two more bites. I don't want you to faint on the dance floor."

"Yes, ma'am," I say, forcing myself to take a few more mouthfuls, feeling like a scolded two-year-old.

Henry and Aaron go to retrieve our remaining dishes from the buffet, which are added to the basket with the rest of our belongings as Mother and Father begin to clear the table.

My spirits lighten as I hear the musicians warming up their instruments. Their tones are full-bodied against the chatter and bubbly voices of those waiting to dance. I turn away from my food to take it all in, only to look back and find the table empty, cleared of plates, silverware, and—my dance card!

Where's my dance card?

It has to be here! I search the basket. Did it get swept up?

Spying Aaron coming toward me I ask, "Aaron, have you seen my dance card?"

Aaron looks down at me, his dark brown eyes smiling. "Henry was looking at it."

I turn; Henry is—there across the room.

"Thank you, Aaron," I say.

There he is, that—talking to the Ewing boys? Why?... Oh, that's mine!

I stand up and approach the boys at a brisk pace, grab Henry's sleeve, and pinch a bit of his flesh in my nails.

He jumps at the surprised pain and turns to me as he yanks his arm free. A hand goes to rub at the tender skin, but a smirk glosses over his lips, as he slides that injured arm of his around me.

"Emilie, let me introduce you to Joshua Ewing. He signed your dance card."

I glare at Henry but turn to Mr. Ewing with the curly brown hair and unremarkable dull matching eyes—and smile. "Pleasure to meet you, Mr. Ewing."

Back to Henry, my glower returns. "How kind of you to secure dance partners for me this evening." I pluck the dance card from his sweaty hand and watch as his smile withers.

"I will meet you on the dance floor, Mr. Ewing."

Not waiting for his reply, I turn back. The musicians are assembling, the floor is cleared, the vast space is opening in anticipation of the caller announcing the first dance. Panic floods over me as I flip through the pages. Out of ten dances, seven are filled. Mr. Hunter, Mr. Ewing, Mr. Byrne, Mr. Hunter again, Mr. Byrne again, Mr. Halle—the younger—and Mr. Green? My heart sinks.

Thaddeus is nowhere on the list.

"Why the long face?" A male voice washes away my anger. I didn't need to see Mr. Marsh, I mean Thaddeus; to know it's him. I turn and look (how could I not?) and erupt into a smile. He mimics the pout on my face for a second and then returns my expression with an undercurrent of affection. His warm deep blue eyes—*Oh how I could just drown in them.* A flutter of excitement rises in my chest, then drops like a stone in the pit of my gut and is replaced by nausea and worse—word vomit.

"Henry took the liberty of filling out my dance card for me. There is Mr. Hunter, Mr. Ewing, Mr. Byrne, Mr. Hunter again, Mr. Byrne again, Mr. Halle—the younger if I may add—and Mr.

Green." I take a gasp. "Why haven't you signed my dance card?"

Thaddeus's brow furrows, "Well, is it all right if I sign it now? Assuming there is still space." He takes the card from my hand before I can answer and flips through the pages with a groan of disappointment. "Guess I'll have to do my best if I'm going to be your last. Now, where is that pencil?"

Watching him search his pockets, he pulls a fresh sharpened pencil from the pocket that also holds his handkerchief and signs his name to the last three dances. The lead snaps, sending the pewter-colored bits off into the air. His brow follows with an arch all its own.

"If I may be so bold to dance the last three dances with you, Miss—I mean, Emilie."

His eyes pin me down in play, but his gaze is soft and holds me afloat, while reflecting the true depth of his nature. He suspends us together in a moment of twilight, and I can't help but think back to last night when he swept me off my feet and over an impromptu dance floor.

"I can't wait for the end of the evening, Mr.—I mean, Thaddeus."

He hands me the dance card, our fingers touching lightly, sending my heart fluttering, my breath catching, his warmth spreading ... Did his finger stroke mine before he let go?

"I look forward to it," he whispers, his voice catching, cracking. A moment of blush creeps over his cheeks before he turns and walks away.

The urge to chase him claws at my insides, a desperate need warring with the rigid corset of propriety that cinches my waist. *How does he do that, make me long to hear his laughter, feel his breath whisper across my cheek?* Perhaps the closeness of our dance will satisfy my flames of yearning, keeping us—me within the constraints of social acceptability.

Returning to our table to sit for a moment, my legs feel weak as my heart mirrors a wild horse's hoofbeats, hammering my chest with unbound excitement. Then I feel a whisper tickle the back of my ear.

"I think he is smitten with you. Did you save a dance for me?"

Turning to the voice, Aaron is holding his hand out to me.

"Speak to Henry," I say, "he filled out the dance card. I am not acquainted with some of these men, so please feel free to cut in."

Aaron goes to grab the card, but I pull it back from his grasp. "But you may not cut in on any of the last three dances." I say, punctuating the last words with a finger to his chest.

He grabs my finger. "I knew you liked him. I'll be sure to watch over you, from a distance."

"Which ladies are you dancing with?"

"A few, but I don't want them thinking I am staying—leaving in a few days remember?"

"Did you have to remind me?" A pout forms at my lower lip.

"No long faces, we are having fun, remember," Aaron nudges me.

I push away his reminder and begin the struggle of putting on my slippers. The corset constrains my movement. Reach ... attempt to breathe ... fail miserably ... turn red. I sit back up with a huff before giving it another go and manage to tie the first slipper in place just as the music starts and the caller summons us to the floor for a Virginia Reel.

On cue, Mr. Hunter arrives.

"Miss Prescott, I'm Timothy Hunter. May I have this dance?" he asks.

I see his arm extend but not his hand because I assume it is hovering somewhere over my head.

Does he not see me struggling down here?

"Good evening, Mr. Hunter," I say. "One moment. I need to get this ... dreadful ... Oh come now—I will be right with you."

Timothy Hunter doesn't speak for a long moment before he kneels to offer to help me slip the shoe in place. He winds the ribbon around my leg with shaky fingers and ties it in such a fashion that I think he fears my ankle will break under any pressure. He's not the only one facing the weight of this close and rather intimate encounter, though. I feel a tide of crimson rush across my face—*then again, perhaps that is from struggling with my wardrobe.*

"Thank you," I say, our eyes meet. His are a deep green. His hair is a brighter shade of red than mine, but our cheeks match in tone. He offers me his hand once more, and this time I take it to stand.

"We best hurry or we will be left out." I feel his other hand low on my back as he escorts me to the end of the line for the Virginia Reel.

My excitement builds as the four-count jig summoned by the fiddles calls to us. Our lines begin clapping as we take steps toward each other, bow and curtsy, retreat, and repeat it all over again in various ways.

"You look delightful this evening." He says, before we move away from each other.

We head back toward one another and hook elbows, "Thank you, and you are a commanding leader."

I catch him looking down and follow his glance down to make sure I am still respectable.

We unhook from one another.

"Is everything all right?" he asks.-

Clap! Turn–2–3 ...

"Yes!" I say as we circle out and around to meet back up.

His hands grasp mine and together we rush under the bridge of hands and arms, only to become a part of that bridge at the end.

"You are light on your feet, Miss Prescott," His voice is a medium tone and a bit out of breath.

"And your dancing skills are just as commendable," I say.

This elicits a grin from him, lighting up his green eyes, and I watch as the red seeps down from his cheeks to his neck.

The reel ends all too quickly, but Mr. Hunter's grace and good charm remind me there are many good gentlemen here.

"Thank you again," I say, as he escorts me back to the table.

"My pleasure. I look forward to another dance soon," Mr. Hunter says. "Until then, Miss Prescott, enjoy your evening." He bows his head and slips back into the crowd. The clatter of the chatter rises as the music of the first reel fades away.

The next dance is the Carolina Promenade. I look for Mr. Ewing but cannot see him until the young man standing in front of me extends a hand that rattles more than it shakes. *If he stood any closer to the wall, I don't think I'd have seen him at all.*

"M-m-m-miss Prescott, may-ay-ay I have this dance?" Mr. Ewing asks. I notice him looking down, not at my chest, but at his feet.

I offer him my hand and a reassuring smile, "The pleasure is mine. Thank you, Mr. Ewing, is it?"

I watch his Adam's apple bounce before he gives a stiff nod, eyes straight ahead, back as rigid as a barn beam, as he escorts me to—I hope a dance? *Though he may be of the opinion it is a funeral march?*

The dancers form several circles as the four-count music begins once again. Mr. Ewing flinches each time the caller shouts, and by the third instruction the poor man trips over his own foot as we step forward and back. By the time I grasp his hand it's slick with sweat.

Perhaps, a little banter will help him relax?

"Tell me Mr. Ewing, what is your trade?"

"Wheelwright." His brow is furrowed in concentration. His eyes are on the couple ahead of us.

"Very commendable," I say counting in my head. "So—"

Mr. Ewing stops and turns directly to me, "I'm sorry Miss Prescott, but I can't concentrate and talk at the same time." Another dancer collides into him, and we spend the rest of the reel trying to either catch up to the instructor or keep Mr. Ewing on his feet, though I think from now on it would be better if he stays off them.

The dance ends without further conversation, much to both Mr. Ewing and my own relief.

"I apologize," he says with a bow, pausing at half tilt. His cheeks burn bright red and then he straightens, about faces, and quickly walks away.

I look down to check my shawl once more. It rests perfectly in place, but I wonder if it is enough.

Walking back to the table, I pull out my fan to cool myself and cover myself at the same time. Looking up, I see Stephen not only standing in front of me but staring at the—fan with that smirk of his and a glint of mischief in his eye. He holds a cup of cold water to me.

"You look positively graceful out there. Can't say the same for Ewing, but that's his loss. So, are you ready to dance with a real man?" he asks. His eyes finally meeting mine with a confident air.

"I don't know. Are you capable of counting to three Mr. Byrne?" I fan myself for a moment as the musicians take a quick break themselves. Looking around the room, I am hoping to catch sight of Thaddeus. *How is his night going?*

Stephen produces an obnoxious sigh of impatience as he stands next to me. I dare say, a goat has better manners. He leans down, breaching the barrier of my fan. His hot breath is on my neck, and a hint of whiskey tickles my nose. "I can count all the way to four, but that's my limit. Think you to instruct me further, Miss Prescott?"

A shiver is elicited as his baritone voice gives lift to the small hairs along my tender neck, moved by his words. "If I had to instruct you, Mr. Byrne, you wouldn't know life without a dunce hat and scarred knuckles."

"Sounds like a good time, but call me Stephen, please." He fixes on me, wrapping me in a vine of possession. He is too confident tonight.

The waltz starts with its telltale one–two–three.

"That's our cue." Stephen takes my cup and places it on the table, while he presents me his other hand and escorts me to the floor. This hand of his guides mine to his shoulder, then rests— on my hip?

I swallow hard and quickly move his hand up to my lower back.

He smirks.

We step.

"Who's counting?" I ask.

"Me. The man always leads, and the woman should always follow." His eyes—Oh yes, they are hazel.

With long, graceful strides, we glide between other pairs until he turns me. I stub my toe against his foot.

"Perhaps it wasn't all Mr. Ewing?" he asks.

"He didn't have big feet to trip on," I retort.

"I'll take that as a compliment," his smirk remains, and for the life of me I cannot figure out why, not that I have much time to consider it. Stephen pulls me closer than he should, and I feel his thigh against the hoop of my dress.

He's too close.

What is meant to be a gentle hand on my back tightens into a grip as his thumb wraps around to the front of my waist.

He's holding me too tight.

His forearm tightens as I lean back in a silent request for space. The flex in his bicep shows, however, as he insists on pulling me closer.

"What's wrong? We've been closer than this, if you remember."

My back aches in protest.

"I remember quite well, but we are in public, and this is not proper ..." I say in a hiss of a whisper.

I trip again, but there is no room to fall, just the crushing pain of his embrace as his arm constricts around my ribs.

"Well, I guess it's only proper to dance with you in your parlor—alone. Is that it?" The last word is emphasized with the spray of spit that may as well be poison, for all the slander it gives.

Fueled by his forwardness, I miss another step, but I refuse to let him see me falter and shift my feet with a quick one–two to get back into the appropriate rhythm.

Stephen chuckles.

Is he enjoying embarrassing me?

"I'm really starting to think I am mistaken about that grace."

I feel him throw his weight, sending my feet to tangle over

themselves.

Oh God, don't let me fall ...

Pushing him away from me, I start to tumble back—back as a hand at my elbow pulls me to—

"Maybe I was mistaken to allow you to dance with my sister," Aaron's dark glare turns to warmth as he looks down at me. "May I finish this dance, Miss Prescott?"

Stephen's features boil up and over his frown as his mouth mutates into a crude scowl. The shock coupled with his indignance is delightful, and though I wait for him to flap back some scathing remark, he appears to have enough decorum not to argue with my brother. Instead, his jaw sets, holding back his venom as he turns and walks away.

Aaron takes up both me and the waltz, and unlike Stephen's his arms play host to me as if I were a delicate feather teetering on the tip of an outstretched branch. Looking over his shoulder, I see Stephen's muddied glare aimed right at me. Aaron steers me away from his visage, and soon we find twinned laughter in the sibling revelry of my brother's heroics. Such laughter twists in my throat, though, spilling out into a muted cry as I am turned back to face Stephen by the tide of the dance.

"What's wrong? Stub your toe again?"

I watch Stephen drink from a flask, his other hand flexing and bunching in a fist with each desperate gulp. Aaron searches my eyes and shifts a bit, activating his broad shoulders and stretching his book-reading slouch out to tower over me like a shield against Stephen's cold stares.

"Never mind him, Em. He'll have to take on all three of us Prescott men to get to you." He turns me with a lift, carrying both me and my spirits up and onward.

I giggle as the floor drops away for a moment. Over his shoulder, Stephen watches us, stoic and hard as steel, unmoved by what he sees.

"What was that all about anyway?" Aaron asks before adding, "He's lucky I stopped Father from cutting in."

"That would have been embarrassing," I say.

"Watch him, Emilie. Mr. Byrne seems to think he's already betrothed to you, and therefore, has rights that belong only to a husband."

"If that is what betrothal is like, then I will never marry. I can't believe he tried such liberties with me!"

"Hush, people are looking at you." Aaron's eyes narrow into sharp edges.

"Well, they have already seen my ankles, and don't get me started on this dress." I whisper back.

Aaron pulls me closer, trying to shield me from the stares. I smell the faint scent of patchouli and feel his chest vibrate with a low chuckle of amusement.

"Don't worry, I won't let you get betrothed to someone like that. Though I do wonder, what is any man going to do with you, dear sister?"

"Give me books and let me teach," I say, a smile returning to my expression.

The dance ends, and I must admit, if only to myself, that I feel better now that Aaron has gotten the dance he requested earlier.

The next two dances are playful. Mr. Hunter returns for a cheerful jaunt of Cat and Mouse, followed by a waltz, with one—Mr. Hunter's stunning green eyes, two—his quiet confidence, three—his tender touch, and repeat.

Stephen did not return for the Quadrille, good riddance, but Master Halle and I had a joyous time with the Broom dance. At the tender age of ten, he brings a youthful playfulness I wish older boys had when approaching the dance floor.

Feeling in need of a small rest, I am not disappointed that Mr. Green doesn't present for his dance. In fact, I find it quite fun to sit at the table with a cup of cold cider in my hand and watch the various ongoings of people around the room. Old maids blush as young men practice dazzling them with lines of poetics, married women become various gaggles of gossipers, while their spouses hobnob about hunting and the year's farming. Beautiful girls about my age are twirled and spun, and dashing—

Oh, it's that Mr. Hunter dancing again. He is going to be a great catch for someone.

Then I see Thaddeus standing to the side with his younger brother, Ian. The poking and teasing of his little brother are accompanied with a nod to a young girl sitting forlorn—waiting, I imagine, for her first dance. With his arm around Ian, he whispers something into his ear. Ian finally grins and takes a few steps toward the young lady, turns back for an extra boost of confidence from his older brother, and then continues his trek into the unknown world of girls.

The nervousness between the two youngsters is palpable, but I can't help smiling when they reach an agreement and head to the dance floor. Touched by the tenderness of brotherly support, Thaddeus and I connect as our gazes sweep back across the room and lock naturally in place with one another. Then he disappears back into the crowd stirring behind him.

How many gents have dark hair?

My eyes flicker from one man to the next, but I can't place him among the many.

If I cannot spot him, does that make me more special to him than him to me?

A waft of bergamot and—lime—yes, its lime that catches my nose, sending tingles through my senses like the subtle current that arrives before a storm.

"I believe the next dance is our first of the evening," Thaddeus is beside me.

"Yes, it is," I say, turning my head to look at him. His eyes linger no lower than my own, but out of my peripheral, I see him present me with his hand.

Our first dance is the Virginia Reel. There is a pep to his every step, a flare of playfulness that reminds me of his youth. Every stolen wink he gives causes giggles to erupt from me in fits of guilty pleasure, which results in him missing a beat and then playing it off as though it were meant to be.

"I'm sorry, I don't mean to interrupt your focus," I say trying to repress the next bout as he approaches me with the same strut as a rooster—head bobbing, knees rising, and arms making up chicken wings.

"Why—bawk—I don't know what you—bawk—mean, BAWK!"

The other dancers around him struggle now, too, and before long everyone is trying a new walk with youngsters joining in too. He makes my corset hurt for a whole new reason, like the stitch in my side, which gets him to return to proper decorum as he moves back over to me with grace and a look of concern.

"Are you alright?" he asks.

I nod, still plagued with the chicken chuckles, which softens his concern with the replacement of a grin as he waits to dissipate and give room for the perfect smile to grace my lips.

His arm scoops around my waist, and excitement tingles through me. Thaddeus spins me about, until the smiling and laughing people surrounding us are whipped into a blur, and Stephen disappears altogether from my view. When we finally stop turning, I am left dizzy with desire, but there is no time to collect myself as we sashay—or rather stagger—like drunks down the line. My right arm passing Mr. Hunter, Mr. Green, and perhaps Mr. Ewing, but I am too enamored with Thaddeus to my left to care.

Another brilliant smile flashes my way, the twinkling of his eyes winking in and out of sight as he closes the left eye and then the right before we join hands, step back from one another and make the bridge of hands when I realize—

"Thaddeus, we are on the wrong sides!" I say. He stands alongside the women and I the men, but this doesn't seem to bother him.

"Says who? For all we know they are the ones out of line!"

The melody of my laugh carries past the music as the song comes to an end, but the musicians pause for only a few minutes before the polka starts up.

Thaddeus still holds my hand as he pulls me in.

"Do you polka, Miss Emilie?" he asks.

"Of course, do you?" I ask, though I'm not sure why as we have already begun.

Hand in hand, he turns me into an inner circle of ladies while he joins the outer circle of men. We dance around each other, before we break off to dance with other partners, exchanging hands again, and again, and again. Then I see him—Stephen— nearing me with his latest partner.

My breath catches, that stitch in my side returns, and I look away for an escape before the stranger I'm with spins me back into the security of Thaddeus's arms. A sigh of relief frees itself from my lungs as the music fades to the final note.

That was a bit too close for comfort, and I need a break.

To my delight, the musicians seem to agree as they call for a five-minute break before the last dance of the evening.

"Refreshments?" Thaddeus asks.

"I thought you'd never ask," I say. "Though you are a wonderful dancer!"

"So long as you are enjoying yourself." He takes my arm in his as we move through the crowd back to my family's table where I sit for safe keeping while he disappears momentarily to retrieve refreshing cold drinks.

"What time is it?" I say, feeling the exhaustion creep into my feet and settle into my low back.

"It's almost midnight," Henry announces. "You are going to sleep until noon after all that dancing."

"I am sure mother won't allow that," I say, bumping my shoulder into Henry's, "but I am not going to exert myself too much tomorrow either."

"Did I hear you admit you are a lazy-bones, Miss Prescott?" Thaddeus asks, handing me a cup upon his immediate return.

"No, you did not, sir. I only said I would not overly exert myself tomorrow after all the chores are done."

I go to take the cup, letting our exchange linger as I feel his fingers brush against mine. He pulls back as he hears someone's throat clear. Seeing Thaddeus's face change, I look up to see Stephen looking down at me.

"Emilie, Miss Prescott, and Mr. Prescott." He pauses, and his eyes glaze over as if chasing some invisible thought. He shifts from one foot to the other. His hands are hidden behind his back.

After a time of this slight swaying, Stephen licks his lips and continues, "Emilie. I'm an idyaht, but you're pretty—in that dress, and I like holding you—in that dress, and I'd like to do it again—in that dress, for the last dance—in that dress." One hand is held out to me as he bows slightly, and sways heavily forward.

One of Thaddeus's hands clasp my shoulder to pull me back, while his other hand pushes Stephen into an upright position—keeping Stephen from face planting into the shawl that shields my bosom.

I steal a glance at the other men around the table, and though they are not voicing their opinion, they are also not moving, just watching and waiting for me to decide Mr. Byrne's fate, which I imagine they hope will involve their fists.

But this is my decision.

I set the cup on the table and stand to face Stephen.

Does he expect me to say yes?

"Stephen, you're drunk, and before you make any more of a fool of yourself tonight, I would like you to go back," I say pointing to the other end of the dance floor, "to take your leave."

For a long moment, Stephen stands there staring, eyes drifting between all of us. Then he grunts, rolls his shoulder away from Thaddeus's steadying hand, stumbles across the dance floor, and out of the barn.

I feel Thaddeus take my hand as the music begins again.

"Thank you for dancing with me." His eyes shift from me to the eyes of the men in my family, "and thank you for allowing it."

"It's not their choice, it's mine, besides I enjoy spending time with you." I say, feeling the weight of the conversation lift.

He chuckles as he leads me to the dance floor, and we take up the waltz position.

"That's why I thanked you first. Anyway, it makes me happy to see you so free. So, any plans for the new year?" he asks.

"Teaching and making new friends. What about you?"

"Working and getting to know you."

His statement feels like a breath of fresh air.

"I would like that," I say.

Our eyes swim in the depths of each other's souls as we turn and swirl around the floor. If I couldn't feel his arm around my waist, his warm hand in mine, I would swear this was a dream, a dream that ends all too quickly as the music ends and the caller announces, "Happy New Year!"

Couples come together and embrace, kissing each other to welcome the new hope and beginning of the year, and creating a wall of longing between me and the man who holds my hand in his.

Thaddeus looks over my shoulder, and I don't have to see my brothers' glares to know that they are there and watching us. Thaddeus gives a nod in their direction, once again unbothered by any threats that come his way. He's got this calm confidence all laced through that boyish grin of his.

Thaddeus clears his throat. "I may not be able to kiss you the way you'd like me to, Emilie Prescott, but I do hope this will suffice." He slips off my lace glove and places a warm soft kiss on the back of my hand.

"To new beginnings," His eyes hold mine, begging for this promise.

"To new beginnings," I echo sealing that promise between us.

New Year New Love

LET OUR NEW YEAR'S RESOLUTION BE THIS:
WE WILL BE THERE FOR ONE ANOTHER AS
FELLOW MEMBERS OF HUMANITY,
IN THE FINEST SENSE OF THE WORD.
~GORAN PERSSON

JANUARY 1861
GETTYSBURG, PENNSYLVANIA

Shoving the books back into my bag, I rush out of the room. Winter break is finally over, and I have so much to tell Sarah—reminiscence of the dance and how I cannot get Thaddeus out of my head. I wonder to myself about Sarah's break and hoping father is ready, I rush down the back stairs, and down the hallway. Is that crying I hear from the kitchen?

It's not like my brothers to cry, and my curiosity getting the best of me, I peek through the doorway to see mother is at the stove and father is sitting at the table comforting a small child who looks to be—Billy Halle?

Well, it looks like Father has this handled, though I suppose I shouldn't interrupt. I guess I can saddle Starlight and go by myself. I head for the front door, hoping to evade the whole mess. My hand is on the door handle, but then I hear him—

"Emilie ..." Father's voice demands. Closing my eyes, *please don't involve me.* Biting my lip, slow to turn, I retrace my steps back to the kitchen doorway to face him when Henry pushes through the back door, and *Hallelujah I'm saved!*

"The wagon is ready," Henry says.

Mother wraps up a bit of toast in a napkin, presenting it to me. My feet slide heavily across the floor like I'm slogging through a bog before I take it from her.

"Mrs. Halle is ill, and Mr. Halle needs you to tend the children while he gets his work done." Mother insists, and I can feel a list of all my blessings accompanied by a sermon to do good charitable work for those who cannot welling up in the silence between us if I dare deny her request.

Deflated by the news, I am obliged to take my position as a "good neighbor" and change my plans.

Sorry Sarah, the news will have to wait.

Dropping my book bag by the door, I pull on my coat and mittens hanging off the nearby coatrack, and gesture to a sniffling Billy Halle to come along.

Minutes later, we are climbing into the back of the wagon and settling ourselves with a blanket shared between us when Father calls to the team to get a move on.

The wagon pulls forward, jostling us this way and that, but this doesn't deter me from opening the napkin. I hand Billy a stack of toast slathered with butter and jelly, just what a boy needs to put a smile on his face and suck the mess off my thumb and forefinger. "Here you need to eat something. A full belly warms the heart."

"Thank you," he says, stuffing a piece into his mouth.

"So, what's happened?" I say.

Billy swallows. "Ma got sick and she's in bed, and I have to do all the chores, and—and change all the diapers, and I mean, and I have to help with all the chores, and Pa and I are tired and worried, and did I mention I have to change all the diapers?"

"Where's Jane?" I ask, my hand brushing a bit of his messy hair out of his face.

"She is doing all the cooking, you know woman stuff, and dishes, and tending the boys, and not changing all the diapers. She makes me do that."

"If it is just a cold, she should get over it in no time."

"Nah-uh, she is coughing real bad. I hear her all night long. She's pale and weak as a calf. She can't move except to ..." his head bobbles, searching for the word, "feed Robert, then she sleeps." His eyes plead with me to believe him as tears form at the edges. He blinks them back, but with a face like that, all covered in butter and jam and crumbs—well, perhaps I deserve Mother's sermon for my earlier behavior.

"What else?" I ask, knowing he is trying to put on a brave face, as it crumbles before my eyes.

"Oh, Miss Emilie," Billy sniffs, "I–I'm afraid."

"She'll be all right. Your mother is strong and brave," I say, placing an arm around his shoulders and giving him a hug as I take a bite of the one piece of toast I reserved for myself, "just like you."

Billy frowns and straightens his shoulders, shrugging off my arm. "Yeah I'm brave, braver than Jane who got all jumpy about some rat," he tilts his chin with defiance. "I'm just worried she—she'll—" His eyes cross and he sticks out his tongue, putting one sticky hand to his throat. But when his silly expression fades, I can see his eyes are still wide with the fear of the word he dare not speak.

"We won't let that happen," I say, my heart breaks for him. As old as he looked the other night, he is so young and vulnerable right now.

Billy nods and stuffs the rest of the toast into his mouth until his cheeks bulge. Blinking faster to chase away any vulnerable tears in his eyes, he tries to focus on chewing everything between his outstretched cheeks.

"How about I help out today? Will that make you feel better?" I say, hoping to elicit a smile from him.

He nods his head as he chews and chews and chews.

"I'll cook, I'll clean, I'll take of the boys, and I'll even change all the diapers."

Billy eyes me, still skeptical, as he did when he doubted my horse handling skills, then he swallows the mouthful of food he insisted on eating all at once and a smile breaks out on his reddened crumb covered face. "Pa and I would sure be grateful, Miss Emilie." Billy wipes the crumbs from his mouth with the sleeve of his coat as the wagon rolls to a stop.

Mr. Halle waits for us with a wave and a smile of relief through haggard, dark smudged eyes of sleep deprivation and worry.

"We brought you some reinforcements," Father says. "Emilie is at your service for the day."

Billy and I step out of the wagon.

"Thank you, Jacob. It's times like this I truly appreciate my wife more and more," Mr. Halle then turns to Billy. "Go help Stephen with the milking. We have work to do today."

Stephen?

My heart drops like a hammer, heavy in my stomach. My jelly toast starts creeping back up my throat.

Maybe he will stay in the barn all day, where he was likely raised on his own homestead.

While waiting for my instructions, the air blows my coat around my legs, creeping up my skirts, biting my cheeks, stinging my eyes, yet they talk on and on. Tears form at my eyes, elicited by the freezing air playing in and around me, but once my teeth begin to chatter, I decide I've had enough of this.

"I guess, I will get started then," I say, letting them battle the cold.

Mr. Halle looks my way. His eyes widen at my appearance, no doubt. My nose is running, eyes tearing, and a shiver of cold is shaking me uncontrollably. "Of course, I will be right in."

My hand on the door, I push through, closing the winter chaos out. The warmth of the kitchen fire surrounds me, caressing my cheeks as I take off my coat and hang it on the hook. Turning around, the kitchen presents me with a jumbled mess Mrs. Halle would never allow. There's a white puddle soaking through the tablecloth with what I can only imagine is sour spilt milk, the floor is scattered with woodchips, bread crust and—crunch. The popping under my boot echoes through the room. Lifting my toe, there is a substance broken into a million pieces, waiting to be swept up.

The sudden sense of quiet screams out for help in a home full of family that hosts no warmth. *Where is everyone?* Listening—nothing, not even a fire popping and crackling in the stove. Opening the firebox, I stoke the coals hoping they don't all disintegrate to ash. A few dying embers glow in agitation. I add a few more pieces to the box, but the wood pile is low. I'll have to coax the boys to bring in more wood from the porch. My hands check the warmth, and a hint of heat teases my chilled fingertips—not all is lost.

My eyes rise to the dishes, strewn from sink to table. The cold, dark, greasy dish water remains abandoned in the tub on one side, a stewpot filled with water and a chicken foot peeking out at me—Does it move?... *Nope, good as dead or drowned. That might suffice as dinner?*

Turning to the dishwater, I move to pluck the basin water out of the sink, turn—

"Hello, Miss Emilie," Jane stands right behind me. I clutch the water basin tighter, so I don't bathe her in dirty water.

"Oh! Where did you come from?"

"I got the boys dressed. They're playing in their room." Jane looks me over, her eyes sunken, face pale, and her body droops like she is about to fall into a heap.

"Jane, are you all right? You look sick," I say, my heart thumps as concern washes over me and I dare to remove one hand from the basin to check her forehead. It's warm. "Let me dump this and then I'll tend to you."

Throwing open the door and using my hip to parry that same door as the wind insists on slamming it back at me, I head to the end of the porch and toss the water with the wind, before I return—frozen—and in need of what little heat the firebox is putting off.

Setting the basin aside, I pull out a chair and guide Jane into it, who plops down like a sack of potatoes.

"Tell me how you feel," I say.

"Sick and sore. I think I have what Ma has. I fed the boys. They are playing the quiet game, so whoever speaks first loses dessert."

Has she ever had a chance to be a child?

Touching her forehead once again, she clearly has a temperature. "How about I tend the house today and let's tuck you back in bed."

I see a flicker in Jane's dim eyes. She attempts a smile, but quickly gives up in favor of a nod in agreement.

"Robby is down for his morning nap. Ma will feed him when

he wakes. She will need help to change him before she—" A fit of coughs begins, but this only pauses her instructions for a moment. "Ma will need tea when she wakes. The boys—"

"And I, Miss Emilie, will take care of everything while Jane sleeps."

Jane nods.

"All right then, the rest is up to me. Let's get you some warm honey and milk for that throat."

"Thank you," Jane whispers, her voice catches as she coughs again, another congested fit.

I fix the milk with a dollop of honey, careful not to scald it as I heat it on the stove. Moments later a warm cup rests in her hands.

"Do you have some flannel and camphor liniment?" I ask, and she points to the pantry.

Retrieving both, I set to warming the flannels on the stove while Jane drinks her milk. When she is just about done, I slather a bit of liniment on the warmed fabric. The scent reminds me of the cold breeze that defied me just outside.

The tell-tale sound of the cup hitting the table lets me know she is done. Keen to get her busy mind at rest before she can make up another list of chores, I turn to say, "Time for you to get to bed."

Up the stairs and down a cramped hall, Jane's room sits vacant and dark. The winter curtains block out most of the light, but with the few rays that do make it through, I can see the tangle of blankets, quilts, and sheets all twisted together. The fire is out in the small fireplace her room hosts, but there are a few logs, thankfully, next to it.

I set the strips of cloth and camphor on a chair and go toss a log or two on the bed of coals, using the poker to encourage flames to return from the sleepy embers. Turning back to Jane, she sits on the bed, with a vacant look in her eyes.

"Let's get out of that work dress, and into a flannel gown," I say.

Jane points with a yawn to a peg holding her night clothing and gives a cough.

Once she is back in her nightgown, I remake the bed and place the liniment-soaked flannels on her chest and back. Covering her with all her blankets and two extra quilts, Jane soon becomes lost in the pile of covers. All that peeks out is her little nose and closed eyes.

"I will check on you around lunch," I say to her sleeping form, as I hear small wheezing snores coming from the blankets.

Down the stairs and back through the parlor, I check in on the boys. They are building structures with homemade blocks and never look up while they try to balance the tower they are building. Passing by the Halle's master bedroom, I hear a horrible cough coming from Mrs. Halle.

Poking my head in, I ask, "Are you doing all right? Can I get you something?"

The bedroom is dark. The form in the bed is bundled under blankets, her voice just above a whisper. "Tea and toast, please." This request is followed by another round of coughing.

"Toast?" I ask, "Do you want it soaked in milk, perhaps scrambled eggs to keep up your strength?"

My eyes adjust to the dark, and I see her nod her head.

"Be right back," I say.

Back in the kitchen, Mr. Halle is waiting for me.

"How is she?" he asks.

"Which one?" I ask, filling the serving teapot with warm water from the kettle, or at least what I hope is warm by this point, before I grab a knife to slice the bread.

"Which one?" he parrots back, as if it is some riddle.

"I just put Jane to bed. Her cough is tight, throat is sore, she's feverish. I am getting Mrs. Halle some scrambled eggs and tea right now. The boys are building structures in their room, and Robert is still napping."

"I didn't realize—" Mr. Halle says. I notice a pained look in his eyes as I glance over my shoulder at him.

"It's been a trying last few days. I'll take care of the meals, and the children, and the sick ones, while you tend to your chores. Chicken for dinner? Soup or roasted?" I ask, trying to give him some comfort through a kind smile.

"I think chicken soup with noodles would be best for everyone. There are plenty of spices in the pantry, and the noodles are already dried. Feel free to look around. I'll be back for lunch."

"Mr. Halle, where are the eggs?" I ask just before he departs.

"Over there," he points to a bowl covered with a towel.

"Thank you," I say.

Just as Mr. Halle reaches for the door, the sound of thundering footsteps races through the parlor and into the kitchen. Van is red-faced and out of breath as Sam chases him around the table. Little Joe stops when he sees his father standing at the door.

Mr. Halle looks down to his sons, "Boys, get your coats and mittens. You're coming to the barn for chores."

A mixture of groans and glee erupt as they rush off to the mudroom to don their winter clothes. With a slam of the door, the house quiets again.

After delivering the eggs and tea to Mrs. Halle, I notice there are two chickens instead of one in the pot, which explains the foot poking out. So, I get to work boiling both with a few carrots, onions, and herbs. The water will make for a good broth. One chicken can be used for the soup, another for a pie, and the bones can be reused for stock.

Lost in my own world, the house quiet and all to myself, the rhythm of cooking, chopping vegetables, and preparing lunch and dinner allows me to hum happily to myself. The fleeting thought of a *house of my own, might not be so bad,* hovers at the edge of my thoughts until I hear a wailing coming from the front bedroom.

Robert's awake!

Looking down at my hands covered in flour and pie crust, I shake the dough off my fingers, turn to dip them in the dishwater, and reach for a towel to dry them.

A baby. How much experience do I have with those? Oh yeah ... None. My mind briefly recalls my promise to Billy about changing all the dirty diapers, when Robert's wail reaches a new ear-splitting pitch.

Rushing into the bedroom, afraid he will wake the whole house, I make my way to his crib next to his parents' bed.

"I'll bring him to you—don't get up." I say to Mrs. Halle.

Peering into the crib, Robert demonstrates his powerful little lungs while his arms and legs flail free of the blankets. His diaper is stained dark with wetness.

"Shh, it's all right," I say, in a feeble attempt to calm the raging fury of pudgy limbs and his pinched face of anger and impatience. I scoop him up and immediately regret this decision as the acrid scent of ammonia hits my nose, and a cold wet bottom sits on my arm. My face must have said it all.

Even in her sick state, I can hear Mrs. Halle's low chuckle through a fitful cough. She extends her arms out to me, requesting the baby.

Gingerly holding him under his arms, the flailing child has taken on demonic qualities—kicking, screaming, red-faced, and at any moment I expect projectile vomit—scary!

Handing him to Mrs. Halle, she lays him down and strips off his wet clothes while instructing me on where to find dry ones. In a matter of moments, the child is changed, clean, and suckling quietly.

"How do you do that?" I ask, unsure whether I said it or thought it.

Mrs. Halle smiles. "After five children, it gets easier. Can you place his things in that borax bucket? Joe will clean it out when its full." She points to a bucket in the corner between the dresser and the wall. I open the cover; my senses are assaulted by an odor reminding me of a day-old chamber pot. Clearing my throat, I quickly add the cloth bundle to its contents, close it, and turn back.

"He will be ready in about fifteen minutes." Another coughing fit seizes her, I wait for it to subside, before she finishes. "The children will be in for lunch soon, then make sure they nap."

"I will be sure to fill their bellies and send them straight to bed," I say. "See you in fifteen." Turning back to her, I pause before asking, "The chicken broth is ready. Would you like a cup when I return?"

"I'll try it, thank you."

All right, chicken from the bone, pie crust in the pan, broth set aside for thickening—a commotion on the porch announces the smaller Halle boys' return from chores. Boots stomping, shouting and giggling precede the opening of the kitchen door.

Bang!

The door slams open, hitting the side of the house, and a rush of cold air swarms around and up my skirts as three little rosy-cheeked boys peer in from the porch.

"Each of you grab some wood before you come in and don't forget to close the door!" I say.

Little Joe with six pieces of wood comes in first. *Bang!*

"Hey!" Sam's voice is muffled behind the door, before he kicks at it.

Little Joe runs back to open it. "Miss Emilie says we gotta close the door when we, when we come in!"

Sam walks in with four pieces and turns back to the door.

An impish giggle bubbles up from both Little Joe and him.

"Don't forget me!" cries Van from outside.

Bang! The door is shut by both boys, right in front of Van's face.

More giggles erupt and Sam goes to drop his wood by Little Joe's stack before returning to open the door just a crack. "Miss Emilie said we had to close the door when we come in."

"Oh." Van slides in with his two pieces in one chubby hand, and then, *BANG!* His, of course, had to be the loudest of them all.

I sigh. *Next time, instruct the last child to close the door. Specifics matter with children. I should have known this from my teaching.*

"We're hungry, Miss Emilie," Little Joe says.

"I think you all need to wash before you sit at my table." I say, pointing to the basin in the sink. I just filled it with warm water and soap.

"It's really our table," Sam points out.

"Ah yes, but who is putting food on it?" I wink at him.

"Ow, that's hot!" Van complains.

"No, it isn't," Little Joe takes his brother's hands and scrubs them clean.

Each boy has a foot on the small stool allowing them to reach the basin, and I know it's only a matter of time before the pushing and shoving begins.

"Don't dawdle," I say.

"What's for lunch, Miss Emilie?" Sam is at my side, holding out his hands.

"Here is some bread, put it on the table please," I say.

Sam takes the plate from me.

I turn around to see everyone in their respective places, ready for lunch. Just as I ladle out the last of the broth, I hear Robert fussing in the bedroom.

"Little Joe, will you please make sure your brothers have everything they need? I must go get Robert."

"Yes, Miss Emilie," Little Joe says, his chest a little puffed, filled with pride at being the bigger brother this time, or so I imagine. I squeeze his shoulder.

Heading into the parlor and then appearing at the Halle's bedroom door, I say, "Is he ready?"

"You are more than welcome to take him." Mrs. Halle offers me the child.

I pick up the infant, and his hands immediately go to my face, exploring me. Little fingers poking and prodding.

"You are all hands," I say. "Quite the wiggly one too. Come on, let's give your mother a rest." Holding him to my shoulder, we leave Mrs. Halle and return to the kitchen. The boys chat amongst themselves with sporadic giggles and laughter. As their tummies fill, they slow their talking, their eyelids droop, and soon they are ready for their naps.

"Who wants warm milk and cookies?" I ask, noticing Van put his forehead on the table.

"Can I dunk my cookies?" Sam asks.

"No, Sam. You spilled your milk the last time ... the last time you did that," Little Joe reminds him.

Balancing the baby on my hip, I take the small pan of warmed milk off the stove and fill three cups with it.

"I know where the cookies are," Sam offers. "I'll get them for you."

"Thank you for your help," I say, as I watch Sam scoot off his chair and jaunt over to the side cupboard, pulling a tin of homemade cookies from the bottom shelf and bringing it back to the table.

"One each," I remind them as their wide eyes and little fingers poke at the cookies in the tin. I continue watching them as they eat and drink their milk, figuring this is as good a time as any to sit in the rocking chair, as my left arm is aching from holding the baby.

"When you finish up, it'll be time for a nap," I tell them.

"I'm too old for naps," Sam interjects.

"Me too," Little Joe chimes in. "Can I, can I read them a story?"

"I was informed by your mother that you need to all lie down," I say, watching the two boys' faces fall into pouts with big bottom lips. "If you are quiet, Joe can read you a story."

"I don't think Van needs one," Sam points to his brother, who is face down on the table.

"I'll get him," Little Joe gets off his chair. "He always does this."

Little Joe goes to his brother's side, picks him up. "Come on, Sam, I'll still read to you."

Sam slips off his chair, following close behind Little Joe and a sleeping Van.

I spy a small, enclosed play area for Robert. His toys are scattered among the blankets. As I sit him down and shake a rattle in front of him, he looks at it, reaches for it, and appears to be fascinated by the toy, or at least keen to put it to his mouth and chew on it.

Stepping away, I turn to the mess left on the table, and begin to clear things away, do the dishes, toss the cut-up vegetables into the pot along with the shredded chicken, and then move it to the back corner to cook slower. I wipe up the table and reset it for Mr. Halle and Billy for lunch.

The broth!

Scooping a cup of broth, I look back to Robert—making sure he's busy and not choking—then bring the cup to Mrs. Halle.

"I almost forgot this," I say, after I notice her awake in the dim room. "Do you want me to open the curtains, or can I get you something else?"

"No, thank you. I am feeling a bit better. I think I'll try the broth and then sleep again before the baby needs to eat."

"All right," I say. "I'll leave you to it." As I turn to leave, Mrs. Halle clears her throat.

"Emilie?"

"Yes?"

"Thank you for helping today. I appreciate it more than you know."

"Your wel—" A cry comes from the kitchen, "Hold that thought!"

Leaving the room, I enter the kitchen to see Robert turned on his stomach and none too happy with this new position. I pick him up and we sit back in the rocking chair to get to know each other.

Turning him to face me, I see his chubby red cheeks puff as he gives me a toothless grin.

"Hello," I say. Feeling silly, I stick out my tongue.

He returns with a coo as his legs kick out straight into my stomach. I lift him to stand, a new position. He tests his legs, bending, standing. His small arm reaches for me. Grabbing my snood, his fingers become entangled in the netting. His grip is strong, as the other arm reaches out to poke at my mouth, nose and—

Woah, wait!

I dodge a finger to the eye.

"You are awfully forward young man," I say frowning at him.

Surprised by his mimicked frown, it looks like he's about to cry.

"Oh, come now. It's nothing to get wadded up about." I make a face at him.

His toothless grin returns. His blue eyes are bright and wondering.

I am entranced by this little human. I feel his legs weaken, so I put him to my chest. Robert settles in, head on my shoulder as a small burp escapes. His fingers tangle in my hair, seeming to comfort him. I begin rocking him, a slow sway, pushing off with one foot, letting the chair ease back into place. Push ... Release ... Push ... Release ... Push ... Relax ... My eyes begin to close.

"She is holding on to him with a tight grip."

I become aware of a weight being lifted off my chest. The cold rushes in as the warmth leaves me. I open my eyes to see Billy and Stephen looking at me as Mr. Halle is leaving the room.

My eyes widen. The bundle between my arms—

Where is he!

Then I notice Mr. Halle entering the bedroom off the parlor.

"Sleeping on the job, I see," Stephen is eyeing me through narrow slits, though that unapologetic smirk plays on his lips.

"No, just coaxing the baby to sleep," I say. His accusation is greeted with my glare. Pushing my way out of the chair, I continue with, "I suspect you all need some lunch?"

"I am starving," Billy says, rubbing his hands together.

"Wash your hands and I will get you some soup. The bread is already on the table."

Billy dutifully walks over to the wash basin, and Stephen stares at me—speechless or defiant, but either way I rather like him quiet.

Mr. Halle walks into the kitchen.

"I hated to interrupt," Mr. Halle smiles at me. "You two looked very comfortable, but I figured the baby could be settled back in his crib to free you up again."

"I'm sorry, I didn't mean to fall asleep."

"Don't worry," Mr. Halle replies, "I fully understand how exhausting my wife's job is. Soup smells delicious."

I set down three bowls in front of them, returning to the stove to stir the soup. "The vegetables didn't get to cook long. They might still be crunchy," I say.

"Will you join us?" Mr. Halle asks.

"I suppose I could use a bite," I say ladling a bowl, looking for a chair, and finally deciding to sit across from Stephen who is quietly eating, looking down at his soup.

Is it good, does he like it?

The savory aroma fills my own nose with the like of carrot, onion, garlic, and chicken, my stomach rumbles its pleas, and I can't help but give in to eating while I listen to the man and two boys talk about their chores.

Mr. Halle talks about how well the repairs to the fences are holding up, Billy adds his two cents about his accomplishments, and Stephen gives a grunt here and there. They are in their world, and I am happy to listen.

However, every time I look across the table, Stephen is watching me, his eyes seeming to look right through me. I hold his stare for a moment, then look away.

Is he even going to apologize for his rude behavior the other night?

Our silent fight goes unnoticed by Mr. Halle and Billy. The conversation lulls as Mr. Halle picks up the newspaper.

I reach for a slice of bread, and Billy slides the butter dish to me.

Mr. Halle breaks the silence, "Well, there goes two more. We won't have anyone left by the time summer comes."

I perk up, "Two more?"

"I'm sorry, Emilie. I know this is your heritage, but two more Southern states seceded from the Union."

Swallowing hard, a ripple of gooseflesh washes over my arms, and I feel the cold start to consume me.

"It's all right, Mr. Halle," I say, biting my lower lip. "They are a stubborn lot. You know farmers." I force a smile, and he returns it with a knowing wink.

"That is idiotic. They won't last six months separated from Washington!"

"Oh, honestly Stephen, you shouldn't talk about what you don't know about," I say, trying to keep my tone level as I feel a sour taste bubble up from my gut.

"Oh, I know plenty, but I'm afraid it is you who doesn't understand politics. Then again, you're just a woman of which little is to be expected."

I see his lips tighten and a hint of rouge touch his cheeks.

Did I touch a nerve Mr. Byrne?

I level my glare at him and say, "I'm sorry, how many newspapers do you actually read Mr. Byrne? I can't imagine, given the sloppiness of your signature on my dance card, you've forgone the X as your mark for very long."

To my left, I hear Billy suck in his breath.

My spoon clinks against the table, though I will myself to stay seated against all my better judgement. A showdown at the Halle residence is not appropriate, but I cannot resist getting under his skin or biting back as he tries to wriggle his way under mine, the snake!

"If you were a man—" Stephen pushes his chair back from the table.

"She is clearly not," Mr. Halle interjects, "so, Stephen, control yourself."

Silence ...

Glaring ...

"Do you wish to clarify your survival statement, Mr. Byrne?" I ask, not breaking our stare.

"What could I possibly have to debate with a woman who hails from a land of stupid, feral farmers who cannot live without their slaves?"

"Try again, and consider your occupation, sir," I say, "as I don't think Mr. Halle is a stupid farmer. Not sure about the opinion you have of yourself—and my father does not own slaves."

"Miss Emilie," Mr. Halle's voice a sharp reminder.

Turning toward the elder gent, "I apologize, sir, I respect farming, unlike someone else."

"All I am saying is that the country should stay together! It is stupid to think splitting up will benefit us in any way."

"I agree, but what else—" I push his argument, as I know he does not understand what I know.

"Why the slaves?"

"Because it takes many hands to manage large parcels of land. For once Stephen, think. Think of all the farmers on Table Rock Road. They all have large parcels of land, and y'all need each other for planting and harvesting. The South's farmers are too spread apart. The mouths they are responsible for feeding exceed far beyond their own, and therefore they have slaves to help them out."

"Why can't you pay them?" A sneer forms at his lips.

"They are paid through shelter, food, and medical care, though I don't disagree that they deserve more like a fair wage and the same liberties as a white man. But slaves have been a part of our culture since before I was born," I say. "I can't change a culture in a day. No one can."

"So, you don't want that to change? You are all right with the culture as it stands?" Stephen asks.

"You are only hearing what you want to hear, Stephen. You know nothing about me or my family," I say, blinking back tears as he refuses to relinquish himself from ignorance. "Do you even know why we are here?"

Stephen stares back at me, saying nothing.

Is he proud of the tears I refuse to shed?

"Stephen, I will not have war break out at my dinner table. Apologize to Emilie. We have work to do." Mr. Halle, taking advantage of the silence between us to end the conversation.

I blink and look to Mr. Halle giving a hint of a thank you through the smallest of smiles to him and stand to clear the table.

Turning back to Stephen, I say, "Since we have no control over how this is going to work out, I suggest we leave it for now."

Stephen looks away, shakes his head, and gets up, snatching his coat from the table. The door bangs as he heads back out into the cold.

Mr. Halle helps me clear the table as he sends Billy back to his chores.

"If women were lawyers, you would command a courtroom, young lady," Mr. Halle says, putting the dishes into the dishwater.

"Thank you, sir," I say my cheeks having eased into a hue of soft pink. "I didn't mean to break out in an argument at your table. It is poor of me, but Stephen can be impossible sometimes."

Mr. Halle grins, "He's just smitten with you."

"So, I hear," I say, reaching in to wash the dishes.

Mr. Halle dons his coat, leaving me to finish my chores. I start a loaf of bread right away, as the last loaf is dwindling from lunch. I pay no more mind to Stephen. If he is "smitten," he has a strange way of showing it.

"The soup smells good," Jane croaks.

I turn to see her standing in the kitchen doorway. Her complexion is pale, cheeks splotched from fever, and her eyes appear larger by smudged dark circles.

"I was just coming to check on you," I say. "Are you hungry?"

"No," she says, as I place a cup of broth at the table and invite her with a gesture of my hand.

"Try some. You need to keep up your strength."

Jane sits at the table and takes a small sip, her face wincing as she tries to swallow the warm broth.

As she struggles to drink, I warm up more strips of flannel and rub camphor into them to replace the ones she already has when she goes back to bed. Turning back to her, I note some color returning to her face.

"I should help you finish up here," Jane goes to stand.

"I think you should fill your belly and go back to bed."

She drinks more of the cup's contents with a scrunched-up face between each gulp, there is no protest from her. She is an easy patient, but unfortunately a sick one too. I usher Jane back upstairs, tucking her back under the covers. As I return back through the parlor, I peek in on the boys. Van is awake, looking around the room.

Motioning to him to follow me, he scrambles out of bed, eager to get out of his nap.

"I'm hungry," he announces as we enter the kitchen.

"You are always hungry. Sit down, and let's get you something to eat—again."

I pull little pie crust pieces off a pan I baked earlier with sugar and cinnamon, serving it to him with a glass of milk. I notice the milk pail is getting low. Just as I pull the chicken pie from the oven, a gust of cold air announces that someone opening the door behind me.

Stephen appears with a pail of milk. "Mr. Halle is requesting you skim the cream off for butter."

"Will do," I say, wanting no more conversation with him.

Our presence in this room together rivals the January cold outside.

I reach for the milk. Stephen pulls it back.

"So that's it?" The question comes out of nowhere.

"What?" I ask.

He stares harder at me, almost willing me to do something. "No apology, nothing?"

"I believe it is you who owes me two apologies."

His fist closes tighter around the pail, his jaw hardens, and his eyes narrow at me.

"If you were a man—I would challenge you to a duel. You embarrassed me!"

"That is all your doing," I say, pulling the milk pail from him and never minding the splatter. "Besides, duels are illegal in most states now."

I turn away from him, setting the milk near the sink. Stephen stands in what I imagine is stunned silence. Turning back to face him, I appear to be correct. He is a statue frozen in his own frustration.

He takes a long-ragged breath. "You are not like any woman I ever encountered before."

"It must be my feral upbringing by the idiotic farmer and slaves, right?" I say, using his words like salt in an open wound.

"It explains why you are not ladylike," Stephen sneers.

"I am just not like the ladies you can control," I say. "As much as you're forthright in your manner, I am outspoken in mine. Kind of similar, aren't we?"

Turning back to the oven, I pull the loaf of bread out to knead down the first rising, hoping desperately I will get this baked before Father comes to retrieve me.

All the while Stephen's eyes remain on me.

I ignore the ice from his glare and cast aside any expectation for an apology from me or him at this point. Flipping the dough on the floured table, and at the sound of the back door shutting, I figure he's given up as well.

It is a victory I am not proud of, but I'll take it. I get the bread back in the oven, just in time for Sam and Little Joe to appear in the kitchen, ready for a snack.

"Do you have any more of what you gots, Van?" asked Sam.

"You mean cinnamon crust? I sure do," I say putting a plate of what I hadn't given Van down on the table for the boys to share and picking up Van's abandoned plate in the process.

Little Joe must have noticed the crease in my brow, "He went back to our room, and is playing with, with blocks."

I smile and nod my appreciation and, after depositing the dishes, return to the table one last time with two glasses of milk before letting the boys tend to their snack as I clean up. It seems only a few moments have passed when I hear Little Joe say, "We better go, go help in the barn."

"I'll go get Van," Sam says.

Turning to gather their plates and cups, I can't help but laugh as I see Little Joe shove what remains of the cinnamon pie crust into his mouth, trying to swallow the last of his milk.

There is a ruckus in the boys' bedroom as I hear shouting.

Racing into the room, I see Van on the floor holding onto his blocks for dear life, while Sam stands over him.

"You have chores," Sam yells to his little brother. "You gotta get dressed now!"

"I wanna build blocks!" Van yells back. He raises his small fist to his brother, wooden block ready to launch at the first indication.

"Van, put that block down, now!" I say not wanting a full account of Cane and Abel to carry out. "Sam, does he really need to go with you? Wouldn't it be easier to get your chores done without him under your feet?"

Sam looks to me and blinks a time or two before the realization dawns on him that being untethered from his brother might be a good thing. A grin spreads on his face from chubby cheek to chubby cheek and then his expression falters into confusion.

"But, Miss Emilie, I am responsible for him," his face turning red in protest. "Ma said so."

"How about I watch him? And don't you worry, I will give him chores, so he won't miss out."

Sam considers my proposal. "All right, but he is a handful. Watch him close."

"I will," I reassure him. Sam runs from the room, and I hear the rustle of clothes before the *Bang!* of the back door.

Hands on my hips, I look down at Van. "When you are finished here, do you want to help me in the kitchen?"

"No, I'm building." Van doesn't look at me as he continues stacking blocks into tall towers.

"When you finish, come help me in the kitchen."

"When I'm done," he echoes.

An agreement made, I leave him be, and on my way back to the kitchen I take a moment to peek into the Halle's bedroom. Mrs. Halle is nursing Robert. She waves me away, so I proceed to the kitchen.

Bread ready for baking, I put more wood in the fire, test the heat with my bare hand, then transfer the bread from the warmer and directly into the oven. Next comes a flurry of ceaseless work: replacing the wash water, drying and putting away dishes I don't plan on reusing, setting the table, wiping down counters, and finally sweeping.

Now that the kitchen is clean and ready for the evening meal, I wonder how Mrs. Halle manages it all day in and day out. It's only been one day and I'm exhausted and ready for home when Van comes into the kitchen.

"Letters," he says, somewhere between a request and a demand, holding out a slate and a pencil to me.

And here I thought I wouldn't be able to teach today.

"Letters? Which ones?" I ask, taking the slate.

"Jane, me, and brothers." His chubby finger points to the slate.

I move the dishes aside as we sit next to each other at the table. Van hands me the pencil.

"Who's first?" I ask.

"Janie," Van watches with intent as the pencil's tip moves across the slate. I draw *J-a-n-e.* Then hand him the pencil.

"You do it," I tell him.

I watch him grab the pencil, wrapping his chubby hand around the thin instrument. He presses it to the slate to the point that his knuckles turn white and that little hand of his begins to quake.

"Wait, gentle," I say.

With a big smile on his face, Van lightens his grip and begins to scribble each letter with a screech in protest from the pencil on every downward stroke. I feign a smile for his sake and suppress the desire to wince.

At least it is not twenty children trying to do this all at once.

The door behind me opens, as a gust of cold air announces their arrival.

"Wagon is here for you," Stephen says.

"I'll watch Van," Billy says, not having been far behind Stephen. "The others are coming in for dinner."

"Perfect timing," I say, getting up as Billy sits in my place.

"Writing names, Van?" Billy asks his brother.

Van nods his head, concentrating on the slate.

"Billy, the bread will be ready in ten minutes. Please don't forget it," I gather my coat and scarf from the rack.

"I won't. Thank you for dinner, Miss Emilie."

"Very welcome. Be sure to call me tomorrow if you need help. *It sure is nice to see the confidence return to that little man.*

I take my leave, stopping at the door when I come face to face with Stephen.

"Excuse me," I say, "I need to get by."

He steps out of the doorway, but his eyes do not pardon me. "Don't let me stop you." His voice is low, and full of unspoken animosity.

"It was a request out of politeness. Running over you would be a job," I say as I push past him, not looking back. I didn't need to look, I feel his stare, chilling my spine despite the warm coat wrapping around me.

The wagon stood in the late afternoon low light, the figure sitting in the seat at first glance appeared to be father, but as I got closer, it was Thaddeus. A smile washes over me and a different kind of tingle rushes up my spine, all the negativities swept away in no time.

"May I escort you home, Emilie?" Thaddeus asks.

"Yes, please, I am ready for an early night," I say, as he takes my hand for me to step up.

"Playing housemaid is hard work, I see." A teasing smile plays at his lips, the very ones that felt thrilling and sensational against the back of my hand.

"I am not ready to be a wife and mother just yet," I say. "It's an exhausting job. Everyone wants your attention and there is no room to sit."

Our shoulders, arms, thighs, knees, calves, ankles, and feet collide and press into one another as we sit side-by-side in the wagon. It is a closeness that feels familiar, comforting, and—dare I think—a bit scandalous?

"Sounds like a classroom. Is it similar?"

"Not at all. I don't have to cook two meals and tend to children all at once," I say. "I just want to curl up in my favorite chair. I lived in the kitchen today."

Thaddeus leans closer to me, breathing in. He exhales and I feel his words hot on my ear, "Smells like chicken and bread. I say, did you use rosemary?"

"How can you smell rosemary?" I ask. Turning to look at him just as he looks away, a gust of wind blows between us, a reminder from the universe to mind my manners.

But who's the universe going to tell if I don't?

"I can't," he confesses, "but I like chicken seasoned with rosemary."

Thaddeus grins, shifting slightly away from me as he turns his attention back to the team, and my eyes follow his gaze to the road ahead.

"I shall remember that, Thaddeus," I say. "Rosemary chicken."

"Was that Stephen I saw at the farm?" Thaddeus asks.

"Unfortunately," I say. "He made quite a fool of himself and blames me for it."

"Interesting," Thaddeus pauses. "I am afraid he likes you, Emilie."

My head turns back to him. "He has a poor way of showing it," I say. "How would he act if he hated me?"

Thaddeus's body begins to shake as he bites his bottom lip, but he can't help the grin.

"Why are you laughing?" I ask, nudging him. "Stephen is as annoying as a fly on a midsummer's day."

Thaddeus shakes harder, finally giving way to a boisterous laugh.

I do not find any of this amusing.

"I don't know why you are laughing at my expense," I say.

"It's just ironic. If he hated you as you wish, that would be easy."

"Easy how?"

Why does he have to have such an amusing laugh; doesn't he know that makes it hard to be angry at him?

"If he hated you, dear Emilie," Thaddeus smirks with a hand wiping the tears flowing from his own amusement, "he would ignore you."

"I wish he hated me," I roll my eyes as Thadeus bursts out in another belly laugh.

"I am glad I can amuse you, Mr. Marsh." I poke him in the side with a pointed finger to try and get him to stop. *I don't want to be a laughingstock around him.*

Thaddeus squirms and bats my hand away, and the horses snort and toss their heads in protest at our antics. So alas, he swallows his laughter.

"I am sorry, I am honestly not laughing at you. I enjoy your company. I loved dancing with you the other night, but more importantly, I want to ask you something."

The sudden change in his sincerity stirs not only forgiveness in my heart but a flutter of curiosity, "It's all right. I am the brunt of all my brother's jokes, so I'm used to it."

"No, you shouldn't be the brunt of any joke," Thaddeus turns to me, his blue eyes pulling my own into his depths.

I smile ... no, grin ... no, sigh? My cheeks flush and I try to release the tension with a soft giggle, but I dare not look away.

He pulls the horses to a stop, drops the reins in his lap, and takes hold of both of my mitten clad hands with his own.

Feeling his warmth through my mittens, the squeeze of his hands in mine. I wait with bated breath, and *I swear if he says something dumb I will hit—*

"Miss Prescott, may I start seeing you?"

My mouth drops and I think my heart pauses only to regain its rhythm as cold air fills my lungs.

"You-you want to see me?"

"New beginnings, right?" Thaddeus's voice caresses me. "I want you to be my new beginning."

He watches me, biting his lower lip ... waiting for my answer.

I watch him, feel his sincerity, and am all too aware this is an important answer, but an answer I must give all the same—an answer I even want to give.

"Yes, I will see you."

Time suspends us between our urges to hug or kiss or—the stamping of hooves from the impatient team brings me back to reality, and unfortunately propriety. So instead, Thaddeus takes my hand, bringing it with my mitten to his lips, and places a kiss in the palm. The heat of such a gesture is followed by the warm squeeze of his hand, which seals our agreement.

And just like that, the most exhilarating moment of my life is over, as he tears his eyes from me, picks up the reins, and calls to the team, "Carry on."

I slip my arm through his for further warmth, or so I tell myself. It has nothing to do with the fact I can't stop looking up at him and tracing the nuances of the happiness that glows from his cheek aching grin.

All we have to do now is tell our parents.

Aaron's Return to Richmond

JANUARY 1861
GETTYSBURG, PENNSYLVANIA

The air, crisp with the chill of winter, carries the scent of excitement. A shiver runs down my spine, not from winter's touch, but the thrill of Thaddeus's words echoing in my ears. His warm embrace, a memory seared on my skin, clashes with the cold reality of school looming ahead. The wagon rattles away, leaving me on the corner of Baltimore and Middle Street to walk the rest of the way to school. My heart, a pendulum trapped between duty and desire, swings wildly as the mud squelches under my boots. Can I keep my promise to Thaddeus, a promise that shimmers bright as the ice coating the mud filled streets, without betraying the path I've so carefully built?

As I turn the corner to school, I see Sarah, my confidant and keeper of my girlhood whims—shuffling, searching, I imagine, for me. The hood of her blue cloak is pulled over her bonnet, and she rubs her hands together while she bounces to keep warm. A smile breaks out when our eyes meet.

"Where have you been? I was worried sick about you yesterday. Are you all right?" Her hands accent her words, as a flash of concern blurs her blue hues before her eyes flit away, chasing after another thought.

"Oh, I can't wait to tell you all the good news and bad news. But really Emilie, there's not enough time in the day to tell you how excited and heartbroken I am!" Sarah slips her arm in mine and begins to pull me alongside her toward the school. "I'm freezing. I hope they ring that bell soon." In the time it takes for her to pause and take a breath, her thoughts have moved on too. "What's wrong?"

I blink and then smile, shaking my head. "Nothing, I'm just waiting to get a word in edgewise," I say with a teasing nudge. "So, about this news, what of it can you share?"

Sarah squeals with delight, "You will never guess who I am courting!"

"You're right, it seems you have a new crush every week," I say with a smirk, but then suspicion creeps up into my thoughts. "Wait, did you and—"

"Thomas! Yes, Thomas! We are courting and if all goes well, I will be married by November! Can you believe it?" Sarah bounces like an excited rabbit, jumping up and down, her eyes brimming with joy.

My grin widens, her excitement intoxicating. "That's exciting. I suppose you are planning the wedding already?"

"Of course! We are having the ceremony at my parents' house, my dress will have one ruffle not two ..." she began and carried on like this for several minutes, occasionally checking to see if my head bobbed in the right moments, which it did. "Oh Emilie, my sisters are so proud of me. I am the third to get married in as many years. Father says he is happy my other sisters are much younger; can you believe he said he can't afford much more?" She giggles, and I hear the muffled clap of her mitten clad hands.

"Great news," I say trying to imagine how my parents would afford three doweries in three years.

"And then there is most dreaded, awful bad news that anyone could ever have. Oh Emilie, promise me you will not be mad at me. Promise me we will still be bosom buddies forever after, and raise our children together, and—"

"Will you just tell me already?"

"Promise?"

"Yes, I promise. Now what is it?"

Sarah bit her bottom lip before letting the words tumble out as if each one were a foul term. "I failed the exam."

I opened my mouth to—

"But oh, Mrs. Irwin is so disappointed in me! But I won't really need my teaching certificate when I am married, right?" Sarah pokes me with her finger, smiling as if she got away with something. Her eyebrows wiggling up and down.

"Wait ... what?" is all I manage to spit out.

"I mean with children, and tending to a home, and tending to my husband, Thomas, and—"

Panic knots my stomach. I can't imagine finishing this without her. We have been together since the first day I arrived here. Alone on the bench, eating lunch by myself, wallowing in withering self-confidence, a burst of sunshine materialized in the form of Sarah. Her summer sky eyes sparkling with mischief, her smile infectious, and her spirit bright enough to draw a gaggle of children to her every word. Though delicate in stature, her sharp wit and determination is enchanting. It was her wit that sparked our first conversation—me, drowning in a sea of unfamiliar faces, reeling from a misunderstanding with a teacher who hadn't seen eye to eye with me, lost and alone. Sarah enveloped me with her infectious chatter, washing away the hurt and forging an everlasting friendship.

"What does that mean? Will we still test together in May?"

Sarah's idle chatter takes a pause, and we exchange looks of surprise—me, at the fact that she actually heard me, and her?

"No, silly, of course. I will need it to teach my children, or maybe we can send them to private school together. He will own his own business, you know." Sarah's light blue eyes sparkle with daydreams of her future. "But the best of it isn't even that! I will have a house in town, and we can decorate it!" Sarah squeals, and I feel our linked arms is the only thing keeping her tethered to the ground.

A wistful sigh follows from her. "Father won't consider me to take the farm. He'll have to choose one of my other sisters for that, but what do I care, so long as there are rose bushes out front."

Sarah's dream of living in town is as important to her as teaching is to me. She is a wonderful confidant, but our life views and taste in most things are as opposite as sugar and lemon.

"Emilie," I feel my arm being shaken by Sarah's pleading grasp, "you're awfully quiet. Does that mean you are not happy for me? Are you cross?"

"Of course, I'm happy your dreams are coming true," I'm still stunned her failure doesn't faze her.

I wonder how I did. I studied, I worked. What if it's not good enough to pass?

"Wonderful, no, stupendous!" Sarah pulls me closer, her body shivering in the morning air. "Now, how was your winter break? What did you wear to the New Year's dance? Oh, and have you met any boys?"

"It was—"

"Stephen?"

I groan.

"Thaddeus?"

A hint of a smile blossoms in my cheeks and I say—

Dong! ... Dong! ...

Saved by the bell.

The school bell sounds as we turn to see one of the male teachers, pulling on the rope.

"Oh, Thomas is lucky I like him so, or he would be next on my list." Sarah bursts into a giggle, as we wade through the bustle of children flying up the stairs, eager to embrace the warmth of the classroom.

"Sarah!" I say, a giggle bursting forth.

"Oh, you won't tell will you, Emilie?"

I shake my head. "No, I won't tell a soul."

"But you will tell me about Thaddeus, yes?"

I shrug and grin, "Maybe."

"Tease!" Sarah pulls me over the threshold to begin our day.

The test results weigh heavy on my mind all day, making it difficult to concentrate. Sarah and I never got back to each other today, so her grim news adds to my fraying nerves. Sitting in the uncomfortable hardwood desk, awaiting Mrs. Irwin's arrival to disclose my fate—

Time slowed, increasing my jitters.

I begin folding my dress pleats between damp fingers.

My knee bounces to a silent jig.

A shuffle of paper and a sigh from Mrs. Irwin occurs before her voice breaks the silence, "You did a fine job this go around, Miss Prescott."

"I did?" The crack in my voice did not sound like my own.

"You did, but—"

I wince at the hesitation, biting my lip, and wipe the perspiration from my hands on my skirt.

"But?" I ask.

A smile breaks out on Mrs. Irwin's face, brightening the accents of her clear gray eyes and defining the streaks of wisdom in her graying hair.

She shakes her head.

"There is always room for improvement," she assures me. "Let's take a look, shall we?"

Mrs. Irwin flips the pages around, revealing an open wound in my life's work. Engraved into the first page in glaring crimson ink is—78 percent.

Failure floods through my veins and hits my heart with a pang.

How could I have scored so low?

Mrs. Irwin, unperturbed by my crestfallen features, ignores my horror to explain, "On the positive side, your strong subjects are orthography, US history, and arithmetic overall. This means you will be a well-rounded teacher, if you study harder in geography and advanced math, like algebra and word problems."

Her news did not ease the need to fly out of my chair and flee to the far west where my failing aptitude might better serve a populace far more ignorant than I.

"How will I ever fix this before May?" I ask, more to myself than to her. "If I don't become a teacher—"

Her hand goes to mine, warm and comforting, grounding me to my seat.

My distant gaze flutters back to her with several blinks, tears tracing the various paths of a broken future down my cheeks.

"Come now, Miss Prescott. There is no need to make such mountains for yourself. I'm sure you will pass in May, because I have a plan for study. And maybe you could assist Sarah—she struggled a bit too."

I wipe my tears with the back of my hand, my cheeks flushing with embarrassment. "You mean you aren't dropping her from the class? You wish to continue with both of us?"

"Well, of course I plan to continue with both of you. You two are my prized students right now," Mrs. Irwin says. "It's why I have high expectations for each of you."

We are her prized students? The world is doomed.

Still, I suppose this reminder is a boost to my confidence despite what it may mean for future generations. Yet, if Mrs. Irwin didn't lose hope, then neither should I. My head bobs in a singular nod.

"Thank you," I say. "I promise to work hard and make you proud of me."

"I am already proud of you, Miss Prescott." Mrs. Irwin then proceeds to discuss the subject outline for the certificate in May with me.

<hr />

Tonight, we gather around the Prescott table for bitter arguments and sweet memories. It is our last evening meal before Aaron returns to finish his schooling in Richmond. The table is lit with candlelight and warmed by the aromas of apple sauced pork, sweet potatoes, and pickled cauliflower as we sit in our known and respective places, and the stark reminder of Aaron's leaving sits visibly with his bags beside the threshold to the back door.

Our laughter still carries through the house, though, imprinting the last remnants of Aaron's good cheer throughout. The scraping of forks and clinking of silver against plates echoes through the room. My eyes trace my brother's visage between each bite, trying to keep his image fresh in my mind, pushing aside the thoughts of his vacant chair come tomorrow night's dinner, just as I push around the pickled cauliflower, trying to bury it under the sweet potatoes.

"Did Uncle William write you back, Aaron?" Mother asks.

"He did indeed. He will be at the station to pick me up."

"Did he say anything about the state of the plantation?" I ask, thinking about Martha and the rest of the family.

"No." Aaron shakes his head. "Not a word, but I'm sure he is keeping his dealings close."

The wheeling and dealing my uncle insist on holding close to his chest invites bitterness into the sweet applesauce encompassing my tongue.

What are his secrets? Are the Blackwells all right?

"We dare not pry into anyone's business down there until it is needed," Father's voice is vacant but firm.

Looks of concern pass between us as our eyes meet but then dart away. No one dares to speak their thoughts, even though I imagine they are all much the same.

I can't help but wonder about the changes there. I don't expect it to be run as Father ran things, but I pray it is decent. My dinner sours, no longer appealing to me, and a pain now resides in my stomach. It is a knot comprised of fear ... Worry? ... The unthinkable? ... I pray all is well for the slaves remaining under my uncle's keep.

As forks return to their empty plates, Aaron asks, "Henry, what are you going to do without me?"

"First, we are going to make your room into a sewing room for the ladies. Then I am going to take everything you left behind as my own," Henry taunts with a grin.

"That's fine by me, so long as all the chores Aaron did become yours, Henry," I say adding a smile of my own.

"No, you're taking Aaron's chores, Em. He said you would," Henry erases the smile from his face, trying to convince me.

"I said no such thing," Aaron replies. "Besides, Emilie has studying to do."

"I have a life too," Henry scowls. "Who needs schooling anyway? Ma taught me all I need to run this farm, and Pa is teaching me the woodworking trade. I don't need no more learning."

I cringe at my brother's use of the English language, "You don't need any more schooling, Henry."

Henry sticks his tongue out at me.

"Henry," Mother warns.

"Since you have the farm, you get my chores," Aaron announces. "After all, no one expects you to teach the cow or horses how to read."

The table bursts into laughter as Mother gets up to clear the dishes, and the dessert she returns with provides the final touch of sweetness to our family meal.

After we finish, everyone retires to the parlor. Silence falls over us as we settle into our respective books. I look up from my own reading to take note of my family residing in harmony. Aaron mindlessly smokes a cigar while watching the fire; his law book rests open in his lap. Mother reads the latest *Godey's Lady's Book*. Father is settled into his chair with one newspaper, while Henry has acquainted himself with another newspaper.

The security and comfort of family is the best feeling of all.

I return to my reading of *The Wide, Wide World* by Susan

Warner. It doesn't take long before I no longer notice the pungent smell of cigar smoke curling through the air or the distant popping of the candles as I lose myself in the world of Ellen Montgomery and her poor sick mother.

Outside of the rustling of paper or the occasional flipping of a page, I sense the first bit of movement just before the mantle clock chimes. Looking up, I notice Mother already standing, having set her magazine aside. Then Henry looks up, refolding his paper and following that with a stretch. Father puts down his pipe, taking care that the ashes within it no longer burn.

"Time for bed Emilie." Mother waits for me.

"I just want to finish these—" I glance down at the page I'm on and check to see how far off the next chapter is. "—last three pages. I will be up after that."

"Well, don't stay up too late. Your brother has an early morning train to catch." Mother steps to the door.

"I won't," I reply.

How is my bedtime going to hinder my brother's sleep?

I shake my head and direct my eyes to refocusing on the page.

"Well, good night then," Mother says.

I hear the parlor door close, but it's the shifting of weight on a cushion I'm not occupying that causes me to look up. Aaron's still staring into the fire, his book untouched from the last time I glanced at him.

"What are you thinking about?" I ask.

"The long train ride back, the plantation, the bar exam—you know, nothing special." He smiles back at me, his eyes playing in the light.

"Oh, I see," I say with a small smirk. "Nothing important."

"Nothing at all, little sister." Aaron takes the cigar from his mouth, contemplating what to say next.

"Can I ask you something?" he asks, just as I find the line in my book I left off on.

Something tells me this something will turn into somethings.

I place the marker in my book and close it.

"Of course," I say.

"I just want you to know," he pauses, taking a deep breath, "I like Thaddeus, and I think he will be an honest match for you. But—"

"I'm quite fond of him too," I say. "In fact, I still have to ask Father and Mother if I can see him."

"Oh?" Aaron turns to look at me.

"He asked me the other day," I say, "and I said yes."

"Before you asked Father? Never mind, that's good, very good. Now—" Aaron hesitates. "Don't take this the wrong way, but Em, you're a stubborn woman." Aaron furrows his forehead, holding up his hands.

"I prefer the term strong willed, but what's wrong with that?" I ask.

"Nothing and everything at the same time." Aaron flinches as he notices my shoulders stiffening and my fingers grasping onto the small green book in my lap. I am preparing for a lecture: *the propriety of a woman when she is in the company of a man.*

"Now, hear me out before you throw that book at me. I only mean this in the best way possible. No sense in getting your dander up," Aaron's eyes on my every minute move as I grasp the book tighter, my nails carving into the stacked pages between the binding, and my eyes already narrowing.

"I will listen, I promise," I say, my voice calm and level.

Choose your words wisely, brother.

"You're an intelligent woman—"

Good start, so far.

"—and I want to save you from heartache, so I feel it is important to talk to you about how men think." He sucks in a breath and releases it with the clearing of his throat. His brown eyes take on the likings of a schoolmaster that Sarah would fall head over heels for, but that I am immune to.

He sets his cigar aside, sits forward in his chair, and claps his hands together, with an elbow to each knee.

I slide the book off my lap but keep it a fingers width away all the same.

His eyes, like a hawk, jerk toward my chosen weapon's repositioning, but then are drawn back to me as I nod for him to continue.

"Men have egos."

I lift a single eyebrow.

"Women who are aware of this said ego and know—how to say—foster it, become successful wives and mothers, with prosperous marriages."

Do I dare mess with him as he struggles to explain the ways of the world to me? Of course!

"Wait," I say, holding back my grin in exchange for a look of pure naïve bewilderment. "You're not in love. How do you know all this?"

The hesitation in his eyes and the touch of natural rouge that graces his features makes me bite the interior of my cheeks so as not to spoil my own fun with a telling giggle. I can see his thoughts reel about my query.

Has he had or does he have a secret love?

"Are you even listening to me?" Aaron asks, deciding to deflect my question all together.

His answer, or lack thereof, does nothing more than bring disappointment. "Yes, go on."

"I am not saying to give up your independence."

"Good because I won't."

His hand silences me. "Just allow him to have an opinion before you decide to give him your own. Better yet, Em, for God's sake, let the man decide once in a while without the benefit of your opinion."

I suck in a breath, considering his words.

He sucks in a breath, preparing for the headache my book just may give.

Finally, I say, "I am not opposed to my spouse being a leader. I am opposed to not having any say in the marriage. He will not make all the decisions without consulting me. After all, marriage is a relationship between two people, and I believe both should have equal say in what happens. I earned the right of being able to discern for myself my own desires and outcomes as a mature, grown individual; I will not depend on a husband as I once depended on my father as a small child."

"That will never work, and your level of maturity is debatable," Aaron admits, shaking his head.

The book flies at his head and hits its target with a Thunk—almost. He blocks most of the damage with his arm.

"What's that supposed to mean?" I ask in a harsh whisper.

"Ow!" The book falls into his lap before he proceeds to pick it up and answer. "My point exactly. Mother doesn't throw books." He gestures with my projectile to make his point. "And now that you have used the last of your ammo, I am at liberty to further my argument."

He smiles at my scowl.

"So, I implore you to ask yourself, sweet sister, what woman, in her right mind, wants to be saddled with such complicated decisions?" he asks.

"It isn't a burden if it is shared. Women are fully capable of solving problems and making decisions. Single women run households and manage finances all the time."

He sets down my book in exchange for his cigar. I let him draw thoughtfully on it, hoping the cigar will clear his mind of such backward thinking, but I get the distinct feeling he is doing the exact opposite in an attempt to build his case—which I will thwart.

Alas, his eyes shift back to me. "What about those who feel you are not following God's laws between man and woman?"

"My marriage is between my husband and I. There will always be naysayers. Although I will concede to making my marriage appear within social guidelines," I say as my hands smooth over my skirts. "It is none of anyone's business, Aaron, and an individual's relationship with God is a personal one. This is what separates us from the Catholics."

"I know and in an ideal world, you may be able to enjoy such privacy, but everyone always pokes their noses in other people's business." Aaron's head tilts to the side as he considers me. I can see the small smile toying with corners of his lips. "Though I must admit, I'm impressed you've thought this through."

"You should try it my way when the chance arises. I am not the only woman who is as strong of mind as you are," I tease back, but maintain an undertone of seriousness in my voice.

"It will be hard to find her. There is no woman out there who thinks like you, Em."

"And yet, I don't think you are destined to get rid of the likes of me so easily brother. In fact, I dare say my independent streak may plague you by the likes of your future wife, daughters, granddaughters—"

The lines of worry soften as his mouth plays with a smile, its corners lifting, his eyes brightening, and his chuckle interjects, "We will see about that."

"I think you mean, I will see to that," I say with a wink.

Thaddeus

FEBRUARY 1861
TABLE ROCK ROAD,
GETTYSBURG, PENNSYLVANIA

Standing at the chalkboard, I erase the letters for the third time in as many attempts. The dust invades my nose, and I cough out my frustration, rather than releasing it with a sigh as I intended. My shaking fingers reach once more for the chalk sitting in the tray. Stiff with nerves, my grasp fails to hold the fragile white writing utensil, and it falls to the floor, breaking in two. Reaching for the largest chunk of the crippled instrument, I look up to see Sarah eyeing me with suspicion.

"What on earth Emilie?" Her eyes survey me up and down. "You haven't been this nervous since the last test. What's gotten into you?"

"Nothing, I just can't—" my excuse abandons me. "I-I'm—I just can't get these lines straight, you know? And I know Mrs. Irwin is a stickler for straight writing on the chalkboard."

Not a speck of seriousness resides in the glint of Sarah's soft baby blues, and I can all but hear stifled laugh as her cheeks help foster a wide smile. "I agree, but she's never been so cruel as to make your hands shake like that."

Curse her observation.

"You're not nervous about the upcoming lesson, are you?" she asks.

This is why she will make a great teacher, always digging for answers from the depths of her pupil's core.

"Not really. Second graders are easy," I scoff.

Sarah moves closer to me. Her eyes studying me like a new-found treasure. "So, it must be that boy—what's his name?"

"You don't remember?" I ask, meeting her stare as I feel my heart begin to crack.

"Of course I do, I'm just testing if you do.," She winks, despite the playful pout she's introduced, not that it stays long given her infectious smile. "Say it with me—"

"Thaddeus," we say together.

Sarah gets up from the wooden desk bench and picks up the long wooden pointer resting by the chalkboard. She turns and points it at me. "I think you have some secret about him you are holding from me." The pointer prods my arm.

"Not from you," I admit, as she turns away from me, pacing the room.

"Then who?" Sarah flips back, pointing the stick at me in accusation.

"My parents," I say, backing away from her and the pointer aimed in my direction.

"Is it scandalous?" Sarah asks, both brows arching as her smile broadens.

"No," I say, fully aware of how she has me pinned between the teacher's desk and chalkboard.

"Then what?" she asks. "Friends tell each other everything."

I look down to her weapon of choice and then back to her.

Her head tilts, my fate is still mine to decide.

I sigh and try to push aside the ruler, choosing the life of our friendship over practice dummy for a teacher in training. "I have to get up the courage to ask if he can see me."

Sarah's eyes widen as she brings the ruler back into view. "Like visit you?" She taps my right shoulder with the edge. "Or court you?" She then taps the left shoulder.

"Whoa, wait," I say, holding up my hands. "No one said anything about courting."

"But we could have a double wedding—" Sarah drops the pointer on the desk. Her eyes foretell a fate much worse than beating.

"Sarah. Sarah!" I say, trying to grab a shoulder, to shake her, to put a hand over her mouth, to—

"Oh Emilie, this is so exciting. We can have matching dresses, and flowers, and we can have it at my house since it's bigger than yours, and make a double layered fruit cake, one for me and Thomas and one for you and Thaddeus, and how will we fit all the bridesmaids in my parlor ..."

My every attempt to hold back the tide of Sarah's excitement for a fantasy I dare not consider fails miserably as the ideas, musings, and rhetorical questions bubble up from an endless fountain composed of a young girl's dreams.

As she skips around the classroom gushing and babbling almost to the point of incoherence, I cannot bring myself to halt her flow, so I wait.

She has to breathe at some point.

And she does, only to turn on her heel and say, "Oh Emilie, you have to tell them, you just have to. How else am I supposed to get the invitations out in time? I'm sure they will be as ecstatic as me. It's every parent's wish to hear their daughter has found a soulmate to share the rest of their days with."

She sighs and I half expect butterflies to magically appear and for the sun's rays to provide her with her own personal halo.

This of course doesn't happen, and neither will the double wedding. I sigh too.

Sarah is right about one thing though. It is my parents' wish that I begin seeing suitors. The promise to my father still hangs over my head—but do they care who I choose?

Thaddeus's pressure for me to tell my parents comes soft at first. However, his insistence to preserve my propriety and court me properly causes him to push harder with each meeting. If I am as strong willed as Aaron proports me to be, then I must admit I come by it earnestly through everyone I know.

So—

"I vow tonight I will tell them, but Sarah, listen to me very carefully. I love you dearly, you are the greatest friend I could ever ask for, but we are not, and I repeat not, having a double wedding. I wouldn't dare impede on such a treasured memory between you and Thomas."

I hold my breath, expecting a facial expression to match that of a kicked puppy from my bosom buddy, but instead I am gifted with strangulation through a bone crushing hug.

"Oh Emilie, you are the most thoughtful, loving, amazing, sweet ..."

"Sarah... Sarah, you're crushing me!" I say, wincing.

"How was school?" Mother asks, as I help her set the table.

"The littles are eager to learn. They read four and five letter words today," I say, "but their runny noses with no handkerchiefs is—well, unsightly."

Pulling the plates from the cupboard, I mindlessly set the table. Fork, knife, spoon, plate, glass—

"We only need four settings." Mother's reminder makes me look back to the table—I set Aaron's place again.

"Right, no Aaron." I take the place setting away, leaving a blank space but not an empty one.

I miss you.

As Henry and Father enter, Mother and I finish the preparations before we all sit down for dinner. There is no small talk, no laughter. Henry, appearing silently lost in his thoughts, eats with his eyes downcast. Mother mindlessly takes in her bites without looking at any of us. In fact, her eyes are diverted to something across the room. And Father—I'd be honored just to sit in his head for a moment, as he nods, holding some secret conversation within. The blank chair mocks us, vacant and cold. Aaron always kept the conversation alive at this table.

I can't do this. I feel our food is warmer than our banter or even idle our chatter—it's time to break the ice.

"I have some news," I say.

My eyes sweep about to the forks held in suspense, hovering between plates and mouths.

Father raises an eyebrow, his interest piqued.

"I want to invite Thaddeus to dinner and a visit," I say, watching their expressions shift to query, like *Who are you and what have you done with Emilie Katherine Prescott, our beloved independent family member?* And yet, Father hosts some spark of hope behind those twinkling brown eyes.

"And for what reason would that be?"

"Probably a hen party, given all the clucking he was doing at the dance. So proud of you Emilie, finally deciding to remain in the coop," Henry snickers.

Father casts him a look of warning, and it is my pleasure to watch him shrink.

"We want to see each other—with your blessing, of course," I say with an exhale.

"What took you so long to tell us, Emilie? This is positively wonderful news," Father says, as a jovial smile breaks out over his face.

Mother adds, "Positive indeed." She looks to Father, and they share a look that borders between pride and reassurance. But before I have a chance to question what that is all about, Mother asks, "When shall we invite him, Thursday? I have just the meal in mind, and we can ..."

"Does Mr. Marsh agree?" Father asks.

"Of course, he agrees," I say. "I am not forcing him to see me."

"I don't know, it would be like a strong independent—"

"Henry!" Father warns.

Henry sighs, "Ya'll are no fun."

"Well, you've been seeing each other in private for some time. I wasn't sure if he was having—" Father begins but coughs as we hear a knock from under the table, and his eyes catch my mother's.

Wait, he knew?

"Invite him for Thursday, and, of course, you have our blessing," says Mother.

I don't respond. I have nothing to respond with! The shock on my face gives Father a satisfied grin as he turns his attention back to me. My face burns red, my eyes wide, my mouth forms that quizzical little *O* it makes when I am positively dumbstruck—he knew all along.

Looking to my mother, she shakes her head, fully aware of what I tried to get away with.

Henry appears annoyed and is stabbing a rolling pea around on his plate with an irritating *clink* at every opportunity. He looks up and snorts a laugh, goes to speak, but apparently feels Father's glare as he looks over to him, "What? I was just going to tell her I didn't know."

"I'm sorry." I swallow hard and look down at my plate. "He is and has been a perfect gentleman."

"He most certainly is, Emilie," Father says. "So next time, don't put him in a difficult position, Emilie."

"But how did you—" I begin to ask.

"Oh, come on, Em. They work together!" says Henry.

I blush. "Oh, right."

Mother and Father exchange glances. The happiness between them shared many times in their marriage now reflects in their eyes. Sarah's words dance through my mind, Every parent's wish.

"If all goes well, we might have a wedding by August and..." begins Mother.

Oh no.

"Julia, the dowery is ready. We could plan by November or December ..." continues Father.

Make it stop.

"Honestly, Jacob, in this weather? A late fall or spring would be best..." Mother shakes her head.

Not listening. Not listening!

"An orchard wedding would be beautiful in fall during the leaf changes." Henry smirks enjoying my rising panic.

I deliver a swift kick to him from under the table.

And now, *I must stop this!*

"No, whoa... Wait." I say, trying to get a word in edgewise, but then there is discussion about flowers and cakes and—

I jump up from my seat, "Can I see him for a few months first?"

Everyone turns to stare at me, a bit taken aback, but then bellies full of laughter erupt around our dinner table.

Father winks at me. Mother offers a congratulatory smile, as a tear glistens in her eye. Henry is grinning with delight at all the opportunities he will now have to tease me, and I suppose it wouldn't hurt for me to laugh a little too.

Then Henry's palm hits the table.

We all look to him.

"So, who's going to break the news to Stephen Byrne?" Henry asks.

In true Prescott fashion, we all throw our napkins at Henry, who tries and fails miserably to catch them all at once.

As Mother and I rise to take up the dishes, I can't help but grin back at Father. "Since you have such bright ideas, Henry, why don't you do it?"

"After all, we were talking about Thaddeus Marsh, not Stephen Byrne, Henry." I roll my eyes and return my attention to mother as we head to the kitchen to wash up and plan for Thaddeus's arrival.

Henry mumbles something, but I don't care.

"Are you nervous, Emilie?" Mother asks as she slips each pearl button through and into its adjacent notch on my visiting dress.

"A little," I say, fingers already beginning to toy with the pleats on my skirt.

"You don't seem quite yourself today," Mother says, brushing my anxious fingers away to smooth the skirt out over my small hoop, inspecting the fabric to make sure it is in place. My silhouette appears to float against the lantern light, accentuating my shape, reminding me of the drawings in mother's *Godey's Lady's Book*.

My room is quiet, except for our conversation. The small photos on the dresser smile back at me, ushering encouragement from previous generations. The fireplace is cold and resting, as the embers won't be stirred from their slumber for another few hours. As the house creaks around us and the wind whistles a tune of winter play just beyond, it feels as though the walls are listening in—each board an interested lady, waiting for the latest gossip to spill forth, holding their breath as I hold mine, praying our first meeting as a courting couple will go just fine.

"Any advice," I ask, biting my lower lip, my nerves pricking my arms until pebbled flesh is drawn forth.

"Just be yourself. If it is meant to be, it will be." Mother's smile is one I've seen before, filled with memories combined with pride and a serene, peaceful grace.

"I like him, Mother." The fabric of my pleated skirt has once again found its way into my fingers. "But what if—" I walk over to the vanity mirror, sitting so she can tame my fly away hairs.

Mother picks up the brush.

"But what?" she asks.

"I don't want to ruin it. He makes me feel all fluttery inside and giddy and nauseous and I don't know if I can do this—" I say my fingers move to grasp in front of my chest as a pang seizes my heart and a knot forms in my gut.

"Here, hold this." Mother hands me a bottle of rose oil. "Put some behind your ears and on your wrists. Wipe the rest of the oil in your hair."

I do as she says, the fragrant oil filling my senses with the whisper of summer rose gardens. At last, I can breathe.

She sets down the brush, picking up a small cameo to pin to the collar of my dark blue and green plaid dress.

"Relax, this isn't marriage. It's a time to get together and get to know each other. Enjoy it."

While it lasts ... seems to hang in my mind like a storm cloud, as if marriage is some inescapable prison on the horizon.

Sensing my nerves are still in play, Mother offers some advice. "You're both developing a lifelong relationship. You will know if it is meant to be."

"And if it's not?" I ask.

"Then it simply won't be."

A shiver shakes me, dusting the nerves off me like snow flurries off a cloak. My mother's hands steady my shoulders. My eyes look to hers in the mirror.

"I hope it will be, though."

I hope it is not a childish fantasy but real ... Thaddeus brightens my world, letting me sample colors, sounds, and smells in a way I've never experienced before—like I am experiencing life for the first time, each breath new and escaping my lungs in search of ceaseless wonders, all wrapped up in him ... No, it can't be real. I am new at this. I am sure everyone feels this way.

My gaze takes up my own image in the vanity mirror and Mother's eyes peering back at me. Our reflection embraces us. She is an older version of me. Our eyes are bright and carry the same almond shape. Our cheeks are high, accenting our noses, while our lips are full, deep pink, and smooth.

She squeezes my shoulders and kisses my cheek before turning away from the mirror.

Deep breaths, or so I tell myself in an effort to calm the buzzing of nerves and dizzying thoughts racing through my mind.

"Time for dinner. Hurry on, Em." I turn around to see Mother leaving the room with a swish of her skirt. A flash of handkerchief from her pocket catches my eye as she uses it to dab at her cheeks.

The knock on the door restarts the buzzing of my nerves, and my stomach flips and bounds into my throat like some over excited puppy. My heart pounds against my sternum like a drum, eliciting my feet to thump out their own jig against the floorboards with the thrill of him.

Henry's hand on my shoulder holds me in place and back from the door as father opens it to let Thaddeus in.

Oh my—

He is dressed in a dark blue coat and matching trousers. His clothes no longer represent the working man I've come to know with his cotton shirt, overworked pants, and scruffy boots, but a man who smells fresh with a whisper of the bergamot and lime cologne, which beckons me closer as our eyes meet. We hold our breath at the sight of each other, embracing each other not with words or faulty limbs but with a smile, his wink, my blush ...

"Welcome, Thaddeus," Father's voice sounds miles away. "Please come in."

I blink.

"Emilie." His voice deep, eyes holding me.

My smile broadens and spills out into a grin. "Thaddeus." My fingers twist the pleats in my skirt, which I don't let go of until Henry pushes me aside.

Becoming slightly off balance, I shoot a glare at him, hoping it stabs him well as he claps Thaddeus on his back, breaking our connection.

He's my guest, not yours, Henry!

Little time is given to fan my ire, though, as Father whisks the lot of us off into the dining room—a serene setting with candles burning on the table, appearing not only set for company, but with the perfection desired from any reader of *Godey's Lady's Book.*

We sit down for dinner where forks and knives clink and clank. Food I've had umpteen times before somehow tastes better, and dessert appears before me in the shape of a man I desire but cannot yet sample outside of smiles, grins, laughter—

As Thaddeus interacts with my parents and brother, he banters with Henry in a familiar male to male conversation that I am certain Aaron would relish. When he reaches for the napkin on his lap, I feel his hand, warm on mine beneath the table, offer a slight squeeze of reassurance. Then a foot—grazes mine?

At first, I look to Henry, but he seems to be oblivious to anything but devouring the spice cake in front of him.

I tap Henry's boot with mine. He looks up.

I eye him. He scowls at me before looking back at the cake in front of him.

Again, his foot grazes mine.

His knee presses against me.

Turning to look at Thaddeus, a small smile plays hide and seek on his lips.

"Is dinner to your liking?" Thaddeus asks.

"Oh yes, how divine you taste," I say. "I mean the food. I mean I cooked it all day, just somehow it's more magical than I recall it ever being, in your presence."

"It's delicious," Thaddeus chuckles. "Though you better eat some more of this magic you've whipped up. I don't want you fainting off into some fantasy without me later."

I giggle, "How ever would you explain that?"

Thaddeus's eyes widen, "Dragons."

I take a fork to a piece of spice cake, slide it through the whipped cream, and sample the taste of his chuckle must have sprinkled over my plate. The sensation of spice, sweet cream, and the tickle of his laughter against my tongue is amazing, and the closest thing I will get to a kiss for what I imagine is some time.

His eyes on me give me pause, and I feel a familiar heat paint my cheeks beyond the rouge Mother had applied earlier.

The music of clinking silver on dishes and cups slows to a halt. Everyone is smiling, satisfied with the meal.

Henry says, "I'll help clean up the dishes. You two have better things to do."

Father clears his throat and claps his hands together. "That's right, the courting candle awaits!" He gets up from the table, heading toward the parlor.

Thaddeus gets up, slides my chair from the table, and offers me his arm. My hand slides into the crook of his elbow, closing the space between us. The scent of him embraces me. His hand secures mine to his arm with a warm pat as we follow to the parlor.

Can he feel how nervous I am?

"I think Jacob, I mean your father, is just as excited about this as we are."

I give a halfhearted laugh that faulters into a sigh. "Let's not encourage him. He just makes me more nervous."

"No need to be nervous, I'll be a perfect gentleman. You have my word."

That's what I'm afraid of...

The parlor doors slide open revealing a warm, inviting cozy space. Father lights a few more candles, and this appears to add to the ambiance surrounding the two chairs which sit center-stage in front of the fireplace.

Orange flames dance in celebration of us as Thaddeus walks me over to one chair, and once I am comfortable, he takes the other. The last candle Father lights is the courting candle, placed at the center of the small table set between our chairs.

"You will take your leave when that flame extinguishes, Mr. Marsh. I trust your two will follow proper decorum, so I won't be staying this evening." His stern voice snaps my head around.

"Of course, Father," I bite my bottom lip, my fingers once more on the pleats on my gown.

"Since you have taken measures of honesty with us about your intentions, the parlor is now available to you both." Father eyes me. "This said, I trust, Emilie, that this will encourage you to discontinue any other private meetings between the two of you."

Thaddeus clears his throat, his eyes on me.

Father's gaze shifts to him. "My daughter is the one who put her own propriety in danger, which means I'm not blaming you, Thaddeus." His hand goes to squeeze the young man's shoulder, a grip I notice tightening as he adds, "Unless, that is, you refuse to offer her the help she so desperately needs."

Father's grin neither stops Thaddeus from snapping his mouth shut, nor ringing his hands.

"Now, we'll be right outside those doors," Father gestures to them just in case there is any confusion. "Have a good evening."

Father's boot steps trail off across the parlor, before he slides the doors nearly shut, leaving a crack wide enough to spy on us, if necessary.

Alone at last, neither of us speak for a long moment.

The time dwindles as the wick burns down.

My fingers fold and unfold the pleats of my skirt, I want to look at him, but I-I'm—

"You look beautiful tonight." Thaddeus's voice, so deep and soothing, sails through my thoughts.

"Thank you. I like that suit on you," I manage to say.

"Between the good food and your father's reprimand," Thaddeus pulls at the collar of his shirt and rolling his shoulders partially back, "it's feeling a bit tight."

"Oh, don't worry about him. He likes you. If he truly did not respect you, he would have thrown you out by now."

Thaddeus swallows hard, "Good to know."

Silence carries on between us once more.

Why's this so hard?

"How's work?" I ask, changing the subject.

Maybe this conversation will be easier.

"Work is busy. New orders coming in all the time," Thaddeus changes the subject. "How is school?"

"Good. I'm teaching reading now, as an assistant." I smile. "It's a favorite subject of mine."

"So, you like to read?" he asks.

"Yes, you too?" I ask.

Thaddeus shakes his head. His hands now rest quietly in his lap, no longer fidgeting. I look down to notice my fingers and let go of the pleat.

"Who is your favorite?"

"A favorite? I'm not sure, but I like to read a variety of authors, especially fiction and poetry."

"Poetry?" His eyes light up.

"Shakespeare, Hawthorne and—" I say, my eyes catch his, and a grin is shared between us.

"I bet you are a Dickenson girl." He teases, sitting forward in his seat.

"Which one?"

He chuckles. "*A Tale of Two Cities?*"

"It's alright. I much prefer *Bleak House*. What do you like to read?" I ask, moving to the edge of my chair, and shifting my hoop to be closer to him. The table to my right is an unwelcome barrier as we begin and continue to talk about poetry.

"... His description of nature makes me appreciate the world around us beyond just an everyday noticing," Thaddeus comments on Wadsworth's work.

"And yet, I imagine it is the everyday noticing that implored him to write what you love most. After all, you have to take time to walk in nature without an agenda to truly appreciate it."

"Agreed. What else must I know about Miss Emilie Prescott to claim that I know everything?"

I laugh. "Are you sure you want to know everything?"

"Sure? No, I only think I do, therefore I must—or is that I am?" he asks.

"A fan of Descartes, I see."

"Yes, but his musings are still not as fascinating as you are to me."

"Well, if you think it, then it must be so."

We laugh until we sigh and find ourselves trapped in each other's eyes.

"Who are you?" he asks.

"I am my own person. Too independent, they say. Too outspoken for my own good."

"What's wrong with that?" Thaddeus still holds me in those deep blues. Our fingers touch, finally making use of that disruptive small table. The warmth between us wants to pull me to him.

"I don't think anything, but—" I say.

"Good, because I can't see a woman such as yourself ever being too much of a good thing. Why, your company is invigorating."

"Me too," I whisper. "I mean—Tell me more about Thaddeus Marsh. Where is he from, when is his birthday, and what makes him happy?" My mouth dries up, feeling the need for water.

Am I being punished for being too forward?

Thaddeus shifts, standing to stir the fire.

The momentary loss of his fingers touching mine causes the tips of my fingers to tingle as I wait for him to return.

He places two more pieces of wood on the fire.

His eyes glance over at the courting candle as he returns to his chair. Sitting on its edge, he reaches for my hand.

I am keen to accept it and let the warmth return as our fingers entwine, connecting us once more.

"Well," He settles in for a more serious conversation, "Thaddeus Marsh, is from the foothills of the Appalachian Mountains. A man who as a babe was placed in a basket and washed down stream, only to be collected by an Indian woman—"

"The truth!" I say, squeezing his hand.

"But I thought you liked fiction?" he asks with a grin.

My head tilts as I fix him with narrow eyes, never mind the smile that gives away all seriousness on my part.

"All right, all right. Let's see ... You already know I have a small family, just my parents, my brother Ian, and myself. I was born and raised here. My father is a farmer, though he occasionally takes odd jobs in town. My mother keeps the house in order and somehow we boys as well. Oh, and my birthday is in August. I'll be twenty this year."

Thaddeus looks down at our fingers, his thumb is drawing a hypnotic circle on top of my hand. "What about you?"

"I was born and raised near Richmond, Virginia. I'm the youngest of three, with two older brothers you've already met. I am going to be a teacher, and I'll be eighteen in September," I say, squeezing his hand.

"Eighteen? So, you are newly seventeen?" he asks.

"As of last September, yes," I say, but his frown alerts my senses. "What's wrong?"

"I pictured you—"

"Older," I say, saving him the embarrassment of stating a woman's age.

"Hmm," Thaddeus's brow furrows, his eyes darken.

"And you are worried I am not mature enough?" I ask.

"No, not at all. It surprises me. I thought you were at least nineteen like myself." He pats my hand. "You're definitely mature enough to lead my thoughts astray and wrong." Thaddeus takes a deep breath, pats my hand in reassurance with his free hand.

"So, tell me, what is your favorite color?"

I open my mouth to answer—

"I bet it is—" His eyes dart to me. "Re ... no ... green ... ah no." He looks deep into my eyes, mining for a hint.

I stare at him, a smile toying with the corners of my mouth, but I say not a word.

He sits back, and our fingers slip apart as he reassesses me from another angle.

"Did it come to you yet?" I ask, a giggle escaping me.

Thaddeus sighs, shrugs his shoulders. "I'll say as yellow as the sunshine in your eyes." He gives me a wink.

"Wrong!" I burst into giggles, smiling so hard my cheeks ache. "Try blue, green, and maroon. And I believe your favorite color is—"

I eye him skeptically, but he will see none of it as his blue eyes beckon me to peer into the pools of his soul and pluck the thought straight from his mind.

"Blue, it must be dark blue. You're not a sky-blue kind of person. You are bolder, more daring," I say.

"Thank you for that compliment, Miss Prescott." The toe of his boot nudges mine. "Though you're not quite right. I'm a burgundy kind of man, but dark blue is a close second."

"What is the difference between maroon and burgundy?" I ask.

Thaddeus bites his lower lip in considers his answer. "I think—I think the difference is that maroon is browner, but slightly more so."

"Brown? It's red," I say, my brows furrowing, trying to remember if I ever compared two fabric swatches of the colors, "What does burgundy have? Black? Purple?"

"Either, but we'll have to compare to be sure."

"I could do that with you," I say, imagining us at Fahnstocks, comparing fabrics, laughing between ourselves.

"Are you asking me on a date, Miss Prescott?"

"That depends. Are you willing to go to the fabrics at Fahnstocks to compare with me Mr. Marsh?"

I sit closer to the edge of my chair, balancing precariously near the edge. I feel numbness settling into my legs. Our joking brings our bodies closer together as he, too, leans forward.

The table between us is no longer a barrier as our knees are inches from each other.

"You smell like a fresh spring day." He leans in.

His breath is warm on my cheek, and I can't help but breathe him in.

"Bergamot," I whisper, my eyes meeting his. I feel his fingers playing with mine, twisting together in a cat and mouse game as the embrace of our palms crosses over into my lap.

"Like it?" he asks.

"It's you," I say. "It's—hmmm."

"At a loss for words, Em—"

Bang!

We jump. Our foreheads colliding into each other, forcing us to raise our free hands to nurture new aches.

"Sorry." Father announces in the company of a smirk. "It's getting late Mr. Marsh, wouldn't you say?"

Thaddeus goes from rubbing his forehead to wiping it away as if there is no pain as he goes to stand.

I don't even notice how our hands are glued together, as I try to do much the same.

Head throbbing, free hand wiping along my skirts, and captured hand squeezing Thaddeus's for support, I go to stand, but my legs give out like a new foal forcing me to sink back into my chair—pulling Thaddeus with me.

"Oh," I exclaim.

"Are you all right?" Thaddeus catches himself on the arm of the chair to keep both distance and my propriety between us.

"My leg fell asleep," I say. Tingling races up my leg, pricking and poking in all sorts of ways.

Father pokes his head back into the parlor as I try to stand and limp with the sleeping limb.

"Emilie, tell Thaddeus good night."

"We're trying!" I say.

Thaddeus holds my arm as we both stifle giggles. He then props me up against the wall as we stand by the door.

"May I call on you again?" he asks.

"Of, course. Thank you for coming," I say, bouncing the feeling back into my leg.

Over the next few weeks, father leaves the doors ajar with the courting candle as our chaperone. Both of us know Father is listening to our visits, but neither of us mind, as he doesn't stop us from our intimate conversations.

Tonight, Thaddeus takes the chair while I sit on the couch. The table is ignored as the candle burns. Facing each other, my hand in his, we begin our conversation in a normal tone, talking about our day, hoping to bore father to sleep.

It doesn't take long before we hear the tell-tale sounds of a snore.

A devious smirk caters to my expression. "Tell me have those lips touched another woman's lips?"

How I yearn to know how they'd feel pressed against mine.

"Only my mother and grandmother's cheeks." A low chuckle erupts from him. "These lips are waiting for the right girl."

"Hmm."

Waiting for him ...

Silence ...

My eyes go to Thaddeus, as I find myself chewing on my bottom lip.

"I bet you are waiting for me to ask who your lips have touched?" His grin plays at his mouth, with a glint in his eye.

"Well, I thought ..." I suddenly feel silly. I look away at the walls, at the furniture, at the books lining the shelves.

"I won't ask because I don't need to know, and it is not proper," Thaddeus states, his pointer finger punctuating the last three words into my outstretched hand, palm up, and willing his caress.

I capture his fingers, squeezing them. "I am saving my kisses for—"

Ahem!

The sound rushes in from the door. I sit back, and our hands retreat to our laps.

"You," I say soundlessly, with a wink when he looks back at me.

Thaddeus shuffles in his chair. Reaching into his jacket pocket he pulls out a cloth covered hardbacked book.

"I have just the thing for us," he says louder. "May I read you a poem or two?"

"May I guess the poet?" I ask, sitting closer to the end of the couch, hoping he will close the space between us. "Is it all one poet or many?"

"Many poets, an anthology," Thaddeus states. He looks thoughtfully at the pages, considering, thinking about how to stump me.

I stand to retrieve a book of poetry off the shelf. Eyeing him over the gray book, I say, "Let's see who knows their poets."

"Let's make it random. I'll close my eyes and turn to a page."

"Challenging," I say, flipping the pages in my fingers.

Thaddeus opens his book, eyes the prose. "Try this."

I sit back to listen to his tenor voice read the prose, loving how he sounds, not wanting him to stop.

Year after year unto her feet,
She lying on her couch alone,
Across the purpled coverlet,
The maiden's jet-black hair has grown,
On either side, her tranced form

Courting Freedom

Forth streaming from a braid of pearl
(Lord Tennyson, Black Beauty, 1842)

"Lord Tennyson," I say, excited to know this one.

"Name the poem."

I scoff, "Black Beauty, of course."

"That one was easy. Your turn," Thaddeus waves his hand at me.

I close my eyes, flip the book open to a page to begin reading.

The night is come, but not too soon:
And sinking silently,
All silently, the little moon
Drops down behind the sky.
There is no light on earth or heaven.
But the cold light of the stars
and the first watch of night is given.
to the red planet Mars.
Is it the tender star of love?
The star of love and dreams,
O no! from the blue tent above
A hero's armor gleams.
(Henry Wadsworth Longfellow, The Light of Stars, 1839)

I pause, looking up from the page. Thaddeus is watching me. His blue eyes dreamlike, a serene look on his face, his mouth turned up into a smile. He is sitting back in his chair, reposed and relaxed, as if he may drift off at any moment.

"Do you need a clue?" I ask.

"No, I just want to listen to you read Henry Wadsworth Long-

239

fellow's *The Light of Stars* to me. Keep going." He waves me on with his hand.

When I finish the poem, he has a satisfied smile on his face.

"I enjoy your voice, Emilie." He sits up in his chair.

"Thank you, dare I say, I almost put you to sleep?"

"No, not in the slightest, as I don't want to miss a moment with you. Sleep can wait. Rather my eyes were closed so I could enjoy the symphony of your lilting—"

"Were you going to say something?" I ask, catching how he abruptly ended his sentence.

Thaddeus looks to the door. Then back at me.

His face changes from pink to a flush of crimson.

"Dare I inquire, sir?" I ask in a whisper, wrinkling my nose, wanting in on his secret.

He shakes his head no.

My eyes widen at him, mouthing the words, Tell me.

He mouths back, *I can't.*

Why not? I ask.

"It's awfully quiet in there!" Comes a reminder from the hall. My father is still awake.

Thaddeus picks up his book saying, in a louder tone than needed, "Last one, Emilie. Goodness, I will go hoarse reading to you all night." His body is shaking, as he silently chuckles.

"Just one more," I say pleading as we exchange winks, and I have to bite my lip to not burst out in peals of laughter.

"Oh, all right. Just this once," Thaddeus makes a face at me. "Now listen."

I watch as he flips through the book, "Oh, this one." His eyebrow raises, a grin playing on his lips.

Courting Freedom

The moonlight fades from flower and rose
And the stars dim one by one;
The tale is told, the song is sung,
And the Fairy feast is done.
The night-wind rocks the sleeping flowers,
And sings them, soft and low.
The early birds erelong will wake;
'T is time for the Elves to go.
(Louisa May Alcott, Fairy Song, 1855)

I don't remember the rest, as I got lost watching his lips forming the words, the timber of his deep voice, imagining him whispering in my ear, drinking him in, imagining, daydreaming ...

"Well, who is it? Any guesses?" Thaddeus asks, his eyes catch mine coming out of their daze. "Emilie, are you all right?"

"I've never heard this one," I say. "I like the imagination, and the fairies sound charming."

"Not charming to some folks, but I won't get into that lore."

"Faries sound delightful." I winkle my nose. "Who is it?"

Thaddeus closes the book, handing it to me. I take it from him, our fingers brush against each other. The warmth, softness, and thrill of his touch races up my arm. We watch each other, holding our connection. The book seems to float between us.

"Thaddeus," I whisper.

"Emilie." His voice sounds far away, lost in his throat.

My eyebrow raises, I glance at the book and back to him.

"Oh, yes," Thaddeus clears his throat. "Alcott."

"Alcott?"

"The poem. It's called *Fairy Song* by Louisa May Alcott. She's

241

new." Thaddeus clears his throat again. "Do you want to borrow this?"

"I'd love to," I say as he lets go of the book.

Thaddeus shifts back into his seat, rubbing his hands on his trousers.

We both look to the candle. It's out.

Thaddeus offers me his hand. We stand and move toward the door—when it slides open. Father is there.

"It's late. Good night, Thaddeus."

"Good night, sir." Thaddeus shakes Father's hand.

We walk to the door. Thaddeus dons his coat and hat.

"Emilie, Mr. Prescott," Thaddeus says, his hand on the door. "May I invite you, Emilie, to dine with my family next week?"

"I would—"

"Thank you for the invitation," Father says. "We will gladly accept."

"I will inform my parents," Thaddeus turns to open the door.

A cold wind blows in, "Good night, Emilie."

"Good night."

Thaddeus gives me a nod, a squeeze of the hand, and then turns and moves away, his fingers sliding out of my grasp, taking with it a part of me and the warmth of our connection. I stand in the window, watching him ride off into the night. I miss him already.

How is that possible?

Racehorse Alley

A HORSE NEVER RUNS SO FAST AS WHEN HE HAS
OTHER HORSES TO CATCH UP AND OUTPACE.
~OVID

APRIL 1861
RACEHORSE ALLEY
GETTYSBURG PENSYLVANIA

Billy Halle reaches down scooping up a handful of dirt. The dirt sifts through his fingers like sand, perfect moisture and density. He watches it float back to the ground. The warmth of the spring sun combined with overnight rains make the roads easy to traverse. Billy looks down the alley. It is well worn—the dirt loosely churned up, perfect for horses to run, and most importantly clear of Mr. McClellan and his men who took their thoroughbreds to the fairgrounds early this morning.

This means it's race day not only for the men, but for Billy and his boys as well. A day that will go down in history once he shows them and himself how well Starlight can run. Billy's skin prickles with excitement.

She'll run well; I will bet my life on it.

His neck cranes to take a gander over his shoulder.

She'll have my friends Johnny and Gates over there to cheer us on, and James will have to shut up about how he knows more than me, because I raise horses and I know horses, especially good runners when I see them. James's apology will be sweet music, and I'll be more than some unsung hero!

"We're here," James says, with dark hair, dark eyes, but skin so pale he looked like he never comes out in the daytime. The nasty scar over his right eye looks more red than pink and enhances the older boy's glare as it passes over Billy and the other boys. Rumor has it he sucks people's blood at night. Billy isn't sure if it's true, but he can't blame James' eight-year-old brother trying to escape his suspenders, as James uses them to keep a handle on his younger brother, Little Tim.

"So, where's this magical horse you're always going on about?" asks James.

"She'll be here," Billy eyes the stick of candy poking out of the older boy's mouth.

Bet he stole it or cheated some helpless kid out of it.

"How are you going to get that horse away from the girl?" James asks. "I never see her without that nag."

"Emilie comes to town every Saturday. She'll be here," Billy turns to Gates, a tiny, sandy haired boy, who follows his every order and every move like a shadow. Annoying most of the time, but useful this time. "Gates, go back to your father's store and watch for her. If she rides up, run back to tell me. Got it?"

Gates head bobbles atop his neck as a gap-tooth grin breaks daylight over his features. "Gots it, Billy. Won't let you down, no way no how. Gots eyes in the back of my head, gots feet as soft as a cat, gots—"

"Gates!"

"Right, on it! See you soon Billy, James, little Tim—"

Billy cuts a glare at the small boy who turns tail and finally scampers down the alley back to the Fahnestock store.

They watch the runt flee like a jack rabbit before James looks back at Billy. "I can't wait to get this over with. If things weren't so boring around here, I wouldn't even bother being here."

"Anyone ever tell you bragging ain't only annoying but wrong?" asks Billy.

"Where did you get that bit from? The mirror?" asks James.

The boys around them begin to laugh and chuckle, fingers already pointing to the loser, him, Billy Halle. But he'd show them.

"Oh, go choke on your tongues. She's faster than any horse around. You'll see," Billy clears his throat. "Well, any normal horse that is. Mr. McClellen's thoroughbreds don't count."

"Right. Fastest nag around. Guess she'll beat Mr. Walker's donkey," James says and laughter from all around continues to plague Billy's so-called friends.

"All you have to do is watch," Billy arms crossing as he looks back down the alley for Gates.

"All right, well look, if this is going to be a proper race, how about we make a little wager?" James asks, taking a step closer, his little brother yo-yoing against the tug on his suspenders.

"I, well, I didn't count on a race, but—" Billy's tongue feels thick as his ears burn red. He can feel the eyes of the other boys and hear the faint whisper of "chicken" ready to flap off their tongues. When his eyes finally fall on his best friend Johnny, the red-haired boy gives him what any friend would offer in times like this—a nod of encouragement. Right. Like hell is he going to let James win this one.

Billy turns back to James, squaring his shoulders, straightening his back the way Ma always wants him to stand in church. "Fine, what you gotta bet?" Swallowing hard, he realizes this could very well be a matter of life or death, but he is a man, and men don't back down—right?

James borrows the devil's own smirk for a moment. "Depends on what you got. And I ain't talkin' about your marble collection. This ain't no childish wager after all." The scar accentuates his features in a way that makes Billy want to shrink up but not cry. Men don't cry.

Billy, not planning on a gamble, can't afford to come up short on this matter, and out of desperation to find something of worth, he reaches into his pocket. His favorite marbles—cat-eye, devil's eye—his trusty shooter, his hankie, a spare rock, some lint, and his most prized possession in the whole wide world— his pocketknife. Having received it for his birthday the previous year, Ma and Pa had spent a small fortune on it, even had his name and the year engraved on the handle.

Billy Halle don't break our parent's heart by giving that away, Jane reprimands him from somewhere in the back of his mind as he pulls the knife out of his pocket, but it's too late—unless he wins that is.

His arm extends, and his palm opens to the sky with the blade tucked closed within the wooden hilt, "This is all I gots. Take it or leave it, James Rogers."

The knife catches the sun, glistening bright and catching the older boy's eye as he reaches for it.

Billy's fingers are quick to close around it, tucking it out of sight as he pulls it out of reach. "But you ain't gots no one to challenge me. So, I may as well just keep it and you can watch her run." He slides the knife back into his pocket. "Also, there be the matter of what I get when I win?"

"I think you mean *if*, and don't worry. We'll find something worthy of beating you and that nag," James says as he reaches into his pocket.

His hand shuffles around for a moment.

His face makes funny expressions with his tongue half out as he shifts around.

"Need my spendies, Bubbah?" asks little Tim, already looking for a way to remove his makeshift leash.

"Take those off Timmy and I'll tie your hands with 'em!" James reaches in his pocket to pull out his playing cards wrapped in twine.

Holding them up for Billy, "I got these."

"No way, that's weak," Billy scoffs. "I am calling this off, unless you got something more valuable, or you can just wisen up and admit I'm right."

James' shoulders slump, but his knuckles somehow whiten even more as they squeeze around the deck, a sight not nearly as terrifying as the smug satisfied grin that follows.

The larger boy, the bully of the block, Billy Halle's arch nemesis takes two steps toward him, "You can have my pocketknife if you win. Knife for knife."

"Deal."

"Good. Now to decide who your racin." James looks around the alley.

"Who?" Billy asks, trying not to shrink in the shadow of the brute.

"She-she's ... the horse ... store!" Gates, arrives breathless and yet somehow finding the lung capacity to shout while waving his stumpy arms as best he can.

Flashing a glare back at James, Billy says, "You know what? It doesn't matter because when I get back, we'll beat 'em. Enjoy what little time you gots left with that knife James Rogers."

Arriving at Fahnestock Store I tie up Starlight, who stretched her neck out after me, smelling mints in my pocket.

"Not now," I say giving her head and the long pleading face that occupies it a gentle nudge.

Starlight stomps her disapproval as I dismiss her needs, perhaps wondering how I couldn't have compassion for a poor round plucky mare like her. And the answer is: giddiness. It rushes through me as I push through the thick wood door with its ornate glass décor and take in the odds and ends of my favorite shop.

Ding! Ding!

I curtsy at the bell's greeting in jest before my eyes drink in yards of beautiful fabric, and my mind plays with the words I read from their fabric sale announcement.

New ballgown here I come!

Oh, I can just see it. Thaddeus and I, hand in hand as he twirls me about and I swish and glide here and there before being pulled directly back into his warm and loving embrace. *Sigh.*

"Good morning." The clerk greets me. A dazzling young woman who I am confident knows her fashion. Mock buttons with their intricate design adorn the front of her dress, which frames her torso in a beautiful pattern, accenting the solid powder blue that forms the rest of her work apparel. I imagine all the women find her silhouette respectable, and yet, all the men would say she is alluring.

"Good morning. I love the lace at the edges of your sleeves," I say, moving to the counter.

"Thank you. I was worried it might be too much. How may I help you?"

As I reach the counter, I notice she appears no more than fifteen. Her brown eyes and dark hair frame her pretty oval face, and her bright smile appears more genuine compared to moments ago.

"I saw your advertisement about the dress patterns and fabrics on sale this week."

"Yes, we just got some great fabrics in. What are you making?"

"A ballgown," I say, suddenly feeling my confidence fading as I say it aloud.

"Ah, Let's see..." She pauses with a finger to her lip.

What if they are out of the fabric that I want? What if I'm too late and all the buttons I've dreamed of are sold out? What if—

"Oh, I know, we have some new selections. Come this way."

I fight to suppress my squeal and try to breathe in the calm and expel the anxiety from my lungs.

The clerk leads me through a maze of fabric bolts, lined up neat and tidy like toy soldiers standing at constant attention. The only difference is the assortment of colors and patterns they offer.

We pause between the silks and brocades.

"These just arrived this week." She says, fingering the multi-colored textures. "I know an excellent seamstress, if you want to pass the work off to someone else."

Taking the fabrics between my fingers, all I can feel is the smooth, glossy shimmer of expensive tastes. Each bolt hosts a blank slate, waiting for a talented hand to create a dress of beauty and grace.

I bite my lower lip, confidence waning once more, slipping into self-doubt.

Perhaps I should ask about that seamstress?

"What's her name?" I ask.

"I'm sorry whose name?" asks the clerk.

I flush from embarrassment, forgetting the world is not privy to my thoughts. "Your seamstress."

"Oh, Miss Bennett. She also has a selection of fabrics on hand. I'm not supposed to tell you that until after you buy, but that doesn't make much sense to me. If you want to have a consultation with her, I can get you her address."

"I'll take a look here first. If I change my mind, I will let you know."

"Let me know what?" asks the clerk.

"About Miss Bennett," I give that sweet southern smile us Prescott ladies are well versed in.

"Fair enough. I'll let you look, let me know if you need anything."

"I will."

I watch as the clerk moves away.

Bless her heart. Pretty as a picture and about as bright as one.

My eyes turn back to the rows, excited to explore. I begin perusing the fabric bolts, exploring their personalities with a touch that reveals the weight, texture, and feel of each.

The dark maroon velvety fabric catches my senses. The smooth texture makes me think of comfort and how I would love to drape myself in it. And yet—

No, too heavy. I don't want to perspire any more than usual, but we can use this as an accent... Oo, I wonder what will Thaddeus think of this?

Fingering a cloth the shade of burgundy, my mind flickers back to our conversation the other night and I make a point to note that it has more purple than brown, the texture is airy, light and—perfect for dancing!

Now this will make him go positively wild for me, though given how he already looks at me I wonder—what was that?

A flash of movement out of the corner of my eye pulls my mind and hand alike from the fabric and gives me reason to move closer to the front window while scouring over the selections.

When another snippet grazes my peripheral, my head pops up to see a boy jumping up and down out front. His arms are waving wildly overhead, obviously wanting someone's attention.

At a closer glance, perhaps his mother?

I look to the left and then to the right of me, even behind me, but outside of the clerk I am the only person here. Turning back to the boy—

Is that Billy Halle?

Once he sees me looking at him, he motions for me in some urgent manner that either spells out a dire crisis or possession.

On my way out, the clerk asks, "Do you need Miss Bennett?"

"I'm sorry, I'll be right back," I say with my hand on the door, the bell bidding me farewell, with the same jingle for hello.

"Billy? What are you doing?" I ask, in my approach. The fact that his hands are already on Starlight does not go unnoticed.

Is he untying her?... He is! Oh, hell no! She is my horse, my best friend!

I go to rip the reigns from his hand, but that little thief, that little urchin, yanks them out of my reach!

Billy's eyes are wide. A frown fills his small face, but his glare is not as dark as mine.

"Billy Halle, you hand those reins over to me right now!" I say in the strictest teacher voice I can muster.

"I can't Miss Emilie, I gotta take Starlight. My friend's in trouble; I'll bring her back I prom—"

The tug at my heart—but wait. He didn't request Starlight. Instead, he told me he's taking her.

He is not taking my horse!

Starlight throws her head back as I grab the other side of her halter, startled by the rough handling. By this time, Billy not only has her reins in hand, but has one foot in the stirrup with the other over her.

"You can't just ride off with her." I say, my eyes wide at the audacity of this imp.

Billy ignores me shifting the reins in his hands.

Refraining from obscenities I say, "If someone is in trouble, as you say, I better come with. I can help."

"No, I-I don't want to trouble you Miss Emilie. We'll be right back."

My hand snatches Billy's leg, giving it a tug and pulling the boy off balance. Starlight throws her head in protest, backing away from me.

A distant voice yells from somewhere behind us, "Awe, she can't come. She will ruin the race!"

Turning to the protest, I see a small child, stomping his foot, kicking up dust.

"Shut up Gates!" Billy yells. "Go tell the others I'm coming."

The boy backs up, "All right, but Ian says to hurry!"

The boy turns to dart off down the street as fast as his short legs will carry him.

Back to Billy, his hands on the reins, me still holding Starlight's halter in one hand and his leg in the other.

"Billy Halle, you get off this horse right now or I will yank you off. You're not racing her!"

Starlight doesn't like my tone and once again begins backing up. "Whoa, easy girl," I say, my voice lower and softer.

My hand becomes pinched between Starlight's cheek and her halter, and I don't suppose my expression is that convincing as she continues to back away. I let go as the pain bites my fingers. Starlight looks at me, before taking a few tentative steps toward me, ears pricked, and nose inching to the pocket where I hold her treats.

I nudge her away from the pocket, but she pushes me back with insistence.

Billy digs his heels into Starlight urging her forward.

Starlight stays.

Billy nudges.

Starlight shifts from one foot to the other but doesn't budge ... Another nudge ... Another shift ...

A kick!

Nothing.

"What is wrong with her?" Billy asks, his brows furrowing. "Why isn't she moving?"

"What's wrong is she's not your horse," I say. Reaching inside my pocket, I pull out a mint sugar cube and proceed to give it to her before walking up to her and mounting her. "And she only moves with motivation."

Settled in behind Billy, I take the reins from his grubby hands.

Billy's mouth opens wide enough to catch flies, and he shifts forward to accompany me, only to look back at me with pleading eyes. "You gotta help me, Miss Emilie or—"

"Or what? Where are we even going?"

Billy motions back toward the alley the other brat ran down. I turn Starlight around following his guidance to the back of the hotel and the alley therein, where we are greeted by a group of eight to ten boys waiting for our arrival.

"Oh, James brought in the others," Billy says looking at one boy standing in front of the others, hushing them as we arrive.

"Halle, I found a race opponent for you," James says, "and we all added to the pot, so that knife," James nods his head to Billy, "you might as well give it over and spare what's left of your reputation, especially if this is the nag you plan on racing."

"She's not a nag," I say. "Now one moment if you will."

Billy grins at James. "She's the best runner in—"

Grabbing Billy's shoulder, I turn him to face me, an edge in my voice that is sharper than any knife he or they may possess. "What do you mean wager? And no, she will not run."

"Come on, Miss Emilie. I bet on her to win. Just this once, please. Please, please, please!"

Billy's big eyes stir what pity exists in my stomach, and then the tussle of boys start arguing throwing insinuations at Billy.

"I told you he couldn't do it," yells one.

An accusing finger gets directed our way. "He is a liar and a cheat."

"Yeah, he is trying to cheat us out of our bets," an older red checked shirt boy shouts.

"Just you wait 'til I meet you in an alley alone." Another glares at Billy slamming his fist into the palm of his hand, his voice hissing a fateful promise dripping with venom.

Billy shifts, swallowing hard. His eyes waver as his confidence withers at the onslaught of their threats.

I sit there as my ears are barraged with the callousness of his so-called friends and the threats being thrown at him. A sigh wells up from within, and my mouth opens. I cannot help him. He must know that, and it is up to me to be the adult and—

A large black horse with a young rider appears. The young boy looks eerily familiar. I just can't place him.

"Hey, let's get this over with, my brother will be looking for me." The boy, sitting astride the large stallion announces to the crowd.

Maybe the beast isn't as fast as he is intimidating?

"All bets are off, Ian. She won't let Billy race the horse," Billy's brother, Sam announces.

The young boy perched atop the stud looks at me. "Aren't you seeing my brother? He told me about you. You're ...Amelia? No ..." His eyes look up trying to remember. His face is screwed up trying to get the thought to surface, but it appears to be neither on the tip of his tongue nor anywhere between his ears.

"Emilie," I say.

"Yeah, Emilie," he smiles at the mention of my name.

"And you must be Ian?" I only recall Thaddeus having one brother.

Ian grins and nods before looking from me to Billy. "You shouldn't race a docile creature like that Billy Halle. Diablo is bigger and faster, unless you just enjoy losing."

Diablo is in fact larger and more muscular. But is he faster? Maybe he has a flaw, a hitch, a limp?

It doesn't matter. Right now, I am certain I cannot race Starlight against him. Even if Billy sits in front of me like a saddened lump of humiliation with the biggest tear-stained eyes I've ever seen.

"Please, Miss Emilie. I have to do this or I'm doomed, I tell yah. I'll have no friends, no one to hang out with. I'll be lost and alone in the world for the rest of my days, an outcast, a bright to my family, a—"

"A blight, not a bright Billy," I say.

"Right. A blight, and a plague, and a demon, and-and-and—"

I find myself looking around the alley as I hear his sniffling begin. There is no one but us and the boys. My eyes trace the length of the alley.

I suppose it's not that long.

"Tell you what, I will race her in your place," I say. "I know her better than you, and under my guiding touch Starlight will win."

Billy slides off her back, his small feet bouncing as they make impact with the ground. His confidence is fully restored, his boasting revived. "I told you she would race!"

Will wonders never cease? How long had he been practicing that cry?

I sigh and reach into my pocket pulling out a sweet treat.

"Here, give her one of these before you head down to the other end," I tell Billy, placing a mint sugar into his waiting hand. As he walks past Diablo, the horse turns his head to the smell, reaching out with a nip, only to be left disappointed as Starlight munches away.

Diablo snorts his discontent.

"What's that?" Ian asks.

"Mr. Perry's mint sugar cubes," I say. "Starlight won't move without them."

Ian laughs, "She's a spoiled one."

"I'll give you some to try after the race, as a consolation prize." I flash him a smile.

"We'll see about that."

Our tit for tat is interrupted by the boys yelling to get our attention at the other end of the alley.

The bigger of the young brutes with the scar over his eye draws a finish line into the dirt.

The boys stand, waiting on both sides of the alley, ready to cheer on the race.

Johnny holds a handkerchief in one hand, signaling the start of the race.

We watch.

We wait for the handkerchief.

The way it floats to the dirt, momentarily I'm amazed at how graceful—

Oh wait!

I jump into a forward position and goose Starlight with my heels, she startles and dances not forward, not backward, but sideways!

The laughter of the boys down the way is embarrassing enough.

"Come on, girl, we have a boy's reputation to save!"

Starlight's ears turn back to listen, and now that I have her full attention, I give her a firm nudge with my heels. She jumps again, surprised at my abrupt gesture to her ribs, but with a snort agrees to my signal and takes off toward the other end.

A commotion stirs behind me, but I pay it no mind, too focused on the finish line. Starlight and I feel as though we are one, as we often do on Table Rock Road. The only difference is there is an audience cheering us on, their shouts echoing off the buildings surrounding us.

Diablo and Ian, once ahead of us, are now beside us.

He must be holding Diablo back, or maybe the horse does have a hitch!

We begin to pass them, inching forward by a nose and then a head.

Out of the corner of my eye, I see a flash of black, sleek, muscle gaining on us. The black beauty's long strides can overtake us at any time.

I spur Starlight to run faster, faster than I've ever asked her to go. It's not enough to run, we must fly. Billy's reputation depends on it! Maybe even his young life depends on how hard those other boys plan to rough him up. No, I can't let that happen. I can't let him become an outsider. I know how it feels. I know—

A tall stern figure steps out in front of us wearing a sleek black uniform and holding a thick cudgel which he smacks against his hand.

What? The constable!

Looking to the finish line, I see two men standing, arms crossed, feet apart, stoic as granite statues.

My desire to race flees in the opposite direction as I now have every desire but to reach the finish line. I pull back on Starlight's reins, trying to slow her pace.

She skips to a halt and shrieks at the displeasure of having her mouth yanked on, but I give her no other choice than to abort the run. Her resistance to listen is displayed in a sideways trot followed by innumerable circles, as she resists my attempts to cease and desist.

"Whoa girl. Easy."

By the time I make it to the dreadful line where I am sure I will be finished, we are at a walk. The two statues with scowls to greet me are of course the constable and—Thaddeus?

I swallow hard.

Ian rides up beside me.

We dismount, and I find my legs shaking, but this doesn't stop me from pulling the lead off the saddle and clipping it to Starlight's halter before throwing the reins over her head.

Starlight blows at me. A slick lather of sweat and her slobber slathers me as she nudges me for a treat, a reward she earned. But just as I reach into my pocket, the constable stops me short.

"Mr. Marsh, this is the third time I've caught you racing down this alley." His sturdy build boasts strength and no nonsense, and his stern glowering eyes shed not so much as a hint of mercy.

"Well, I don't know about that," Ian says. "I mean—it's been," he looks down and begins to count on his fingers.

"Two months!" The constable confirms. "Mr. McClellen has been patient with you. He asked you boys to stop running behind this hotel. Did he not?"

I steal a look at Thaddeus. His eyes are narrow, jaw set, shoulders square, and arms crossed, uninviting, cold, distant.

I'm sorry.

My mouth remains clamped shut, concealing my thoughts. Not wanting to feel his anger toward me, I look away.

Ian sighs but doesn't answer the constable—just remains silent. A wise decision given that the constable could very well use whatever smart remark Ian has to offer against the boy.

"I am charging both of you with trespassing and endangering others with your irresponsible behavior. I hope this is the last time I see either one of you in this situation." He scribbles on his pad, rips the paper before rinsing and repeating the action until we are both left standing there with a sheet of paper in our hands.

The angry marks scribbled are loud and clear on the ticket, revealing my fate. My heart sinks. This will cost me a good portion of my ballgown.

"You, young lady," the constable addresses me.

I give a little jump and look up to meet dark eyes and big red blustering jowls.

"I don't know you, but I see you are trouble. Someone of your upbringing? Racing with boys! Let this be your warning, and I pray that I will never see you like this again. No propriety, no decorum." His reprimand booms loud and trails off down the alley, but his words still scald my ears.

"I apologize sir," I murmur. "It will never happen again."

"I should hope not," the constable mutters as he turns to leave. "No proper lady should be riding ..."

I look around. The cheers and those who made them are nowhere to be found. The young boys skedaddled at the first sight of trouble, and the alley is empty. Well, not completely empty.

My gaze goes to Thaddeus, whose wistful blue hues now host dark rain clouds and flash with an uncanny fury. His face is redder than the fabric I sampled earlier, and his jaw is wound tight, not a grin in sight.

"Start walking," Thaddeus says, his tongue lashing out at his younger brother, "and you best think of a good story to tell our parents."

Ian's lips purse, but he goes to grab Diablo's reins.

"Leave Diablo. I'll pick you up when I am finished here."

My heart drops straight into my gut, and the intestines within knot around it. The tone of his voice gives me chills and causes prickles over my scalp and down my arms—not the good kind.

He turns to me, or at least I think he does. I can't bring myself to look up.

"Do you mind telling me what just happened here?" Thaddeus's words lash out at me. His sharp eyes poke holes deeper into my fear.

"Long story," I whisper.

"I can wait." There is no smile in his voice.

"Well, the-the Halle boy attempted to steal Starlight to settle a bet. I refused to let him ride her, so I took his place instead." I suck in my bottom lip, biting it as my fingers toy with the pleats of my skirt.

A long moment of silence stands between us, and my eyes catch his hands as they drop to his sides, opening and closing into fists.

What is he thinking?

"Let me get this straight. You risked your reputation for a ten-year-old boy, who you have no relation to, and is also a horse thief?"

His weight shifts from foot to foot.

His fists unclench only to regain purchase.

"I'd ask what you are thinking, but you're obviously not capable of thinking at all."

"Well, I couldn't let Billy—"

"ENOUGH!"

I jump, but this gives him no reason to pause. "Is the childish desires of a small boy worth your reputation, your career, our relationship?"

"What—wait, I'm confused." My head shoots up, eyes searching for his as I question every decision I've made in the last hour.

"Who's going to know about this? There is no one here," I say, "and what does this have to do with our relationship?"

The pain of my admission sends a nervous, dizzying energy

through my body, rooted here, unable to move or think.

"This is Gettysburg, Emilie. Everyone knows everyone's business; I can't have you so frivolous with your reputation or mine." Thaddeus shakes his head. "I worried about it at first, but maybe you aren't ready."

"Ready for what?" Panic sets in, and his anger grows. My heart thrums in my ears.

Is he really saying what I think he is saying?

"For us." Thaddeus's voice cracks and so does my heart, but his words continue to carve. "I need a partner not a child."

Wait! No!

"I'm not a child!"

"Yet today's actions would suggest otherwise." The steadiness of his voice hosts a bite. "A woman thinks before she acts. She is not impetuous and does not go galivanting off without considering the consequences of her actions." Thaddeus takes a step back. "But if you insist on being a petulant child, I will leave you to nurture relations with the likes of Ian and that Halle boy. May you find better company and a better future with them than me."

He smooths the crease in his vest, ridding himself of the alley's dirt continuing, "and—"

Please don't leave.

"You may consider our dinner plans cancelled tonight."

No!

"Thaddeus, wait!"

He turns and walks away. He doesn't look back. He leaves me—has left me—alone in this forgotten alley way.

Had he slapped me just now, it would not have hurt as much

as this. My heart crumbles to pieces with my legs, much faster than the old, weathered brick around me; yet we are equally exposed for anyone to witness.

How am I going to fix this?

Rumor Mill

APRIL 1861
GETTYSBURG, PENNSYLVANIA

Embarrassment and shame follow me home, my own personal storm cloud brewing over my head, invisible to everyone else but electrifying every frayed nerve I possess as self-deprecating thoughts batter against my skull, sending tears raining down my cheeks.

Thaddeus is right. I completely neglected my reputation ...

Thaddeus is right. My careless actions may ripple, causing harm to those closest to me ...

Thaddeus is right. I've brought shame to my family, the teaching community, and worst of all—

" ..." His name hangs in the air before deteriorating in the silence, and my sobs chase after him, but all I catch is my own foolishness and Starlight's neck as I wrap my arms around her.

We are on Table Rock Road, nearly home, and I can't bring myself to take another step. I played right into a fool's errand all to prevent some silly boy from becoming an outcast and now look at me. I'm the outcast, unfit to be a teacher, and now doomed to be a spinster. It is the worst possible feeling anyone must endure.

Starlight gives a soft nicker, and I feel her fuzzy lip ruffle my hair in what I hope is compassion but must admit is the hunt for another treat. My flushed cheeks press against her neck. "Can you just be my friend, just this once?"

She throws her head as she shifts her weight, forcing me to let go of her, but my head still hangs low. Lower than dirt. Lower than the shoe on Starlight's hoof, which she refuses to put pressure on?

Wiping my tears away, I frown and run my hand down her foreleg. The coolness of her knee contrasts with the heat of the tendons running along the back of her cannon.

What have I caused now? My poor decisions trickle down to everyone. My pride is hurting those I love most. Damn me.

Rising back up, I give her a cube out of pity and a quiet apology.

"Let's get you home so I can wrap that for you," I say, as Starlight groans and looks away from me when I force her to take another step.

"I guess I deserve that," I say to her, stroking her neck.

My day is heading from bad to worse at an accelerated pace, unlike our walk home. A new wave of tears breaks through as we start up the driveway home.

How can I lose Thaddeus and my horse in one day?

Once inside the barn, I untack her and put together her feed of oats stirred with a little bit of molasses. Starlight is content to eat dinner while I rub her down with a towel and wrap her leg. My voice, though not the best, sings to her and myself, soothing both of us.

"Father will see you in the morning," I say once I finish up. "Take it easy girl."

Starlight gives a soft knicker or a snort. I'm not sure which as her head never leaves the feed bucket.

She hates me.

The warm light of the kitchen invites me into this sanctuary of comfort I need right now. How do I hide my awful day from the prying eyes behind this door? Maybe they're all reading in the parlor? Brushing the last of the tears away with my damp sleeve, I open the door to not only my family, but Stephen Byrne—standing in the kitchen, waiting for me.

Dear God, have you not punished me enough?

My mother turns with a pleasant smile, and I watch it morph into a horrified gasp when our eyes meet.

Henry's smirk likewise vanishes when he eyes me, questioning everything.

Do I look that bad?

I look to Father, always warm and welcoming. He peers over his newspaper but then proceeds to cloak his expression behind the black and white words held between his hands.

Tears well up again, and I fear my sorrows will drain me until I am nothing more than a husk. Of course, they do not wish to look at their shameful daughter—why?

Because the words of the man who stands before me, bouquet of wilted weeds clutched in his hand echo through my mind, *Everybody knows everything about everyone else.*

Stephen holds up my pity prize, drooping in all its misery, for being the grandest loser in all of Gettysburg—no, in all of Adams County, Pennsylvania!

"What now?" I ask with a sniffle. My nose is running again, I don't have a handkerchief, and I'd use my sleeve but cannot withstand another reprimand, especially from Mother.

"Mr. Byrne came to see you," Father says from behind his paper, a shield against my lack of propriety.

A handkerchief that appears at my elbow. It looks to be Mother's. Under normal circumstances, I'd be able to inhale the comfort of her perfume, but I can't because I-I ...

My snotty nose takes refuge in the cloth, ruining it like I ruin everything and everyone else.

Stephen clears his throat. "Emilie, I couldn't wait to ask you."

Silence fills the room, and I look at Stephen from behind the hanky, then to Henry, and finally to the paper in front of my father's face.

No help from them. Abandoned during my ugliest moment, so desperate they are to throw me into the arms of any man who approaches, now that I have destroyed any chance with my darling, Thaddeus ... Thaddeus!

"No, no, I can't. You can't. How could you? Why would you ask me anything right now?"

"But—it can't wait." Stephen insists as he presents me with the wilted flowers.

The weight of the day—tears spent and self-recrimination—wells up, rising from a deep pit within me. The bombardment of his relentless insistence, his untimely intrusion, his torrent of words, his presence with the audacity to think today of all days, I am going to give him the attention he demands!

His face, his presence, his needs, his wants—creates fissures in what remains of my resolve. My grief doesn't vanish. No, it boils and begins to roil, and spit, and sputter with my words as a tide of anger from the pit of my knotted guts, plagued with the frustration of everything—tumbles forward, outward—

"It can wait, and by God, Stephen Byrne, it will wait! I may have lost my propriety today, but that does not excuse you from the rules. God forbid, you send a calling card." My shouts echo off the walls and ring between my ears as I push him aside, leaving the kitchen, leaving Stephen Byrne standing, leaving my family, or at least trying to.

There is a *thud,* the tight grasp of a large hand wrapping around my arm, halting me and threatening to bruise me if I don't comply.

"I sent you a card last week announcing my arrival today," Stephen says with a forced hiss.

"Let go of my arm," I say, turning to him with a hardened stare. "You are hurting me."

I yank.

His grip tightens.

There is a pinch of pain from elbow to shoulder.

Stephen's eyes pin me down. "Don't tell me no!"

"I will tell you what I please," I say. "Now, let go."

Over Stephen's shoulder I see Father's paper hit the table, but before he can rise, Henry appears behind Stephen, his hand on Stephen's shoulder.

"I think my sister is telling you to leave. Let's visit another time, shall we?"

Stephen releases my arm. "This isn't finished." He turns heel, allowing Henry to walk him to the door. Their voices converse in low tones and murmur, until Stephen is on the doorstep with our door shut before him.

Henry turns to me asking, "What was that? I don't know if you know this Em, but he likes you."

"Thank you for pointing out the obvious!"

I'm so tired of this. I'm so tired of everyone. I just want this day to end!

"I am going to bed."

The echoes of foot after foot stomping up each stair is greeted with the slamming of my door.

Finally, I can retreat under the covers, blocking out the world and all its horrors. My best intensions have blown up and with them, the casualties of my life. Horse and love gone in five minutes. I don't know how to fix it all, and after hours of worry, my eyes close. The images of Thaddeus's cold anger haunts me from my memories into my dreams as I drift off to sleep wondering if I will ever see his soul smile from those deep blue pools again.

The clouds of self-doubt leave me, with the help of the sun's warm rays announcing a new day. Fleeting wisps of sadness try to obscure my determination, like the bits of winter clouds trying to block out the sun, and my worry chases after the remnants of yesterday's emotional fog. However, like the clouds, they cannot hold the light forever or smother my hope in eternal darkness.

Granted, I don't know if Thaddeus will ever forgive me. However, he is right. I am no longer the girl I was a few months ago. I have a relationship and career worth saving and responsibilities to tend to. If I wish to achieve my greatest desires in life, then I need to chase those dreams and drag them into reality, rather than entertain the girlish whims and challenges that do not matter.

"I hurt him, Mother," I tell her over dried toast and cold coffee. "The pain in his eyes is still unbearable to endure from memory, and I can't tell you how sorry I am—or him for that matter."

"You don't have to tell me," Mother says, "and it may be best if you wait for him. If he truly wishes to build a life with you, he will be back for your apology."

"Are you sure?" I ask, biting my lip.

"Long term relationships take work. I cannot speak for Thaddeus or see the future on your behalf, but I hope this has you thinking about what you need to change."

"Endlessly, over the last ten hours," I say, pushing breakfast aside.

Mother's eyes hold a message, something between, 'I'm sorry,' and 'It's time to embrace your womanhood.'

"I better go see Father. He will have to take me into town," I say, picking up my dishes and depositing them by the water basin.

Then I go back to my room to gather the sum needed to pay for the fine and for this undesirable lesson. The fine is the easy part. Not knowing how I will make things right with Thaddeus is the hard part.

When I arrive in the barn, Father is preparing to hitch the team.

"Can you look at Starlight for me?" I open her stall.

Father places a collar over one of the work horses' necks. "I already did. Looks like a ligament strain. She will need time to heal, so we will be going to town together for the next eight to ten weeks or so, which means a time schedule. You will not make me late for work."

"You're right Father, I won't," I say, "because things are changing for me."

"We'll see about that." Father works to finish buckling the last few straps to the team. "I better get the team hitched."

"All right, I am ready to leave when you are," I say.

The journey to town is quiet. I can't tell if Father is disappointed in me or not. Come to think of it, I'm not even sure he is aware of what I have done. I just assumed, and there doesn't appear to be room within the silence between us to ask further. He drops me off on the corner of Baltimore and Middle Street before turning the team back toward the carriage factory at the edge of town.

Sighing, I smooth out my skirts, lift my chin, and cross the street to the courthouse. Looking around in momentary pause, I hope no one will see me go inside. The town seems to be stretching and waking from the night's slumber. A few travelers, wagons, and horses pass. Mysterious hands appear and disappear as signs turn in the windows of businesses, signaling the start of a new day, a new me. The decreased crowd in the early morning makes me hopeful to get in and out without being spotted by gossip mongers. I don't need another stain on my already tattered reputation.

The wood door framing a pane of glass opens without an announcement or a bell. The front counter has two people waiting in line. I step up behind one of them and wait my turn. The tall lanky man ahead of me has stringy unkempt hair that hangs in his eyes. He needs a bath with strong lye soap and a good soak because he smells of an old tavern and sweat. I try to breathe through my mouth to give my nose a break, but his stench is palpable. Henry's dirty old socks are not a taste I care to entertain, and yet here I am.

"Oh, another ticket? Honestly Adams, if you stopped donating to the town, you could afford a bath." The clerk seems comfortable berating this man.

The man mumbles something as he reaches in his pocket to

pull out the sum of the fine.

"Let me give you some advice," the clerk announces. "Drink at home, so the constable can't ticket you for being so useless in public."

The lanky man shakes his head, turns, and walks away.

The clerk is in fine form this morning. This poor man is the second person to be publicly humiliated today, which I suppose will make me the third?

I step up to the counter and slide the paper and the money toward the clerk. He greets me with a leer and a hardened stare. His blue eyes rake down my form and then back up to my face, never staying too long in one place, and yet the fabric that adorns me feels useless under his gaze.

A chill rushes over me, as his stare slithers over his glasses and coils around my form. His prim tight lips and small beady eyes have a hunger to them that I don't like. And his tongue—does he have to lick his lips? His eyes do not meet mine. Despite the height difference, they settle lower—lower than I'd like.

Is he looking at my bosom?

He licks his dry cracked lips again, painting the crevices with saliva, teasing the corners of his mouth into a lecherous grin.

"Excuse me, I'd like to get this handled."

He clears his throat and pushes up his sleeves, delivering a pungent waft of sweat and body odor.

"Paying this fine for your brother I see," the clerk mumbles, sweeping the fine and coins toward him. "Couldn't pay it himself?"

The clerk looks up from the slip of paper in hand. His eyes tour my figure once more without a hint of discretion, darting here and there, his tongue slithering from his lips and tasting my scent as it mingles with his own stench.

I clear my throat.

"No, the fine belongs to me," I say, tapping the countertop. The coins are just out of my reach.

"I heard about you." He smiles, revealing yellow crooked teeth, and presses into the stiff wooden barrier between us, causing me to take a step back. "The racetrack is looking for jockeys, but then again, I bet you don't ride anyway but sidesaddle, being the fine morsel that you are." He almost chuckles. "I bet you don't let anything between those legs of yours."

My face burns with shock, and again he is outwardly staring at my chest.

"That, sir, is none of your business," I say as my thighs clench beneath my skirts, not about to entertain the thought of him— or him, for that matter.

The clerk dismisses me with a laugh, his own private joke.

When he looks down, I touch the buttons on my gown discreetly, checking, searching for an opening, trying to hide any weakness the barrier of fabric might offer when I recall my coat and draw it close over my bosom. But the cold wet sucking of leeches all over my skin doesn't give in. My flesh crawls beneath the cloth, trying to evade his devouring gaze, his intension, his ick. Its intensity chokes me, like those blood sucking slugs I swear are somewhere on me, have somehow burrowed into my guts, and now exist as the lump in my throat. I'm not sure whether to swallow or throw up.

His scribbles scratching across the page of what I pray is the receipt, scrapes against my thoughts, and when he proceeds to slide it over to me, I snatch it up before his grasp can strike.

"Thank you," I say and turning on my heel, I rush out of the office as I hear a low chuckle mocking my hurried escape.

Outside the air fills my lungs. I franticly search for a private place, any place where I can—

Ick!

My body screams against the memory of that ... that ... whatever that was. Certainly not a man. A wave of cold sweat follows the nausea. My eyes continue to search for something ... A wave of dizziness threatens to turn day to night ... Anything?... My hand goes to my stomach ... *Please wait* ... Cheeks puff out as I feel a burning sensation coat the back of my throat, an acrid sour taste coats my tongue, my stomach churns and clenches. I lean over a mound of old discarded crates and vomit—not once but three times.

Once my body is done raging over that distasteful encounter, my knees weaken, and I slide down the vacant wall to sit on one of the old crates not covered in bile.

I close my eyes. My head rests in my hands. Waiting ... wondering when—sucking in the cool air ... forcing a shaky exhale—for the panic to subside.

A few minutes pass—

The day must go on, and I must dare to try and walk the rest of the way to school, keep my feelings locked up tight, not say a word to anyone—they'll just say it's my fault.

All my good days lately are tarnished with the black marks of bad events. Not only did I have an unpleasant encounter with the clerk, but Ginny had to take leave, leaving me in charge of her class by myself. And the children took full advantage of it, making their behaviors and the endless distractions from them the death of my very last nerve. Between notes passed, spitballs flying, and chalk dropping to the floor, I am ready to go home, back to my bed with its sanctuary of covers, and lock out this insane world.

But no. I had to deal with incidents such as Frank Bowden putting sassafras candy in little Josie's hair, causing her to scream as she flailed about, wrapping the sticky candy deeper into her dark brown locks. Then somehow a black snake—and yes, Mr. Warner verified it is real—found itself in the depths of the outhouse. As if dealing with one cold blooded individual wasn't enough today! This left me with a classroom of children jumping up and down, unable to relieve themselves for fear that a coiled monster would strike their exposed bottoms.

Though days like this one may lead to future fits of laughter, this is one day I would rather forget because the tale of Slither-Me-Shivers only marks events up to lunch, which I skipped. I cancel with Sarah as I hold six boys in from recess as punishment for putting bullets in the stove pipe before I arrived earlier this morning. The dents are likely never to come out.

Finding what I hope is a responsible eighth grader to watch the students for a few minutes, I can't help but seek out Mrs. Irwin for refuge. I find her sitting in her classroom reading over papers and knock as I tiptoe just over the threshold, waiting for her to acknowledge me.

"Mrs. Irwin?" I say, quiet at first. "May I have a moment?"

She raises her finger, putting a pause on that moment while she finishes reading a paper. A satisfied smile on her face, she looks up and motions for me to sit in the chair at the side of her desk.

"How may I help you today?"

"I seem to be having discipline problems with the children. They are causing trouble, yelling out, messing with the younger students. I think one of them might even be possessed."

I see her frown. "It is Maggie? She often has odd fits," She sits back considering my dilemma.

"Odd fits? What do you mean? That last bit was a joke!"

"Oh, nothing we can't call Father McIntyre about should it happen again." Her smile makes me wonder, no hope, that she too is joking.

"Have you tried the corner?" she asks.

"With four in the room, I'm afraid I've run out of corners to put them in."

"Anyone staying after class?"

"Right now, I have six staying in for lunch and an eighth grader watching them for now."

"Which eighth grader?"

"Daniel,"

"Oh dear."

"What?"

"Well, it's too late now. You'll just have to deal with the damage when you get back. Hmm." Mrs. Irwin pauses. "The detention won't help their energy this afternoon. Have you tried an interactive lesson?"

My mind reels, not sure how worried I should be about the rest of the day.

"Miss Prescott?"

I blink, returning from my thoughts, and after a moment I say, "You mean a spelling bee or arithmetic showdown?" Thoughts of how much fun I had in challenges with my brother bring me a glimmer of hope.

"It might help," Mrs. Iwin says. "I knew you would think of something. Remember, classroom management is one of your biggest challenges as a teacher."

"I will try it," I say with a renewed sense of hope. "Thank you for the advice."

Mrs. Irwin smiles at me. "That is what I am here for."

I stand to leave.

"Oh, Miss Prescott?"

"Yes?"

"You may want to take this. The appearance of it often has a lasting effect, and once you put one of them back in line, the others tend not to step over it."

My eyes look down at what she holds—a paddle.

Three o'clock took its sweet time to arrive today, and though I detest the idea of using such an awful contraption as the paddle, I will not have a repeat tomorrow. Looking frayed and frazzled with wild hair, flushed cheeks, and chalk-stained skirt, I finally step onto the street to walk toward home with Sarah.

"Was it me or were the children a-b-o-m-i-n-a-t-i-o-n-s today?" Sarah asks.

"Worse. They were awful. Also, why are you spelling?" I ask.

"Was I? Oh dear, I must still be in shock," says Sarah.

"Over the snake in the outhouse?"

"Over Petey having a meltdown about broken chalk, Jeanie refusing to say anything without spelling it, and—" Sarah begins.

"And Daniel tying up the children I left him in charge of over lunch to their desks, Jimmy and I having a chase around the room after he used his sling shot to aim a marble at my bottom, and then Maddie made Betty cry over her freckles, having convinced everyone it was the plague!" I finish for her, recalling the second half of my day while stepping over a rut, trying not to trip.

"I don't know. That tying up bit sounds rather helpful, but now I see why you weren't at lunch." Sarah knocks into me while she skips over a pile of manure. "I missed you."

"You and me both. Are you sure you want children?" I ask Sarah.

"I'm sure I do not want them today."

"Did you leave them tied up the whole forty-five minutes?" Sarah asks, her eyes glinting with excited intrigue, as if this were a marvelous way to solve all her future problems.

"I wish, but with pity in my heart, I had Daniel untie them and then made them all write. The six younger children wrote, 'I will behave in class so I don't miss my next marble tournament at recess,' and Daniel wrote, 'I will not neglect my responsibilities by tying younger students to their seats,'" I laugh at the memory of the daggers in their eyes.

"Did they actually write it?" Sarah asks. I am sure she is taking mental notes to use later.

"They did, especially after I informed them that the one who has the least amount written will have to return to continue tomorrow. Though if you use this technique, make sure they are far enough apart that they cannot sabotage each other's work."

"Oh, that's a good point."

Smiling to myself, I give a nod. "I've never seen such frantic writing in my life! Though if tomorrow is anything like today, I don't think I will spare the rod."

Sarah grabs my arm, gasping. "You mean you would use the paddle?"

My head tilts as my eyebrows give lift, amazed by her shock. "It's either that or I call a priest. Besides, Mrs. Irwin states classroom management is key, right?"

"Oh right. It just seems so awful is all."

"That's because you don't have brothers, Sarah."

Sarah gives it some thought. "Suppose you're right. Oh, here's my street. See you tomorrow?"

"Of course," I say, waving to Sarah as she disappears down the street. And I promptly step into a pile of manure, or at least that is what I hope it is.

Sarah, the bright light in my life who erases the darkness from my day, is definitely...gone. I groan, heading over to a step to shave the excrement off my boot before I continue my walk to the carriage factory to meet Father. And maybe Thaddeus, who I am half tempted to avoid, because why would he forgive me today of all days?

My elbow is snatched, and I'm pulled out of the street, into an alleyway. The harsh jerk causes my feet to stumble, trip, and tangle beneath me as pain shoots up my arm and into my shoulder. A cry catches in my throat, stunted by the brick wall I'm shoved against.

Head spinning as my eyes try to collect my surroundings and whoever has me, it takes me a moment before recognizing the broad shoulders, dark hair, and hazel eyes filled with determination. And if I'm frank, I don't know if seeing him is better than seeing a scraggily vagabond.

Dear Lord, have you not punished me enough for my transgressions?

"What are you doing?" I say struggling against him. His other hand encircles my free arm with a familiar pinching grip, preventing me from shoving him back. I have no choice but to look up at him as he towers over me. His shoulders, broad and strong, pulling at the seams of his jacket and releasing an odor of sweat contaminated with a frustration that mirrors my own.

"No, what are you doing?" His fingers punctuate his words as they dig deeper into my flesh, his breath hot and sour with fury. His hazel eyes have nearly vanished as a turbulent darkness consumes them.

Desperate for an escape, I try to strike out with my knee, but he blocks it with his own. I can hear the straining of the stitches in my coat, the rustling of my skirts, the amble of people passing by, unaware that I need their help. I fear Stephen is beyond reproach, as beads of sweat draw over the vein bulging from his temple.

Is this just because I refused him last night?

"Vandalizing private property, gambling away your family fortune, consorting with younger boys, seducing a county official, and now scouring the streets unattended like a common whore."

A frown ripples over my brow and my mouth opens out of confusion, but I can't seem to make anything come out.

He shows restraint but only in his voice—his eyes feast on the rise and fall of my chest tucked beneath layers of form fitting fabric. His thumbs brush over my arms as he restrains me with his grip. His breath is hot against my skin and shouts of whiskey.

"It's no wonder Thaddeus discarded you. In fact, it's a blessing you still have a man such as myself to spare you from your wicked ways, to save you before all is lost."

"And what of us alone in this alley? What will people say now?" I ask, narrowing my eyes at him. The angry knot in my belly begins to rise up into my throat. There is no question as to whether I will spew words of hate or actual vomit all over him. It's only a matter of when and which will come first.

I try to roll myself out of his grasp. Then match his grip by digging my nails into his forearms as I struggle against him, my nails trying to inflict pain. He stands firm, grits through my grip, and holds me fast against the rough brick. The wall's exterior feels like shards of glass, despite the barrier of my clothes, pulling at wisps of loose hair, burning me as I scrape against it in my need to escape.

As my efforts become futile, the remaining heat baked into the wall by the afternoon sun now transfers to my neck and cheeks. Anger, getting me nowhere, is replaced by an intense recollection of this morning and the events that accompanied it. The clerk's eyes, undressing me with his thoughts. His serpent tongue, slithering past his lips. His words, treating me like nothing more than some prized pig.

Stephen's lip cocks up in a sneer, and his hot breath brands my skin as his words pour salt into my mind's fresh wound. "I could have my way with you," Stephen's voice is slippery and confident. "and no one would stop me. In fact, if we are betrothed, they will think nothing of it."

He leans into me, closing off the gap between us. His mouth on my neck. His knee forces its way between my clothed thighs. His hips press hard against me, and I feel what I hope I'm not powerless to deny.

"See? No one stops me, not even you."

"No, please no. Stephen, please. This isn't you. Please, please stop." My words fumble and tumble out as spittle crowns my mouth, hot tears carve down my cheeks, and snot makes it near impossible to breathe. All my fighting has accumulated into uncontrollable shaking.

Please dear God, please, please make him stop. Please. I'm sorry Thaddeus, I truly am.

Stephen lets go of my right arm, too tempted to explore other parts of me and thinking I have already broken completely, but I am more than willing to take advantage of the small gifts God grants me.

SLAP!

My hand strikes, claws, and cuts into his cheek as his free hand strays to my breast to give it a squeeze. A curious grasp becomes a grip, but this doesn't stop me from striking him again and again, anywhere I can manage to hit!

"No ... No ... Get off ... Get off me!" Red lines cover his neck, tufts of hair come loose from his head. He tries to snatch my wrist and renew his efforts to carry out his plan. But gaining slight freedom, my hitting progresses to pushing, squirming, biting, and even attempting to kick, which is useless as I am still trapped by his knee.

Then his hand clamps around my throat. His fingers begin to press in warning. "Be still."

My teeth grit, my tongue swirls, gathering, swishing—*spit*!

"If I am betrothed, it will be to Thaddeus, not you," I say as I watch the gob of saliva from my protest drag down his cheek.

His hand leaves my throat to wipe it away and regaining an inch of freedom, I go to gift him more pain. But I am mistaken. It is a bluff I did not consider. As he releases my throat, he snatches up my wrist mid swing.

Dragging both wrists up over my head, he joins them together in a single grasp, pulling them up higher to make my body stretch. My shoulders burn—a reminder that I am useless, powerless, and should be afraid.

His teeth bite at my lobe. His tongue drags along the edge of my ear. His words are only for me to hear. "Do you really think he will risk his reputation on the likes of you? Spinsters can't be choosers."

"If I am to be a spinster it will be because of you!" I yell, refusing to go unheard, and renew my struggle, anyway that I can, trying to get free.

The more I struggle, the tighter he makes his hold. My fingers tingle until I can't feel them. The brick bites and claws at the back of my trapped hands. His strength is far more than my own.

I pray for someone—anyone—to care as I force air into my lungs and prepare to—

His mouth seizes mine, his lips closing off the scream, letting it transform and die on my tongue in a muted shriek. It is a wrestle of his will over mine, but I manage to break free if only to turn my head away while his lips lay claim to other parts, nipping at my jaw, biting into my neck, sucking like a fiend and not caring if I have bruised flesh.

"HELP! HELP ME!" I shout out to the carts rumbling, horses passing, and denizens shuffling by as they chatter and go on without a care. A few cast a weary look my way, but as soon as our eyes meet, they carry on, not wanting any trouble at the end of their day.

"Anyone?" I ask, voice retreating into the back of my throat as the beast before me continues to play the devil's role. I feel my dress loosen and look down.

One button—no, two—are now undone, with Stephen's fingers fiddling with the third. My heart pounds in my ears and I begin to squirm and make his task more difficult.

He might think he can take what he likes, but I will not go down without a fight!

That's when the third button flies.

"You jerk! Do you know how expensive that button is?"

"Had you been a good girl and submitted to my will, you'd still have it." He says in a low tone.

"I will never speak to you again if you continue this, Stephen Byrne. Just wait until I tell—"

"Oh, running home to Daddy?" he asks. "Just how are you going to explain this? Father, I was walking the streets like a common whore. Heh, I'm sure he will see it for what it is. You deserve this."

He readjusts his hold on me. Pain bites the tender skin, a warm flow of blood trickles down my wrists.

"This is a man's world. The choice is not up to you." Stephen's nostrils flare, as his thumb flicks the last button out of place, and he sees more of me than any man ever has. My bosom rises and falls, swelling beneath my stays as cold air ripples across exposed skin.

My eyes well up with tears. Stephen glances up and shakes his head, a hint of kindness returns, a moment of caring as his large thumb brushes away a drop of my pain.

I gasp in hope.

Has the devil released him? Has sense returned?

"No, you don't get to do that. You don't get to disarm me with your tears, because you will never refuse me again." His words demand through gritted teeth.

"I hate you, Stephen Byrne, and I will never forgive you for this—"

I crumble to the ground, as Stephen's hands reach for his throat. His collar is pulled tight, making his eyes bulge. I try to get up, but stumble to the side, my legs no longer working. My hands, down to the tips of my fingers, shiver. But at least I can subdue them into rebuttoning myself as I try to shield my image from whoever has Stephen—a rescuer and not someone worse, I hope.

My pounding heart fills my ears, blurring out the rest of the world as I struggle to breathe, to see. Drawing my knees into my chest, curling up and tucking myself away from the world, I try to block everything out, try to stop the shivering, the weakness that is me. Each breath is strangled, caught in my throat, unable to fill my lungs.

Lightheaded and dizzy, I suck down more and more air but can't seem to get enough. The sensation of needles under my skin pricks me from within. The shadows around me encroach upon my vision, closing in. My clothes are still on me, and yet I still feel exposed as if I am naked and abandoned in a snowstorm.

If I can just get this button in, maybe it will end, but the black and purple surfaces of my wrists meet the streaks of red caused by the droplets of crimson still oozing from the back of my scraped hands.

Perhaps it is best to succumb to oblivion, to let today and ever after to be over with. Perhaps I am truly broken. How could Thaddeus ever want this? What if Stepehen comes back and tries again?

As I sit on the very ground proclaimed to hold my worth, the strong odor of varnish and paint carry a familiar sensation and I dare to choke out a word, giving up what little prized air I can grasp. "Father?"

Out of the corner of my vision, I see something move toward me and flinch, pulling away.

"Emilie?" The voice, though masculine in nature, is gentle and holds no anger. "Are you all right?"

I shake my head no. I am everything but all right.

"Emilie, can you move?"

A flood of tears is my response. I don't know.

He crouches down to my level, but I dare not look at him.

I'd be happy if I never saw another man for as long as I live.

"Those scrapes on your hands look painful. Can you let me see them? I won't touch. See, my hands are right here."

Through blurred vision I see that his hands are holding his elbows, which poke out from his makeshift lap formed by squatting. So I unfurl my fingers and present my hands an inch or two past myself, ready to pull them in if need be.

The man takes a deep breath and exhales an anger that is so palpable I shrink. "I'm sorry this happened to you, Emilie. I should have never been cross with you. I should have been here to protect you. I—I don't expect you to ever forgive me, but can you at least let me clean your hands, bring you home, get you somewhere safe?"

His words filled my ears and silenced the racing thoughts, letting them drop off into a void of nothingness.

Never been cross?... Forgive?... Protect me?...

My breathing, my beating heart, the rattling of my bones ease as I try to puzzle out who would say such things. Aaron is away, Henry and I are on good terms, and those are not Father's shoes.

"Thaddeus?" I blink away the tears as I dare to look up.

"Yes, it's Thaddeus, you're safe now."

A sob breaks free, and my mouth opens to try and explain everything, to say everything at once, but the words don't come out—just my voice as I babble on and on and on.

He pulls out his handkerchief and puts it between my hands. His touch is warm, soft, and loving, even as I fall apart. I grasp not only him, but his sleeve. And though knights of days old no longer exist, he moves to shelter me in his arms.

"Shh, no one's going to hurt you, now that I'm around."

"But I-I'm sorry, and-and I-I—"

"Shh." He rocks me back and forth as he sits beside me and kisses the top of my head. "It's all right. You'll be all right. I'm here. I'm here Emilie."

He lets me cry into his shoulder as he holds me close. He doesn't ask me to repeat what's occurred. He doesn't utter a single harsh word. Rather, he is patient as the minutes pass into what feels like infinite time.

On occasion, his hand strokes my hair, his lips plant the softest of kisses atop my head, and his hand cups my shoulder, insisting on keeping my form together despite its fragile state. When I grow quiet, he asks, "Can you look at me?"

I blink.

Was I drifting to sleep?

I look up at him, daring to dive into his twin pools of sadness and concern.

"Thaddeus." My voice cracks as a smile attempts to show itself.

Thaddeus smiles in return, "Yes, it's me."

"I'm sorry—" I begin, but he places a finger to my lips, and I look down at it as its warmth caresses once wilted petals, bringing me back to life, back to a reality I can live with.

My eyes drift back to his and he tentatively takes that same finger to push a stray hair behind my ear.

"You have nothing to be sorry for, but I want to tell you something. Do you think you're ready to listen?" he asks.

My head bobbles in a nod.

"I'm sorry for yesterday. I was rash, and I realize—"

My lips go to part again. "No it's me who—"

That solitary finger of his returns to my mouth. "Listen."

But I was stupid, I fell for a boy's tricks just to prove I could win. I would take it back a hundred times, but I can't because—

"Listen." He repeats, somehow seeing the thoughts racing through my mind.

I nod again.

"One of the things I enjoy about you is how kind and considerate you are to the needs of children, and it would be wrong of me to fault you for displaying a trait that I adore. So, consider this forgiveness and an apology for not realizing it earlier."

My mouth goes to open again, but the presence of his finger

still lingers, and I look down at it before looking back at him.

One more thing and then I'll let you speak."

A crease forms in my brow, but I wait.

Thaddeus clears his throat. "I have to ask—" I feel his hand on my shoulder drop down to caress my fingers, rubbing small, soothing, hypnotic circles, careful not to irritate the broken skin. "I need to know—"

I watch him fight to keep his composure and feel myself tense beneath his touch as I wait.

"What happened here?" Thaddeus asks, swallowing hard.

My chin quivers as I take a breath and look away, not wanting the tears to return with reinforcements. "Honestly?"

"I want nothing less from you," His eyes reach out to me with compassion, and my gaze is drawn back to him.

Licking my lips, finding my voice, I begin. "Stephen showed up at my house last night, unexpected. I-I sent him away," I say. "After school—"

I take a deep breath.

He waits a long moment and is rewarded when I exhale and start speaking again. "I walked Sarah home. I was on the way to the factory to meet Father when—" I feel my throat constricting. "I—I was hoping to see you."

My hands begin shaking as a cold chill slips up my spine, stripping away my confidence.

Will he believe me?

Stephen's words echo through my mind.

"Go on."

"Stephen grabbed me, trapped me here, said awful things about yesterday—today. That I'm worthless, and no one will marry me, and that I asked for what the clerk did this morning ..."

I suck in my bottom lip and bite down hard, squeezing my eyes shut while praying the pain will hold off the tears long enough for me to finish.

"I-I tried, honest. I wanted to get a-away. But-he-he's so strong."

The memories swell up from the back of my mind, and I work to shut them out by pressing my fingers into my closed eyes until vibrant colorful splotches appear behind the lids. I can't risk opening them and seeing the pain in Thaddeus's expression. I can't bear to hurt him again and think this is my burden to suffer alone.

I feel his hand gently pulling my fingers away from me.

Small chinks form in the dam holding back my hysteria. "I wanted to come to you. Tell you I am sorry, tell you I learned, and ask for your forgiveness. And then he just grabbed me. He grabbed me and-and-and—"

I look up at him, and he gives me a weak smile as his emotion lay naked on his face, tender but vulnerable.

"Please forgive me," I whisper, begging his heart to hear me.

"God help me, Emilie Prescott, there is nothing to forgive." His voice rumbles with the distant thunder of vengeance, but the promise of spring for me—for us—resides in the forefront.

I smile.

His smile lifts a little higher, making my heart sing.

"Are you going to kill Stephen?"

"Don't worry about that."

He leans forward.

Instinct screams at me to retreat. A nervous terror rising from moments ago resurfaces.

He stops, a flicker of concern in his features changes to remembrance.

"I'm sorry. May I kiss you, Miss Prescott?" he asks, his tone cushions the request coming from his heart. The vulnerability in his eyes mirrors the tangled mess of emotion churning within me.

"Only if it means we are together again," I say, needing to hear his pledge as I won't be taken for a whore ever again.

"Without a doubt, you are mine and I am yours, and may I be strong enough to endure us." His voice is just above a whisper before his lips meet mine, hesitant at first, a mere brush against my skin.

My own hesitancy melts away. The kiss deepens. The dam within me breaks for a completely different reason from what I expected as what rushes out is a tangle of emotion—surprise, confusion, a blooming joy threatening to burst from my chest.

When he pulls away, a breathless laugh escapes us both. My head spins and the world around me becomes a hazy blur. In this moment, in a forgotten alley, apologies, forgiveness, and something entirely new blooms between us. A seed is planted with his touch and is nurtured by our tears as his eyes churn with storms I've never seen, revealing a question I can't decipher. But does that matter? The warmth in his gaze speaks volumes.

Uncertainty Wakes

APRIL & MAY 1861
GETTYSBURG, PENNSYVANIA

The kiss ...

A sigh ...

I look up into his sapphire pools, a glint, a smile as he pulls me into his chest.

His embrace is warm, protective, and intoxicating. My head rests against him as I enjoy the gentle *thump-bump* of his heart, the hypnotic beat singing a peaceful lullaby of calm. Thaddeus rocks me, his chin rests atop my head, he breathes deep and lets out a low sigh of his own. His closeness smells of musk and mingles with sweat. Nestled in his arms is a perfect paradise despite sitting in the dirt in the middle of an alley for everyone to see. I look up. The late afternoon is giving way to evening. The light will soon change from blue to yellow and orange before nightfall. A rogue wind kicks up dust in the alley and urges us to go. The sky, darkening with clouds of gray, warns of further trouble if we choose to delay.

"I'd better get you home." Thaddeus's voice rumbles in his chest. He moves me to arm's length, smiling.

I smile back.

"Now that's the woman I know."

Thaddeus stands and reaches for my hand. Temporary pain shocks my wrist as he grabs it to help me up, but I swallow it down, knowing he meant no harm. Dusting off my skirt, I turn around to look for my book satchel.

"I better find Diablo. Wait here."

Standing for the first time since Stephen was pulled off me, I look around. The alley is a typical place for barrels, crates, and discarded trash—a forgotten space no one cares to use except as a shortcut from one busy street to the next. I turn to face the wall, the accomplice to my struggle. My body shivers. My stomach clenches as the hair on the back of my neck pricks up on guard, ready to defend.

I swallow hard, narrowing my eyes, my resolve clear.

That will never happen again.

Turning away, I see my bag discarded on the opposite side of the alley. I walk over to pick it up as Thaddeus rides in on Diablo.

"Ready?" he asks. "Don't need your father to come looking for the wrong man." He flashes me a smile, his blue eyes dancing with a smirk on his lips.

"You are the least of his worries," I say, the banter we misplaced over the last twenty-four hours tugs on my playful ways.

Walking up to Diablo, I say, "Hello, buddy, good to see you again." Thaddeus helps me up as he settles in behind me.

I feel his lips in my hair, his breath on my ear—I giggle—and then let my body fit into the curve of his chest with my shoulders just inside his and his sinewy arms around me—a slight squeeze. *Ah, his closeness returns.*

"What's this?" His voice turns hard and demanding. The comfort disappears.

"What?" I say, trying to turn to him. I flinch as a flash of pain in my shoulder flickers under his touch. "Ow!"

"Did he bite you?" Thaddeus asks.

His fingers pull the hair off my neck inspecting the bits of pain with a poke and prod. The pain in my neck comes back in a flash, remembering being pinned beneath Stephen and needled with his harsh words, hot breath, tongue slobbering along my ear gnawing, biting.

My body answers Thaddeus with a shudder.

Thaddeus exhales, and with it his arms return me to his calming embrace. "Don't go back there," he whispers. "I'm not angry with you."

"I-I'm sorry, I—"

"Stop apologizing. I don't blame you."

I can only nod, as I struggle to reign in the emotional hurricane threatening to make landfall, and weep, proving I'm not a woman but a child. Sucking in a breath, I shake my head, dismissing such thoughts as I feel him relax behind me, his legs nudging Diablo forward.

We ride together, but the silence unnerves me.

"How was your day at the factory?" I ask, reaching for some normalcy.

"Busy all day."

Seconds pass into lingering moments—

"How were the children today?" he asks.

"Wretched. I swear, I wanted to leave as soon as I arrived," I say. "Thankfully, Mrs. Irwin gave me some good ideas for discipline."

I feel his chest rumble with a low chuckle. "That bad? Did she give you a ruler?"

"No, a paddle, but I fixed them without having to use it. Provided the snake is removed from the outhouse, there shouldn't be any problems—at least for a week."

"A snake? You really have had quite the day. Emilie Prescott, the snake charmer and child tamer extraordinaire!" The shock in his voice, proceeded by such showmanship, makes me giggle yet again.

When we arrive home, the sun is well on its way to passing its vigil to the moon of the night sky. Orange and red fade into shades of pink, purple, and an ever darker shade—the evening blue I expect to see is masked by thick clouds of gloom. This makes the comfort of the warm light glowing in the front windows of home appear even more inviting.

As Thaddeus helps me down, his hands stay on my waist. He looks around, then pulls me to him. I sigh. His arms encircle me, his warmth comforts me, his strength reinforces my own.

"May I call on you later this week?" I feel him kiss the top of my head.

"Yes, I look forward to seeing you," I say as the gap between us grows.

"Good night, Emilie." His hands squeeze mine, share his warmth, and offer his tender heart with a slight brush of his fingers as we part.

He turns to Diablo, remounting.

"Thaddeus?"

He turns back, gazing at me, waiting.

"Can you show me again?" I ask, recalling our kiss in the alley, giving him a raised eyebrow and a smirk.

"Someday, I wish to show you a thousand times a day." He erupts into a chuckle. "Good night."

"Good night," I say feeling a sense of renewed excitement for us.

❧❁❦

Silence greets me at the kitchen door. The kitchen is spotless, everything back in its place as if dinner had never occurred. Yet, one place setting remains on the table. I smile and try to keep quiet as I search the warming oven for my supper, but I cannot muffle the creak of the floorboards under my feet, the faint sound of water dripping from the pump, or a soft sob?

Low whispers trickle in from somewhere.

Reaching to retrieve my dinner, I strain to hear more. The same sounds return. The voices are not typical conversation, but distress.

Closing the oven door, leaving dinner behind, I listen intently. There it is, another sniff, men's voices—Father? Henry? Where's Mother?

My footfalls echo down the dark hall to the voices in the parlor. The door is open as the lights shine bright, inviting me in from the vacant hall. Father is holding Mother's hand, kneeling beside her chair, his face imploring her—but for what?

Henry clutches the newspaper in his hand, the usual smirk and playfulness abandoned. Whatever this is, it matters to Henry too.

Mother sniffs, dabbing her wet cheeks, her white handkerchief a surrender, if not a warning of the onslaught of emotion streaming down her face.

"What is this?" I ask as all eyes turn to me.

"You didn't hear?" Henry asks.

"I just got home," I say, turning to my parents. "Mother what's wrong?"

Unable to speak between her tears, she shakes her head. The raw emotion carved into her face is something she fails to tame.

"It's Aaron," Father's voice cracks.

I look back to the chair occupied by mother. This is the last place I saw Aaron, talked to Aaron—the night before he left. His laugh, his scowl, his interest in my words ... Our dinner conversations, his jokes, his teasing, the playful glint in his eyes, the flash of his smile ... Henry's reactions to all his antics—Aaron the leader, mother and father's eldest, Henry's brother, and my hero.

I turn, noticing an acrid oily odor not familiar to the parlor. The side table, a usual place for family treasures, now lies dirty and cluttered with old newspapers spread across its top. One of father's rifles is scattered in pieces on one side, while a can of black powder and a neat stack of thin square papers wait to be assembled. The smell is gun, oil, and powder.

Layer upon layer of fear, anxiety, and worry—a culmination of today's emotions—ricochets through me, sounding alarms of danger, twisting my stomach, squeezing my dread to the forefront, which I'd previously calmed.

"Someone tell me what is going on with Aaron before I scream!" I say, the fear gripping me threatening to strip away my security, my sense of family, and—Oh please not my Aaron. I begin quaking and feel lightheaded.

Henry stands, rushing over to me, guiding me to the couch, and settling me firmly next to him.

"Whoa, Em, please. We just got Mother to settle down. I can't have two women hysterical within ten minutes time." His hands are on my shoulder. I stiffen and rip his hands off of me, my own still stained in blood.

"What the hell!" Henry snatches one of my hands for closer inspection. "Who did this?" Henry holds my hands up for our parents to see.

Father looks up, anger flashing in his eyes.

Mother gasps at the sight of blood and bruises, and then the calamity of questions and demands begins all at once, a clutter of nonsense as far as I'm concerned.

"What about Aaron!" I command, standing so they will listen. "Is he hurt, is he coming home, is he dead?" My hysteria crescendos, choking me and throttling my nerves until tears shake loose. "I can't lose my brother, I can't, I won't. I'm sorry, I'm sorry for everything, dear Lord!"

Father stands, rushing over to me.

"Emilie, sit!" His hands firmly pressing me back down to the couch. "Aaron is not hurt. We got some disturbing news that will affect us all."

Henry flips over the latest *Gettysburg Compiler*. His finger lands on the headline: "Bombardment of Sumter—Progress of the Battle." The rumors that have taunted us through the papers over the past months have finally come to fruition, tumbled into our laps, and now rot—leaving a sour, gagging taste in our mouths. My hand goes to stifle a cry. Grim faces return my look of shock.

The realization of the war stares back at me—a monstrous entity, it shadows stretching across the land, threatening to engulf everything it touches. Emptiness, uncertainty, and doubt solidify them into a heavy darkness in my gut. A culmination multiplied—I have family on both sides of the Mason Dixon line.

What will happen to our neighbors, the slaves, the plantation? What will happen to the boys here, going off to fight each other?

Where is Aaron, will he come home, or will he be swallowed up—lost?

Where do my loyalties lie?

A tapping on the window, a rhythmic insistent beat, breaks our silence. A broken branch is the first casualty of the storm that is coming. The wind outside whips up in response to the thunder's mournful growl echoing through the valley, leaving an icy dread in my heart.

Tap-tap-tap goes the splintered twig against the glass, knocking of an omen. I can't help but hold my breath.

The spring rains brought about fresh swarms of mosquitoes. They whine an incessant song, a new annoyance joining the clatter of war fever that closes its grip on Gettysburg. Gone are the sleepy days of apple blossoms blanketing the town with sweet perfume. Now, the air is thick with the bitter tang of arguments, heavy with words like "States' rights" and "a house divided cannot stand." Every conversation, every headline in all three newspapers spout the same dirge, each a verbal bombshell exploding in this once-peaceful town.

The wagon navigates its way down the street, as Father and I pass the townspeople sweeping their front steps, but rather than a hello—

A shrill pronouncement from a woman with broom in hand claps against our ears, "Abolish slavery, it's the only way to keep this country together."

Two doors down an older gray-haired gent shouts back, "The only thing them Rebs understand is the end of a barrel."

The back-and-forth argument continues as we pass by unnoticed.

"Our neighbors are drawing lines and taking sides."

"We can't say it wasn't coming."

Is this the storm Father talks about?

"I hope Aaron sends a letter. It's horrible and hurtful enough being from Virginia, much less not knowing if he is okay." My mind begins to play a scene I don't wish to see.

"Be patient Emilie. Your brother is trying to finish school, and I am sure your uncle needs help tending to the family legacy with all this uncertainty. I am sure he will write soon."

"Do you think he would enlist without telling us?" I ask.

"God, I hope he is smarter than that. Besides, if he does, your mother will be scarier than any battle he'll encounter," Father's face pinches as if he bit a sour cherry. He breathes out a long sigh. "And yet, he's an adult, so whatever he decides, we won't be able to stop him."

"What if Mother locks him in the cellar?"

"Don't go giving her any ideas, Em."

The wagon pulls up to the corner. School is half a block away. After the incident with Stephen, my father and brother are my personal security. I am not allowed to go to school or town by myself for now, which suits me just fine.

Sarah spots me as soon as I round the corner of the building. She's waiting on our meeting bench, watching the children mill around the school yard. The school bell should ring in about ten minutes.

"Have you heard from your brother yet?" Sarah asks, biting her lip. Sarah dragged the news of Aaron out of me the day after we found out. I apparently was not happy enough for her, so she interrogated me until I told her what was on my mind.

"No news yet," I say plopping down next to her. "No letter

yet."

"Well then, I've got some good news. My father says, if it comes to war, it will be done by Christmas!" Sarah smiles at me and waits with hopeful cheer for my smile to reflect black at her.

"I don't know about that," I say, "The South is pretty set on—"

Sarah's hand goes to my arm, her eyes wide, as she bites her lower lip. "Oh but it will. My father's always right, mother says so." Her hand grips a little tighter and I wince before mustering a small pat to her hand, in hopes that she will release her grip and her excitement that comes with the daily Sarah and Thomas news announcement. It arrives at the same time every day, at precisely three ... two ... one!

"Did I tell you my father has enough money saved for my dowery, so Thomas and I can get married sooner if we want." I watch as her face lights up at the prospect of marriage, and her prattle begins to rattle on as she speaks of her duty and responsibility to be wife and mother.

"That—"

"So I was thinking, if the wedding is it to be earlier ..."

"Sarah—"

"And I'm not sure if we should go with daffodils or ..."

"Yes, good news indeed," I say, though I am fairly sure she doesn't hear me, so I try a different tactic—a mournful expression, a picture of sorrow carved into my features as if the world around me is surely about to crumble—which it very well might despite Sarah's father's predictions.

"Oh dear. Oh no, what's wrong Emilie? Oh please, you must tell me. I insist, as your bosom friend and confidante, it is my absolute responsibility to make sure that you—"

I put my finger to her lips forcing the last utterance from her to turn into a squeak. "Good. Now, I have a question for you."

She nods her head, big blue eyes staring at me in curious empathetic wonder.

"Does Thomas know you are planning to move up the date?"

No sooner do I remove my finger from her lips then does her answer begin to spew forth.

"Well, not exactly. Father only told me last night. And I haven't—"

My finger goes back to her lips.

"So, you're breaking it to him when?" I ask, removing my finger once more.

"Tonight, of course," Sarah begins as the bell cuts her off from anymore news of the one and only Mr. and Mrs. Fletcher. "See you at lunch."

"See you then."

Sarah gives me a sharp glance.

"I promise to meet you right here."

Sarah gives me a wistful smile, and we file into the school to begin our day.

I watch a tangle of boys march around the playground, struggling to keep in line with a military formation as the self-proclaimed leaders bark orders. They salute each other, with serious scowls on their faces, their play a trickle down to our youngest citizens from the rumors and talk of the country's troubles.

A hand touches my shoulder, and I jump.

"I made it," Sarah comes around the corner of our usual bench on the playground.

"How did your morning go?" My lunch is already set in my lap.

"The fourth graders are challenging," Sarah sits next to me with her lunch basket in her lap, fishing around in it for a sandwich. Plucking out her stomach's desire, she unwraps it and proceeds to take a bite without finishing her story.

My gaze turns back to the boys, who break from their formation to huddle together, their heads bowed, intent on their own conversation.

A younger boy, Fredrick, with dark brown wavy hair and big eyes in a green checked shirt jumps up yelling, "Oh no, I'm not going to be a Reb!" *His face grows red as he kicks the dirt, and his friends who are expected to suffer the same pseudo fate soon join him in the protest.*

"If my Pa found out I even played a Reb, he would send me to the woodshed," Nicolas says, his red hair and freckled face matching the bluster of his scowl as he links arms with Fredrick in a show of camaraderie.

"We're not allowed to even talk about my relatives in North Carolina. Pa says they are dead to us." Fredrick chimes in.

"Yeah, they're dead to us," pipes up a yellow haired boy with black trousers and gleaming white suspenders. "We're not playing dead Rebs."

My hand covers my mouth, "Oh dear Lord, how could anyone—"

"What's wrong?" Sarah asks, as she reaches for a bottle of lemonade to wash down the sticky sandwich.

"I can't believe parents are actually taking children to the woodshed for speaking about the South, and worse yet, instilling that their Southern relatives are dead to them," I say.

"What's wrong with that? It's discipline, and who knows what families dispute about. They might deserve it."

"It's family, Sarah!" I say. "Family is the most important blessing one can have."

"Well, if that's the case, Emilie, you're one lucky girl, 'cuz I don't know that everyone would agree," Sarah says, unwrapping a piece of cake. "I know my relatives are questionable. I have an Aunt Becky ..."

I turn to watch the boys again, turning out Sarah's prattle about all her relatives—dead, alive, and some of which she claims are in a state of in-between. The older boys in the group have put their heads together once more before announcing they will all draw straws to see who will play the respectable union and who will play the enemy. The younger boys cheered at this, drew straws, and scattered to make plans within their respective groups, resulting in each boy searching the playground and wood pile for sticks to be fashioned into weapons. The way the news of our country is seeping down into the minds of our young children in such a barbaric way makes my stomach churn.

"... And then there is Uncle Rosco, we're not quite sure—Emilie? Have you heard a word I've said? Em—Now what are you looking at?" Sarah asks as she spoons another mouthful of cake into her mouth.

"The boys," I say, my chin pointing in their direction. "They are emulating their fathers and uncles and every eligible male in their household."

Sarah turns and her eyebrows raise as the boys march in two lines at each other with sticks pointing at the enemy.

"Huh, well, will you look at that. I wish the war would have started sooner. This will probably be a great benefit toward discipline in the classroom. Look, they're actually following orders!" Sarah notices as she puts her leftover cake back into her basket.

My mouth drops as my dear friend leaves me truly flabbergasted, but rather than try to point out the flaws of her logic, I decide to change the topic. "Why aren't you eating that? Is it spoiled?"

"No, I was just thinking about how I don't want to fill a doorway when I get married," Sarah pinches her middle. "You know, watching my figure."

"Don't be silly. Whether or not you fill a doorway will depend on how many bones you want in your hoop, not cake."

"You're not helping," Sarah nudges me. "Now, as I was saying, I expect there to be more of that behavior because Governor Curtain just called for thousands of Pennsylvania's finest, and everyone who is anyone is scrambling to enlist to get this skirmish over before it turns into an all-out war."

"Skirmish? Where did you hear that?" I ask. "I thought we were at war."

"Not according to the paper. My father talks endlessly about this; I've memorized all the details better than my orthography lessons."

"I'd refocus on orthography," I say. "You can't get your certificate in May knowing all the details in the newspaper."

"But the paper is much more riveting! There's a meeting at the hall, for new recruits next Saturday." Sarah giggles. "All the young strapping men will be there because someone is looking to form a company, the first of which to leave this area. I wonder what sort of business they'll form to help President Lincoln. Oh, do let your brother Henry know. He certainly fits the bill."

I smile back at Sarah, "Bless your heart, Sarah." I don't have the heart to tell her that the sort of company they will be forming is not *a business, nor do I want to think of my brother as a prospective bachelor.*

The boys enter the classroom after lunch all excited about what happened on the playground. Fredrick and Nicolas spout off about all their "kills" and bemoaning the fact they are too young to enlist.

"My Pa says, as soon as I'm twelve, I can serve our country. He'll give his blessing and everything," Fredrick puffs his chest like a peacock. "He told me fighting will make a man out of me, put hair on his chest just like his."

"Great, I'll just run away and tell them I am twelve then," Nicolas says from his perch on top of his desk, where all the other boys flock around him.

Tapping my ruler on the desk, everyone turns as I direct them to their seats. "I think it is time for a new lesson," I say. "I want all of you to take out your slates and draw me your ideas of the military and this so-called war you all are dreaming about."

Josephine giggles. "Miss Prescott, you talk funny. Are you a *secesh?*"

Turning to the dark-haired girl, I ask, "Tell me what 'secesh' means, Miss Josephine. Go on, please stand and tell the class what you know about this. If you are going to call someone a name, you must be sure of its meaning." I give her a stern look.

The girl swallows hard, reluctant to stand, but my gaze does not waver and with everyone staring and the help of the bench desk, she finds her feet.

"Loud and clear please," I say.

Josephine looks at the desk with her slate, red washing over her face. "Well—my Ma said—it means you like the South." Josephine looks up at me with big watery eyes.

"That is correct," I say. "A secessionist is one who believes in the Southern cause." Josephine's eyes light up at my approval of her definition. "But," I begin, my finger halting the conversation that is beginning to grow from a murmur to rumble, "how do you know that is where I stand?"

Josephine sinks down into her desk chair.

"Josephine, you have not been given permission to return to your seat. Back on your feet. Do you know my political views or are you just assuming I believe in the Southern cause?"

The girl's eyes widen, she bites her lip, shaking her head, dark brown ringlets smacking her cheeks.

"I'm sorry, I didn't hear you. Speak up," I say.

"No, Miss Prescott, I do not." A pout forms at Josephine's lower lip.

"All right then, do you think it is proper to judge other people by what you don't know for sure?"

"No, Miss Prescott, it isn't." Josephine says.

My expression softens to one she and the class are more familiar with, and I give her a wink to bring back her smile before turning my attention back to the rest of the class, the tip of my ruler resting in my palm.

"That is how misunderstandings and bad things happen. When others judge people by what they do not know for sure," I say. "All right, you may be seated. Let's return to those slates."

My attention flickers back to the boys. "Nicolas, tell me what you drew. What is your idea of this army you want to run away to."

Nicolas springs from his seat and announces, "In this new life, I will get to be the drummer who calls the men back from the fight. I am their guide when the field is smokey. They will hear my drum and come running. They will praise me and tell me what a good job I am doing." His smile says it all. The boy's story is a yarn spun for him by someone he admires.

"So, you are safe on the field, and nothing can happen to you?" I ask.

"No, you can't shoot the drummer boys," Nicolas boasts. "Everyone knows that, Miss Prescott."

"Nicolas, have you ever seen a dead person?"

"Yes, my grandmother was laid in her parlor about six months back," Nicolas says. "I touched her." He grins around as the class 'oohs,' a smile playing at the edge of his mouth as the class feeds into his bravery and the next words to come out. "She was cold, and her skin felt like—"

"Once she died, did she ever come back to life?" I ask, before Nicolas can elaborate any further.

The class erupts into laughs and giggles, knowing well the answer.

"No," they all say in unison.

"Exactly, dead is dead. No one comes back to life. There is no picking up your toy guns like after you play in the school yard. Soldiers do not shoot each other then all get up and go have dinner, do they?" I ask.

All twenty pairs of eyes were on me, and for once, the loudest noise came from my steps as I paced about the classroom, giving them more than my words to follow.

"What I want you to remember is a fight on the battlefield is permanent. Once someone dies, and it does not matter which side or how old—" My walk about the classroom takes a pause as I look to Nicholas. "—they will never get to come back." My hand goes to his shoulder to indicate he can take his seat.

The boy's boastful expression wilts under my gaze, and he slides further down in his seat.

Resuming my walk I ask, "How many people would miss you

if you died?"

A few hands pop up.

"Percy?" I say calling on a quiet boy in the back.

"Everyone."

"Yes, everyone, including family, neighbors, and community. Because you and you and you," gesturing at random with my ruler, "and all of you are important to them, and they equally to you."

I pause, watching their faces, and realize I am on the precipice of making an entire class of fourth graders burst into tears. Good, because I'm not quite done yet.

"I want you to remember this too. The men on both sides of the North and South have family, loved ones, and communities who will miss them if they don't come home."

Their faces change from dismal to thoughtful, brows furrowing, faces squinched. Their innocence is teetering on reality. Will my message be enough?

Out of my peripheral, trained—as some would believe—to see what is behind me, I see a boy mouth something to the effect of, *But that's the enemy. We're not supposed to care*, as my words sink into his little heart.

"We need to pray this skirmish won't happen, as there will be many sad people as its result," I say as I turn to look at the child. "Do you understand, Charles?"

He gulped the question of just how I saw him ricocheting between his bright red ears.

I return to the front of the quiet classroom. The students drained of their enthusiasm for war, and I pray, wrestling with a glimmer of understanding within their innocent minds on the tragedy that is likely to befall us all. I do not wish to blanket the room with such facts, suffocating their jovial childhood optimism, but I also fear what will become of them if I allow them to maintain their ignorance.

After a moment of reflection, I say, "All right, shall we have a spelling bee competition? I have a piece of candy for the winners."

The class breathes a heavy sigh of relief as smiles return, and the seriousness of our lessons dissipates in their excitement for the spelling bee. Chatter buzzes to life again, with laughter and carefree conversations. I allow them to return to this state of innocence, but I know remaining oblivious will not remain an option for them. Not when the coming fight our nation is determined to have, standing brother against brother with a fervor threatening to tear families apart and pitting patriotism against love, is standing on our doorstep. Will duty and honor shatter us all or can we weather this coming storm ... together? I pray to the Lord for help to keep a brave smile as we carry on with the lessons—for today.

Calling All Troops

EVERY CITIZEN SHOULD BE A SOLDIER.
THIS WAS THE CASE WITH THE GREEKS AND ROMANS
AND MUST BE THAT OF EVERY FREE STATE.
~THOMAS JEFFERSON

MAY 1861
GETTYSBURG, PENNSYLVANIA

The creaking of the wagon is a counterpoint to the happy song of birds celebrating today's fresh air as they flit and flap throughout the warm promise of spring. Henry sits beside me, silently focusing on the road ahead, trying to avoid large potholes from the recent rain. The last thing he wants is to jostle me out of the wagon, or worse, get a wheel stuck.

Word from Aaron states he is trying to get home but doesn't know when. The South is recruiting for the Confederacy, and he is interested in what is happening. He also reports that Uncle William is anxious and angry, his focus is on the next crop and money, so in other words, nothing new.

"Why are you so sour today?" I ask. "It's a lovely day, and you get to escort me to town rather than being stuck at home doing—"

"I'd rather be plowing the upper field," Henry scowls. "Have you tried to get this wagon through town on Saturday? The crowds, no place to park—its maddening."

"I promise we'll be quick about it," I say, smiling and nudging my brother whose pout persists and eyes narrow. "We only need a few items from the grocer and a quick stop at Fahnestock's for some sewing supplies."

"That's what you told me last time, then we ended up—wait, sewing supplies?" Henry bemoans, "There goes the day. I may as well plan to eat a late dinner and go straight to bed thereafter."

"Oh, don't be so dramatic" I say, ruffling his hair.

"I'm not being dramatic," He pulls away from my hand and tries to swat away my insistence. The wagon lurches and he struggles to get back to his task as I let out of a shriek of a giggle.

"Are too!"

"Am not! Look Em, when it comes to women shopping, it is an all-day affair. Can't we stop at Bobble and Knot-Interested another day?"

"We could. Which day would you like to bring me back?"

"The day after never," he says. "Besides, at some point, I have to get up to the Welty's to help plant their fields."

"Maybe I should go by myself. It's been weeks," I say, trying to ignore the telltale thumps of my heart echoing the misgivings of Stephen Byrne. "It's about time I become independent again."

"What are you, a glutton for punishment? I'd sooner drop you off at that convent Aunt Jenny is always going on about."

Henry's question hangs between us. Weeks of waiting, feeling locked up like Starlight in her stall, wanting to be free, to run, and in her case, to roll in the dirt.

Then again, maybe if I rolled in the mud not even Stephen would want me, but Mother would seal my fate with the laundry.

I sigh. Though I know they mean well, my father and brother's protection are stifling.

"One of these days, I will need to return to my independence."

"Not today. Let's get our things and get back home."

We drive past the center of town. Baltimore Street is already congested with people, horses, and wagons. Everyone seems to have things to do today.

"Start looking for a place to park," Henry says. My eyes begin searching for a place and—

"There's a spot," I say pointing to a wagon leaving the front of the grocer.

"Huh, maybe you're useful for something." He grins.

"What was that? You want me to spend two hours in Fahnstock's?"

"Did you bring the list of items needed?" Henry asks as he maneuvers the horses to a stop.

"And the eggs to sell. I will get this started."

As soon as he sets the brake, I hop out of the wagon seat and grab the basket of eggs.

Outside the grocer, the window is decorated with patriotic banners and slogans about duty and honor to serve our country. Neatly arranged military buttons, fabric bolts of union colors, haversacks, mess kits, shoes and boots, pocketknives and matches, sewing repair kits, and anything else a man may need outside of his military issued equipment sits behind the windows. An array of advertisements, all of which include a nod to the country's skirmish, litter any blank spaces that do not inhibit the display of goods. Flyers ask for Pennsylvania volunteers—Three-year enlistment and Home Guard to protect the city. Another notice speaks to the women of Gettysburg to join the Ladies Relief Society meeting at the Methodist Church.

Pushing through the door, a jingle greets me, but it stutters as it is grabbed by—I check behind me weary of who may have followed.

Henry closes the door and I smile.

Perhaps he is right. Perhaps I'm not ready for independence.

My attention turns back to the counter, where I see the clerk smiling, no doubt from all her sales today. She has the body of a twig with a long-drawn face and brown hair so straight I wonder if her mother took an iron to it.

Poor dear. I don't think any number of layers could help her, but maybe a few ribbons and some fancy plaiting?

"How can I help you?" the clerk asks, and I blink, realizing how easily my thoughts trailed away.

"Sorry, good morning," I say. "Are you in need of more eggs?"

"How fresh are they?"

"Plucked them from the chickens an hour ago." I present her with the basket filled with brown and white eggs. "For some reason, we have more than we can use."

"Fifteen cents a dozen?" she asks as her gaze grazes over them, counting, "How many do you have?"

"Two dozen," I say. "We have a list of items we need also."

"Wonderful, let me help you with that," she puts her hand out and I give her the list.

With a quick once over she says, "All of this looks to be in stock. Do you know where to find these items?"

"We'll manage," I say, and she hands the list back.

Turning to Henry, I say, "I need you to grab ten pounds of flour and sugar, and a pound of salt. I'll get the rest."

"Do you see how bossy she is?" asks Henry with a grin to the clerk.

"You want bossy? How about: do it now, Mr. I-don't-want-to-be-here-all-day," I say.

The clerk stifles a giggle as Henry sets to gathering. By the time I am done, he has the flour, sugar, and salt stacked on the counter and is talking up the young woman who I overhear asking, "Are you going to the recruit meeting at the hall today?"

"No, ma'am, I wasn't planning on it.".

"Why not? You know they'll be looking for strapping young men like yourself." Her eyelashes fluttering in appreciation for—the sting of bile rises in my throat—my brother, like a new bolt of much needed muslin.

Though I doubt there is enough muslin in the world to cover that mouth of his.

"That as it may be, I can't leave the family right now to settle a skirmish," Henry says.

"Skirmish?" she asks, her brows knit together in confusion. "Oh, my dear, the papers are saying this it's an outright war." Her eyes narrow with a hint of pity for his ignorance, perhaps thinking all bronze and no brain.

"Surely, it will be over in a few months. And if that's the case ,why trouble myself to take on another man's concern, when there are fields to plant and mouths to feed?"

"So, your family is more important than your country's wellbeing?" she asks, her sweet demeanor swept away by a flash of anger this storm appears to stir up in everyone. "Don't you care that this country you call home to is being torn apart by loudmouth rebels, who don't give a wit about anything but making money off the backs of poor negros?"

I see the indentation of Henry's cheek, as he bites the inside of it. His lower jaw hardens, his face brightening to a soft pink hue. At last, he clears his throat, "That's a personal decision, which is none of your concern, ma'am." His tone is level, though he works to blink away the narrowing of his eyes and returns to his casual self. "I am sure this skirmish will work itself out with or without my help."

The clerk pushes a paper toward Henry. "I just want you to know the facts."

Henry pushes the paper aside. "Found them all already, can you believe it?"

Setting the arm full of items on the counter, I look at the clerk. "Can you please deduct the thirty cents from the bill?"

Henry turns away, pretending to look at the pocketknives on display, his back turned to the counter.

The silence of their standoff hangs between me and the clerk as she adds up our items and packs them up. I hand her the requested sum, saying, "Thank you, have a pleasant day."

Her return smile is anything but natural, and sweeping up what groceries I can carry, I turn to Henry. "A little help?"

Henry turns away from the pocketknives. "Hmm? Oh, right." He takes up the flour, sugar, and salt, nods to the clerk, and uses his body to push open the door. The only thing pleasant about our exit is the bell's *jingle jangle* as we free ourselves from the clerk's otherwise scrutinizing looks.

At the back of the wagon, Henry lets down the back gate, and we pack the items into small crates.

"Now you have a taste of the inquisition I went through the first day I was here," I say.

"But the store has changed hands since we arrived," Henry points to the new script in the window.

Shaking my head, "I don't know. Maybe it's us who brings out confrontation in everyone we meet." I hand him the coffee.

"I'll tie these down, if you want to walk down to Fahnstock's and get started on your shopping," Henry says, dismissing my concerns.

"I'll meet you—" He pauses at the sound of a cacophony of rumbling heading our direction.

My eyes follow his gaze down the busy road, widening with understanding. Now I know where the children get their ideas. A large group of men and boys push through the streets, whooping and hollering, filling the air with angry music, off-key and peace shattering.

"Shoot those Rebs!"

"Let's show 'em!"

"Johnny Reb won't be welcome across the Mason-Dixon line!"

"We'll show 'em steel!"

"Sign up boys. We need to give them all we got!"

"Hit 'em hard, so we can be home by Christmas! Wassail!"

The revelry passes by us, kicking up dirt and stirring up the seeds of our future like dust devils in the fields. As the last of the stragglers, young men with barely a whisker on their chin, follow along, one of them stops beside Henry.

"Hey friend, did you sign up yet?"

My neck cranes up to the young behemoth's face, red from yelling and running through the streets. His sandy hair is tousled by the comradery of his brethren, friends, cronies who first crowd and then tower over us, leaving no room for escape. Their limbs are thick and strong like oak branches, knobbed at the joints and scarred over like bark from years of hard work. They stand far too close for my comfort, and yet as my back meets the side of the wagon, the most unsettling part of all this is the questioner's beady brown eyes. They appear void of all common sense but filled to the brim with mischief—and speak of a desire to seize my own flesh and blood.

My hand reaches for Henry's arm, which bends at the elbow, but remains taut.

Henry, eye-level with their chests, stands his ground. "Not yet."

"And yet time has passed, so how about now? No time like the present, am I right boys?"

A cheer goes up as two men grab Henry under each arm before he can respond, before I can cry out in alarm, and just like that, he's gone, swallowed up by the beast of war and all its stupidity.

No one even looks back, not even Henry.

My heart pounds in my ears, drumming out the cadence of my fear. Chills start to prickle up my arms, filling out my form, leaving me wondering for a split second if bugs seize my scalp, leaving me wondering—no, disbelieving for a moment longer than I should have—*what's going on?*

I look around, my skirts pinched up in my hands, giving my legs room to join up with—*Who?* Everyone is going about their business as if my brother had not been abducted, as if the young men in their lives have not been hustled and bustled out of their sights.

Isn't anyone going to stop them?

If he signs those papers—Will Henry and Aaron be on opposite sides of the war?

Images of my mother crying flit through my mind, and the spur of reality strikes like a lightning bolt, shocking my feet into action toward the maelstrom of hate.

Saving Henry is not something I do often, but I'll not seek cover from this storm like the rest of the townsfolk. The crowd is several blocks down the street by now. Reaffirming the grip of my skirts in my fists, I rush to catch up before I lose them and more importantly, Henry. Passing onlookers and window shoppers, dodging manure in the streets, a fast walk turns into a light jog. Interrupting carts and horses, ducking under delivery men with their arms full, breaking through bosom buddies in luxury, I pick up the pace and begin to run. A crowd stands in front of a store, all talking and mingling. Skirting around them doesn't appear to be an option. I am swallowed up whole.

"Excuse me ... pardon me ... I need to get through," I say trying to be polite, as my throat tightens.

Henry's crowd disappears from my sight.

I begin to push people aside, letting their remarks of *"Hey, watch it!" and "An excuse me will do!"* fall to the wayside.

Freed from the tangle of bodies, I flee down a street to who knows where, and yet everyone but anyone is there. The crowded streets block my view, but not a one of them makes up a motley crew. I brush by a father and son, emerging from a store with new rifles in hand. I interrupt small children running in circles with sticks, pretending to shoot each other. I cause ladies talking about the next relief meeting to pause and I'm sure gawk. I don't stop to look, to apologize, or to plea for help. Everyone seems to be on the war bandwagon, willing to jump in without concern.

Struggling to catch my breath, I slow to a walk again, one hand releasing my skirt to pinch the stitch in my side. My stays feel so confining; I can't take a full breath. At the end of the next block, I pause to take a rest. The town seems to have thinned out, except for a large group of men gathering at a home.

There they are. At least, I hope.

Walking over to the small yard, there appears to be a celebration, complete with men smoking cigars and slapping each other on the back. The front door is wide open, inviting guests to enter no matter who they are. Yet just as I step up onto the porch, two men come out and if I didn't step to the side, I'm sure they would have run me over.

"We did it now," says the tall man in a full beard. "Now we just got to tell the wives."

"What do you say we stop at the tavern, before we break the news," says his counterpart, a shorter, stockier man with lines etched in his face, the hair sparse atop his head. "We're going to need some liquid strength."

They pass by me without a second glance, and a second is all I give them before I step over the threshold and directly into a wall of bodies. A haze of smoke hovers above everyone, the tobacco burning adding to the hot and stuffy features of the room. I bring my arms into my chest giving myself protection as they shift about shoulder to shoulder, unconcerned if someone gets hurt. My eyes looking left and right, searching through a sea of brown, gray, black, and blue for Henry.

I wish men were as colorful in their wardrobe as women. They all look the same!

Two men look down as I have no choice but to bump into them. They smile as if I'm their lucky day.

"Hey girl, want to give a kiss for good luck against the Rebs?" He grabs my chin and angles my face to get a better look.

My scowl is first to greet him. "No thank you I'm looking for someone," I say, pulling away, smacking into his friend who pushes me back into the center of attention.

"Oh, I bet she's married and gonna take her husband out by his ear." The friend whispers from behind.

"Can we stay to see it?" asks the lout.

. All I want to do is shrink and fade away, an expression I must be wearing because the man from behind reaches past me and grabs his friend's shirt. "All right, all right, come on. We're scaring her. Better get out of here before that husband of hers finds her."

They tip their hats to me as they leave.

Is this how the rabbit feels when the hounds start baying?

Everywhere I turn, shoulders, chests, and sweat surround me in a sea of patriotic fever. Jostled back and forth through the crowd, bodies press into me, nearly fall on top of me, drowning me in a current I have no desire to be caught up in—but Henry. I keep pushing through the crowd of shirts, smoke, and shouts.

The heat causes my own sweat to boil to the surface. Overcome by the stench of men, tobacco, and the fields they both come from, a wave of nausea rushes up into the back of my throat, flooding my tongue with the sting of bile and its bitter aftertaste. Following this, a tide of lightheadedness shifts into my awareness along with a tapping on my shoulder. I blink, gasping for air, unwilling to drown in this sea of unfamiliarity while simultaneously struggling to stay afloat.

A shrill shout, like a bird's call, sounds above the crowd and is followed by men laughing.

Where's it coming from?

I turn around and around.

The crowd parts at one point. An elbow crashes against my stays. I push back, nearly toppling myself, until my hands rest upon a broad back. The gap of space has come and gone, my chance to be free of this body-trap slips away. Up-righting myself, the current of limbs carries on as my nemesis.

"What were you thinking?" A familiar voice breaks through the haze.

I search through the chaos around me and wonder if he could really be here?

"Henry!... Thaddeus?" I call out.

Strong hands, broad shoulders, a scowl I remember, and blue eyes drift in and out of my vision.

"Thadeus!"

The man pauses in his pursuit of fresh air to breathe, a sack of trouble in his grip. When he turns in my direction, he's holding his little brother by the scruff of his shirt.

It is Thaddeus!

Ian of course looks displeased, his face red, his eyes narrowed into arrows tipped with anger, as he squirms about like a scolded puppy who doesn't know when to give up.

Maybe they can help me?

Thaddeus wades through the sea of men.

"What are you doing here?" he asks. One more sharp tug, and he pulls Ian over to close the distance between us.

"I—I lost—" I say, as the demand of sensation knocks harder, lightheadedness spins me in an invisible whirlpool, and the tide of nausea crashes into my throat. The receding wave pulls the color from my face, followed by beads of exertion as I am washed up between rocks of muscle. A chill whips around my battered form. The room starts to darken—

In the distance, I hear Thaddeus.

But isn't he right next to me?

His voice, far off, calls to me, "Emilie ... don't look good."

The crest of my vision folds over, crashing against the surface of my mind as darkness pulls me under. To the world I am blind, the voices around me no more than distant thunder. "Help ... Henry ..." I resurface in a sea of black wrapped in a blanket of weightless comfort, free to float away, let go of reality, feeling it slip from me, leaving Henry, Thaddeus ...

I am floating in the serenity of the deep dark, drifting along like a wayward jellyfish in a current of bliss. A breeze caresses my cheek, my head is cradled in the steady rise and fall of endless waves. The rest of my body lays relaxed against something hard?

Water's not meant to be—hard?

I try to shift, to move, wondering if I can swim toward a light. My fingers brush up against textures of linen and smooth skin. I work to blink away my confusion and regret this decision the second my eyes are assaulted by the early afternoon light of the sun. My hands, feeling twice the weight of any brick, rise up to shade my eyes, and the buzz of murmurs around me stops.

Who's—who was talking?

Hands reaching my face drop heavy with my groan. Eyes semi-covered with my hand, I try again. This time I am able to see—

"Ow, the light ..." My rock hard pillow shifts and I sense the presence of someone's lap? A flash of Thaddeus before darkness had consumed my world materializes in my mind.

"Are you Thaddeus?" I croak, my throat is parched and raw.

"The one and only."

My whine trails off into a whimper before asking, "Did you rescue me again?"

Thaddeus's knee shakes as he chuckles. "Why so cranky? If it helps, I didn't intend on saving you. But here we are, and if you don't want me to, I won't tell anyone."

"Even Henry?" I ask, dragging my free hand up to my throat.

"Don't think you'll have to worry about that," he says. I can hear that lopsided grin of his.

"What are you doing here?"

Thaddeus looks down at me. "Saving my brother from breaking my mother's heart." His tone becomes gruff, just as we manage to make eye contact. Turning my head, there, with two sets of brown eyes upon me, are Ian and Henry.

Henry!

Pushing myself up, I say, "You didn't sign anything did you?"

Henry's hand goes to my shoulder to ease my wibble and wabble. "Easy, Em, and no. Thaddeus here lied about my age, telling them I am too young to enlist." Henry smirks. "Heh, never thought I would be thankful for being younger."

"Speak for yourself," Ian grumbles. "I was going to sign up before Mr. Gloom came to tattle. Now I'll miss the whole row!"

Thaddeus turns to his brother, his ears a shade of anger. "Don't be stupid, Ian. Do you have any care for our mother's heart? It would break if you left without one word!"

"I'd have written a letter or two, once I killed some Rebs," A sheepish smile plays on Ian's mouth. This is received with a swat upside his head, the pain of which Ian tries to rub away.

"Honestly, Ian, you need time to mature before you run off and get yourself killed."

"Why? So Ma and Pa can pay for a bigger coffin?"

SMACK!

At this point I wonder if the poor boy's ears are ringing.

"There is a lot to think about before committing yourself, Ian. I am afraid your brother is correct," says Henry, appearing distant, serious—nothing like the brother I know.

"You are all talking like this is an all-out war," I say. "Last time I checked, it was just a skirmish."

Is it wrong of me to embody Sarah's hopefulness?

They all laugh, amused, much to my surprise.

"No, dear Emilie, it's war," Thaddeus confirms my fears. "The government is calling for troops, money is being budgeted through congress, and the Confederacy is taking a strong stand that they will not return to the Union without a fight." He looks at me, a heaviness in his eyes accompanied by a silent apology.

My heart begins to hammer.

"What about you?" I ask, not sure I want the answer. "Will you stay home?"

Thaddeus pulls me into his arms. I feel his breath in my hair and a kiss on my head. "I have too much to do here to think about signing any papers just yet." I feel his arms tighten around me. "Like a certain red head who needs constant rescuing, orchards that demand pruning, and then, of course, there is my family that needs me. Besides, someone has to make sure this one doesn't poke his eye out with a stick."

"That was once, and I still have both eyes!" says Ian.

"Three times, you just forget," Thaddeus reminds him.

"Guess we aren't the only ones who bicker, Em." Henry chuckles for the first time all day.

However, I find little amusement. In fact, my heart sinks. He is not saying he will stay forever. "Does this mean you will go eventually?"

Thaddeus, his finger under my chin, turns my face to him, and I look into his deep blue eyes. My resolve begins to erode faster than the roads in a rainstorm. He winks, a note of reassurance. "It is my duty to fight, just not yet. We'll talk about it later, yeah?"

Speechless, I nod my agreement as worry floods my mind, the runoff flowing throughout the rest of me. But—

He kisses my forehead, to seal the promise, and then nuzzles me.

The comfort of the Prescott dinner table becomes a place of strategy, where we not only work to shield ourselves but fortify our family against the harsh realities we face. Reeling from the enlistment office scare, Henry and I get a moment to breathe and reassess the predicament we are in. The dark clouds of war, once a distant rumble, now shadows our doorstep and demands the Prescott family make decisions—minus one member.

Aaron remains an enigma along with his loyalties, but even if his loyalties were here, how long would he reside? This reminds me of a new worry gnawing at me—Thaddeus. His determination and loyalty to serve his country could hinder our future together. Is it possible to have a cannon ball, comprised of all the world's troubles, in the pit of one's stomach?

Henry's mood also has been pensive and quiet since we found our way back to Table Rock Road. I can tell he's worn down by thoughts plaguing him by the way he has been picking at his peas since he finished the potatoes and ham.

"They picked me up and dragged me to this man's house to enlist," Henry says. "I couldn't talk them out of it—tried to make every excuse, but they weren't having it."

My hand reaches for his, a tender squeeze. "It was scarry to see you dragged off like that, but I wasn't going to let you go, Henry."

"What is all the fuss?" Mother asks as she gestures for another slice of ham. "Last I heard, this wasn't lasting long. I am sure you'll be able to stay home, Henry. Grown men know better than to rush into things without thinking it through, right Jacob?"

I look to Father just as he delivers another mouthful of potatoes to himself.

"The newspapers are now saying this is an all-out war. We know how the South won't give up their stance, and the North is determined to make them."

"No, they're determined to make me sign away three years of my life, so that I can make them give it up," Henry says. "It should be illegal to fight against your brother."

"Nonsense. Aaron is too smart to get involved in all of this," Mother says.

Father clears his throat. "Loyalty is a tricky thing. It presses a person to find their true self without falling prey to social pressures."

The *clink* of Mother's fork draws everyone's attention to her, but she is not looking at Henry or me. Rather our parents are having one of those silent conversations.

The newspapers would have quite the time trying to figure out who is winning this skirmish.

The tense emotions at this table sour the savory taste of ham and potatoes. I push my plate aside, and neither of them seem to notice.

Henry puts his fork down, once again not so much as a side glance from our parents. He pushes himself back from the table. "I don't see what you two are glaring about. I'm the one expected to take a stand that may end my life. I grew up in the South, I live in the North, neither by choice. So, tell me, which should I do, kill my brother or burn down the farm?"

Mother stands and begins to clear the dishes, the scraping of uneaten food matching that of pencils on a slate. She doesn't even take care to stack them with care, a rattle—and what I hope is not a crack—occurring as she piles on one plate after the next.

"I think this is a conversation for men." She says the carving knife still in hand. Her glare stabs Father, his name sharp on her tongue. "Jacob."

Father's mouth opens to address Mother, and for a moment I hope it is some joking banter, but he appears to think twice. Instead, he looks at Henry.

"Let's go chat about this in the barn, son. Man to man, so we don't upset the ladies."

Henry nods, standing to hand Mother the gravy boat but is quick to set it down after she slaps his hand. He sighs, mutters something under his breath, and follows Father out the door.

Why do I have to stay here? She's still got the knife!

Walking out to the barn to have a father-son discussion weighs heavy on Jacob's heart.

I fully understand her need to protect him. But as a man, I must educate him, make him think for himself. We can't keep him behind if he wants to go.

Jacob's eyes track after his son who moves ahead of him, still in some ways the little boy, who tagged along everywhere—except now he has long straight strides and the confident swagger of a man who desires to take the lead.

Where did all the time go?

Arriving at the barn—they're greeted by the horses, cows, and lazy cats—watching as mice scurry across their path in search of food. Once seated on their familiar talking stumps, Jacob pulls two cigars from his pocket, cuts off the ends, and hands one to Henry.

"What's this?" Henry asks, taking the fat cigar.

"Since you have a man's decision to make, I figure you might as well experience the whole thing. Here let me light that for you."

Henry imitates drawing on the end of the cigar and promptly sputters and chokes.

Jacob can't resist a chuckle but waits until his son regains his composure before saying, "You asked about loyalty, right?"

Henry's face reddens, holding back a small cough. He licks his lips as the tobacco dries out his mouth.

"I—I did," Henry pounds his chest, coughs, and looks at the cigar, trying to decide if he wants to try it again.

"Go on," Jacob says a small smile playing on his lips. "A man doesn't give up after the first bad taste in his mouth."

Henry tries again, inhaling the smoke of the cigar, resulting in another fit of coughing.

"Loyalty is a tricky business. A man must be sure of where he stands because he'll have others trying to sway him to do what they want," Jacob watches Henry take another draw on the cigar.

This time he doesn't cough. Instead, a smile of success appears along with the swelling of his chest.

Henry's eyes meet Jacob's as he asks, "So you are telling me, smoking a cigar makes me a man?"

"No, just makes you look like one," Jacob pokes his chest, resulting in another sputter of coughs from his son.

"The man's beneath the fog of expectations, beneath the posturing. He doesn't have all the answers, but he's got a strong understanding of where he's going."

"But that's the thing," Henry says, following his next attempt at recovery. "I don't know where I stand. My Southern roots tell me to fight for the plantation, our home, and our wealth.

But we have neighbors—I've made friends here—who feel vastly different about my home. They don't understand the love I have for the plantation. I mean, we both agree slavery should be abolished but—" Henry draws on the cigar, a cough erupts, and his nose begins to run. "If I fight, can I not cherish both— which side do I take up for?"

Jacob watches the anguish in Henry's eyes. His son fully understands his position, and as a father, he doesn't envy him. Still, Julia's glare, begging and crying from their discussion this evening, ripples through his mind.

Talk some sense into him, Jacob, her eyes plead. *He's my baby.*

A deep inhale helps him calm his own nerves.

"Henry, you are of legal age to sign up and fight for who you choose. It's a man's decision, despite me being forced to tell you to stay home."

"What?" Henry asks, a frown of confusion ripples through his brows.

Jacob clears his throat. "Listen, your mother doesn't want you to go, and I don't want any harm to come to you either, but it's your choice, as a man. This choice is as harsh as that cigar there."

"This isn't helping me decide," Henry says, now taking another draw as he blows a puff of smoke adding to the hazy cloud between them.

"Let me give you some advice."

"I thought that's what this was," Henry says, laughing— coughing.

"Listen up, when you know exactly why you're going to war, then it'll be just as unpleasant as that cigar you're smoking. But like a man, you'll be confident in your choice. No smoke will cloud your judgement, not from bragging, not even the smoke on the battlefield. Trust your own instincts, and don't let anyone sway you like they tried to do today. Being a man, son—it's a tough decision to make, but it's easier to swallow when you know you're doing the right thing and you're clear about your reasons."

Jacob watches a younger reflection of himself ponder over this talk, sending a sense of pride racing through his veins. As a selfish father, he doesn't want him to go either. He wants to keep him safe, right by him and his mother's side—but as a man, he'll respect his son's decisions as long as they're made with a clear mind and pure heart.

"So, I don't have to decide today?" Henry asks.

"Are you clearer than this barn in your thinking?" Jacob asks, the smoke hangs heavy over their heads like a foggy summer morning.

"No, sir," Henry's eyes are red from the cigar, but a flicker of hope sparks in his eyes.

"Then not tonight."

"Hey, can you show me how to blow a smoke ring?" his son asks.

Jacob chuckles.

At the sound of the door latching shut, I turn to my mother. Her shoulders are tense, as she has surrendered her rage to the sink where she's washing dishes with unusual vigor for this hour. Plates, silverware, and bowls clanking and clinking, and I expect any moment something will go flying or crashing.

I walk over to her, pick up a towel and ask, "Mind if I help?"

Mother shakes her head, continuing to lather, scrub, rinse, and haphazardly hand the dishes off in my direction. I take a plate to dry before she decides to abandon its fate to the floor below us. Three dishes later, I ask again, "Did you and Father have a fight?"

"No, yes, sort of—" Mother bites back what she really feels.

"Is it about me?" I ask, trying to remember if I had any transgressions that would have caused them to argue.

"No," she whispers. A tear falls from her cheek, rippling in the wash water. Her shoulders shake as she tries to hold back. Her wrists wiping away what she can. When there are no more dishes to wash, Mother is still standing frozen in front of the wash basin. Her silent tears mix with her sweat.

Daughters need mothers as mothers need daughters.

"I hope when I'm married that I'm able to argue as quietly with my husband as you do."

"Hmph." The smallest hint of a smile appears at the corner of her mouth, but fades just as quickly as it arrives.

Thoughts race through my mind.

What else can I do? What would she do?

I gently take mother's hands from the wash water, give her a towel, and steer her to the table. I set the kettle to warm, gather teacups—sugar—and pour milk into the serving pitcher.

"What are you doing?" she asks, as she watches me place the tea set on the table.

"Having a heart to heart with my mother," I say, returning to the stove to pour the water into the pot, steeping the tea. Upon returning to the table, I take the towel from her, seat myself, and watch her.

"What's got you so upset?" I ask.

Mother's eyes, dark red from crying, still hold a spark of clear blue as she looks at me. She tries to smile, but it fades away.

"Your father and I are concerned about your brothers. They are both of age to make decisions on going to war."

"But Henry doesn't know what he wants. I am sure he's smart enough to stay out of it," I try to sound hopeful.

"But Aaron," she whispers. "He's my baby, too, my first born. He's going to do it, I can feel it." Her drying cheeks wet again as the anguish of her realization washes over her. "Emilie, you don't understand. You don't have children, but mothers are not supposed to see their babies die." She begins wringing her hands, her eyes escaping to the window. There is a strong effort made in taking long steady breaths.

Picking up the towel, I give it back to her and wait a little for her to calm down. I pour the tea, my hands shaking, rattling the teacup against the spout of the pot.

"You're right," I say, "but as much as he's your little boy, he's also my brother—my hero. I mean, as a sister, my pain would be different but just as great—I imagine."

Mother looks to me, a knowing in her eyes. "What do you suggest we do?"

"Support our family and community? I saw a Ladies Relief Meeting at the Methodist church—coming up—w-we could make socks and other items to send," I say, not sure how to make a difference with Aaron, but maybe—this could be something?

"Oh, yes, Mrs. Halle informed me that we're creating our own committee. We'll be meeting at the Welty's, at some point," Mother's features brightening, a glimmer of hope returning.

"That's a splendid idea," I say. "If there's one thing we Prescott women do, it's love thy neighbors."

"Oh, Emilie, we certainly do," Mother grabs my hand to give it a squeeze. "As hard as it is for men to go to war, it's even harder as women to stand by and watch."

"I'm here for you. Daughters need mothers as mothers need daughters."

"I like that," A smile tugs at Mother's lips.

"What do you think the boys are talking about?"

"Your father better be telling Henry he's not going to war," Mother eyes narrow as a cloud of fear covers over the sparkle there.

I nudge her gently. "Your tea's getting cold."

Patriotic Celebration

TRUE PATRIOTISM HATES INJUSTICE IN ITS OWN
LAND MORE THAN ANYWHERE ELSE.
~CLARENCE DARROW

MAY 1861
GETTYSBURG, PENNSYLVANIA

The white cloth is a stark contrast to the vibrant florals and checked textiles we normally hem and haw over during these meetings. Scraps of fabric lay tangled over chairs and scattered throughout Mrs. Welty's kitchen, waiting to be rolled into bandages. Mounds of muslin are spread out over the family table therein, catering to the constant snip-snip of scissors as Mrs. Welty cuts and moves more muslin from the kitchen over to Mrs. Halle's waiting sewing machine in the dining room, where the thump-thump of the sewing machine treadle is set to endless work. Once Mrs. Halle finishes the shirt, it goes to Mother's hands as she deftly sews tight buttonholes with precision, before passing it off to Mrs. Byrne who adds the finishing hems. Their rhythmic clatter of needles against thimbles adds to the cacophony, before production is moved to those of us in the parlor.

The parlor has its own song that floats on the warm spring breeze, flowing through the open windows, leading the fresh clean scent of spring throughout. The shirts land in little Jenny's lap where she proceeds to sew three pristine white buttons in place. Her work meeting the whirr of the spinning wheel used to turn wool into yarn, which is then taken up by the clicking and clacking of knitting needles belonging to Louisa and me as we make wool socks. All of this for the sake of stitching comfort into the hearts of our men, a tangible act of love amidst our growing fear of what is to come in the months ahead.

I shoo a tiny tabby out of my sewing basket as Louisa snatches an errant ball of yarn from a fluffy orange kitten's claws. Our conversation is a bit more active as Louisa and I do not have to concentrate as hard on socks as the others do on seams and sewing, which I suppose makes our task a little less dull.

"I don't know if I have the patience to knit a dozen socks. I have been knitting since I was seven, and socks are my least favorite," Louisa talks as she deftly knits together blue and gray strands as she sits in a lady's chair across from me.

"Knitting with friends is less tedious than knitting alone," I say, trying to lighten her mood. "Besides, I'd rather knit then sew shirt hems or buttonholes."

"Or cuff hems," Louisa says, "Why do they need wool in the middle of summer anyway? My fingers are going to be raw after ten pairs."

I laugh. "I have an answer for that."

"Do I really want to know?" Louisa asks, meeting my eyes with a mischievous glint.

"I read it in the paper," I say.

"Can't believe you read that dreadful bore," Louisa rolls her eyes and wrinkling her nose. "What a waste of time."

"Not really," I say. "In last week's news, there was a veteran's tip for new soldiers."

"Oh, this should be good," Louisa says, looking back to her socks.

"It recommended wool socks over cotton for marching because they prevent blisters by being soaked in tallow. Can you imagine how far you'd have to march in a day to get blisters?"

"So do we soak them now, or write a note about the tallow?" Louisa asks, scooping the orange beastie out of her basket and placing him on her chest, as she proceeds to stroke his fur. The kitten snuggles into the braid resting over her shoulder, before finding a better use for it as a toy.

"And the break is over." She untangles the ball of fluff with teeth from her now ruined braid before plopping him on the floor. The bundle of mews proceeds to pounce on his sibling, and we can't help but giggle watching them.

"Probably best to write notes," I say. "Tallow can go rancid, and I don't want to ruin a perfectly good pair of socks."

Louisa holds up the pair she just finished. "Are these big enough for Aaron?"

His name plucks a heartstring of tender memories. I swallow. "They are his favorite colors," I say. "But—you didn't—"

"Emilie, if I am going to knit socks, I'd like to have a say in who I'm giving them to," Louisa throws the pair in my direction, before reaching into her basket and launching another pair at me. "These too—for Henry."

I lift up my arms in defense at the bombardment of socks. Kittens start jumping without a chance of catching the flying bundles, but the fun and games is cut short when I hear Mother's throat clearing from the dining room. My smile wilts. I sigh and looking down at the socks now in my lap, knitting needles set aside, my throat begins to tighten with unfamiliar emotion.

"Thank you, Louisa, really," I say. "But they haven't enlisted."

"Not yet. I'm sure they will though." Louisa smiles, and then eases into an expression of regret, lips flat lining.

"What?" I say, seeing my world begin to blur as my eyes get a bit glassy.

I'm not crying. I'm fine. The country's at war, they aren't. Not, yet?

Louisa reaches for my hand, giving it a squeeze. "I'm sorry, Emilie. We'll be here for each other though. Fortunate as I am to not have brothers, I'd be happy to trade away some of my sisters, but the Army won't take them either."

We burst out laughing.

Jenny looks up with a pout, "Louisa!"

"I didn't mean you, Jenny. Mind your own business."

We both giggle again and I give a little stretch with a sigh before taking up the socks in my lap again. "I'll make sure they know these are from you." I say folding them and tucking them into my basket, under a sleeping black and white fluff ball.

Louisa casts on another set of soon to be socks. I wait, concentrating on my knit rows, so as not to interrupt her count. Once she finishes, Louisa asks, "Are you going to the ball?"

"I hope so," I say. "I don't exactly have a dress, but I plan to alter one of my mother's."

"I wish I had an extra one to give you," Louisa says. "Mine are all hand me downs."

"Hand me downs are better than showing up in a chemise and drawers," I say.

We giggle.

"Does your brother have a bevy of girls he's going to dance with?" Louisa asks, diverting her eyes back to her needles.

I pause mid-knit, smiling to myself as I watch a flush of red race up her neck.

She's not forgotten him from Christmas.

"Would you like me to make sure he signs your card?"

"Emilie, you wouldn't!" Louisa gasps. "What would he think of me?"

"He wouldn't think anything of it, after all he's Henry. He doesn't think," I say. "Besides it's payback for all the men he got to sign my dance card at Christmas."

Louisa's eyes widen, brightening her cheeks with the thrill of gossip.

"Didn't I tell you?" I ask, knowing full well I didn't.

Louisa edges forward on her seat leaning in.

"He paraded my card around the event, getting any lad he could find to sign it," I say. "Well, I say any, but in truth he chose the worst boys, but luckily, I snagged it from him, getting at least three dances with Thaddeus. You know we're courting, yes?"

A ripple of confusion forms across her brow, her eyes narrowing, her mouth forming an O. "What? I—I was told—" Louisa bites her lower lip, eyes adverting.

"Told what?" I ask, my head tilting.

"Oh god, I shouldn't listen to gossip, but—" Louisa looks to me and then her eyes dart away again.

"Louisa, what were you told and by whom?" I level my tone as a chill flashes through my body. My needles rest in my lap, less they become tools of confession, as I wait for her to answer.

Louisa's face blushes deep red. She clears her throat, gathering courage. "I heard, uhm—"

She looks down to my lap and takes my knitting needles, setting them beside her chair, a lifetime of sisterhood no doubt having given her wisdom beyond her years. Her eyes dart around to see if anyone is listening before she leans in and takes up my hands, giving them a reassuring squeeze or making sure I can't strangle her?

"How bad is it, Louisa?" I ask, squeezing her hands in turn.

"Not too terribly bad, I wouldn't think, so long as you're okay with Stephen Byrne looking forward to—" I squeeze harder. Brothers have made me stronger than I look. "Ow! Ow! Ow! I heard him tell my father and a group of friends he is courting you."

"He what!" I let go of her hands in shock, and she in turn covers her mouth as if she had just spoken in the Devil's tongue.

The snipping, the thumping, the clicking, the clacking, the whirring, and the hushed murmurs all come to an abrupt halt.

I feign a smile that all is just fine, as dandy as the springtime, and although my now audience seems unconvinced, the majority of them return to their tasks.

Looking back to Louisa, I scowl, whispering, "When did you hear this?"

"About a week ago." She squeaks. "I suspect—"

"You suspect right," I say as my fingers twist the pleats in my skirt up into knots. The truth is finally out. Stephen thinks I am going to be his betrothed and has told everyone but me.

The audacity of that man!

My glare turns back on Louisa. "He's a liar, and a cheat, and a scoundrel, and a—

"Fathead foozler?" asks Louisa, catching onto the joy of insulting.

I frown. "No, nobody uses those terms anymore. Louisa, it's the 60s."

"Sorry, heard my grandpa say them. Always wanted to try it myself."

I roll my eyes and sigh. "The point is, I am closer to being engaged to Thaddeus Marsh than I ever will be to Stephen Byrne. What a windbag."

"I am so sorry," Louisa's eyes cloud over with regret. "But I'm happy for you and Thaddeus." She attempts a smile.

"Me too," I say. "Sorry about your fingers."

Louisa shrugs. "No worse than the cramps from knitting, though with a grip like that you'd be a real danger at pinching. When my sisters annoy me, I get them right here." She says, gesturing to her arm.

"Oo, I should try that on Henry! He's always annoying me," I say.

Louisa looks crestfallen.

"Don't worry, it's just a brother sister thing. If he ever annoys you, just tell me."

We both giggle and carry on with the day gossiping, sharing secrets, and well, I just may have another means of getting to know what my dear brother Henry is up to these days.

Knitting with Louisa and talking about the upcoming ball set me to resolving the gown problem the eve before the dance. Sitting in my underpinnings, surrounded by piles of discarded multicolored dresses, I long to be that innocent twelve-year-old that can fit into my Christmas dress. It holds so many memories that it's hard to let go, but as mother says, I have blossomed, and I refuse to blossom out of this dress in public. The more dresses I try on though, the more disappointment creeps in, whispering, I guess you can't go ...

What will Thaddeus think when I tell him I won't be there?

Picking out a blue-green dress from my mother's trunk, I struggle to get into the bodice. It hangs off me—too big. Pulling it off, turning it inside out, I inspect the seams, the thought of ripping these stitches and re-sewing them blooms but then wilts.

It will take at least four days to fix it. What about the skirt?

Pulling the skirt out of the trunk, I fluff it out, watching the puff of fabric catch air and billow into a big cloud. It's plain, no ruffles or embellishments—easy enough to tailor. Sliding my hands over it, there are no holes or stains either.

"What's going on in here?" Mother asks, poking her head into my room.

"Trying to see how late I'll have to stay up to ensure I go to the ball," I say, a frown forming at the corners of my mouth. "Do you have anything else in your wardrobe?"

"This room looks like Mrs. Welty's parlor had a fabric explosion," Mother says, picking a dress off my bed, to re-fold it.

"At least it's not muslin," I say, trying to find a bodice that just might work with the skirt.

"We should donate some of these. I can't wear them, and I gather they don't fit you."

"Where did we get these?" I ask.

"I grabbed them from the plantation," Mother smirks, and gives a little shrug. "I didn't want Jenny to have them."

We giggle.

"Well," I say, "this is all I have. I figure it'll take me four days to fix it, and with your help—" My eyes look to my mother, filled to the brim with as much love and adoration as I can muster. "I might have a dress to wear?"

My eyes then shift down to the blue-green bodice in my hands.

I need a miracle.

There are sweat stains in the armholes, frayed crinkled ribbons at the back, and tattered holey lace. My heart sinks.

How will I ever feel beautiful in this?

"I better break the news to Thaddeus."

The bodice slips out of my hands.

I reach for my skirt and top to re-dress but pause when Mother's hand clasps my wrist.

"Come with me. I might have one in my wardrobe."

Eyeing the suspicious smirk forming on her lips and her outright optimism, *Didn't I just say I wasn't going? I could use some empathy here, not some mother-daughter talk about—*

Mother starts out of the room, dragging me along, not letting go until we reach my parents' room. Moments later, she has her wardrobe door open. Father's clothes exiled to the dresser drawers.

"I thought—" Her voice muffled by the yards of fabric as she sifts through her dresses.

I sit on her bed, unimpressed, beginning to rehearse exactly what I will tell Thaddeus. I look down at my hands and discover a hang nail.

"Emilie."

"Did you find something?" I ask, picking at the nail.

"I may have—"

Silence.

I look up. Hanging on the outside of the wardrobe is a dress I've never seen before, and it's stunning, like an ethereal tapestry, giving off a lunar glow when the light hits it just right. The soft cotton blue fabric is embroidered with a damask pattern of white silk, on top of which sits floral imagery stitched with a beautiful dark blue thread. Each flower is accented with a pearl where the bud should be. Then there is the neckline—ruffles made with matching soft blue ribbon, hemmed with delicate lace, will encircle my neck and shoulders.

Oh yes, here it hangs just waiting for me to grace it with my presence.

My mouth hangs open, my fingers twitch with desire to touch such perfection, feel it cascade over my body. I stand up.

"Where's your hoop?" Mother asks. "I may need to hem it to dancing length."

"Be right back!" I say, bounding out of my parent's room and into mine, grabbing the hoop, crossing the hall, and dropping it on the floor. I need no further direction as I step into the center, scoop it up, and cinch it around my waist. My arms raise overhead, and I wait.

Mother laughs before she gathers the skirt and floats it over my head.

Swish.

The curtain of fabric falls onto the hoop.

Bounce-bounce.

A few jumps and the skirt slips into place over the cage around my waist.

"I need a petticoat under this," I say.

"This will be fine; I just want to see—" She pulls the skirt from the hoop allowing it to settle in place beyond what my bouncing allows for.

"When did you make this?" I ask, admiring the details.

This took hours to make.

"You spend many hours in school and studying in your room." Mother says, as she buttons the skirt, it fits perfectly secured by two double buttons on the waistband. Waiting patiently, I turn with a gentle push from her hand.

"Is the bodice front or back lacing?" I ask, dancing a small jig, the excitement bubbling over as relief washes through me leaving behind the glistening sparkle of joy—just like my dress!

"Arm ... Arm. Hold the bodice in place."

I feel her tugging at the back of the bodice, she is lacing this together without me holding my breath or praying it will close. I feel her warm hands on my shoulders. "Ready?"

I nod, too excited to speak.

Mother turns me to the full-length mirror. Our reflections smile back at us. Hers a smile of pride, mine of pure joy at a dress she made for me, it is a perfect size, color, and fit!

Mother tugs at the sleeves of the dress positioning it so a hint of shoulder to either side is revealed. The lace collar waterfalls over my upper arms and chest. Not a hint of indecent flesh to be found. The skirt is full enough to make Ginny jealous, even without ruffles.

Mother turns to her vanity for a moment, and when she turns back, she has a matching fabric and lace neckband in hand.

"How can I thank you enough, Mother?" I ask, admiring the ensemble in the mirror.

"With a new beau, comes a new dress," she says. "Besides I wanted you to be the most beautiful girl at the ball."

I throw my arms around her. "Thank you. I'm thankful for you."

She hugs me back, but it only lasts a moment as she tries to relinquish herself from my grasp. "One last thing, the length.

Step back."

I step back, turning slowly in a circle, watching her eyes scrutinize the hem. "Are you wearing shoes?" she asks.

"No," I say. "My slippers have a tiny bit of heel."

A satisfied smile crosses her face. "I think it'll work."

The carriage rattles to a stop; the gaslights of Gettysburg flicker against the twilight sky. A knot of apprehension stabs my stomach. Tonight's fundraiser isn't just about showing support for the troops—it's a beacon of unity, a stage for Gettysburg to raise its voice and its purse for the brave men marching off to war—but there is a gnawing ache echoing. Am I turning my back on Virginia?

Anticipation hums in the air, a mix of excitement and unease. Every smile, every dance, feels like a declaration beneath the watchful gaze of the Ladies Relief Society. Henry offers me his hand, his touch a familiar anchor in this sea of uncertainty.

"That dress is beautiful." His eyes twinkle as they catch the light of the lamp. "Much better than Christmas." His grin arrives, the missing piece to his forementioned compliment.

"Thank you, brother," I say, my hand sweeping over the blue gown, inching over the skirt, no pleats to entangle my fingers in.

The air holds the sweet tang of spring, a welcome contrast to the mud and chill of the past few months. Father helps Mother out of the carriage as we stand looking up at McConaughy Hall. Stepping into the hall, we are met with a symphony of sounds. Laughter mingles with the excited chatter of citizens, a far cry from the usual stoic murmurs accompanying Gettysburg's work attire. The military band's nonsensical music while warming up blurs with laughter.

Women in vibrant gowns, a stark contrast from drab cotton dresses of everyday life, flit past, their arms overflowing with platters of baked goods. Gentlemen sporting their best suits nervously adjust cravats with calloused hands. The stark utilitarian hall has undergone a transformation. Gone are the bare walls and plain furniture. Instead, streamers of red, white, and blue adorn the room, transforming the once austere space into a vibrant hall of patriotism. The floor creaks under the weight of so many guests, each step echoing a silent pledge of support for the men and boys leaving for war.

To my left is a table decorated with a red cloth, hosting neat tidy rows of bookmark-like dance cards. The chords and tassels are red, white, and blue. A short pencil rests next to each one. Picking a red chorded card, I slip the chord over my wrist. Attached to me, there is no way Henry will get ahold of it this time. It flutters as we move to an empty table at the other end of the hall.

Henry drops my arm once we arrive, turning to leave.

"Henry," I say, watching him turn back. "Aren't you going to escort me, to fill my dance card?" A small pout forms at my bottom lip.

"Where's Thaddeus?" Henry asks, looking around for the hero of the hour to save him from this daunting task.

"Haven't seen him." I say, "Oh, by the way—" I pull on his sleeve, soften my gaze, and widen my eyes just a bit more, using my talents as a little sister to beg.

"What now?" Henry asks, the impatience is evident in his eyes.

"When you find Louisa Welty, will you give her a dance?" I ask, "Please?"

Henry's eyes narrow, but his hesitation says he is at least considering my request. Finally, he offers a counter, "Clean the stalls tomorrow?"

"No, I have school in the morning," I say, offended by the thought of tonight's splendor juxtaposed with tomorrow's shabby work wear and manure. "I'll collect the eggs in the morning, before school. Be a dear and just put a smile on a girl's face, please?"

"I'll think about it," Henry says, disappearing into the crowd before I can ask another favor of him.

I watch him leave, then look around for Louisa. Maybe I can pull a "Henry" and just sign his name, but I wouldn't want to embarrass Louisa if Henry stood her up. Just then, a scent of bergamot and lime wafts past my nose, eliciting an uplifting smile as a shiver runs down my back.

His proximity warms me, and a deep whisper thrills me. "You look breathtaking this evening."

Turning to face him, I'm met with those deep blue, smiling eyes and his strong jaw under a close-cropped beard. The hair atop his head, though, refuses to play nice. My hand reaches up to fix stray wisps, until he reaches out to catch my hand, clasp it, and entangle our fingers together. He gives my hand a squeeze and follows it up with his signature wink. A tingle courses through me.

"Looks like you are ready to dance this evening," He leads me into a spin before pulling me back to him.

"The dance card is open; would you like to sign every line?" I say, feeling dizzy and dazed as a flood of pink races over my cheeks.

His eyebrow arches at this, a glimmer of sapphire sparks in his eyes, and a rumbling chuckle creeps up his throat. "You'd like that wouldn't you?"

"I would," I whisper. Thaddeus guides the dance card off my wrist, pencil at the ready. He looks from me to the card, and back, teasing me with pauses as he scribbles. "All right so the first dance goes to Honest Abe, the second to that guy over there—"

I give his arm a playful swat and he laughs. "All right, all right, if you insist, I'll put the president on all of them."

His grin broadens as he finishes writing and hands the dance card back to me, his name scribbled in every imaginable way throughout the booklet. *Thad ... Thaddeus ... Mr. Marsh ... T. Marsh ... Thaddeus Marsh ... Emilie's one and only.*

I giggle and look up, but his attention is redirected toward my father.

"Mr. Prescott, would you like a dance with your daughter?" he asks. "She has room right about ..."

Father looks at him, saying, "Well, I was hoping you would fill in for me. I am distracted by this beautiful woman."

Mother swats Father with her fan. We laugh.

"Maybe her brother would like to fill in for you, if you can't keep up," says Father.

Now it is Thaddeus's turn to look shocked.

Our jovial scene is interrupted by a call to order by the master of ceremonies, a tall man dressed in a military uniform.

"Ladies and gentlemen—" The crowd hushes. "We are all gathered here tonight to help our country battle over a disagreement between the states that is threatening to tear our united nation apart."

A chill settles over me. Bumps along my arms and legs rise in protest.

"... tonight, the newly formed Home Guard along with our lovely Ladies Relief Society hope to raise money so all our boys going off to this war will have clothes on their backs, socks on their feet, and food in their bellies. Please consider opening your purses to support our boys in blue ..."

A sudden unease follows the chill—*what about Virginia?* Thaddeus's other hand is at my lower back as his fingers remain entwined in mine. His silent support, willing me strength. I squeeze his hand—*thank you*. The warmth of his body seeps into my shoulder, his intoxicating scent blankets me into a secure bubble.

"... so tonight, have fun, enjoy the dance, and merriment as our boys will be forever grateful for all you have to offer." The Master of Ceremonies finishes his speech, as clapping and cheers burst forth from the still silence of the room. "Let me introduce our dance master tonight ..."

The buildup of anticipation and worry threatens to overwhelm me. I breathe deep, allowing all of it to pass. We don't know what is going to happen in the future, but tonight, I plan to enjoy this time like no other.

The caller announces a Grand March, and the evening is off to a great start. Thaddeus rubs the small of my back and leans down to me. His breath warms my ear. "May I request the first dance from the most beautiful girl in the room?"

My answer is, of course, "Yes!"

The floor fills with couples parading around the room with poised steps and the swishing of skirts. A smile settles onto my face, the joy of such movement seems to melt away the worries hiding in the depths of my mind. Thaddeus and I are separated for most of the March as the partners change hands time and again, but as the next number, the Quadrille starts up, we are reunited with each other.

Thaddeus takes my hand as we line up in squares of four couples. His hand warms mine as we look forward, counting silently to ourselves, while making faces at the other couples to see who will mess up first. We briefly turn to each other—a bow and curtsy, and it doesn't take long before the rest of the dance becomes a blur. Our hands touch and fall away as each couple takes their turn in the square. The music fades away, we turn to each other, a final bow and curtsy before he escorts me off the floor.

"I like the Quadrille," I say, as he steers me toward the refreshment table.

The crowd thins around us, and Thaddeus stops short. I look up to see Stephen standing there, staring in our direction. He is dressed in his Sunday best, if one were to consider the pub afterward. No tie, his neckline hangs open. My feet feel like they are stuck in invisible mud.

"I really don't need anything." My throat suddenly dries up as a knot in my stomach clenches tighter than my corset. My hand goes to Thaddeus's arm, pulling him back. "Let's ignore him."

"I am right here, beside you." Thaddeus squeezes my hand. "I won't let anything happen to you."

My eyes search for his, the promise spoken in the sparkle right at the center of his twin sapphire gaze.

I take a deep breath, "All right," I say, "But—"

Thaddeus shushes me. "Come on, Emilie."

I follow his confident steps toward the refreshment table. Stephen smiles at me, his eyes lighting up briefly then dim in a haze.

"Nice of you to come this evening, Stephen," Thaddeus shakes his hand.

"Pleasant evening. Look at these good folks ready to support the cause and keep this country together." Stephen gestures to the room before turning back to us. "So, Thad, what say you and I sign up, get these rebs back in their place, and get on with life back at the farm? Then I can beat Mr. Locher at his own made-up war stories." His eyes are red, and a faint waft of whiskey tickles my nose.

"All in good time," Thaddeus pats Stephen on his back.

"We could capture a few of 'em. Can't be any more difficult than snaring rabbits. Make heroes of ourselves all in one go, and then this celebration won't be for nothing," Stephen tosses back a lemonade in a quick gulp, he blinks as his stare shifts to me—and lasts a bit too long.

My lips purse to keep my fury from erupting and my insults from spewing.

"Don't worry, no harm will come to your family unless they're rebs. Then they're fair game—dead rabbits."

A sharp gasp escapes me, my eyes widen and then narrow at his audacity. My hand drops from Thaddeus, my arm swinging back—

Thaddeus catches my wrist.

My chest rises and falls trying to steady my breath.

"You're awfully quiet there. What's wrong? Finally learn your lesson from the alley?" His hazel glare grows dark, suffocating me, causing the hairs on the back of my neck to bristle. "Glad you understand—women are meant to be seen, not heard," Stephen sneers.

My left hand flies up and a sting ripples through my palm as I slap Stephen.

Well worth it.

Stephen grunts, his hand coming up to his face. Then he grins, licks his lips, and takes a step toward me.

Thaddeus pushes me behind him, shielding me from Stephen. His jaw is clenched. His fists are up.

Stephen returns the stance in kind, left fist guarding, right fist making the first punch. However, because of the alcohol swimming through him, he's less stable on his feet and slower with his movements.

Thaddeus sees the hit coming a mile away, blocks Stephen's fist with his left arm, and his right arm crosses over to seize Stephen's left. He then yanks it around his back and upward, forcing Stephen to bend over and putting Thaddeus in control.

"Outside, now!" Thaddeus pushes Stephen toward the door.

Stephen's eyes widen. He winces in pain as Thaddeus tightens his grip.

"Emilie, back to the table."

I blink, never having seen Thaddeus like this, but I sure do want to watch what happens next. What other marks outside of the red handprint emblazoned on Stephen's cheek will Thaddeus reward him with?

"Emilie—" My name comes out in warning.

I sigh and nod, turning away, back toward the table my family has claimed for the night.

Why do boys get to have all the fun?

At the table, I sit down, my arms crossed with a momentary pout as I watch the men disappear past the doors of the hall. I look to my mother who is smiling as she watches the dances. It doesn't take long, though, for her to acknowledge my stare.

"Was that Stephen, Thaddeus was with?" Mother asks.

"Yes," I say turning back to the dancers on the floor. They are floating together in a waltz. My mind steadily counts along with the music.

One-two-three, *I hope he decks Stephen,* one-two-three, *makes him pay dearly,* one-two-three, *wipes that smarmy smirk right off*

his mug. Oh, but dear Lord, please don't let either of them get ar-
rested.

A flash of memories one after the other fuels his anger—the rumors Stephen's spread about her ankles while atop her mare, the rumor he's heard that Stephen's telling everyone he's court-ing her, her broken spirit lying on the ground of the alley— It gathers, cumulates, and is unleashed by Thaddeus's fury. Every fiber of his being screams at him to make Stephen pay for in-flicting Emilie's pain.

"Time for a lesson in manners," Thaddeus turns Stephen around and slamming him against the building, delivering a quick jab to his gut.

Stephen folds over and responds with a wide swing to the ribs.

Thaddeus grunts, having forgotten to keep his elbows tucked in, but he doesn't give Stephen time for a second hit. Instead, he grabs Stephen by his throat, and lets his fist do the rest of the talking.

The first strike aims for Stephen's nose, but Stephen turns his head, and his ear takes the blow.

Anticipating his second strike, Stephen moves his head again.

Thaddeus's knuckles clip his ear, smashing into the brick. A grunt of pain surfaces from Thaddeus, but it's nothing his adrenaline can't take. "GOD ALMIGHTY!"

Stephen chuckles, "Why don't you fight like a real man, in-stead of pinning me against the wall. Too afraid I'll win?"

Thaddeus let's go of Stephen's throat.

Stephen comes off the wall with an upper cut. It turns out a few hits is enough to sober him up and get him back to being light on his feet.

"Son of a—" Thaddeus staggers back, grabbing his jaw as Stephen bounces about him, showboating.

"Prick," murmurs Thaddeus, putting his fists back up, watching, waiting, reserving his energy.

Stephen circles him trying to land jabs and get him to put his guard down. He manages a few hits, but nothing Thaddeus can't brush off.

Come on, tire out you big oaf.

The more Stephen moves, the faster he becomes, the more jabs he gets. To the arms, to the shoulders. Stephen's toying with him.

"I thought you wanted to fight like a man, seems to me like you fit in with those rabbit rebs," Thadeus says.

He drops his arms slightly, relaxing, waiting for the fight to begin. He doesn't expect the hit right underneath the sternum, which sends him to his knees, or the hand that comes to grip a fistful of his hair forcing him to face the next fist that will seal his fate.

The waltz ends with a final chord as the dancers take their leave and the musicians take their first break.

Louisa and Henry approach our table. Both with a smile and pink cheeks, though I imagine Louisa's complexion is from more than the exertion of dancing. It suits her though, matches her bright eyes just as she matches my brother's strides, her arm cradled in his elbow, which he pats.

"I see my brother has followed through with his promise to me," I say.

Henry nods his head and looks to the table of ladies as a whole as he ushers Louisa into a seat. "May I get you a lemonade?"

"Yes, please," Louisa beams with joy.

Henry nods toward Louisa and then looks to me. "Where's Thaddeus?"

"He's outside, teaching Stephen some manners," I say, my expression souring.

"I see. Louisa darling, hold that thought on the lemonade. I think my beloved sister's beau may need my assistance," Henry takes my friend's hand and kissing the back of it.

I stare at him in shock.

Darling? What book did he get that out of?

I've never seen him act like such a gentleman.

Who is this woman, and what has she done with my brother?

My brother, who doesn't even take the time to admonish my expression with a tease, makes quick, long strides away from the table before disappearing out of the hall.

Henry's eyes are drawn to the fight in the desolate street like a mosquito to a flame, and he's keen to get a bite of the trouble when he notices it's Stephen about to get the final say. He charges forward, bull rushes the man, but Stephen doesn't let go of Thaddeus, and they all go tumbling down in a pile of muscle and limbs.

"Oh man, what the hell?" Stephen says, trying to get back up. "This isn't about enlisting, is it?"

"Don't even think about moving," says Henry.

Thaddeus blinks and then grins. "Good of you to join us, Henry. And no, it's not about enlisting. Stephen's just learning that harming women is not gentlemanly."

"So, I take it you were playing the woman's role just now?" asks Henry.

Thaddeus grunts saying, "Do you want to hear about how he almost struck your sister, or how he almost raped her?"

"Is that why she had bruises on her neck?" Henry turns to Stephen.

"Nothing she didn't deserve to get."

Henry takes Stephen by the arm and hauls him up. Thaddeus scrambles to his feet to help him. The men disappear around the corner into the shadows of a side alley.

Henry shoves Stephen against the cold brick wall.

Stephen stumbles back, his head hitting the brick with a sickening thud. His hand goes to his head, his eyes cross in pain.

Henry lashes out with a right hook. The blow connecting, sending Stephen reeling. A bewildered yelp escapes Stephen's lips as he tastes blood.

"I thought we were friends, Henry."

"You overstepped your bounds." Henry's voice is steady despite his taut nerves egging him to punch the man again. The twitch in his hand is ready to deliver.

"I never overstepped anything," Stephen reaches for his flask. Henry plucks it from his hand.

"What? Give me that." Stephen reaches for it again.

"No, you're going to feel every bit of emotion you forced Emilie to face in that alley," Thaddeus delivers a punch once more to Stephen's gut, causing him to double over retching, spitting.

"Did you rape my sister?" Henry demands, his level tone giving way to anger.

"No, we never got that far, and if we had—"

Henry throws the flask down, rushing Stephen to deliver a rapid succession of punches not caring where they hit so long as they land. "You son of a bitch."

Thaddeus' hand keeps Stephen held fast against the wall.

Henry's emotions tumble out, inflicting on Stephen the pain he can only imagine his sister felt. The guilt of not being able to protect her strengthening each strike.

Have I failed as a brother?

Stephen holds up his hands.

"Come on, wait—wait," Stephen finally manages to cover his battered and bloody face with one arm.

"I don't know what she told you, but I was just teaching her a lesson. I didn't violate her. She's still a virgin, ripe for the taking."

Henry pulls back his fist.

"Hold on!" Stephen says, fear creepin at the edge of his shaky voice.

Thaddeus holds Henry back

"I just wanted to scare her, You know, teach her this is a man's world, and she can't say shit about it."

"Oh yeah, well you're fixing to be the one that can't say shit about it because I'm going to close your mouth forever," says Henry.

Thaddeus lets him go, and Henry delivers the final blows, laying Stephen out flat in the alley.

Louisa and I talk between dances, while waiting for Thaddeus and Henry to return. Two dances go by before Louisa taps me on the arm, pulling my attention back from a couple arguing in the corner.

"They're back," she whispers, leaning into me.

I look up to see two men striding across the floor, heads held high and confident. What happened to their clothes? Their hair! There's blood!

Thaddeus' blue eyes meet mine along with one of the goofiest of smiles. His eyebrows rise up and, giving a pat on Henry's back, the two of them stride over in three quick steps.

With his hand outstretched he says, "I believe I owe you a dance." His voice is deep and mesmerizing—and wait, no!

"Thaddeus, Henry, what happened?" I ask.

Henry shrugs. "We tripped."

I frown and look behind them to the door they came from. "And where's Stephen?"

"That's who we tripped over." Thaddeus smiles.

The boys snicker and exchange some sort of congratulations between them as Louisa, and I stare at them in disbelief.

"And how did he get on the ground?" asks Louisa.

We all stare at her in disbelief, but Henry grins and scratches the back of his head. "He was drunk; he fell. Come on, let's get that punch you were wanting earlier, yeah?"

"You mean lemonade?"

"Yeah, that." Henry, extends his arm to Louisa.

I briefly notice his swollen knuckles but say nothing of it. Instead, I look to Thaddeus with concern. "Are you all right?'

"Never felt better." Thaddeus, beams.

"You don't look better."

"I'll be fine, Emilie. Besides, it's not like I could ever hold a candle to the most beautiful girl in the room." He extends his hand once more, that grin of his playing on his lips, beckoning me to lay aside my worries and dance away with him.

My hand floats up to meet his, a light grasp on his swollen, bruised knuckles as he sweeps me out to the floor for a waltz.

The dance allows us to be close for a conversation. The strength of his arms around me fortifies me, protects me from the outside world, securing me to him. Our hearts race together from the exertion—or is it our closeness? The deep timber of his voice and feeling of the heartbeat in his chest. *Is this intimacy? A thrilling flutter answers—Oh yes! And I never want to stop feeling this with him.*

"So, you won't be seeing Stephen again for a very long time."

My head snaps up, peering into his eyes, watching him.

"What actually happened?" I look down at his hand, a bruise is peeking out on his second and third knuckle.

"Is he still breathing?" I ask, not wanting to say it.

"Yes," he says, "It's just a lesson, not a hanging."

"Well, it could have been. You realize—"

"No more questions. I told you; he will be all right—in a day or three." Thaddeus's voice softens. His shoulders relax a little as his hand gives mine a squeeze in reassurance.

"If he wants to enlist, I won't mind you know, but I'd rather you stay right here with me." I wiggle my eyebrows at him. He breaks into a grin, and pink rushes to his ears.

Thaddeus pulls me closer. Feeling the weight of worry settle between us, he takes a deep breath. "Em, you know it'll be only a matter of time." My finger goes to his lips shutting off his voice. I can't bear to hear it.

"What about us?" I question.

"I see us together for a long time, with a farm, children, and—" Thaddeus stops and clears his throat. "Do you want to share that with me?"

"I do," I say, lost in the count of the dance, falling deeper into his eyes, as our souls timidly touch, in that thrilling moment.

"Good, then I hope you'll wait for me."

I sigh and look away, not wanting to think of it—only wanting to be with him.

"I can't wait to steal another kiss from you," Thaddeus whispers, as he dips me over his leg, our faces inches from each other.

I gasp, giggle, feel his breath mingle with mine. Just a little more, my lips ache.

"I know," I say, with a mischievous nose wrinkle, and a dare in my eye.

Setting me back onto my feet, our fingers slide together, dancing as our feet once waltzed. Thaddeus holds my gaze in his as he turns my hand, raising it to his lips, our eyes locked, souls waving at each other.

He blinks.

His warm kiss seals again the desire between us.

I sigh.

We come out of our solitude only when another couple bumps into us. They mumble their 'excuse me' and 'sorry', as they flow past us.

My hand still in his, we walk to the table following the last dance of the evening.

I look around, confused, as everyone gathers their coats, waves good-bye, and files out of the hall taking the jovial mood with them. The band is packing up their instruments.

The mood of the space shifts from jovial to somber as the room quiets, footsteps echoing across the wood floor. Mother places my cloak over my shoulders. As Thaddeus pulls me along, I look back just as a patriotic banner flutters to the floor. A wave of finality washes over me.

Family Returns

BUT FRIENDSHIP IS THE BREATHING ROSE,
WITH SWEETS IN EVERY FOLD.
~OLIVER WENDELL HOLMES

MAY 1861
GETTYSBURG, PENNSYLVANIA

The dark halls echo, the sound bouncing off walls, doors, and glass. Sarah's and my footsteps sound like faint whispers continuing the conversations left by the children who were let out early for summer break. Everyone's gone home to plant gardens, tend fields, and say good-bye to loved ones. How different will they all look when we come back next fall? We step out into the bright sun and walk toward the stables.

"Just a few more days, and the exam will be done," Sarah hooks her arm in mine. "I can't wait to never look at another book—until fall!"

"I plan to read for pleasure," I say. "My library is waiting for me. Just think, reading for pleasure. No tests to follow."

Sarah stops to look at me, a faraway look in her sky-blue eyes. "I can't remember the last book I read for fun. Hey, do you want to walk to the post office with me? Maybe there's a letter from Aaron?"

"I suppose," I say, loving the idea of her company. "I'll pick up Starlight on the way back."

We continue to the post office. The trees are leafing out, starting to add shade to the sparsely foliage-lined street.

As we turn the corner, Sarah pulls on my sleeve, saying, "Oo, look at all the people at the courthouse."

We see couples standing, milling about, waiting, and talking. The men appear dressed in Sunday suits and the ladies' dresses are the telltale fancy gowns for marriage, as no woman would dare dress this way on a typical day of the week. Some of the women are holding small bouquets of lilacs in their hands.

"Are they all getting married?" I ask.

"There's another train of recruits going out at the end of the week. I heard Thomas talking about it the other night."

My eyebrow arches. "Well, we can walk on that side of the street to ask if you're so bold." I nudge Sarah, who giggles and yanks our linked arms, pulling me across the street.

I shouldn't have asked; then again, would it have made a difference if I hadn't?

We barge into this group of couples headlong, and with Sarah in charge, we soon learn all there is to know—just as a few of them learn more than they probably ever hoped to know about Thomas. Regarding the couples that don't wish to talk, we weave in and out of the crowd, eavesdropping when allowed. Somehow Sarah always catches what is being said aloud.

As Sarah pulls me into the crowd, I overhear a man hugging a woman, saying, "Be sure to plant a large garden this year. I don't know how sparse food will become."

"Who is going to help me weed it?" She asks. "There will be no one left after you leave."

We casually slip in and around others, as I overhear another man speaking, "Remember this is temporary. I think it best to pick up a job while I'm gone. I don't know how often or how much of my pay I can send to support you."

Meanwhile Sarah has met a lovely young woman whose name I've all but forgotten and time is ticking onward. Before we know it, we won't make it to the post office before it closes.

"Sarah—"

"I'm hoping myself for a wedding in August with my dearest sweetest fiancé Thomas. I hear August is a month for good luck. Oh, it's such a shame you two can't have an August wedding, but if you could, what kind of flowers would you—"

"Sarah!"

Sarah pauses and looks at me without the faintest clue as to why I may be interrupting her. "What?"

"The post office. Do you still plan to go?"

"Oh, yes. Oh, that's right. Right you are, Emilie. This is my friend Emilie, Emilie Prescott. She is courting Thadd—"

"Yes, and I do hope you two have a wonderful wedding and a happy marriage. Come along now, Sarah," I say, it now being my turn to tug her with our linked arms.

Once we break through the crowd, Sarah and I take up walking on the other side of the street. A boon to the various couples' ears, I imagine.

Sarah turns to me. "They're all having quick weddings before the men go off to war." Triumphantly, she bobs her head, feeling proud of her antics.

"You don't say?" I ask, a smirk playing on my lips. "I have to say, that crowd is holding more men than I have seen in the past two weeks," I add.

"Or that I've seen in church," says Sarah.

"Yes, but doesn't it alarm you that there is a train leaving every few weeks?"

"Don't worry Emilie. We have plenty of old men and boys to protect us."

Sarah's words leave an impression in my brain. Will we truly be without men to protect us? Looking back at the couples outside the courthouse, I wonder, *Should I marry Thaddeus before he leaves? Are we ready for marriage?*

No one's waiting in line at the post office. Sarah gathers her mail, and I stand waiting to see if there is a letter for me.

"I'm sorry Miss Prescott," Mr. Buehler, the middle-aged postmaster says. "I have no letters yet."

"Thank you, Mr. Buehler. I'll check back another day," I say taking my leave.

Pushing through the door, Sarah is waiting for me, thumbing through the letters.

Sarah looks at me with a hopeful tilt of her head and wide eyes, waiting for me to confirm her prediction.

I shake my head, disheartened. "No mail for me."

"Tomorrow. I know the letter will arrive tomorrow." Sarah's optimism is infectious.

We walk back up the street. Sarah leaves me to fetch Starlight as she continues to her home a half-block away. The courthouse appears emptier than before, with one lone woman pacing in front of the building, looking and waiting. She carries a small bouquet of flowers in her hand, looking forlorn, gazing up one side of the street and down the other. The strange stillness around her sends a chill up my spine. What is to become of Gettysburg's citizens when its strength and security leave?

Starlight finally decided to hurry as soon as she saw the driveway to home. A lazy walk turns into an animated trot, and it is all I can do but hold her back from a gallop once she sees the barn. Briefly, I notice an oil cloth covered wagon but think little of it when Thaddeus greets me with a wave.

"What took you so long?" Thaddeus asks, already having her lead rope in hand.

"I stopped by the post office. Still waiting on a letter from Aaron."

"I see." He hands me the lead rope. We walk Starlight into the barn. She immediately starts looking for food, pawing impatiently, neighing, and protesting as it takes a second longer than she desires.

Thaddeus fetches some hay and alfalfa to put in her stall and a scoop and a half of grain for her bucket.

Not a moment goes by when she isn't dancing in her cross ties as I go to untack her.

"How was your day?" I ask, pulling off her saddle and blanket, her bridle already slung over my shoulder.

Thaddeus takes the tack and puts it up.

I pick up the towel and begin to rub her down.

"It went well enough," he says. "Nothing new to report. Are you putting her out back or in the stall for the night?"

"Out back," I say, "but put her in her stall to eat, and I'll come get her later after dinner." Looking to him, I see a suspicious grin on his face and ask, "What's going on? It looks like you want to say something."

"Of course, you didn't tell me about your day." Thaddeus follows me around Starlight as I start to comb out the wood shaving and twigs and—

How does she accumulate this much debris between the stall and home?

"Oh, well, it was interesting." I look back at him, almost as if I am afraid he will disappear.

"How so? The children didn't want to leave for summer break?" Thaddeus asks, a grin breaking out on his face, a wink interrupting the glint in his eye.

"Not that," I say. "When Sarah and I walked to the post office, we saw couples waiting outside the courthouse."

"Really? That's odd, don't you think?"

"Well, I thought so," I say, "until Sarah told me that Thomas told her another bunch of recruits are leaving in a few days." I bite my lip.

Do I dare voice what has been plaguing my mind since the ride home?

I set down the comb, take Starlight's lead, and unhook her from the crossties. I'm not sure why I use the lead. This mare practically drags me into her stall, or at least halfway, as her rump sticks out in the aisle. All she needs is a bucket.

"Starlight, all the way in."

I hear a snort in protest as I push at her hindquarters.

She tells me exactly how she feels about it with a pile of manure before complying.

Thaddeus laughs and goes to get a shovel, as I unhook the lead rope, tie it to the stall door for later access, and close it.

"Here you are, madam." he hands me the shovel.

"Awe, what a gentleman."

"I do what I can."

I begin to clean up the mess of my darling best friend, when I feel his arms slide around my middle. Thaddeus closes in on me.

"Please stop me if I am too forward," Thaddeus's breath warms my ear, his strong arms pulling me to his side. The shovel clinks before I manage to prop the handle up against the barn wall.

"As long as you don't think less of me," I say, turning toward him and putting my head on his shoulder.

"I wouldn't dream of it, even when you have hay in your hair, and are shoveling manure," Thaddeus grins. He's hot—there's a bit of sweat beneath his shirt. What little of our skin is exposed sticks to each other, limbs kissing.

My eyes swim into the depths of his blues, wishing some other part of us could—

"I can't stop thinking about it," he murmurs.

I look up at him, his blue eyes roiling with passion. I can feel it, the tingling warm sensation rushing through me. All the etiquette books say what I'm doing is wrong, but with him, it's so right.

Why does society want me to deny my feelings and make him pretend he doesn't exist? What do they know?

Our eyes connect and in that moment in time, his lips draw closer to mine, my arm reaches around his neck pulling him in to taste the sweet sensation of his kiss, the kiss I miss, long for, and have dreamt about. A sweet sound of longing escapes me, as he pulls me in, deepens it.

Feeling a rush of heat from him, I ask, my lips brushing his with each word, "Do you want to marry me?"

When my own words dawn on me, I pull away and stumble back. "I'm sorry, I didn't mean to imply—"

Thaddeus's eyes widen at our sudden distance, "Watch the—"

I step in Starlight's manure and the shovel that holds it, the handle of the shovel popping up to *thunk* me on the back of my head, "Ow!"

Is this God's punishment for indulgence?

Thaddeus stands there with his mouth slack. "I shouldn't have. I'm sorry."

We stand apart, looking at each other, confused.

"So, you didn't want to kiss me?" I work on using the side of the shovel to clean off my boot, feeling very foolish.

What have I done?

"No, yes, I mean ..." Thaddeus stumbles over his words. "It was my fault, I shouldn't have—but Emilie ... God, you drive me crazy."

I can feel the frustration in his eyes as he watches me.

If I can just get this bit off—ugh, it stinks.

"Look, I didn't mean to—" I say. "I'm not that kind of girl, I mean—" I pause and look at him. "I like you more than I should." I bite my lip, hoping against all hope he does not think less of me.

Thaddeus turns away from me, walks over to the wall of the barn, stares at it, kicks it, takes a deep breath, and begins to hop.

I jump as he spits out a word of pain. "It's made of oak, you know."

"I know, I just—"

We both stare at each other for a long moment, him holding his foot, me feeling the knot grow on the back of my head.

"You don't think less of me because I kissed you just now?" Thaddeus's face is a deep red. He's breathing hard, unsure of this situation.

"So long as you don't think less of me for kissing you back?" I ask.

We both laugh.

"How's your head?"

"Better than my boot. How's your foot?"

"Nothing I can't handle."

"What do we do now?" I ask.

"I think we should go inside." His boyish grin returning, "Forgot to tell you, I have a surprise for you."

"A surprise?" My eyes widen, a giddiness bursting from my chest, stealing all the remaining anxiety with it.

"Sorry, no—um what I meant to say is, there's a surprise for you." Thaddeus looks at the ceiling, then the floor with what I believe is an attempt to gather his wits, as he shifts his weight to his better foot. Then his gaze returns to me, that deep blue appreciating gaze.

"So, should we not touch for a while?" I ask. "I mean since it is hard for us—I mean, me—or us to control our feelings?"

Thaddeus clears this throat, considering for a long time.

I wait.

His deep blue eyes look into mine. He sucks in his breath.

Biting my lip.

I can't interrupt this time, I just can't.

Blinking.

"I never want to stop touching you—" he says. "But, I will not be responsible for ruining your reputation, so—"

I feel the pain of this decision and offer, "How about we keep our distance for now. At least—until these feelings subside?"

I have no idea what I am saying, and I don't believe it either.

"That's a plan for now." He nods. "I'm not sure it will last, but if we stay here too much longer discussing it, they will come looking for us." Thaddeus's jaw is firm with resolution. If he is feeling an ounce of what I am right now, his resolve is as fragile as a sandcastle when the tide rolls in, waiting to disintegrate at any moment.

"All right, shall we go inside?"

Thaddeus gives me a stiff nod. We turn, walking the length of the barn side by side, our fingers touching, wrapping around each other's until we separate at the door. Our hands separate with a longing for each other's warmth. Sliding apart, his hands delve into his pockets and mine tuck into the folds of my skirt for now. I walk ahead of him as he opens the door to the house.

An odd stillness surrounds us as we enter the kitchen. The table is set with six plates, a fancier setting than usual. I open and close the warmer, lift lids to pots and peek into the oven and on the stove. Dinner is still cooking.

Well, then where is the family who intends to eat it?

I turn back to Thaddeus.

He stands patiently behind me, smiling, waiting.

"Do we have company?" I ask. "I mean, other than you?"

A slight nod of his chin, the glint in his eyes return. "Might I suggest checking the parlor?"

We venture down the hall. The parlor doors are closed.

I turn back to him with a scowl on my face.

He grins back at me, an arch to his brow.

I pull open the pocket doors to a room full of family, and—

The men in the room are all standing.

"Seth? Aaron? Aaron!" I rush into my brother's arms, throwing myself at him. "Oh, you made it home!"

Aaron wraps me up in a bear hug, trying to squeeze the life out of me. Picking me up off the ground for a moment, my cheek scratches against his face and neck.

"Did you miss me, dear sister?" Aaron asks, his deep voice rumbling in my ear, before he spins me around and sets me down.

"More than you know. I have been worried sick about you." I swat him on the shoulder. "Did you forget how to write?"

"And spoil the surprise? Look, I brought Seth home to see you," Aaron says, as if this will make up for his lack of correspondence.

It's a start. We'll discuss letter-writing later.

I turn to my longtime friend, a brother at heart.

"Seth!" I say outstretching my arms to him.

"No, Miss Emilie." Seth's arms outstretch to stop my advances. "It ain't proper with your beau—I mean, it ain't proper no how."

"It's no big deal, really but— All right." I stop in front of him holding out my hand hoping at least he will give it a quick grasp.

He hesitates as he reaches for me, but for a brief moment his hand encloses over mine. It's calloused from work, large like his father's. Even his shoulders are broader. He stands much taller than me now—muscular. My childhood friend is now a man, as I am a woman. No wonder he didn't want to hug me.

I give him a quick squeeze of reassurance then let go.

"I'm happy to see you. How're Martha and Big Jim?"

A flicker of pain appears in his eye, but it is soon covered by a smile.

"They miss you bad, Miss Emilie, bad as I do." Seth looks away from me.

I turn to Thaddeus, pulling him into the circle of family saying, "Seth, this is Thaddeus—Thaddeus, Seth. He's my other brother, from my other mother. We grew up together. Seth was my first student."

A big smile breaks out on Seth's face, his eyes light up at the memory. "She taught me how to write the letters and read 'em too. Haven't been the same since. Even got me teaching Ma and working with some of the children too."

My heart catches when he mentions teaching the plantation children.

"Pleasure to meet you, Seth," Thaddeus, reaches out to shake Seth's hand. Once again there is hesitation from Seth, and I wonder if he thinks such an invitation may be a trap. Our eyes meet, and I give him a reassuring nod, so they shake.

There are smiles all around, and I notice Seth's shoulders swell with a bit of pride.

"It's great to hear you're teaching as well. I'm sure you and Emilie will have lots to catch up on. But, why not all the children?" asks Thaddeus.

A heavy silence falls over the room and Thaddeus looks at me, a question in his eye, wondering if he has overstepped.

"Because slaves ain't allowed to write, read, or teach, Mister Thaddeus. Some of the fine folk I work with, well, they worry what might happen to their families if they be caught." Seth was never one to shy away from such truths. But then again, I suppose his life does not offer the luxury of ignorance.

A flicker of pain flashes through Seth's deep chocolate eyes.

Thaddeus swallows, glancing from me to Seth, then back to me. "Emilie, it sounds like you've been teaching a long time then?"

I feel his hand at the small of my back, warm and encouraging, but is it for me or for himself?

"Yeah, Miss Emilie. Aaron told me you got some other youngins you be minding. Boy, do I wish I was they."

"And I see we aren't done with your elocution lessons, Seth," I say with a smirk.

"But you still understood me. Besides, we all know what happens if I sounds too smart. Say, Miss Emilie, when me and my folks get here, you think I could be a teacher like you?" Seth asks.

"I don't see why not," I say.

"Well, I think that's a swell idea," says Henry. "There are lots of free blacks who could use an education. Come to think of it, I don't recall seeing any black kids at your school, do you, Emilie?"

"No, unfortunately not. But a black school would be a fine institution to start here in Gettysburg, and who better to start one than our Seth," I say, feeling pride swell my heart. "I will help you. Somehow, we will find a way together, Seth."

"You saying 'I will' instead of 'I'll' for my ears?" asks Seth.

"We all have to start somewhere," I say with a tease and a wink.

He smiles back at me, and we exchange looks of mutual appreciation for our long-time friendship.

Father clears his throat. "But until then, be careful, Seth. I know my brother's temper." Father's warning is one we are all too aware of, save for Thaddeus, bless him.

The conversation quiets as we all turn to Seth, holding our

breath in double-edged encouragement for his bravery. The shackles of slavery are like a thunder cloud in the sky, the crack of lightning the telltale sign of an overseer's whip.

"He ain't caught me yet," Seth says, a bit of mischief tugging at the corner of his lip. "Besides, ain't got no time as of late. We been workin long hours to get the crops in. Makes a man too bone tired by the end of the day to even speak but not eat."

"Oh, how I miss Martha's cooking. I mean, we do our best to replicate her recipes, but sometimes we just don't have the seasonings," I say.

There is a rumble of agreement throughout the room.

Mother clears her throat. "Why don't we all eat, before dinner overcooks."

"Splendid idea," Aaron says. "I've sure missed your meals Mother."

"Mmhmm, don't act like you weren't spoiled by Martha's cooking," I say back to Aaron.

"Right—right you are, Emilie." His hesitation didn't go unnoticed. "But my stomach doesn't care who cooks it, so long as its good food."

We add another plate and squeeze another chair into our table arrangement. Mother and I set out a scrumptious spread of ham, potatoes baked in a cream sauce, green beans with bacon, a basket of warm rolls accompanied with butter, and pickles. Everyone stands around the table save for one—Seth is missing. Looking around, we notice him in the doorway, a worried look etched into his expression.

"Seth," Father holds the chair out to him, "come join us."

Seth's eyes widen, his mouth hangs agape. He begins to back

up, saying, "Sir, I—I can eat over here." Seth points to the empty hall.

Father looks down at the table of food and then back to Seth.

"But we want you to sit at our table. While here, you are a good friend, family even. And friends and family break bread together. Now, come sit here next to Henry and Aaron."

Seth swallows hard, "Yes, uh—" Fear flashes in his eyes.

"Mr. Jacob," says Father, warmth filling his tone.

Seth bobs his head, swallows hard again. "Yes sir, Mr. Jacob. Thank you, Mr. Jacob. I'm grateful for your hospitality, Mr. Jacob." Each statement is accompanied by a few tentative steps toward the table until he stands between Aaron and Henry, who add their smiles of warmth. He looks around, discomfort still evident as everyone takes their seats.

I can't imagine what is going through his head, this being the first time he's been in our company as family, but whatever he fears seems to dissipate as we all take hands to say grace. The familiarity of faith and prayer unites us all as we thank the good Lord for the safe return of our family and the bounty of the feast that rests before us.

The clinking of silverware against dishes ensues as we pass food around the table to each other with little conversation, save for Henry and Aaron who want to make sure Seth is eating well.

"Seth, that sliver of ham is so small you might as well call it a bit of bacon. Here," Aaron puts two more slices of ham on Seth's plate.

"Thank you kindly, I just don't want to—"

"Lose all your muscle? You will if you don't have some of this." Henry adds more potatoes.

"And you all need your green beans," Mother passes the dish in their direction.

Seth smiles and takes it from her, "Thank you kindly." He piles his plate with the good stuff. "Smells just like my Ma's, just don't tell her I said that. Here," Seth adds a healthy helping of vegetables to both Henry and Aaron's plates.

"Like to share, is all I'm sayin." Seth grins.

Henry and Aaron's expressions both sour at the green beans now filling a third of their place but not wanting to be rude or risk Mother's wrath, they are quick to brighten and share in the abundance of food.

Aaron passes the green beans to Thaddeus. "Here, have as much as you like, they're great!"

When the last dish is returned to the table, we take up our forks for the first savory bites.

"I passed my bar exam."

All eyes look to him and we raise our glasses.

"Congratulations!" Father says. Murmurs from around the table continue with similar sentiments from all of us.

Henry looks to Aaron saying, "Got another smart one in the house, though I suppose you won't be sticking around the farm much longer."

Aaron clears his throat. "Well, I have a few things in mind, but I think it best to discuss family matters later this evening. Tell me what's happened around here?"

The men discuss the upcoming planting and plans for the season. Thaddeus interjects a few things about his farm and tips on how to combat the climate, while I sit back and listen. I notice there are subjects being avoided, such as the upcoming war, and Aaron is keeping his political views to himself.

"Did you finish your fields?" Thaddeus asks, as I feel his fingers searching under the table for my hand.

I entangle mine in his, the warmth of his touch a calming sensation.

"Father and I finished planting yesterday," Henry says. "We are off to lend a hand to the Welty's. How's yours coming?" Henry pushes his plate aside, the ham and potatoes all but gone, and the green beans like an island all their own.

"We have another day's work in ours. I am teaching Ian the finer points of farming," Thaddeus adds, "Mostly the hard work part. He is not taking kindly to it."

I feel Thaddeus squeeze my hand as I try not to smile as to give ourselves away to the family around the table. "If Mr. Welty needs more hands, I'll be happy to volunteer Ian and myself."

"I'll inform Mr. Welty," Henry says. "I'm sure he won't say no if he needs it."

I notice Mother looking at me, an indication we should gather the dishes for the dessert course. Giving Thaddeus's hand a quick squeeze, I release him and stand to clear the table.

"I'll help you," Seth offers between bites.

"No sir," Mother stops him. "You enjoy the men's discussion. Emilie and I will take care of dessert. We'll need six small plates, unless Henry decides to finish his green beans."

Henry grumbles, and there is no mistaking the clink that comes from the stab of his fork for a mouthful of greens.

"Yes, ma'am," Seth says. There is a lost look in his eyes.

I suspect it is his unrest about the sudden change in roles. Here he is not a servant, field hand, or slave. He is a friend, a family member, a free man, and I pray his new roles eventually become ones of comfort for him.

Mother cuts and serves the spice cake, while I fetch the whipped cream, working together to dish and pass out dessert to everyone—even Henry—before we sit.

Silence falls again over the table, as the tinkle of silverware to stoneware sings of the joys of spice and sweet cream. We fill our bellies with good cheer and nourishment. When the last fork sets to the plate, Aaron says, "Henry show Seth and me around, while the ladies tend to the dishes."

"Come on, Seth, I'll show you around."

The men get up to leave.

Thaddeus stands, addressing my father, "Thank you for the invitation to dinner. I best leave you to family business and catching up with Aaron."

"You are always welcome, Thaddeus, may I show you out?"

"Yes, sir," Thaddeus says, then turns to me. "Em, I'm going to let you get reacquainted with Aaron and Seth. Can I call on you in a few days?"

"I'll enjoy that more than you know," I say.

Thaddeus takes my hand, gives it a reassuring squeeze, and leaves. I watch him say good-bye to my father and brothers out the window. As he turns around, the family goes back to their conversations.

"Emilie, the dishes," Mother pulls me back to the task at hand.

"Right," I pick up another plate to dry.

Long days travelling is a tax on anyone. As soon as the sun goes down, I notice Seth is feeling the weight of sleep. His head bobs, he startles himself, and his eyes open again for the third time.

"Seth, would you like to turn in for the evening?

"I am sorry, Miss Emilie," Seth says. "This chair is comfortable, and I like all your talkin, just—" He yawns. "Don't know why I can't keep my eyes open." A big stretch follows.

"Emilie, see to it that Seth is set up in the trundle bed in Henry's room," Mother says. "I put bedding and towels up there, but you will have to make up the bed."

"Yes, Mother," I say. "I think I will turn in early also. It's been a long day."

"Good night then," Mother dismisses us, as I stand motioning for Seth to follow me.

I turn back to Aaron, "You'll still be here in the morning?"

"Of course. I will see you at breakfast. Sleep well." Aaron bids me good night.

"All right then," I say. "Good night, everyone."

A chorus of good night follows, as Seth and I head upstairs for the night.

Up the stairs, Seth follows me to Henry's room. I immediately see to the bedclothes, making up the bed. Seth stands at the other side of the bed, to help me smooth out the covers while we add the layers of a sheet, blanket, and finally a light quilt to the bed. I pull a pillowcase, grab up the pillow, give it a shake and stuff it into the case, and then plop it at the head of the bed.

I watch Seth smooth his hands over the covers and poke at the pillow. He looks at me, his face scrunched in thought. He picks up the pillow and listens.

"This pillow doesn't make noise."

"No, it's full of goose down," I fluff the pillow for him. "You should sleep like a king."

"It's strange. What if I don't like it?" Seth asks, holding the pillow close to him.

"What if you do? When you and your family come at the end of this season, I hope you will finally feel freedom and live the life you should have always lived—a life like this one."

"I don't know about that, Miss Emilie," Seth looks away.

"I meant what I said about helping you become a teacher, Seth. I will do my best to get you connected to the school."

"But it won't be your school."

I bite my lip, looking down, saying, "No, Seth, it won't be my school. Segregation has not changed up here. But we will be closer, and we have a free community here that needs a school—and you.

"I hope it happens. Theres a lot that can happen between now and then."

Red flags wave in my head. I knew something was going on. "Seth, tell me what you mean by that."

"I can't speak out of turn. I could get a good lashing if they find out. Already said too much."

"Too much? You just volunteered that you are teaching. What more could you possibly say that would be worse than that? Teaching could get you hanged."

His eyes now avoid me.

A chill races through me. Now that I asked, I can't take it back. His reality hits me hard, like a splash of ice water, and I immediately hate myself for throwing his life back at him in a careless unfeeling way. In a soft voice, I say, "I'm sorry, but know we are friends, and you can tell me anything. I'll keep your secrets, like I always have."

Seth swallows, struggling with what I know nothing of, but I can see the cloud of pain that fogs his gaze. And I do know the agonizing life he leads, recalling what secrets he has shared with me, which could mean life and death for him should they ever spill past my lips.

"Seth," I say, "I promise to keep your secret. Just please tell me you and your parents are all right. I need to know."

"We're fine, Miss Emilie. It's just—just things ain't as you re- member it, and Pa told me to keep our business ours 'cause it no longer concerns any of y'all." His hand mindlessly smooths the pillow on his lap, like he's petting a dog.

"I want to help—"

"We don't need saving. Pa says if we let you save us over and over again, then we still ain't free. So, we'll manage on our own. Besides, plantings almost done. Should be packing up as soon as I get back."

My head begins pounding with the echoes of unknown truths he keeps to himself.

"All right, fine, then. I—we won't save you, but I'm sure as the day is long, Seth Blackwell, my uncle will follow through. And I promise, I won't say anything to my father, but you must find a way to tell me if you need our help. Do you promise me that? As a friend? As a brother?"

Seth meets my eyes.

"I only want you to be safe," I whisper.

"This ain't a safe world for negros like me." The scars of his pain hide in the shadows of his eyes.

"I know," I say, reaching for his hand. He pulls back.

"And when you going to learn, us black folk can't touch a white girl?" he asks, leery and suspicious.

I huff, sigh, apologize. "Right, it won't happen again. It's just hard to forget we're not children anymore." I remember our days of playing carefree without worries over an innocent touch. We played tag, clapped hands, shared morsels from Martha's kitchen, and if they made Seth work, I threw the biggest temper tantrums. It's not like I had many friends.

"No, we're not. There's responsibility weighing on our shoul- ders now." He gives me a quick smile that fades with the weight of what he feels he must bear alone.

I guess all men are stubborn.

"Please, think about what I said?" I plead as my eyes meet his.

We nod, sealing the understanding between us.

"Sweet dreams, Seth," I say, standing to leave.

"Sweet dreams," Seth echoes, as I close the door behind me.

Seth's words echo in my mind, we will never be free if you keep saving us. The truth of this statement is as daunting as their rights as free citizens, which they have even less of compared to me, a woman. A sense of helplessness taps me on the shoulder. I am forced to keep a secret, with no way to change what may be happening in Virginia.

I walk into my room, stoke the fire, and ready for bed. I take the diary out of my desk and begin writing myself into exhaustion. Maybe a solution will be clarified tomorrow.

Aaron stares up at the parlor's ceiling, listening for the click of Emilie's bedroom door, waiting. The conversation they are about to have has already thickened with mistrust as his parents are getting closer to uncovering the secrets he holds dear to his heart. Yes, the bar exam went well, and he's now able to practice in the state of Virginia—

But will there be anything left of Virginia if the North comes knocking at her door?

The papers, debates, and general contention of the South is to hold fast to our beliefs. We will hold them hard and vow to die doing it. My only choice is to keep my uncle's secrets, lest I break my father's heart with the news, and tell them what I am determined to do. What if—

"Was that her door?" Henry asks, he looks to Aaron, holding his breath.

Father draws on his pipe.

Mother sits stiffly, her hands nervously twitching in her lap. Her eyes are close to tears that she bravely holds at bay.

They've all been waiting for this conversation; one they chose to keep Emilie out of—for now.

"Well, are you going to tell me what's happening?" Mother asks. Behind her glassy eyes, there sits a glare for Aaron.

"I—" Aaron begins.

"Aaron Fredrick Prescott don't give me that! You have been hush-hush about everything since you walked in that door," Mother's tone is not to be tested.

Aaron's eyes flee his mother's, flickering over to Henry, who bites back a snort of laughter by chewing on his bottom lip. Henry has a smirk and a glint of mischief in his eye, but then he receives a glare from their mother, who sits on the couch across from him. Henry swallows, shrinking back into his chair.

Their mother's glare returns to her eldest.

Under his mother's ire, memories flood Aaron's mind all the way back to the age of five. Despite his size now, she still scares him as much as she did when she towered over him with her wooden brush. Not the decadent metal one she used to untangle her hair, but the one she used to untangle her children when they were naughty. His head tilts to the side, peering at her hands and at the cushion. There are knitting needles for stabbing but not a brush in sight.

Hopefully she hasn't gotten better at hiding it.

"Julia," his father interrupting his mother's inquisition, "let the man speak."

"Oh yes, speak! Speak! By all means, share with the common-wealth, Aaron. I'm not stopping him. I'm not the one waltzing up into our home, acting all prestigious with that awful cigar hanging out of his mouth. I tell you Jacob, I don't care if he is the President of the United States or the King of England, I'm his mother, and he will tell me what he is keeping from us. Do you hear me, son? Speak!" Her cheeks already having boiled to a hue of scarlet, but there is fear behind the fire. Aaron sees it all too clearly, and it brings a pang to his heart.

Why must she make it harder than it already is?

"Shall I get the wooden brush, Mother?" Henry asks, his smug smirk rising to the occasion at Aaron's expense.

"Only if you wish to feel it too." She promises. It's not a threat, it's a promise. Her eyes never waiver from Aaron. Her chin is set. She holds her breath.

Henry's mirth is smothered by their mother's words and the heaviness of the air that sits between her and Aaron. He shrinks further down into his chair. It's his turn to be afraid, but not as afraid as Aaron.

Am I still a man if I look her in the eye when I break her heart, or does that make me a monster?

Father clears his throat. "Let's start with the plantation—anything new?"

"There's plenty new," Aaron rubs the back of his head, looking away from his mother as her glare continues to bore into his soul. "Uncle William has changed everything and is looking for profit. He doesn't care about the labor or laborers. It cannot be denied that—the place was so much better under your command."

"Thank you, son." His father says. "But there's no going back now. I promised your uncle and Jim, too, that I wouldn't interfere. So neutral it is, for as long as I can."

"Fair enough. So, I won't expound on the plantation, except to say it is profitable according to Uncle."

Father nods.

The clicking and clacking of Mother's knitting carries on. She knits and purls like a pro, her fingers unbothered by emotion, thought, or the weight they both carry throughout her dower expression, which remains poised on Aaron.

Henry squirms in his seat.

A dull ache spreads through his shoulders. He squeezes each in turn, sighing.

Click-clack, click-clack.

Aaron pulls a cigar from his pocket, cuts off the end—

Click-clack, click-clack.

He looks to his mother, licks his lips, looks away to the fire, and then casts a side glance back to her. It's easier to face her this way than head on. "Do you mind if—"

"Mind? Me mind? Are you actually being considerate of how I feel? About the roof we have provided over your head. About the sweet, loving, comfort I've worked hard to preserve for the sake of you having a place to call home and rest your weary head without fear or worry of what is to come? What do you think, Aaron? Do you think I mind?"

Aaron sighs and sets down the cigar.

The mantle clock ticks away the remaining time. If he delays this any longer, she's likely to need of a doctor for hysteria.

"How long are you staying?" Henry asks.

Aaron turns his head, squinting at his brother.

I'm the one in trouble and yet he's the one planning an escape route.

"I have to get Seth back in three weeks. He's only on loan, according to Uncle William, but we can stay for another week,"

373

Aaron gives another side glance to his mother for any sign of a truce.

Click-clack. Click-clack.

"Did he threaten you?" Father asks, his eyes narrowing.

"No, he took no such liberties. Only stated he would send bounty hunters after Seth, if I didn't return him in time," Aaron says. "I brought him with me, saying I needed a strong man to help with the crates."

Click-clack. Click-clack.

Best to tell them before she finishes knitting that straitjacket for me.

"So, I want to tell you—the other reason why I'm here."

"How did the graduation go? Do you have a girlfriend yet? Any job offers that could provide you with political clout?" Henry asks the questions spilling out as he sits forward, elbows to his knees, with extreme interest.

"Henry, I know what you're trying to do, but I need you to stop," Aaron says, sharing a moment of compassion for his younger brother who, through some degree of frustration, followed him about more than his own shadow.

The brothers' eyes lock as Aaron filters through the memories, starting with the curious moment he pulled on Henry's blanket, excited to see the baby. Ah yes, his little snot-nosed brother who teethed on his favorite wooden toys, caught frogs with him by the creek and suffered de-leeching afterward, and who he taught how to carve a wooden bird, so the brat could have a gift for Mother on her birthday instead of stealing his. Henry, who disappeared the second they broke Mother's prized vase. Henry, who could sweet talk his way into Martha's jar of cookies night or day. Henry, who agreed for the sake of not having to disagree and always tried to see the glass of milk he had with those cookies as half full.

Henry gives him a weak smile, full of hope and a plea, but Aaron knows this is one bit of music they must face as a family. To not do so would be cowardly.

"No and no. I graduated, passed the bar, and I plan—" He looks at his mother. "I'm going to enlist."

Click—

She's as still as a statue. Her expression appears fractured. Small trembles break out of taut muscles all over her beautiful face. A quiver in her lashes, the pursing of her lips, the tightness of her chest— Her back, rigid and straight, like the soldier he hoped to be, and yet he worries the battle they are about to have will be the death of them both.

"Which side?" Henry asks.

Aaron blinks, but all he can manages is a hushed whisper in reply. "The South." His focus is still on their mother. His hands wanting to reach out, as he sees her own visibly shaking, alone in her lap. She is beside herself, biting back the pain of his words as she sucks in her bottom lip, holding back for what he imagines is a barrage of fire worse than any Union brigade, and knowing he deserves every moment of it.

"Mother I—" A spark of wetness dampens the tender skin just under his eyes.

I don't want to hurt her; I just need her support.

"No," she says. "No, you're not thinking. You're being ridiculous, silly, foolish, and we raised you better than this Aaron. This is not a game, this is real. These men you claim to fight for, regardless of the side you pick, care nothing of your life. Not like me who carried you for nine months, brought you into this world, and is the very reason you sit as you do now as a young man, a young man who has many long years ahead of him, who will not remove himself from my life—possibly forever."

"Are you looking to be a man?" Henry asks. "Because Father

can teach you that, you don't need to join a fight to prove it."

Both Aaron and Mother glare at Henry.

Henry frowns. "I was just trying to be help—" He sighs and curls up in his seat with a pout.

Aaron turns back to his mother. "I'm not taking myself from you Mother, nor do I need to reconsider Henry. I'm doing this to save our heritage and despite what you may think, I'm not a little boy anymore, but man enough to figure this out for myself."

He looks to Father, as he knows he can depend on his level head and male opinion. However, Father's face is drawn, his jaw set. So far, he's said nothing, just sat back watching the two of them, like a boxing referee. Alas, Father takes a deep breath, looking to his wife then back to his eldest son.

"This is going to be an unpopular opinion. Aaron, you are schooled, a lawyer who is able to practice law in the state of Virginia." Father pauses, swallows, blinks. "I don't want you to fight, but if this consideration is due to an honest, well thought out conclusion, we—" He looks to his wife and then back to Aaron. "—will support you."

Aaron takes a deep breath, not realizing he was holding it for a long moment, "I have thought this through, and with everything I know and understand to be true, I cannot allow the Union to stomp all over the rights of the Southern people."

"What about Uncle William or the plantation? Are you defending them?" Henry asks. He is now sitting at the edge of his seat, his courage, Aaron imagines, renewed by their father's words.

However, their mother is still fuming, and he struggles to look at her for any length of time as she sits in stoic silence like a fractured statue ready to crumble. He knows he'll have to deal with her sooner or later.

"Henry, I am not defending Uncle William. I would rather free the slaves and figure out another way to make the land prosperous. Times are changing. It behooves us to consider changing with it. But when all is said and done, the economic policies the Unionists have tried to enforce on Southern States at a federal level is unconstitutional, and slavery is a front for their shenanigans. The South holds our family's legacy, and we mustn't turn our back on it or we will lose it."

Aaron watches for Henry's reaction, seeing not just his brother, but a blooming man full of ideas, strength, and passion.

"Henry, have you decided if you are going to fight?" Aaron asks, not daring to look at their mother.

"He is not going," Mother says. "I will not lose both of you to slaughter."

"That's Henry's decision, Mother." Aaron insists.

Mother's glare shifts to her youngest son. "Are you going Henry? Do you wish to break my heart too?"

Henry opens his mouth, but nothing comes out as he looks between Aaron and their mother. Finally, his eyes rest on their father, a plea for help.

Father clears his throat. "You are both of age to decide your fate. What your mother is saying is that this is a difficult decision that should not be taken lightly. We beg that you both consider and reconsider what is in your hearts."

Henry exhales, his hands rubbing against his thighs, wiping the nerves and sweat on his trousers. He looks first to Aaron. "I've not decided what to do," Henry says. "Just know, I will never take up arms against you. You're my brother and my family. But, if you're fighting for our legacy, then it makes sense that I would join you."

"So, help me, Henry Arthur, I will lock you in your room until the end of this damned war!" Mother shouts, standing now, her knitting falling in a knotted mess at her feet. "I'm done listening to this foolishness. I don't deserve this, from any of you!" She takes a moment to look at Henry, at Aaron, at their father, as tears traverse the cracks in her composure. "Shame on you, Jacob Prescott!"

She storms out of the parlor.

There is a slam from the back door.

Silence.

Aaron sighs and retrieves his cigar, lighting it with shaky hands. He loves his mother but—

Will I be going alone?

He looks over to Henry, who is avoiding looking at anyone, staring into the fire, trying to escape the scolding that still paints his ears red.

Father's sigh draws the boys back to the parlor, their heads and eyes toward him, a leader of men, Prescott men. They wait for some command from him, both at a loss for what to do next.

"We raised you to make good decisions. All I can do now is give you my blessing and pray to God to keep you safe. That said, you better make damn sure that whatever cause you decide to fight for is worth giving your life." Father looks at both of his sons. "We love you both."

Aaron watches him stand and stretch the knot out of his shoulders.

"Where are you going?" asks Henry with wide eyes.

"To make amends with your mother. After all, I can't go off to battle with the pair of you, and I'd rather my next meal not keep me in the outhouse."

Father leaves Henry and Aaron in the parlor.

"You don't think she'd poison him, do you?" asks Henry.

"Not without first making it look like a mistake," Aaron says. "But at least I've made it through in one piece."

Henry gives Aaron a look of confusion.

"What?" Aaron asks.

A lopsided grin takes hold of his brother as he says, "Oh Aaron, you have been gone too long."

"What are you talking about?" Aaron asks, trying to determine what he missed.

Henry gets up, walks over, and takes the cigar from Aaron's hand. He takes his time drawing in, hacks and coughs the remainder out, but still manages to stand up straight like a man in the aftermath. "You've still got to tell Emilie."

Jacob leaves their pride and joy, boys they've raised into men, in the safety of the parlor as he steps out on the porch to face someone far scarier than any army—his wife.

"Do you know why they don't want women to enlist?" he asks as he moves with caution to take a seat on the swing beside her.

"Mm?" She won't even look at him.

"Because then the war would never end," Jacob says.

Julia turns to face him, not with a smile but a scowl.

He'll take it and he gives her a warm smile. "You women." A hint of exasperation lacing his voice. "Never forget a thing. You let those memories simmer and the people in them, well they linger like ghosts. You plot and you plan things with such deliberation, such care—even the masterful tactician Alexander the Great or Caesar himself couldn't hold a candle to your strategic finesse."

Jacob looks to his wife, attempting a smile of truce before continuing. "And speaking of plotting, my own dear mother is probably at it right now, concocting the perfect tongue lashing for my return—heavenly arrival, God willing, not too soon of course. She's still mad about the time she caught me, a teenager no less, kissing a pretty teacher from a small farm family in our stables."

Julia breathes deep and looks away, not wanting to give him the victory of a smile. "That was love—this is war."

"So, choose love, and not war," says Jacob. He, too, feels her pain, the fear and loss for what may come of this country's decisions.

She shakes her head, breathes deep, and squeezes her eyes shut. It doesn't stop the tears, just rings the sobs out of her body, causing her to break down and convulse once more.

Jacob wraps his arms around her and holds her close as her body and soul heaves with heartache. He kisses the top of her head and waits as she starts to take long deep breaths.

"I—I am the—the one who chose—I-love, they chose—war!" she cries. "Why can't you—make them stay?" She looks to him with sad pitiful eyes that shatter his heart.

"Hey, hey, shh," Jacob says. She is clearly not ready, so he takes a deep breath with her and waits.

Finally, her breathing is slow and steady, she has stopped hiccupping, and his shirt bears the brunt of her runny nose, salty tears, and spittle. He feels her nuzzle into his shoulder.

"Henry's not going anywhere," Julia pushes herself away from him. "I swear to God, Jacob. I will tie that boy down. If I have to lose one, I won't lose the other! Do you hear me?"

Now she is trying his patience.

"Darling," Jacob, pulls her back to him, "if Henry wants to go, we must allow it. It will break him as a man to force him to go against his judgement. We raised them right; it's now time to allow them to follow their path."

"I'd rather break his heart than bury him in a casket." The cold realization surfaces in her voice.

"No, I won't see my son regret such a decision for the rest of his life. We will not undermine him that way. It's like cutting off his legs and not teaching him how to adjust. As parents, we must honor his decision."

"I—can't. I won't lose my babies—I won't!" Julia begins to cry again.

How does she have any tears left?

"Julia Prescott, we are in this together, as we promised in our wedding vows."

For the first time in this conversation, Julia looks into his eyes. Her eyes say it all. His wife's determination is nothing to try to sway or change. It is as sturdy as the mountains.

He sighs. "Julia, you may not have a say in the war our country is in, but you have a say in whether there is war in this household. Do you really want to add to their fight? Or do you want this home to remain the beautiful, safe refuge you've made for them?" He pauses. She is still listening, he hopes. "Understand, love, I don't want anything to happen to our boys either, and I'll do my best to make sure they are well prepared, given whatever decision they make. But I beg you Julia, choose love, not war with our sons."

Jacob kisses her on the forehead, and they rock on the swing until they are ready to sleep.

Celebration & Tears

CHAOS IS REJECTING ALL YOU HAVE LEARNED.
CHAOS IS BEING YOURSELF.
~EMILIE M. CIORAN

JUNE 1861
GETTYSBURG, PENNSYLVANIA

All the work over the past six months leads up to this day. Today I will earn my ticket to freedom as a woman, with the independence and skills to earn a living on my own. The bright morning June sky greets me with a warm sun. Riding into town to take my teacher's exam feels like an accomplishment mixed with anticipation and anxiety. Can anyone feel ready for such a life-changing event?

Once there, my head is pounding after three hours of staring at an exam book. The questions feel eerily similar to those I saw a few months back. My fingers ache from grasping the pencil too hard, but I am proud to have only broken one and worn down another. The rest of the pencils sit unused and at the ready.

Stretching my back and neck, I look around the room, most of the chairs are empty. The clock ticks on, ten minutes remain.

Do I go through it one more time?

Turning the booklet over, I review everything, name, date, page one ... five, everything looks correct. Still, worry creeps over my limbs sending a shiver, causing my head to ache with a dull pounding.

I better not change an answer unless I know for sure.

I turn to the last page.

Let out a sigh.

Standing, a sense of calm washes over me as I walk the test over to the instructor.

Remember, just put it down this time.

The top of the instructor's head is all I see. She never looks up, but then again, she isn't Mrs. Irwin. My hands shake, fluttering the papers as I suspend the test over the desk—I put it down.

I wait a moment—and turn to leave.

Pushing the door, I see Sarah sitting on the brick wall, while Thomas and Thaddeus are talking. They're waiting for me under the tree.

As I approach, Sarah is telling Thaddeus, "Don't worry, she's the slowest test taker I know, last time she took a test—"

I clear my throat.

They all turn to me.

"How do you do, Emilie?" asks Thomas. He towers over Sarah by about three inches, his hair is fair, and his light skin is reddening in the sun like his fiancé's, given the tree's limited shade.

"I'm well, and how good it is to see you Thomas, I didn't think anyone could make Sarah shine brighter than she already does, but you've certainly managed it somehow."

"What no greeting for me?" Thaddeus asks with a wink.

"That depends. Were you talking about me?" I say with a playful pout.

"Only about how thorough and studious you are," Thaddeus greets me with a smile as he hands me a wildflower.

"Congratulations." Our hands touch briefly as we pass the flower between us.

I bring it to my nose, inhaling deep, a smile breaking out on my face as our eyes meet again, in a familiar greeting between us. "Is that what Sarah was saying?"

"Actually, I was saying—"

"How nobody's left yet," says Thomas.

Sarah beams. "Maybe that means we all passed?"

"When did you get done?" I ask Sarah, her blonde hair catching the light.

"Awhile, I thought the questions were a repeat of the last one we took, didn't you?"

"I am sure they were similar, but not exactly the same," I say. "Now, all we have to do is wait."

"A watched pot never boils," Thomas reminds us.

"Like your mother has ever had you watch a pot. They should be calling those who didn't pass inside soon." Sarah begins to pace again. "Oh, Emilie, what if they don't call us? What if we don't get called during graduation either? What if they forget we even took the test?"

I turn to Thaddeus, his amusement with Sarah's anxiety shows in the glint of his eye and his bemused smirk.

Thomas put a hand on Sarah's shoulder in assurance. "Sarah, I am sure that won't happen; besides they do this every year. They know what they are doing."

Sarah looks up at him, with those big blue eyes that make all of us melt at her naivety, "So, they won't forget to call us?"

"I doubt it," Thomas says, as Sarah's smile brightens her face. Their gazes lock for a moment, and finally I see my best friend take a deep breath.

Miracle of miracles.

The door to the school opens as a school board official stands to ring the school bell announcing our assembly for the graduation ceremony.

"Already?" I ask. "That was fast."

"They just needed your test results," Thaddeus chuckles holding out his arm. "Shall we?"

"Learn my doom together?" I ask, giggling at the scowl on his face. "Will you still desire me if I fail?"

"We are in it together." He pauses. "Yes, maybe, I don't know. I think Miss Floyd is a wonderful catch, what with her stooped over back and all three of her teeth."

Sarah gasps. "But she's likely to croak before there's a chance to marry."

I elbow him.

Thaddeus laughs.

"I don't think he was serious, Sarah," says Thomas.

Thaddeus leans over, his warm breath bathing my ear. "You. I only have eyes for you."

Everyone assembles in the largest classroom the school has to offer. The close confines have ladies' fans working up small breezes in every direction, despite the room's windows being open to allow as much summer air as possible. Men's brows all show beads of sweat forming, some trail down their cheeks. School officials stand at the front of the room and one of them begins to read the graduates' names.

My heart is pounding in anticipation.

What if Sarah is right? What if they don't call my name?

Sitting next to Thaddeus, his knee touching mine, we wait through the A's and C's.

"How many took the test?" Sarah asks, leaning over to Emilie.

"I don't know but this alphabetical order is nerve wracking," I whisper back as I feel Thaddeus tap my shoulder.

"Emilie Prescott?" repeats Mr. Kind.

Thaddeus nudges me, and I stand, my heart quickening. Mr. Kind gestures me forward. The crowd watches as I walk to the front of the room and shake six hands, each belonging to a school board member congratulating me before I receive my teaching certificate at the end of the line.

"Congratulations, Miss Prescott," Mr. Kind shakes my hand. "The school board will be looking forward to receiving your application."

"Thank you. I mean yes. I mean, it's an honor, sir," I say, accepting the certificate.

Turning back to the crowd, I see ahead of the sea of faces, Mrs. Irwin standing in the front row, applauding.

My smile broadens to the point where my cheeks hurt as I walk over to her. She grasps my hand. "Congratulations. I knew you could do it."

A tear rolls down my cheek. "I couldn't have done it without you," I say.

Returning to my seat, more voices of "congratulations" come my way as I dodge and weave through people and legs to get back to my chair. Thaddeus is standing and clapping as well, though his smile says it all. Sitting back down together, he slips his arm around me giving me a quick squeeze.

"Poor Ms. Floyd. She'll be heartbroken when I break the news?" He grins.

He pulls me into him kissing the top of my head as the crowd continues to cheer for the next group parading to the front of the room. My heart flutters, my thighs squeeze together.

So much for our no-touching rule, not that I'm about to remind him.

Sarah squeals, "That's my name! They called my name! Did you hear them say my name? That's my name!"

"Yes, Sarah, now go up there!" I urge her from her seat.

"Oh, right," Sarah apologizes and excuses herself to every single person she passes, shaking hands and kissing babies.

"If she wasn't a woman, she'd make a fine politician," Thaddeus says in my ear as we stand and clap together for her.

It takes Sarah a good five minutes before she let's go of Mr. Kind's hand, shaking the circulation right out of it as she profusely tells him what I can only imagine is words of thanks, that she has a fiancé, what she ate for breakfast, why her parents couldn't attend, and whatever else might have bubbled up in the moment—but eventually she does make it back to Thomas's side.

Another twenty minutes pass and my palms sting from all the repetitive congratulations. When the ceremony is over, we burst through the doors and back onto the playground, much like the pupils we desire to teach, full of mirth and a desire for fresh air. However, everyone's energy melts away as we are greeted by more of the summer's heat.

The crowd mills about as people begin moving away, everyone getting back to daily life. We walk together until Sarah and Thomas turn to continue to Sarah's house. Wishing them farewell, Thaddeus and I head to the boarding stable to get Starlight.

"Do you want a ride back to work?" I ask.

"No, thank you. It is a lovely day to walk."

"All right. See you tonight for dinner?" I ask.

"Looking forward to it," Thaddeus holds Starlight's reigns, as

I mount up. Once I settle into the saddle, he adds with a wink, "Can't wait to see you."

Thaddeus pats Starlight and we are off to home.

After a jovial Prescott dinner full of giggles, jokes, and good food, we all retire to the parlor for cake and coffee. A celebration for two graduates in one year—Aaron a lawyer and me as a schoolteacher.

"You did it Emilie," Seth says. "You told me you were gonna become a teacher and you did it."

"A lot of hard work Seth, but that's nothing new to you."

"Soon as we set foot here in Gettysburg, I'm gonna take you up on your offer."

"I look forward to it."

"You know I'm looking forward to you opening those presents we got you," Mother says as she gets up to bring a chair to the center of the room.

Aaron immediately gets up, "I've got that for you Mother."

"It's all right, I can do it—just as I was able to do it before you left," Mother then looks to me with a warm smile patting the cushion of the chair. "Sit here Emilie."

I look between her and Aaron, but they both give me vague smiles as to what all the fuss is about. Rising from the center cushion of the couch, I take a seat in the center of the room, Mother to my left, Aaron to my right. The small table in front of me, which usually hosts the courting candle for me and Thaddeus, has three presents with boxes and packages of all shapes and colors.

Which do I pick first?

There is a package of green paper and bows, plain brown paper, and last, an ornate, wooden box with a large, decadent bow on top. I look around to my loved ones' faces, each filled with anticipation. Smiling, I am flooded with gratitude and support that I once doubted.

"Are you going to look at them or actually open them?" Henry asks, his cup still in hand.

"Well, I don't know which one to pick."

"Just close your eyes and pick one already," Henry begs already bored with the celebration.

I close my eyes, my hand over the table, as I reach for a package. I open my eyes to see the one wrapped in bright green paper with a large bow on top. It is heavy but not too thick, and through the paper I feel the telltale signs of binding.

"A book?" I ask looking around the crowd watching me.

Thaddeus nods, "From yours truly."

I hesitate. A general rule is that a lady should not accept gifts from the man she courts, as it could be considered a bribe for her affection. Despite none of that being the case here, I decide to follow protocol, for once.

Looking to my Father I ask, "Do you approve?"

Father scratches his chin in thoughtful jest, and then with a grin, he nods.

"Thank you," I say, looking back to Thaddeus.

"You haven't even opened it yet."

"Maybe if we give it her late—" Henry begins, and the telltale sound of a thwap from Mother finishes it.

I look down to the package and carefully open the edges. Inside is indeed a book, bound in maroon leather. My fingers trace over the gold lettering that reads "*Fairy Tales* by Louisa May Alcott."

"You read me her fairy poem," I say, as a flood of memories warms me.

"On our second night."

He remembered.

"It a compilation of all her fairy and flower poems," Thaddeus informs the others. "I hope you will enjoy it."

"I hope I'm not the only one to read it," I say, caressing the pages, turning them carefully, before I look back to him. Our eyes meet, touching each other the only way we can right now.

Aaron, still standing beside me, clears his throat.

Setting the book in my lap, I reach for the brown paper package.

"Finally," Henry says, sitting forward in his chair.

I shake the present at him. "This from you?"

"Yes, and Aaron and Seth too," I shake the gift, looking at each giver.

Seth smiles, biting his bottom lip and leaning forward, much like Henry, as I begin to peel back the wrapping to reveal a bar of sandalwood goatmilk soap, a stack of stationery, and a wooden plaque with Miss Prescott engraved into it.

"Gentlemen," I say, "thank you. I will use all of these and think of each of you."

They nod and smile back at me, with murmurs of your welcome and congratulations, Henry and Seth patting each other on the back.

Am I difficult to find gifts for?

One last package remains on the table. I pick it up, looking to my parents. They nod for me to open it.

The presentation of the gift alone shows off both my parents' handiwork. The wooden box is a canvas for intricate carvings that remind me of Virginia and one I will cherish as a keepsake for as long as I live. The bow that tops it is crafted of blue ribbon with puzzling loops and detailed beading at the center—if I am careful enough in its removal I could perhaps sew into onto my dress as a centerpiece.

Slipping off the bow, I open the box, where a velveteen cover rests. Pulling the cloth back, my eyes drink in a silver chain with a heart-shaped locket. I gasp at its beauty. It's decorated with filagree scrolls, and my initial resides on the front. Inside there is room for two pictures. I carefully close the box and set each of the gifts on the table before rising to my feet.

The first hug goes to my mother.

"Thank you," I say into her neck, catching the waft of her lavender perfume.

"We believe in you, Emilie," she whispers in my ear as she hugs me back.

I fling my arms around father next. He chuckles as he braces himself for impact but hugs me all the same.

"We knew you could do it." He pats my back, before unraveling my arms and sending me back to my seat.

"When do you start teaching?" Seth asks.

"Well, I have to apply to teach at the school, but once I get hired, I hope as soon as possible, but enough about me. I'm not the only one we should be celebrating," My neck cranes until my eyes meet Aaron's. "Have you taken anyone up on practicing law yet?" I ask.

Aaron's smile fades.

Is it just me, or did the light in the room dim?

My eyes flicker to the window, looking for a sign of rain, but the sun shines away. Then I notice Father looking stoic and Henry avoiding eye contact. Seth gives a shrug, Thaddues too.

"Mother?" The word slips out before I can stop myself. She looks like she's about to cry, if not give Aaron a direct scolding here and now.

What has he done?

A crease forms in my brow as I look to the other side of me to Aaron.

He clears his throat, attempts to say something, looks away, clears his throat again.

I look back to mother. My hand instinctively grasps onto hers. She sniffles, shakes her head, won't look at any of us.

My eyes strike Henry, who's looking at the ceiling. My gaze jerks over to Seth and then Thaddeus, but they look as confused as I am.

Father's calm assertive expression guides me back to Aaron.

"Tell her, Aaron."

"Tell me what," I demand more than ask.

"I had two offers, but it looks like the conflict between the states is delaying my future a bit." Aaron's finger pulls at his collar as his Adam's apple bobs.

"What do you mean?" I ask. "Folks need a good lawyer. What's stopping you?"

His eyes meet mine. "I am enlisting Emilie."

The color washes from my face, chased by a thousand prickles uniting into a cold wave, dousing me into a sea of doubt and betrayal.

"But you don't have to, not now anyway. You can wait this out like Thaddeus. He's going later because he has responsibility and family, like you. You have responsibility and family. You can't go. Not yet. You have to wait. You must. You need to—"

"I am leaving with Seth in a few days. I have to return him, or Uncle William will send bounty hunters," Aaron says, not waiting for me to stop, not thinking to stop, not thinking!

There is a gasp of shock from someone behind me. Aaron looks over my shoulder and perhaps addresses Seth. "You know I won't let that happen. I told you I'll keep you safe."

But this is beside the point. Of course we won't let anything happen to Seth, just like I won't anything happen to Aaron.

"No, no Aaron, this is stupid," I say, my hand waving about at something, anything, so I don't try and knock some sense into him. "There are plenty of jobs up here, and there are plenty of jobs in Virginian. You can make good money anywhere. You are smart and talented. You have a family who loves you, needs you. I need you— Why would you want to throw that all away for a bullet? Why is a bullet worth more than me, than Mother, than—"

"Emilie, our legacy is in the South. And besides I don't fit here."

"Uncle William is taking care of our legacy, and you haven't been here long enough to find out whether or not you belong," I say. "If you'd stop running, for a change, you might find you like it."

"Emilie, the Southern cause needs me more," Aaron's voice still level, and emotionless. "This family is strong enough to get through this. I have to do this."

"No, you don't have break this family's heart. You're choosing to, and I want to know why!"

"I have thought this through—"

"Oh really? This should be interesting. Go on!"

"I can't allow so many to suffer from the over stepping of this government. You know me. I will never sit by and watch injustice happen."

I blink. "Whose suffering? Our uncle in his lavish mansion? Our neighbors the Sprees in their equally wealthy estate? Or the slaves who the North wish to free?"

Aaron's mouth drops before he closes it, gritting his teeth, his face turning red, his fists balling. "Huh, here I thought you were going to school to become a teacher, but it looks like they've scrubbed your brain of what is truly home to this family."

I stand up, squared shoulders, eyes determined. "Home is wherever this family resides—the family who knows you by name, who loves you all the same, who you are choosing to walk away from to fight a war dreamed up by politicians!"

"Don't delude yourself sister! This war isn't about slavery or even politicians, it's about commerce and how the North desires to control the way the South carries out their business operations. You yourself stated the working conditions of the lower class in various manufacturing plants is just as barbaric, if not crueler than the plantations that sustain this country and make it a force to be reckoned with throughout the world!"

"Are you saying our dear Uncle is as kind and gentle as a lamb?"

"I'm not doing this for him."

"The Sprees?"

"Or them."

"Then who?"

"I'm doing this for—You know what? Never mind, I don't have to explain myself to you, Emilie. I'm going and that's final."

"Coward!" I yell before looking to Father. "Talk some sense

into him!" I shout. It's all I can do to keep the influx of emotion at bay and my fists from pummeling into this stupid brother of mine.

"Emilie, we've talked," Father says. "He has our blessing."

"That doesn't sound like talking to me," I struggle to see how anyone with a lick of sense could agree to this. But that's not the only quandary rattling around in my head.

"Why wasn't I in on this?" I demand.

Henry pipes up, "Because of this."

I wheel around on my heel to see Henry's hands making a broad gesture over my display, and the smirk on his face, sending me from angry, to incensed, and back to desperate.

The tears begin to flow, and I turn back to Aaron. "For as smart as your supposed to be, this is the most foolish thing you can do to us," I say, shaking at the realization that he is right. He owes me no explanation, there is nothing I can do to change his mind, I have no control over his decision—no power to sway, not even my love for him. It hurts.

Long graceful arms hold a hidden strength wrap around me. "I know," Mother whispers to me. She kisses the top of my head before she pulls away, walks away, out of the room. Seeing her tears only accentuates my pain, knowing my sense of abandonment is nothing compared to hers.

I look back to Aaron.

"Please?" I ask, my voice cracking. "We need you here. Please, don't go."

But Aaron's eyes have hardened with his resolve. He shakes his head no. His mind is made up.

Exhaustion floods my body as a bitter taste bathes my tongue. "Fine. I hope your proud of yourself."

Like Mother, I, too, decide to leave the room. Stopping in the privacy of the hall, my legs are shaking. I lean against the wall to offer myself some support before I slide to the floor and curl into a ball, hugging my knees, nursing my pain. My lungs beg me to gasp for air while my mind grasps for another reason to make him stay.

Footsteps draw near as I sob into my hands.

A hand, large and warm, clasps my shoulder. "Em," Thaddeus says in a gentle whisper. "I'm sorry."

Looking up our eyes meet, his watery blue, mine a watery blur. "Why Thaddeus, why can't he be like you?"

Thaddeus shakes his head. "Because I'm Thaddeus and he's Aaron. Look Emilie, no man wants to disappoint their family. Please understand me when I say he's not doing this to hurt you."

"I'm not disappointed. I just think his decision is wrong. Why the South?"

"He is fighting for your legacy, Emilie." Thaddeus clears his throat and gently takes my hands, easing me back to my feet. "I know you are angry now, but do not let your brother leave without some understanding between you. He's leaving—he's made that fact clear. The fact that you have to consider now is you don't know if you will ever see him again."

"What?" I ask, not knowing if he wants me to apologize or say I agree with Aaron. "I can't say I agree with him; I don't like what he's doing."

"Then agree to disagree," Thaddeus holds my hand between his, his deep blue pools imploring me to understand. "Just tell him you love him; he's going to need to know he's not on that field alone."

I sniff and look away, arms crossing as I consider what my brother's harsh word.

"Do you love your brother?" asks Thaddeus.

"I do love him," I say, sniffing, my eyes being drawn back to his, feeling calmer under his hypnotic gaze, his tenderness, his gentle touch.

"Then make sure he knows it."

"I will," I say. "In a day or two, when I am not so—angry."

Thaddeus kisses my fingers between his, before pulling me into an embrace, right there, in the hall, only caring for my comfort now. Enjoying his embrace, feeling his warmth, languishing in his heartbeat dancing with mine, I open my eyes. Over his shoulder, I see Aaron standing against the door of the parlor, a cool measured stare, his jaw set, lips firm. He's hardened by our fight, and his actions speak volumes as he turns his back, disappearing beyond the threshold and abandoning me first.

Promise Me

THERE ARE NO GOODBYES FOR US. WHEREVER YOU
ARE, YOU WILL ALWAYS BE IN MY HEART.

~MAHATMA GANDHI

JUNE 1861
GETTYSBURG PENNSYLVANIA

The days press on toward Aaron and Seth's leaving. Several times, I try to make amends with Aaron, but I can't bring myself to do it. His outright abandonment of our family in lieu of his patriotic duty irritates me as the heavy weight of betrayal follows close behind. Unable to escape to town, as I no longer have school, the grip of the chains holding our family to unhappiness tightens. This stifling sense of discord dampens our moods, sending us all into bitter arguments, snapping and biting back words that could have lasting consequences.

One last strike to it with my fists, flailing arms, and kicks, I startle myself awake to blackness and quiet as I lay twisted into damp sheets around my legs and my chemise tightly wrapped around my middle soaking wet against my skin. My hair is dripping with sweat. The only sound is my breath, panting away the fears of the nightmare and the dread of it coming true.

I lay under the gauze canopy locked in from the night bugs as my windows rest open to the night air, hoping to relieve the humidity of June. I listen.

Stillness.

Waiting.

A shuffling. A crack of wood?

Grating.

Is that the stove lids moving?

I could use some water.

Kicking my bedclothes from my legs, untwisting my chemise to set it straight, I don my wrapper and pad down to the kitchen.

If someone is there, good. If not, I'll get a drink of water, then back to bed.

A dim light in the kitchen emits from a lamp. The sink sits quietly, as the *drip drip,* from the pump seemingly talks and answers itself. Embers sit within the stove, a small fire warming the kettle.

"What are you doing up?" Aaron's deep timber interrupts the stillness.

"Nightmare," I say, walking to the cupboard for a glass. "You?"

"Thinking too much," Aaron says, taking a short glass of amber liquid. The bottle sits nearby in case a refill is needed.

"Are you warming water?" I ask.

"Yes, I need some tea. This brandy isn't helping. Want some chamomile tea?"

I pump water into my glass, drinking a long refreshing sip straight from the well.

"I'll join you," I say, filling my glass with more water before sitting across from him at the kitchen table.

"Looks like you and Thaddeus are getting on just fine." The smell of brandy wafts in my direction, its warm rich scent playing with my nose.

"We're getting on wonderfully. We like each other a lot."

He pushes the glass in my direction. "Want some?"

"I thought you prefer whiskey," I say, becoming interested, recalling the only use of brandy being the brandied cranberries Mother makes for the holidays.

Aaron watches me, a smile playing on his lips as I consider the drink. Taking it to my nose, the tang is stronger, deeper, and warmer. A single gulp—the liquid bites my tongue, grabs my throat, and seeps into my nose with a warm rush of a cough. My nose wrinkles at the offensive sensation. Then a calm warmth rushes behind in a whisper. My eyes water. Another cough.

Aaron rescues the glass from my shaking hand.

"That's nice," I say, "after it tries to kill you, that is." I reach for the glass as Aaron pulls it away in warning.

"It's too dangerous for you; it will get you in the end." He is smiling now, a glimpse of amusement in his eyes as he refills his glass.

Confusion sets into my eyes. I blink. My nose and lips have a warm fuzzy sensation, like after Thaddeus kisses me. I smile.

"Thanks," I say, as we laugh together.

The tea kettle rumbles on the fire. I get up, feeling unsteady and grabbing the chair.

"Easy, Em," Aaron warns. "See, too much brandy will render you useless."

"I got it," I say back to him as the steadiness returns. I pick up the kettle, pour the water over some chamomile, and take it back to the table to wait.

Aaron is still lost in thought.

Thaddeus's words come back to me. *Don't let him leave without your forgiveness.*

"How are you holding up?" I ask.

"It's hard. I feel like my opinion doesn't matter anymore." His eyes retreat to a slow blink. I reach out for him, my tiny hand over his large, calloused fingers.

"That's the thing Aaron," I say. "Everything about you matters to us."

"I don't know, Mother is so angry she can hardly speak, and you have been giving me the cold shoulder and icy stares all week. I should just leave early. The only one who supports me is Father, and I still see sadness in him every time we look at each other."

I grab his glass and drink the rest of the vile concoction, choking before I say, "Let me clarify something for you." I cough again, grab the water, and swallow the less offensive liquid before speaking. "Mother still sees you as a small infant who was given to her, a gift she's grown to love and cherish. Somewhere she thinks if you do this—" I wave my hand as the words slip from my mind, "—war will take you from her. I admit, I am with her on this. It scares the hell out of us."

"No more brandy for you," Aaron says with a bemused smile. "Go on."

"Father is both proud of you and wishes you wouldn't go— But he is proud just the same that you are holding fast to the Prescott legacy." I take a deep breath, not knowing exactly why I am speaking so fluently. Up until now, I have been trying to rehearse this speech all week. "And—I have no idea how Henry feels. He's been too busy with Seth to tell."

I reach for the tea and pour some for both of us. Adding a dollop of honey, I push a cup of hot chamomile toward Aaron. He is still frowning.

I take a sip.

Silence.

"What about you Em?" Aaron asks. "How do you feel?"

I bite my lip.

Take a drink of tea.

Wish there was more vile liquid in his glass, as my eyes rise to meet his.

"I don't want you to go," I say, swallowing hard, biting back my tears.

"Don't you understand?" Aaron begins.

"I understand you are the most honorable man I know. I understand you will fight for every injustice there is, especially when it comes to human injustice. I understand that you love our home, our culture, but hate slavery. I understand you're well schooled in the politics of our nation; the one you love and vow to serve," I say, as a tear rolls down my cheek. "But Aaron, do you understand how your absence shakes my world off its foundation? What if something happens to you? It will profoundly affect my outlook on life."

"I am not married to you Emilie. You'll replace me with a husband of your choosing. You'll find a foundation elsewhere."

"No one will replace my brother. I support you Aaron, I just don't want a world without you."

"Be strong for me. Support me," Aaron begs me to listen. "Our parents taught us family is everything. I need you."

His dedication to his country rings clear to me. Politics and justice are just as important to him as teaching is to me.

"I will," I say. "I won't like it, but I support you, Aaron. Because I need you too. I need you to come home, and I love you."

A smile brightens Aaron's face. He squeezes my hand, takes a deep breath, and reaches for his tea. When we finish, our eyes are heavy with sleep as the first light of morning peaks over the horizon.

Aaron turns to me saying, "Thank you, and just know I'll do everything in my power to come home."

"I know," I say. "And know I'll be writing to you non-stop until we hear from you."

The tension between us begins to lighten a bit as departure day arrives. None of want to say it, but the inevitable comes anyway. We share a big breakfast together, Seth fitting easily into the woven fabric of our family. Everything is packed and loaded into the wagons—presents for Big Jim and Martha, clothes for Aaron, and food for the trip back to Richmond.

I notice Henry disappears after breakfast; he is nowhere to be found.

Up the stairs and down the hall I stop at Henry's bedroom door, I hesitate, then knock.

Is he sulking?

"Henry?" I say, pushing the door open to find my brother's room a mess with scattered clothes and other things I dare not ask about.

"What are you doing?" I ask.

"What does it look like, Em?" Henry avoids my stare. He throws some socks my way. I touch them, wool. "Throw those in the bag, will you?" He says, while searching through his bureau.

"Not until you tell me what the hell is going on!" My voice is just this side of shrill.

"Convent!" Henry shouts back, his usual warning to my lack of decorum and spicy tone. I ignore him.

"Do you even know how to use these?" I ask, shaking the socks at him.

"Yeah, those are socks." Henry looks at me as if I am daft.

"You better unpack now!"

"Hey, keep it down. I haven't told Mother yet." Henry turns to me, taking the socks out of my hand, stuffing them into the bag, and flipping it onto his shoulder with a sigh of accomplishment.

Taking a ragged breath and trying to calm my nerves, I push Henry back onto the bed. He falls over the mattress, looking like a fish out of water. I stand over him. "Speak!"

Henry turns a deep shade of crimson; I am unsure if it's because I pushed him or because of what he is hiding.

"I made up my mind."

"That's obvious," I narrow my eyes at him, then push him back as he attempts to sit up.

Silence.

Henry's eyes search the room for escape out of this predicament.

"Henry!" I shout.

"Gosh, Em, keep it down. I don't want them to know until we leave," Henry lays back defeated.

"You're leaving?"

"I won't take up arms against Aaron, and I have to see one of us comes home so Mother won't have a broken heart."

"You leaving will break her heart enough, stupid," I say, offended he didn't think this through.

"You get the house to yourself," Henry says, trying to find something positive. "'Sides, nothing will happen to me. I'm looking after Aaron. Let me up."

I step away from the bed, feeling a cold numbness wash over me.

"Come on, I better break the news to Mother and Father."

"Wait!" I say, pulling him to me. "Please come home safe and sound."

"I wouldn't dream of staying away," Henry smirks. "You'd wilt if I didn't tease you."

I embrace my brother and get a warm hug in return. "I miss you already. Wait here. I have some extra shirts and socks for you."

I rush to the open boxes in Mother's room and pull from the supply we've been creating for the other soldiers. I created these; I will make sure my brothers are clothed. Returning to Henry, I say, "Here, take these with you."

He does just before he heads out his bedroom door.

Once Henry's room is empty of him, the only thing left is his bed and his lingering scent—a combination of cut wood and sweet hay from the animals he tends to.

Everyone is waiting for us when we arrive to the yard. Father turns to see Henry with a packed bag. He pulls Mother in for a close embrace as Henry walks past and drops his bag in the back of the wagon.

"Henry?" Mother asks. "What on earth?"

Henry walks back to Mother and Father, shakes Father's hand and goes to give Mother a hug. She pushes him back, glaring.

"Where do you think you're going?" Mother demands as she begins visibly shaking and her face turns white.

"I am going to see that my brother comes home safely," Henry says, his tone level as he meets Mother's eyes. "I won't take up arms against him, so I'm going to make sure we both come home to you."

The shriek that arises from Mother is both bone chilling and haunting. A mother not only losing one but two children—who are not men, but children in her mind right now. Aaron rushes to her side, hugging her close and whispering into her ear, as Henry shakes Father's hand, whispers of support exchange between father and son.

Aaron lets go of Mother, shakes Father's hand. "We will write as soon as we can." Aaron motions to me.

I rush in for a hug, determined to stay strong, as Aaron asked me to do the other night.

Feeling the security of being wrapped in his embrace, memories of us flash through my mind: Aaron teaching me how to dance, how to catch frogs and fish, how to ride, our dances at the ball, and our late-night conversations—his smiles, his laughter. He is my foundation.

"Hurry back. Promise me you will keep each other safe," I whisper. His shoulder muffles my voice. "Please don't let go." My resolve is beginning to wash away. I hug him tighter. "Oh, God, Aaron, this is hard."

"I need you to be strong for Mother. Help Father. He's going to need it. Love you, sis," Aaron says, and with that he sets my feet back on the ground, pulling away from me.

A rush of heat floods though me as the dam of emotions surface. I hear Mother yelling at Father, "You promised Jacob!" Mother's sobs, yelling, sorrow, and pain. "You promised to keep him here!"

Mother is hugging Henry in a tight embrace, sobbing into his shirt. The pain in his eyes—I look away as Father pulls them apart.

I look to Seth, tears running down his face. The torment of my family is written all over him. I pull Seth in. "I am sorry to hug you," I say. "It just looks like you need it."

I let him go quickly saying, "Seth, we made a promise. Give our love to your mother and father."

"I will, Miss Emilie," Seth whispers, as he steps away from my quick embrace. He retreats to wait in the back of the wagon. He waves to us as Aaron calls to the team.

Henry, Aaron, and Seth disappear down the drive, and with their departure is a flood of emotions.

"Jacob!" Mother yells. "You just allowed our babies to go off to war! I hope you are proud of yourself!"

"Julia ..."

Their voices trail off as Father follows Mother into the house. Silence engulfs me into a suffocating reality, making me want to flee for my life. Alone in the yard, I am left for the first time as an only child. All the chores now fall to me, as well as the haunting words of my Aaron. Stay strong for Mother Em.

How am I to stay strong for someone else when I don't know if I have the strength to be strong enough for me?

A wave of nausea washes over me.

Looking around the yard, the emptiness taunts me. I must leave. I can't stay. I need to run—anywhere but here.

Rushing to the barn, I saddle Starlight and ride.

My first fleeting thought is to ride to town to distract myself from this dismal life of abandonment, but as Starlight arrives at the end of the drive, she turns up the road taking me to another destination. As we pass the road between the Welty's fields, I remember the place Thaddeus told me about—Rock Creek and the willows. A perfect place to get away until my parents come to terms with Henry and Aaron's new life choices.

A low grassy path leads us to Rock Creek. As we get closer to the water trickling over the tiny rock falls, it welcomes me in for a moment of solace. Just as described, several tall willow trees anchor to the shore, their long wispy branches whisper in the summer breeze.

I untack Starlight and tie her to a tree, close enough for her to eat all afternoon. I lay her blanket over a place to sit and think. I take off my jacket to hang it over a branch and let my hair out of the pins, enjoying the wind playing and tugging at the auburn locks. I shed my shoes and socks, wiggling my toes in the sun. The sound of the water floods me with memories of catching frogs and fish and playing along the shore with my brothers.

What is left of my family doesn't know if or when my brothers are coming home. All we can do is carry on with life as usual and wait for our reunion. It is daunting to know I will have to be both daughter and son to my parents, with loads of work and other responsibilities.

Will I get to teach?

Hiking up my skirt, I walk into the creek to enjoy its cool waters and play with the wildlife there. Frogs jump, diving from the shore to water. The rocks they hide beneath are slippery, but as I continue to explore, I feel myself give way to relaxation and joy again. Small minnows dart in and around my ankles, nibbling on me. Their little bites tickle: I giggle. The water washes away my fears and worries, for now at least.

When my hems are soaked heavy with water, I wade out of the stream, and settle back on the blanket, drinking the warmth of the day—the solace and peace. Gathering grass to braid small bracelets and wreaths, I think about Sarah's wedding, and question if I'll have one. The grass beneath me is a soft mattress for me to lounge on as I look up through the trees, enjoying the vast sky through the branches. I close my eyes.

Whish.

I open my eyes, listening—more movement. I look to Starlight; she whinnies an alert. I roll over to spy on the intruder.

Shading my eyes from the sun, I first see his trousers and boots. Then I note who it is. Thaddeus with a silly grin on his face.

The tenor I hear in his voice makes me melt. "No bonnet today, Miss Prescott?"

"Not today," I call back. "The sun is delightful. Want to share some?"

"You are a scandalous woman, allowing the sun to touch your delicate skin," Thaddeus steps closer to the blanket. I scramble to sit up, patting the blanket and indicating a spot for him.

"A bit undressed by the looks of your toes." Thaddeus can't help but chuckle at the playful inviting grin I give him.

"Will you save your reputation and run Mr. Marsh, or will you be scandalous with me?" I meet his blue eyes with an inviting look of mischief. His answer is a shake of his head. He removes his coat to hang on a branch next to mine. With a grin and a devilish glint in his eyes, Thaddeus sits beside me.

"You are a dangerous woman."

"I have no weapons, sir," I bat my eyes, holding out my hands.

"Not ones of hard steel, but weapons enough."

We consider each other, eyes meeting, a tilt of his head, his hand in mine.

"Hard day?" he asks, seeing through the façade of laughter.

I nod, biting my lip. "Henry left with Aaron, mother is beside herself, father is in the doghouse, and I ran away from it all."

My eyes sadden as vulnerability peaks from behind the shield of strength bestowed upon me by Aaron. "I am clearly not the brave one here."

"You are the bravest woman I know."

I look at him for a long time, enjoying the sight of him.

"Though I didn't realize you had a dog with a house to share. It's supposed to rain tonight." He looks up at the clear blue sky, holding his hands out to catch rain that isn't dropping.

I push him and he falls back, then grabs my hand, kissing the back of it as he uses me to draw himself up again.

"How did you know where to find me?" I ask, watching his fingers play in mine.

"I told you this was my place to run away to, if you remember correctly." He kisses my fingers.

"You did. I hope you don't mind me borrowing it."

Thaddeus shakes his head No then asks, "Tell me, what bothers you the most?"

"There are forces around me I cannot control. I'm helpless, defeated."

"Those are the last words I'd ever use to describe you, dear Emilie," Thaddeus pokes my knee as we sit close. "You don't realize your own strength."

I shift around, so he can't poke me again, and lay my head in his lap.

He resorts to playing with my hair, a slight edge of his nails soothing my scalp.

"I've never seen your hair this red. It's beautiful in the sunlight."

"Is that my strength?"

"Beauty is a strength, but you have more than that. You are capable of anything, you know? You achieved your teaching certificate and managed rooms full of children. If that isn't brave—"

"I'm sure you think so," I say. "It's nothing. I'm talking about my family. It breaks my heart to see them go."

"Men have this thing about duty and honor. Remember how I told you about God, country, and family? It is what men do."

"I call it abandonment. Why not family before country?" I ask.

Thaddeus chuckles. "Because if we have no country, we have no laws or rules—just chaos."

"What do you think this country is going to look like if this goes on?" I ask.

He pops the head off a dandelion, sending the fuzzy seeds flying over to me.

"Good point, but a country can't run on chaos. There must be rules, and one of ours is country comes before family."

"And as an only child, how am I going to find the strength to do their jobs—be both daughter and son—and have time to teach? It's too much."

Silence falls between us, my chest rising higher with overwhelm and falling lower into a valley of worry.

"I'm sorry," Thaddeus says, as a cloud of sadness passes over his eyes, turning them deeper blue. He blinks. "I know everyone expects you to have strength, and I am sure you don't know where you'll find it, but believe me, you have it."

My eyes open meeting his cerulean deep pools, adoration warming them as they skim over my relaxed repose. Thaddeus takes a breath as our gazes enjoy each other. I'm safe in this space, just Thaddeus and me. From my vantage point, I see his chin, the close-cropped beard, his mouth that has a perfect shape, full and inviting. A smile plays on his lips, mirroring the ease that settles in my chest.

The sound of his voice deep, warm, and calming to my ears, a soft rumble that sends shivers down my spine, a melody up and to the point when he says—

"... because you are amazing, smart, and strong, and that is why I love you."

"Tell me again?" I ask, unsure if the words that tumbled from his lips were a dream or reality.

"Which part, love?" Thaddeus asks, chuckling. "No, let me show you."

I feel him move his knee as I sit up to face him. Our knees brush once more before he leans in. He cups my face, his touch feather-light, before his lips meet mine.

The kiss—a slow and deliberate exploration of melding textures—the gentle press of his lips, the sweetness of his breath against mine, the comforting rasp of his beard, the heady scent of him, bergamot and lime, fills my senses. In that kiss, our racing hearts find a shared rhythm, a lullaby that soothes the worry gnawing at me, blanketing me in security and comfort, speaking soothing words through his actions. His heart and soul whisper the truth we dare not admit to each other. His mouth teases my lips with small, tender kisses when I hear him say, "I love you," again.

Our hearts sigh as one, a shared exhale speaking volumes louder than any spoken word. Our eyes meet, a pause as understanding passes between us, no longer a dream, but reality sitting here in front of me, confessing his feelings.

"How long have you been keeping this from me?" I ask, with a quirky smile, wrinkling my nose at him.

"Hmm, since the first day I saw you, in the sleigh ride home, at the New Year celebration, and—

"Don't forget the ball," I say with a smirk.

"And all the other times too."

"Even after the horse race in the alley?" I ask

"Even then. I can't stop thinking about you."

"You always turn my world right side up when I think it is upside down," I say. "I cannot imagine my life without you. As a matter of fact, I want to keep you with me forever. Do you think you can tolerate me forever?"

"I'd like to try," Thaddeus clears his throat. "I mean—if you are willing to have me, that is." A crimson hue floods his cheeks, rushing to his ears. He looks at me then looks away, grinning.

Now it is my turn to surprise him. I lean in, my arms around his neck, kissing him with a long playful meandering of my lips on his. His hands disappear from me in surprise, then come back to pull me close to him. We plant short kisses across each other's faces and lips, but I pull back while still holding his face close to mine.

"I love you, Thaddeus Marsh. I never want you from my sight for more than a day's work. Say you will stay with me."

Thaddeus winces, biting his lip.

"What is it?" I ask, fearing I offended him with my forwardness. We sit up to face each other. He takes my hands in his, kissing the fingertips peeking out from between our grasps.

"I have to tell you this," Thaddeus says, looking down to our hands joined together. Our foreheads touch, as he begins saying, "Like your brothers I have a responsibility to my country, to see it through."

I sit back, pulling my hands from his, eyebrows arching, waiting.

"But what about Ian?" I ask. "Just a month ago, he ran loose in the streets. He can't be ready this soon."

Thaddeus shrugs saying, "I assure you he is doing better than I expected."

Thaddeus takes my hands back into his. "Emilie, I need you to listen before you speak." He shakes his head asking me to mimic him. "Promise me, you'll listen."

"I-I promise?"

Thaddeus sighs, looks at me, looks away, then back to me.

He clears his throat. "I think it best for our future that I first ask you to marry me, then enlist for a two-year commitment."

"Two years!" I say, pushing back from him.

Thaddeus watches me closely, as I purse my lips closed, committed to my promise. "So, I can get back as soon as possible."

My scowl says everything.

"If I don't do it now, I may be enlisted to the end. I'd rather come right back to you."

"Don't say it," I whisper. "I can't bear it again, not today."

"I want you in my life, Emilie Prescott," Thaddeus says, forcing me to look at him with his finger under my chin. "I want you to be mine forever, build the farm with me, raise my children. And I promise you this—I will love you more every day, until our last days together." He swallows, deep breath, then asks, "Will you live this life with me?"

"Are you proposing to me, Thaddeus Marsh?" I ask. His bittersweet proposal has a daunting echo. My mind is a heavy cloud of confusion, two emotions fighting for dominance. Looking down, I concentrate on the emotional confusion.

His finger under my chin, Thaddeus lifts my head to meet his deep blue eyes, warmed by adoration, imploring me to speak to his soul.

"I don't know what I would do without you," My voice catches, opening my thinly veiled resolve.

"We will be doing it together," Thaddeus pulls me close. "I promise to come home to you. We will pick up where we've left off. Will you wait for me?"

"I want you now," I say, thinking about the myriad of meanings, none of which I would be opposed to as long as it is with Thaddeus.

A knowing smile plays on his lips, the glint in our eyes flirting with each other.

"I better ask your father's permission first. Before we go too far, because once I marry you, it will be harder to let you go."

"Too late. You are already mine, and no one will ever replace what we have."

"Is asking him tomorrow too soon?" Thaddeus asks.

"You'd better wait a few days."

Thaddeus furrows his brow, forming a question.

"My father needs to get into my mother's good graces first."

Proposal of Love

BEING DEEPLY LOVED BY SOMEONE GIVES YOU STRENGTH
WHILE LOVING SOMEONE DEEPLY GIVES YOU COURAGE.
~LAO TZU

JULY 1861
GETTYSBURG, PENNSYLVANIA

The woodshop has not been the same since Henry left a few days ago. Jacob misses the companionship; their long father-son talks. Still, he has the comfort of his tools, which hang neatly on a rack, gleaming in the afternoon light. In the center of the room, a large workbench with a partially finished cupboard takes up most of the space. The scent of sawdust and heavy oiled leather hangs in the air, a familiar comfort to him.

Rolling up his sleeves, Jacob continues his work on the soft rosewood, carving into it an intricate leaf and ivy pattern to create a trim meant for the top of the cupboard. Finishing this will get the commissioned project to its owner on time. Time, which he easily becomes carried away with as he focuses on the task at hand.

A soft rap at the woodshop door alerts Jacob. He pulls the chisel and mallet away from the pattern and looks up.

Thaddeus is standing in the door, waiting to be invited into his sanctuary.

"Come on in," Jacob motions to Thaddeus. "Take a seat, I'm just finishing this up."

"Thank you, sir," Thaddeus says, a formality in his voice Jacob is not accustomed to as co-workers and friends. Thaddeus's face is serious, a small twitch to his right eye, as beads of sweat glisten on his forehead. He wipes his hands on his trousers.

Jacob smiles to himself recognizing the man's discomfort as his own back when he was in his prime with Julia.

"Seeing Emilie tonight?" Jacob asks, pulling at why Thaddeus is in his presence instead of entertaining his daughter on the porch swing this beautiful summer evening.

"No sir, I mean—if it's permitted—meaning, I didn't make it an official night to see her," Thaddeus released a heavy sigh.

"Sounds like you have something else to say," Jacob says, picking up a discarded rag to wipe his hands, and sitting next to Thaddeus. "So say it. I'm listening."

Thaddeus takes a deep breath; a smile graces his face as his deep blue eyes soften.

"I want to ask you—" Thaddeus clears his throat and tries again. "I want to ask you for Emilie's hand."

"I think she needs that hand more than you, son, but if she's willing, I'll grab the axe," Jacob smirks at his wide-eyed question mark written all over Thaddeus's face. Jacob chuckles.

"That is not what I mean," Thaddeus tries to fix the confusion. "I-I want to marry your daughter and I'm asking your permission—sir!" Thaddeus's chest rises and falls as he tries to catch his breath and kidnapped nerves. His hands tremble and a bead of sweat races down his temple.

"Did you struggle this hard when you asked her?" Jacob asks, his smirk unwavering.

"Not quite sir. Emilie is a whole different nervous for me."

Thaddeus clears his throat, redirecting his eyes for a moment as a red tinge soaks his cheeks. "You see, I have enlisted. I would like to marry her before I leave." Shuffling his feet in sawdust on the floor, his shoulders have a slight slump. "I figure, if I sign up for two years, I can get home quick, and we can start the homestead my father has waiting for us."

The boy Jacob has come to admire as a young man looks at him, eye to eye, filled with a chest full of hope. "I promise, sir, I'll do right by your daughter—I love her."

Jacob eyes the nervous man. This is quite different than their day-to-day interaction. He didn't expect to have so much power over Thaddeus's life. Sure, with his daughter, this decision was bestowed upon him at her birth, but today another man is asking to take his position and care for her. They already agreed to some extent in casual talk and his blessing in allowing Thaddeus and Emilie to court but enlisting—this adds another complication to the situation.

"You realize my sons are fighting on the other side of this war," Jacob says, as he moves to pick up a bit of sandpaper and begins to run it over a slab of wood in need of his attention.

Thaddeus swallows hard. "I know, Emilie told me. I can only pray we never meet as I do not wish to take up arms against family. Jacob—Mr. Prescott, I have no ill thoughts with their decision. I just want to do my duty for my country. It is my job to heed the call, even though it pains me to think of taking up arms against our own countrymen."

Jacob listens but continues sanding.

"I will be back as soon as I can. I look forward to a good marriage to your daughter."

Jacob, thoughts weighing heavy on his mind, alas shakes his head. Stands upright. Sets the sandpaper aside.

He looks over to Thaddeus.

"The problem with this plan you two thought up is neither

of you know what'll happen in the next two years," Jacob says. "Do you love my daughter so much that you're willing to leave her a widow?"

Stillness.

Silence.

Heaviness.

Jacob sees the color drain from Thaddeus's face, beads of sweat forming and now dripping down his cheek.

"No, that is the last thing I would ever do—I'd rather stay home than leave her saddled with widowhood."

Jacob puts a hand on the man's back to steady him.

"One more question. Do you love my daughter so much that you would be willing to wait? Wait until you are safely home to give her everything you plan?"

"I worry about her security sir," Thaddeus clears his throat. "If we are engaged, it will give both of us hope in the days ahead." Thaddeus bites his lip and rubs his hands together, trying to get comfortable in this situation.

Jacob waits for him to look back at him, and when he does, he speaks. "I am proud of both of you. There is no denying you seem happy together, but Emilie will stay under my guardianship, where her future will still hold promise no matter how the conflict ends. When you return, I'll happily walk her down the aisle to be at your side."

"Sir," Thaddeus's face lightens with hope as a grin plays on his lips, "may we at least make it official and become betrothed until my return? She needs the security, and I need the hope."

"My wife and I'll be more than happy to meet both of your needs with the engagement," Jacob shakes Thaddeus's hand, before pulling him in for an embrace. "Welcome to the family."

Crickets chirp a relentless chorus as the last gasp of summer light surrenders to the sky blooming with an infinite sprinkling of stars. The air hangs heavy with humidity, clinging to my skin despite the approaching night. The Marsh's stone and clapboard farmhouse looms up the dusty road after the Welty's and the Byrne's, but before the Halle's.

The invitation to the Marsh's hadn't come directly from Thaddeus, but from Father after a late return from the woodshop. I suspect Thaddeus confided in him during the day, but Father's memory at times resembles a leaky sieve. This dinner, my first at their residence, holds a weighty significance now that Thaddeus and I have confessed our love.

A quick grimace as I glance at my hands that reveal the telltale signs of a hard day's work and the reminders of the alley—the backs red from exertion and the faint pink impression of old scrapes. I hasten to pull on a pair of cotton gloves hoping to disguise the evidence. A flicker of excitement flutters in my chest.

Taking a deep breath, looking to Father's waiting hand, its reassuring callouses a stark contrast to my own trembling fingers. I slip my hand into his, the familiar warmth calming my jitters. Together, the three of us step out of the carriage, the soft crunch of the gravel underfoot the only sound.

The ivory organdy three-piece dress feels cool against my skin, the light blue and white lace adds a touch of summer elegance. My hair cascades in long auburn curls, while a braided crown encircles my head. The final touch—a delicate cotton-lace shawl draped over my shoulders. Tonight, I will leave a lasting impression, be seen in the best possible light.

"Well, well," Father voice is filled with mock surprise. "Look at the thorn between these two beautiful roses."

The comment, accompanied by the rustle of our dresses, elicits a giggle from Mother.

A giggle escapes me, "Father, you always say that."

"Do not." Father feigns offense through the twinkle in his eye as the creases of laugh lines deepen in his cheeks.

"As long as I can remember," I counter, the familiar banter easing a smile onto my own features.

Mother's warm laugh fills the night air. "Oh, Emilie, that is truly a long time—seventeen years to be exact."

Father's firm knock on the Marsh's front door draws our attention back to the present.

"When will you be back to fetch me?" I ask as Father continues to host my hand on his arm. "I am sure Thaddeus won't mind escorting me home."

A chuckle, an exchange of looks between him and Mother. "That won't be necessary. We're all invited this evening."

"Oh?" I say, holding back my surprise. "That'll be lovely. I wasn't expecting—"

The solid oak door creaks open, revealing Thaddeus, his face a reflection of my own nervous excitement. He looks handsome, as always, in his best and only suit, and the smile he musters is warm and genuine.

My breath hitches as his gaze sweeps over me.

"Emilie," Thaddeus's voice tickles my ear with its deep rich tones. "You look—" His smile falters for a moment, his throat working as if struggling to form the right words. "—a picture of beauty tonight."

"Come," he says, recovering and ushering us inside. "My parents are right this way." Thaddeus takes my hand in his, the warmth of his touch whispers, *I'm home.*

His hand in mine, Thaddeus leads the way through the vestibule and to the parlor on the left. Lamps and wall sconces are lit, filling the room with a warm evening glow. Bookshelves line the walls and reside on either side of tall windows where light curtains blow gently as the summer breeze filters in.

"Father and Mother, may I present the Prescotts," Thaddeus says, as Mr. and Mrs. Marsh stride over to shake Father and Mother's hands.

"Thank you for inviting us to your home." Father shakes Mr. Marsh's hand.

"Yes, what a beautiful home you have," Mother compliments Mrs. Marsh.

"And if it isn't the beauty to our beastly son." Mr. Marsh grins as he moves over to me, sweeps up my free hand, and plants a gingerly kiss on the back of my glove, "How are you Emilie?"

"I'm well," I say with a smile that can't be helped.

Although I've met Thaddeus's parents in brief, it seems only now that I realize the resemblance between Mr. Marsh and his eldest son. It's remarkable. Deep blue eyes, chiseled jaw, and his tall muscular stature—Thaddeus is just like him, a reflection of the Marsh reputation as men of hard work and steadfast pride.

"Oh Edward, be kind. Our son isn't that hairy," teases Mrs. Marsh, a pleasant looking woman who matches her husband in height and hosts light brown hair atop her head. Tanned skin and lines of hard work are beginning to show around her clear blue eyes, and the laugh that follows from her dances carefree above the room and sets a smile on everyone's face.

"Nor do I have tusks yet." Thaddeus adds winking at me, not about to let his parents outdo him in witty banter.

I giggle again, feeling a heat rise in my cheeks.

"You hear that, Emilie? Key word, 'yet,'" says Mr. Marsh before he lets go of my hand and gestures to everyone. "Please take a seat. It's a lovely occasion, and we've been looking quite forward to the evening."

Lovely occasion, I thought this just a dinner?

"Quite, but no time for me to sit. Dinner will be ready in a few minutes," says Mrs. Marsh. "Please, though, get comfortable. Make yourselves at home."

"Caroline, do you need help?" Mother offers.

"Oh, no-no, that won't be necc—" Her head starts off shaking, then begins to wobble, before nodding, "—on second thought Julia, yes, come right this way. You see, I'm just not accustomed to receiving help with a house full of boys, not with the cooking anyway. And good thing! They'd poison us all."

Thaddeus lets go of my hand and goes to sit with the men as I take a step forward toward Mother, who nods for me to follow Mrs. Marsh and her across the hall, through the dining room and—

Before Mother and I pass through the swinging kitchen door, I pull her to a stop.

"What's going on?" I ask.

"I don't know what you mean, Emilie," Mother nods for me to follow. "It's just dinner with the Marshes."

She puts her hand on my elbow and guides me into the kitchen.

A tapestry of aroma woven into marvelous dishes greets us. The warmth from the stove they bubble and roast away on would be stifling except for the evening breeze toying with the curtains on either side of the room.

"Ian should be in from the chores any moment," Mrs. Marsh

says, handing me a pitcher of water to set on the table. "Then we can sit down."

"Dinner smells delicious," Mother says, looking around for something to help with, but nothing comes her way. Mrs. Marsh flits from pot, to pan, to oven, to dish saying here and there, "Oh, I've got that ... Don't worry about it, I'll handle it ... No, it's all right. Your company is nice enough!"

Bang!

We jump.

But it's just the back kitchen door flying open.

"Ian! You scared me half to death," Mrs. Marsh shouts.

Ian pokes his head around the door, "Sorry, I didn't want to be late for dinner."

"And if my door flies off its hinges, you won't have a dinner."

Ian smiles big and immediately turns his attention to us, the guests, who he waves a hand at. "Hey Miss Prescott and Mrs. Prescott, You hear that? She beats me five times a day and sends me to bed without supper!" Ian looks back to his mother, a silly grin on his face as he disappears into the mudroom.

As Ian scurries through the kitchen and up the backstairs, Mrs. Marsh calls after him, "We are setting the table with food right now!"

A muffled response is heard over the stomping of footfalls, as he hurries up the steps.

Mrs. Marsh then turns to us, "I don't starve him or beat him, just another one of his tall tales he likes to spin."

Mother and I exchange a knowing smile and laugh.

"Oh, we know," says Mother.

"We have a Henry."

Mrs. Marsh's smile broadens at our shared empathy. "Shall we serve the food?"

After a solemn moment of thanks to the Lord, the dining room fills with conversation as we take our seats.

I move to sit next to Thaddeus, only to have Ian try to bump me out of what he considers his place.

"Ian," Thaddeus says, "Emilie is taking your place. Sit over there."

Ian looks at me, a wave of confusion crossing his brow, before pulling out the chair opposite his usual seat.

Laid out on the long dining room table is a symphony of delights. A regiment of pickles lay in a crystal dish next to baskets of fresh golden rolls, still warm from the oven. Their aroma begs for butter, every pat stamped with a flower shape and sitting not too far from each setting. Next, a vibrant bowl of blue and yellow hosts an equally colorful coleslaw with purple and green ribbons of crisp cabbage and hints of sweet carrot shavings, tossed in a tangy vinegar emulsion. Then, nestled into a cast iron dish is a bubbling treasure—scalloped potatoes, creamy and with crisp browned edges. Its richness promises a velvety taste I can already feel on my tongue. Finally, at the head of the table, Mr. Marsh starts to carve the golden roasted chicken, its skin glistening with a fragrant glaze. Tendrils of steam, with whispers of rosemary and thyme, dance upward as the knife pierces the golden skin, carrying the promise of mouth-watering bites.

We pass dishes around the table, and the sound of forks clinking against plates fills the air. Each of us is silent, wrapped up in the enjoyment of the dinner before us. Seated next to

Thaddeus, I notice he feels stiff and more formal this evening. His hands remain in his lap never straying as to our usual foray of hands touching under the table. Not even his foot brushes against mine in silent comradery. I miss it. I miss him.

When the adults are all engrossed in their own conversations, I whisper, "Are you feeling all right?"

"I am fine. Are you enjoying the evening?" Thaddeus asks, raising his glass to his lips.

Across the table, Ian is watching us closely.

I smile at him. He looks down at his potatoes.

"I feel things are different somehow," I say, a slight nudge to his shoulder.

A smile plays at his lips. "Don't worry, yourself. Everything is fine. Trust me." Thaddeus puts his glass back on the table near his plate. His hand drops back to his lap and grazes over mine.

"What a lovely dinner," says Father. "Thank you again for inviting us. Mrs. Marsh, my compliments."

"Oh, please, call me Caroline. But thank you." She covers her smile with her napkin.

In fact, everyone is smiling, looking at each other, holding something back.

I look to Ian, hoping he will give it away, but he only clamps his mouth shut and looks away from me.

My hand yearns for another tender touch from Thaddeus, but everyone is starting at us.

I squirm.

"What's for dessert, Ma?" Thaddeus asks, trying to ease the tension from us.

"Dessert can wait," she declares staring at us, beaming, unblinking.

Mr. Marsh places his napkin on the table and sits back in his chair saying, "Yes, it can, my dear Caroline. But Thaddeus my boy, there is no time like the present to get this off your chest."

All eyes go to Thaddeus.

Well, that certainly took the tension off of one of us.

I look to Thaddeus.

He is looking down at his lap. Then he swallows, pushes his chair away from the table, and stands.

My eyes move to Mother and Father, who are still grinning. I shift to Ian, who is watching wide-eyed while Mr. and Mrs. Marsh sit back in a moment of adoration.

Thaddeus clears his throat, wipes his hands against his trousers.

I look back to him.

He turns to me saying, "Emilie, we are gathered here to make it official."

Official? Official! How's my hair? Am I wearing the right outfit for this? Is this protocol? Tell me I have nothing on my face? If I dab with the napkin will that seem unsightly?

He takes my hand, pulling my fingers away from the pleats of my skirt, drawing me out of my head and into his gaze.

"We have grown together, and before I go to war, I want to ask you if, when I get back, will you be my wife? And as a promise, to wait for each other—" Thaddeus reaches into his pocket and pulls out a box. He opens it revealing a multi-stoned flower shaped ring, "Will you accept this ring that I will come home and marry you soon?"

The puzzle of strange events start to piecing themselves together. Father and Thaddeus meeting, the announcement of the dinner at such a late hour, Mother avoiding my questions, secret looks, smiles exchanged, and now—this. Thaddeus renewing the pledge we made to each other at the creek, making my heart blossom in my chest as his promise rings true and his heart speaks to mine.

Still, I look around. Everyone's eyes are on me.

Am I taking too long?

My eyes travel back to Thaddeus, his sky-blue hues meeting my earth-brown gaze, though he also bites his lip, waiting for me—holding his breath.

"I will wait for you," I say, my voice whispers. "I will wait forever and always if it means I get to be your wife."

I stand as Thaddeus plucks the ring from the box and slides it over my left ring finger. The gold band feels strange, but the warmth of his hands in mine does not. Our eyes meet, sealing this promise between us.

The dining room bursts into cheers and clapping. I look to Mother and Mrs. Marsh who quickly tuck away their small flags for sentimental tears back into their dress pockets, blinking back their pride and bittersweet memories of their girlhood.

Mr. Edward stands. "Shall we have dessert in the parlor? I think Jacob and I could use a drink."

Everyone moves out of the dining room, leaving Thaddeus and I still standing next to the table.

"This is beautiful," I say to Thaddeus.

"Not as beautiful as you, but I say you both complement each other well," Thaddeus takes my hand to admire the ring. "I want you to remember, my hope and my desire is to return to you safe and sound. Your Father promised to walk you down the aisle to me as soon as we are reunited."

"That sounds like my father," I say, admiring the ring. "What is that stone?"

Thaddeus looks down. "Well, the jeweler told me this ring spells 'Dearest'" He studies me a moment. "So, the center is a diamond, emerald, amethyst, ruby, use the emerald again, sapphire and tourmaline."

"Thinking over the spelling and the sentiment. "I hope to be your dearest for a very long time."

Thaddeus pulls me to him. I feel a kiss near my ear as his warm voice imprints into my mind, "Forever, my Dearest Emilie."

Duty Calls

WHEN DUTY CALLS, THAT IS WHEN CHARACTER COUNTS.
~ WILLIAM SAFIRE

JULY 1861
GETTYSBURG, PENNSYLVANIA

The air hangs heavy with the scent of blooming lilacs and fresh cut hay, a symphony of summer clinging in the twilight. Fireflies begin their nightly ballet in the long grasses at the end of the porch, blinking like celestial winks against the inky July sky. Thaddeus and I sit together on the creaky porch swing, its rhythmic *moan-groan* a comforting counterpoint to the disquiet in my heart.

Reality is closing in as we spend these last precious days together. Each push of the swing is a stolen moment, like a tick of the clock from the relentless sands of time. A long yarn of conversation spins in my mind. His calloused hand grazes mine.

"What are you thinking?" Thaddeus asks.

He startles me out of the thoughts.

"Just of the news I read today," I say. "It bothers me."

"Which news?" he asks. "The paper is full of information."

"Virginia split into two states," I say. "They elected a man named Francis Pierpont as the provisional governor of the area.

I guess there's no name for this new state, but why would Virginia separate?"

"I am sure the article mentions—" Thaddeus begins.

My eyes meet his as I nod. "It was rhetorical."

"Oh."

I feel his hand caress mine once more; the comforting warmth holds me, suspends me, and grounds me to him. My gaze drifts off to the crescent moon in the sky, shining bright, and yet like our love it, too, has yet to fully bloom, held back by the inky unknown of the dark and lonesome. It looks like fate is cruel to everyone these days, to the families of Gettysburg, Virginia, my own, Thaddeus and me—even the moon.

"I feel like I've known you for a lifetime and many more lives, if that's possible," I say, "and yet, not long enough." I wait, needing to hear him as much as I feel him.

Thaddeus reaches for me, pulling me into his chest. His touch is a silent promise, a vow whispering in a language of stolen glances and lingering touches.

Will this be enough? Will these memories forged in the quiet moments of unspoken love be strong enough to bridge the vast distance that looms before us?

"Do you think there will be enough time?" I ask, whispering into his chest.

He kisses the top of my head, tightening his arms around me, his touch sending warmth blooming in my chest despite the night's chill settling in.

"Enough time for what, my love?"

"Enough time for everything," I say my voice choking with panic, as a tear breaks free, sliding down my cheek. "To know each other, to love each other to—" I stop before the pent-up hysteria bubbles over. Biting back my rambling, my lip catches between my teeth.

"I'm coming right back to you." He promises with a smile. "Two years will pass by in the blink of an eye. Well, maybe two blinks if you let Sarah's chatter fill the silence. I'm sure she'll love helping you plan the wedding, which we'll have twenty-four hours after I arrive back home."

"Why twenty-four hours?" I ask, a hesitant smile winks at him.

"I want to smell good, and besides I don't think I'll be able to wait any longer," Thaddeus's voice is low and inviting as his eyes warm with desire.

He cups my cheek in his hand, his thumb brushing away the stray tear. His deep blue pools submerse mine.

"Emilie," his voice thick with emotion, "we may be miles apart sooner than we like, but you'll still be in my heart, every beat, every breath."

He leans closer to me; his lips brush mine in a kiss that is achingly sweet, a desperate plea to hold onto this fragile moment. Our hope is that it will give us both the strength we need to endure what lies ahead.

"I wish you could marry me now," I say, a whisper on his lips. Thaddeus pulls me closer, as close as either of us dare.

"Soon Emilie, soon."

The floorboard creaks with heavy footfalls.

Is it possible?

Unfortunately, Father is coming to end our evening.

Can I convince him otherwise?

Thaddeus is on his feet, offering his hand to help me off the swing before a protest can escape my lips.

"Time to leave, sir?" Thaddeus says, as Father rounds the corner.

Father nods. "Good night, Thaddeus."

I watch Thaddeus disappear into the inky night as the fireflies continue the second act of their ballet. I pray there is a second act for us, a light at the end of the war's dark and lonesome night and hold onto his promise that we will be strong enough to meet each other at the end—two years.

Why can't I marry him tomorrow?

Thaddeus may be satisfied to wait, but the waiting gnaws at me, an irritation sharp as glass under an unsuspecting foot. Walking through the kitchen, the light in the parlor is still there. Maybe I can change his mind.

Father sits in his favorite winged back chair, the paper perched straight in front of his eyes. His pipe dangles between his teeth.

Mother must have gone to bed already.

I step into the room; he doesn't acknowledge me, but I'll make him. I'll make him listen or at least answer me.

"Why won't you let us marry before he leaves?" It comes out more a defiant demand than a request.

The paper does not move; his eyes never leave the page.

"Father? Father! Father, I don't know how I am going to get through the next two years without him."

His eyes remain on the black and white print, a slight wave of a page as he turns to the next bit of reading.

"Is this just a closed subject?" I ask. "Not up for discussion?" I cross my arms, my frustration growing, with each flicker of non-reaction from him.

His eyes glance to me, narrowing.

"For a man against slavery, I don't see why you would treat

your daughter as one, something to barter with, rather than ask the permission of. It's my life! Why don't I get a say in what I want?"

Father's chest rises and falls before his gaze darkens and turns back to the doom and gloom reporters and their readers feast upon.

"I just don't understand," I say, sinking into the couch, biting my lower lip.

If he's just going to sit there, I might as well spill my heart to the gaping chasm of the generation between us.

"This is truly cruel to keep us apart. I need him. Father, don't you remember how you wished Mother was by your side? How you could do nothing about it until the preacher gave his blessing?"

I let out a long sigh.

I know he hears me, but how can I get him to listen?

"Have you had Mother for so long, that you no longer recall what it is like to suffer her absence?"

Father lowers the newspaper; his eyes soften. Is that a smile I see playing on his lips, as if he understands the cadence of my heart?

So why? Why must he torture me?

He gives a long-drawn-out sigh ... of frustration?

Yes, frustration. That's what I feel. All the frustration!

He folds the paper, reusing the creases before setting it aside on the table. Then he takes the pipe from his lips, placing it in the tray beside the chair before his eyes turn to me.

Dare I breathe? Can a truce be had? Will he at last set me free?

"Perhaps my old, hardened ways are cruel to your young hearts," Father says, "but someone has to be the voice of reason within the noise of your befuddled minds and elsewhere. As your father and guardian, I am tasked with that job."

"My guardian?" I ask. "But why does that make a difference now that I'm an adult?"

"The difference is I remain your guardian until you marry," Father's tone hardens. "If you are widowed, my job becomes more difficult to help you control your own affairs as a single woman."

"But Thaddeus will take care of me," I say turning the ring on my finger, keeping myself calm, while knowing I'd rather have one night with him than risk a lifetime of longing, not knowing the touch of his love.

Father looks to the ceiling; my gaze follows after his.

"Did it work?" I ask.

"Did what work?"

"Your prayer."

Father chuckles, "Well, this conversation isn't quite over yet." Another sigh follows though, his jaw hardening.

The next words he speaks—rise barely above a whisper, "What if something happens?"

My heart races in my chest, saying, "What if nothing happens before something does?"

"Emilie, I am not going to negotiate this with you." Father's voice deepens with a sharp edge.

"But is it not the words of poets such as Tennyson, who says 'Tis better to have loved and lost, than never to have loved at all.' Does not such men of art know more of man's heart than all others?"

"A modern tale from the books in which you pour yourself does not make for reality Emilie. I'll not pick you up broken and ruined for marriage if you become a widow, not because I don't want to, but because by law I won't be able to."

"How could you think like that?" I say my voice rising with the panic coursing through my body. "Can't you be delicate about it?"

"Reality isn't delicate, it's harsh. I've tried to protect you from it, but you aren't listening, and like your brothers, seem bound and determined to suffer from it."

Silence.

"I can learn to handle Thaddeus' affairs; I'll have to while he's gone anyway."

"I said no! For Christ's sake, is losing two sons not enough? Must I lose a third and my only daughter as well? Am I the only one in this family who bares patience!" His face is red with vexation, but his brown eyes hold a depth and a pain I cannot dispute as a tear draws down his cheek.

"So, the final answer is no, I have to wait," I say, barely above a whisper.

"I'm afraid so," Father settles back in his chair, looking away from me, pinching the bridge of his nose between forefinger and thumb. "I would change it if I could, but this is best."

I nod and lean over to hug him, kissing his cheek. "Sorry, Father., Thank you for listening," I say.

"Emilie," Father's arms wrap around me and he rubs my back followed by a tender squeeze, "he'll be all right. Thaddeus is strong, smart, and he has you to fight for. I know he will do everything to get back home to you."

I pull back.

Our eyes meet. Father does know my heart. I nod and slip off to bed.

The hourglass of sand slips to the last grains hanging on the edge before dropping to the bottom, signaling the end. Thaddeus leaves tomorrow.

Poised at the vanity mirror, I pull a strand of my long auburn hair to the forefront. All I have on hand is a pair of small embroidery bird scissors. At the nape of my neck, and behind my ear, I measure out the strand and snip it off. Using a thin burgundy ribbon, I tie the lock together. Once it is secure, I wrap it around my pinky finger in a tight circle, hold it between my forefinger and thumb, and place it into the locket before sealing it shut. I just need to—

"What are you doing?"

I jump.

Looking up, I see Mother standing in the doorway and then walking into my room. Questions form in all the creases of her quizzical expression.

Still holding the locket in my hand, I say, "Packing items for Thaddeus."

She spies the lock of hair in one side of the heart and an old photo of me cut down to size nestled within the other side of the locket. A smile graces her lips.

"That was our last family portrait at the plantation," Mother says. "You were fifteen and a half."

"I'm sorry, it was the only likeness I had of me. Do I look too young?"

Mother's arm slips around my shoulder, pulling me close to her. "He won't care. It's still you, and I imagine there will be many nights where he'll look at this and remember you as he knows you now."

"I wish I could go with him," I say, putting the locket in a drawstring pouch and spraying it with my rose perfume. Walking over to the desk, I pull out stacks of paper and pencils, tying each together with another burgundy ribbon.

"So, this is where all my ribbon is going," Mother's brow arches.

"For good reason," I say, finishing the packing.

"Did you pack him some extra shirts and socks from the supply?" Mother asks.

"I did. Thaddeus will be well dressed and have warm feet. Even packed a bit of tallow."

"Tallow?"

"Just a bit of advice I read, for the blisters."

Latching the knapsack secure, there is nothing left for me to do but say goodbye.

"I don't know how to do this, Mother. I don't know when I will feel his hand in mine again. I don't know when I will smell his cologne or hear his laugh. I don't know—"

I move away from her plop down on the bed, my face in my hands. "I try not to dwell on it, but how can I be brave, when I don't feel brave enough to face tomorrow?"

Mother moves to sit beside me. I feel her arms around me, enclosing me in her protective embrace, saying, "We are Prescott women. We have the strength to endure the most difficult times." She is rocking me. "We're not alone in worrying over our boys. We'll endure this together. We'll worry, cry, and be strong together, holding this vigil until they return to us. Praying that the Lord brings them back—"

"Brings us together," I say.

Mother smiles and nods, giving me another squeeze. "Be sure to kiss him 'until next time.' When you get back to the house,

I'll give you twelve hours to miss him, but then we have work to do. It's the only way to make the time pass. Watched pot and all that."

Her words soothe me like butter on a burn. Her confidence roots my resolve and strength. A small seedling at first, but with time, I will come to bloom again, like a daffodil, carrying my seeds of hope into the horizon.

"Thank you," I whisper. "I can do this."

"You can, and for it, you'll be a stronger braver woman in two years' time. Thaddeus will be impressed."

"Oh, he promised to marry me in twenty-four hours after coming home," I say, a smile gracing my mouth.

"Well then, we have two years to plan a wedding."

"The best wedding!"

I woke before anyone else this morning; I want to get the day going. It is a bittersweet day of lasts for me until Thaddeus returns home. After dressing, I opened his knapsack to unpack it and repack it, making sure I put everything in there that he needs.

The velvet pouch containing my locket and handkerchief sprayed with rose perfume. His housewife kit for repairs, a jar of tallow, three shirts, and four pair of wool socks. A written note about the tallow and long marches per the veteran's account in the newspaper, a letter to him filled with encouragement, promising I'll be here—ready—with open arms when he returns. The paper smudged with one lone tear that I couldn't avoid or wipe away fast enough. Latching the bag closed, I stand, ready for the sun to rise and the trip to the train station.

Captain McPhereson came back to Gettysburg a short while ago to recruit a few more men to complete his regiment of Gettysburg boys. Thaddeus is one of them. "At least I will be among my neighbors," he said one night.

The sea of people is overwhelming. They flow past me, some jostling me with their bags or shoulders. It is hard to pick out one face as a river of faces stream past me. Promising soldiers and hopeful citizens fill the platform, bustling and jostling and dodging each other as people wait to board the train. Small children and women with ribbons of red, white, and blue wave the colors, sending off their loved ones. The hustle and bustle of the train station heralds a scene of celebration for the men who have chosen to leave for West Chester. No one is shedding tears, except an unhappy child wanting to run instead of being held hostage in his mother's arms; his red face pinched in anger, his shriek echoing off the platform roof and the brick walls of the adjacent building.

And then there is me.

I don't feel patriotic or proud today. I feel lost, sad, and left to wait for an outcome in my favor. Despite my conversation with Mother yesterday, I struggle to forgo my anxiety and fight to keep it locked away as I force smiles of bravery and support for Thaddeus, once I find him.

Where is he?

"Emilie!"

My name comes through the crowd again, "Emilie!"

I listen. It doesn't sound like him. Perhaps because it isn't. Perhaps because—I turn to see Stephen walking toward me, his eyes filled with excitement, an eager smile gracing his face.

His hair is trimmed, face clean shaven, and his clothes appear fresh—even pressed.

So, he is going. Good for him.

I don't return a smile to him, only a slight nod of my chin.

"I take it you are not here to say goodbye to me," Stephen says, trying to elicit a smirk all the same.

"Good-bye, Stephen," I say, trying to keep ill thoughts from entering my head. "Stay safe." I turn away from him, still looking for Thaddeus, craning my neck, stretching my toes, growing more nervous as the train's whistle blows.

"Emilie," Stephen's voice is softer. "I want to apologize for—"

I turn back to him.

"No, Stephen," I say. "Keep it to yourself. I don't need your sorry attempts."

And I refuse to let an awkward silence stand between us. My eyes return to their vigil, praying for Thaddeus to arrive. I see his arm waving to me!

In a few quick strides, his faint cologne whispers a tickle to my nose.

"How long have you been waiting?" Thaddeus asks as his arms envelop me into an embrace. I hug him back. He kisses the top of my head, keeping a tight hold.

Can't we just stay like this?

I continue to hold him, treasuring this moment, praying I will never forget the rush of excitement, the thrill of him, and how my body responds to his touch.

"Let's just stay here," I say into his jacket, "just like this forever."

"That would be my first choice." Thaddeus points to the strap over my shoulder, I feel the knapsack move and hear him ask,

"What's this?"

He releases me.

"Oh, it's for you," I say. "Made it for you to carry your things, extra socks, tallow, some memories of me—"

His eyebrow arches, "Oh, what kind of memories?"

"You'll have to look later," I say, relishing the playful side of him.

"Do you think it's big enough to fit all of you?" He says, opening the clasp, peering into the sack. "Hmmm, not your size." He eyes me with a wink, which makes me giggle.

"I wish it was," I say, "For I would be a dutiful wife and wash your clothes and keep you warm at night." Thaddeus pulls me back into his arms, close enough for my own breath to warm his ear. "Your sole job is to bring yourself and whatever is in that velvet bag home to me. I expect both of you in two years."

Silence falls between us.

"A bath and marriage," he winks at me.

"I'll be ready, my love," I whisper.

Holding each other, not caring about anything, we remain locked, unbreakable in each other's arms. Breathing him, feeling his warmth, listening to his heartbeat, I memorize and hold tight.

We startle as the blare of the train whistle marks the last grain of sand dropping to the bottom of the hourglass.

Time to go.

We continue to hold each other.

The crowd noises quiet around us as he cups my chin in his hand, raising my lips to meet his in a kiss. A bittersweet farewell, a desperate collision of salty tears and lingering sweetness. The lingering warmth of his lips, a brand, a memory that will surely be imprinted in my dreams and revisited in two years.

Two years. I can do this. We can do this.

His arms press us close, sealing his promises near and dear to our beating hearts.

"I have to go—" His hand grabs hold of the rail to the boarding steps of the train.

"I will check the post office daily," I say, the tears streaking my face, a glimmer of a forced smile.

"Be strong, my love. I'll write soon."

Our eyes meet, our souls—

"I love you, Emilie Prescott."

"And I love you, Thaddeus Marsh."

I reach to grasp his spare hand and close my fingers around his. A desperate squeeze, a plea to my memory to hold onto his touch, his chuckle, his grin, his blue eyes meeting mine—

"Young lady, you must step back from the platform. The train is fixing to depart," says a porter.

"It's okay, Emilie. I'll be back for you."

No, no. Not yet. I'm not ready to let go—of our awkward sleigh ride, the ease of our dances, his silly serenades, his confession of love, his lips pressed to mine, the way he softens when he talks of our future—

The train begins to move, the porter's hand grips my arm pulling me back.

Thaddeus's grip loosens, brushes, fingers slide away, taking the warmth of him from me.

"Let go! Stop!" I pull myself free. "Thaddeus!"

But my steps fall short, knowing I cannot race the blurring image of the train receding into the distance, or fight the trail of acrid oily smoke it leaves behind.

"Thaddeus ..."

His parting words echo through my mind, a promise etched into my heart, a lifeline—miles long, *I'll be back for you.*

The train disappears. The bustling station, once a symphony of sound, now reflects a hollowness, mirroring the emptiness inside of me. I take a deep breath and clench my fist. His ring bites into my skin, the pain a reminder that our love is real.

Lord keep him safe. Bring him home.

Soldiers' Life

EVERY CITIZEN SHOULD BE A SOLDIER.
THIS WAS THE CASE WITH THE GREEKS AND ROMANS
AND MUST BE THAT OF EVERY FREE STATE.
~ THOMAS JEFFERSON

JULY 1861
TRAIN STATION
GETTYSBURG, PENNSYLVANIA

Two years and I'll be right back.

As they pull out of the station, Thaddeus navigates through the train car. He needs an open window, just one where he can see her one more time, but the seats are already filled with men, women, children, and recruits going off to West Chester and beyond. His heart pounds, as the locomotive's appetite for the track ahead grows. Sweat breaks out on his brow, his breath trying to keep up with the thoughts racing through his mind.

Maybe this is a mistake?...

What if I can't make a difference?...

One single man against an army?...

Is this a fool's errand?...

Will her memory of me be enough?...

Smoke filters into the car as the train's whistle blows.

"Thaddeus! Thaddeus Marsh!"

Thaddeus looks up. Stephen is waving to him.

"Here, you can see her from this window."

Thaddeus moves into the row of seats occupied by Stephen who, after taking Thaddeus's bag, moves to allow him closer to the grimy dust laden window.

Thaddeus reaches for the latches, struggles, a pull, push, wiggle ...

The window won't open.

Thaddeus slams his fist against the window.

Passengers eye him with suspicion, and he blinks back the tears he dares not shed in front of them.

Stephen nudges him aside and wipes the window with his kerchief, clearing away some of the soot as more of the train's black smoke rushes by.

"Here, she's pretty as a picture," Stephen says. "Go on, take one last look."

Thaddeus presses up against the window as the train pulls away from the station, from home—from his future wife. His heart drops when she fades from his view. He sinks into the train seat—numb and aching. He prays it will subside sooner rather than later.

"Looks like you could use some of this," Stephen reaches into his pocket.

Out of his periphery, he sees the flash of Stephen's silver flask.

"Nah, I'll be all right. It'll just take some time, I guess."

Stephen chuckles. "Desperate times call for desperate measures." He opens the flask, and the scent of whisky wafts past.

"Maybe one sip won't hurt," Thaddeus thinks aloud, watching Stephen take a swallow.

"It'll put hair on your chest," Stephen pokes him, "and from the looks of it you need it."

Thaddeus grabs his finger.

"Watch it. Or I'll find another alley for us."

Stephen looks taken aback.

Thaddeus cracks a grin. "I joke. It's all behind us. Did you ever get a chance to apologize to her?"

Stephen looks down at his hands and shrugs. "I tried—but she wouldn't hear it."

"Can't say I blame her; she's stubborn," Thaddeus pushes Stephen's shoulder. "But we're good, yeah?"

"Yeah," Stephen says. "Though one question: I know Emilie's become a teacher and all, but—did she teach you to punch too?"

"No, but your Ma did."

The men look at each other before breaking out into boyish laughter. Flashbacks of the schoolyard they had left behind with all their childish dreams fills Thaddeus's mind. Shortly after they finished eighth grade, their boyhood friendship gave way to work, farming, and responsibilities. However, as they sat together, it appeared they picked up right where they left off in yesteryear's whispers of camaraderie.

"I'm happy to step away for a while," Stephen says, after another taste of his flask. "My parents are relentless."

"I wish it were that easy for me. Between my mother and Emilie, my nerves are frayed." He reaches for the flask.

Stephen gladly hands it to him. "You think they'll let us bunk together?"

Thaddeus thinks for a moment and then shrugs. "I guess I'd rather bunk with you than a stranger."

Thaddeus and Stephen are plunged into a new reality as soon as they arrive at the train station in West Chester, Pennsylvania. Orders bark from all different directions, as seasoned recruits assist in pushing and sometimes pulling the fresh meat off the train.

"Stand in line!"

"No talking!"

"Slackers volunteer for latrine duty!"

They're shoved into a side-by-side formation, two by two.

Thaddeus looks behind him.

"Eyes front! You're not here for sightseeing boys." The demands come from a man with three stripes on his uniform in the shape of a V, his blonde mutton chops covering his chiseled jaw. His narrow green eyes cut into the young men.

Thaddeus flinches and looks back to the front, or at least to the man in front of him.

Stephen who stands beside him gives a chuckle—

"You think that's funny? You think war is funny? Well, I got something funny for you funny-boy. It's a shovel for shit. Aren't I funny, boys?" asks the same man with the three-striped V.

"Ha! Ha! Ha!" Mechanical laughter from the soldiers doing the organizing fills the air.

"I don't hear you new recruits laughing!"

"Ha! Ha! Ha!" Echo the greenies, including Thaddeus, who can only imagine how red Stephen's face is right now.

From his peripheral he sees a soldier with two stripes in a V on his uniform, runs up and hand the one who seemed to be in charge a large shovel, which is then handed to Stephen.

The two of them don't even glance at each other after that but instead bide their time as everyone is rounded up.

At last, the train station grows quiet, save for the bark of the three-V-striped soldier, "All right boys, welcome to the Union. I'm Sergeant Dickerson, and even though your Pa didn't make you a man, I'm about to. That said, save your tears for your letters because your Ma's not here to dry them. When I say, 'Ready, march,' you're going to step forward with your left foot." He lifts his arm as he walks up and down the formation, "This is your left side. When I ask if you understand, you will respond to me with, 'Yes, sir!' Do I make myself clear?"

"Yes, sir!" everyone says in unison, with a handful of delayed responses.

"After your left foot, comes your right foot. I will count to four. The odd numbers of one and three are for when your left foot hits the ground. The even numbers of two and four are for when your right foot hits the ground. Do I make myself clear?"

"Yes, sir!"

"All right. Forward, march!"

Whoever said marching is easy, did not have to march next to Stephen Byrne, who kept getting his numbers mixed up, and nearly hit Thaddeus in the head with the shovel three times. All by accident, of course, as he kept trying to talk to a soldier moving by them to check what number they were on, or to chat with the men behind him when there were no superiors to reprimand him.

Half an hour later, the cacophony of noise from rifles, horses, and cannon barrage drowns out any banter Stephen has to offer. The reverberation enters through their boots and sends chills up Thaddeus's spine as they arrive at Camp Wayne, a small bustling military training camp near West Chester, Pennsylvania.

Upon arrival Stephen and Thaddeus are herded into a line

where they wait for their uniforms and equipment to be issued.

BOOM, BOOM!

Every new soldier in line ducks down, taking cover, arms overhead, hands clamping over their ears. The recruits looked like frogs in a snake pit. Wide-eyed and shaking, their faces covering every shade of white.

Thaddeus hears Sergeant Dickerson say to some other soldiers, "Good on them, they're still scared. Now we just got to teach them not to run."

He dares to look over his shoulder. The two officers, cigars in hand, nod to each other.

Keep it moving," he hears someone yell, "Nothing but a little thunder boys!"

A laugh comes from the cigar pair as they puff and shake their heads.

Rising back to their feet, Thaddeus takes this as a chance to get his bearings on what else the camp has to offer. Their living conditions have changed from clean and tidy to dirty and rough. Some men are seen sleeping on the ground, others are hauling straw to pad the tents, and a few others are minding their blankets for lice as they sit around campfires, just outside large and small tents.

"Camping in the woods overnight was never this bad," Stephen says, taking the proffered uniform and accoutrements as the crowd pushes him onward to receive the rest of his military equipment.

"We don't get to run back to the house in a rainstorm either," Thaddeus glances up to the storm clouds brewing above before following Stephen in collecting his issued equipment. Each of them is weighed down with tools, clothing, items for fighting, and items of survival, which they are expected to carry and maintain with their haversacks from home. Thaddeus carries their two rifles as Stephen manages the other supplies they accept before receiving direction to their sleeping quarters.

As Stephen and Thaddeus step over the ruts and mud holes in the path that leads the way to their assigned tent, the sights and sounds of the camp further mangle their senses. A mix of gunpowder, sweat, and body odor are all baked into the humidity of July.

Thaddeus shakes his head saying, "Are we sure this is what we signed up for?"

"No, but we're here now, and I swear, if someone yells at me again just for a look, I'm going to start swinging," Stephen shifts the pack of belongings from one arm to another.

"Level heads will prevail," Thaddeus warns. "We have to learn the rules in order to get out of this all in one piece."

"Yeah, but did you see them? They were all looking at us, like we were a bunch of hookers dressed in candy dresses," Stephen says. "Where the hell is our tent?"

"Row twelve, tent twenty-two," Thaddeus rereads a piece of paper in his hand. "It should be—right here. This row."

Surrounded by larger tents, a small A-tent comes into view.

"Are you kidding me?" Stephen asks. "How are we fitting in that?"

"Same way we got here. Side by side," Thaddeus says, sizing up their living quarters.

"No wonder there are no secrets in camp." Stephen lets out a whistle. "Damn thing is so small you'd smell a cricket fart."

"And an ant belch," says a soldier watching the spectacle of new blood sizing up their living conditions. "I hear winter quarters are tighter yet. Hope you like the smell of feet."

Thaddeus and Stephen look to the soldier and then turn to each other. Disdain and an eye-bulging shock gives way to doubts in Thaddeus's mind. Stephen, however, still has a mischievous twinkle, as if this is some grand adventure. Thaddeus hopes he'll eventually be able to play along because two years seem like a millennia from now.

Standing at the front of the tent, Stephen looks to Thaddeus. "Ready to move in?"

"I don't think movement is a choice. But I'm not sleeping with the mosquitoes."

"Right then," Stephen says, as each of them grabs a tent flap and flips it over the entry of the tent. When they step inside, they stand chest to chest, and only at the center of the frame.

Stephen lifts an arm to measure the height over his head saying, "At least we have that. I'll take this side."

After procuring a bale of straw, each man tries to move in their things, laying out blankets, setting their knapsacks in one corner, and hanging their belts on inside hooks already present.

"Oh, sorry," Thaddeus bumps into Stephen.

"No problem," Stephen puts down a blanket, his hand nearly smacking Thaddeus. "Oh, no, I didn't mean to—"

Thaddeus brushes it away with a wave of his hand. The tango of dodging and bumping goes on when Stephen says, "I swear we'd have more space in our mother's womb."

Thaddeus laughs. "Well, I guess that makes us twins."

More laughter follows before Thaddeus finds a solution. "How about I start us a fire while you finish moving in?"

"Good plan. Then I got to take a leak," Stephen says looking around.

"It's over there beyond those trees," Thaddeus reminds him.

Stephen waves him off with a nod of the head, "I know, got the shovel and everything, remember?"

After dinner, Thaddeus sits out by the fire, when he remembers the pouch Emilie spoke about. Retrieving his knapsack from the tent, he pulls out the velvet drawstring pouch. It reminds him of a small purse his mother might have had. Pulling the strings apart, the scent of rose oil—her favorite perfume— hits his nose. Normally, he'd think it a bit strong, but compared to the scents around him, the fragrant waft of rose is a boon. He carefully pours the pouch's contents. The silver locket, given to her by her parents upon graduation, is the first item to land upon his hand. Using his thumbnail, he opens the heart, sees a lock of her hair, and a photo of a girl younger than the one he knows, but it's her. Thaddeus sighs as a tightness overwhelms his chest.

"Please don't let this be a fool's errand," Thaddeus whispers. The fire crackles and pops in response.

Using his finger and thumb he fishes her handkerchief out, and brings it to his nose, inhaling her scent, recalling her laugh, her smile, her blush, her endless line of questions—one letter will not be enough.

"What's that?" Stephen says intruding on his thoughts.

Thaddeus sighs, tucks the items back into the purse, and looks up at Stephen, his eyes a bit puffy and red.

"You can't start moping over her now, we just got here," Stephen gives him a firm pat to the shoulder. "Stay focused. Get busy proving ourselves. Do not let her distract you."

"I'm not moping, I was just curious about what she gave me, and then the smoke got in my eyes," says Thaddeus.

"Yeah, sure you were," Stephen shakes his head. "I'm turning in. The bugle sounds at first light. Don't let that smoke get you too worked up." He then walks past Thaddeus and into the tent.

Thaddeus listens to him shuffling around as his thoughts drift back home.

Ellyn M. Baker

What's she doing right now?

I hope she's holding up better than—How am I holding up?

He shakes his head, trying to shrug it off. *It doesn't matter. There's no turning back.* She'd never have a coward for a husband, and so his commitment to his country must be his first objective. Besides, any wavering of his duties will endanger himself and others. Standing up, he moves to bank the coals of the fire. As more smoke rises, he takes note of the low murmurs around them, the snoring, and the singing of crickets—but no bug farts.

I suppose I should get some rest, while the night is still cool and before Stephen's snores beat the cannons at their own game.

Brothers in Arms

EITHER WE WILL LEARN TO LIVE LIKE BROTHERS,
OR THEY WILL DIE LIKE BEASTS.
~MAX LERNER

JULY 1861
SOMEWHERE IN VIRGINIA

If only Aaron could quiet his mind, for just a moment. The creak and moan of the wagon is better than the chattering and giggling from the boys in the back. Seth and Henry have talked nonstop since opening their eyes this morning. Oh sure, the small reprieve around twelve was nice, but it didn't last long.

Another burst of laughter breaks out behind Aaron, as the boys are currently lying in the back of the wagon, propped up on the baggage, carrying on like gossiping schoolgirls. At least the conversation is entertaining enough to chase away some of Aaron's boredom.

"Who taught you how to woo a girl, Seth?" Henry asks. "If you want to get a girl's attention, gotta tell her."

"You don't get it Henry," Seth implores Henry to listen. "I can't tell a girl nothin' because if Master Will finds out, he'll do something crazy 'cause he can't stand the sight of happiness."

"Sorry, I didn't think of it that way. Just you wait until you come back. We'll find you a nice girl to court the proper way."

"We'll see," Seth says. "I don't know—"

"Oh! Do I detect you are sweet on someone already?"

"Hey, stop! Stop!"

Aaron sees a broken twig fly past his shoulder and frowns, turning to look behind him.

Henry is throwing bits of twig at Seth, and another, and another, searching for more when he runs out, all for the sake of trying to get the truth out of his friend.

"Henry, you throw one more thing and I'm making you walk!"

Seth's cheeks grow hot, but then he grins.

Aaron watches his little brother shrug and begin to poke Seth. Rolling his eyes, Aaron shakes his head and turns back toward the road ahead. "Children."

"Your secret's safe with me. I won't tell you're sweet on—"

A pause between them.

Ah, a bit of silen—

"Oh, I know," Henry pipes up. "It's Millie. Yup, she's a dutiful little thing. I can see it."

Seth chuckles.

"What?" Henry feigns surprise. "I bet it is Corsica, Betsy, Hazel, Josie, Ruth, Sari—"

"Sari?" Both Seth and Aaron say.

"She's three years old!" Seth throws a twig back at Henry.

"Oh, I think I meant Sena!"

"That's better, but no."

"All right, but really, who is it?"

Seth sighs, "Hey, Aaron is he always like this?"

"Every waking moment," says Aaron.

"Henry what you trying to play at? You ain't nowhere near as cute as your sister. That face you making just makes you look plain dumb."

"Well then just tell, and I'll spare us all!"

Aaron hears a whisper but can't make out the words.

"Lucy! She is b—beautiful!"

Aaron nods. *Leave it to Henry to let the cat out of the bag.*

"Lucky you. Does she like you too? I mean, have you confessed to each other in private?"

If only Emilie could hear him now, gossiping like this is some tea party.

"That's personal," Seth says.

"You're right," Henry says. "But no worries, I'll go to my grave with your secret."

"You better, unless you want us to share a grave," Seth chuckles.

Aaron rolls his head, stretching his shoulders. He's had the reins in his hands since before first light. The roads are dry and cracked from no rain, the humidity lessened by the winds. The tree cover is comforting, but the heat is relentless. He shifts, uncomfortable on the hard wooden seat that now feels a part of his anatomy.

A pang of worry is ever present as the deadline inches nearer to Seth's return. Uncle William is not to be tested. He's argumentative and cranky about his uncertain future and has no qualms about making everyone else suffer his ill moods. But at least they are making good time. Another day and a half, and they should be home.

A sign announcing a tavern up the road appears and is the break Aaron has prayed for since dawn. They can stop for a decent meal and then find a place to camp for the night.

"Hey, when are we stopping? I gotta piss," Henry asks.

"Stop now or at the tavern in five miles?"

"Now, if that's all right. We need to stretch our legs anyway," says Henry.

"Now it is," Aaron pulls the wagon over.

Water for the trees, water for the horses, and water for the men, thanks to the barrel and bucket they keep in the back. Half an hour later, they pile back into the wagon. The sun shows late afternoon, a perfect time to eat and travel a bit more before nightfall.

"We're stopping at the next tavern for some food, and hopefully a good drink."

"Water?" Seth asks.

"No."

"Cider?"

"Not exactly," Henry says. "It's ale, Seth, good old ale. Since I am enlisting, I should be able to drink like a man." Henry's tone rises to get Aaron's attention.

"I heard ain't nothin' good about that stuff. Mama says spirits is the devil's work. I don't need him beatin' me about the head too. Got enough of that."

Tavern sounds of clinking, and shouts seep out of a small cabin-like building.

"That won't happen here," Aaron assures them, as he steers the wagon under a tree upon their arrival.

"Whoa," Aaron sets the brake. "All right, let's get something to eat."

They all clamor out and head up to the shabby establishment. Henry leads the way with Seth and Aaron not far behind him.

The front windows are fogged with smoke and road dust. Yellowing curtains keep out nosey peeping Toms not allowed in. The sign, decorated in peeling paint and dangling by one chain on the entrance, announces—*Miss Maggie's Copper Penny, and beneath that it reads, No Niggers Allowed on the Premises.*

Seth stops, taking two steps back. Aaron bumps into him.

"What is it?" Aaron asks, his hands going to Seth's shoulders to keep them both from toppling.

"I can't go in," Seth swallows hard.

Henry stops and turns just as his hand reaches the door, frowning, "Why not?"

Aaron's eyes follow Seth's taking a moment to read the sign before he nods and says, "I'll bring you some food and drink—"

"None of that ale," Seth says abruptly, holding his hands up as if to stop the suggestion.

"No ale. Got it. How about lemonade?" Aaron asks.

"That would be all right," Seth shrugs out of Aaron's hold on him. "I better tend the horses Mr. Aaron."

Both Aaron and Henry find themselves blinking at the formal use of their names. It's a reminder that makes them both swallow hard, as they watch Seth hurry back off the property of Miss Maggie's Copper Penny. Both of them wait until Seth is settled into the back of the wagon, peering over the edge only to offer them a wave that he's alright.

Aaron gives a stiff nod and turns back to Henry. "Well, you going to stand there all day thinking about being a man or actually bother to become one?"

Henry nods, offering his brother a small smile. "Yeah, right." He opens the door.

The small smoke-hazed tavern teams with shoulder-to-shoulder patrons, men of all shapes, sizes, and ages, military and local alike. The air is filled with the merry tune of a flutist and the shrill sound of women's laughter. The low note of old leather and sweat supports the perfume of debauchery. The sour scent of spilled stale beer, mixed with the tangy overtone of Virginia tobacco gives way to America's cologne. However, none of these wrap themselves around Aaron's tongue as well as the savory hint of meat: roasted pork, chicken, and beef.

Aaron pulls Henry behind him as they dodge and move around the tables hosting crowds of shouting men and raucous laughter. The creak of the floorboards moan under their feet, glasses clink spilling copious amounts of ale the brothers have yet to drink, and hushed conversations share secrets Aaron wants no part in.

"I'll order food," Aaron says as they arrive near the bar. "Keep an eye out for an empty table."

"Don't forget the ale. I'm parched."

Aaron shoulders his way between two patrons and waves down the barmaid, a tall woman with dark brown curly waves, wearing a simple grey dress and a multicolored apron that, with a longer look, he realizes is maroon with many stains.

The woman turns, her green eyes captivating Aaron. He smirks and winks gesturing with two fingers for her to come hither his way. She smiles, and his brow gives rise. A gap shows between her front teeth, but what a woman lacks in her mouth could be a man's boon, not that he'd ever admit to experiencing such a thing. His eyes trail further down her form as she heads his way, unable to deny the draw of her ample bosom, much thanks to the dress that hangs off her shoulders.

Hmm, which will happen first, her dress falling off, or her breasts spilling out? I'm sure the men around here have odds on a bet.

"Welcome to me establishment, I'm Gap Tooth Maggie. What

can me get you with, darling?" She asks.

He is quick to move his eyes back to her—lips, which she bites as she returns the not-so-subtle glances of appreciation over his form. Wait, did she just wink?

Aaron clears his throat, reminding himself to keep eye contact, not lip contact or bosom contact, lovely as they may both be. "What's on the menu tonight, Miss?"

"Yeah, I like your menu Miss," says Henry from behind him.

Aaron suppresses a groan as he feels Henry, pressing to his back, trying to peak over his shoulder.

"Awe, ain't you sweet," Gap Tooth Maggie winks at his idiot brother. "We gots brisket, potatoes, greens, and corn. Although if you like I mights be able to offer you a bit more."

Aaron notes how her eyes shift back to him as she leans forward exposing—

His eyes drift back to the blessings the good Lord gave her, and then back to her waiting green eyes. "As much as I appreciate the service, ma'am, gonna have to pass. But we'll take three meals, two ales, and one lemonade, if you please."

"Oh my, manners too. What a rare treat you are. Shame that's all you be wanting though. I'll see what I can do," Gap Tooth Maggie turns back to pour their drinks, but delays in delivering them. A small pout still sits on her bottom lip as she lingers, appreciating a stolen moment for fantasizing, though about what, well, Aaron can only imagine.

He winks at her.

She sets down the drinks, and he leans closer.

"Excuse me, Maggie dear, but what are they doing over there?" Aaron nods to a table of uniformed men appearing to be officers milling about a table.

Maggie leans closer, noses nearly touching, "Oh them? They

be enlisting horse soldiers and walkers. But if it be a job you need, I'd be happy to put you to work."

Aaron smiles, and as he pulls back, he taps her nose with a teasing grin, "Maggie dearest, I'd hate to give you more reason to toil. A woman like you deserves some time off her feet."

Gap Tooth Maggie smiles all the wider as Aaron grabs the drinks and steps away. He notices her eyes turn back to Henry who is grinning and making anything but eye contact with her display, his mouth agape.

Aaron elbows him.

Henry blushes and wipes the slobber from his chin.

"Aww, well, he ain't just a little greenie," Gap Tooth Maggie reaches over the bar to ruffle Henry's hair then slips her long fingers to squeeze his cheek. "He barely got whiskers coming in."

This comment elicits a low chuckle from Aaron and a grumble from Henry who reaches up to hold her hand to his cheek.

"Just shaved is all," Henry says.

She pats his cheek, giving Henry a wistful smile. "I'm sure you did honeybun, but it's all right. I'll play Mammy. Just sit tight and I'll be back with dinner. Though if you be needing any dessert, just remember to address me as Maggie."

Her gaze sweeps over to Aaron as she gives the price, and he responds with a reach into his pocket, an act he notices she watches with great interest.

"Would you mind bringing the meal to that table over there while I go see those gentlemen?" Aaron asks nodding back over to the table of enlisters.

"You looking to join?" Gap Tooth Maggie asks. "What a shame. A beautiful man such as yourself wanting to get killed—"

Aaron slips some money into her hand. Maggie looks down

at the coins and bats her long lashes back up at him. The coin is secured within the crease of her bosom with a nod of understanding. She throws a wink at Henry and disappears into the kitchen.

Aaron hands the drinks off to Henry, "Go sit."

He watches Henry walk over to claim the recently opened table, setting the drinks down and clearing away the dishes to one side before settling in. With his brother out of the grasp of potential trouble, Aaron approaches the officers' table. He takes a moment to peer out a nearby dirty window, making sure Seth is all right while he waits for a lull in the men's conversation about numbers.

"What do you want?" asks a deep voice with a growl.

Aaron turns to see the burly full-bearded man with a barrel chest glaring up at him. He stands a bit taller, trying not to look nervous, as he quiets his tapping foot.

"My brother and I are looking to sign up for the Virginia Cavalry, sir."

The man sizes up Aaron, turns, kicks a dull copper spittoon closer to him, and spits. Misses. He grunts, snorts back a loogie, and looks up.

"Hey Maggie," he shouts above the crowd that quiets momentarily as all eyes turn to him.

"Yes, Captain," Maggie shouts back. "What can I get for ya, ale, whiskey, or me?"

Shouts and laughter follow her call, and the captain's cheeks flush red.

"Just another ale," orders the captain, turning back to Aaron, glaring at him for the grin he is wearing. "Who's your brother?"

Aaron gestures to Henry, who sits watching the crowd, still

waiting for their meals, and then looks back.

The captain shakes his head, "Looks like he just got weaned from his Mama." He turns to have another go at the spittoon; a glob runs down the side—another miss. He grunts.

"He's eighteen, and I'm twenty-one sir."

The captain looks to his ledgers as he chides, "Oh, well, lookie there. You can count. Can you ride too or does that ass need a cushion and a silver spoon?"

Aaron draws a deep breath. His jaw flexes, but he smiles. "Yes, sir, we can ride—no cushion needed, bare back if we must, no silver spoon required for either of us."

"Yeah, must have recently fallen off and hit your heads too," the captain looks over to the bar. "Maggie! Where's my damn drink!"

"Let's put it this way," Aaron says, closing in on the table. "I've been a Southerner since birth. I am a lawyer who believes in our rights and firmly disagrees with the shenanigans of the North which will bankrupt us all." Eye to eye the men stare at each other. "I have a plantation to keep in our family, and I'll be damned if I let any Northern scallywag think he can come in and make a disgrace of it. You need men, I'm looking for a fight, and we are going to put a stop to this mess because I'm just the man to help!"

Aaron's hand slams on the table, making the captain swallow, inhale—he chokes on his chew.

"So, when are you ready?" asks the captain.

"I have to stop home to drop off a slave, then we'll be ready."

"Shame. A bullet in a negro is one less bullet in my men," the captain narrows his eyes.

"Where do I sign?" Aaron asks, arms crossing, eyes narrowing at the captain.

Captain looks him up and down and decides to keep his next opinion to himself.

"All right, bring yourself two good horses, not no nags. Army ain't starving yet. Meet us in Ashland. We'll add you to our rosters." The captain pulls out two documents, points to where Aaron should sign, then he turns to yell, "Hey Maggie, bring me that whiskey, make it a double on accounts you are slower than molasses!"

"Just a dang minute, can't you see I got my hands full!" Aaron notices her arms balance plates of food, and a pint of ale as she heads over toward Henry.

Turning back to Aaron, Captain says, "Get your brother's signature and we will see you in Ashland in a week or so."

"Thank you, sir," Aaron turns from the captain's table.

He makes his way back to Henry, the steaming dinner waiting for him and Henry deep within his ale with a second one at his fingertips.

Lemonade, his ale, my ale. Where did he get the third ale from?

Henry has eaten half his meal, but the ale is the focus of his little brother's attention right now.

"This is amazing. The food is great. Eat before it gets cold." Henry motions to the plate of brisket. His eyes in the light are bright and glassy.

Aaron spots two empty mugs, one of which where his own should be, and a third full mug of ale which Henry is already reaching for.

"Who paid for the third ale? And what happened to mine?" Aaron asks.

"You—you know there's food, drink, and pretty ladies offering me dessert, Maggie told me a second one will put hair on my chin," Henry's speech is becoming more slurred by the sentence. Henry leans in whispering, "One let me touch her bobbles." This elicits a giggle from him, as he slaps the table.

"Henry, look at me! You have to sign these papers sober; you hear me? This is an official document enlisting you. Do you understand what you are signing?"

A confused look falls over Henry's face, he touches his finger to his nose, patting it.

"What now," Aaron asks, staring at his brother, who appears childlike with a silly grin and wide eyes.

"My nose? Is it still there?"

"Yes, now, focus Henry. The papers—do you want to sign them?"

"Oh, sure. Do I get to serve with you?"

"Yes, as far as I know."

Henry picks up the document and appears to read it over. How much he understands is doubtful, but he grabs the pen, and signs his name, surprisingly legible and clear.

Aaron feels a swelling of pride, bitten by a pang of fear. Will he be able to keep his little brother, his friend, and now his comrade in arms safe?

Henry pushes the paper back to his brother saying, "There, now you better eat. I need another ale."

Just as the words left his mouth, Gap Tooth Maggie shows up with two more mugs. "Here, I saw he drank yours, so two more on the house." She stands inches from Aaron, leans right over him, so he can see her bosom heaving as she speaks, among the musk of toil is a faint smell of honeysuckle.

Honey, suckle indeed ... No, this is business!

Henry's hands are eager to reach for another mug.

Aaron pushes it out of reach, while holding the papers in the other hand. Then he takes hold of Henry's half eaten plate, pushing that in front of him.

"Eat this before you take another drink. Or you'll be walking the rest of the way to Richmond."

Henry eyes his brother suspiciously.

His hand slides forward.

Aaron slaps it back, presenting Henry with a fork.

"But I have to save room for dessert," Henry says, looking over at a red head. "Can you tell that pretty one in the green dress, I'd like her dessert."

Maggie giggles. Aaron is left with his mouth open.

"Looks like you have your hands full here," she says. "I'll bring these back to the captain. Feel free to watch me hand them over."

"That would be mighty kind of you," Aaron looks into Maggie's evergreen eyes.

"Don't think another thing about it," Maggie plucks the documents from Aaron's hand, walks to the bar, grabs a glass, then walks to the captain. The captain waves the papers back at Aaron, who waves back before turning to Henry.

Henry's arms are folded. He slumps deeper into the seat, inching his fingers toward the mug of ale.

"What are you doing?" Aaron asks.

"Waiting for des—dessert," Henry says, managing to snag that fourth mug of ale and taking a hearty gulp.

Aaron spies Seth's plate and lemonade sitting on the table. He picks both up.

"Wait, where you goin?"

"I am going to get this to Seth, before he starves. You keep waiting for dessert," Aaron says, "and that last mug of ale better be full when I get back or you are dead! Got it!"

"Whoa, Aaron," Henry raises his hands in surrender. "No violence needed, man. I'm the property of the Confederate government now. You don't want to piss them off by killing me." Henry's grin is still absurd, and Aaron chooses to ignore it as he leaves the table.

I should threaten to write Mother.

Aaron pushes open the door, hitting someone just on the other side. The lemonade splashes back on his shirt. He pushes again, the door gives way to a crowd of patrons, yelling, shouting, and stirring up the crowd.

"He's trying to stow away in that wagon!"

"I bet he's a runaway!"

"Let's put that nigger out of his misery and hang him!"

Aaron looks to the wagon. Seth is not there. He turns to the shouting crowd, straining to see over and around the people. Two men have Seth, one by each arm. Another has a rope he's currently making into a noose.

"There's a tree!"

Aaron's heart plummets to his stomach. Plate in hand he yells at the top of his lungs, "What is going on here!"

The crowd tries to ignore him. Aaron persists, pushing his way into the group.

"What are you doing with my nigger!" Aarons voice booming, the men stop and turn.

"He's trying to stow away."

"No, he's not. This boy is tending my things like I ordered him to," Aaron says. "Unhand my property, or do I need to get the law out here?" Aaron stares down the crowd, and they begin to retreat. "Go on, get. Get the hell out of here!"

The crowd disperses, scattering in staggered steps and tripping over themselves to mount their horses and ride off.

One young man says, "Well, gee, mister. We just trying to help."

"Mighty obliged, but your kind of help is not needed, good night gentlemen!"

Aaron is left with Seth crumpled to the ground, shaking for his life. Aaron crouches down, saying, "I'm sorry Seth. I didn't mean to imply."

"I know you didn't mean it," Seth looks up at him, tears in his eyes. "It's the only thing they understand."

"I'll say anything to keep you safe," Aaron says, "and its only for that reason—to keep you alive, safe. I bet you're not hungry after this, huh?"

Seth shakes his head no.

"Let's take this to the wagon and put it on a dish to eat later maybe."

Seth stands and walks with Aaron.

"Had more lemonade but ended up wearing it." Aaron says, handing him the lemonade, which Seth gulps down. Once Seth is sitting in the wagon, Aaron takes a plate from the basket and puts the food on it.

Seth, by now has changed his mind and begins eating.

"I'm going to send Henry out to sit with you, so there's no more trouble."

"Thank you, Mr. Aaron," Seth takes another bite of brisket. "These greens are close to what Mama makes."

"Glad to hear it," Aaron says, a smile gracing his mouth, "I got to go save Mr. Peach fuzz from himself and the girls in there. Try to stay out of sight. These men are drunker now, and we already know what kind of trouble they're capable of stirring up."

"Yes, sir, I'll cover myself until Henry comes."

He pats Seth on the shoulder, they nod to each other, and Aaron turns back to the tavern to fetch Henry and hopefully a good meal—and there had better damn well be a full mug of ale.

Inside the tavern, the jovial banter continues. The crowd is now less coherent as the drink flows free. Henry is slouched at the table, snoring.

"Henry!" Aaron gets no response, "Henry Charles Prescott!"

Henry's eyes pop open, and he looks around at the unfamiliar surroundings.

"What?" Henry says, "I'm waiting on des-dessert!"

Aaron spies another mug of ale empty with one partially full sitting next to Aaron's untouched plate.

"Henry! I told you not to touch my ale!" Aaron grabs Henry by the scruff of his neck, walking him to the door and pushing him out with a boot to the butt. "Go sit with Seth."

"But—"

"Not listening, get out now!" Aaron's tone makes Henry scramble, stagger, and crawl across the road to the wagon. Aaron slides into the cahir near the window, and pulls the curtain over to make sure his brother makes it to the wagon.

Henry looks like a man walking in a windstorm, but thankfully Seth is there to jump out and assist. Aaron shakes his head as he watches Seth pile Henry into the back of the wagon like a sack of potatoes.

Settling back to his cold plate of dinner, Maggie appears at Aaron's table with a fresh mug of ale.

"You look like you need this." She slides full ale in his direction. "Anything else?"

"Some sanity, I sent my brother out to the wagon to watch things."

Maggie gazes out the window. She shakes her head, asking, "Is that so? Who's supposed to be watching who?"

"Only the devil knows," Aaron says with a heavy sigh. His hand goes to the mug of ale. "Or so I am told."

Home to Richmond

ALL CHANGE IS NOT GROWTH,
AS ALL MOVEMENT IS NOT FORWARD.
~ELLEN GLASGOW

AUGUST 1861
PRESCOTT PLANTATION, VIRGINIA

The jovial spirits of the three travel companions curdled into a heavy silence the closer they got to the Prescott Plantation. They were now two days travel from the tavern. Thanks to several mugs of ale, Henry had spent the first day recovering from his dance with the devil. The second day, his head was left reeling from the possibilities that he never pursued regarding the barmaids' winked promises. Henry looks around the wagon, looking first to Aaron, whose eye rolls and short answers do nothing to play into Henry's sense of adventure.

Wonder if he's got travel fatigue?

Then he looks at Seth who is daydreaming again, staring off into space; his humor having gone as cold as a rotten fish since daybreak.

Henry pokes Seth, saying, "Do you think that brunette will remember me if we go back there?"

"Oh, how could she forget? You're the one who missed her dessert," Seth's grin plays at his lips. "I bet she's crying about you, what with you not having enough room after three mugs of ale."

"You should have seen it," Henry brags. "I bet she wasn't just saving me pie." A smile curls his lips, his eyebrows wiggle tantalized by the idea.

"I gotta say, glad I missed it." Seth's grin continues to light up his eyes. "I got no interest in watching you spill your cream, when she turns on her charms, calling you—what did Aaron say, Peach fuzz?" Seth chuckles to himself, then laughs aloud when Henry's face turns as red as he imagined.

"Well, I don't see you growing a beard anytime soon," Henry reaches out to rub Seth's chin.

They begin to push at each other, Seth saying, "I don't have peach fuzz. I got manly whiskers, and not just in one place, but all over."

The playful banter continues as the streets become congested with horses, wagons, and pedestrians. Richmond is in the grasp of a business day, with shades of gray from uniformed men smattered throughout the citizens and slaves, each person bustling to accomplish their tasks. Posters and signage mar the beautiful, decorated shop windows, advertising goods for the soldiers and encouraging Richmond's finest to enlist for the Confederacy. Wanted posters for runaway slaves boast rewards for their safe return.

Henry looks to Seth. The wanted poster steals his smile and darkens his eyes; his Adam's apple bobbles as he visibly swallows. It just goes to show Henry how much his friend can read and comprehend.

Silence returns.

The midday heat, punctuated by the cloudless sky, raises the humidity to uncomfortable temperatures. Henry desires the relief of lemonade or well water to quench his thirst. He imagines having his drink in a cool parlor darkened by curtains with open windows to the river. But what about Seth? He had never really thought about it before, but he supposes the dark corners of a horse barn would be the only way to stay out of the oppressive heat—if a slave is allowed to dream.

He looks back over to Seth, who has moved to the other end of the wagon, looking pensive and quiet. Henry dares not to ask how close they are, but it has been so long since he's traveled down Plank Road, he's not sure of the timing anymore. They pass the other plantations, and sooner than he would like, a familiar gate comes into view, announcing by metal sign his family's name, *Prescott Plantation*.

"What happened here?" Aaron asks. "The gate hinge is broken."

"The pillar is missing chinking," Henry says. "Someone must have hit the gate." The comment about the fence fades as soon as the wagon turns up the drive.

The big house appears haunting and dismal, saddened and dark.

Henry listens—*Did the birds stop singing?*

Passing by the big oak, Henry notices his swing now hanging by a single frayed rope, the seat swaying listless in the breeze. A memory of his childhood—broken and discarded. This is not the home Henry remembers leaving.

A wind whips through. This brush of cool air wraps him like a cloak left in the cold—an omen?

His head rises to the dark gray cloud hanging over the big house. The only storm cloud in the sky, or—

"Is that smoke?" Henry asks, watching the cloud.

"Don't know," Aaron says.

"Nah, unless they are burning grass or something's on fire," Seth turns back to sit down. It's the first peep Henry has heard Seth make in a long while. He tries to offer Seth a reassuring smile, but his friend is looking back from where they came.

Watching the freedoms of the last month disappear, I bet, as he steps back into this cage of slavery.

Henry can only imagine what it's like to hear the *click* of the lock, and the *tinkle* of a key.

Will the home we've had here ever be a positive experience for anyone, again?

"It's a rogue storm cloud," Aaron surmises. "We get those all the time—pop up showers and then they leave."

His big brother then pulls up to the house and sets the break. Simon, a middle-aged gentleman, steps out with a limp on his right due to a stiff hip. He greets Aaron and Henry.

"Welcome home. Mister Aaron, your aunt is awaiting your arrival. Master Henry, how you changed. Welcome home."

"Thank you, Simon," Henry watches the gray-haired servant give Seth a sharp look.

Seth jumps out of the back and takes the reins from Aaron.

"I'll take care of the team," he takes the reins from Aaron while keeping an eye on Simon.

"Your Pa is in the fields, boy," Simon says. "He expects to see you when you finish with the horses."

A silent nod of understanding is given to the old man.

"Don't forget your bag," Henry hands Seth's satchel to him. "And tell your parents I'm here; I'll come see them later tonight."

Henry shares the briefest smile with his friend, watching the returned gesture, once as bright and as welcoming as a sunrise, flicker to a dying ember.

"Of course, Mister Henry, I'll tell them," Seth mumbles. The carefree spirit that once animated him is now a distant echo—the jovial man replaced by a shell burdened with servitude.

Aaron takes a deep breath, putting an arm around Henry saying, "Well, should we go see Aunt Jenny?"

Henry's eyes meet Aaron's, and they exchange doubt and unease.

"Let's get this over with," Henry takes a deep breath and bites his lower lip. With that, the two Prescott men walk up the stairs and into the house.

The house is dark despite being open to catch the summer winds. A breeze blows through the entry way, the lace on the receiving table flutters.

"Mrs. Prescott will greet you in the parlor," Simon says. "I will inform her you are here."

"Thank you, Simon."

The door closes as Simon excuses himself.

Hats in their hands, gritty and dusty from travel, Henry wishes he could go to his former room to freshen up. They step into the parlor; it is unchanged from the day they left. The piano sits waiting in the corner. Henry smiles at the memory of Emilie playing the same tune repeatedly, and him covering his ears with pillows to block out the monotony. His grandmother's rocking chair has a hoop of embroidery laying in the seat, a discarded project from his aunt.

"Did you bring back the boy?" Aunt Jenny asks.

Henry turns as she glides into the parlor, noting that she looks taken aback at the sight of them, then again so is he. She looks years older. Still, she presents the role of the lady of the house, dressed in a light grey linen gown beset with rings, a pearl choker at her neck, and matching earrings. Not a hair is out of place, as the scent of roses follows her like a cloud.

Maybe the posh lifestyle she leads has not been kind to her?

"Please have a seat. I will order some refreshments." Aunt Jenny's hand goes to the bell, summoning the help.

"Sorry, auntie," Aaron says. "We're filthy with road dust. We wouldn't want to—"

"Nonsense, Aaron you are such a dear for your impeccable manners. It's a joy you're here." Aunt Jenny pats the sofa insisting Aaron and Henry sit despite their state of dishevelment. The boys look at each other then take a seat on the edge of the sofa, polite to follow orders of their elders.

A thin young girl sweeps holding a tray with a pitcher of lemonade, and glasseses. She sets down the tray in front of Henry and Aaron, with a curtsy, then her attention turns to Aunt Jenny.

"Would you like me to pour the lemonade for you, ma'am?" Her big brown eyes and dark skin stand out against the crisp white apron. Her hands shake as she clasps them under the starched white cloth, a pale attempt at hiding her nerves.

"Will you spill it like you did last time?" Aunt Jenny asks, her eyes narrow at the girl, her tone sharp as shattered glass. "How long did it take to get that stain out of the carpet?"

The girl blinks, her face red with heat as embarrassment flushes up her neck. She bites her lower lip.

"Leave, Corslina, before I consider sending you back to the fields."

"Sorry, ma'am—I'll do better, Mrs. Prescott, please," Corslina begs. "I—I—"

"Leave or I'll send you back this afternoon!"

Corslina dips a quick curtsy, fleeing from the room before Aunt Jenny's wrath can manage to wrap itself around her throat.

"It's near impossible to find good help these days. Even the breeders turn out a useless crop."

Henry's mouth goes to open.

Aaron bumps Henry's knee—but why?

Why should I be quiet? She's just a woman. Still, suppose it's not our business, not anymore.

Henry bites back his comments, painting a smile on his face.

"I'll pour it, auntie," Aaron offers a distraction to Aunt Jenny's stare that chases the girl out of the room.

"Mm, yes Aaron, you might as well. That thing is a disaster waiting to happen."

Aaron notices a hiss of irritation that shudders through her small frame. Aunt Jenny turns back to her nephews, as Aaron pours out the lemonade, offering her glass with a smile.

"I suppose you are leaving right away?"

"Yes, auntie," Aaron sits at the edge of the sofa. "Henry and I have business in Ashland the day after tomorrow. We need to purchase some horses in town, and then we'll be gone."

"Thank you for allowing us to lodge tonight," Henry says, accepting a glass from Aaron. "It will feel good to have a bed again."

Aunt Jenny raises an eyebrow at her nephews. "I'm sorry to hear it has to be such a short visit. I mean, Henry, you've been gone for months. Of course, I didn't expect to see you ... but even in the briefest of moments, what a treat."

"I go where my brother goes, auntie." Henry puts his glass on the tray. Forgetting about his clothing, he sits back on the sofa.

The glasses empty, Aunt Jenny's gaze returns to the hall several times. She sighs, hands dry ringing in her lap, before looking back to the boys. "Well, I am glad you made it safe. You are of course welcome to stay—longer if you wish. Dinner will be at four-thirty. Your Uncle should be home by then, God willing."

"Thank you, auntie," Aaron places his glass on the tray. "I better go make myself presentable for dinner."

"Yes," Henry says. "I am looking forward to washing and walking about before dinner."

"Be my guest," Aunt Jenny stands to take her leave.

Henry stands, picking up the tray. Aunt Jenny turns back, a confused question mark written across her delicate features. "What are you doing?"

Henry stops. "Taking these to—"

"Henry Prescott, you will do no such thing!"

Henry hurries to set the tray back on the table. The glassware clatters. He swallows hard. "Sorry—I forgot."

Aunt Jenny bites her lip. There's pity in her eyes. "Oh, you poor dear. Your parents ruined you." She shakes her head. "And those northern brutes say we are uncivilized, but at least we do not waste our time with meaningless work. Try to remember that under my roof. You are a Prescott, after all."

Aunt Jenny turns. There is a swish of her hoop followed by the *click-clack* of her every step, echoing her biting words as she departs the room.

Ghosts of his former life inhabit Henry's vacant bedchamber. It is certainly larger than the one he has back in Pennsylvania—it could sleep five or six children. Henry shakes his head.

What a waste.

He starts to search for towels and water for the washbasin. A soft knock sounds on his door.

"Master Henry?" The voice rings of familiarity. A smile graces his features—Lucy—Emilie's former ladies' maid and one lucky man's love.

"I'm decent, please come in."

Lucy pushes open the door. Her arms are loaded down with towels, a bar of soap, and a bucket of warm water.

"The missus said you are in need of freshening up," Lucy smiles at him, a smile he can't help but return as warm memories dance in her eyes. "Do you need assistance?"

Henry blushes, blinks, and coughs, shaking his head, "No, no, I mean, I know you mean anything else, but roads, they make your brain—Heh, this is assistance enough," Henry tries swallow the redness racing up his neck. "Thank you. I will take it from here."

Lucy's smile eases into a thin line of worry as she sets the armload of supplies at the wash basin, neatly laying out the towels. She moves to leave, but then—

"How is Miss Emilie?" Lucy asks, biting her lip.

"She's a teacher now, and believe it or not, in love with someone, not a book." A smile of amusement plays on his lips when the maid's eyes light up. "I know, I can't believe it either."

Lucy giggles. "Well, I'll be. Our girl has grown into a woman."

Henry and Lucy look at each other. The room falls silent.

Lucy shifts, clears her throat, and glances down at her skirt. "Well, I will leave you to it then. Just put the laundry in the basket there. I'll have those clothes washed and dried by tomorrow."

"Lucy, we will be leaving in the morning." He notes the drag in her expression. Worry kidnaps her momentary happiness.

But then her jaw sets with the resilience he knows her for. "I am sorry to hear it. I'll have them dried by this evening." Lucy turns, pausing at the door. "Hope you and Master Aaron have safe travels, wherever you're going." She leaves the room, closing the door with a soft click before Henry can respond.

A quick wash and change and Henry finds himself looking at his reflection within the cold wash basin clouded by dirt and what suds are left from the soap. His gaze shifts over to his dirty clothes, crumpled in a pile on the floor. Guilt whispers in his ear, *Maybe I should at least fold them?*

He sets to his task before leaving the room, journeys down the stairs, a quick jaunt through the dining room, out the back door, and into the kitchen. Henry stops at the door, a flutter of excitement in his stomach—Martha!

He checks the buttons along his shirt and sleeves, smooths his hair back with his fingers, and pushes through the door—

The kitchen fires are burning, pots bubbling, and the Dutch ovens baking. All of it hosts dinner, and all of it is at the hand of a woman he admires, who turns to him, her tall thin figure, hazel eyes, and wait ... Henry blinks, not sure who he's seeing, as the woman wears a scowl, warning against his intrusion into Martha's kitchen, even though she is definitely not Martha.

Henry takes a step back.

"Who are you?" Her voice sounds of salad greens and nothing of delicious bacon grease.

"Where's Martha?" Henry asks, his voice is vacant of emotion. The rest of his body fears the answer.

Her eyebrow shoots up. Her hazel eyes pierce him, a flash of irritation, even the thunder of her voice doesn't fit the world he used to live in. "I see you didn't get the news. That heifer's been replaced. Don't ask why. Ain't got the time, ain't got know how anyway."

Her words rain down on his ears, and Henry turns away, walking out of the kitchen, dumbstruck.

Things have changed.

Changed how?

Guess I can find Limerick or Jim, they'll know.

The words push Henry's boots onward to the stables. *Limerick will know.* Henry's heart pounds in his chest, the eerie feeling confirmed with every step that gathers into a jog. Before long the sweet smell of hay and horses greets him. Henry breathes a momentary sigh of relief at the familiarity as he walks along the open face aisle, looking for Limerick. He doesn't want to spook the horses or wake the gentleman if he's taking a moment to himself. The barn is calm. The horses poke their heads out, nickering in greeting, whinnying for something else to eat, calling out as Henry searches. A few even make a game of trying to nip at his clothes. All their ruckus pulls the old stable hand into view.

"Limerick? Is that you?" After the kitchen incident, Henry worries about the answer that will echo back.

"Hello, down here, and that's me, sir," comes a reply. "But do my eyes deceive me, Master Henry?"

"Yes, sir! I mean, no, sir! I mean, it's me, sir!" Henry hurries to the end of the row.

The men clasp hands in a hearty handshake, but Henry pulls the man to him further giving him a hug.

"Oh, heh, Master Henry. My, you've grown. Only been some moons since last seen you." Limerick doesn't hug him back, simply pats his back and waits to be released.

"I'd say the same of you Limerick but looks like you've gotten younger."

Limerick laughs, "Now you telling tales as long as the horse's. But good to see you, anyway. Been worried 'bout you. How your folks?"

"At least I'm not pullin' on them tails anymore, so no need to worry on that front. Thanks, by the way, for not letting me kill myself. As for my parents, they are well and send their regards."

"Oh, it's no trouble, Master Henry, no trouble at all. Though you the only boy I knew who thought to climb a horse's tail to get on. But good to hear, good they doin' well." Limerick turns to walk to the other end of the barn, where he likes to sit and whittle throughout midday. Henry knows to follow.

"How are you and the family?" asks Henry.

His mentor's smile breaks into fractions, reflecting a broken man. A tear draws down his cheek and travels down the gutters formed by worn sunlines in his expression.

"Limerick?" Henry's heart pounds in his ears.

Limerick wipes his face with his sleeve, breathes in a sniffle, and stoops on the old stump, shoulders slumping in defeat.

Henry tries to stay patient. He shifts from foot to foot, but he can't stand seeing— "Wh-what happened?"

Limerick's words come out in a croak, "Master William sold my family two—" His voice catches in his throat. "—two weeks ago." Henry seeks to ease Limerick's pain, placing his hand on Limerick's back.

Henry sucks in a breath, his own words sinking into his gut with his heart. He struggled to pry something out. "All—all of—"

Limerick nods, "All different families. Scattered to the wind, or so that's what the devil told me."

Henry allows the tears, hot and raw, to streak his face. "Why?"

Limerick shakes his head, finally saying, "Said we needs new blood here—too many mouths not enough hands—business, you understand." Limerick whispers the last words, stinging both of them more than any lash could.

The two men sit, silence stretches between them.

Henry wants to be comforting, even though their world wants them apart.

"Hannah ... well, we done never been apart, not for a day," Limerick's eyes are wet, while only his tears are free. "Lena, Juno, and Lunah—just blossoming into beauties, I c-can't bear—" Limerick breathes deep, shaking his head. "Not after seeing what happens here." His exhale comes shaky, a rattle in his chest. "Amos, George, and Peter gonna be fine. They strong, even Peter, and he's but fourteen."

Limerick rubs his hands on his thin slave cloth trousers.

Henry rubs the man's back. The injustice of his uncle's last poor business move sets Henry's head reeling in a whirlwind of sadness, twisting his thoughts into disaster. Even his hands shake from shock, a reaction he tries to combat, clenching his fists, turning his knuckles briefly white hot.

A deep breath though and he releases, finally asking, "What else has gone on here?"

Limerick shakes his head, aware that the truth could mean a harsh punishment, but with no family— Limerick's eyes harden. He dries them on his shirt, nodding, swallowing back the misery. "Let's take a walk, Master Henry."

Henry and Limerick stand and leave the shade of the barn trek through the plantation's many paths, Henry finds himself bearing witness to his biggest fears. A cascade of bad decisions and chaos surround him. Sure, the crops have grown with excellence and are now being gathered in droves, but as they walk down the path, Henry notices just how business is done.

Standing alone in the woods—

"The church?" Henry asks. The windows are boarded up, a padlock and chains crisscross the door.

"Master William feels happiness don't produce, just blood, sweat, and tears, so services been cancelled 'til the crops go to market," Limerick leads them into the slave community of small cabin homes. All eyes turn to Henry. He doesn't recognize the new faces as they peer at him, curious as to why he cares to visit their sanctuary.

Would they gawk so openly if Limerick was not beside me?

New wood dresses half of the homes, which he is fairly sure did not exist before he left. They are accompanied by crooked windows without coverings, and doors that won't shut because of shoddy hinges. His father would not stand for such poor quality.

"Who built those?" Henry asks, inspecting one of the shacks. The gaps in the walls are evident as light passes in scattered rays, along with cold drafts, come the end of summer days. "How does he expect you to stay healthy through the winter?"

"No doctor," says a voice from behind a curtain.

Henry walks over to the curtain, pulling it back to reveal a woman with three children clinging to her skirts. They're wide-eyed. Mouths hang open, perches for the flies. Fear from their minds dances on their faces.

"Did you say no doctor?" Henry asks. The woman only nods, too afraid to speak. Henry lets go of the curtain allowing it to flutter back and keep them in hiding.

Stepping out his eyes bounce from one new house to the next. No gardens, and the old ones appear overgrown with weeds.

"We lost a man to a snakebite last week. Master William wouldn't call for a doctor. Poor man died within days. Couldn't even host a funeral. No singing, no dancing either. Doubt many will make it through winter, extra foods no longer spared."

Henry notices Limericks slumped shoulders, not from age, but defeat?

"This isn't right. I'll send word to my father," Henry feels the stab of injustice fraying his last nerve. "Someone must know what's happening here."

Limerick's hand squeezes his shoulder. "I knew you'd grow up respectable like your father."

The men walk back to the barn. Henry offers to help with the feeding, but Limerick shoos him away.

"Your talking done me enough, Master Henry. But you best be getting to supper, or you won't get none." The old man shoos him away, but Henry stops him and offers his hand.

"I miss you, too, Limerick, more than you know. Promise me you'll take care?"

Limerick looks to the hand, takes a quick glance around, and then shakes on it saying, "Godspeed Henry."

The glow of the lamps and candles cast shadows on the dining room walls. The dishes, a fancy array of China and polished silver, are set for a dinner party. Each setting hosts two glasses, one with water and one with a deep rich red Bordeaux. The aromas mingling throughout the room tantalize the most finicky of eaters. The sideboard is filled with the evening's spread—collard greens, corn, pork, and stuffing, with cold relishes and pitchers of water to quickly fill emptying glasses. Servants stand at the ready, each dressed in black with crisp white aprons.

Henry smiles at the memories of his grandparents full of pride and the fancy clothes they all wore to impress those milling about them. He was only leg high to the guests and family at the time, but the pomp and joyous laughter danced through his memory even now as a young man. Those memories are a stark contrast to the somber, business-like manner of this meal.

Uncle William had already arrived home by the time Henry returned from his visit with Limerick. The tall man with dark hair and dark eyes hosted an equally dark shadow over the head of the table. With his uncle's presence comes the lack of Prescott joy and banter that affords Henry a thoroughly enjoyable dining experience. If only his father were here.

Henry's eyes dart around the room as the servants move about placing and clearing dishes as needed, pouring wine and water for the family. Aunt Jenny sits across from him, dressed in an evening gown of a different color than she had worn this afternoon while he and Aaron sit to the left of their uncle.

"So, when are you two leaving back to Gettysburg?" Uncle William asks, with a forkful of pork poised at his mouth and sharp narrow eyes set on them.

"We're not going back north, uncle," Aaron says, setting his water glass back on the table.

"Oh, well, where will you be off to then?" Aunt Jenny asks, dabbing the corner of her mouth with a crisp cotton napkin.

"We are expected in Ashland in about two days for training. Henry and I will be meeting up with a Virginia unit."

"Well, I'll be," Uncle William smiles for the first time this evening.

Is that a twinkle of pride in his eye?

"Henry, my boy, did your brother arm wrestle you to join the great Confederate Army or did you just get sick of those damned blue bellies?" Uncle William turns to his nephew, a grin twisting his lips.

I'm certainly not doing it for you or those like you ...

Henry swallows his anger and clears his throat. Pulling himself straighter in his chair. "It's like this, uncle—I can either do nothing, take up arms against my brother, or fight alongside him. I choose family—so we're going together."

Aunt Jenny claps her hands together. "I knew you boys would do the right thing. That's why we're proud to call you family. See, something good came of it after all, William."

Aaron's jaw becomes firm, and he struggles to chew his dinner.

Henry says a silent prayer to the Lord that dinner's end will come swiftly.

"No need to worry about your birthright, Aaron. I'll make sure the plantation is waiting for you when you return. I dare say I've got this place running as efficiently as one can, now that I've weeded out all those nonsense extras your father insisted on having," Uncle William waves a servant out of his line of sight.

"For me? But—" Aaron clears his throat, looking from his aunt to his uncle, not wanting to broach the subject.

"Well, we don't think the good Lord will bless us, you know," Aunt Jenny stiffens with a quick glance to her stomach. "Not to say we haven't tried. We have, many times, nightly even with no result." Her face glows pink as she discusses such a sensitive subject.

Uncle William clears his throat. "Well, hold on now. I'm still in good health. There's nothing wrong with me, so don't get your hopes up too soon."

Henry bites back a smirk with another mouthful of pork. His uncle's discomfort on the matter trumps his own.

Aunt Jenny gives a small laugh, "Forgive me, Willie. But think of it this way, boys. It'll give you something to fight for."

A smile plays at Aaron's lips. "It's something to fight for, and I'll take over when you are ready, uncle."

"Yes, Aaron, how thoughtful of you to consider giving our dear ole Uncle Willie a rest. Fine idea. Aunt Jenny, did I mention this meal is exquisite?" Henry's lie tastes bitter on his tongue, but the blush creeping into his cheeks isn't just from the wine as he watches his Willie at the head of his table fluster and bluster.

"You mean, when I'm dead? No one needs be in such a rush. Let's enjoy what we have here as a family."

Whatever you say, Willie.

Uncle William raises his glass of Bordeaux in the air as a toast to his family.

"Here, here, to a safe return of family, and a win for the Confederate States of America. Let's not let those damn Yankee bastards pull us into bankruptcy. By God, they started this war at Fort Sumter, trying to claim their ill-got taxes, but we will finish it."

I could have sworn I read that the rebels were the first to fire, but I suppose there are two sides to every coin.

"Now William, it's not right to speak of our Lord in such a way, though we do our best to protect what he decrees is the right way." Aunt Jenny bites back the rest of her speech when she catches her husband's warning glare.

"Don't talk of religion to me, Jenny. Not when they are out to scorch God's green earth, stealing and pillaging to feed their greed because we refuse to sell our goods for a fraction of what they are worth and pay taxes that will only go toward helping their poor. They claim we are cruel for having slaves, but God decreed that it was Noah's third son, Ham, who would be a servant to his brothers, Shem and Japheth, just as God decreed the ten commandments—which they seem so keen to break, one by one."

Henry has to resist a roll of the eyes as his mind thinks back to Moses, but he dares not start a battle of biblical rhetoric at dinner.

After the glasses return to the table, dessert is placed in front of each of them—bread pudding smothered in caramel sauce.

"Thank you," Henry whispers to the girl he knows as Corslina.

She continues her work, but he notices a small flicker on her lips—a hidden moment of appreciation.

"Uncle, can you tell me where we might procure some horses?" Aaron asks.

Henry narrows his eyes, questioning his brother. Aaron looks back, a slight shrug to his shoulders.

Suppose it's worth a try.

"Horses? I can take you boys up to Ashland if you need a ride." Uncle William's brow furrows.

"Um—not exactly, we joined the cavalry, so we need good stock or we will be demoted to infantry."

Aunt Jenny gasps, "Oh, that's dreadful. It'll be the death of you, for sure, and I can't imagine what will become of the horses." She pulls her fan from her lap, waving it franticly to ward off either the thought or a fainting spell.

Uncle William swallows the last of his wine and then continues to consider the boys' quandary with a furrowed brow. "I've got two mares I planned to sell. They are strong and fast, but also a bit flighty, and I don't have the muscle I used to for training. The old nigger I have down there says he can tame them, but I'm not about to bother with his delusions. He's lucky I didn't sell him with the rest of his lot. Still, you're welcome to them if you want them."

Henry takes cover behind the dregs of his wine glass as he feels the heat of his uncle's gaze shift from him to Aaron in those final words. It's all Henry can do not to launch his dinner knife at the man.

Drink, for Limerick's sake, drink and shut up.

"We have money to pay you for them." Aaron shifts in his seat, looking back to Henry.

"How much?" Uncle William asks. "I don't want those Union bills, won't do any good down here."

Aaron shakes his head. "Sorry uncle. I don't have access to that kind of money."

Uncle William pulls his shoulders back, smiling at the boys. "Don't worry, Aaron. How about I gift them to you as tokens of my appreciation for your commitment to fighting back the Yankee aggression. It's the least I can do."

"Thank you, uncle." Aaron places his napkin on his plate.

"Yes, thank you, uncle." Henry does his best to smile.

Aaron stands and Henry follows, as they rise with their uncle, thrusting out their hands to shake on the arrangement.

"Now you boys make us proud," Uncle William grasps Henry's hand as their eyes lock. "God's watching."

Guess that means you're going to hell, uncle.

Henry squeezes his uncle's hand back, hoping his malice for this man and his useless willie isn't scratched across his mask of appreciation.

"We will do our darnedest to make it happen, uncle."

"Good, now let us retire to the parlor for a cigar and whiskey to celebrate this occasion and talk business."

A Different Kind of Homecoming

I HAD A RIGHT TO, LIBERTY OR DEATH;
IF I COULD NOT HAVE ONE,
I WOULD HAVE THE OTHER.
~HARRIET TUBMAN

AUGUST 1861
PRESCOTT PLANTATION, VIRGINIA

Seth walks next to his pa, Jim. It's high time they return home after finishing the fieldwork for the day, or what is left of the night, before starting again at first light. Seth's arms ache, and his back has tightened, too, in protest from the constant bending and squatting demanded of him. He's gotten soft during his stay with the Prescott's, and as such, his body's grown lazy to the expectations of a field slave. Pa, however, knows of no such luxury, and towers beside him, remaining the same old mountain of security Seth's known all his life.

"Ma be home?" Seth asks, watching his Pa's slumped shoulders.

"She best be home, God willin'. They kept her for two days straight, last week. She missed you."

"Missed you both," Seth steps aside, so his father can ascend the two stairs to the cabin that is about the size of Mr. Prescott's parlor back in Gettysburg.

Pa pushes the door open into an abyss of darkness.

Seth hears the creak under his feet as he steps over the threshold, and together they depend on their knowledge of where things lie to maneuver around. The familiar scent of the room is plain, no fancy flowers or cooking to mingle in the air. Just old pork grease and burnt coals, a faint smell of laundry. It must be hanging on the other side of the room left to dry from a quick morning rinse.

"Candles in the center of the table; matches right next to it," Pa says, "Get it lit. I'll fetch the firewood."

His Pa's footsteps *creak and groan* across the floor before becoming muffled by the dirt path beyond their door.

Seth feels the table in the dark, careful to move slowly, so as not to knock the candle or the matches on the floor. His fingers find a match, and his other hand searches for the cold feel of the wooden holder. Once secured, he shuffles to the fireplace feeling about for the striking stone.

The bright orange flame comes to life, and he touches it to the blackened wick. The room begins to glow in hues of amber light.

Seth, bending down despite the ache in his back, places the candle on the hearth and begins to stir up the embers dying within the remaining ash. He pulls some wood shavings and gathers a few twigs from a nearby bundle to bring the fire back to life. The candle, already lit, reserves what matches remain as there is only enough for a month. If they run out before then, they'll have to beg for more.

Seth holds the candle's flame to the wood shavings and dried twigs. He blows a soft steady wind on the fragile flame, encouraging it to ignite. The fire leaps; the flames grow stronger under his steady hand.

"No embers left?" Pa asks, handing him some small wood.

"Hardly." Seth murmured. "Ain't minded during the day." He places just enough of the small wood on the fire to keep it glowing until morning; then fills the tea kettle and places it on a trivet to heat.

Pa takes a bucket of water and sloshes it in a basin to wash his face and hands, before searching for bits of food left over from last night's dinner.

Seth notices too that all they have is dried bread, three chicken eggs, and wilted green beans.

"Your ma needs more time home. Too many mouths to feed round here; little enough going round as is. We stretchin' what we gots."

The men each toast a slice of bread and fry an egg, saving the beans for another meal. They eat in silence, both watching the door, waiting for Ma to walk in.

Seth eyes his Pa as lines of worry etch deeper into the man's forehead, becoming more pronounced as the wait drags on.

"How the Prescotts?

Seth's grin bubbles up, but he tempers it due to the absence of his Ma. "They well, Emilie's a teacher now. Got herself a beau."

Pa smiles, and his teeth catch the light of the candle. "Well, I'll be damned. That girl all grown up. I remember you two sleep'n in the same cradle."

"Ain't fittin' in no cradle no more." A flicker of humor plays at the corner of Seth's mouth. He misses the playful banter he and Henry exchanged through the day.

"I should say," Pa chuckles.

"Mr. Prescott lookin' forward to us comin'. He ask about you, and Mrs. Prescott sent me home with some things." Seth looks to his empty plate, despite his stomach growling for more.

"First we gotta see how this works out," Pa pushes his plate aside. "Rumor be families be split and sold again. Hope we ain't one of them."

"But," Seth's stomach clenches, "we-we gots papers."

"Papers don't mean nothin', you know that. If the white devil decides they false—they don't exist."

"Mr. Prescott—" Seth begins, but his Pa's hand stops him.

"Mr. Prescott's not here."

The warning coils in the pit of Seth's stomach, tight and cold like his unrelenting hunger. His pa snaps a twig of tobacco in half, and hands it to him. They chew on it to ease the pain of their reality.

"Mr. Prescott agrees, this our business we handle it on our own."

"You ain't handlin' it," Seth feels his hope devoured by the coiled serpent in his gut. "We at the mercy of the man, who's evil, and we ain't got no say." Seth folds his arms in front of him and stares ever harder at the door, wishing Ma was here to talk some sense into Pa.

When the door finally creaks, both men shift their glances to see Seth's Ma, Martha, standing on the threshold. Her body sags with defeat. Her hair falls out of its pins, her dress is disheveled with buttons open at the neck, her sleeves are pushed past her elbows, and the basket in her hand dangles precariously at the ends of her fingertips.

Two chairs shout an alarm as they scrape across the floor. Both husband and son move to her side, each putting an arm around her and guiding her to the table to sit.

Seth takes the basket from his ma's hand and sets it near the dry sink.

"Good Lord, Martha. What happened to your face?"

"Seth," Ma ignores Pa, "When'd you get here?"

Seth moves back to his Ma's side, his hands going to her shoulders until he notices her flinch, so his hands retreat, and instead he fetches the candle to inspect the injuries of her flesh. Her beautiful full face resembles a distorted mask. Her cheek is swollen—

"Seth, this ain't no way to greet your ma," Martha begins.

"Ma, please—"

"He got a right to be concerned," Pa says, intervening on the simmering discussion.

"Fine," Ma says, her hands warding off any questioning advances. "Seems my opinion don't matter to nobody. Not ya'll or Mrs. Spree."

"Mrs. Spree done this?" Pa asks gently, eyeing his wife with more suspicion.

"Well—not exactly. They all done say, I gotta work the Sabbath for the next six weeks," Ma waves with a fan of her wrist over to the pitcher. "Seth get me a cool rag for my cheek."

"The Sprees?" Seth asks. "Why you not in the Prescott kitchen?"

"I know you heard me, boy." Ma asks.

Seth closes his eyes for a moment and presses his lips together, but he places the candle on the table and retreats to do as his Ma asked, all the while continuing to listen.

"Little Miss Suzie givin' favors to the Master, making him think I got no use in his kitchen."

Seth comes back with the cold rag. He notices her body shaking at the injustice.

"They's be carryin' on for weeks. She even done told the Missus I done stole food, and that I was too bossy. Like the Missus didn't notice what they be doin' in that pantry.

The nerve.

Can't be blaming chickens for all that mess. Now, I works for old lady Spree. Can't say I knows what's worse."

"We leaving," Seth says. "Get them papers, let's go."

Seth's parents look to him, surprised by their son's declaration. They then exchange looks with one another, before training their gazes back to their son.

"Boy, what's gotten into you? You been infected by them white folks, talkin' all them nonsense like the overseer ain't just waitin' to hang a nigger. Shut your damn mouth."

Seth bites the inside of his cheek, feeling caught between two worlds—one he is born to and one of promise. He's tasted freedom, and now his invisible shackles feel heavier and tighter than before.

"Ma, freedoms right there. We gots papers. We gots to get to Gettysburg. The Prescotts be waiting for us."

"Seth, wake up," Pa says, "Papers or not, you think Master goin' to let you walk up on out of here?"

"Pa, why didn't we leave with the Prescotts when we had the chance?"

"Why? So, the Master can hunts us down for sport?"

"Mr. Prescott wouldn't let that happen. I ate at his table, he treated me as a—"

Seth begins to unravel his adventure as he paces the room, his energy flooding him with emotion while the memories stir the air.

"Seth!" Pa claps a large hand on his son's arm. "Sit! I know you itching to go. But we ain't free. Them papers don't mean nothing to them white devils keeping us here."

"You best change back to a slave by morning, boy" Ma's warning and her inability to listen sending tears dripping down

Seth's cheeks. "All this talk getting you in a heap of hurt, and I ain't about to watch. Now you going to lay low." Ma places a calming hand on her son.

Seth looks away from his parents—refusing to believe his taste of freedom could be his last. A joy his parents have never known is now being suffocated by the reality of his life. He longs for Gettysburg and the accepting arms of the Prescott family. Even Emilie and her hugs, as strange as they are, make him feel included and connected to something bigger than himself.

"You wanna know 'bout my visit?" Seth asks.

Ma sighs, "Guess we should have started with that."

Seth feels her fingers trace his head, and her thumb strokes a tear from his cheek as she guides his chin back to them. He breathes deep but nods and sits down, accepting her apologetic smile.

"The Prescotts miss us. Miss Emilie gots a beau. Gots to meet him and all. Slept in Henry's room. Mr. Prescott didn't want me doin' no chores, but I insisted, so we all did them together." Seth's face brightens as he licks his lips, hands rubbing together. "They even let me eat at the table every night. Mrs. Prescott and Emilie are mighty fine cooks, if I say so myself. Uh, but not as good as you, Ma."

"Hmph, well that's a change. I couldn't get that girl to cook one thing much less a meal."

"Her biscuits are the best."

"Now that's my doing." A smile graces Ma's bruised lip.

"Yeah, they second best compared to yours, Ma. Oh, Mrs. Prescott put a little something together for us." Seth gets up to retrieve the brown paper package from his belongings, warmed by the memories and the promise he gave her.

Tell your mother, I miss her and your father too. Safe travels

Seth.

As her words flood his memories, he can still feel her hand on his, bidding him a safe return.

"You making us guess what's in there?" Ma asks.

Seth blinks, feeling a heat food his ears and cheeks. "Sorry." He sets the brown paper package on the table. There's a small rip at one corner, but the twine still holds everything else in place. He pushes it toward his ma.

"Here, Mrs. Prescott wants you to open it."

Ma pulls the package toward her, unknots the twine, searches for the ends, and then slowly unwraps the gift.

"Well, I'll be. How did she know?" Martha pulls up a large green and brown checked shirt and it wasn't of slave cloth. "Jim, I know this is yours. It's so soft," Ma hands it to Pa, who takes it into his hands as if it were the finest of silks.

"She's a mighty fine seamstress." Pa admires the new textile, holding it up to himself, measuring the sleeve length and shirt length. "Even gots some fancy buttons on it too." He fingers a metal button with a star stamped into it. It holds fast to the fabric.

Ma pulls a second article out to find a dark yellow and brown checked skirt flutter open, "Oh, now ain't this a beauty and a waste all rolled into one. Now where will I wear something like this? There's no service to attend, and it be too fine to replace that old skirt of mine that caught its last snag on a boot scraper."

"Martha, I'm sure instead of having something nice to wear it will work just as well as scraps. Let me just—" Pa goes to reach out a hand toward the skirt, but Ma is just as quick to smack his hand away.

"Don't you be startin' all that foolishness, Big Jim. Good Lord be sayin' times always be changing and believe me, I'll find time to change into this." She smiles, holding the skirt to herself, checking length and fit. "She done a mighty fine job with this." Ma whispers.

Finally, the last item left in the wrapper is a blue and green checked shirt for Seth.

For him, for Seth, how did she know?

A genuine smile breaks out as he remembers admiring the fabric Mrs. Prescott sewed, but he didn't think to ask who she was sewing the shirt for.

"That's mighty kind," Pa says. "Best be getting to bed soon. The day still be coming."

"Mm, don't need no remindin' Big Jim. Old Lady Spree be on me all day tomorrow. It's polishing day. First let me tidy up those vegetables. Then I'll turn in."

"Told Emilie I would practice writing every night. Going to work on that before bed."

"Get that candle off the corner," Ma says. "Don't need no one seein' you practice anything."

"Promise." Seth has an idea forming in his head. An idea that just might push his Pa and Ma to act instead of waiting for a miracle they've already been blessed with, freedom.

Seth gathers his powdered ink made of crushed coals, grease, water, and a few sheets of paper Emilie gifted him, which he keeps hidden in a box. The low flat box fits between his husk mattress and the ropes of the bed.

Sitting in the corner, he begins composing a picture of a family: a large man, a woman, and a child, all crying. The dark flames behind them threatening to swallow up the family. Seth hopes Emilie will understand it. The only thing Seth needs to do is safely get it to Aaron and Henry before they leave.

"Let me put this on your eye," Jim gently soothing the salve over his wife's bruises with his big thumb. Her lips are swollen, her eye is bruised.

He wonders how he is going to keep his family safe in this uncertainty.

"Boy's tasted freedom," Martha says. "How we gonna get ours?"

"Don't know," Jim inspects his work. "We gonna be sold, like Limerick's family. Ain't showin' Master papers; he tear 'em up."

"What about the Prescotts—" Martha holds her husband's wrist with both her hands.

Jim shakes his head, "Told Jacob to stay outta our business. We gots to do the rest on our own. Don't need no white man savin' us." Jim pulls his arm back and releases a heavy sigh. "We got our own dreams, freedom, and I strong enough to get us outta here."

"James Blackwell, strength ain't got nothing to do with it!" Martha jaw tightens as she struggles to control her voice. "William Prescott has our hands tied and our backs strapped. The heaviness of these shackles gots us nailed down like Jesus himself."

Their eyes meet, each holding fast to their argument.

"Now your stubbornness, gots something to do with it, insisting we stay here, for what?" Martha shakes her head. "Pride goeth before the fall, James Blackwell, and our freedom, our papers, our ticket outta here. Jacob Prescott held up his end of the deal—it's you being a damn fool keeping us up in here."

Jim blinks back the emotion welling up in his eyes. "Martha, how you expect me to leave? William woulda ran this place down if we done left. Taken what little our souls own. London, Hector wouldn't be here, but I showed them how to work a forge. The Jones never have a roof over their heads, we put it there. If it weren't for you, Mary would have lost that baby —"

Martha sighs and reaches out a hand to cup Jim's strong jaw, "Everyone can't be saved. You done taught many a man to fish, they gotta do the rest. We gots to let go. We won't be a family if you don't do right by us. You hear me, Jim? They already done loaned me to the Sprees. So, you gonna do what needs doin. Swallow that lump of pride. Seth's gonna write that letter to the Prescotts." Martha watches her husband, while Jim fights with his pride, his body shaking.

"He gonna get caught," Jim whispers.

"No." Martha wraps her arms as best she can around his bulk. "Give that boy a chance. No one thinking less of you for it, 'specially me. Besides, Seth deserves a better future then what this place got."

As big as Jim is, he can't help but fold into her loving embrace as her calloused fingers offer a tender stroke, easing the pain in his heart that is as big as the rest of him. Yes, big and stubborn as an ox, but no less of a man, a man of integrity. No white man will ever take that from him.

"We be safe, Martha." He looks up into those soulful dark eyes and for a moment they share pleasure in a kiss, but just a moment before his attention turns to his son.

At the light of dawn, Seth stole off to the barn to help Limerick with the morning chores. His hand from time to time dipped into his pocket, testing to make sure the bits of paper hadn't slipped into a stall's fresh bed of wood shavings.

"Good to have you back Seth," Limerick says, interrupting the whistle he's always maintained with his step. "Can you get those mares tacked up and ready to ride? Mr. Aaron and Mr. Henry will be out after breakfast. They're leaving today."

"Yes, sir." Seth's heart begins to pound louder.

"Packs them a tack kit with extras. Gotta makes sure they come on home."

Seth nods, unsure if Limerick is talking about Aaron and Henry or the mares.

The bay is a spirited creature, rambunctious and full of nonsense, dancing in the cross ties, refusing her bit, and trying to pin Seth's toes to the aisle. Meanwhile the chestnut is sweet with a kind expression to her eyes, until he turns his back. Then she wants to bite.

The morning is bright and sunny, a good day to travel. Seth's nerves play good idea, bad idea with him as he fingers the blankets. Should he stash it here or in the tack kit?

"Hey Seth."

Seth jumps near out of his skin, startling the mare in the process.

"Sorry didn't mean to scare you," Henry brow furrows. "Was just going to ask if you can secure these bags to the mares? We are leaving in thirty minutes."

"Yes, sir," Seth takes the bags from Henry. "Which one do you want?"

"I don't know. Haven't gotten to know them. Which one would you take?"

"I like her," Seth points to the chestnut. "She's gentle, so long as you don't turn your back."

"That's a first. Looks a bit like Starlight, wouldn't you say?" Henry stops, noticing Seth is not himself today. "Hey, are you all right?"

Seth nods. "Yes sir, just getting back into work," his eyes glisten as he bites his lower lip.

Henry studies him for a moment, both men trying to decide what to say next.

"Well, stick around. I know Aaron will want to see you before we leave."

"If I'm not pushed off to the fields. I'll be here."

"Good," Henry claps Seth on his shoulder. "See you."

Seth watches Henry leave, wishing he was riding away with him. A vacant lost feeling swells in his belly compromising his hunger, but his mother's warning fills the void.

You best change back to a slave by morning, boy.

Seth breathes deep and sighs quietly, slowing his heart beating out of his chest, and prying the paper from his pocket.

Forty-five minutes later, Seth is holding the horses, waiting for Aaron and Henry to arrive. They appear at the door, hugging the missus, turning to wave one more time before heading down to meet Seth.

Aaron is all smiles, clapping Henry on the back as they say something to each other.

"Hey Seth," Aaron greets him. "Which one is mine?"

Seth returns a smile to Aaron and holds the reins of the bay toward Aaron.

"Oh, good choice, Seth."

Seth shuffles from one foot to another, swallowing the bitter nerves. He reaches into his pocket and pulls out a slip of paper, tapping Aaron on the arm.

Aaron turns to Seth.

They look at each other.

Aaron tips his head, waiting for Seth.

"Open it later," Seth whispers. "It's just something to remember me by."

As the letter passes from one hand to another, a larger hand pulls it out of Seth's hand.

"I'll take that. Had a feeling you would try to do something sneaky, nigger. They can't be trusted, Aaron. Don't let your father's naivety become a habit."

"Uncle," Aaron steps back. "I'm sure it's just a token of thanks for our hospitality."

Seth nods his head yes.

"I think it's time for you two to leave." Uncle William says nothing more until Aaron and Henry mount up and ride off.

As Seth starts to walk away, he feels a pinch on his arm, tugging him back.

"Get back here boy! What is this, a measly plea for help? No one cares about a nigger." William's voice is like the crack of a whip, but Seth holds his tongue as pieces of paper rain down around him. The bits left to disperse in the wind.

Seth feels his heart pounding in his ears.

"Get the overseer!"

Life's New Changes

THERE ARE MANY WAYS OF GOING FORWARD,
BUT ONLY ONE WAY TO STAND STILL.
~ FRANKLIN D. ROOSEVELT

AUGUST 1861
GETTYSBURG, PENNSYLVANIA

Henry's scratchy clothes and heavy chores leave a gaping hole of absence. His work pants cinched around my waist, hanging from the suspenders that slip off my shoulders, are too big to tighten further. His boots, accustomed to the muck of the stalls and dirt of the garden, shield my feet in a clunky cavern tied tight and fortified with two pairs of socks. The August sun, a tyrant even at dawn, beats down on my neck as I wrestle with the heavy wheelbarrow. Sweat plasters the stray tendrils to my face, clinging like a forgotten dream.

The air hangs, thick with the earthy scent of manure, the rough feel of the feed bucket in hand to the crunch of straw under my feet reminds me of the endless work, of being an only child now—the only constant in all the changes over the last month.

"Oats for you, Starlight," I say, hooking her feed bucket in place. "Eat up, we're going into town today. Maybe, just maybe, there will be a letter for me today."

Starlight nudges me aside as she plunges her face into the feed bucket without one note of thanks. My stomach growls to remind me I need to feed myself. Still, one last chore remains as I pluck the eggs from the hen house. The chickens cluck happily around the enclosure in their constant search for grubs or worms. My hand goes into their nest under their warm feathered bellies to retrieve each egg.

"Thank you, Henrietta," I say as the chicken ruffles against my intrusion. "Wonder if you got any double yolks today?" Henrietta jumps out of her nesting box and waddles off, clucking to herself, ignoring my question. Outside the henhouse, I wipe the sweat off my brow, inspecting my arm for signs of anything I do not want on my face.

I sigh. Chores are done for now. Walking toward the house, I scrape my boots and remove them on the porch. Looking over the tree line, the air shimmers with heat, blurring the distance, making the trees appear farther away. It's going to be a hot August day today.

"I will never get use to you dressed in your brothers' clothes."

I look over my shoulder.

Inside the door, Mother watches me, as she adds, "Well don't dawdle, go get changed. Breakfast is almost ready."

Passing through the kitchen, I take up a clean bucket of warm water and towels to wash away the grime of the barn and transform myself back into a lady. A flicker of hope ignites as I put on a clean chemise, light petticoats of linen, and a light cotton dress. Smoothing my skirt, turning one last time in the mirror, I pluck my latest letter to Thaddeus from my bureau and take it to the kitchen with me. On the way down the stairs, the smell of fresh eggs and bread sets my stomach to request food again. I walk into the kitchen just as my parents are sitting down. Aaron and Henry's chairs remain vacant. Memories of their laughter whisper through the room. Meals are not the same anymore.

"Eggs?" Mother asks, passing the bowl to me. The scrambled eggs glisten with butter and flecks of black pepper.

"Yes, please," I say taking a seat at the table.

"Going into town today?" Mother asks, as I set the letter next to my plate in exchange for the bowl of eggs being offered.

"So, how many letters does that make, Emilie?" Father asks, taking a bite of toast and chasing it with a sip of black coffee.

"Three," I say. "But I didn't send the other two." Looking down at my plate, reaching over to stab a slice of toast with my fork, I pull the butter and currant jelly closer.

"Why didn't you send them?" Mother asks, taking up the conversation.

"They were too sappy, depressing," I say. "No one needs to hear me lament over how much I miss him or how lost I feel without him."

My parents resound a collective, "hmm," before returning to their papers and meal.

"I mean, I wouldn't want to read that mawkish sentiment," I say wrinkling my nose. "But it's so hard to miss someone all the time. When I'm not working my fingers to the bone, I can't bear the quiet."

"Maybe you could work on a project that is going to take a long time to finish," Mother says.

I look around the room pondering her suggestion, "I don't know," I say taking the last bite of eggs. "I'll think about it."

"Don't forget, I have some letters for you to mail," Mother points to the sideboard that holds a white cotton table runner, our fancy soup tureen set, and a vase of wilting garden flowers.

"I'll put them in my bag," I sit back and enjoy the end of my tea, which mother poured for me.

The sound of Father's paper rustles in his hand. The stove fire pops, as I watch Mother stare off, her mind heavy in thought. Setting my teacup on my plate and gathering my utensils, I push away from the table.

"Well, I better get going. I don't want to be late for my visit with Sarah. I'm sure she has gobs to say about the wedding."

"It's too bad you could not stand for her wedding," Mother says.

"Well, with such a large family, it makes sense why they couldn't invite too many outside guests. I mean, she has five sisters and only four sides to her, so I doubt there is little standing room to be had," I say, though a ping of regret surfaces despite my good humor over the whole thing, as I do wish I was invited.

"Weddings are expensive affairs," Father says, from behind the newsprint.

"A truth you will learn soon enough," I smile at them.

He grunts in response, as I depart the table to wash up the few dishes I have before heading to the door.

"Don't forget your hat," Mother calls to me from the hall. "You're going to turn into a giant freckle!"

"No, I won't," I grab the straw hat, the letters, and my saddle bag. "See you later."

Dust devils chase across the subdued street in town as Starlight and I clop down Baltimore Avenue toward the post office. Barely past noon, I wonder if Mr. Buehler received the mail yet. The faded storefronts, adorned with tattered enlistment posters, serve as reminders of Gettysburg's sacrifice. The patriotic displays, once vibrant, now seem to shrink, replaced by advertisements hawking more practical wares. The streets, devoid of men's usual presence, feels oddly vulnerable. Women and children walk unescorted. Gone are the strapping lads whose laughter once filled the taverns. Now, only relics of a bygone era remain—men weathered and worn, too old to fight or burdened with duties too vital to abandon. Occasionally a figure in mourning black, veiled in silence, can be seen peering through a window—a stark testament to sons and husbands already swallowed up by the distant war.

Securing Starlight outside the Post office, I turn to the sounds of sobbing and murmurs. A bereft middle-aged woman, shaken by a letter clutched to her chest while holding a handkerchief to her nose, is guided steadily out of the post office. Both women wear lines of distress as they quiver, biting back their anguish. My heart pounds at the reality that this can be anyone at any time.

Thaddeus.

Standing in line, shifting from foot to foot, I watch Mr. Buehler give and receive packages from patrons. He's a tall man with a gentle face, kind words, and a smile for his customers. He is noted to be well educated as he holds many positions in town including editor, lawyer, and postmaster.

"Miss Prescott," he says to me, "I'll take your letters."

I look down at Thaddeus's letter and find myself leery about sending it off into the world. What if it brings him more sorrow than joy? I bite my lip and silently wish it farewell as I place all the letters into the postmaster's waiting hand.

"Good day, Mr. Buehler," I say. "Did the train come yet? Are these the newest letters from today, I mean?"

A smile plays on his mouth as he shakes his head saying, "I haven't sorted today's bag, though you're welcome to come back after one o'clock today." His eyes shift to empathy as a frown turns down my mouth.

"I will come back," I say, resigning myself to waiting.

"Very well, Miss Prescott," he pauses, nodding in my direction. "If you please, there are folks waiting."

I startle at the realization, and quickly sputter an apology, "Forgive me, sorry." Turning to go, I say a quick apology to those waiting on me and push my way back out the door.

Untying Starlight, I hope Sarah has some refreshments waiting for me, and I ride back to Chambersburg Street where a mix of businesses and homes all mingle together.

"Which house is it, Starlight?" I ask in search of Sarah and her now husband's new residence.

She answers with a shake of her head, or maybe that is in response to these annoying flies. I, too, try and swat them away in between looking left and right.

"What a funny way to greet someone! Is that the way people are waving in your etiquette books now, Emilie?"

Smacking the air once more, I pull back on Starlight's reins and look around. There Sarah stands on the steps to her house, waving every which way but proper.

"Am I doing it right? This is kind of fun!"

I groan but also chuckle before hopping off of Starlight, only one house away from where my bosom buddy stands making an absolute fool of herself.

"Sarah, stop, stop. It's the flies," I say.

Sarah stops, a small pout adorning her expression, "What a shame. I felt like I was really getting the hang of it; it was quite liberating, all that movement. We could make it something you know, it being a time for big changes and all. I'm sure kids would love it. I know I didn't like having to sit still in those frumpy dresses my mother used to make me wear ..."

Sarah prattles on as I secure Starlight. She's still much the same as I recall from when we last spoke. Then again, I'm not sure what I expected. Is there any difference between my young friend and a newly wedded woman? As her lips flap, I take in any outward changes about her. Her hair is pulled up and back, her schoolgirl ringlets gone. Her dress is as expected—a splash of bright brilliant colors to match her clear blue eyes and straw yellow hair. Her cheeks are bursting with pink from what I assume is nervous anticipation of my arrival.

"Oh, but enough about me. Come, come," she grabs my hand, pulling me over the threshold.

A narrow entryway surrounds us, and directly behind Sarah are a set of steep stairs to the upper rooms.

"Do you want to see the house?" Sarah asks, biting her bottom lip as her body bounces and spills the overflow of her excitement. All it takes is for me to open my mouth before the words are back to bubbling up past her lips.

"I can't tell you how splendid it is to live with just one person and weird at the same time. I've never had brothers, so maybe you'll be able to answer my questions about some of Thomas's peculiar habits, like why he can't find things that are two inches in front of his nose or why he leaves his clothes in piles around the various rooms or the fact that he snores loud enough to wake the neighbors. Also, I thought when boys become men that gross things no longer fascinate them, and he seems positively obsessed with my bosom," Sarah pulls me into the room to the left.

My mouth, which I realize is hanging open, now closes, but there is no room for me to give my own two cents on these matters as it appears the hinge on my jaw moving in the slightest fashion is some que for Sarah to continue gabbing.

"Isn't this room delicious?" Sarah asks. "I've already set out the tea, but first the parlor."

She sweeps her arm in a presentation, and I have to wonder if she has cajoled the sun before my arrival into its participation. Sunlight streams through the lace curtains, casting a dappled pattern across the worn velvet upholstered sofa.

Dominating the room is a round walnut table, its surface gleaming with a fresh coat of beeswax. A crystal vase overflowing with vibrant flowers rests at the center. Flanking the table, a high wingback chair and a mismatched lady's chair invite guests to sit a while.

Even the walls, stark of pictures or paintings, have not escaped Sarah's vibrant personality with their floral striped wallpaper. Above the cold fireplace sits a mantal clock whose incessant ticking is swept away by the melodious babbling of my friend. Though to accompany her vocals, the air does hum with the faint scent of lavender potpourri and pipe tobacco, a subtle blend of domesticity and masculinity.

"It's cozy and I can easily get around. It's perfect for two or three, which I imagine there will soon be three, shortly, however long it takes to make a baby. Do you know anything about the time it takes to have babies? I imagine you would, given how well you are so acquainted with farm animals. Though I do hope it is not too much like the way of an animal, though Thomas does like to behave like one in the bedroom. Oh, I'm so glad I have someone to talk about these things with. So, what do you think?" Sarah asks, but once again I cannot respond, "But wait there's more!"

She leads me to the kitchen at the back of the home, saying, "It's got everything I need—

It is at this point I grab her shoulders, shocking her enough to make her pause and even squeak. "Breathe," I say.

I wait for her to nod, and I smile, leaning forward to kiss the top of her head before ushering her into a chair at her small table. "I'm just going to look around the kitchen, all right?"

Sarah's head bobbles.

I smile and release her before inspecting the open cupboards and the new dishes stacked within. The dining table Sarah sits at is set for two. A stifling wave of heat rushes over me. I look to my left, a closed window and the back door.

"The window?" I ask, pointing to the closed window holding back a breath of fresh air.

Sarah sits there like a tea kettle about to scream. She rises quickly to open the window, by placing a stick of wood to hold it in place. A warm breeze rushes in, playing with the tendrils at her cheeks.

"Sorry. Thomas doesn't like the windows open. Says it lets the flies in, though I agree this is much better." A smile of satisfaction plays at her pink mouth. "Let me check the bread." Sarah pulls the bread out of the oven. A waft of warm yeast and butter dances through the room.

Martha's voice rings through my mind, *Child, you're baking bread and you ain't gots no windows open?* I stifle a giggle as I think about Sarah then misinterpreting the old saying of having a bun in the oven.

"What's so funny?" asks Sarah.

"You're just adorable. Come, let's have some of that tea you prepared."

"Not before I show you the rest of the house!"

Escaping the sweltering kitchen, Sarah takes me up a narrow set of stairs. To the left is a room holding boxes, crates, and a sundry of possessions needing a home. We pass their bedroom to the window at the end of the hall. Sarah turns to me, "That's it. A quaint start to our marriage."

Start to our marriage. Does she know how lucky she is?

"A quaint start? Sarah, it's a great start, a lovely home," I say. "Is this not everything you've dreamed of?"

"Yes, of course, I have to finish unpacking, as you can see, but Thomas and I talked about our future more than ever on our honeymoon. Shall we now go back to the parlor?"

"Yes, though don't you think it's a bit too soon to talk about the future? I mean, you're still getting together your present," I say following her back down the stairs and into the parlor. Sarah sits across from me, smiling back at me.

I wait, but my question seems to have gone unnoticed or uncared for.

"How was the wedding?" I ask, ready for a barrage of details, but instead Sarah shrugs.

"It was beautiful and all, but family is too much," Sarah frowns. "Thomas's parents didn't want anything to do with celebrations after the service, so they left early. Then my extended family is exhausting, my uncles pressuring Thomas to enlist, then teasing him in bad taste when he stated he has no intention of fighting."

Sarah reaches for tea, pours it out, drops in some sugar, and adds milk in mine. There's a good stir before she hands it to me.

No intention?

Accepting the cup, I blow on the tea, perched just below my lower lip.

"You mean, not yet?" I ask. "I understand you just married. What man would want to leave his new wife, especially you—so soon?" I ask, smiling, hoping she cannot see the cold shroud of disappointment behind it.

Sarah narrows her eyes, she swallows, "No—Thomas isn't going—at all."

I set the teacup down, blinking. Sarah's statement swirls around me in a confusion of questions and emotion.

"I see."

"Emilie, Thomas needs to get the business up and running. He's going to run the butcher shop while his family raises the meat. Is it not just as important to feed people as it is to protect them?"

I nod. Sarah will never know the heartache of her husband being taken away, the questions of how he is every minute of every day. Will she ever really be able to empathize with me?

Not wanting to be the storm cloud on her day, I say, "Good for both of you," then "When will you be returning to school?"

"Did you get a position this year?" Sarah asks, blowing on her tea.

"Haven't heard yet," I say. "It is getting dreadfully close to the start of the year. I honestly don't know where I'll fit in teaching with all my other home chores."

"What do you mean?" Sarah asks, sliding a plate of delicate jumbles twisted into heart shapes toward me. I take one. At the first bite, the sugar and rosewater mingle together on my tongue.

"Between the chores and helping my parents run the house," I say, "I don't know how I'll run a classroom too."

"You will have to tell me about it. Thomas decided I won't be going back. He wants me to be a wife at home, as we are starting a family as soon as possible."

"But you are so good with the children," I go to put my cup down with clink to the plate.

Sarah smiles, "It's all for the better. Is there nothing more splendid than a husband and children? You know, I only got my certificate in case no one wanted me. That way as a spinster, I would have a way to support myself. But soon I will be blessed with both man and child."

"You honestly thought you wouldn't marry, Sarah?" I ask, shaking my head. "You are so vibrant and alive. That's why you need to be in the classroom with those children. They need you, and you need them, Sarah." My voice trails into a whisper, my heart breaking at the thought of anyone telling me I could never teach again.

Will the differences in our lives now put a wedge in our friendship?

Sarah shrugs her shoulders, then reaches across the table. "It's a good decision for us." She places a warm hand on mine.

"But are you happy to give it all up?" I ask, biting my lower lip, wanting to cry for her loss.

"I'm not giving it up. I'm just trading it for my destiny." My friend studies me. "Come now Emilie, I am not doomed. If anything, you should be crying tears of happiness for me."

"I'm happy for you," I say, despite being consumed by disappointment. The mantle clock chimes once behind me. I turn to look.

One o'clock.

"Do you have to be somewhere?" Sarah asks, pulling the dishes back to the tray.

"I've a few more minutes," I say. "I'm going back to the post office to see if Thaddeus wrote to me."

"How many letters has he sent already?" Sarah asks, interested in the gossip even though she has not shared any newlywed gossip with me.

"None," I say.

"Are you joking?" Sarah gasps. "I would be so angry with him."

"He's busy, Sarah. It's not like he's off doing nothing," I say.

"I'm sure there is much to learn in the ways of war, and he is doing his best, so he can come home to me."

"Oh, thank God, I don't know how you do it, Emilie. I would be positively beside myself."

"I am," I whisper, blinking back the emotional stew boiling inside of me.

Sarah comes around the end of the table, throwing her arms around me, squeezing me into her, the scent of lavender in her hair making my head swim. "I love you more than a sister," she whispers in my ear. "I am here for you."

"Thank you," I squeeze hers back. "I just want you to be happy."

"I am and you will be, too, as soon as he comes home."

Sarah lets go of me. As I stand, she walks me to the door. "Now, you hurry off and get that letter. Come visit me soon and tell me all about it, yes?"

I step over the threshold turning back, "Soon," I say.

"Good. Next week then, same time," Sarah waves to me.

I leave Sarah smiling and waving to me from the front porch.

The post office door shuts with a bang, as the wind catches it, seizing it from my hand. Mr. Buehler jumps at the noise, looking over his spectacles at me. The waiting area is empty.

"Miss Prescott?"

"I apologize for the door sir," I say, pointing at the door as a blush races up my neck. "The—wind grabbed it." Looking back to him, a smile and shake of his head says he is not upset about the door, so I hurry to the counter.

"Any news?" I ask, taking a stack of letters from his hand.

"Look for yourself."

I flip through the letters, hopeful—*Father, Mother, Father, Mother from Aunt Carrie*—hope is dwindling—*Mother, Mother*—I hold my breath, as I flip the next letter forward—

I squeak, trying to contain my excitement. I look up to Mr. Buehler saying, "Thank you, thank you, sir. You made my day!"

"So happy for you," the postmaster grins ear to ear. "There's nothing like being in love."

"Oh, I am," I say. "Can't you tell?"

"It's very obvious, Miss Prescott. I hear there's a storm coming. You best hurry home before the wind whips up anything else."

"Thank you again," I rush from the post office. "See you later."

If the door slams on my way out, I don't notice between the clapping of shudders, and the creaking of hanging shop signs.

Securing the letters in my pack, I mount Starlight. Looking to the sky, I see the dark clouds churning and mixing into grays, black, and white. A rumble of thunder set the two of us off urgently to seek shelter before we get wet, petrichor in the air.

The rain starts first in big swollen drops, here and there. As soon as we pass the Locher house, a flash of lightning perks Starlight's ears and the booming thunder makes me hold her tight as she twitches under me, ready to flee.

"Let's get home in one piece, please," I say to her.

Starlight shakes her head and snorts, chomping on the bit.

"I promise two cubes, if you don't drop me in a ditch." I watch her ears twitch. "Yeah, I know you heard me. Let's go, girl."

The rain and thunder came in earnest as we ran down the

driveway, water beading off her mane, soaking my dress. I dismount and walk her into the barn, untack her, dry her off, and give her two peppermint cubes as promised with her dinner. The rain clatters against the barn roof, but shields me from the wind, keeping me safe and dry. I check on the other animals, feeding them as needed.

Bright flashes of lightning and grumbling thunder has me trapped here in the barn, or at least I decide to wait for it to let up before braving a run across to the house. Sitting on Father's stump, I open the satchel, deciding to read the letter that is more precious to me than gold.

The feel of the paper in my fingers. Putting it to my nose there is a faint scent of woodsmoke, but nothing more. Careful to rip open the envelope, the thrill of the scrawling words, his handwriting greets me with happy swirls and curves he's perfected in school.

Dearest Emilie,

I hope this letter finds you well. Life here at Camp Wayne is a far cry from our evenings reading poems and enjoying the porch swing together. Our days are filled with the constant drone of drilling and marching boots. Every hour caters to the meticulous instruction of rifle maintenance, formation marches, and the art of battlefield maneuvers. By nightfall exhaustion sends us to our bedrolls to the solace of sleep until the bugle calls the next day.

The company Stephen and I joined has already gone through their paces. They are waiting for us to complete our training before we move out to Camp Carroll to be mustered into service. Mustering brings a strange mix of trepidation and a grim sense of purpose to this duty. Stephen and I spend our time reminiscing about our school days, sharing memories that seem worlds away from the regimented world we now inhabit.

I haven't received a letter from you yet. I know you must have written at least five, but for some reason you did not send them, or maybe they were lost? My mind conjures countless reasons for your lack of letters. My heart clings to the hope you haven't forgotten me amidst your daily trials and tribulations. Don't spare my feelings, my dear. I need your words to soothe my soul. I want to see through the window of your lovely written curves. Don't pout, I can see your lips as I write this. How I long to kiss them. Oh Emilie, please know I am teasing you in the best way possible.

Though my words are insufficient to capture the depths of my longing, let me share a glimpse of what I miss about you. I miss the gentle furrow of your brow when you ponder a complex issue, that infectious lilt of your laughter ringing in my ear, and the way your eyes sparkle in their own peculiar way when you look at me. Above all, I ache for the comforting scent of rose on your skin and how it whispers through your hair.

Rest assured, my love, I remain safe and sound. Worry less, my darling, for a soldier must endure hardship. Your prayers are a constant shield protecting me, and my thoughts turn to you with each sunrise and twilight.

Give my warmest regards to your family. Until the next letter, know you remain ever present in my heart.

With unwavering devotion,

Thaddeus

His words feel like he is right here, closing my eyes, I reach for the memories of him lost in the moment of joy, feeling his warmth, his body, listening to his whisper and chuckle, the comfort ... joy ... security ... and then—it turns cold, fading back into reality, leaving me sitting on this stump—alone—in the barn, with the rain trickling, like my forlorn tears.

How am I going to get through the next two years?

Waiting Game

SUCH IS THE STATE OF LIFE THAT NONE ARE HAPPY BUT BY THE ANTICIPATION OF CHANGE: THE CHANGE ITSELF IS NOTHING; WHEN WE HAVE MADE IT, THE NEXT WISH IS TO CHANGE AGAIN.

~SAMUEL JOHNSON

JULY-AUGUST 1861
CAMP WAYNE
WESTCHESTER, PENSYLVANIA

The screech of a woman's voice is not an uncommon sound in a camp of men, but this ear-piercing sound followed by a deeper counter shout, only means Stephen's in trouble with a one of the temptresses again. The arguing two-some, Stephen and his Ruby, are coming down the row of neatly filed tents, fighting like an old married couple yet again.

Ruby, a fiery red head with a sharp-tongue and a cutting glare, makes the largest of men cringe. Her temper juxtaposes her sweet demeanor, whispered sweet nothings, and sugary kisses—or so the rumor goes.

"Fine, I can find another wench to wash my clothes and sew on my buttons," Stephen sputters, "and you ain't getting none of this either." His hands gesture over his cut-for-battle figure.

"Oh yeah, well you ain't never touching these again!" Ruby squeezes her ample breasts in Stephen's direction.

"Who wants those saggy things anyway?" Stephen zigzags toward his tent thanks to the drink, though if Ruby had a gun, perhaps it would be for other reasons.

"Son of a bitch," Ruby's pitch sends spines tensing. "Pay up or I'll plant pins in your drawers next time!"

Stephen turns back to Ruby who faces him. Inches stand between them, her eyes holding his. Her pink tongue gliding around her lips as her hand slides to his pants, gliding up his leg. A quick squeeze. The phantom of release. She slips her hand into Stephen's pocket, taking his flask from him, dangling it away from his reach. A grin fills her cheeks as she taunts him, nimble fingers unscrewing the cap, as she tips the flask over, threatening to pour the contents out.

"None of this either," Ruby laughs as she changes her mind with a flip of her bedraggled hair she enjoys a swig instead. When she's done, she caps the flask and shoves it between her tits. "So long asshole."

Her head snaps around, as she stomps off to warm the tent of some other lost soldier boy.

"Oh, no you don't!" Stephen reaches out to grab her long braid, winding it around his fist, pulling her to him.

Ruby lets out a spine-shattering screech, but it is far too dramatic to bear anything more than amused glimpses from onlookers.

"That's mine, and I don't want any more of the swill your selling—ever!" Stephen reaches between her breasts to fetch the flask, as if her body were nothing more than his personal sack. He gives the flask a shake and then tucks it back into his pocket.

She turns as best she can, slapping him as his hand dives down her flesh. "Paws off!

He curses, but refrains from returning the blow, instead letting go of her braid and shoving her forward and away.

"Pig, I'll see you when that's empty." She ignores the crowd, pointing to his pocket.

"When hell freezes over."

"Go to hell!" Ruby yells back.

"I'm already there, thanks to you!"

The two part ways, with Stephen stumbling toward Thaddeus. The uneven ground exaggerates his sway and missteps.

Onlookers, who have a front row seat to this disaster of a relationship, cheer and then volunteer to take what she is giving.

"Hey Ruby, darling, I'll keep you warm tonight."

"Ruby, sweetheart, won't you come chat with me? I'm more pleasant than that lush."

These gestures toward his girl only make this spectacle more irritating to Stephen who is swearing under his breath and kicking logs he hasn't stumbled over before plopping down next to Thaddeus.

Thaddeus is propped against a makeshift reclined chair, ink pot at his side, pen poised in his fingers. The crisp yellow paper lays flat on a writing box he borrowed from his campmate, Paul. He looks up from the letter he's penning to Emilie.

"Alley cat got the best of you this time?" Thaddeus asks, grinning at this friend.

Stephen breaks twigs between his fingers, throwing the pieces into the fire.

"I don't know what's gotten into her," Stephen grumbles. "She's been impossible all week, asking for more money. Do I look like a bank?"

"Sounds like she is no longer accepting withdrawals on credit." Thaddeus bites back his grin.

"Well, at least I am seeing more action than you," Stephen says. "All you do is sit around and get writer's cramp."

"That's not the only thing my hand cramps from, but if it were, I'd still be getting more action from this nib and ink than you are with the ladies," Thaddeus bites the inside of his cheek. "But if you're looking to get even, the tent's free."

Stephen's jaw tenses. "She's so frigid. With a mouth like that, I bet she ain't gonna get action from anyone. She'll be begging for my fire."

Thaddeus looks at Stephen, whose eyes narrow as they both look to the tent two a-frames away where a giggle and soft whispers linger in the night air.

"Sounds like she is getting plenty of action from Paul and I hear no begging." Thaddeus nods to the tent.

"Yeah, well, what do you expect from that kind of girl anyway?" Stephen stands, waivers, and holds out his hand to steady himself. He unbuttons his fly and waters the fire, but it does nothing to ease the ire inside his gut.

"When you're sober, maybe I'll share some secrets about women."

Stephen scowls and buttons up, or tries to, before he heads for his cot, only to trip over a tent stake.

"Stephen?" Thaddeus asks.

"What?" Stephen looks up from the ground, confusion written all over him.

"Those tent stakes are dangerous." Thaddeus smirks.

"Fuck off," Stephen grunts as he raises his hand in surrender.

"That's what your hand's for, though I suggest you sleep whatever this is off before morning," Thaddeus shakes his head as Stephen gets off the ground. "And drink some water. I'm not about to listen to your bitching over a headache when the bugle sounds."

Stephen staggers off to the tent, battling the rope in front of the door before shuffling around in the dark and settling in.

Thaddeus dips his pen into the ink and begins again. The night has turned inky dark, only the small orange and yellow campfires light the path between the tents. In the background, a lonely fiddle plays a slow song, beautiful and enchanting. The camp is settling in for sleep. Snores can be heard from tents; Stephen has given up for the night.

Thaddeus figures perhaps he should too. Putting the cork into the ink pot and wiping off the nib of his pen, he begins to put the supplies back into the drawstring bag when his fingers brush against the cool silver locket. An ache rushes through him—Emilie.

Thaddeus closes his eyes, his fingers tracing the locket, as memories flood through his mind.

God, I miss her every moment of everyday.

Thaddeus's tender memories are suddenly disrupted by the barking orders, "Roll call—line up!"

Thaddeus looks up, to see a group of officers ordering everyone out of their tents.

"What now?" Thaddeus sighs, rolling out of his chair, as he gathers his things, dreading the task of waking up a lumbering beast like Stephen.

Just as Thaddeus turns to the tent flap, the officer yells, "Marsh, now!"

"Yes, sir." Thaddeus drops his things standing at attention.

"Where's Byrne?" the orders bark from Huxby, an aide to the drill officers.

"Sleeping, sir."

"Get his ass out of bed. We have a deserter to find."

So, what does one do with a drunken soldier? Drown his head in a bucket of water! Stephen is awake and not happy about it as Thaddeus grabs him by the back of his wet shirt and shoves him out of the tent, leaving his friend to fall before the boots of their superiors, and doing his best to yank him to his feet. "Come on, officers, look sharp."

"What the—sir, reporting to duty, sir!" Stephen tries to blink away the sleep and drink, saluting as best he can.

"Wrong hand," mutters Thaddeus.

Stephen quickly switches as Captain McPherson's fire encircles them, both waiting for orders as the camp crawls, groans, and shouts to life. Once the commotion settles, a small band of select men shift back and forth waiting for orders.

"We have a deserter from camp," says the captain. "You all have been chosen to go find him. He was last seen at dinner this evening. Since we recovered his weapon, you need to track him down and bring him back. Remember men, we are all in this together, and to desert the Union is to desert your country and your loved ones."

Grumbling from the crowd ensues, as men exchange looks.

"Now, I highly suggest you bring justice back to this camp, if you want so much as a wink tonight," the captain says, pacing up and down the line. "Any questions?"

"A wink? All I got was a blink. Can't I just go back?" Stephen says to Thaddeus, his furrowed scowl darkened by the firelight.

"Byrne, you got something to say?" The captain stops in front of him.

"No, Captain."

"Good. Then shut your yap. Now everyone, split up!"

The search party spreads out in all directions. Thaddeus and Stephen head off into the woods, wading through the dense underbrush. The heavy foliage is shrouded in shadows so thick with black they seem solid. Their feet tangle in roots as they scramble to keep from tripping. Thorns grab their clothing, poking skin and snagging exposed skin.

"Where the hell are we going?" Stephen asks. "I can't see anything." He jumps back as the brush under his feet rustles.

"What was that?" Thaddeus asks, righting Stephen before he falls into the dense brush.

"I don't know and don't wanna know."

They walk on, or try to, until the underbrush gives way to an open pine grove with tall trees, a soft blanket of needles with sparse twigs snapping underfoot. The night air whispers through the pines. The near full moon lights up the forest as their eyes adjust without the light of fire as their guide. The shadows become recognizable trees and brush, all cloaked in well-defined dark outlines.

Stephen walks around, looking behind trees, listening, twitching at every branch snapping under his feet. He mumbles to himself.

"What are you doing?" Thaddeus asks. "Quiet down."

"I gotta take a leak," Stephen announces.

"Again?"

"What goes in, gots to go out," Stephen wanders off, shuffling through the wood, his adventure echoing through the night air.

"If he gets eaten by a bear, he won't get me killed," Thaddeus mutters to himself, doubting Stephen has ever hunted in the woods before. He stands still, listening for noise, obscure movement, but all he hears is a forced stream against a tree and a loud sigh.

A snap of a twig ... a trip ... a tap on the shoulder and Thaddeus jumps!

Thaddeus turns around ready to strangle—Stephen!

"Dammit, Stephen!"

"What? You said be quiet."

"Stephen," Thaddeus breathes deep, and then looks at the vague visual trappings of his friend. "Remember how we played in the woods as boys?"

Stephen's face screws up making him look disfigured in the shadows.

Thaddeus dares to continue his course with his logic. "Ten paces, remember? This way, then that." Thaddeus demonstrates the direction drawing a square on Stephen's chest, trying to force the memory to the front of his friend's mind.

"Yeah, yeah. Who made you the boss?" Stephen asks.

"I'm the sober one, remember?" Thaddeus continues, "If you mark off one hundred paces in a square, you'll be right back here. Don't get lost. And for damn sake, look for the guy. Be sure to stop and listen. He may be in a bush, behind a tree, or even up a tree. Got it?"

"Is this some sort of test they conjured up?" Stephen asks.

"I'm sure it is. So, let's find this guy, so we can go to bed."

Stephen nods and wanders off counting his pace to himself.

Thaddeus listens to the wind in the pines, he can still hear Stephen's clumsy footsteps, tripping over fallen branches. Three, that's how many times Stephen has fallen. Thaddeus looks up; the tree branches are easy to see as the moonlight filters down to the forest floor.

Where is this guy, and how fast can he travel at night?

Thaddeus takes ten steps in one direction.

Listening.

Watching the shadows.

Looking up ... Nothing.

As he continues to walk in the same methodical pace and direction, he turns as something falls to the forest floor.

Thump

Crack

Thaddeus turns his head to the sound; his heart starts pounding in his ears. Narrowing his eyes, praying for better eyesight, a deep breath to calm his heart from pounding in his ears, so he can listen ...

Thaddeus notices a lump next to a tree. Animal, object, or Stephen?

Standing in the shadow of a tree, Thaddeus watches the object for a moment, no movement. Looking up into the trees, the light is obscured. Is that limb moving?

Squirrel?

Stepping closer he watches for movement, listening. The whisper of the pines, the brush, a hooting owl—otherwise nothing.

Where is Stephen?

Thaddeus moves closer, trying to get to the object under the tree. Picking up a long stick, Thaddeus shoves the stick at the mound.

Nothing, it's solid.

Thaddeus tiptoes over to the base of the tree to pick up the object—a haversack. His eyes avert up into the tree.

"Hey," Thaddeus waits.

No movement.

"You in the tree, what are you doing up there?"

Perhaps, the man is most likely sleeping or dozing off? Thaddeus listens closer, there are more twigs snapping. He hears a horse whinny in the distance. They must have gotten some cavalry to join the search.

"Soldier!" Thaddeus's voice cuts through the silence. "We're looking for you."

The form shifts in the tree, sending pine needles and bark floating to the ground.

"Come on down before the whole camp hears us."

"Who's asking?" a voice says.

"It's Marsh. Do I know you?"

"Don't know you—go away."

"Why are you running?"

"Feet hurt, back aches, haven't had a good meal in weeks. I don't wanna to be in Lincoln's war anymore."

Stephen comes up from behind, patting Thaddeus and saying, "Looks like you're a hero. Now get him down, so we can sleep."

Thaddeus waves Stephen away.

Stephen grunts, but leans against a tree, waiting—dozing.

Hushed whispers, murmurs, and more twigs snapping. A crowd has been alerted to the shouting, but they are slow to trickle into the clearing.

"What's going on?" the voice says from the tree.

"We've attracted some attention. Come on down, so we can clear up this misunderstanding."

"I ain't misunderstood nothing," he says. "I ain't going back."

"Look, I'm sure we can get you some medical attention."

A voice from the gathering crowd shouts, "You signed up for

this. Stand up and pay your dues, so we can all get some sleep tonight."

The crowd begins to rumble agreement, the tone growing deeper with discontent.

"I don't believe of a word of it." The form shifts on the branch.

Crack.

His arms are seen as a shadow, grabbing for branches as he catches himself to settle on a branch below.

"Better get down before you fall," Thaddeus's warning echoes through the forest. "Did you talk to the surgeon? He might be able to deem you unfit. You could go home honorably. Wouldn't you want to do this with dignity man?"

"A medical discharge?" His voice brightens. "That be nice 'cause my joints hurt. Feel like I'm ninety."

"Well then, come on down. If you fall and break your back, you'll go home an invalid. Best you hurry. We're attracting attention."

"All right, I'm coming," he says. The shadow in the tree begins to move. "Here comes my other pack." The weighted bag drops to the bottom of the tree as the crowd takes two steps back. The man twists and turns himself through the branches, lowering himself to the ground.

A flash. *BANG!*

The horses protest the sound with stamping hooves and strangled whinnies.

The body seems to fall in slow motion, bouncing from limb to limb, tumbling headfirst before resting half slung over a heavy low branch with the head and feet toward the ground. The canteen dangles from the shoulders; the kepi falls to the ground.

Thaddeus stares in horror at the man's lifeless body and then turns his eyes seeking justice. Three men on horseback aren't far behind him and those who have gathered. All are staring at the body while one man holsters his gun.

Thaddeus strides over to the officer. Sargent Stewart, a light haired, opinionated, wealthy lad with officer training, born with a silver spoon and an attitude of nobility dripping from his persona, glares down at Thaddeus.

"What the hell did you do?" Thaddeus asks, as the anger ravages his shock, sending his blood boiling. "He was turning himself in!"

"He disobeyed orders," Stewart says. "I was following them. Now, pick up the body and get him back to camp. I'm tired."

Stewart and his companions wheel their horses around, leaving the rest of the search party in the woods to ask questions and mill about.

Thaddeus turns back to the crowd, stunned. Silent.

A few of them walk over to the body, trying to release it from the tree.

They shot him. He was turning himself in, and they took his life. His whole life, gone. In a flash. In a bang! In cold blood. There was no reason for it. Had they not heard what he said? He was turning himself in ...

"Hey," Stephen taps him on the shoulder. "Are you walking back? They got the body."

"This is wrong," Thaddeus bunches his hands into a fist. "He was following orders, and they just shot him."

"What's done is done. We can't do anything about it now."

"There has to be some kind of justice," Thaddeus says, as Stephen pulls him through the underbrush and out the other side.

"Can we talk about this in the morning? It'll be clearer in the morning."

"I'm not sure it will," Thaddeus says. The numbness spreads through him as his mind grapples with the death of a fellow soldier and the wrongs committed by an arrogant officer whose foot has never felt anything past the iron of his stirrup.

They stop at their tent row.

"Are you coming?"

"No, I need to puzzle this out. You go on. I'll be right there."

Stephen gives a shrug and a grunt and turns in.

Thaddeus walks toward the officer's tents.

Watching the ground and where he is going on the uneven terrain, Thaddeus comes upon a lone officer sitting outside the captain's tent. The man is leaning back in a chair, his long legs stretched out toward the fire as he ponders, smoking a pipe and staring into the hypnotic flames.

His eyes move up to Thaddeus, assessing him with a small frown forming. He removes his pipe from his mouth. "State your business, private."

"I would like to report a murder," Thaddeus says, standing taller. "Who do I speak to sir?"

"Murder, eh? We ain't even mustered in yet." The officer sits up, pulling his legs under his chair. "Who did you kill?"

"I didn't—"

"What's your name?"

"Private Marsh, sir, and who do I have the pleasure of addressing?"

"Lieutenant Huxby,"

Thaddeus nods, still unsure of what to say, knowing "pleasure to meet you" may not work in this man's army.

"Sir,"

"Lieutenant will be enough; I am not your girl's father or yours, for that matter."

Thaddeus clears his throat.

"Sit. We'll talk man-to-man."

"Thank you," Thaddeus sits on an empty stump, trying to calm his nerves in front of his superior.

"State your concerns again, Marsh," Huxby sits back and returning his pipe to its perch in his mouth.

"Well, I was sent out on the search for the deserter."

"Oh, that guy," Huxby nods. "Can't say he didn't get his wish. He's going home—in a box."

"That's the thing, sir—Lieutenant. He was shot down by a cavalry man while following orders. He didn't deserve to get killed. I had him convinced to come back and follow procedure."

"You did, did you?" Huxby asks, considering Thaddeus with narrowed eyes. "What did you tell him."

Thaddeus looks to the fire, gathering his courage. He steps on the toe of his boot to stop his leg from shaking. Swallowing hard, he finally says, "Well sir, I told him if he physically could not do the job of a soldier, he could see the surgeon to discuss the matter. See, it wasn't right for him to lose his life, when he was willing to return peacefully."

The silence grows between them.

"Maybe I wasn't clear, Lieutenant—"

Huxby clears his throat, sets his pipe next to him, and then leans forward. Grounded brown eyes meet baby blues.

"This is the army, Marsh. As an individual, you're going to think there are many injustices here. However, as a piece of the unit there is something you need to get a grasp on. The deserter put this camp in danger by forcing us to leave our posts. He did it once, and he'll do it again, maybe even when the men we're up against are on the other side of that tree line. They could catch him then, torture him, and that spineless welp could cost us the damn war."

"But he has—"

"Yes, he does, but he also signed up and is only a few weeks from taking his oath to serve country first," Huxby says. "That oath is above anything and everything else that makes him an individual."

Thaddeus takes a deep breath, hearing his own words to his beloved echo back at him. He has no choice but to nod at the logic, adding to the Lieutenant's wisdom. "One man cannot win a war; therefore, the group becomes more valuable."

"Now you're getting it," Huxby's grin surfaces and the pipe returns to his lips.

"Thank you, Lieutenant. I better understand the mentality necessary now."

"Good, it'll save your life someday," Huxby pauses. "You the eldest in your family?"

Thaddeus looks at the officer, "Yes, why do you ask?"

"I can see it, Marsh. You have leader qualities."

"Thank you, sir. I'd love to—"

"But you're not ready to use them. Good night, Marsh."

"Good night, Lieutenant."

The camp once again at peace, Thaddeus's new perspective begins to sink in as he walks back through the grounds, listening to the night sounds of camp. Snores, whispers, low voices, giggles, and moans mix in the night's song.

The morning bugle call cannot be ignored. When the sun rises, so does the heat in the tents. Stephen opens his eye, only to feel a stinging drop of sweat roll into it. He wipes at his brow and cheek before he's up and out of his cot, throwing back the tent flap, praying for a cool sip of air. Instead, smoke from their campfire assaults his lungs.

"God—" Stephen bites his tongue, not sure if it is Sunday as he steps out of the tent in his drawers.

Thaddeus looks up from the rifle he's cleaning. "That's a good look on you."

Stephen glares at Thaddeus, hawks a loogie, spits to the side. "Yeah, that's what your Ma said too." After grabbing his pants and jacket off the line outside, he ducks back into the tent. He shakes out his coat and pants. There's no help for it. The uniform stinks and laundry day is next week. Luckily, everyone smells the same, wood smoke and days' old sweat. Running his fingers through his greasy hair and giving his beard a good scratch, he steps out of the tent for the day.

"Ready for the last day of training?" Stephen asks Thaddeus, who is now picking up the rifle cleaning supplies.

"I am ready to move on. This place is a mess. New surroundings may do us some good."

"Rumor has it, today is going to be the worst of it all," Stephen says. "We'll be pushed to exhaustion." Stephen notices the shadow and brisk breeze before looking up to the clouds, building in the west.

Hope that's not some kind of omen.

The relentless curtain of rain lashes down on them just after noon, transforming the parade ground into a muddy quagmire. Stephen slogs through the ankle-deep muck, his boots squelching with every step. His wool uniform clings to him like a second sodden skin, with the commands of Sergeant Hooten droning on in his waterlogged ears.

Sweat, now indistinguishable from the rain, trickles down his face, stinging his eyes, blurring the rows of his fellow recruits in front of him. Every muscle in Stephen's body protests, and his shoulders burn with the weight of the rifle as their second round of endless drilling commences.

Shoulder arms, presenting arms, firing blanks that echo like mournful cries in the flooded air. The commands seem endless. Hours blend into one another. Company drill morphs into battalion drills. The monotonous cadence of "Left, Right, Left, Right, Hay foot, Straw foot, Hay ..." pounding a rhythm into his skull, which throbs back its own cadence in an echo.

There's a stabbing pain in his left heel as the blister lets go. The world around him swirls into a mass of yelling, gray, wet, blurred, fatigue, exhaustion ...

An ear-splitting *CRACK,* followed by a hair-raising flash splits the sky, momentarily drowning out Sergeant Hooten's roar, "... in the park, keep those lines straight. Step it up. It's only a bit of mud!"

The faster they try to move, the more the mud sucks down their boots, their calves—deep into the ground, demanding they have an early grave. Stephen's legs burn with exertion.

He begins to long for the workdays in the orchards, following his father, tending the animals. His mother's cooking—although it wasn't his grandmother's cooking—it is sure better than the slop he's gobbled up over the last month.

As the line turns to fold in on itself, Stephen's sees Thaddeus and he realizes he is not the only one questioning the path they've chosen, yearning for the comforts of home and family, worlds away from this muddy purgatory.

It feels like eternity before Sergeant Hooten finally bellows through a raw voice, "Dismissed!"

Their bodies are weighed down by rain-soaked wool. Their fingertips are wrinkled by the endless deluge. Stephen and Thaddeus stumble toward their tents, each step an attempt to shake off the mud encrusting their forms. A puddle of water lays over the ashes and half-burnt logs of their fire, which has long since been extinguished. Neither of them cares as they trod over to the tent, Thaddeus being the first to pull back the tent flap.

Inside the thin canvas that offers little protection from the cold, each of them strips off their wet clothes, careful not to touch the rain-swollen walls. Within their sacks are still damp yet drier set of clothes to wear. Under the cover of the wool blankets stretched across each of their cots, they lay in silence, their bodies relaxing into the lumpy straw, praying for the rain to stop, the mail to arrive tomorrow, and for sleep to pull them into their only day of rest before a three to five-day march to Camp Carroll—somewhere near Baltimore. Stephen's eyes begin to close, not wanting to think about being mustered into service.

"Tomorrow, we will be marching from sunup to sundown to Camp Carroll in Baltimore, so pack up your things and clear your tents," Sargeant Houten paces the line of recruits, before rattling off a list of items they must complete before their departure.

Stephen shifts his weight to his toe, giving his left heel a reprieve from the stabbing pain. Socks. He could use some more.

"... take advantage of today's reprieve to wash out your clothing, air out your bedding. If you spot the beasties, get your things washed promptly. We will not be welcoming them to our next camp. Also, take care of your feet and request bandages from the surgeon if you need them. No one will be left behind, so if you slow down this march, you will be prolonging everyone's agony ..."

The list of orders drones on for a long time as Stephen's mind begins to wander off to other things.

Will the mail come today? ... How difficult will the march really be? ... Will we have larger quarters at Camp Carroll?

"Private Byrne!" Sargeant Houten yells. "Stand at attention, so I can dismiss the lot of you."

Stephen forces his heel to the ground as his face winces.

"Byrne, report to the surgeon when you are dismissed."

"Yes, sir."

As the lines dissolve into tangled groups, all scattering in different directions, Thaddeus pulls on Stephen's sleeve. "I'm going back to the tent to begin packing and washing some clothes. Meet you there."

Stephen gives a nod and joins Thaddeus after he visits the surgeon, with rolls of bandages and salve for the blister. Their tent is completely empty as the blankets are on the line, and the straw from their mattresses is drying in the sun. Thaddeus has his haversack emptied, too, with all the items laying out, waiting to be repacked.

"How's your foot?" Thaddeus asks, looking up at Stephen. The wind blows his hair into his eyes.

"He says I'll live. What can I do to help here?"

Thaddeus stretches, looking over the array of items on his extra blanket.

"You can wash your clothes; I left the pot of water on the fire. Other than that, I'm ready to go. I just need to write to Emilie and let her know where we're going, so her letters keep coming."

"She writes to you almost daily," Stephen feels pang of jealousy stabs his heart.

"She is amazing at keeping up my spirits," Thaddeus laughs to himself. "She always has something good to tell me. I can't wait to get home."

"Hardly mustered in and you're ready to leave?"

"Well, life with her has to be better than this," Thaddeus opens the drawstring pouch, reaching in for her locket. The shiny silver catches the light, blinding Stephen for a moment. He watches Thaddeus open it, looks inside, and smiles.

"What's in there?"

Thaddeus turns the locket to Stephen. Inside the heart is a young Emilie—her innocence is breathtaking to him. A lock of her auburn hair sends a rush through him, the smell of rose—a flash of her and him against the wall in the alley. So close to her, he felt her tender skin on his lips, her hair intoxicating. But she shuns him, refuses his apology. Perhaps—Ruby is right?

"It's Emilie," Thaddeus sees Stephen's reaction, a blank face with no hint of recognition.

"Oh, that's right," Stephen turns away. "Treasure that. I would love to have my love's locket."

"Then we should talk about your approach to women," Thaddeus nudges Stephen.

"I suppose we should. As you can tell, I am not the best at wooing."

"Well, step one, it's a devoted woman you're after. Not a girl."

"What's your secret with this one," Stephen asks gesturing to the locket.

"This one is one of a kind," Thaddeus beams. "She's smart, funny, resilient, and when I recognized that and fell in love with her for her free spirit, she and I became inseparable."

"Free spirit? You mean independent and non-traditional?" Stephen asks. "You must have had something incredible to get that woman to agree to a role such as wife. Or did you master hypnotism while she slept?" Stephen eyes Thaddeus, while giving him a complimentary teasing jab.

"Not really. We just fit. We listen to each other and love being together."

"Did you get her to marry you?"

"Her father said yes, after I come home," Thaddeus has far-away look in his eyes, remembering all he knows intimately about her. "Truth be told, I should have stayed back with her."

"No, you'd then resent her later in life," Stephen warns. "Believe me, you're doing the right thing. You know it and I know it."

"I suppose you're right. But I would be devastated if something happened to me. I couldn't bear to know I ruined her life."

"Not sure you can be devastated in a box," says Stephen.

"Mail's here!" A recruit announces, running down the lane of tents.

Stephen sees Thaddeus's eyes light up.

"Shall we?" Thaddeus stands brushing off his pants.

"How wonderful it must feel to be punch drunk on love. But sure, I suppose another guilt trip from my parents wouldn't hurt."

"At least it is something from home."

"Let's just hope someone doesn't scream letters amidst battle. Then you're sure to get shot." Stephen as he puts an arm around his friend and squeezes the man's shoulder. "Come on, Romeo."

The crowd gathers as everyone waits for their name to be called. Packages, letters, and gifts from home are doled out like an ongoing birthday party. The wait feels like an eternity for some, as the mail is separated into companies before being handed off to each man with a call of his name.

Stephen receives two letters and a package.

Thaddeus, a lovesick pup, turns back with two packages and two letters, one of which he brings to his nose, savoring, no doubt, the scent of rose.

Figures.

"Let's read these back at the tent," Thaddeus says putting the letter to his nose.

Stephen knows Thaddeus isn't the sort to hoard such happiness.

But does he mean to rub his giddiness in my face?

Once settled near the campfire, Stephen opens his package first. A letter from his parents, baked cookies, horehound candies, socks, a scarf, and drawers. A small smile peaks at the corner of his mouth.

"These will help," Stephen says, holding up the socks. He stops and opens the sock to pull out a small piece of paper, which he reads aloud.

"We hope these socks keep your feet warm. If you soak these in tallow, it will help keep your feet from blistering on long marches. The Lady's Relief Society of Table Rock Road prays daily for your safety and safe return home. God speed."

"Emilie complained how she and Louisa Welty knitted, as she

says, hundreds of socks. Do they fit?"

"I'll try them on. What did you get?"

Thaddeus opens both of his boxes, listing off their contents, "Socks, a shirt, a bag of lemon drops, and oatmeal cookies. Not counting the letters from my family and Emilie."

When Thaddeus peers into the socks and pulls out the note a slight tinge of pink blankets his cheeks.

Stephen snatches it and notices that this one is signed by Emilie with a heart. He rolls his eyes and hands the note back to Thaddeus who clutches it like it's the damn woman herself.

I hope I'm never that desperate.

They each sample a piece of candy and settle into reading their letters from home. Stephen delves into the pages from his parents, each bridge between his present duty and the life he once knew.

Ah yes, each letter is masterfully crafted with emotion, the words sewn together with a stiff thread of guilt. The design is meant to underscore his selfishness in his quest for freedom from his parents' stifling grasp. *We are proud of you*, the letters proclaim, yet the inked lines speak of their longing for him to be present. The same general message echoed between them, *we understand your allegiance to our county yet yearn for you to prioritize family first.*

Stephen hmphs.

Perhaps, I should tell them what happened to the deserter. That'll change their tune. God's speed, they'll say. Arrive home safely. We are blessed to have a son as brave as you, they'll say.

But that will never be the case. The bittersweet symphony of their actual words resonates deep within him. While he treasures the connection to home, Stephen craves the connectedness and blissful attachment to family that has eluded him from the start of his teenage years, before his parents began to see him as a commodity, not a son. However, the truth resides with him now and cannot be shaken; he is nothing more than a means to carry on the family's tradition, reputation, and wealth.

A giggle. A small chuckle.

Stephen looks over to Thaddeus who is deeply engrossed in reading his letter from Emilie—grinning like a fool. His heart aches for the experience and joy that lights up Thaddeus's countenance, while simultaneously, the flames of envy smolder within him, a slow-burning torment, a ceaseless fire consuming him from the inside out. Is it not agony enough that he must be aware that Emilie irrevocably belongs to Thaddeus? Must he bear witness to it too?

What does she say to him? His curiosity about her letters gnaws at him.

Until now, it was easy to forget her. He had drink, he had Ruby. Now, he has these socks in his hands—

"Marsh!"

Both look up to see Sargent Houten's stocky short frame with broad shoulders and thick arms and legs to match.

Thaddeus stands to greet him, discarding the letter inside the box. "Yes, Sargent?"

"Lieutenant Huxby wants to see you now," Sargent Houten says, an arm sweeping beside him.

"Now?"

"No, next Tuesday at two o'clock," Houten rolls his eyes. "Yes, now, you idiot!"

Thaddeus stands to follow the Sargent when he turns back to Stephen. "Can you put that on my bedroll? I'll take care of it when I get back."

"Sure thing," Stephen watches Thaddeus walks down the lane with Sargent Houten.

What does Lieutenant Huxby want with him?

Stephen turns back to the package. He bites his lip, struggling with his conscience for but a moment, and then gives in, picking up Emilie's letter.

My darling Thaddeus,

As I write this letter, I realize it is a flimsy barrier between us, and yet the only bridge I have to reach you. Therefore, I will cross this bridge every moment of everyday if it means I can hear your words echo off the returning page.

Your last letter challenged me to name three things I love about you. My three things, among many more, include—your chuckle, your voice when you read poems to me, and your silliness that makes me laugh when I want to be angry.

Daily life here is much the same except for the longing for the missing loved ones. Father seems to be shrinking away, the smile gone from his face as he worries about work. The factory is reducing hours. I guess no one needs a carriage during war. He spends a lot of his hours in the wood shop thinking about Aaron and Henry. Mother busies herself with harvesting and preserving food for winter. My heart aches for them. I am a poor substitute for the boys. I miss them.

I have to tell you, I dreamt of you last night. It was vivid, and you were warm. I was nestled against you on the swing, a blanket covering us, shielding us from the outside cold. We shared the most amazing kiss; it makes me smile to think of it now. Imagine, my darling, if you could feel my arms around you now, a silent promise of strength and comfort I long to offer you. How I yearn to feel you against me like that again, to be truly held by you.

Sarah's wedding looms like a bittersweet reminder of everything the war has taken from us. She confides Thomas won't enlist after their vows. A selfish part of me burns with anger and jealousy. They will experience everything while we wait tethered to the outcome of this war. I am sorry for being so petty, but this is a confession from my heart.

Let's see, what else is there to tell you?

The upcoming school year is approaching. I have a faint hope I might still be chosen to teach, but as each day passes, it is hard to stay positive. If I don't teach, maybe I can fill in. I long to get into the classroom as a distraction from missing you. This is because I do not think keeping myself busy with the multiple sewing projects Mother insists I do will be enough to keep away my longing for you.

I hope this letter chases away the grim realities of camp life. Are you moving on to Baltimore? You mentioned in your last letter, you were marching that way soon. I put some socks in your box from me. As you know Lousia and I have been assigned to the task of keeping all the men's feet warm and dry, but it is your feet I think of most.

Write soon, my love. Tell me about your days. Knowing what you might be doing will soothe my worries.

Know every day without you stretches like an eternity. But with each sunrise, I hold onto the hope that someday soon, I will hear you chuckle, have the song of your voice to complete my poetry, and your silly words to keep me from strangling dear Sarah.

I pray you are well and safe.

All my love and devotion,

Emilie~

Stephen reread the final line of Emilie's letter; the words blurring before his eyes. Shame wraps around his neck, tightening.

He's the fool, driven by a twisted mix of insecurity and the desire that Emilie bend to him. He projected his insecurities onto her, and yet she was strong enough to hold fast. Good. The woman who wrote the words in this letter is kind, strong, fiercely loyal, and exactly what he craves by his side. But does he deserve her even now—as a friend?

Forgiveness feels like a distant mountain peak shrouded in a heavy wet mist of tears. Friendship, that bridge Stephen so gleefully burned, seems impossible to rebuild with her. Could he even approach her again? Should he? She had refused him once. What would stop her from doing it again? Or stop him from recklessly abusing the gift of her presence?

Stephen's renewed desire for Emilie burns a small hot ember as a plan coalesces in his mind. However, it will require truth far more raw, more vulnerable than any lie he's ever spun. But will it be enough?

He looks down to the socks still in his hand. Could they have been knitted by her? Could they be a piece of her he can touch until he is able to win over her friendship at last? Stephen vows to hold them close and not let them fall to ruin like everything else he has touched.

The ride through Richmond is a blur of cobbled streets bustling with nervous energy. Military wagons rumble by with soldiers barking orders, and anxious women clutch handkerchiefs to their lips. The city drums with frenetic energy that heightens the gnawing anxiety Henry feels about his new life ahead.

Two hours into their journey north toward Ashland, however, is uneventful, a monotonous blur of green fields and dusty small towns. Dust devils dance on the parched earth, churning up the turmoil in their hearts as they carry the weight of the family's secrets.

Henry vows to write to his father, telling him about everything he saw, tracing the grim echoes of the plantation they left behind onto a letter, provoking his father to act. After all, he has nothing to lose, and the plantation has everything to gain as Uncle William won't be able to bring his wrath down on Aaron or him. A fair bargain Henry reasons to himself.

"Let's grab something to eat," Aaron says shaking Henry out of his thoughts. "I need to get off this horse."

"Agreed. I'm famished."

They dismount beside a gurgling creek, the sound of cool water a welcomed melody for horse and rider. After watering the horses and stretching their stiff limbs, Aaron searches through his provisions packed by Aunt Jenny. She insisted they have good food for the road.

"Aunt Jenny damn near packed us enough food to feed the whole Confederate calvary for three days," Aaron says with a wry smile, pulling out a thick slab of ham and a loaf of bread.

Henry digs through his own saddlebag, a growing frown marring his features. He fumbles past extra tack supplies, leather, polish, and a worn horseshoe before his fingers grasp and pull out a clean white envelope.

"What's that?" Aaron asks, taking a bite of bread.

"A letter addressed to Emilie," Henry turns the paper over in his hand. The script on the front is unmistakenly Seth's, clear and precise with the Prescott's address flawlessly written below. A slow grin spreads across Henry's face.

"Seth, you sly dog," Aaron chuckles, handing Henry a slice of bread. "Seem he's taking matters into his own hands."

A glint of pride lights Henry's eyes. "He's a clever one, that's for sure. We need to get this to the nearest post office and on its way to Gettysburg."

A tense silence settles between them.

"Ready to get back on the road?" Aaron asks, a hint of impatience in his voice.

Henry feigns protest, shoving the rest of his bread and ham in his mouth, "Barely even had a proper bite."

"Ashland waits for no man, little brother. Let's go."

With a shared glance, they mount their horses and continue their journey with a bit more haste now that the weight of the plantation feels lighter on their shoulders, and the unexpected discovery of Seth's letter sparks a glimmer of hope.

Letters Home

LETTER WRITING IS THE ONLY DEVICE
FOR COMBINING SOLITUDE WITH GOOD COMPANY.
~ LORD BYRON

AUGUST 1861
GETTYSBURG, PENNSYLVANIA

Another day, another trek into town, another set of unanswered questions. Father and I arrive around noon, our errands almost finished for the day—his last stop the feed mill, mine the post office. The line in the post office is longer than expected.

The dust motes dance around the window slats, the sun lighting their impromptu stage performance. A quiet hum whispers through the room as conversations between patrons carry on. Behind the counter are stacks of mail and newspapers. The scent of the old paper and faint tang of printers' ink floats along with the motes.

I tap my foot, mostly to distract myself from the heat of the room. My fan flutters a breeze on this late August day. This, mixed with the anticipation of letters, sends a fidgety current through me.

The customers in front and behind me shift impatiently, waiting—just like me—for any news the mail will bring. Aaron and

Henry have not written. I haven't received a letter from Thaddeus since before he marched off to Baltimore, and then there's the waiting to see if my teaching application was accepted. School starts in a few weeks.

The man and woman ahead of me step aside.

Mr. Beuhler looks up to me.

"Miss Emilie," his familiar smile creases his features, sparking a glimmer of hope in my chest.

"Good day, Mr. Beuhler," I greet him, our conversations becoming less formal with our daily familiarity.

"You're right on time; I just finished bundling your letters," he reaches behind him to present her with a trussed stack.

A genuine smile breaks out on my face, a rare sight these days. "A bundle?"

"It must be your lucky day. See you next time."

"Thank you," I say, moving away from the counter.

Thaddeus's letter sits on top—*finally!*

Outside the post office, I sit on a bench and pull off the twine binding the post.

Careful not to tear the paper, I rush to connect with his words.

Dearest Emilie,

The march to Camp Carroll was tiresome. Long days of moving one foot in front of the other for hours on end. No one's feet are the same after four days of endless marching. The men are plagued with blisters, callouses, and sore feet. My feet, however, survived as I received a note in my socks telling me to soak them in tallow before we left. The handwriting looks suspiciously familiar. Do you know of these mysterious note writers?

Our regiment was mustered into service the day after we arrived in Baltimore, so I guess it's onto the next months in Mr. Lincoln's army, but my only concern is the countdown until the day I will see you again.

Orders came today. We are marching to Annapolis to attach to Dix's command. We were promised, if anyone can believe that around here, this march will be about two days if we are not forced to rush. I guess my socks will return to the tallow. I don't know where we are going from Annapolis, but I will write as soon as I can.

I hope this letter finds you smiling. Know I think of you every moment of the day and sometimes you visit me in my dreams. I long for our nights visiting on the swing. I miss reading Hawthorne to you. How is the Alcott book? Did you finish it? Continuing our game of what I miss most about you—your cooking. I would love some jumbles or oatmeal cookies from you. I miss kissing your head and waltzing with you, how your forehead scrunches when you are keeping count, and how big your eyes get when I dip you. Your turn, what do you miss about me, my love?

I cannot wait to hear what is going on at home. I think of you all often. We do our best to keep busy here, but a home cooked meal and a smile from our loved ones is what we miss most. Keep me close to your heart and know you are never away from mine. When you need me most, close your eyes and imagine a kiss. May the whisper of these words brush against your tender lips.

Write soon,
All my love,
Thaddeus

I hold his letter to my chest, cherishing his words, feeling his passion. It makes me long to be in his arms again. Staring at his handwriting, I begin to remember the small things about Thaddeus that make my heart dance a thrilling jig.

A couple across the street holds hands, discreetly intertwining fingers as he pulls her along. They laugh and smile at each other.

The stack of letters slides off my lap, fluttering in all directions as they scatter on the ground. Returning to reality, I look down and begin to pick up the letters.

Where did I leave off? Who wrote this?

The handwriting is not one I've seen, but I open the letter anyway, searching for—Stephen? I'll skip this one for now.

Third letter. The school board finally made a decision. Just as I expected, I have been passed by for a teaching position this fall. The board states they are impressed by my professionalism as a student teacher and would like to see me apply in the spring. Folding the letter, I tuck it back into the stack, disappointed, yet hopeful, for spring is not too long after fall.

I turn over the next letter, the script neat and professional— Aaron, a smile returns.

I wonder how Aaron feels about his decision; did he change his mind?

Opening this letter, I begin to read.

Dear Family,

Henry and I arrived to Camp Ashland within twenty-four hours of dropping Seth back at the plantation. Thankfully, Uncle William found it in his heart to gift us two mares, so Henry and I could pursue our duties in the cavalry. Nelly is a beautiful bay. She is disciplined except for squirrels. Gunfire is no problem, but Nelly fears the bushy tailed bossy squirrels, I fear the critters will be the death of her or me.

Camp is much as I expected. I take my responsibilities with ear-

nest discipline. Father taught me leadership, and this is proving to be helpful in my work. I am making great contributions to training and helping to manage the troops.

Henry is my constant shadow. Who knew his constant companionship when we were kids would pay off? He takes his responsibility seriously, is becoming a man overnight, and will make a great soldier. He is doing well in marksmanship and using signal flags. However, we took him off bugle duty as he sounds like a forlorn cow and cannot read music worth a darn.

We both miss all of you dearly. When you are sleeping in the elements with rain and thunder overhead and the only protection is the thin canvas of your tent, home never sounds so good. We are both thankful we are not in the infantry. Our clothes are cleaner and less tattered than those poor boys. Still, know that we are both healthy and doing a fine job here.

Our correspondence may be vague, as we cannot risk divulging any secrets, since we are on opposite sides of the war. Despite this, please know I am on your side as your son and family member. Thank you for understanding my need to be here. I will make both of you proud and we will come home as soon as this is over. We pray you are all well.

Your devoted son,
Aaron

Picking back through the stack of letters, I pick out the odd one from Stephen.

What could he possibly want to write to me about?

I roll my eyes, but tear open the letter anyway; it is neatly scripted with his best handwriting, no doubt. I take a deep breath and read his correspondence.

Ellyn M. Baker

Dear Emilie,

Believe it or not, I miss you. I bet you didn't think that would ever happen. But training changes a boy to a man.

After I arrived at camp, I started to think of all that happened between us and since you refused my apology on the train platform, I also decided to write to you in hopes that after all your boredom—you will read this letter and know that I am sincere in my apology to you once more. In fact, this letter has not one but two apologies, but you will have to read on if you wish to know of both.

I am sincerely sorry for the way I have treated you. I am wrong to argue with you for the sake of argument. I am wrong to try to force you into a role you not only disdain but wish to comply to in an untraditional manner. There are many others who are untraditional but are still good people.

There is Ruby for instance. She is a camp follower who cooks, washes, mends our clothes, and tends to other duties that our tired and weary bodies have no energy to expend upon after training or marching—always with the marching. Yet, she is not a wife nor even thinks about marriage, but still she is a good person nonetheless, like you. But not like you. The good parts of her are like you.

I digress. I can neither take back what I said nor did in the past. I know you probably hate me for the comments about your family. And yes, that was plain stupid and hurtful of me to say, which was the intention. But the Lord's honest truth, I said those words out of spite. I do not wish harm to you or your family, Emilie. In fact, I never wish to see you cry again, and ask special forgiveness for my foul behavior. If you cannot find it in your heart to forgive me, I will settle for another one of your harsh slaps. My other cheek misses your strike.

Knowing you and Thaddeus are engaged to be married, I am

pleased to hear you are happy with him. I'm sorry for spreading rumors about us. As you might have guessed, I desperately wanted to be the one to court you. Alas, my stupidity leaves me empty handed, but worry not, I'll not come between you. I simply ask your forgiveness and to call a truce between us from here on out. Can you not let me be the friend I should have been from the beginning, when we met on the Halle porch?

At this point you are probably wondering about my second apology, and to show you I am a man of my word, I will write that you deserve more than words, and yet words are all I can afford to give you. So, as a second apology, I am sorry there is nothing but this letter to offer you for my ill behavior.

If you choose not to write to me, I will accept that my apology and, gather, that this method is not acceptable. But know I will not cease to find a way to earn your forgiveness. Perhaps I can fashion you a fabric bouquet from threadbare socks, though I doubt much can be done for the stench. Anyway, I suppose all comforts must come to an end, like writing this letter to you does for me. I hope it, too, provides you with some comfort, a small smile. Please know, I wish you the best every day, and I will be sure to keep Thaddeus safe. Take care of yourself, Emilie.

Sincerely,
Stephen Byrne

Stephen's letter leaves a blank hole in my thoughts. I don't know if I can ever forgive him. He did some unforgivable things between us. I commend his letter, but I am not sure I will write to him. On the other hand, what am I to do with a bouquet of threadbare smelly socks? Either way, he can afford to wait.

A letter from Henry is next, this one is thicker than the others. I open the letter, and there are pages crammed inside. Henry's the sort to scribble only half the grocery list and try to remember the rest. Surely, he did not write four pages worth of paper.

The script at the top of the letter warns, *To whoever reads this, make sure father sees the second page.*

My heart stops, my breath catches, but I begin with what Henry has to say, hoping he will explain himself before I reach the second page.

Dearest Family & Em,

Well, we finally made it to Camp Ashland in one piece, though Aaron nearly took a tumble from his mare, Nelly, when a particularly enthusiastic squirrel crossed our path. Let's just say Nelly and the squirrel didn't see eye to eye. Thankfully, Uncle William gifted us two beauties, Nelly and Millie. Emilie will be pleased to know, or maybe jealous to know, Millie looks like Starlight, but Limerick promises Millie is not from the same line, and she's certainly not addicted to sugar or as bothersome a temperament as Starlight.

Camp life ain't all peaches and cream, though. The tents are draftier than a politician's promise and the food, well, it's bland, and lumpy, but it keeps us going. The good news is I am a natural sharpshooter. Turns out, Aaron's and my hunting back home paid off. I'm also learning all about signaling with flags—they chose someone else to mind the bugles. Though come fall I think my bugle calls could attract some mighty fine venison.

Speaking of learning, Aaron seems a shoo-in for an officer position. That fancy degree seems to impress the bigwigs around here. Maybe if he gets promoted, I can be his right-hand man? Imagine me, the dashing aide-de-camp! That's French! Just picture it Mother—a shiny new uniform, a fancy plume on my hat, and the authority to boss everyone around, except for Aaron of course. Life here is a far cry from mending fences and dinner with all of you.

One thing hasn't changed—missing all of you something fierce.

Especially you, Em. The men are no fun to tease, and they promise to punch me if I try. There's no one here I can steal a dance card from either. Don't do the chores too well. I don't want new expectations when I get home.

Don't worry Mother, Aaron and I are sticking together like glue—well, at least until they slap those shiny officer bars on his shoulders. Until then, I'll just have to rely on my charm and good looks from Father to get by.

Speaking of Father, I tucked a letter in this envelope from Seth. He is telling the truth; the Blackwells need some help, as I don't think Uncle William will free them. I can also vouch for the changes back home. It's not what anyone remembers. Please check on them. I don't think they will arrive in Gettysburg as promised if you don't.

Write soon and tell me all the gossip from home. Every little thing is a welcome distraction from the endless drills and dust of this new life.

All my Love,
Henry

"Damn you, Henry," I say, as tears drip into my lap as my heart aches for his laugh, teasing, and constant presence in my life.

Turning to the second page, the script changes again. The elementary practiced letters written straight, tight, and carefully practiced—*Seth?* I begin to read what I have dreaded.

Dear Mr. Prescott,

Thank you for mI visit. I like tIm with yor family. Please tell Mrs. Prescott her kindness is the best a-round.

I write two you as Miss Emilie made me keep my word. We are in danger of being brokin and sold. Many are gon from the farm, while new ones are hear. My Pa wont ask for help, but I fear pa-

pers dont matter. If you help one more tIm, Id be greightful not to be torn from mI Ma and Pa.

Seth

The words crash through my senses. My skin pricks with chills, a rush of blood from my face follows close by while a dizzying, nauseating wave expels from my stomach. Folding the letter, tucking it back into the stack, I look up as I see Father's wagon pulling up to the post office.

"That looks like some good mail," Father says, as I step up into the seat next to him.

"We have to talk," I say, my eyes holding his, my jaw firm.

"Bad news?" he asks, turning the team around to home.

"What did Aaron tell you about the plantation?"

"He said things changed," Father seems surprised at my sudden inquisition.

"Did he tell you how bad it is?"

"He—told me it was different from when I was in charge—why?"

Silence falls between us.

"I don't think the Blackwells are coming," I say, watching his face. His eyes harden and shoulders tense.

"Did they decide to go elsewhere?"

Is he playing dumb?

"No Father!" I say my voice demanding. "Uncle William is going to sell them!"

"Em, I think you are over-reacting. Jim has their papers."

"And I have papers that say otherwise," I demand shaking the stack of letters at him. "We have to save them!"

"We'll do no such thing," Father's voice is calm and uncommitted. "I made a promise to Jim I cannot go back on."

Why is he not taking me seriously?

I turn away from him. I must control my temper, make him understand.

"Promise to who?" I demand more than I am getting from him.

Why is he so non-committal?

I shake his arm, Father's head snaps around to me. Our eyes glare at each other in mirrored stubbornness, glinting like sharp spears aimed at each other. "Make me understand."

"Emilie—" Father's voice is a warning that I am overstepping, but the fire within refuses to cool. "I said no. I promised as soon as I stepped foot off the land, I would not go back."

"It's your family, the Blackwells—" I plead with him to listen.

"They are fully capable of handling your uncle. I will hear nothing more about it."

When we arrive at the house, Father sets the brake and gets out of the wagon, leaving me fuming.

I get out of the wagon, stomp into the house, and slam the kitchen door, throwing the letters on the table.

"What on earth?" Mother asks. "Emilie?"

"He is a pig-headed stubborn fool!" My voice is raised for all of Table Rock Road to hear.

"You best not be talking about your father, young lady."

"Then you best talk some sense into him," I say fully aware of my insubordination. "I am banishing myself to my room!"

SLAM!

The fact the doors didn't fly off their hinges meant the sound did nothing to quell the fire burning inside of me. Somewhere, something happened to make my father suddenly not care about anything that is important to us.

Did the sun make him sick? Did he have a bout of apoplexy, suddenly wiping out all the tender emotions he had in his body? I pray Mother will read the letters and set him straight. If not, will the Blackwells be gone from my life forever?

Tears break through, hot and angry, overflowing, drenching my cheeks in salty pools. My nose runs, adding to the mess, bathing me in a pool of anger and dread. I wipe it all away with one pass of my sleeve, then search for a handkerchief, to no avail.

Slumping onto the bed, gasping for air, my chest heaves. My breath refuses to move as my heart is clenched in the constrictive grip of my emotions and the knowledge—sharp and undeniable—the Blackwells are in trouble and my father is abandoning them. This betrayal twists my world into a mess of confusion and worse—dread. *How are we equals if we leave their fate to useless papers they cannot decipher?*

Return to Richmond

I HAD RATHER BE ON MY FARM
THAN BE EMPEROR OF THE WORLD.
~ GEORGE WASHINGTON

SEPTEMBER 1861
GETTYSBURG, PENNSYLVANIA

Jacob heard his daughter's shriek coming from the house as he moves the team into the barn. The flash of stubbornness between them pains him as he sees himself in his daughter's eyes. How will he get her to understand? He completes his chores as if someone else guides him through the tasks, while his mind ticks off all the possibilities. His heart is broken, betrayed, and overflowing with rage, not at his willful daughter, but the real pighead in all this—his brother.

Should have known, he'd betray them ...

William Prescott, the baby of the family, a daddy's boy since he was able to walk, the two of them as alike as twins. Mother coddled and spoiled him like a fragile baby as a boy, as an adult—until her death. William was always *too young to know better,* and Jacob was always expected to have patience with your baby brother. Then the argument, as they were young men, when William shoved his silver spoon up his pompous attitude, scoffing at Jacob's plan to free the slaves.

You're too softhearted ...

You are going to ruin our legacy, and I will never forgive you for it ...

You are a disappointment to our father!

The words echo in his head, beating him down for his stupidity and blind trust in someone who proved time and time again to be untrustworthy, devious, a liar, a scoundrel, a cheat, a fool ... The animals leave him to his thoughts. They make no noise except to shuffle about, maybe feeling pity for this man, this fool who buys the feed, who serves the soiled hoof—but not the freedom of my neighbor. With the last of the chores complete, not a single solution comes to him, a blanket of shame his only comfort.

I promised Jim I wouldn't interfere ...

You promised Jim, before that, as boys, you would make him a free man ...

I gave him the tools ...

Tools you never taught him to use, before you walked away never to return ...

It was Jim's decision ...

And now you have a decision: which promise are you going back on? What will your best friend think of you? What must he think—

Jacob's fist crashes into the barn's wooden exterior, shattering his thoughts with pain and yet, as he tries to shake the burn out of his nerves he looks back at the house—

What will I have to face there? An angry daughter? Julia. What does she know about this?

Reason knocks at his skull, hardly dazed by the physical burdens of his world. *Read the letter, listen, then decide.*

Jacob takes a tentative step toward the house, looks down at his hand, already beginning to swell and soon bruise. He shoves his hand into his pocket, spits, kicks dirt over the saliva with the ball of his foot, and then with a roll of his shoulders figures—

Best to face this music than let the Devil control the tune.

Jacob closes the door behind him. The kitchen greets him with smells of dinner cooking on the stove and baking in the oven. But there is little to savor at the moment, his stomach has already flipped to sour.

Julia is paging through the letters on the table. She looks to him. Her brow furrows, her clear blue eyes glisten, holding back fear and tears. A bite of her lower lip. A shake of her head. A quiver of her darling stray curls—

"I-I haven't gotten to the boys' letters yet, sh-should I—" She pauses, gives a stiff sniff, and looks away.

Jacob frowns, runs her words through his head just like he runs his swelling fingers through his hair. Pain clogs his thoughts. He sucks in a breath and with it smells his wife's fear. Women are complex creatures, which he hardly understands, but he figures he might as well take a shot in the dark. At this point, it's all he has.

"Are you—are you worried that Emilie is upset over something that may have happened to Aaron and Henry?"

He hit the nail on the head noted by the widening of her eyes and the clarity of their whites. Jacob almost had to laugh, but he had good sense to swallow and just shake his head, "No, no Julia. I don't know what's in their letters, but last I checked, I'm pretty sure the post does not take correspondence from the dead."

"Then, what the devil was that about!" Julia snapped at him, gesturing to the stairs where he guesses Emilie's head rests or conspires with ways to exact her rage.

Dare he wonder if they were both moody for womanly reasons?

"I'm sure she's overreacting," Jacob glanced at the stairs before he pulled a chair from the table to sit. The table is strewn with letters; he recognizes Aaron and Henry's handwriting. The others are addressed to Emilie.

Julia's lips perse and her eyes shoot him a withering glare before she reaches for the letters from their sons.

Jacob watches her as she reads, trying to read her in the same breath, wondering if he'll be sleeping in the barn once all is said and done. Eventually she tucks her hand into her lap as she passes on a short quick letter, the handwriting different from his sons'.

"I don't think so," she says. "Read."

Jacob's eyes read the letter. His heart pounds in his ears.

Why isn't Jim leaving now? Surely, he or Martha knows some abolitionists. He's let them off the plantation to run errands plenty of times, but what if William—

"What are the chances William will sell them?" asks Julia. Her question is pointed and stabs at his insecurities.

He lowers the letter and looks at her, his chest swelling with stubbornness more than pride.

"I promised Jim—"

"What do you think is the going rate for the price of flesh?"

"Julia as I told Emilie—"

"You told her what? That this is no longer your business, but William's?"

"No, but—"

Julia's words lash out like a serpent's tongue, casting venom into his thoughts, making his veins pulse. "He must know by now Seth can read and write. Jim is strong and knows the land, and Martha is a superb cook. Surely they'll fetch enough to warrant Jenny's new ball gown—"

"ENOUGH!"

"Then do something about this!"

"I can't," Jacob voice is tight. "I promised Jim his freedom, and I am not going to come to his rescue every time. The man has pride. Am I to be the one to break him of that too? Among friends there is honor, and I will honor his wish to be his own man. I'll not be his white savior!" Jacob pushes his chair back, the scraping of the legs on the floor punctuates his frustration. He stands in the kitchen, his head bowed, body shaking. One foot in front of the other to let it out as he paces the floor, pulling out his pipe from his vest pocket, lighting it, drawing in rapid successions. The kitchen is filling with smoke, worry—fear for his best friend's family.

The judgement from his wife's eyes haunts him. By now his pipe smoke is giving the train station competition. He hears Julia move, glancing in her direction.

Pushing herself away from the table, Julia quietly opens all the doors and windows.

He sighs. "I should go outside."

"You should go wherever you want, but might I suggest the plantation."

Jacob shoots her a glare.

Julia scoffs. "Don't give me none of that. By and by, I know you, Mr. Prescott, and you be goin' because the good lady says it."

"You sound like Martha."

"I'd rather hear her say it than me."

Jacob grunts, blows smoke, but his shoulders finally sag. Women.

"Well, that settles it. And you should take your daughter with you."

"Why aren't you coming?" Jacob asks, trying not to fully commit to her suggestion.

"I am going to gather items to make sure the Blackwells can move into their home as soon as possible." She looks at her husband, pushing her plan—the plan—further into his mind and heart.

"I see. Not that I agree." Fingers scratch the shadow on his chin. He sets his pipe down and crosses his arms, wincing as his injured hand brushes against his sleeve. Never mind, he leans against the counter. "But if I were to go, why do you think my daughter would want to accompany me?" Jacob asks. "She hates me right now."

"Well, I see where she gets her flare for dramatics from," Julia pulls his bruised and swollen hand free, not asking, just tending. "Jacob, she doesn't hate you. She is angry because you are a pig-headed fool."

He frowns, cheeks growing flush.

"Her words, not mine," Julia smirks. She releases his hand to grab the liniment and a cheese cloth. "But trust me. When you two talk about it, she'll go."

"But what about Jim?" Jacob asks. "I'm doing exactly what I promised I wouldn't do."

"You promised to be a good friend, first and foremost, Jacob," Julia returns reaching for his hand. "Now, would you rather get them safe, so Jim can be the man he deserves to be? Or have their backs split, their family carved, and them wondering why you abandoned them?"

Jacob resumes the fight from earlier in his head, while his wife tends to his hand.

"Jacob, your brother needs to be put in his place. The plantation is still yours and your sons' legacy too. We cannot let it fall apart; I will not have Aaron put his life on the line for shambles."

He grunts as she pulls tight on the cloth, but her point does come across as he looks down at his hand and then over to his beautiful, doting, stubborn, insubordinate—and right wife.

Jacob takes Julia's hand, pulling it to his lips, kissing the back of it. "You win. I'd rather Jim be angry with me, than me never seeing him again."

"Good. Now can I get that in writing?" Julia asks with a playful smile.

Jacob rolls his eyes, but grins. "I think I'd rather face the wrath of our daughter." He sticks out his tongue.

"Well then, you do that. Maybe she can give you some pointers on how to handle William."

They both chuckle as Jacob pulls Julia into his arms, burying his face in her neck and hair. They share a hug of understanding and bonding, strengthening their marriage.

"Please bring them home," she whispers.

They hold each other for a long time.

When Julia pulls back, he has to stifle a yawn. She's so warm and plush and flush.

She steps away, clearing her throat with a pat to his chest.

"Well," she sighs, "I better get you two packed up."

"Did she really call me a pig-headed fool?" Jacob asks.

Julia bites her bottom lip trying to suppress a giggle as she begins to set the table. A nod is all he gets.

His expression shifts into a pout, which she ignores, brushing by him as she prepares the food for the table. Brown eyes track her every move. "But I'm not, am I?"

His wife doesn't answer, just breezes by him to stand at the bottom of the stairs, calling up, "Emilie, dinner."

"Julia?" asks Jacob.

Julia looks to Jacob. "No. Now go sit." Her attention then returns to the quiet stillness from upstairs.

"Emilie!"

Silence.

"Emilie Kathryn Prescott!" Julia yells.

"That girl. If she thinks she can out stubborn me ..." Julia's voice fades under the stomping footsteps of his wife up the back stairs.

The familiar stomping of mother and daughter puts a smile on Jacob's face.

"Well, if she gets her dramatics from me, then she gets her stubbornness from you," he says to himself as he sits down at the table, taking a piece of bread and butter. Resolving this may take a while.

"Emilie Kathryn!" Mother yells through the door.

The rapping on the door means business.

"Come down to dinner."

"No, thank you. I'm staying in tonight."

The door opens. Mother's face is adorned in a mask of no-non-sense.

"No, you will not. We have things to discuss ... Now!"

Embers of anger flicker between us.

"Did you talk some sense into him?" I ask.

"You can't avoid speaking to your father because you don't understand his decisions."

"I can and I will," I say. "He is abandoning the Blackwells. I'm going to get them." I push back from my writing desk, cork the ink, and wipe off the nib. Thaddeus's letter will have to wait.

"Really?" Mother asks, her hands on her hips. "And how do you plan to do that and with whom, I might add?"

"Well—I—I—" I take a breath, but it gets caught in my throat. My gaze turns down to the floor. I hadn't thought of that yet.

But I'll figure it out when it's time!

"I will go by myself, if I have to," I say.

"And for the plan?" Mother asks, looking at me as though I were seven and not seventeen.

"I won't let the Blackwells be sold. We will never find them again. I can't—if no one will—" I begin rambling, tumbling toward hysteria, only to be stopped short by her demands.

"Emilie Kathyrn, you will do no such thing. You are acting out of emotion, which will be your ruin if you don't control yourself. Now, enough of this. Walk with me to the table and you will apologize to your father."

"But he—"

Mother shoots me the look.

Great. Now I have no choice but to follow her or risk the penalty of death.

On the way out, I grab another handkerchief, just in case I need it, as I am sure I will.

Father waits for us in the kitchen, rolling the crust of his half of the bread to put another glob of butter on it before popping into his mouth with a satisfied smile. I look away from him as he tries to make eye contact with me. His chipmunk impression was cute when I was seven, but not anymore!

The embers of emotion from before reigniting, twin flames glowing in my dark coal eyes, before settling into a smolder.

He swallows hard and tries a grin.

"I'm not hungry," I say, scowling at him.

"That's fine. Will you at least have a seat?" he asks, his hand gesturing to my place at the table.

My arms fold.

"Sit down now!" Mother says.

I huff but slide into my chair, arms still folded in front of me.

"We had a discussion."

"It seems that you were not, in fact, overreacting," Father says.

"Can I get that in writing?"

Father glances at Mother, and I turn to look at her too.

Weird. She looks like she just sucked a lemon.

Father clears his throat, and my attention resumes on him.

"Aaron kept his secrets while he was here, but the letters from your brother and Seth confirm my suspicions."

My scowl lightens. "So, why won't you save them?"

Father sighs, pushing back his chair. "I made a promise to Big Jim that I wouldn't interfere in his life once I gave him the manumission papers. His freedom means he gets to call his own shots, and we will not save him or them from trouble."

"That doesn't make sense. He has no say as a slave. He's not free yet. Uncle William's made sure of that. How can you expect Jim to stand up for himself and his family when—"

Father put his hand up. "If you shut your mouth and open your ears, dear daughter of mine—"

Mother squeezes my shoulder. "This is a bit more complicated than we thought. We didn't think Uncle William would take it this far."

"Has the air around here affected both of you?" I ask. "Uncle William is horrible, a monster—and the Blackwells are as good as sold if we don't act now!"

"A prom—" Father began.

"Damn your promises, Father—" I say, but Father's eyes sharpen, cutting my words off at the throat.

Then my parents looked at each other, leaving me paralyzed by their silence. I cannot tell if what I said is sinking in or if they are thinking about a thousand and one ways to punish my insubordination. When they finally decide to acknowledge my existence and turn back to me, I cringe.

I'm in for it now.

Father smirks.

What?

"Emilie, remind me to warn Thaddeus about your debate skills," Father says reaching for more butter and bread, only to have Mother swat his hand.

"What?" He is taken aback.

"You'll ruin your dinner. Now stop dawdling and ask her."

"Ask me what?"

"Ask you if you want to come to the plantation with me to bring them back," Father asks almost absentmindedly, as his attention turns back to Mother. "Now woman, let me have my—"

I throw my arms around him as I squeeze him tightly, kissing his scratchy cheek. "You're the best! You're the greatest! I love you! I—wait, what about Mother?" I ask as Father is caught between me and trying to reach for the butter that Mother, just after taking her seat at the table, pulls out of his reach.

"I am going to take donations for them to set up a house," Mother says. "Besides, someone has to keep the farm running."

"I wish Aaron were here. He would—"

"But he's not here, and I need you to keep my temper level," Father says. "You've always kept me sane."

"I thought that was Mother's job?"

"She keeps me humble and starving. Julia, please pass me the butter."

Mother passes him the string beans instead. He takes the dish with a reluctant grunt, spooning some onto his plate, before he looks over his shoulder at me, who's still wrapped around his neck. "If Aaron were here, he'd pass me the butter. But what do you say? Will you come with me?"

"I will," I kiss his cheek again before taking my seat, my appetite having miraculously returned.

"Good, and Emilie, could you be a dear and pass me the butter?"

"Nope."

Mother smiles at me and then puts her hands out to both of us. "Good, it's settled then. Let us give praise for this meal and a safe journey for you both. I will have you ready to leave within the next two days."

Family Conflict

FAMILY QUARRELS ARE BITTER THINGS.
THEY DON'T GO BY ANY RULES.

~F. SCOTT FITZGERALD

SEPTEMBER 1861
RICHMOND, VIRGINIA

The train lurches to a shuddering halt, jolting me back to a reality far harsher than the rhythmic clatter of the past twenty-four hours. The realization of life's cruel mutability settles heavy in my gut, a weight of unfamiliarity, slammed into me with the forced stop of the locomotive—life, that fragile porcelain doll we cradle in our illusions, could shatter at the blink of an eye.

My bag is packed and sitting under my watchful grasp, waiting for the aisle to clear of bodies disembarking from the train. Richmond. My dear Richmond, once a bustling haven of familiar streets and friendly faces, feels like a stranger in a tattered cloak.

"Stay close," Father's deep voice reminds me, his warning jostles the weight sitting in my stomach. I nod as I can't turn to answer him; we are pressed in a crowd of bodies moving to the station doors. The vortex of activity flashes before me as the crowd surges us with a tide no individual can control, not even Father, who brought and carries a gift from his father, a polished walking stick.

Goodbyes are now a sharp painful business, fracturing families by the call of war, each clinging to the other's embrace, a silent plea for time to stand still. A ping, the first drop of an incoming storm, hits my heart and echoes my own memories as these families force me to relive my own goodbyes.

A woman, her face etched in a mask of stoic determination, smooths the stray hairs of her teenage son clad in a miniature soldier's uniform.

"Remember," her voice hoarse with emotion, "you fight for us, for our way of life. Fight with God in your heart, and know you'll return home a hero or rest with the Lord in heaven."

The boy—barely a whisper of manhood—stares up at his mother, trying not to cry, his eyes wide and unblinking. The look they share is one that lingers, gives me pause, breaks my heart as they share a nod—one of determination, the other of silent prayers. He turns to board the train, leaving his mother on the platform. I watch the back of her hand, brush away a single tear, a single act of vulnerability in a performance of unwavering faith—*In God We Trust.*

"Emilie!" Father calls me.

"Coming!" I say, moving back to his side, though my eyes can't help but soak up the changes to a world I thought I knew. Father takes it upon himself to steer me through the station doors, while the cacophony of shouts, pleas, and fervent sermons hammer my skull.

A preacher, his voice amplified by the cavernous station hall, bellows about the righteousness of their cause. "The fate of the South rests on your shoulders!" His roar is encouraged by claps and shouts. "Don't let those heathen Northerners tread on our

God-given rights and steal our livelihoods! Fight for your family, for your freedom, for your very souls. For if they win, we are all damned to hell!"

Stepping onto the walkway, the familiar air of Richmond is thick with the pungent scent of ammonia, and I am quick to put my rose aroma handkerchief to my nose.

"Is it just me or is the odor of waste stronger?"

"Nitrite. The ammunitions factory up the road is using urine to help make gun powder," Father says.

My nose scrunches as what I am experiencing doesn't mix well with the spicy taste of Virginia's famous tobacco that tickles my tongue from every pipe on every corner. Gone are the quiet days of ambling through the streets. Instead, there are throngs of soldiers. Some have fresh faces full of bravado and a hunger for adventure. Others have grey whiskers of wisdom, already educated in the ways of war. One guides the other, shouting in their reprimands.

I suppose this is what Thaddeus meant when he said they were taught to work as a unit; they must think alike down to their very step. I wonder how Stephen got on with that.

Across the street, a motley crew of beggars and drunkards mingle through the crowd, hands outstretched in a constant plea. Their desperation is a stark contrast from the military swagger.

One man in ripped clothing, face and hands smudged black with dirt, cracked and caked on his shaky knuckles, approaches us.

"Please sir, I only require a few cents to eat tonight."

Father shields me from him with a brusk, "No thank you," as we walk to the livery stable to rent a wagon and horse for the ride back hom—to the plantation.

Another tries a different approach, a smirk coiling his lips.

"I'll take that fine girl off your hands." A boney hand that reeks of rotted fish and oozes with white puss reaches for me. I pull back, mortified as the sharp acrid taste of my own vomit stings the length of my tongue.

Thwack!

"Back," Father's voice is as sharp as the crack of his walking stick across the man's hand. The filth shrinks back into the crowd—whimpering, sniveling.

I rearrange my grasp on my bag, so it is not only close, but in front of me.

"What is happening to my Richmond?" I ask, as Father's confident step guides me through the chaos, his walking stick clearing the way of unsavory pedestrians.

"Richmond has war fever. Everything's changed. Stay close and be careful. The stable is up this way."

I look back over my shoulder at the crowd swaying behind me, a hypnotic woven scene of certainly some form of fever and righteousness besets my eyes. Shrill voices condemn the North, painting them as monstrous heathen invaders. The air crackles with a desperate urgency, urging men and boys to join the Confederacy, fight for the Cause, defend against the Northern aggression. A suffocating sense of guilt hangs heavy, a weapon used to bind these citizens to a cause that feels increasingly hollow in my mind.

"Protect your women and children!" bellows a man, his voice raw with fervor.

"The North would have us collect crumbs for their feasts and have us pay for the wet nurses of their bastard sons! As Marryat said, 'There's no getting blood out of a turnip,' and yet those Yankee bastards will not stop until our soil and every cobblestone beneath your foot at this very moment, turns crimson. Mark my words, greed is the cause of this war, and justice will be the end of it if we fight for what is right!" says another who stands in front of an office of law, drawing in an even bigger crowd.

The unwavering belief of the mother I witnessed earlier echoes in my mind, a conviction that sends chills down my spine. Her son, she declares, will find salvation only through fighting. It is a skewed reality from the one I experienced months before. As the crowds disappear from sight, a question begins to nibble at me: *What is everyone really fighting for?*

We arrive at the stable where Father secures a wagon and two horses for a few days. Dropping our bags in the back, I climb up into the seat, ready to leave this now foreign land called Richmond. Father guides the horses out of the city toward Plank Road.

After moments of silence tick between us, I ask, "Did you send word to Uncle William about our arrival?"

"No, I don't believe your uncle will be keen on seeing us, so we are going unannounced," Father's brows are furrow with his own remembrance.

I leave him to his thoughts as I reacquaint myself with the scenery. The city itself is nothing as I remember, but once we reach Plank Road the familiar packed dirt road transpires into a peaceful undisturbed path. Here the air is fresh with a hint of autumn's chill. My excitement grows with each passing mile. I miss many things about home, but mostly the people. A flutter in my chest bubbles up as the excitement builds, anticipating a happy reunion with the Blackwells and Limerick and Lucy and ...

When the black iron gate comes into view, it is open and inviting, and I can hear my heart announcing our arrival in my ears. The oak and pines remain ever vigilant sentries along the long drive. The front of the house sits as proud as the family occupying its walls. Even the rose garden is in full bloom with pink, yellow, and red blossoms, pricking my lips with a smile warmed from my childhood memories.

Home!

"I'm going to find Martha and Big Jim," I say, my legs bouncing, my body springing into action before the wagon even stops. "I'll tell them we are here to take them home."

My arm is snatched up by Father's grasp, pulling me back to the seat we share.

"Just tell them we are here," Father says, his voice low.

My head whirls around to face him, and I see a shiver race across his shoulders. My eyebrow arches in a question mark.

"I want to speak to Jim myself; do you understand me?" His abrupt warning is out of place.

"Yes, Father. I'll just—tell them we are here." I will respect him.

Father pulls the wagon up as a footman, hunched over and walking with a hitch in his gait, comes to greet us.

I stare hard at the man, trying to remember his name. He's familiar yet different.

"Oh God. Is that Simon?" Father asks.

My eyes widen, a flash of memory depicting a much younger Simon with a smile of sunshine and a good, humored joke fades away to the man, standing in front of us.

"Mr. Jacob," Simon's face brightens with flicker of familiarity. "Good to see you again, sir." Turning to me, he offers me a gloved hand for my departure, his face warm. "Miss Emilie, all grown up and more beautiful the missus's roses."

I blush at the compliment. "Thank you, Simon."

"I wasn't told you were coming today. The missus is napping. Shall I wake her, sir?"

Father sets the break, steps down from the wagon, ties off the reins, and unhitches the team. "No need Simon. Let dear Jenny sleep. I'll take care of the team. We'll wake her after."

"And the wagon?" Simon asks.

"Leave it. Can't make the place look worse than my brother has."

Simon's eyes widen, caught between the orders of the two masters.

"If—you say so—sir," Simon swallows hard before adding, "Are you sure you don't wish me to call on a stable hand, sir?"

"I'm sure. Though if you would like to take our bags from the wagon and deliver mine to the guest room and Emilie's to her old room, I'd greatly appreciate it, Simon."

Simon brightens as he goes to fetch the bags. "Yes, sir. I can do that."

"Oh, and one other thing Simon. Is that old coot Limerick still in charge of the stables?" Father smiles, and I can't help but feel he is trying to ease the man's worry over our surprise arrival.

Simon returns the gest with a chuckle. "Still as ornery as ever, Mr. Jacob, but I'm sure you will make his day, sir."

"Simon, where is everyone today?" I ask, interrupting the banter.

"Well, I suspect the men are in the upper field—the old wheat field—getting ready for the next planting."

"Thank you," I stifle an urge to rush away as I look to Father, wondering if I'm dismissed.

"Out and back. I would like you to greet your aunt with me."

"Yes, sir," I say as we walk part of the way to the stables before I take the other path up to the slave quarters, then out to the fields. "Give my regards to Limerick."

"You better do that yourself. You don't want to disappoint him by not stopping by."

"I'll stop and see him after I see the Blackwells."

Down the uneven dirt path and through a small windbreak of trees, the sights and smells of the sharp pine pitch mixed with the tantalizing aroma and spices of the smokehouse greet me with the comfort of memories and happiness of days gone by. The summer kitchen's chimney even has a small plume, as I am sure the maids are busy with dinner.

Around to the left, the double rows of wooden slave quarters sit in their own community with the center open for laundry, cooking, and gathering. The new residences show a stark contrast of weathered wood and paint bare doors, a telltale sign of their shoddy construction. Some of the doors are ajar. I wonder where everyone is. The cabins are eerily quiet for such a usually bustling community.

Taking a closer look at the new cabins, there are no new garden plots. The garden plots were a staple to these homes. After an outbreak of diseases due to poor nutrition, we planted fruit trees and everyone got small gardens. It happened when I was eight or nine, and even at that young age, I can recall how seeing their happiness felt overwhelming to me.

Searching for the only cabin with window boxes, I see Martha's and Big Jim's home and walk up the steps. To my left, the window boxes lay vacant. No splash of flowers this year and the dirt is dry. Rapping my knuckles on the thin plank door, I wait.

No one is home. Then again, it is the middle of the day.

Turning away from the door, I search for any signs of life. The laundry cauldron sits atop a fire, boiling water. The flames lick the bottom of the large cast-iron pot. Someone must be close enough to watch this fire.

"Hello?" I call into the wind. A slam of a door to my left. A giggle of a small child to my right. I turn to see a middle-aged woman staring at me from the threshold of one of the open doors. She stands about four to five inches shorter than me. Her tiny frame boasts a dark orange and brown skirt, and matching top covered with a dark holey apron.

Excited to see a human inhabitant, I wave and begin to approach her. The closer I step, the more her deep brown eyes narrow as she stands steadfast in the door, pushing the small children behind her.

"Can I help you?" Her voice is clear, yet the hint of suspicion punctuates her words.

"Yes, thank you. I am looking for Seth and Big Jim. I suspect Martha is in the kitchen, so I will see her when I go back to the house." I ramble on as if we are old friends. The enthusiasm rushing through me can't be helped, what with the idea of seeing the men again.

"All the men are in the fields out back. They's busy."

I cringe at her pronunciation, trying to stop myself from correcting her wordage. Her usage no fault of her own. If only they could receive a proper education, but such thought is a distraction from her other words that make me grimace.

"That overseer is a mean one. You don't wanna be causing them pain, do you?"

My father's words echo loudly in my memory. *Tell them you arrived and nothing more.*

"No, I don't, but they aren't expecting me, so it is important I speak with them," I say. Just as the words escape my mouth, the woman's crooked finger points at me as if to tap out the reality of the memory.

"Are you that Emilie child that left a while back?"

"I apologize, ma'am, I don't remember you." A warm blush

rushes up my face.

"I don't suspect you would. You weren't here when I arrived." A genuine smile graces her beautiful dark face, lighting up her chocolate eyes.

"I'm Emilie Prescott, niece to William and Jenny Prescott."

"Pleasure to meet you, Miss Prescott. I'm Phibe. I take care of the children and tend the washing. They says I'm not fit to be a house slave."

"Why's that?" I ask. "It appears you know the work, as it seems the same job you are preforming here." I gesture to the laundry hanging on the line, and the little curious faces peering out from behind her skirt.

"I can't say as I would want that job."

"Long hours?"

Phibe's face sours as if she ate a lemon.

"No, miss. Long hours is nothing round here. It's that the job comes with more expectations than just cooking, is all."

"But I am sure Martha would welcome you in the kitchen," I say. "She taught me everything I know."

Phibe tsk's me. "Poor child. She didn't teach you everything she know. Then again, you just got here, didn't you?"

"Yes, ma'am, I did. And I would love to talk, but I need to find Big Jim and Seth." Returning to my original mission, I look around. The children are peeking out from behind Phibe's skirts, but there is still caution in their eyes.

Their fear is disturbing. What has Uncle William done?

"Like I told you, they are in the field, but you had best stay away. You don't want them in trouble with that overseer."

"Don't you worry, Miss Phibe. I will set him in his place if he sasses me," I say, waving good-bye. "Nice to meet you, Miss Phibe, and all of ya'll too." One final wave to the small faces looking at me with wide eyes and I can't help but smile as they finally gift me with their big grins and shy waves.

The growing fields are situated at the far back of the property, behind the slave houses and a row of trees. The crack of whips snapping like thunder echoes through the air. The fields are mounded, neatly turned over soil by horse and plow. In the middle of several rows, thirty to sixty men, women, and children old enough to be in school are equipped with hoes. Currently, they chop away at clumps and weeds, working the soil, removing rocks and roots, turning over the tobacco fields. The heat of the early fall sun bakes them between the sky and the earth.

Hiking my skirts just above my ankles, I hop over the mounds of dirt, making my way out to the field of men. Three men sit astride horses, each holding long snake-like whips and canes, shouting anything but encouragement.

"Keep that hoe moving, we got a whole field to turn over."

"The slower you move, the later your dinner be."

"Get on there. You been leaning too long." The crack of a whip to the man's flesh stops me in my tracks. A scream I fail to stifle turns everyone's head to me.

The slaves flicker a quick look before moving their tools into the dirt, but it is long enough for me to take in their suspicion. I can only imagine their thoughts. *Who is that? ... She's parading around just to watch us work. ... Is she fixin' to make our day worse?* Every one of them had to question why I am standing in a wheatfield far from the comfort of the parlor.

Approaching the husky overseer closest to me, his horse snorts and lifts a hoof to paw me and then the earth. At least the brute of a stud is smart enough to back up before I can swat its knee

Ellyn M. Baker

for such rude behavior.

"Tell me where Big Jim is," I say.

A smile graces the overseer's lips before he licks them. I can tell just by his eyes that he has about as many manners as the horse he rides.

"You got yourself lost darling?" he asks. His voice is soft, melting away the anger for a moment, but those lecherous eyes dragging down my form make it easy for my scowl to return.

"If you value your job, you will keep your eyes and your appendages, including that whip, to yourself and tell me exactly where I can find him," I say, placing my hands on my hips. "Or do I need to bring the indecency of your gaze to my uncle's attention!"

The man swallows, averting his eyes after one last lingering stare. He clears his throat. "Second row, far end. Go on and state your business, then get out of my field."

"You mean my uncle's field."

The overseer doesn't respond. Rather, his attention has moved on to someone he can control, another slave. "I say, get hoeing, or you'll be wishing you was dead."

Rushing over the mounds to reach the row indicated, I race down the smooth dirt, passing by whispers.

"Get out, missy."

"You ain't got no business."

"You bad luck, girl."

Their eyes avert from me as I look at each one, and stop short, at the former frame of a large man, who is now thin and gaunt. Big Jim is a far cry from the muscular strong man I last laid eyes on. Now he wears a torn shirt, ripped trousers, and stands barefoot. Still, he towers over me, and I smile, glad some things haven't changed.

"Miss Emilie!" his voice is sharper than I remember. "You best get back to the big house."

"Big Jim, I've come to tell you we are here," I say, my smile broadening, hoping he will return my excitement or at least understand my meaning by it.

"I see you. Now git, 'fore I get a lashing."

"But—they can't lash you—"

"Hell, they can. I'm still a slave!" Big Jim has never raised his voice to me.

I feel a hot bubbling anger rise in my gut. *How dare he? Wait til I tell Martha. She'll set him straight.*

Seth appears at his father's side—*or maybe his son will set him straight.*

"Hey Seth!" But my smile fades as I notice the fear in the whites of my friend's eyes.

"Hey Emilie," he whispers. "You have to go, or they'll lash us. Please." Seth's eyes beg. His demeanor is nothing like the carefree man who visited. He is now thin, gaunt like his father, with healing angry lash marks on his right forearm.

Is this necessary? Father didn't allow such cruelty. Why is Uncle William? Looks like he is doing more than ripping families apart.

"But I told him—"

Seth gives me a look that warns me I'm doing that thing I do, where I don't understand how things really are. Things that I now realize my father sheltered me from and his slaves from, back when they were his and not Uncle William's.

"All right," I say, shaking my head as the realization of all my hopes for them never hatched. They remain locked into a hardened jail of bondage.

"Stop standing there, woman," Big Jim says.

I jump, shrink into myself.

"Get out of this field," he hisses with a harsh whisper, and as if he were a snake coiled in his chains, I heed his warning, fleeing from the field. As the men on horseback turn, I can feel their eyes burn into me, a bemused chuckle at my failed attempt for a warm greeting, the brief embrace of family, as if they knew what I was originally after. Regardless, there is nothing but the harsh realities of slavery and the unbreakable chains holding them to this land to welcome me to the place—not home, but hell in the flesh and blood of my friends.

Reeling from the inhospitable greeting in the field, I run back to the kitchen. *At least I know where Martha is. Surely things have not changed so much for her ...* The path to the kitchen is a mix between flat steppingstones and gravel. The door is open to let out the cooking heat. Moving up into the threshold, I stop short. My eyes fall upon a tall thin woman. Her hair is braided in rows encircling her head like a crown. A bright red kerchief holds everything in place.

Who is this? And what is she doing here?

A squeak of surprise escapes me, alerting the woman to turn around. She presents me with a young beautiful face and a protruding pregnant belly, but her glowing appearance stops at her dark eyes, glowering at me—unwelcoming and sharp.

"Where's Martha?" I demand.

"She doesn't work here anymore. This is my kitchen now."

The smile on the woman's face is not only out of place, but drips with vengeance, a pure evil that is both frightening and disconcerting.

The mix of emotions embroils me at this minute, flooding through me with a mix of fear and anger. The audacity of—I swallow my words. My eyes trace over the kitchen, each section holding some form of memories of mixing, baking, and preparing meals together. It all adds to the flames of fury, until the maid looks through me.

"I don't tell tales, but she's probably sold by now." A smile snakes over her mouth, as a wave of mortification consumes me. Does she know how she fuels this horror by her turned up nose?

"Now if you'll excuse me. I have dinner to prepare." She turns away from me.

Aunt Jenny, that bitch!

I don't know if it is my racing heart fueled by fear that sets my feet running from the kitchen, around something on the path, into the dining room, through the foyer as the parlor doors jump out of the way!

My hands itch, screaming for my fingers to wrap around the delicate skin of her neck, the desire to stop the throbbing of the vein taunting my fury. Her screams, her breath, her claws tear at my forearms. *Squeeze!* My thumbs obey the command as my nails dig deeper into the ivory thin flesh, only to be satisfied as the blood oozing out, her eyes bulging out, her mouth gasping out a tiny plea. *A plea Martha didn't have a chance to give. A plea Big Jim and Seth will have to sleep with because you forced her to leave!*

Something around my waist pulls, a pinch on my wrist forces my fingers to unfurl. NO! I want to keep hold. I want her to suffer. I still cling with my other hand as a voice unlike my own screams profanities and demands justice.

"You bitch, you deserve—" Something large, calloused, and slick covers my nose and mouth. I go to bite it. I want to scream into it, so I gasp, my world goes black.

My eyes flutter open. The world is a blur of light and color as I surface. A soft breeze glides over my face as a soothing, deep voice calls to me. My vision sharpens, and I find Father's eyes staring at me with concern as he fans me. My body is reposed on the duvet in the parlor.

It must have been a dream—No—

"I had a nightmare! I dreamed Aunt Jenny sold Martha and—" My gaze falls onto my aunt, her throat imprinted with red bruising and scratch marks. Her eyes wide in horror at my statement. Her hand goes to her throat.

"D-d-d-did I—do that?" Do I apologize for something—I don't remember? Looking to Father, his firmed jaw and raised eyebrows confirm my nightmare as reality.

"Yes, you did, Emilie."

"I-I'm sorry. I-I ..." My gaze diverts back to Father, another dam of sorrow threatening to break.

If I attacked Aunt Jenny, then is what happened to Martha—

"Where's Martha?" I ask. "Just tell me she's all right. I promise I won't do it again. I promise ..." My voice shakes, my hands quiver, and my body begins to rattle over my second mother's safety.

I feel Father's arms around me, pulling me close to him, protecting me, comforting me.

"We'll find her," he whispers in my ear. "She will be all right. I promise." I feel a soft kiss on my head, our moment interrupted by a huff from grandmother's rocking chair, where Aunt Jenny sits, now fanning herself.

"I don't see what all the fuss is about," Jenny's face is pink with irritation. "Over a nigger, no less. What about me? Your heathen daughter almost strangled me, Jacob! She is positively feral, and I blame you for taking her out of this genteel South, where she at least knew of manners and her place."

"Jenny, if you'd be so kind, I would like a moment with my daughter—alone." stare wilts my aunt's composure. "I prefer to do my parenting in private."

Aunt Jenny stands, huffing and fanning herself with an air of indignant pride and self-pity. "Well, if you ask me the only father that girl needs is Jesus, and I know just the convent for her, an all-girls school of sorts. Oh yes, there will be beatings, but the nuns there know ..."

"Leave!" Father barks, pointing to the parlor doors.

Aunt Jenny starts with a squeak as she scurries out of the room like a mouse being stalked by a cat. The parlor doors slam behind her.

Sitting up, I face my father and the punishment I know is coming my way. My eyes are wary, but I meet his gaze. But— blinking, I look again. There is no anger in his expression. Disappointment maybe? But it is certainly empathy and worry that consume him.

"I didn't mean to," I say just above a whisper. "I am so scared for all of them. Big Jim is thin and weak, Seth is holding up, but Martha—she's not in the kitchen."

Father continues to hold me, and my head rests on his chest. "Emilie, I don't condone what you did, but I understand why you did it."

Pushing myself away from him, "I didn't mean to. I thought it was a nightmare."

"Shh—It was fury and anger so hot it knocks out all of your senses," Father offers an explanation. "But we have to figure out a plan to get out of here with the Blackwells."

"He abuses them, Father," I cry, a crack shakes my voice. "Big

Jim and Seth are in horrible shape. What if Martha—"

"I will take care of that. What I need you to do is help me stay strong and not lose my temper." His eyes plead. "I brought you here to help and this is …"

Watching him think, watching him take a deep breath, "You muster up the bravery to help get us through this, and for God's sake Emilie, no more physical violence."

Swallowing hard and biting my lip, "I'm sorry."

Silence falls between us, both of us mustering the endurance to make it out of this mess, intact and with the Blackwells.

SLAM!

The noise that set the crystal tinkling on the wall sconces made my heart start like a scared jackrabbit. The commotion in the hallway cannot be mistaken, as my uncle's voice can carry miles long.

"Is this any way to greet your husband after a long day at the auction house …"

Murmurs and a shuffle.

Uncle William's voice booms, "Good Lord, Jenny what happened to you? You look as if you were attacked by a pack of wolves!"

"Oh, far worse than wolves, Willie. That dreadful niece of yours attacked me, and your brother seems to have taken her side. And she even called me … Oh, I dare not say it, Willie. It's dreadful! Truly, dreadful!" Aunt Jenny's shrill voice set my nerves on edge, but the pity she is vying for awakens the anger simmering in my gut, and I can't help but roll my eyes.

Father's hand settles on my arm.

"What's he doing here? When did he arrive?" Uncle William let out a barrage of questions, further flustering Jenny. "Simon, where are they?"

Simon's voice is muffled.

Father and I stand to receive my aunt's and uncle's arrival into the parlor.

We wait.

"Speak up, nigger!" Uncle William demands. "I can't read your dreadful mind."

The parlor doors open at Simon's touch.

Uncle William walks in, pulling off his waistcoat, unbuttoning the top and lower buttons of his vest, and then loosening his neckerchief. The man is determined to be relaxed in his own home.

Aunt Jenny follows behind him, tight as a shadow, pointing a sharp bony finger in my direction. "See? That sniveling wench is right behind him."

This sniveling wench didn't strangle you hard enough.

I glare back at her as she shrinks back and then turns away to fix refreshments from the decanter, offering one to my father who is now coaxing me to shift behind him as a shield of protection.

"Brother, I hear Martha is missing," Father accepts the glass from Aunt Jenny's shaking hands.

"I hear your daughter is a raging lunatic," Uncle William says. "Surely the state of my wife is more important than some nigger."

Father takes a long sip of the amber liquid, before answering. "My daughter's state aside, Martha is our family, so her wellbeing is important. But that is something you'd never understand."

"You're right, Jacob. They are slave property. A means of getting business done. And what a business we have, now that I am running things the way they should be around here. Keeping the strongest and renting out the weakest. I dare say, that Martha of yours is getting a bit long in the tooth."

Uncle William enjoys his beverage, his eyes never leave my father.

It's at this point I don't mind shrinking into the wallpaper.

"That being said," Uncle William continues, "I contracted her out to the Sprees, as any white blooded American would see right to do." His smile drips with sour satisfaction.

I bite my lip hard to hold back the outburst poised in my chest. As the tide of anger resurges, my limbs twitch, my hands ball into tight fists. My breath quickens. I feel my father's hand on my arm.

A warning?

Comfort?

I wince as the iron taste seeps from my tongue.

"Business what business? All I see is the mess you've made of our family's legacy," Father sets his glass on the side table, lest, I imagine, he uses it as a weapon. "The slaves on this plantation are in poor health and starving. What little profit you have made will be eaten by the cost of replacing them. What did you do with their gardens? Why are they not properly clothed?"

Father did not allow Uncle William to answer. "Their homes are in disrepair, their spirits are broken, and this—in your mind—is going to make for better production? On top of that, we Prescott's have always been men of our word. We pay our debts. We keep our promises. Neither of which you have done, and worse yet, you claim yourself to be a man of God when you are like Cain, betraying your own brother. The only thing I've seen you bring to this business, to this plantation, and to this family is shame."

Uncle William's face flinches but he recovers in a flash as he hands the empty glass to his wife. "At least I didn't abandon this family," he sneers. "I am making something of our father's legacy as a smart businessman, who understands how politics and business go hand in hand. I am doing everything I can to make sure this farm is profitable, and if that means cutting corners, that is my decision!"

The brothers stand with a table between them, staring each other down, waiting for the other to strike.

All I can do is wait.

Aunt Jenny slips a full glass in front of her husband and shrinks back to the parlor doors.

"You can't overwork something and think it will always maintain performance. Those gardens are a means of food and health for them. When was the doctor last here?"

"Just a few weeks ago," Uncle William takes a long draw from his glass.

"Little too late from what I hear. The man died," Father keeps his voice level. "If you want to talk numbers instead of human lives, then explain to me, how is losing three-hundred and fifty dollars profitable? Isn't that what they are going for nowadays?"

Uncle William shrinks back from his older brother's narrowed sharp eyes. "In abandoning your responsibilities, you left me with little choice. It's your fault we are in dire straits."

"I will be at fault for ever thinking you would be responsible enough to take care of what has been given to you," Father lowers his voice to a smooth, poisonous tone. "But, little brother, you always did manage to break your toys. So, here's what is going to happen ..."

Uncle William winces, a twitch appearing in his right eye.

Am I holding my breath?

"You will repair the slave quarters by fixing the drafts and adding windows and doors that close. Preventing illness is cost effective, wouldn't you say? Nod your head, and keep your mouth shut."

I take a deep breath, silently cheering Father on as he continues his list of demands.

Aunt Jenny looks aghast, but I'm starting to think this is her natural disposition.

Uncle William appears to have a slight tremor in his hands.

"You will give each home a variety of seeds to plant for next year's gardens and reopen the church, giving them rest on Sunday as God wills it. You will bring in a doctor to see to their health once a month, more so if there is an illness, as I imagine there already is. I will return in six months to make sure these requests have been completed, and if they are not, then you will no longer be the master of this plantation."

"You're bluffing," William's voice cracks.

"No, I'm not, and I'm not finished. I am going to retrieve Big Jim and Seth, and then I'm going to obtain Martha from the Sprees; you will not stop me. Is that clear?"

Uncle William begins with, "But you-you can't—"

"What right do you have to say anything about God's will when you and your family abandoned his decree to own slaves?" Aunt Jenny found her soapbox. "It's a hard business, managing those savages, but we as good Christians, are doing our duty to endure the tasks God has placed on us. And what thanks do we get? None, just the heathen ways of your beloved North, possessed by greed, trying to turn all of us into destitute Paddies, paving our road to hell because they care not for God's word!" Aunt Jenny's face is pinched red with a glisten of sweat at her temples. Her head bobs, emphasizing her points—but it is nothing more than a regurgitation of what we heard at the train station.

I look to Father; he's amused at her tiny frame gesticulating this way and that with her pointed fan.

"As a good Christian woman, didn't God decree to treat others with kindness and love? Are the men and women who work at this plantation not your neighbors? You have both bought into the rhetoric of someone else's agenda, whether it be politics, economy, or a skewed religious mangling of God's word. There's no reason to make any man a slave," Father's point stuns the parlor into silence. "Have you ever considered treating them as fellow human beings? You might find they are rather cooperative, intelligent, and just want to live their own lives."

"I want you and your niggers gone by dawn," Uncle William's face is beet red with anger. He looks to the door, his only escape route.

"Fine, but I have one more task for you, brother. Locate Limerick's family and buy them back." My father's words make Uncle William jump.

"How did you ...?" Uncle William asks, gasping.

"You know damn well how, and if I find you've done something to Limerick after I leave, you and your wife might be finding what it's like to truly be among the Irish—to do the work no master would allow their slaves to do. Remove that luxury cloth you shelter yourself in, and our red hair becomes a dead giveaway. So don't forget, William, you may be the so-called master here, but respect, even among slaves, must be earned," Father glowers at his brother, who now shifts uncomfortably under his gaze. "Trust—it's a human thing."

Free at Last

FREEDOM IS WHAT YOU DO WITH
WHAT'S BEEN DONE TO YOU.
~ JEAN PAUL SARTRE

SEPTEMBER 1861
PRESCOTT PLANTATION

Jacob is comforted by this familiar scene as his boots crunch along the gravel path on his way to the stables. The bright sun warms the crisp morning air, as a veil of mist stubbornly clings to the low-lying fields. As he walks down the open-faced shed row, he is met with the rich and earthy scent of hay, mingling with the comforting aromas of leather. This familiar perfume soothes his soul, with past memories of a simpler life. These thoughts are much needed after a restless night of worry. The plans he sifted through came to him only after the crickets slept. Now, all he needs is someone he can count on.

The horses greet him in a welcoming chorus of nickers, whinnies, and snorts. A chestnut mare, her coat gleaming in the nascent light, whickers to him, nudging him with her head, seeking attention. He reaches out a hand, scratching her between the ears, her velvety muzzle nuzzling into his palm looking for a treat he doesn't have.

Limerick walks toward him with two feed buckets in each hand.

"Mornin', Mr. Jacob," Limerick's voice is low and gentle in the early light. "Do you want me to hitch the team right away?"

Jacob takes a bucket of feed from Limerick, saying, "I thought we could talk while I help with the chores."

Limerick stops, giving him a curious look.

"I don't mind the work, sir," Limerick says. "Though you're welcome to follow along if you need to get something off your chest."

"Very well," Jacob follows the man to into the mare's stall.

"What's on your mind, sir?" Limerick asks, pushing the mare out of his way to pour feed into her bucket.

Jacob pauses, working his tongue around his words. "I see what is happening here." He pinches the sniffle from his nose, looks away to blink, then back. "I never meant—" He swallows hard. The lines on his face pull down with worry.

"No one here blames you."

Jacob shuffles the straw under his foot. "Thank you, but I have a plan."

"I got ears."

"It'll be dangerous if William finds out."

Silence.

Limerick steps out of the stall with the empty bucket in hand and they carry on to the next stall.

"You ask'n if I'll help," The resolve in Limerick's eyes darken to a deep russet brown, "I got nothing more to lose. He already took my kinfolk. So, what you need done?"

Jacob winces at the truth of it, which increases the thrumming nerves coursing up his spine.

"Have you discussed your freedom with him?" Jacob asks.

Limerick chuckles, shaking his head, "Not to brag, but I know too much. He'll keep me here until I die. So, you best tell me this plan, so I can help the others."

"Yes, right you are. You've been a blessing to us—teaching the boys to ride, caring for the stock ..." Jacob says, comforted by the memories.

"Well, the good Lord says we all gots talents," Limerick smile brightens his expression.

Jacob hands Limerick the bucket in his hand, exchanging it for Limerick's empty one.

"I'm going to contact an abolitionist vet I know in town. I'll set up correspondence with him to be my eyes and ears here. He'll make regular visits," Jacob says, laying out his plan. "I'll ask him to speak directly to you about the bull. He'll report back to me what you tell him."

Limerick furrows his brows. "We sold the bull last summer."

Jacob smiles. "It's his name. If you need the veterinarian, speak of the bull and he'll know you are talking about William. You'll have to speak in code, but I think it'll work."

Limericks face brightens and a laugh erupts. "Very clever," he says, "but what happens if I'm sold?"

"If I don't hear from you, I'll assume the worst and come, but please be careful."

"No, sir. I keep all the secrets of the living and dead around here."

"I wish it could be more," Jacob says, dreading the idea if things do not improve. What will be his next steps?

"Anything is an improvement," Limerick says, as he steps into the next stall to deliver breakfast to an inpatient gelding.

"Limerick?"

"Sir?"

"I told William to buy back your family. I can't promise he will follow through, but—"

Limerick blinks. "Thank you. I pray he'll do it."

"I wish it was more."

"It's more than I expected to hear today," Limerick says. "Now let me tend your horses, so you can get home to your dear Miss Julia."

"Much obliged," Jacob shakes Limerick's hand. "I'll be back as soon as I rouse Emilie."

"I'll have the team long ready before then," Limerick chuckles and takes the empty bucket from Jacob.

Emilie seats herself in the wagon as Jacob hands her a towel of wrapped biscuits and bacon.

"I missed you, Limerick."

"I sure miss you buggin' me all the time. Now how's that stubborn mare of yours?" Limerick asks.

"She is spoiled, but I'm more concerned about you. You'll take good care of yourself, promise?"

Limerick nods to Emilie before he turns to Jacob.

"Thank you for everything," Jacob says. "I'll see you in six months."

"Safe travels to you both," Limerick watches Jacob step up into the wagon seat.

"Thank you, Limerick," Emilie waves to him.

Limerick nods to her as Jacob calls to the team.

The horses pull them toward the cabins, as Jacob reaches for a biscuit, eating it on the way. Staying up all night makes a man hungry as worry consumes him. The rows of cabins sit quiet in the early morning. The fog is heavy, and light in some areas give the land an ethereal peace it lacks in the full light of day. Puffs of wood smoke curl out of each chimney, chased by the comforting warm smells of firewood, as everyone wakes for the day.

"I hope they are waiting for us," Emilie says. "I want us to get Martha as soon as possible."

"All in good time. Save the rest of the biscuits for the Black-wells. I want them to have something to help get them through the day."

"I will," Emilie folds the towel around the still warm break-fast. As she takes in the sights of the plantation. I wish we could take them all with us."

"I do, too, but it isn't practical," Jacob clears his throat to ease the tightness growing there. "It will bankrupt your uncle—we could lose the land forever."

"I don't know if we can save it," Emilie turns to him, searching for a sign of his quiet strength. "The land feels cursed, ruined by his greed."

"The person who runs it is what brought these dark days." Jacob nods, his jaw tightening to hold back his burning disap-pointment. "I know things will be different once Aaron steps up. He will bring it back to life—if he gets the chance."

"I pray you're right," Emilie says, resting her head on his shoulder for a moment. "Great grandfather had such hopes for this land."

"He did," Jacob halts the team and sets the brake. "I'll call you when we're ready for your help."

"All right. I'll be here," Emilie says, already looking around at the others emerging from their cabins.

Up the two stairs to the porch, Jacob's boots announce his arrival with clear heavy footfalls. He notices Martha's windows lack life, a reflection of the fruitless circumstances here for everyone.

His hand goes to the door, rapping three short knocks.

He hears movement inside, the scraping of chairs and low murmurs. Jim's voice, deeper than his son's, an unclear warning—the doorknob turns and creaks open as Jim peers from the other side.

"Jacob?" Jim greets him, "I thought—"

"Let me in. We have to pack. We don't have time," Jacob orders.

Jim's expression hardens, "Now, wait a—"

"A deal is only good when all parties keep their word. Besides, you'll have to take it up with Julia. She sent me."

This elicits a hesitant smile from Jim, saying, "And Emilie—"

"Is my shepherd. Now, come on. We don't have much time. In fact, the hard dawn is already on our tails, and soon, I imagine, the dogs will follow."

Jim nods, "You mean—"

"We have to be out by sunrise," Jacob says, looking around at the sparse cabin holding two beds, a table, wet sink, and three chairs.

How could he let it get this bad?

"Where's your furniture?" Jacob asks.

"Good morning, sir," Seth says with a huge grin on his face. "I see you got my letter."

"Good morning, Seth. That I did," Jacob raises a brow at him.

"Very brave of you."

"It only cost me a few lashes," Seth says, his shoulders set with a nod. "Well worth it."

"Seth," Jim orders, "get your things in order. Hurry up."

His father's urgency widens Seth's eyes. "But—I know nothin' about packing. Ma does that stuff."

"Well, it's about time you be learnin'," says Jim.

Seth scurries around picking up items, setting them down, biting his lip in confusion. He looks like a lost puppy who can't find a way back to his home.

"Let me call Emilie. She might be able to help."

Relief washes over Seth.

"She's waiting in the wagon—" Jacob starts to say, but Seth is already opening the door.

Jim smiles as she walks in.

"Need some help?"

"Yes, we do," Seth says.

"Pull out that trunk," Emilie orders. "Grab your belongings. Don't worry about the dishes. Mother is gathering all your household goods back home. Pack what you need, keep it tidy. Don't forget your personal items: keepsakes, things you can't replace."

The men look at each other, silent, unsure.

"You know, clothes, grooming supplies." Emilie's hands fly about, then. "Anything considered illegal—we don't want anyone punished."

The men blink, exchange looks.

"Now, let's go!" Emilie says.

They snap into action, like soldiers, going from milling about to gathering everything they could put their hands on, flinging the items half haphazardly at Emilie, who puts the items into the trunk, while other items, such as a bar of soap and forks and spoons are set aside. When Seth brings her a large pot, Emilie looks at him.

"Seth?"

"It's Ma's favorite. She cooks everything in here," he says. "She'd be lost without it."

His eyes fill with sincerity Emilie can't deny. She takes it from him, inspects it, and lovingly places it into the trunk with everything else.

Emilie closes the lid. "Is that everything?" she asks. The bare cabin had nothing left on the walls. What little furniture exists sits silent.

"The rocking chair?" Seth asks.

"It's too big. All we can afford is the trunk," Jacob says. "I am terribly sorry."

"We'll get her a better one," Jim voice trails off as he stares at the lone rocker. Jacob can only imagine the memories that flood through his friend's mind, but they are memories that can be enjoyed from the wagon.

"All right, let's go," Jacob says.

Emilie opens the door, and the harsh light of dawn slaps them in the face.

"Jim on the count of three: one, two, three—" Jim and Jacob lift the trunk with a dueted groan and then haul the trunk into the wagon.

Jacob then gestures for everyone to get in as he climbs up front, and grabs hold of the reins. He can already see the overseers making headway on their horses toward the cabins, blood hounds trailing after them on a leisurely morning stroll—or a warmup as the overseers kick their mounts up a notch to greet them, to hunt them?

"Well, looky here. Looks like we gots a nigger lover. Where you think you going with them niggers, nigger lovers?" asks the overseer who has a crop of mangled jet-black hair, a woman's bush on his chin as an excuse for a beard.

"I've got papers that say they are free. William has given me his word he will not stop me from removing them from this property."

"He done also said you needs to have them out by dawn, and the sun already done come up," says the other overseer as he spits a wad of chew off to the side of his mount before sharing a tobacco-stained grin, the bulge of his tongue chasing clumps stored in his cheeks and bottom lip.

Jacob's hand goes to rub the back of his head, squeezing the back of his neck when he feels something cold and hard press into his back. He frowns, but lowers his arm to switch positions, as if checking his shirt tail, but in truth he takes the weapon offered, and then points it at them, pulling back the hammer.

Click.

"So, which one of you wants to die trying to stop me?"

All the overseers look down to the whips at their hips. It's enough to quail an uprising, but not enough to rob the plantation of its property.

"Mind you, whichever one of you survives, will no longer have a job after my son replaces my pathetic excuse for a brother. So, what'll it be? You two going to draw straws in a race to meet the Devil, or let us through?"

Jacob watches them grow as stiff as statues, a pale hue of grey lapping up their complexions.

Alas one of them nods. "Come on Curt. Ain't no use stirrin' up trouble before we even get the day started."

They ride around the wagon, splitting to either side, dogs whining and following after with tails tucked, but Jacob keeps his weapon trained on one of them just in case.

"Emilie," Jacob says.

"Yes?" Her voice is small.

"Take this," he hands her a gun.

"But I—"

"Point and pull the trigger if they so much as touch anyone in this wagon," he says loud enough for everyone to hear.

Jacob hears shuffling in the wagon, and as he commands the team into motion, he checks over his shoulder to see Jim and Seth pressed into the side of the wagon opposite Emilie and most definitely behind her.

Jacob turns back to the team and the path ahead as he rounds about to the long driveway.

"This is heavy. Is that normal?" Emilie asks as she looks back to the men.

"Hey, watch where you're pointing it!" Seth dodges the barrel.

"Emilie, keep it aimed at the overseers until they are out of sight, and then hand it back to me. Jim, get up here with me—please," says Jacob.

Jim nods and climbs up front. They ride in silence for a moment, everyone's nerves on edge until they reach the iron gate. A sigh of relief escapes them as they begin the rickety trek to the Sprees.

The gun is dangling in Jacob's peripheral between his daughter's finger and thumb.

"Emilie, it is a gun, not one of your brother's socks. Always hold it with purpose."

"Yes, but I don't want it. You take it."

Jacob sighs, hands the reins to Jim, and takes the weapon. "Remind me to teach you to shoot one of these days."

"No, thank you."

Jacob looks down to the revolver, and pointing it away from everyone, horses included, he slowly, draws back the hammer a little further and squeezes down on the trigger before controlling the release of the hammer back to neutral. Then he looks over to Jim, who stares ahead with sweat dripping down to his chin, eyes locked on the road. He was fairly certain he knew who handed him this gun.

"Jim—" Jacob frowns dumbfounded by the idea he has such an item in his possession. The fears of exchange of power is paralyzing among plantation owners. If any slave owner has any inkling that a slave could shift that power, they will justify death without question.

"I have to protect my family. You keep it, at least until we get back to Gettysburg. 'Sides, you might need it to free my wife," Jim says, his eyes staring ahead, unblinking.

"I hope it's not necessary. Do I want to know how you got it?" Jacob slides the gun into the inside pocket of his jacket.

"Nope."

The Sprees' home is about a half mile up, and the quiet of the crisp clear morning stuns everyone to enjoying the peace of the moment. A moment that is shattered when the Sprees' home comes into view. Jacob turns to Jim.

"Stop the wagon at the far side of the drive. Don't set the break. We need to be ready for a quick ride out of here," Jacob points to the stopping spot, "as I'm sure they won't be happy with me."

"Bring her back to us," Jim looks to Jacob. "I'm counting on you."

"I will." Jacob says patting his jacket, where the pistol stays warm against him.

The big house with a wraparound porch and a small turned-out balcony on the second floor appears elegant indeed. The Sprees' reputation boasts of great wealth and upper-class status, but the reality of this house and its occupants are not as robust as the airs they put on for their friends and family, especially now that both Constance and Horace Spree are getting up in age, and Horace's reputation as a shrewd businessman as well as a heavy-handed slaveowner, leaves little desire for others to partner with him—less they find their hands tied in the court room.

After the third knock, the front door slathered in black paint begins to move with a slow deliberate creak, revealing a hunched butler with near-white cotton hair and stiff starched gloves to match—dressed for receiving guests. However, his expression offers no comfort, and instead his eyes narrow as he takes in Jacob's appearance.

"May I help you?"

"Is the gentleman or lady present?"

"They are having breakfast, sir. If you would like to wait in the parlor, I'll announce you."

"No, thank you. I will see myself in." Jacob pushes past the butler, thinking nothing of it, knowing that under a roof such as this, with a lavish marble entryway and a large winding staircase, slaves are meant to be seen but not heard.

Before he passes the receiving table in the large hall, Martha appears, descending the stairs, folded linens stacked atop her arms.

Their eyes meet, and as her mouth opens in surprise, she breathes a silent *oh*.

Jacob addresses her in a short, curt tone. "Martha, get your things. We're leaving now."

A disbelieving smile blossoms on her expression, but it soon falters. Jacob notes her slender form slipping like a whisp of smoke back behind a swinging door, fresh laundry her visible excuse for parting ways, though hopefully she is going to grab her belongings as he bade.

"Jacob Prescott, you have no right ordering my help around." Horace Spree's cheeks appear like twin puff pastries and are as red as the sour grapes. His intoxicated breath reeks of—all for the sake of five simple steps from his custom-made dining chair. The girth of his waist fills not only his shirt but also spills into the doorway like a smushed jelly roll. His porcine eyes welcome only one guest, greed, and there is no doubt in Jacob's mind that this could become a very sticky situation.

"Well, that is the thing Horace. I have come to inform you, with all due respect, that Martha is no longer in your service, but is a free woman, and I have the papers to prove such."

Horace wheezes, jowls flapping, waddle rippling. The sight of the man's ire rising makes Jacob wonder if the viscous liquid is likely to ooze from his nose, ears, and eyes if his blood pressure gets any higher. All in all, it's a pitiful sight from which he can't quite bring himself to look away.

"Did William approve this?" The glutton's hand grasps the door frame to steady his knobby knees.

"In a way," says Jacob.

The shrill voice of Constance further divides what little peace resides between the two men and their strained discussion.

"What's the meaning of this? Who's going where?"

"I'm taking Martha with me."

"He's stealing our cook!"

The mahogany door, leading to the downtrodden passages where only the slaves' feet trample, flaps open, shielding Martha as she moves behind Jacob, making herself scarce in the sanctity of his shadow.

"No, I'm not a thief. I'm taking Martha with me, now that she is a free woman. Good day to you, Mr. and Mrs. Spree. God's speed to you both." Jacob gives a small tilt of the head to them and begins to back up toward the grand entrance, aiming to make a subtle exit. One hand reaches back to Martha, silently requesting she keep behind him, while his other hand clasps the lapel of his coat, a thumb stroking over the cool surface of one of his plain brass buttons.

Constance's face, which is as long as her hair is high, peeks over her squat husband. Her hand on his shoulder could be the straw to make Horace's knobby knees crack. However, he saves himself from such embarrassment by swatting her away like the flies that now join the fray—buzzing around his head, drinking in his sweat.

"You have no proof."

"Yes, I do," Jacob speaks to him in the same manner he would a small child.

Creak.

Martha must have managed to pull the door open.

"Liar! You have no papers. No right!"

A ray of light spills into the foyer.

"The wagon's at the end of the drive. Go," Jacob whispers over his shoulder.

He listens, hears her feet, and watches the silhouette of her shadow in his peripheral—elongate, thin out, and disappear. Meanwhile, his hand dips into the interior of his coat, fingers grazing nickel plating.

We sit, waiting in silence, praying for Father and Martha to come out of the house. We cannot hear anything as the wagon rests at the end of the drive.

A blanket of pensive worry shrouds us.

I turn to Jim. He is biting his fingernails, watching the door. His jump turns my attention back to the house as the door opens.

I sit next to Seth, frozen in a lake of suspense, holding my breath. But as I see Martha, a grin traces the cracks in my lips as we watch the flurry of skirts while Martha sprints to the wagon.

"Come on, Martha," Jim says. "Run for your life, girl!"

All of us silently cheer her on.

Jim reaches an arm down to hoist her up into the wagon, Seth grabbing her belongings from her the second she's in reach of warmth, comfort, and her husband's arms.

Despite her weary form lashed by the cold grip of this place, her eyes are alight with a fire I cherish, and she briefly grabs my hand and gives it a squeeze as our gazes meet. "Good to see you, Little Miss!"

"If you give me one moment, Horace, I will show you her manumission papers."

Horace squints. His wheezing increases.

Constance squawks, trying to help her husband save his breath. "I don't understand, Mr. Prescott. If you want that nag so badly, why not just buy her from your brother?" Her expression brings to question whether she hosts a mustache on her upper lip or horse dung.

"She was never owned by my brother to begin with, Mrs. Spree." He begins to slide his hand out of his pocket, hand grasping—

"Never mind what he says, Constance. This is all hogwash, as I have a contract too, legally binding, that says she is mine to rent until I outright own her!" Horace states. "So, if you think I'm about to let my own neighbor steal from me, thanks to some falsified paperwork then—" His features are pinched, while his veins bulge. His blood must be at a boil by now. "Mr. Prescott, you may have better legs, but I guarantee you I've got a better aim. My gun, someone get me my gun!"

Jacob shakes his head, his hand letting the papers slide back into his pocket, exchanging them for the harsh metal he rather not use—but if there is no choice ...

Click.

His other hand clasps the door handle behind him, pulling it further open. "Now, Horace, I don't want any trouble."

"You got trouble when you decided to seize my property, which you'll either return or I'll shoot!"

Jacob, slowly backs into the opening he's made for himself, "Horace, I can't—"

BANG!

Jacob goes down, his large frame halfway out the door.

A gunshot echoes!

My eyes shoot over to the front door to see my father's form lying across the threshold.

I scream, grab the side of the wagon, one leg over the edge—

Large hands wrap around my arms, pulling me back.

"No, no, Father!" I yell again, flailing against their grip. "Please, please—I must—"

A trail of blood pools around the corpse.

Silence grabs hold of everyone.

Their eyes fill with the visage of death.

Constance folds herself over her husband's lifeless form with a wail.

When Jacob finally manages to pull himself up from the nightmare that will forever stain his mind, he hears someone shout, "Get out!"

Jacob doesn't need to be told twice as he clamors to his feet.

The Sprees' door is left open to freedom—in case the butler holding the shotgun dares to claim it.

Father's form begins to move, stumbles to his feet, pauses, turns, and then he's running like a teenager straight toward us.

Jim moves over, grabs the reins, as Father jumps into the seat beside him.

"Hup! Hup! Let's go!" Jim slaps the reins, calling to the horses. Their jolt into action sends me falling into Seth's lap. Scrambling away, I apologize and sit while holding the sides to steady myself.

My back to the wagon's front seat, I hear Jim ask, "What happened in—?"

"Mister Jacob, your arm," Martha's eyes widen at the display.

"What the hell?" Father looks down to his sleeve splattered in blood.

"Emilie, find me a clean shirt."

Struggling against the wagon's jostle to stand, I hold the back of the front seat, poking my head between their shoulders. "Are you hurt?"

"I need a new shirt," Father demands. "Don't make me ask again."

Father's strong tone makes me turn to the bags, shifting between Martha and Seth, both holding the side of the wagon as we hit another bump in the road. I fish out the shirt and pass it between them, then turn away.

The wagon slows and stops at the edge of the road.

"Why we stopping?" Martha asks. "We ain't to Gettysburg yet."

"We ain't much better off with a dead white man either. Take a look at Jacob's shoulder," Big Jim looks back at her and then notices me.

"Not that I think he's gonna—" begins Big Jim.

"I'm fine, not a scratch. Just a murder I'd rather not be associated with," Father changes shirts and tosses the bloody one back at me.

I grimace at the shirt. "If it's not your blood, then—"

"None of our business, that's who, Little Miss. Now, let's best get a move on, less you want me driving," Martha takes Father's shirt from me as the wagon lurches forward.

"I thought the goal was to get out alive, not wrecked," says Big Jim, and I can see the pearly whites of his grin as he coaxes the team back into action.

The Blackwells watch the world shift around them, a tempting place to enjoy—but the trepidation that all of it could be ripped from their hands and replaced by shackles is never far from Martha's mind. Still, the new sights and sounds are something her dark eyes are pulled toward as her husband guides the wagon under Mr. Jacob's direction.

Martha isn't sure what she expects of a place like Richmond, having not been here in a long time, but it certainly doesn't look as rich as she had once imagined. The streets smell as foul as an outhouse, with the latest incense to roll through being that of good ole Virginia pipe tobacco. An acrid taste tickles her tongue that she can't quite place, and she fights to hold her breath, pulling a small handkerchief to her mouth and nose.

Laughter from drunks and squeals from half clothed white women mingle with the pigs and other livestock herded through the cluster of streets. The loud proclamations from preachers, street hawkers, and anyone who has an opinion about the war threatens to drown out such a ruckus. All in all, it is a whirlwind of confusion in a strange foreign landscape known as a busy city.

When Jim parks the wagon, he gets out to offer a hand to Martha.

"We gettin' out?" she asks.

"To catch a train, yes," Mr. Jacob reassures her.

Martha blinks, her eyes shifting between her husband and son before she looks to Little Miss and back to Mr. Jacob who offers a reassuring smile.

"Come on, Ma. It will be an adventure!" Seth jumps down.

"Unless you want to stay here?" asks Jim.

She knocks her husband's offered hand out of the way and clamors out of the wagon, never minding his chuckle in response.

Seth hands Little Miss her valise and then hands Martha her basket just after she takes a moment to rearrange the shawl over her shoulders. He then grabs Mr. Jacob's bag, and Jim and Mr. Jacob lift the trunk—with a grunt and a bit of strain.

"What all you got packed?" Martha asks.

"Oh, you know, just your pot and a few essentials," says Jim.

"My pot?" Martha lifts a brow at her husband.

Jim leans into his wife, whispering for her ears only, "Make a big deal about the pot. Seth thought it important. He really wanted you to have it."

Martha matches her voice to his. "That's because that boy is always hungry."

They navigate through the streets to the train station, sticking close together. An observer might see this entourage as a normal affair of owner and slave, but to Martha and her family, this is their first walk of freedom. A freedom stained in segregation and leery looks, but freedom none the less. Then Martha feels Jim's hand, guiding her between and somewhat in front of Mr. Jacob and him. This puts her and Little Miss between the men and yet never out of their sight, with Little Miss leading the way to this so-called train.

She looks back at her husband questioningly and he gives her one of his secret winks before they pass a wagon that splashes who knows what from the street onto his pants.

A soft blush blankets Martha's cheeks, but she says nothing— not so much as a smile teases her lips, just the scrunch of her nose and a passing thought about laundry.

As they arrive at a lengthy building with plumes of smoke rising out of its backside and there is more noise and clatter than Martha ever thought possible, Mr. Jacob gestures to a bench. "Sit tight. Emilie, stay with them."

Martha watches Mr. Jacob with a close eye as he moves over to a line that leads to a counter.

A hand touches her shoulder, and she jumps, the whites of her eyes seized by what ifs.

"We'll be alright," Jim, leans in to kiss her temple.

"You'll love it, Ma. These trains go real fast, faster than any wagon!"

Martha figures she will be the judge of that but says nothing to either of them, just keeps her hands on her basket and her eyes on guard as she goes back to looking for and then at Mr. Jacob.

Wonder what all the fuss is about? ... Hope he don't shout no louder than that. People will start starin' ... What if those papers Jim's got means nothin'? ... Dear Lord, see us safe.

Time doesn't fly, it crawls. It sits about for a bit of tea in some parlor she dares not enter. She's held her breath so long her chest begins to hurt, a fact she doesn't even notice until Mr. Jacob returns to them wearing the aftermath of annoyance in his scarlet features, but looking pleased, nonetheless.

"We have tickets for the late train. We are on the same train, but not the same car or the same waiting room."

Martha and Jim exchange looks.

"How will we know they made it on the train?" Little Miss asks.

"Because I have a schedule here." Jacob hands Jim the train schedule and three tickets. "We board at 4:00 p.m. and will travel through the night before we will meet again in Washington."

"Four o'clock," Seth announces looking at the clock. "I will make sure we are on the train."

"Jim, you have the manumission papers I gave you?" Mr. Jacob asks.

Jim nods.

"Good. Keep them close, show them if requested, and if there is any trouble I will be in the next car over."

"Car?" asks Jim.

Seth points to the train, "Each one of those box things is called a car."

Both Martha and her husband nod.

"I need to go see someone, since we have four hours to wait."

"I'll stay with the Blackwells."

Mr. Jacob hesitates.

Little Miss moves closer to the Blackwells.

"Go on Mr. Jacob," Jim nods. "We will watch over each other until you get back."

Long Cold Flight to Freedom

I CROSSED THE LINE. I WAS FREE; BUT THERE WAS
NO ONE TO WELCOME ME TO THE LAND OF FREEDOM.
I WAS A STRANGER IN A STRANGE LAND.
~ HARRIET TUBMAN

OCTOBER 1861
SOMEWHERE IN VIRGINIA

Martha looks to Seth as her annoyance with him grows. Her underlying nervousness interrupted by her son marking the passage of time every half hour while Little Miss's continuous chatter aims to maintain morale.

When Seth announces half past three, Martha decides she needs to see to her personal needs because no one's told her how train travel works, or maybe that is what Little Miss has been rambling on about, but for some reason Martha has a hard time imagining all the things the girl describes, like cushioned seats and comfort enough to sleep.

Martha leans over to Jim. "I gotta find that outhouse,"

Her husband looks around and then at Little Miss. "You know where that outhouse is, Little Miss?"

Martha's cheeks glow hot, and she pinches Jim's arm, but Little Miss thinks nothing of it and gestures to an area they had seen others come and go from all afternoon.

"Over there, but I need to find Father. Oh, one more thing. Here's the map of our journey."

"When'd you find time to mark it up?"

"Before we got here. Now y'all have a safe trip. See you in Washington," she says with so much sunshine and optimism Martha is fairly sure the temperature just went up a few degrees.

Seth looks at the map, offering a preoccupied murmur of thanks before he folds it up and shoves it in his pocket.

"Seth, accompany your Ma over there," Jim nudges his son.

"Over where?"

"To the toilet."

Martha hits his shoulder. "You ain't gotta say it so loud!"

"Woman, we all do it," Jim shakes his head.

"Come on, Ma. We have to hurry. Train leaves soon!" Seth stands up and escorts her to the privy.

"Don't you be telling me like I don't know that, and you best be waitin' for me when I come out." Martha's nerves are taut with irritation.

"I will," Seth says, walking beside her.

He escorts her past other people, and her gaze traverses them briefly, wondering where they are going.

Probably prayin' this "freedom" won't be snatched away ... Land of milk and honey they say. Well, I'm the sweetest I've ever met and I'm damn near sour at this point ... Ain't no sense in gettin' my hopes up, not yet anyway. Oh Lord, what kind of sty is this?

When she arrives at the bathroom there isn't much in the way of privacy like the single occupancy of an outhouse. However, Martha does her best to hurry about her business, keeping her eyes to the dirt floor as she sits on one of the many holes offered by the long bench. Old newspaper is the softest comfort this shithole has to offer for cleaning purposes.

Suppose free or not, kindness can't be expected from people who see you as property. I'd like to see how splintered Mrs. Spree's ass would get from the likes of this ... Maybe Seth would like somethin' to practice them letters with. Then again, we don't need none of that foolery. Don't know when it's not a crime. Best just finish up my business ...

It isn't much longer before Seth and she returns to the bench where they all wait in a room that grows ever more cramped. At first, it's not so hard to tell the difference between a slave and someone who is free. The free ones dress better, but as the room gradually fills to capacity, there becomes an indistinguishable mix of gray between those who are newly free and those who are escapees. Every moment that ticks by as they wait and listen for something to happen makes her tense.

Martha's eyes dart to the door Little Miss and Mr. Jacob had left through.

How long has it been? ... How long will it be? ... It'll be all right. They just through that door.

But they are a lifeline she does not want to need. The dream of freedom still dangles at arm's length, but Martha is unwilling to fall for this false hope.

Lord Almighty, if these white people got any sense, let it be now—

"Can't you see I'm praying?" She snaps as a big hand clasps over her bony shoulder, ushering in a warmth that she's not quite sure what to do with, especially with her husband's wide brown eyes and all the amiable nature a stag has to offer looking into her own.

"Sorry? You look a bit tight—"

"Oh, do I now? What was your first hint, Jim? The fact that we in a room full of strangers like a bunch of pigs in a pen waiting for slaughter! I cook chitlins, I don't become them!" The feeling of eyes on her made her stiffen even more, as if vocalizing her fears could somehow summon them forth. The creaks in the floorboards echo while the tobacco smoke filtering in from barred windows choke any remaining banter out of the cramped room.

Martha swallows hard, "Why y'all starin'? We know we be thinking it."

Her words deteriorate into mutters, but the whole time Jim keeps his big arm around her, and soon his deep baritone laugh fills the air. "I didn't marry no meek misses. I like my women the way I like my eaten, full of soul."

"I know that's right," came one person and soon murmurs of agreement spark into idle conversation, but Martha does not join in. She's seen it too many times—the runaways returned in exchange for money and pain.

Dreams for other folks, not us. We ain't got that pleasure of dream. They dissolve into nightmares of death—

"You goin to be all right?" Jim asks, the heat of his breath blanketing her ear, offering momentary relief from all the pins and pricks of every sound that comes their way.

"Ain't gots no choice."

Another squeeze. A kiss to the temple. "You gots choice. We gots choice. You just don't know what to do with it yet. Now, come on. Looks like we gettin' a move on. Seth, wake up."

"How that boy be sleepin?"

"With one eye open." Jim chuckles.

"Hmm?" Seth rubs his blurry eyes.

"Come on, Seth. Help me carry this pot your Ma be insistin' she needin'."

Martha shoots Jim a glare, but he winks, smiles, and heaves his side of their life up off the ground.

The Blackwells move with the crowd to the platform. Everyone's ticket is inspected and papers shown before they are allowed to step up into an old livestock car. A wooden box on wheels, filled with desperation. The closed walls and rudimentary wooden crates stacked here and there, waiting for them—no comfort, just necessity.

"You can guard the pot," Jim pats the trunk with a grin.

Martha is given their trunk as a seat. "Boy, I'm tired of you actin a fool about that pot."

Jim smirks if only for a moment, and Martha follows his eyes to a woman holding a small baby, who stares at them with a big gummy grin.

She looks back to Jim who is making funny faces, to the child's and other passengers' delight. She has no choice but to sigh and shake her head.

Dear Lord, you done gave that man one too many saving grace.

"Ain't you glad we got you a pot?" asks Seth.

"Sit down before there ain't be no room."

Seth smiles and he and Jim pull over two more crates to make seats for themselves.

Martha watches, and waits ... A closed in sensation squeezes her lungs as the car fills with men, women, and children in the barest of clothing, as compared to some better suited—*Perhaps they be free or just wrapped up like gifts, presents to another family?* The air hangs with the body odor of these strangers, a cocktail speaking of laundry that needs doing, sweat with an ample dosage of stress, and the rotten fruit of their labor. Their faces are filled with worry, anticipation, and silent prayers—except gummy baby, bless his innocence.

A man with a cap shielding his eyes, a grizzly beard masking his face, slides the large door closed stealing the light from everyone inside. The finality of the lock sliding into place plunges everyone into darkness. With no windows and strange sounds surrounding them, infants begin to wail as panicking parents' hushed murmurs punctuate the growing chaos.

The bleeding screech of steel grinding on steel causes groans.

The wrapping of a fist on a boarded-up wall with utterances from the outside commands silence.

The collective feeling of the air being sucked out of the black as the train announces its departure with a loud, shrill whistle, throws Martha and those she collides into, off their perches.

Martha grabs onto someone. "Seth? Jim!"

Jim's big hand finds her, steadies her, and helps her to her seat.

Martha's nerves begin to settle, when gummy baby starts to howl. His cries tug at Martha's heart. How many babies have she comforted? Aaron, Henry, Seth, Emilie and countless more who were born free and into bondage.

"We gettin' through this," Martha whispers she then begins to hum. The lullaby blossoms from her heart as comforting memories of the song gives hope to the weary travelers and hushes poor gummy baby to rest peacefully in his Mama's arms.

The tune, familiar to all of their ears, leads to a chorus of voices, which brings them together as a community if only for this moment in time. When Martha's voice fades into the darkness, and the last echo of the chorus gives way to wheezes and soft snores, gummy baby is quiet.

Martha breathes a sigh of relief and reaches for the security of Jim's hand.

Seconds pass by, minutes creak by, and hours groan by. Exhaustion, fueled by anticipation, and reeling from the day's uncertain events gnaw at Martha while the rocking of the train car with its rhythmic heartbeat becomes a hypnotic lullaby, coaxing her to close her eyes.

Click-clackety, click-clackety, click-clackety...

As it begins to win out, Martha's eyes give way to images of the plantation, her kitchen, and the joy of cooking for people she loves, the flow of hollandaise as it pours in ribbons off her wooden spoon, the smell of fresh fertilizer as she nurtures seeds into something worth a belly full, the rustling of sheets hanging on the line, a line that coils into a noose, segways into shouting, and becomes a canvas for shadows and gunshots and— She wakes with a jolt.

The train's stopped—why?

The doors slide open, and a group of men appear in the entrance, demanding, "Tickets and papers!"

They step up into the railcar, their faces etched with suspicion and a keen eye as they hunt for runaways, false documents, meaningless drivel—

What if the papers ain't nothing?

What if they expire?

Lord I pray this ain't the end—

Martha clutches Jim's arm, her knuckles whiten as they approach, and a pale hand is extended.

Jim puts his hand on hers, giving a gentle squeeze of reassurance, and she dares to watch his other hand reach into his pocket to produce their documents.

"Sir, papers right here." Jim's voice is steady despite the tremor in his hand.

The official snatches the documents from his hand, scrutinizing them with narrowed eyes. "Who are they for?"

"Sir, the papers for the three of us," Jim motions to Martha, Seth, and then himself.

"I can read," the officer snaps. "Can you?"

Jim's mouth clamps shut, but he sits straight, refusing to shrink under the man's iron gaze.

"Where are you going?"

"Gettysburg."

"What's there for you?"

"Sir, we gots family waitin'," Jim stares straight ahead, without a flinch or blink.

The officer grumbles under his breath.

Martha can't make out his low mumbles, but after what feels like an eternity, the official grunts, "All right, leave them be. We'll be checking everyone at the next stop."

The white man tosses the papers back to Jim, then moves down the aisle. His presence continues to cast a dark shadow over the passengers.

Martha watches him go, then lets out a shaky breath as relief in the form of sweat washes over her. She looks back over to Jim, who gathers the flutter of pages that have fallen to the straw covered floor and retrieves the three longer pieces they know to be their tickets. Yes, all three of each document, present, accounted for.

She knows this because she insists Jim lets her count them off—multiple times—just to make sure nothing is missing before she allows him to slip them back into his pocket. Her hand smoothing said pocket, patting it, just in case her fatigued mind desires to trick her, say she never put it there, but a slight *crinkle* of paper offers a satisfying enough sound to her that she finally feels it is safe to exhale and get another gulp— *Best to get fresh air while it's for the taking.*

Martha's eyes skitter about, drinking in the scene just beyond the tracks as her eyes adjust to the brightness of dusk. She leans over to Seth, "Where we at?"

Seth yawns and pulls out the map Emilie gave them, unfolding it, turning the paper trying to find a direction.

"What's wrong? Don't you know what you lookin' at?"

"Mr. Jacob says we don't get off til Washington and this ain't no station. "

"I know that." Martha asks. "But how can we depend on you, when you can't read that map?"

"We don't need it." Seth folds the map and slides it back into his pocket. " Washington station. Grab a train to Baltimore, another to H— I know it gotta be with an H—" Seth pauses to think harder before he pulls the map out, his finger traces, a smile. "Wait! this one here Han—"

Their attention snaps to the shrill pleas filling the air with desperate words for freedom—now extinguished—transformed into cries of pain as the mother and gummy baby—once full of smiles—are physically dragged by limb, by hair, by any means necessary off the train.

"But I got my papers! There right here! Please!"

"Shut it, nigger. Your master done wants you back. Says he misses the brat, now that his wife done up and kicked it over, fell sick, and died."

"Is that so?" asks his companion, never minding the woman's claws digging into the floorboards, grabbing onto the many limbs and clothes she is forced to pass. The baby squalls, as scrapes and splinters brandish them both all the way out into what is becoming the chill night air.

"What I heard down in the watering hole," says the first man, who lights his smoke and then the woman's papers, setting them ablaze before slamming the boxcar door shut.

Martha holds Jim and Seth's hands, the image burning into

her mind, as her stomach boils over with a wave of nausea. Despite their every right to be here, the stark reality is—

Jim nudges her, squeezing her hand with his own large, calloused warmth.

"That life ain't ours anymore," he says. "Besides I don't see William claiming Seth as his, do you?"

Martha glances up in the direction of Jim's voice, sheltered in the comfort of his confidence, but she knows as well as he does: if the white man wants an excuse, then by God, he'll make it.

The door slides shut with a bang and a click, the whole car is awake and alert as whispered prayers for the woman and her child are sent to heaven in an urgent plea.

Is this the price of freedom? Will we ever be truly free?

When the lump in Martha's throat dissolves and the wave of nausea is no more than a bubble of anxiety, her memories flood forward of the song her mother and she sang in the cold, dim lit cabin through the darkest of the night when her father made his run for freedom, to save them all, or so he promised. It brought her comfort then and now she just had to try to bring herself and the others comfort. With a prayer to her mother and father for guidance from the heavens, Martha's voice was accompanied by the huff of the train and the grinding of the steel wheels.

By the heavens we go walkin'
To Jesus's steps we are flockin'
Braiding our path to the Jordan's waters
We go walkin' up toward Canaan
Lord, lead us the way
Sitch a path to dreams you will
Wrapped up tightly in your quilt
A bow tie, God's glory brings
Double up your wedding rings

Courting Freedom

Lord, has shown us the way
By the heavens we go walkin'
To Jesus's steps we are flockin'
Passin' dead trees to Jordan's banks
We go walkin' toward Canaan
Lord, lead us the way

Her voice fades into the stillness of the void; Martha sighs with relief. She feels better and from the sounds of the quiet, they do too. The gnawing promise of their papers being checked at the next station keeps her eyes wide awake, waiting for another promise to be broken. With nothing but her thoughts, her son's snoring and Jim's warm hand in hers; Martha keeps vigil throughout the rest of the ride, keeping track of every noise, breath-filled breeze, and shuffle.

When Jim drifts to sleep, his small snores remind her that in some respects, this time is like all the other times in her life they've spent hunkered down together—minus a bed. These sounds are Martha's constant companion through the night and into the early morning light.

What few winks she gets of sleep herself becomes indistinguishable from the reoccurring nightmare that is the checkpoints. The car is roused awake by officials. They give her scrutinizing stares, and make her hold her breath each time, every time, they pass by. Tired and exhausted, Martha waits and watches for the promised land of Gettysburg to come into view.

Will it be enough? ... Will we be enough? ... When will enough be enough?

Martha's mind casts back to Mrs. Julia's smile, Little Miss's optimistic sunshine, and Mr. Jacob's quiet confidence. She prays someday she and her family will not depend on them, but she also supposes she should be happy to experience the friendship and the joy they bring, joy that is, as of now, still a distant memory.

.

Home to Celebrate

EVERYONE IS KNEADED OF THE SAME DOUGH
BUT NOT BAKED IN THE SAME OVEN.
~YIDDISH PROVERB

OCTOBER-NOVEMBER 1861
GETTYSBURG, PENNSYLVANIA

Click-clackety, click-clackety, click-clackety ... The humdrum of the train falls to background noise barely perceptible in her mind as Martha waits with bated breath for this journey to end. Though where it will end is something she is still unsure of. Save for what a bit of ink has cyphered on a slip of paper, nothing in this world is certain, not even the paper, which she has seen burned as dreams go up in smoke.

The view beyond the cracks of the boarded railcar reveals a foreign and therefore hostile landscape beyond. When the train finally stops and the sliding door is pulled open, unveiling a larger canvas, Martha squints past dawn's light and takes in the sight of a train station that is similar in structure to the one in Richmond, but not quite matching in design.

"Washington? Anyone stopping in Washington?" says a man in a stiff navy-blue uniform with brass buttons lining his coat and a mustache chiseled out of beard wax. "Anyone heading to Baltimore? ... I repeat, anyone heading to Baltimore?"

"What's the hold up, Ralph?" calls a distant voice from beyond the frame of the doorway.

"Got another car of witless darkies! Scared stiff, the lot of them!" calls back Ralph.

Martha feels a hand shaking her out of her thoughts, the anxiety having run off with her again, with that mother, with gummy baby who smiles no more. She looks to her right to see the twin of the hand that grips her on Jim's shoulder. Then chances a glance behind her to see Seth.

He smiles, somehow still filled with hope and excitement. She doesn't know whether to envy him or consider him a fool.

Her son's hand gives her another squeeze.

"I'm up. I'm up," she says, thinking back to those sunny days when they gave the Lord praise and in return he gave them one blessed day of rest, but Seth in all his youthful glory still thought she and Jim needed to be up before the morning rays. Some things never change, and the briefest smile blows across her lips, but then it is back to business, back to reality, back to her feet.

Moments later all three of them are standing, plus a few others. All of them daring to claim their destination as Baltimore and brazen enough to step off the train. Not that it matters all too much to the porters who herd them like cattle from one car, stamping their tickets as they cross a platform, and guiding them into another car—still dark, still stark, still the bare necessities, before the iron door slides shut and they are consumed by their blackness once more.

Click-clackety, click-clackety, click-clackety ...

Martha once against begins to dose off, but no, she can't. Not yet anyway. Sleep waits for fear to release its illusion of waking up—what if this was a nightmare disguised as a dream to freedom? If she gives in to sleep now, will she open her eyes to find herself faced with another day as a slave?

She fights it, but her body demands it, and at times, she even succumbs to it.

Why is freedom so hard to embrace?

The morning was filled with three more transfers from Washington to Baltimore, and Jim and Seth do their best to guide her tired body from train to train while sleep claws at her eyelids, attempting to drag them down. Hands, both big like Jim's and wiry like Seth's, try to wrestle with her through every stumble. Her defensive and sour mood persists until finally, on the last train to Hanover, the Blackwells see something besides the eternal night of a railcar and smell something beyond fear and feces.

They breathe sighs of relief as they sit in a passenger car with boards bolted down for seats and a window with a beautiful view on their last train.

"Next stop Gettysburg," Seth brightens with excitement. "Emilie said this trip be less than an hour. I pray Julia be waitin' for us."

"Seth Blackwell best you best not have left your manners in Virginia," Martha scolds. "Mrs. Julia not be waitin' on you ever."

"But she asked me to call her —" Seth begins.

"I don't care what she asked you to call her. I'm telling you what you gonna call her, and that call starts with misses, you hear?" Martha scowls at him, too tired to show him the back of her hand.

"Yes, ma'am," Seth turns away to look out the window before adding, "I pray she be at the train station."

"We be walkin' if she not." Jim says. "How far is it?"

"Is what?" Seth asks as he wrinkles his face, trying to decipher the question.

"To the Prescott's, boy—walkin'?" Jim asks. "You been there."

"Oh, not far. A ride is better. That trunk is heavy."

"Well, we couldn't leave your ma's sturdy cooking pot," Jim

grins.

"One more word about that pot and you'll be wearing it instead of eating from it, Jim Blackwell!"

Jim chuckles.

"Oh, you think that's funny. We'll see how funny you think it is when it gives you a knot up your nappy head. Lord, why'd you go packin' that thing anyway?" Martha asks before remembering the conversation between her and Jim the day before.

"Thought it was your favorite. The pot is part of you Ma, its what gives your food soul. I'm hungry." Seth grins. He receives eyebrow arches and head shakes in return for his humor.

"You always hungry. I know why you wanted it. I'm tryin' to understand why pa allowed you to take it?"

"Because I'd rather lug a pot around in a trunk, than give you a wooden spoon to keep in your pocket woman. Figure you can only throw the pot once, that spoon's a whole 'nother matter."

"You mean to tell me you brought a pot but no damn spoon!"

"Would you look at that view?" Jim asks, turning away from her as he pulls a few twigs of tobacco out of his pocket, offering one to her and the other to Seth. "Here try this. Just don't go spitting it all over the place."

Seth waves off the twig.

"Then don't go complainin' you hungry." Martha grabs one of the offered twig.

Their gazes go off into different directions, as each of them waits out the last of the train to Gettysburg.

Click-clackety, click-clackety, click-clackety...

The screech of brakes, train whistles, and black smoke are the worst sounding orchestra in town, but also the most celebrated where it concerns the Blackwells as the train pulls into Gettysburg. Small cheers of celebration, started by Seth's clapping as he stands, ripple throughout the train car from young men and women with more happiness than sense.

"Seth, sit your tail down."

"Oh, come on, Ma. We here. We made it!"

Martha scowls. "We ain't made nothing yet."

However, Seth is already working to pull their trunk out from the luggage stacked in the back.

Martha sighs and feels Jim's arm envelope her into a side hug. "Keep looking over your shoulder, you ain't never goin' to be free."

He kisses her temple, and she turns to him in response. Their lips meet. Her breath catches. He still makes her heart sing. When he pulls away, she has no choice but to breathe as his thumb grazes her cheek, sweeping away a budding tear.

"It's sweat."

"I won't tell."

A steady flow of bodies presses out of the train car, and when Martha gets the opportunity to step out onto the platform, clean, fresh air delivers a cooling balm to her lungs. This strange place is nothing like the land of milk and honey she imagined. The white folks here still stare, point, and whisper at them. Maybe this was a bad idea, to plummet themselves into a strange place, knowing so few people and former slave owners at that.

Her body tired and exhausted makes walking feel akin to slogging through a swamp, the weight of the past pulling at her— *Don't look back.*

Dear Lord, please let Mrs. Julia be here. Never thought I'd think it; I miss that crazy white lady. She be the only person around here that I know can cook half as decent as me.

Porters of the railway escort the Blackwells and other people of color through the sea of passengers on the platform, around the building that is the train station, and out onto the street scarred in wagon tracks.

"Big Jim! Martha! Seth!" Julia waves from her perch, then she tries to clamor down until her dress snags on something.

Martha bares the smallest smile, shaking her head. *It's a miracle she can get herself dressed without me.*

"You made it!" Little Miss's voice cheers from behind with Mr. Jacob in toe, carrying all their luggage past the doors of the station.

Little Miss hooks her arm around Martha's, tugging her along to the wagon where Mrs. Julia still wrestles with her skirt.

"What's the fuss?" asks Mr. Jacob.

"My petticoat." Delicate hands fight with the hardy nail. "It's caught. I thought you had them all tacked down?"

"Well Julia, wagons by their nature move, and on roads like ours, something probably came loose." Mr. Jacob loaded his and Little Miss's bags into the wagon. Then he turns to help Jim hoist the trunk, before setting out to rescue his damsel from the crude metal.

Martha isn't given much time to digest it all as once Mrs. Julia's within reach, this crazy white lady encircles her in a hug. Then the yammering begins, "Oh, it's so good to see you, Martha! I've missed you so much and have been dying for some of your greens. I've tried to make them your way countless times and just can't seem to get the seasoning right—"

"That's okay, Jul—"

Martha stiffens.

"Oh Seth, and Big Jim!"

"Yes, Mrs. Julia. It's us, and as I was sayin' Ma brought her secret ingredient for all her cookin'."

I did?

"Her pot!"

"Oh, what an interesting secret. Did you season it different?"

Martha rolls her eyes, but Julia pays her no mind as she proceeds to throw her arms around Mr. Jacob, who has freed her from that rusty dagger of a nail. Next comes Little Miss, Jim, and then Seth—everyone gets a hug! Whether they want one or not.

When the Missus turns back to Martha she can't help but ask, "Mrs. Julia, no hug for the horse?"

Mrs. Julia laughs and hugs her all the more, squeezing what little energy Martha has right out of her.

"You made it, you made it, you made it!" Mrs. Julia bubbles over with enthusiasm, rocking the two of them back and forth. "I can't say enough how worried I was about all of you."

The embrace of her long-time confidant is once again jarring and yet still a strange comfort. This public display brings on whispers, looks of intimidation, and pointing fingers from strangers.

We still in the South?

"I bet you're exhausted. But it will be alright once we get home. A good meal in your bellies and a warm bed; it's just the cure for a long travel."

Martha pats Mrs. Julia on the back ever so lightly before straining to separate herself, pushing back against the woman's arms with her body.

Mrs. Julia steps back, concern creasing her brow, covering over the pure delight she is feeling. "What's wrong?"

Martha looks to the crowd and back. "They be starin' at us. They gots no manners?"

A young girl is yanked away from walking too close to them. The girl squeaks in surprise tripping over her feet, when her mother lifts her by the arm. The woman snubs her nose at them, with a loud pronounced exasperation.

"Ain't they seen a black person before?" Seth asks.

"Boy, I thought you been here?" asks Jim.

"No, not here, here. Just Table Rock Road, where the Prescotts live."

Little Miss giggles. "Oh, don't worry about them. They judge everyone, even me. Let's load up in the wagon. Martha, will you tell me how your trip was?"

"Oh, Little Miss, we just got off that box of bolts. Can I tell you later?" Martha asks, her face drawn long, with muddy smudges under her half-closed eyelids. "Got a terrible headache."

Mrs. Julia frowns. "I can't imagine how difficult your trip was, being your first one and all. Of course, we can talk later, and I bought some coffee earlier. We can brew that up when we get home. Should help with the headache."

Little Miss and Mrs. Julia both extend their reach to help Martha into the wagon. Seth hops in with the ladies, while Jim attempts to get in, too, but Jacob stops him.

"Join me up front?" Jacob asks. "Let the womenfolk chatter."

"It's all right. I'm use to sitting in the back."

"Well, it's time you get used to being your own man and sit with the men." Jacob nods toward the front of the wagon. "Come on, I want to give you a tour on the way home."

Julia's optimistic air and contagious smile is what Martha needs to let her own lips relax into an upward curve for the first time since they left the Sprees. Her friend's infectious behavior also helps build Martha's excitement as they ride out to the Prescott home.

"So, I worked for the last few days to make sure our home is comfortable for y'all. It'll be tight for a while, but you and Jim will have your own room, and Seth can take Henry's room. I know it's only temporary, but I'm so excited to have you home with us. Please consider our home yours. I insist. I mean, you will, won't you?" Mrs. Julia's hand reaches for Martha's giving it a tender squeeze.

Martha feels her back go rigid at the gesture, not only because she is not used to physical gestures of affection—from a white woman no less—but—well, in all of Martha's years, words like Mrs. Julia's have never been spoken to her directly. She stares, afraid to blink less sleep con her into believing this is some dream.

This gotta be a dream. Do I really belong here?

Martha sighs. "Oh well, I guess I be doin' the cooking and cleaning. Lord knows, Jim and Seth be doing the chores outside to earn our keep." The thought of work overwhelms her as the lead weight of exhaustion presses on her lids.

"That's not expected anymore. You're welcome to help, of course, but it isn't your sole responsibility now."

Martha continues to stare, no longer knowing what is expected of her. "Well, I'll be—"

"Oh, thank God," Little Miss says, her face brightening. "You mean I don't have to muck the stalls anymore and do Henry's chores?"

"You ain't suppose to do that anyways," Seth shakes his head. "You a teacher and a lady."

"But I have to help out now that the boys are gone."

"I ain't say'n you can't do it, just sayin' you don't have to."

"Thank you, Seth," Little Miss has a blush on her cheeks, touched by his protective sentiment Martha supposes.

"Little Miss, I sure like to see you in the kitchen with me again. I hear your biscuits are better than mine, you know how I feel about tellin' tall tales when you're only half the size," Martha says with a wry smirk.

Emilie's mouth opens, and her eyes widen as her head shakes in denial, "I-I never said."

"No, you didn't. I got that from his mouth, and if it ain't flappin, it's eatin!" Martha points to her son, that smirk of hers broadens as she sees the heat fill his ears.

"Well, you taught me everything I know." Little Miss says.

Seth shifts, his expression darkening into a solemn pout.

Martha playfully bats his arm, "Scrub that look off your face, boy. You had us lug that pot all the way here. You best believe I ain't goin to let that hard work go to waste."

Seth grins, "That means I get the first biscuit?"

"Mmhmm."

Martha places her hand on Little Miss, giving her a reassuring squeeze. "Thank God we be together again."

The motion of the wagon turning stops the conversation as they roll up the drive. Once the parking break is in place, the men hop out and walk around to help the ladies out of the back.

"We'll tend the horses and do the chores," Jacob says. "Will dinner be ready soon?"

"Just need thirty minutes and we can eat. Do you need Emilie with you?"

"No, Mrs. Julia. I'll do her work," Seth smiles at Little Miss who gives him a wink in thanks.

"Jacob, I have Seth in Henry's room and Jim and Martha set up in Aaron's room. The trunk can go into Aaron's room." Julia turns to Martha. "If that's where you'd like it?"

"That'll be just fine," Martha says.

The men turn to tend the barn chores, and the ladies turn back to the house.

"Let me show you around," Julia guides Martha into the house.

Inside, the kitchen's aroma pulls them into a warm embrace: chicken stew, pumpkin pies, and fresh bread fill the space.

"Feel free to hang your outside things here." Julia takes Martha's hand for a quick tour through the house with Little Miss in tow.

"The parlor is in here," Julia continues, "and look at this."

In the corner of the room are stacks of pots, pans, dishes, glassware, tools, quilts, mattresses, and everything else needed to set up a home.

"What on earth?" Martha asks. "Where did these things come from?"

"I asked for donations, and all our friends and neighbors gladly gave us items they didn't need. I'm afraid it's not brand new, but it is all in good working order. I inspected everything."

Martha backs away from the items, hand going to her temple, hoping to ease the spinning that has overcome her from the resulting generosity.

Are you all right?" Little Miss takes her elbow and steers her to the couch. "Let's sit down, Martha."

"Emilie," Julia orders, "go get her some water."

Little Miss pops up like a daisy the moment her butt hits the couch cushion, and she scurries out of the room; the sounds of her hurried footsteps trail off.

"Do they know?" Martha asks. "Do they know it's for us?"

"I told them we have a dear family who is moving up here. All I said is y'all needed some things to get you started. Everyone gladly pitched in."

"Why?" Martha asks, eyes narrowing. "We don't need no charity."

Julia's eyes widen, her mouth opens then closes. "It's not charity. It's a little help to get you on your feet. We value your independence, and we want to get you there as fast as possible. Think of these as welcome gifts." Julia reaches for Martha's hand.

Martha looks at her, reaches into her pocket, and pulls out an old, tattered handkerchief dabbing the tears in her eyes. "No one ever been this kind to us except you and Mr. Jacob when you could."

"It's the least we can do." Martha feels Julia's hand squeeze her shoulder followed by a whisper, "Welcome to freedom."

The cook dries the wet stains on her face and takes a deep breath. A weak smile peeks at the corner of her mouth.

"I'm afraid," Martha confesses. "I don't know life without being a slave."

"And I don't claim to know what it's like to be you. But as our friend, we're here for y'all, if you need us that is."

Martha nods, acknowledging Julia, her words lost to concerns about fitting in and the learning trials that lie ahead. Yet a small glow of resolve within her and the realization that this moment is a gift, fortifies her determination. She musters a smile, her eyes light on Julia's clear blue pools. "We must be truly blessed," she squeezes Julia's hand, and they share a moment of reassurance.

Martha sighs, packing away her emotions. "Alright, alright enough of this. Dinner ain't gonna put itself on the table."

Julia laughs. "Shall we?"

"Where is Emilie?" Julia asks as she and Martha enter the kitchen. She is nowhere to be found. Julia looks over to the sideboard, the stack of letters is missing from where she placed them a few days ago.

"Surprise, surprise, Little Miss duckin' out of the kitchen again. Bet Little Miss done lost her way to the waterin' hole. Should have known Seth was just tellin' tales about her cooking." Martha picks up the cover from the Dutch oven. Steam from the chicken stew curls out of the pot. "Mmm—Mrs. Julia, smells like you got all the right stuff in there. I'mma taste it to be sure."

She touches the bubbling stew with a callous finger, popping it into her mouth. Her eyes squint in thought, chin shifting— she nods, "Needs a little bit more— " Martha looks around for that something to add.

Julia, smiling to herself, loves that Martha is making herself at home in the kitchen. In fact, she takes a seat at the table, knowing that trying to help her friend would merely result in getting in the woman's way. She points to the pantry, "Everything you need is in there."

Martha pushes aside the pantry curtain, burying herself in its contents and many shelves before stepping out with a jar that Julia can't quite make out, and it doesn't help that Martha's grasp conceals the label.

"What's that?" Julia asks as Martha takes up a spoon to open the lid to add the ingredient.

"None-yah," says Martha.

"None-yah?" Julia is not sure she's ever heard of that ingredient, and then it dawns on her, "Fine, keep your secrets."

Martha chuckles and goes about her business, stirring away.

Julia looks around, realizing that she, too, is not used to sitting around, doing nothing. Only a minute has passed and she's already itching.

Suppose I could set the table.

"No collard greens?" Martha asks.

"The bugs got them," Julia says as she sets to her own task. "We have a new crop coming, but I'm afraid it won't be a lot this year."

"Maisy showed me just how to get rid of them critters." Martha's carefree demeanor is 'the Martha' that Julia loves.

"Is that so?"

"Mmhmm. Get yourself some cayenne pepper, a bit of water, and oil. Then spray them darlings so they up and leave."

The ladies laugh.

"So, when do I start cooking for you?" asks Martha.

Julia sets down the final place setting, looking up. "Start? For me?"

Martha stops, turns, and their eyes meet. "Ya'll don't wanna hire me?"

Julia clears her throat, licking and biting her lower lip. "Martha."

The woman's smile vanishes.

Julia sighs. The only word she wishes to say is yes, but— "You worked for me for a long time. You taught me not just how to cook but how to be a mother, and for that I am forever grateful but—"

"What? I ain't good enough no more?"

"No, no, not at all. You're great. You're the best! I just—I just want you to make your own way. Open a market stall and share your blessings with the rest of the world. Become your own woman. Experience all the joys of freedom."

"Mrs. Julia, I know nothin' 'bout that."

"You don't have to know everything about it. I'll help you, if that's something you want to do. That's what friends are for, and it's Julia, not Mrs. Julia. I don't want you as my slave. I don't want you as an employee. But I do want you as my friend. I need you as my friend."

"How—how am I gonna make it without work?" Martha's eyes shift as the muscles in her face quiver, but Julia knows the woman well enough that she will not resign to crying.

Julia smiles. "If you want to be a cook, I will certainly put in the best word for you with the kindest employers I know. That's what friends are for. They help each other out. They visit each other's kitchens, but they maintain their own independence."

"Mrs. Julia, I understand." Martha nods, the tremble in her expression echoing in her voice. "Guess I'm still trying to figure out being free."

"It's Julia and give it time."

"Mrs. Julia, I will."

"It's Jul—"

"It's freedom of speech."

Smiles are exchanged and laughter follows.

Martha sets the spoon down, rolls her shoulders, and stretches her arms out. "Gettysburg don't know what's coming, but their noses sure will by the time I'm done cookin'.'"

Julia and Martha share a laugh.

"Now, where's Little Miss?"

As I lay on my bed, I pull the paper to my nose. A faint musty, inky smell adds to my disappointment for his bergamot-lime cologne. How I long to bury my nose past the paper into his neck, right in that soft tender space just behind his ear. Pulling the letter back my gaze scrolls across the handwriting. The loops appear to be rushed, the curves sharp, the words tight—as if holding his breath for him. Odd.

My darling Emilie,

Your recent journey to Virginia has weighed heavily on my mind. While I understand and support the reasons behind it, I fear for you and your father's safety. When you return home, please write to tell me you are safe.

The days without you feel empty, my love. I long to hold you in my arms once more, to breathe in the scent of your hair, and be lost within your presence, not just the faint dreams I have of us together. Though I admit, it is these dreams where I find solace and comfort amid the challenges of camp.

We are firmly entrenched here at Camp Pierpont at Langley outside of Washington for the winter months. The routine of camp duties and efforts to ward off the cold are monotonous. We are in need of more socks, scarves, and other warm essentials. If you have time amidst this busy holiday season, I would be grateful for both. I lost my last scarf and now resort to layering socks to combat the cold constantly nipping at my feet. Oh, how I miss the warmth of your parlor's fireplace and the joy of your company within it as we read poems and shared our news of simpler times.

Worry not though. I am thankful to report my health remains robust, though some comrades have fallen ill with the season. We bid farewell to a few of those who departed for their final rest, but I assure you I am taking every measure to stay safe and healthy.

The quilt sent from the ladies has been a cherished companion, keeping me warm during these colder nights. Receiving mail and gifts from home is a lifeline to me, my love. I look forward to your letters, it is the best part of my day.

Do you remember our first Christmas? That magical day is forever etched in my heart as the moment I fell deeply in love with you. The memory of the last waltz on New Year's, and how I had to wait to kiss you remains a cherished treasure for me as well. I can't wait to make more memories with you when we are back together, face to face at our wedding. We will have a new life together.

My dearest Emilie, I carry your love with me always and find my strength in the thought of being reunited with you. Dream of our kisses and write to me whenever you can. Your letters sustain me through these lonely times.

Forever Yours,

Thaddeus

Socks and scarves? Looks like I will need to create those quickly over the next week or so. But a quilt being his prized possession? I will make him a better one, the only one he will ever need. One that will provide him more than comfort as he wraps himself up in my stitches instead of some piecemeal, shoddy craftmanship from the dirty hands of a stranger.

I look to my fabric trunk calculating how long it will take for me to craft such a masterpiece.

Setting my hand in my lap, the crunch of paper reminds me I have another letter to read. Turning the letter over, I look down.

Stephen's letter—I should go help with dinner.

But then I might never get to it. I sigh.

Best to get it over with.

I open the letter wondering why he is writing to me after the cold reception I gave him at the train station. Didn't he say in his last letter that if I didn't respond he would accept it as a sign and would cease in his correspondence? Then again, I have never known Stephen Byrne to give up on anything he puts his mind to, including making my life miserable.

Dear Emilie,

I sent you a letter earlier, but upon further speculation, I realized that it may have conveniently become lost and therefore the words within forgotten to time or a fire. Therefore, I have decided to write to you again in hopes that you will at least read this one and kindly or even unkindly respond.

As I am not sure as to whether you have read the previous one, there are a few things I would like to reprise from the previous letter as well as add to this one. Firstly, I hope you do not think it too forward of me to write, but in my defense, not that I deserve any, I did ask Thaddeus if he minded our correspondence.

You see, I only have my parents' letters to entertain me here and they are not nearly as entertaining as stories from the letters you send Thaddeus. Not that he shares many of them with me. Still, Thaddeus, being the generous gentleman that he is, understands my plight and has approved of my desire to write. How is that for poetry?

I must admit, I am grateful that Thaddeus and I are friends again just as we once were in school. Though just as it was in school, he is outperforming me and getting promotions. I suppose some things never change but worry not. He'll come home with so many medals he'll look like the earring rack at that bobble and bits store you're so fond of.

Anyway, we are keeping our noses clean of the death snots and trouble here as we settle into life at camp in the winter, where we are supposed to be until the corpses start popping daisies. The quarters here are cold and drafty, so as you can imagine many of the men have already caught their death.

We have little in the way of responsibilities outside of picket duty, where we guard trees. I am happy to report that none of them have yet to get up and leave. Thaddeus and I spend a lot of our downtime playing cards, making bets, staring at dwindling fires, counting specks of dirt, and reading letters from home.

I've read the letters from my parents so many times that I find the dirt and the flurries that blanket them a better form of entertainment. Would you have me suffer longer?

Of course you would, and I don't blame you for it. I was a monster to you in days past. An angry boy who did not respect the gift of your friendship. For that I am truly sorry, Emilie. Please accept this as a partial apology, as I will one day stand before you and ask again.

So once more, I ask you to please consider writing to me. I promise you I am working to become my best self—thanks to your Thaddeus's guiding hand. If you do not write, I will consider this an unacceptable method of apology and will try another way. I will also consider that you have used this letter as fodder for your parlor's fire and will write again.

Have a safe and healthy season. I hope this letter gives you warmth whether it be from the words within or the kindling it gives.

Respectfully,
S. Byrne

P.S. If this letter displeases you, I apologize but do remember to send all your blame to Thaddeus for granting such permission and a few more pairs of socks to me. Your threadbare bouquet of stink is coming along nicely.

Sitting with Stephen's letter, a concoction of emotion stirs my gut.

Why should I forgive him? ... How do I trust he won't be as contemptible as he's always been? ... Can I ever trust him? ... Do I want to trust him? ... He's a good guy when he wants to be but—how often is that?

"Ugh," I say to the empty room.

Bouquet of stink, stink of my mood! I should have read Thaddeus's letter last.

Mother's voice barges into my irritation. "Emilie, dinner!"

"Coming," I say, folding his letter and tucking it in my desk drawer—out of sight, out of mind, still considering whether I will or won't deal with Mr. Byrne.

A Place to Call Home

For to be free is not merely to cast off one's chains, but to live in a way that respects and enhances the freedom of others.
~ Nelson Mandela

DECEMBER 1861
GETTYSBURG, PENNSYLVANIA

The urgency for warmth and comfort did not escape the Prescotts or the Blackwells this season. The snow and bitter cold blankets the town by the second full week of December, and the women of the two families—and Seth—do their best to keep warm within the confines of the house. Meanwhile Jacob and Jim use the quiet of the chilled air to their advantage, keeping their secrets within a shroud of whispers as they work in the woodshop attached to the barn.

Jacob and Jim push gritty sandpaper over their latest project, causing bits of cedar dust to powder the air, releasing hints of citrus and an undertone of camphor, fooling their tongues into thinking they might taste something better than bland flecks of wood.

"Don't know how to thank you for all you done over the time we been here," Jim says as he massages the paper over the wood with care.

"It's my pleasure," Jacob continues to follow along the curve of wood before him. "We've enjoyed your company and as excited as we are for you to eventually get settled, we will miss having y'all as our guests."

"The money you offered is too much to ask—" begins Jim.

"Don't think another thought about it. William owes you that as part of your freedom, and I'll be sure to collect the money from him one way or another."

"He told me he'd never pay. His exact words were 'over my dead body.'"

Jacob chuckles. "That can be arranged."

Silence follows—save for Jacob's own smoothing of the wood within his reach.

He looks up to see Jim staring at him with wide eyes.

"I tease, partially. I'll just beat it out of him. Consider it tough brotherly love. He deserves it, but never you mind that."

Jim smiles, shakes his head, and sets back to work.

Their pride and joy sits upside down. Its two long armrests are clamped onto sawhorses placed at either side.

"Jim, we've always been in an unusual situation. You've been with me since childhood, and I know we can both agree that we got in trouble more times than either of us can count, though it always bothered me when you ended up suffering the whipping for something we had done." Jacob puts aside his sanding, his mind casting back to the past, snagging memories and luring them to the forefront.

"We know that be reason enough for them to let us socialize," says Jim.

Jacob nods.

Jacob's father knew that his eldest son was the sort who would volunteer to suffer the worst of a whooping to ease the hardship of someone he cared for. It didn't take much to recall one of the many times his father publicly humiliated Jim while forcing Jacob to watch as punishment—in hopes of hardening his son's tender heart. He winces as the memories flood forth. He can hear the crack of the lash, smell the copper in the marks that still streak Jim's back—gaping with a quiet cry and shedding silent tears of blood as Jacob is forced to stand by.

"I'm sorry," he whispers.

"Sorry for what? Like I done said before, you ain't the one who done me dirty. Besides experiencing life with you—closest thing I had to freedom—to a brother."

Jacob looks up, his cheeks a tinge of red as water surfaces at the lips of his lids, threatening to spill over. He nods. Sniffs. Looks back to their craftmanship.

"We should probably shellac her."

Jim nods. "Yeah, protect her from the weather, but she'll need time to dry."

"Good time for us to go into town."

Jim nods again, and Jacob turns to the various shelves that line his shop, looking for the shellac, talking all the while.

"You and your family's perseverance—" The words die on his lips in exchange for murmurs as Jacob shakes his head, turns to Jim in brief, nods, and then goes back to his search.

His tongue licks his lips.

He sucks in a breath, "I guess what I'm—"

He sighs.

His fingers lift up to scratch an itch, but it recedes out of reach, into his thoughts, so he rubs his stubbled chin instead, then caresses the back of his neck with a squeeze, trying to coax the tension out.

"Jacob, you gonna spit or shit if you don't get what's off your chest."

Jacob plucks the jar of shellac and two brushes off the shelf, turning to Jim. "All I'm saying is that—that without you we wouldn't have been able to run that plantation, and I know no one's ever voiced it, but I want to.

"In fact, I want to do more than that, and this is how—your family's freedom, the money, all of it. I don't just want you to have it. You deserve it; you've earned it. So, don't thank me for paying a debt that's long overdue."

Jim smiles, gives a nod, chuckles to himself, and then shakes his head as he accepts one of the offered brushes. "We were troublesome, weren't we?"

Jacob cracks a grin at the same time he unscrews the lid to open the shellac releasing a perfume of cleanliness mixed with the sharp tang of a saloon. Both melodies of the nose overpower the sweet notes sung by the wood.

The contents of the container are offered to Jim before Jacob allows himself to dive in. Each in turn, they dip their brushes into thick, sticky goop and set to work slathering on the protective coat.

Jacob starts with the rails. "I'll never forget when we planted firecrackers in the parlor's fireplace that New Year's Eve just to see if the burst of color came out the chimney top."

Jim's face broadens, showing off his smile as he works on the smooth curves of the rockers. "Remember that time we painted Ole Pokey in shoe polish to look like Black Jack, so them Kents won't buy him for that brat they called a daughter?"

"Ah, yes, but that plan wasn't exactly fool proof, was it? If I recall it rained, and Pokey dragged an inky trail all over for days—"

"—yeah, black and brown Miss Kent's white dress was after Ole Pokey dumped her in that mud puddle. Serves her right for all the beating and kicking she was doin'."

"I still say we did her a favor. Black Jack wouldn't have just dumped her, he'd have trampled her. Shame Father wouldn't listen to reason." Jacob begins to work on the seat.

"Did he ever?"

The men exchange a snort and laugh.

"Got to say, it was worth polishing your father's boots for a month."

"Glad you still think so, but poor Pokey, I miss that plucky pony."

"Came to an end when we got a bit of fuzz on our chins, didn't it?" asks Jim, moving to the stretchers and then the legs.

"Yes indeed, no more running around together, coming back with ripped trousers and missing buttons, causing my mother fits that would have her dipping into the laudanum. Father began to teach me the business—"

"—and I gots put in the fields," Jim says. "Suppose that be for the best. Never was a good houseboy; must say, them fields saved my life."

"But I'll never forget how you saved my hide in those early years."

The men step back to examine their handywork.

"Think Martha will like it?" asks Jacob. Now that the shellac's offensive odor permeates his whole shop and the masterpiece that sits before them, Jacob seals the jar.

"If she don't, I will." Jim hands his brush over to Jacob.

Jacob takes the brush in hand with his own. "We'll let that dry and then turn her right side up when we get back from town. Mr. Lawton wants to meet us to go over the paperwork. Did you tell your lovely wife what you're up to?"

"She's got enough in her pot to handle. Gonna keep this secret dear and beg for forgiveness later."

"On one knee or both knees?"

"Already done one knee, now look where that got me?"

"Beg for forgiveness it is. Let's hitch the team."

The desire to see the home—see what needs fixing—sits at the forefront of Jim's mind. However, Jacob insists there is paperwork to be had—paperwork he don't understand a lick of. Nerves bubble up in his gut as they drive into town to Mr. Lawton's office located on Chambersburg Street, a quaint building jutting out from the attorney's home with a separate entrance.

They pull up to the residence, and Jacob sits back, waiting for ...?

Jim waits too.

Jacob looks at him.

Jim asks, "Ain't you coming out of the cold?"

"It's plenty warm here," Jacob assures him, pulling his coat tighter around himself. "Besides, it should only take you a few minutes."

"So, you just goin' to wait here?"

"I am. This is your business," Jacob says, rubbing his hands together, shuffling his feet. "Now you better hurry on before I catch my death."

"What about—" Jim starts to say.

"Death catching."

Jim casts a look back, searching for a sign of a smirk on Jacob's face, wondering if this could be some sort of prank, but it would appear his friend has curled up within the depths of his coat, head receded beneath the collar flaps, and hat pulled over his eyes for a nap.

"Alright then." Jim disembarks from the wagon.

Sighs.

Shaking his head and wiggling his fingers just to check they still work, he steps up to the door and knocks.

Thump-thump. Thump-thump.

His pulse is louder than the soft rapping that comes across the door.

"Louder," calls Jacob from the depths of his coat.

"What, you heard it."

"That's different. I've got children."

Jim grunts and goes to knock on the door again, but his fist hits air as the door opens to reveal a startled woman, petite in size, whose eyes betray that she thinks him a giant—a big black giant.

Jim relaxes his shoulders until they curve off his neck and hunches his back a bit before he speaks with a real soft voice, "Ma'am, how you do? I'm here to see Mr. Lawton about some property I'd like to buy."

She looks past Jim and then directly at him once again. Her eyes remain as wide as slices of coined sausage before she gives a nod of her head and opens the door—wider, even wider, all the way, ducking back behind it to allow him through.

Jim smiles so wide his cheeks hurt as he steps inside.

"Ma'am, thank you kindly."

Jacob peels an eye open as he hears the door open once more. He's not sure how long it's been but what he does know is Jim looks ten years younger as he practically jogs his way back to the wagon, dangling a key from his large fingers and shaking the documents in his other hand.

The wagon shifts as his friend steps up, and Jacob adjusts his hat and resituates himself, gathering the reins.

"It's done. It's finished. Jim Blackwell, that's me, owns his own home!"

"Congratulations, Jim. Now, where to?"

Jim unfolds a bundle of paper and then stares at it for a moment, "Washington, Washington some—," he begins before handing it to Jacob.

Jacob flips through the document reading over the provisions of ownership. The price of the home and the address is listed. At the bottom of the contract resides Mr. Lawton's signature, Jim's X, and the date. A paid stamp is imprinted in the lower corner. No funny business. The paperwork is in order.

Good. Seems like the little talk I had with Mr. Lawton the other day had an effect.

"South Washington Street," Jacob says as he hands the documents back over and then calls to the team, setting off to inspect the house.

Jim nods and neatly folds the papers back before tucking them into the inside pocket of his jacket. "Washington Street."

"South Washington Street, and no worries, Jim. Seth will have you reading in no time. Did you have any problems with the transaction?" Jacob asks.

"No, sir. Mr. Lawton be very kind. He explained everything in the contract real nicely. No questions. He says there be a church nearby; he assured me they a welcoming bunch on Washington Street—South Washington Street."

"Soon you'll be so busy with new friends, I'll have to send a calling card ahead to get on your calendar for a visit," Jacob nudges Jim's shoulder.

"True enough," Jim says, nudging him back. "Is there a black-smith in these parts like me?"

"Sure is, Mr. Warfield has a great reputation. I would use his services but he's out on the other side of town."

"I be sure to make his acquaintance. He might have a job for me. Otherwise, tenant farming." Jim pauses and sighs. "Not too keen on that."

"No, you should be free from the fields."

The steady *clip-clopping* of the team fills the remainder of their ride before they pull up to the house.

Jacob turns to Jim. "What do you think?"

"Well, I'll be damned," Jim says. "This ours?"

Jacob puts out his hand, "Let me see the papers again?"

A bit of rustling and a minute later Jacob is taking the papers from Jim's hands. He looks to the property, then back to the papers, and nods. Reaching over, he touches Jim's arm with the paperwork as he hands it back.

"Yes, indeed. It's all yours."

Jim sits there with his mouth opening and closing like a fish.

Jacob chuckles. "Unless you want to live in this wagon, I'd advise we get out and look around."

Jim nods and then scrambles out of the wagon so fast he comes close to falling.

"You alright?"

"N-never better!" Jim approaches the two-story brick home, the key scrapes up against the door as he works to calm his nerves.

Jacob waits behind him, knowing eventually Jim will unlock it.

When they step into the home the place is void of furniture but boasts plenty of room for some as it hosts a dining room, parlor, and kitchen. Walking into the kitchen, the small wood stove, pantry, as well as a dry sink and pump greet them.

Jim walks over to the stove opening all the doors. The fire box is small, but the stove has no rust or holes.

"Oh no."

"What is it?" Jacob asks, his hand on the pump encouraging water to flow.

"Stove's too small. Glad we gots one. But she ain't gonna go for this. She prides herself on what she cooks and this ain't it."

Jacob laughs. "Well then, I guess those who want a helping of good eating, outside of you and Seth, will have to pay a fee. Hang a sign up for the world to see: Martha's Kitchen."

Jim joins in on the laughter. "Not a bad idea."

Jacob asks, "Well, what do you think?"

Jim nods his head. "The house looks good, looks ready to move in."

"Martha will be decorating and fussing over it in no time." Jacob watches a broad grin spread over Jim's face. The excitement spills from his friend's whole being, his steps lighter, his confidence boosted by ownership and independence.

"Now, how are you going to keep this from her?" Jacob asks.

"They too busy decorating to care what trouble we be up to." Jim chuckles at Jacob's raised eyebrow of disbelief. "Haven't you been listening? The women been going on and on about traditions I ain't never heard of decorations I hardly seen, and good eatin', which I've only dreamed."

"I am sure you will know them all by the beginning of the new year," Jacob looks at his watch. "Oh, the post office. We best get going. I don't want to face my daughter if I come home empty handed."

I never enjoyed leaving the kitchen as much as I did just now. The parlor chair welcomes me with the comfort of its woven tapestry and sturdy frame, enveloping my weary back and aching shoulders. Martha put me through my paces in the kitchen preparing for the holidays. We made cookies, pies, and planned the Christmas dinner today.

My eyes drift over to my sewing basket. The yarn is a blur in a waterfall of colors from various projects waiting for me to tend to them: scarves, mittens, socks. The laundry list of supplies for the winter camps are endless, not to mention Christmas gifts I am making.

I sigh. There is no chance of me picking anything out of the basket today. It will have to wait.

Closing my eyes for a moment, sipping in the solace, listening to my breath, thinking about Thaddeus. I become subtly aware of the soft pad of footsteps, tentative, then faint.

"Emilie?" the whisper floats to my ear. "You sleepin'?" Seth asks, his voice is a bit louder.

My eyes pop open to Seth standing before me with a bowl of popcorn, cranberries, thread, and needles. I sit up when he says, "Mrs. Julia asked me to ask you to—"

"What do you need, Seth?"

"What do I do with these?"

"We string them for decoration." I say, thinking back further and further into my memories.

Seth stares at me with a blank look on his face, and I motion for him to come closer to the table.

"When was the last time you were in the big house in Virginia?"

"Uhm, when I was five? They allowed me in the kitchen to haul wood and clean the fireplace. Ma let me play in the garden but kept me back saying I'd break things and get in trouble. Then when I was ten, they sent me to help Pa. Grew up in the fields ever since."

"Do you remember how we decorated in December?"

"No, I 'member Ma coming home tired all the time. Complaining about dinner parties and guests all month long."

"I see. Come, let me show you how to string those, and we can make some new memories," I grab the bowl from him and set it on the table. Then I take up a needle and thread to show him how to make a long string. Pausing, I look up to see Seth pop a few kernels of popcorn in his mouth.

His face screws up, his mouth immediately trying to reject what he thought would be a treat.

I stifle my giggles.

"This is terrible." He looks for a place to spit it out.

I bite my bottom lip and point to the small trash can.

Seth rises and goes to spit up the half-chewed corn, wiping his tongue on his sleeve.

"It's not supposed to be good. It's over a week old, that's why we use it for decorating," I tell him. "It doesn't break apart when you string it. Now watch me."

Seth moves in to watch me take a berry, push it onto the needle, and then repeat with a piece of popcorn. His focus is trained on my fingers until I have a string of popcorn and berries worth presenting.

I hand him my string. "There. Your turn."

Seth takes the needle into his larger fingers; the berry-popcorn strand swings between us.

"You don't eat this after, do you?" Seth asks, his focus on pushing a piece of corn onto the needle, but he squeezes it too hard, and the corn pops off to the corner of the room.

"Not at all," I say. "We put it in the trees outside for the animals. Here try again." I have another piece of popcorn ready.

"Last I checked, don't think them squirrels or birds mind if their meal comes with strings in a fancy pattern."

"The decorations are for us, Seth."

"They won't last if we put them outside."

"That's why we put it on the tree inside before we put them on the trees outside."

Seth lowers his needle and thread to meet my eyes. "So, that's why we hauled that bush up in here."

I frown. "It's a Christmas Tree."

Seth glances over my shoulder and my eyes follow his to the round table in the corner of the parlor and the tree that sits upon it, sparsely decorated with a few paper ornaments and soon our garland of popcorn and berries. "It ain't a tree. It's a bush sittin' on a table."

"Well, it behaves like a tree and come Christmas there will be presents underneath it, but none for you if you don't get back to stringing."

Seth gives a grunt, and we fall silent as he goes back to concentrating on the corn-berry cadence.

A faint jingle of bells grabs my attention, and I look up, listening for the door. A knock in four short sharp raps soon follows. Then footsteps, rushing down the hall, as Mother goes to answer it.

Martha steps out of the kitchen, coming into the parlor.

"How's it coming?" she asks, craning her head over our shoulders.

Seth shows her his hands; the sticky cranberries having reddened his fingers.

"It will be festive when we finish," I say, looking to her, as the needle pierces my finger. "Ow!" Dropping the needle into my lap, the weight of the garland is sliding off my skirt to the floor.

Seth and I both reach for the string, and—

Thunk!

Seeing stars, my hand flies to my head.

Then I feel a hand on mine and blinking back the cosmos, I notice it's Seth's hand.

"Miss Emilie, blood."

I frown.

It wasn't that hard of a head knock, was it?

I look up as if expecting crimson to drip down into my vision, but he pulls my hand to him, inspecting the source—my pricked finger.

Something between a shriek and gasp of surprise comes from the doorway.

We both turn and are greeted by the vision of Mrs. Maura Byrne, who stands next to Mother, her mouth stretched so wide, I wonder if we may need to send word for a priest.

"What is that boy doing to your daughter?" Mrs. Byrne asks.

Thunk.

The package in her hand drops to the floor, and for a moment I hope it is not breakable but then dismiss such a worry as Mrs. Byrne is not the most giving of our neighbors.

Seth stands, backing away, but staying in front of his mother.

I stand to greet her. "Mrs. Byrne, how wonderful it is to see you in such good cheer," I say reaching out for her hand, but she withdraws it as if I'm some lepper.

"H-h-how dare he! How dare he, be so-so forward as to-to-to touch you," Mrs. Byrne sputters.

"He's concerned about me," I say. "We bumped heads, and I pricked my finger."

I show her my appendage—stained maroon—and give it a wiggle, before popping it into my mouth to suck away the wound.

Mrs. Byrne's eyes grow even wider, and mentally, I dare them to pop. But wonders do cease, especially as I notice Mother giving me a disapproving glare.

Mother bends down to pick up the dropped parcel and asks, "Is this the donation we talked about?"

Mrs. Byrne looks to Martha, who is staring at her. "I didn't know you hired help."

"She's not help," I say. "Martha and her family just moved here."

"Oh. Oh, I see. So. Well. So, the donations, the donations are for-for—" Mrs. Byrne backs up to the door. "Are they staying with you, by chance?" Her face has doubled in wrinkles as confusion deepens the crevices in her brow and scratches at the crow's feet around her eyes.

"Yes," Mother says.

At this point Mrs. Byrne's back is to the door, her hand feeling around for the doorknob. "Well, what will the neighbors think when they find out their generosity is for—" Her chin points to

Seth and Martha as she looks to Mother.

Perhaps, I will write Stephen afterall. He might be amused by this.

"Is it not the good Christian thing to provide for those in need? Is it not of the ten commandments to honor thy neighbor?" Mother asks, narrowing her eyes, her full lips pulled tight into a thin line.

I, on the other hand, must suck my bottom lip in and bite down hard to stifle all my inappropriate manners, because Mrs. Byrne looks to have turned a new shade of white at the word neighbors.

"Well, of course," Mrs. Byrne begins, "but—"

"You were perfectly willing to donate your items. Did you change your mind?"

"Well, had I—" Mrs. Byrne's tongue is tied as she struggles to unknot the words.

"Let me say," Martha addresses Mrs. Byrne, "we don't need what you be givin' if you done changed your mind. Certainly don't want you feelin' any kind of way 'bout it."

Mother and Martha look at Mrs. Byrne, waiting for her answer.

Mrs. Byrne squirms, her mouth rippling with indecision, twitching at the corners. At last she gulps, gives a stiff nod, and wipes her shaky hands over her skirt.

"No, no, I suppose you are right, Julia," Mrs. Byrne says. "I hope they can use these things that I have so charitably offered out of the kindness of my heart." Another stiff nod follows, as her eyes dart around the room, but then relax in relief as her hand finally finds that doorknob.

"Well, I mustn't keep you." Her face is licked red with embarrassment. "Be seeing you at the next meeting?"

"Yes, of course." Mother wears a polite smile that hides what she's really thinking. "Emilie and I will see you in January. Shall I show you out?"

"Right. Yes, of course. I mean, no. I have it, right here. Thank you. Good-bye, Julia, Emilie, and—yes, well, good day to you," says Mrs. Byrne as she manages to open the door and slither on out of our sights.

The door shuts.

"Bless her heart." Mother blinks, shaking the incident out of her head.

Martha shakes her head too. "They goin to talk about this till Judgement."

"Let them, then God can judge them. You know better than I do, people don't change overnight," Mother says. "But change has to start somewhere, so why not here, now, with us?"

"Mrs. Julia—"

"Julia."

"Woman, I'll call you what I damn well please."

Mother looks to Martha, for a moment shocked, and then she begins to laugh.

"Mmhmm, you go right on kickin' up them giggles, stirrin' up those white folk you call neighbors like a fox in a hen house. You ain't innocent."

"Why, Martha. I have no idea what you're talking about."

"I'm talkin' bout you wastin' your time trying to get the pity of white folk, only to get your feelings hurt when they don't understand and don't care to."

Mother sighs, her merriment falling away. "Oh Martha, I neither see a need for pity, nor do I see you as a charity case. I see you as a friend and more importantly a family member—" She looks to Seth who has rejoined me on the sofa threading garlands for our bush—I mean tree.

It's a tree.

I am more in tune with watching the women navigate this jagged terrain of conversation than Seth is and elbow him to get his attention.

He looks up, meets eyes with my mother, then Martha, and then freezes. Perhaps he thinks if he doesn't move, they will disregard his existence.

"I want you both to understand this is how I wish I could have treated you in the South."

"Isn't that nice?" I ask, trying to ease the battle of wills.

Seth uses my interjection to flick a bit of popcorn by *mistake* and excuses himself to go after it.

Both women are back to staring at each other: Mother begging for Martha's understanding, Martha unwilling to change her belief about people's state of mind.

"You did your best given the circumstances," Martha says. "I know you did."

"I wish it could have been more," Mother's voice cracks as the emotion rises, "but I'm sorry if this isn't enough."

Martha's head tilts for but a moment before she sighs and moves to grab Mother's hand. "Come here you crazy white lady. Our friendship is all I really need, you got that?"

Mother half laughs and half sobs.

Martha pats her back as she looks to the pile of donations. "But the stuff you done got for us—Julia, that's more than I ever hoped for."

Mother draws back, pausing, "Did you just call me Julia?"

Now, it's Martha's turn to laugh, and even I can't hold back my own chuckle, "Don't get used to it, my crazy white lady."

Mother now laughs too—a full hearted belly chuckle that challenges her stays, as the tears erupt in both women's eyes.

Before I know it, they are pulling out handkerchiefs, dabbing their tears.

"I love you, Martha."

There is a silent moment between them, and they both look down to their hands, clasped in one another's.

"I love you, back."

"I'd be lost without you." Mother sniffs.

"Don't I know it," says Martha.

Then we all hear a rumble and grumble from Seth's stomach.

"What? Staring at all this popcorn is making me hungry," Seth pipes up lowering his garland in progress.

"Hush up, boy. I just fed you this morning and you ain't hardly done a thing since." Martha puts her handkerchief back into her pocket, brushing away a stray tear. "But them collard greens ain't gonna cook themselves, so we best get ourselves back in that kitchen, Julia."

Mother nods, adding Mrs. Byrne's package to the pile of household goods in the corner of the parlor. "Yes, yes, I believe you were about to tell me that secret ingredient of yours."

"And I believe that's in your dreams," Martha calls back from the kitchen.

Seth and I laugh as Mother returns to the kitchen. Our minds and our eyes turning back to our own work in earnest.

"I thought Mrs. Julia said this would be fun," Seth said.

"What? Stringing popcorn and cranberries? It isn't, but the drama that goes on while you're doing it? That's a whole other matter."

Christmas Traditions

TRADITIONS ARE THE THREAD, GLUE, AND MORTAR
THAT BIND FAMILIES THROUGH THE GENERATIONS.
~EMILIE PRESCOTT

DECEMBER 1861
TABLE ROCK ROAD
GETTYSBURG PENNSYLVANIA

The whirlwind of celebration sweeps us up in earnest four days prior to Christmas. Martha put Mother and me to work cleaning the house top to bottom, polishing silver, washing the fine dinner dishes, and pressing the tablecloth and napkins. Once the house was spotless, we returned to the kitchen to create the scent of the season with all the recipes she cooked for us back home. And us women folk aren't the only ones under Martha's command. She sent Big Jim and Father to run errands, picking up supplies for the dishes and has forced Seth to add his weight to the chaos by handling all the tall chores around the house.

"Did you have traditions for the holidays?" I ask, as I stir the stuffing with a large wooden spoon.

"Christmas be a good time for restin'," Martha says.

"If this is rest, I'd hate to see what you consider work." I wrinkle my nose.

"The rest be comin' after the work be done. We did look forward to receiving gifts from y'all before Mr. Two-Inch Willy—sorry, I shouldn't have said that."

But it's too late. I'm already giggling, Seth bites his lower lip, and Mother is doing her best not to smile, an attempt that fails when her melodious laughter breaks into the air outdoing us all.

Martha relaxes and lets her own laugh join the fray as well. "Not that I ever saw it. But let's just say Maggie had room to complain."

"Ma, you wrong for that." Seth shakes his head trying to stifle his chuckle.

"Lord knows if I be omittin' the truth I be tellin' a lie."

"Well, like Ma sayin', what little time we got off be the best time for us."

"Mmhmm, Mr. Two—, I mean we got four days off." Martha begins and the giggles renew, "Of course, Mrs. Prescott, your Ma and even your Grandma made sure them meals were simple and easy —but not that fool that's there now—."

"I remember bringing gifts out to all of you on Christmas day," I say, "The children would chase me, capture me, and yell 'Christmas gifts!' until I gave them some." My smile broadens as their little faces flash through my mind. "Handing them small gifts and candy, made me happy."

Martha smiles, warmed by the memories. "Mrs. Julia, remember that time Mr. Jacob gave us all chickens for Christmas meal?"

Mother laughs, "He scurried to get twenty-five chickens that year. He was so proud to deliver those. Did you enjoy them?"

Martha laughs. "Well, I ain't sure who did more scurryin' the chickens or him, but them tough birds met our stew pots and let me tell you, it was all over from there."

Mother frowns. "Oh, were they tough? What a shame, I should tell Jacob, we can roast some chickens for New Years."

Martha shakes her head. "Roast? Have you done lost your mind? Don't you go tellin' Mr. Jacob nothin'. We be grateful for them birds and besides a roast lasts a day or two, but you put some good eatin' in that pot and that meat will last you a good month and make that forever-stew even richer when it's all gone. Just got to keep it bubblin' and add fresh water as people come to empty it with their mouths."

"You all were teasin' and playin' when I insisted Ma have her pot," says Seth.

We all laugh.

"The Lord blessed us with Mr. Jacob." Martha began. "He allowed us to celebrate our traditions, with dances and storytelling. Gave us gardens and chickens to raise. Even understood that the better he treated us, the more we could offer. Kept to the golden rule, he did."

"Y'all made us feel like we mattered." Seth goes back to slathering white frosting on another cookie.

"What was your favorite part of Christmas, Seth?" I asked, only knowing the parts of his life I was allowed to participate in.

"A whole day to celebrate, just us. Our community celebrations were the best with music, dance, and the Jonkonnu parade."

My mind casts back into my memories. "Is that what you call it? When you danced about in all those costumes at our front door until Father gave one of you a coin?"

"Those costumes were part of the celebrating our traditions. What's left of them. Like the Jonkonnu parade."

"And what's that about?"

"Makin' fun of white folk." Martha laughs.

"Ma!"

"What? That hat that looked like a big house didn't look like none of our cabins, did it? And the costume with the bull whip? Who else you done seen with one of those? Ain't one of us any normal day. And when you see me wearin' one of those big ole patchwork dresses with the wooden hoop?"

"It's all right, Seth. This all sounds fascinating."

"You ain't offended, Miss Emilie?" asks Seth.

"What's there to be offended about? We live in a country that expresses freedom of speech, Martha's allowed to speak her peace." Emilie smiles watching Seth's countenance light up with excitement as he gives it some thought.

"Well, we'd spend all year collecting items. Scraps of cloth and burlap for the costumes. Pots that done wore out their use. Bits of wood with hides stretched over for drums. Dried out gourds with seeds for shakin'. Stuff like that. Then we got to groovin'.

"It starts a little like this." Seth reaches out to any and every surface, drumming up a beat. At first it starts out real soft before getting louder and louder until his next words come out just below a yell. "And then you start moving, like this!" He lets the rhythm shake him all the way down to his feet.

"It be like the *'Ring Shout'*, *'Buck and Wing'*, and *'Jig'* all in one dance!"

My eyes spread wide at the display, a smile dancing across my face.

It's so lively, so different.

"Come on, Miss Emilie. Gotta let the beat move your soul. You got this, too, Mrs. Julia. Don't be afraid. Feel it in your toes!"

Mother and I laugh at the idea of me trying this out.

But why not? Who is here to judge us? This is home.

"Come on, Mother. No one's here to watch!"

I take her by the hands and as such, take the lead, starting to bounce on the balls of my feet.

"There you go. Now get your arms in it, shake it all out. All that stress, all that expectation, all that neccesitation."

"But that's not a word!"

"Ain't no time for thinkin', Miss Emilie, just feelin'." Seth carries on with the *pit-pattering* and the *tip-tapping* on every surface between him and where Martha stands, bouncing and swaying but staying in place at the stove.

Under Seth's direction, the drawers and cabinets have voices. The crockery sings its own *clink-clank*. It's as if the kitchen has its own life, its own heartbeat, and it matches my own, racing as I wiggle and I jiggle and I giggle my troubles away.

"And when we get hot and tired; the women come by and pour us a bit of drink, a bit whiskey, 'till all our troubles pass us by."

Mother grins. "I can do that."

When I look over to her, I can't help but think of a loose board being battered by the wind. Unable to shake off the stiffness of society but trying all the same—if I didn't know any better, I'd think she is having a fit.

Is that how I look doing this?

"We've got a bit of whiskey. I'll just—" Mother continues as she heads to the pantry, but Martha grabs her arm and gives a shake of her head.

"One nip won't hurt us," Mother says.

"Mmhmm, I see how you get at your own Christmas parties, Julia. Now let's stop all this foolishness. We still gots work to do, and I ain't about to be the only sober one when the men get back."

I've never seen my mother pout, but in witnessing this moment, with her crestfallen features and big oval eyes, I realize I might be her daughter after all.

Martha shakes her head. "We be having drinks with supper."

Mother perks right up and wriggling out of Martha's grasp, she heads over to the pantry saying, "I know just the thing."

"Some things ain't changed." Seth's smile dissipates as he goes back to frosting the cookies.

Despite being a little out of breath, my curiosity still lingers. "What do you mean by that?"

"He means the fun's gotta end, and that be New Years Day." Martha's demeanor is no longer bright. "Heartbreak Day. They put us back in our place, reminded us we still slaves, forced us to leave all that happiness in the past."

"Heartbreak Day?" Mother asks. "I don't remember that."

"Cause it didn't start till last year. When Mr. Jacob's brother sold four families with a smile and took back control."

Silence falls over the kitchen.

I reach over to Seth, who looks down at the cookies and frosting in front of him, blinking. I touch his hand; he looks at me.

"I'm sorry that happened," I whisper pulling my hand back to my work.

"Behind us now," Seth whispers.

The latch clicks on the kitchen door, and we turn our heads to see Father and Big Jim return with two crates of supplies, but it is the letters in Father's hands that make me drop my spoon to greet him.

"Letters!" I say, relieving the small bundle from his grasp. I flip through them, ignoring all but two.

"Who are they from?" Mother asks, while unloading the crates and putting the supplies away.

Father and Big Jim make some excuse under mumbles and grumbles—something about chores, I imagine, and slip out of the kitchen.

"The boys and Thaddeus and others," I say. "Do you want me to read the one from the boys?"

"What about the one from Thaddeus?" Seth raises his eyebrow with a smirk.

"Who's Thaddeus?" Martha asks. "And why ain't I heard of him if he's writing you letters Little Miss?"

"He's her fiancé," Seth teases, as my face floods with a rosy blush.

"You sound just like Henry," I snap at Seth, who is laughing at my expense.

Mother appears from behind the pantry curtain.

"Save the letter from the boys. We will read it on Christmas day," Mother says. "Em, try to put down Thaddeus's letter, and set the table."

"But I—" Mother gives me the look and I sigh. "Yes, Mother."

A small pout forms on my bottom lip as I move to set the dining room table. Father, of course, will sit at the head of the table, with Jim, Martha, and Seth to his right. Mother and I sit to his left, which leaves two empty chairs, one to my left for Henry and one at the opposite end of Father for Aaron.

When I come back, Seth has disappeared, most likely out for evening chores as we set out the Christmas dinner.

"Little Miss spinster found herself a mister," Martha says when I return to the kitchen. "How long you been hiding that from me?"

"Not long," I say.

"I see. And when's this Thados, Thadaous—whatever he's called, coming to dinner?" Martha asks.

"Thaddeus," I say, "and not anytime soon, I'm afraid. He's off to war." Looking to the sideboard where his letter lay, discarded for the moment, my fingers move, wanting to pick up his words, capture the mustiness of soldier life, be with him.

Dinner on Christmas Eve is spread out on the table, which is lit with candles. The light dances off the crystal glasses. The goose is steaming in front of Father's plate at the head of the table, while wisps of steam curl from the fresh biscuits, candied yams, giblet stuffing, and collard greens wrapped in Martha's secret seasonings. Gingerbread cookies iced with odd clothing thanks to Seth, and fruit cake saturated in three times more brandy than Martha's recipe suggests—I misread—awaits us for dessert along with mulled wine.

We all take hands as Father leads a prayer, then Big Jim says a prayer, and we all say one thing that has blessed us. It's sweet, but not as short as I'd like.

My stomach growls in anticipation, and I let it shout as I cannot unlink my hands from Mother and Seth.

Seth eyes me with a quick smirk as he notices my stomach's declaration.

Finally, the word *Amen* is spoken, and we can all commence eating.

"This goose is prepared perfectly, ladies." Father picks up a knife to cut into the bird.

"At least it's not a chicken." Mother smiles looking at Martha who shoots her warning eye.

"Oh, yes, remember that year everyone got a chicken?" Father asks. "I hope you all had a good Christmas that year."

"It was a Christmas celebration," Jim says, "although, those chickens were more for stewing than roasting." Jim jumps when what, I presume, is Martha's boot strikes his shin.

Father's knife stops. He looks up, frowning. "You mean they were old?"

"No, he means stewed is how we like it. Makes the meat last longer," Martha chimes in, giving warning glares around the table.

"That was then," Mother declares. "Tonight, we share a meal with all of you, as family." She lifts her small glass of brandy in toast.

Glasses raise with hers. "Here, here."

Everyone sips and returns to passing dishes to each other.

Once Father is done carving and doling out the goose, he begins his own meal. After a few bites, he stops and says, "What do you say we exchange gifts tonight?"

Mother stops and sets down her fork, asking, "Why tonight? We always exchange gifts on Christmas day."

My eyes take in the reactions around us. Everyone seems confused except my father and—Big Jim, who is hiding a smile behind his pressed napkin.

Martha eyes her husband, a scowl of confusion creases her brow.

"It's settled then," Father insists. "We can all enjoy dessert, coffee, and then presents in the parlor after dinner."

"But-but I've been trying to teach Seth about traditions this whole season," I say. "What reason would we have to break it now?"

"We have it all planned. A hearty breakfast and then we open presents, tomorrow morning," Mother frowns.

"This year is different. After our hearty breakfast, we will all be taking a ride into town."

"Why? Who are we visiting?" I ask, ticking off any number of dresses I could wear for such an occasion.

"No, we are not visiting anyone, so don't dress up. Wear your everyday clothes."

"On Christmas day?" Mother protests. "Honestly, Jacob."

Big Jim chuckles. "This what it's like be outnumbered?"

The men's expressions shift as they glance at each other.

Martha looks her husband up and down, then shoots a look at my father. "Well, don't you two look like cats in a mouse factory." She turns to Big Jim. "What's your secret?"

"Whatever it is," Seth says, "explains why they leaving me with the women."

"James Blackwell—" Martha begins.

"Don't you start on me, woman. It's a secret worth waiting for."

Martha gives him a withering glare, but clamps her mouth shut.

Something tells me they will continue this conversation later because an explanation never comes as Father and Big Jim refuse to say any more.

Father, Big Jim, and Seth retire to the parlor, and we clear the dishes and clean up. When the dishes are all back in the cupboard, Martha sees to the coffee, and I pull the plates and forks out and cut the cake. It wiggles and wobbles like the drunk I've made it to be, and I have to stifle my giggle as I bring myself and the servings to the parlor.

Over the last two months, Mother, Martha, and I have been busy making gifts for each other and the men, so it was no surprise to us when everyone opened them as we had all seen them before. Mother and I made sure the Blackwells had clothes, so they could discard the ones they brought from the plantation.

I gave Seth a slate and my primers to practice with to prepare him for school, a scarf for Big Jim, and I helped Mother finish a sontag and crocheted dish cloths for Martha. The colors match her dress mother made earlier this year. For Mother and Father, I made him a shirt and purchased lilac perfume for her.

"Why, this is what you folks do on Christmas?" Martha asks. "It's a lot of work."

"That's the joy of it," I say. "I love making presents for my friends and family."

"You did a fine job," Big Jim raises his glass.

"Miss Emilie, when can we start learning?" Seth asks as his fingers scan over the pages of the primer.

"How about tomorrow?" I ask, excited to teach again.

"How about the next day," Father suggests. "Better yet, how about some cake?"

Mother and Martha get up to pass out the cake when I remember the boys' letter.

"Can I read the letter now?" I ask, once we are all settled back into our chairs, the cake, sitting on the table in front of me as I open the letter.

"You've already opened it, so I don't see why not," Mother says.

Seeing my brother Aaron's handwriting sends a tight squeeze to my heart, a longing for him to be right here with us. I glance at Henry's chair. Seth occupies it now. Turning back to the letter, I begin to read aloud:

Dear Family,

As the holiday comes closer, we are both missing each of you dearly. We hope all is resolved back in Virginia and the Blackwells are safe and enjoying the holidays with you. If only we could be sitting with y'all now. Alas, this letter will have to suffice.

Henry says he misses teasing Emilie and wishes she could come for just a day. He talks about her all the time, and I suspect he is trying to find her a husband. I've reminded him of Thaddeus, but he still brags about you, Emilie, to some of the men, who finally appreciate his humor; they are always together.

Don't worry, Mother. I am keeping Henry close, and thankfully, he has a knack for avoiding latrine duty and other disciplinary measures, being his happiest self when following orders and keeping away from the girls. Though, I'm not entirely sure he's figured that out for himself yet.

Father, please know, Henry is working hard to earn rank with me. It is more difficult for him as he does not have a leg up on education as I do. As for me, I have moved up the ranks to corporal.

We are well-fed and free from disease as the winter months are keeping us in the plentiful South for now. We have meager chores and picket duties, but mostly leisure time to write and receive packages from loved ones.

This is not to say that we haven't seen any skirmishes, just that as of now, we are mostly out to gather information regarding the whereabouts of the enemy. This said, the South has been fortunate to win many battles,

We hope to end this fight soon in the Spring. All of us want to get back to our lives and families.

Henry and I wish all of you a merry Christmas and a blessed New Year, and good health through the next year. We will be there next year.

Godspeed, your faithful sons,

Aaron & Henry

My voice cracks as I read their names, and tears drag down my cheek. I miss my brothers; it is not right they are not here today. I place the letter back in the envelope. The room is quiet, reserved, as everyone is lost in their thoughts, remembering Aaron and Henry in their own way.

It is a somber way to end the evening, but when Big Jim murmurs, "Bless them boys, and may God return them home."

Everyone whispers a united prayer.

Early in the morning, the house began to fill with activity. Footsteps and shuffling press me to dress quickly, engaging my curiosity as to what all of last night's fuss was about. My gaze crosses Thaddeus's letter just as I am set to leave, *I'll get back to you, my love.*

Breakfast is already laid out on the table, as the men arrive from the barn almost the same time as I step into the kitchen.

"Merry Christmas," I say to Mother and Martha, as I am handed a bowl full of scrambled egg to place on the table.

Martha sweeps past me with a neatly stacked plate of toast in one hand.

"We're ready," Big Jim sits down, looking like he is holding a hive of bees in his pocket, his knee bouncing away. Everyone, save for Father and Big Jim, looks at each other—*ready for what?*

I watch the men. They eat without a word, fork to mouth in a hurried fashion, and I worry they'll forget to swallow.

"Make sure to drink some coffee," Father says in between shoveling his food. "It'll be a cold ride."

"Seth, fill the foot warmers by the stove, and place them in the carriage for the ladies," Big Jim, scrapes up the last of his breakfast with a piece of toast.

"Yes, sir," Seth says, as he looks between his parents.

The men finish eating, taking their plates to the sink, washing, and then drying them in a hurry. Father takes the pans off the stove and cleans those too.

"Jacob, what are you doing?" Mother asks.

"Just helping us get to our destination." Father smiles, picking the pan up off the stove.

"I know you ain't helpin' by puttin' that cast iron in the soap," Martha scolds. "Cause if that be what you fixin' to do, Lord knows, I'll have to season that pan again and then beat you with it!"

I snort back my milk as Father puts the pan down and backs away from the stove.

Big Jim pulls on his sleeve. "We best get the horses ready."

The men nod to each other, don their coats, hats, and scarves before heading out the door. The door closes with a distinct *thud*.

Mother and Martha turn to each other.

"They be taking us to church?" Martha asks.

"Well, if they are, where is a mystery to me. We haven't joined a congregation yet," Mother says.

"Why not? Never mind, we'll talk about that later." Martha's eyes are still on the door. "I don't know about those two. They up to something. They be acting like boys again. Jim don't tell me anything. He can chew and chew but he don't say a word."

"If it helps, Jacob wouldn't say anything to me either."

"Seth," Martha looks to her son. "Go on see if you can pry it out of them, you hear?"

"You think they'll tell me?" Seth shrugs.

"Did I ask what you think?"

"No, ma'am."

"Then what you still be doin' here?" She takes his breakfast out from under him and gestures to the door with a glare.

Seth takes a moment to pout but sighs and gets up to grab his coat. "Yes, Ma."

Martha takes his plate to the bucket, and with a knife scrapes the leftovers off. "This ain't happenin' the only secret in this house is what I put on the plate. Walking around here giggling, acting up, bein' fools on Jesus's birthday. Shame on them. Shame on all them."

And I'm not about to disagree with her.

The ride into town was beautiful on Christmas Day. A fresh blanket of snow whitened the landscape in a pure crystal scene of peace. Bundled under blankets, I sit between Mother and Martha to keep warm. Father drives the carriage, while Big Jim and Seth take the wagon filled with who knows what under a large oil cloth.

Martha tried to peek, and it almost looked like a new game in the making with the way Seth and Big Jim tried cutting her off each time she so much as thought of reaching out for the wagon.

We pass into town and down Baltimore Street then to High Street. I listen to Mother tell Martha, "This store here is the best place for supplies, and that one there has a large selection of fabric ..." I smile at the tour Mother is giving her. "... and when you have a place of your own, this is the best ..."

I return my gaze to what's ahead, wondering where Father is taking us.

We turn down South Washington Street past a beautiful church.

"Oh, Martha, there's a church for you," Mother says, recognizing it as a place for blacks given how the Holy Spirit poured past the walls with lively music, clapping, and merriment.

"Good, y'all need Jesus." Martha looks around. "Those are some mighty fine homes over there."

The carriage slows, and Big Jim pulls up beside them. The grin on his face is as bright as the sun above us, which reflects in the excitement in his eyes. He jumps out of the wagon, unties the oil cloth, and announces, "Merry Christmas!" He strips it back revealing the donated items, the trunk they brought with them, and—

I don't recall Mother collecting any furniture.

Turning to Martha and Seth, I see them exchange looks with each other before returning their eyes back to the wagon.

"Well, now Jim, I know about the—but wait is that—but why out in the middle of—what you playin' at Jim?"

Big Jim walks over to Martha and extends his hand to her in a request that she step down.

Eyeing her husband, she takes hold of him. "Alright, alright. I'mma comin'. Seth, you comin'?"

"Yes, I mean, no, I mean, I'm comin' ma."

"Boy you know about this?"

Seth shrugs.

Mother and I lean in a combination of forward and back, equally curious as to why they stand on the dirt road and why we are piled in the carriage in a part of town I am most certain none of us have ever been to.

"Welcome home, family!" Big Jim sweeps a hand behind him to the two-story house.

We all gasp, except for Father who's got a grin as wide as Big Jim's.

"Oh Lord, Jim. What did—what you mean—what?" Martha's words trip and stumble over the cracks in her voice.

"We made it. A home of our own."

"This ours?" Seth asks, the excitement making his body quiver.

"Sure is. Bought it from the white man myself. Paid in full. And Seth—Seth! You get your room. You hear, Martha? He got his own room!"

Seth hugs Big Jim, who lets out a belly laugh before looking to Martha. "Hold it. Looks like your Ma needs a seat before she falls down, and I gots just the thing."

He hands the key over to Seth. "Go on, unlock the door. I got your Ma." He scoops Martha up bridal style and looks back to Father, Mother, and me. "Y'all comin'?"

Mother and I step out of the wagon with Father and follow them up to the door as the family, our friends, step across the threshold of their new home.

"Jacob Prescott," Mother scolds. "Is this what you have kept from us?"

My father beams with pride, a glint in his eye as he blinks back his emotions.

"Can you blame me, Julia? This is Jim's surprise. I only helped when I was needed."

I throw my arms around my father who looks down at me with surprise and a small laugh. "What's all this about?"

"I knew you'd do the right thing. I love you," I say.

A tear escapes, running down Father's cheek, and he hugs me back. A sniff is heard. "I love you too, Emilie." He kisses the top of my head.

"Emilie, Julia, come see!" Martha, finally having found her voice and feet, comes rushing out of the house, grabbing Mother's hand, and pulling her inside.

Mother and I exchange glances of joy and we giggle, rushing to keep up with Martha, who enters her family's new home, a dream come true, and a wish achieved—maybe even a miracle from their view.

The small entryway opens into a cozy parlor. Despite the chill in the air, the bare bones interior still has a sunny disposition. The walls are painted in a cheery yet palatable mustard yellow with matching delicate lace curtains covering the windows. Wood accents the trim with a large fireplace to warm the room.

The only furniture to fill the empty space thus far is a rocking chair.

"The chair?" Mother asks, pointing to the new piece still giving off a faint scent of shellac.

"They replaced it!" I say, remembering the dilemma back in Virginia.

"Sure did." Martha grins. "It's a Christmas present from Jim, thanks to your husband." She goes to sit down in it. "Rocks so smooth—not a sound to be heard."

Mother looks to us, unsure of the context.

"Seth wanted to bring her chair from Virginia," I say, "but we had to leave it."

"Let me show you the rest of the house!" Martha bounces up like a spring chicken and has Mother by the hand once more, dragging her into the kitchen with me trotting behind in an effort to keep up.

Seth is in the process of starting the fire in the stove, as we enter. "And when you're done, we'll start unloading the wagons. Julia, look, look—"

Martha whisks us through the house, showing us around the blank canvas that will soon reflect her hand and personality. After the tour, the house is quick to warm with love, mirth, and the swirl of activity as we come together to move the Blackwells's things into their home. Martha dictates where she wants the odds and ends with the same energy as a hummingbird, though as late afternoon arrives, we find her slumped in her new chair, snoring away peacefully.

"Am I putting her to bed?" asks Jim.

Mother shakes her head grabbing a quilt and laying it over her friend. "No, let her dream in peace, and then give her some liniment for soreness in the morning."

We say our farewells to Big Jim and Seth, before Father and I clamor into the carriage, and Mother takes charge of the wagon on our way back home. I cannot wait to be invited back to visit soon.

Freedom's Enduring Struggle

IF WE ARE NOT OUR BROTHER'S KEEPER,

AT LEAST LET US NOT BE HIS EXECUTIONER.

~MARLON BRANDO

DECEMBER 1861
FAIRFAX COUNTY, VIRGINIA

Bullets buzz past like a hoard of angry bees, ricochetting off rocks and splintering bark off of trees.

"Keep your head down!"

The whistle of shells screams overhead, exploding into the ground. *BOOM!* The earth shakes and rains up from the impact. The shrapnel from the explosion embeds itself deep into the bowels of the hard, cold, black dirt, missing soft, warm, pink flesh—this time.

Fueled by adrenaline, Thaddeus' heart pounds, chanting the familiar drumbeat of war, an alarm, a plea: *sur-vive, sur-vive, sur-vive.* His hand grips the smooth steel of his gun, while his other fumbles at his side to pull out another cartridge. Ripping open the bit of paper with his teeth, the familiar taste of battle—a nip of gun powder—bites his tongue. He knows the motion by now, loading and shooting is like breathing. One doesn't think, just allows himself to do it. He quiets himself and takes aim.

The phantom enemy weaves in and out of the trees, taking

cover in a fog of smoke that burns his eyes. Wait—

The enemy is lining up, right in his line of—

A sharp yank at his sleeve—

BANG!

He misses. "The fuck!"

"Come on," says Stephen. "They're behind us!"

Thaddeus clambers to his feet. "How did they get behind us?"

"Damn smoke!" Stephen's body moves out of Thaddeus's periphery. "Get down!" His friend's dead weight pulls him to the earth as a deafening boom thunders to their right, to their left, and—

Thaddeus' hand searches for his accoutrements, finds everything in place. He looks over to the back of the blue uniform beside him. Still, unmoving.

"Stephen!"

The whizzing of invisible projectiles shatters the oak tree above them.

"Stephen?"

Thick splinters and thin slivers rain down upon them.

"Stephen!"

The cries of wounded men, some mortally, serves as a reminder that they are back in the thick of it. The company continues rushing forward, sweeping around them and through the tangle of undergrowth.

"Dammit Stephen, answer me you yellow-bellied bastard!" Thaddeus kicks at the heap of soldier beside him.

The body coughs, groans, and dares to move.

"Shit," Stephen says, picking his head up off the ground. "That was close." His face and uniform are layered in dirt; the whites of his eyes are the cleanest part of him.

"Good, you're alive," says Thaddeus.

"Double quick men, keep your lines straight and fall in behind the sixth," the sergeant barks, his voice rough as gravel. "The enemy is through those woods; our reinforcements are in front of us."

"We're surrounded?"

"We will be if we don't get across that road. Now up!"

Like quail flushed from the brush, they spring up, brothers in arms, rushing toward the clearing, holding their line tight among the sea of men, ready to face whomever is at the other end.

Another round of artillery rings through the sky overhead. Generations of old stalwart hardwood shiver under the god-like thunder of guns answering guns.

Then while under the cover of trees, playing a deadly game of hide and seek from bullets, an ominous realization dawns on Thaddeus at the edge of the clearing. Once they cross the road ahead they will be within a whisper of the rabid curs, who are the rebels currently breathing down his neck. He will never get used to this.

Henry's hand steadies his horse as he feels her twitch and shiver under the reverberation of cannon in front of him. He directs his spy glass to where the cannons are aimed at the line of woods in front of his infantry. The smoke rises from the rifles firing at the unseen enemy hiding.

He squints and peers through it ... The enemy placed at least eleven guns in two adjacent hills on the beloved high ground beyond the thicket of trees. The artillery is over the heads of his troops at the tree line and not anywhere close to his artillery. A smirk plays at the corner of his mouth.

He sweeps the spyglass left ... The smoke in the forest is thinning out—enough to see the bodies of men still fighting the unseen enemy in the woods.

Back to the right ... More of his men are flushed out of the timbers, heading his way.

Looks like the reconnoitering troops sent to rustle the enemy from the woodland are retreating back across the road. Wait ... Is that another Union body moving across the road and into the tree line? Must be reinforce—

"Any orders yet?" Corporal Riley asks, nudging Henry, knocking the spyglass from his view.

"Last I heard, we were to hold this ground until further notice."

"There you are!"

Henry turns to the sound of galloping behind him.

Aaron slows his mount. "I'm taking a few cavalry around to gather men from the woods before they get captured. Stay here until I return."

"Don't you need help?" Henry asks.

"I gave you an order, didn't I?" Aaron says with an icy edge.

"A useless one."

"They are only useless when you don't follow them."

"Well, I want to be helpful," Henry says turning away from his brother.

"You're only helpful when you stay out of the way." Aaron doesn't wait for Henry's retort as the sound of hooves beating the earth peels off to Henry's right.

Great. Here he is forced to wait again just like before, since the beginning of time, back when Aaron used to climb trees and leave Henry stranded on the ground. Why? His legs were too short, and his arms couldn't reach the branches. Then there was the time he was forced to sit with his mother and sister, while his father and brother left for the smoking car.

Henry narrows his eyes as he trains the spyglass on Aaron moments later, gallivanting across the battlefield on that nag he dares to call a mount. One moment the man charges one way, the next moment he's riding off in the other direction

He doesn't even know where he's going.

"What's gotten into him?" Riley asks after an awkward pause.

"I think he's lost."

"No, I was referring to your brotherly skirmish."

"Oh, that? It's nothing. Unfortunately, he's been like that his whole life." Henry shrugs and peers back through the glass.

"And do you like being treated like a little brother?"

"What do you think? Not that it matters. As he outranks me I have no freedom." Henry's jaw sets and he lowers the spyglass. "Looks like we might be falling back. Although I can't imagine they are dumb enough to come through those trees with us sitting here."

"I've seen dumber," Riley says as he shifts in his saddle, reaching into his haversack to pull out a twig of tobacco.

Crossing the road is the easy part as reinforcements have begun shooting the enemy behind them, allowing the company to finally be free of their pursuers. When Thaddeus and Stephen emerge in the field, they fall in behind the chaotic swirl of the

Sixth currently in battle with the enemy, who hides in yet another layer of woods beyond.

There is loading, running, shooting, ducking, and taking cover. There are dodging bullets, marching over the fallen, and stepping on the wounded as well as over the debris that litters the once pristine field. Time blurs the events, but they are always moving forward, pushing the line toward slaughter as they face the furious storm masked in smoke, dirt, blood, flesh, projectiles, and debris. All of it greets them, raining down upon them and, in an all-too-frequent occasion, bringing one man or another beside them—down.

Vengeance is sought. Fury meets fury and gunfire is exchanged for screams and moans as death claims one more brother, son, and husband without bias. Each strike adds an empty chair to holiday tables, wood for another grave marker in the family plot.

In the dying's chorus of pleas to the Almighty, his invisible hand comes down to muffle the fight as the guns lower and the shooting stops. The pounding in Thaddeus's ears decrescendos to a whisper. His heart begins to slow. His mind peeks out from behind its protective layer as he roots his back against a tree. He slides down to the ground, diving under the thick, heavy, gray smoke to breathe.

Looking around, everyone is moving in slow motion except for the array of bodies that never made it to the other side of the tree line. Come to think of it, how did he make it this far?

Am I actually all right or am I dreaming?

In his exhaustion the ethereal swirl of smoke lifts in a way that makes him think sleep is upon him, but despite this his hands search his person for crimson wetness.

Then through the dense haze of smoke, he sees men running past the refuge of his tree. Wait, are they his men? ...

They are, but why? The enemy does not pursue them, no one

is chasing them, they are just fleeing.

Did the line break?

Should he run too?

A bugle sounds in the distance.

Is it ours or theirs? What's the command?

The call came again.

Retreat, retreat … The enemy is retreating. They haven't retreated all summer. So, why now?

Listening harder, Thaddeus also wonders harder.

Is this a bad dream or wishful thinking?

"Who authorized a retreat? God damn it!" the gruff officer shouts, not giving a damn who hears him. "We don't bow down to those damned bluebelly bastards!"

Henry smiles to himself as he returns the spy glass to his eye, scanning over the engaged troops in front of him. The devastation is typical of battle as the lines dwindle, leaving gaping holes in the ranks and men strewn in pieces all over the field like discarded branches after a windstorm.

"Dammit! Quit standing around!" The only one apparently listening to the officer is his gelding, who becomes antsy on his feet at all the yelling. The officer starts to rein his mount, pulling him in tight circles while continuing to give orders. "Pull in the cavalry to cover those cowards. We will not retreat! You got that Prescott?"

"Sir?" asks Henry.

"Don't just sir me, Prescott! Ready your men with torches and move to the trees. It's time we smoke those hornets out of their nest."

"Sir, I believe you have mistaken me for my brother."

"Prescott, are you trying to weasel your way out of my orders? Because if so, I'll shoot you myself here and now."

Henry's face turns the darkest shade of crimson he ever wishes to experience, and he swallows hard. "No, Lieutenant! Sorry, Lieutenant! Yes, Lieutenant!" He then looks to the rest of the men, who sit idle on their horses, waiting for a solid plan. "Ready your weapons!"

After shaking themselves from the initial shock at what they are witnessing on the field, the men who reside on their mounts along with Henry check their weapons in preparation for the ride ahead. There are the carbines holstered on the right of their saddles, the sabers strapped to their belts on the left, and their backup steed—colt army revolvers on their left hips. Finally, checking their personal cartridge supply they maneuver their horses into formation.

Turning to Corporal Riley Henry says, "Come on, looks like we got our wish, and you're up front with me."

"About time!" Riley nudges his horse and rides with Henry.

As they ride up the front Henry calls out, "Ready your torches! You heard him, we're smoking them out!"

He and Riley each grab a blazing torches from privates on their way to the front, and once in place Henry calls back, "Move out!"

The clinking of brass, the creaking of leather, the palpable roar of the various fires, all play on the wind of the well-orchestrated cavalry as they head down the slope, across the field, and toward the tree line that worries the officers on the beloved high ground.

Given the carnage that greets their senses, where innards are seen as much as outtards, this is not the worst battle Henry has ever experienced. In fact, it will probably be reported as a mere skirmish in the papers tomorrow. However, even scuffles such as this have their fatalities, and Henry is not keen on him or his company adding to the final roll call.

"Keep yourself moving and ready your guns once you discard your torches. We're hunting rabbits today, boys!"

A cheer follows up from behind in response as they ride to the edge of the trees. They toss their torches into the dry brush here, there, upwind, and down yonder. The flames lap up the kindling, engulf saplings, and feast on mature trunks before moving forward, onward, never stopping as they take advantage of what it means to be a constant moving target for their enemy.

The birds take flight first. The critters scurry into the surrounding fields second. And eventually—Henry loops his reins around the saddle horn and reaches to withdraw his carbine— their real prey reveals itself, a flashing of blue uniform in a haze of gray.

He brings the gun to his shoulder, cocks the hammer, aims, but hesitates. A tingle races up his spine, prickling the fine hair on the back of his neck. Something is wrong.

But what?

His target, once present, disappears like vermin into the tall grass of the field as Henry rides by.

Hell's bells!

Perhaps his mount will trample the bastard when he turns back. In the meantime, the explosion of trees in combination with the black powder is music to his ears when it meets the screams of the men within the woods.

"Henry!" Riley calls out, riding up beside him. "Your brother is looking for you."

"How many times do I have to tell you? Its Lieutenant Prescott, not 'your brother.'"

"Right, because bullets and shrapnel give a damn about who you are. You're lucky I even found you!"

Another flash of blue arrived, but his horse's head is jerked to the left. "What the hell!"

Henry turns back to Riley, who's steering his mount away from the trees, the smoke, and the zip of bullets that whiz through the air mere feet from where he could have been.

"You almost got fooled by the short straw!"

"You think they'd sacrifice one of their own to—"

"Listen to yourself! Of course they would. Adapt, distract, overcome!"

"Watch out!"

A man comes screaming from the woods, his back ablaze.

Henry shoots him as they gallop past while Riley directs their mounts out of the fallen soldier's way as the fire that consumes the dead continues to rage.

"Prescott!"

Henry looks over his right shoulder to see Aaron closing the distance between them.

"I thought I told you to stay on watch!"

"Turns out you're not the only one who can give me orders. Besides, looks like I got more done than you today."

Under a layer of smoke and deep within the brush of the tall timbers that now crackle and crack above him, Stephen thought the one thing he would be safe from was—*Shit!*

The searing sting comes before the warm ooze, and his hand covers the ever-growing crimson stain seeping through his coat sleeve. His eyes narrow, trying to see through the choking fog.

A cavalryman? Bastard! Why don't you hop off that Shitland you call a horse and fight me like a real man.

From beyond the tree line the niggle of a familiar voice pierces his thoughts. "... I got more done than you today!" the coward says to one of his pouf buddies who had ridden up to his aid, perhaps?

Stephen has half a mind to pick up a rock and get that horse bucking on the retreat, but the pain in his arm pulsates, throbs, and sears in hot anger.

"Stephen?!"

"Over here!"

"You're bleeding." Thaddeus crouches beside his friend.

"You run off and"—a coughing fit erupts from Stephen's chest—"receive a promotion, Captain, while I—" The cough returns as Stephen waves Thaddeus to help him.

"Captain? Like the ring of that." Thaddeus begins preparing a tourniquet.

"Shut up and help me bandage the damn thing."

"What do you think I'm doing? Why are you in here? Didn't you hear the order to retreat?"

"Heh, I'm not retreating until I take out one of those Videttes on horseback."

"Four legs against two? You're just plain stupid. Come on, before we become prisoners."

Stephen growls, turning back to peer through the branches and out into the field once more. The two cavalry men are still there, arguing from the look of their silhouettes.

"Stephen? What are you—"

"I'll be right back." He drops to his belly and crawls forward through the brush, letting the fire, smoke, and fleeing wildlife excuse the snapping of twigs beneath him.

Just need to get a closer look ...

He grits his teeth as the pain bites down on his arm, but eventually he gets close enough to register that the tall, thin one looks more authoritative with his arms gesticulating in punctuated motions. When the second one, the one Stephen reckons who shot him, turns his horse away, the side profile of the cavalryman sends a cold rush of familiarity, chilling the marrow within Stephen's bones. Sweat slicks the back of his neck.

"You com—?" Thaddeus' words become strangled in his throat.

Stephen turns to Thaddeus as he pushes his body back against the earth. "Come on, my arm hurts." He swallows hard, the color drained from his face.

Thaddeus blinks and clears his throat. "But do you think that's—"

Stephen is already on his feet and heading into the heat. "Doesn't matter. We have to go."

Stepping out into the field opposite the opposing forces' cavalry, Stephen and Thaddeus walk through the thinning smoke. Behind their own stench and their singed nose hairs resides the smell of putrid bowels mixed with the copper tang of blood making its home in the back of their throats and sitting on their tongues.

The air still threatens to strangle them, their trudging boots halt. The two men draw gasps, cough, hack, and empty their guts among the carnage.

Stephen turns his head to a low moan rising from a nearby body leaning against what's left of a tree. He walks over, bends down on one knee in front of the wounded man. His right hand cups his chin, raising the man's face to meet his eyes.

"Carter? Carter Davis?" Stephen's voice strangles in his throat.

The man not six months younger than Stephen himself, searches for the voice. He locks eyes with Stephen's. The grimace attempts to hide the wave of pain coursing through his body.

"Ah, Stephen. Of course you'd be the one to find me." Carter coughs and a small spurt of blood burbles from the gut wound saturating the front of his shirt. Carter grabs Stephen's hand leaving a red stain as he squeezes hard. "I need you to tell my wife, I died for the cause ... and ...I-I love her. You hear?"

Stephen swallows hard, blinking. "You can tell her yourself, Carter. Come on, get up I'll take you to the sawbones."

Stephen hands Thaddeus his rifle, then with a grunt, hauls Carter up to stand. He shoulders him as Carter lets out a grunt of his own.

"You'd better hurry before the grim ..." Carter's legs give out from under him as he falls unconscious.

As Thaddeus and Stephen trudge on pulling Carter along, Stephen becomes lost in thought.

After a few long moments Thaddeus asks, "How many times do you think we've made this walk together?"

Stephen looks up to see Thaddeus move ahead and answers, "Too many times."

"Really? I'd say not enough."

"You like seeing the aftermath of battle?"

"No, but I do like having you by my side."

Stephen stops. "What the hell?"

"Boy, you sure know how to ruin a moment," says Thaddeus as he moves beside his fellow brother in arms and peers down.

The lifeless body lays face up. Unseeing eyes looking to the heavens.

It's George," says Stephen.

George's frozen expression beseeches the Lord to take him away from this nightmare, and Stephen hopes the good Lord has mercy enough to answer.

They had stayed up all night with George in an effort to win all of Stephen's losses.

"He still owes me money," Stephen says.

"I'm sure that was the first thing on his mind when he got shot. Speaking of shot—your arm."

Stephen looks over to Thaddeus with a pensive stare. "Was shot by one of her brothers."

"Her?"

"Emilie, the girl you're marrying!"

"Well, we don't know for sure," Thaddeus says.

"Yeah, right. How long have you known?"

"Known wh—"

"Known that her damned brothers are Rebs!"

"Stephen, there are thousands of men, what are the actual chances it was them?"

"So, you don't deny they are damned Rebs?" Stephen swallows hard as the needle pricks of reality stab into his brain, stamping the truth there: the Prescotts are still Southerners.

"All I know is they left together. I am not privy to where they went." Even as Thaddeus says it, Stephen notices his fellow man cannot look him in the eye.

"I can't believe this. You are going to marry the enemy!"

"She is not the enemy; she is going to be my wife."

"Not if her fucking brother kills you first. Jesus, Thaddeus! What are you even doing here?"

"What do you think, Stephen?" Thaddeus turns to face Stephen, exhaustion plaguing his expression. "I'm fighting for my country. I'm fighting to get home. I'm fighting to get back to her!"

"Her, a woman who will choose your killer over you. Heh, and I always thought you were the smart one out of the two of us." Stephen shoulders Corporal Marsh with his good side as he marches past.

"You would do the same if it was your ring on her finger!" Thaddeus calls after him.

"My ring wouldn't be caught on her corpse," says Stephen, making headway for the medical wagons, refusing to turn back.

Yes to Freedom

THOSE WHO EXPECT TO REAP THE BLESSINGS OF FREEDOM MUST
... UNDERGO THE FATIGUE OF SUPPORTING IT.
~THOMAS PAINE

NEW YEARS EVE 1861
GETTYSBURG, PENNSYLVANIA

Nestled into my favorite spot, snuggled in a warm wrapper with a dense crocheted blanket over my lap, I look up to the crackling fire, relieved we are not out in the biting, cold snow of this blustery New Years Eve. My thoughts drift back to Thaddeus, Aaron, and Henry, praying they are warm and safe, even though we should be here, together.

"Hot chocolate?" Mother's hand offers a steaming cup before she sets a plate of leftover cookies on the table between us.

I shift as I take it from her. "Thank you, will you join me?"

She sets her cup on the table before taking a seat. "What are you thinking about?"

"Last year. It was such a flurry of activity, unlike the quiet welcome of this one. There was love, and music, and ..." I sigh.

"Freedom."

"What?"

"Freedom."

"Mother, it's snowing outside, I'm trapped in this house, and if I dare to remove this blanket I'm sure I'll—"

"Still complaining? Julia, I thought you said she would out-grow this stage?"

My head whips around. "Father!"

"Pretty fast movement for a girl claiming anything not un-der layers will freeze." Father smirks as he picks a cookie off the plate, sampling the corner.

"Woman," I insist, wrinkling my nose at him as I disguise my disdain behind the rim of my cup. The warm milk, chocolate, and sugar concoction makes me forget our banter for a moment.

"Mm-hmm,." The glint in his dark eyes either means he had a jolly time with the Blackwells or one too many nips from his flask as a way to ward off the cold on the ride home.

"Now you sound like Martha."

"As he should. How are the Blackwells settling in, Jacob?"

"Living quite the different life from a year ago, but I heard no complaints." Father settles into his favorite chair near the fire-place, the one where Aaron loves to sit when he is home.

"Not even about the pot?"

"Not with it filled up, or maybe I should say partially filled up. There is a crock of stew on the stove, Julia."

"Oh, she didn't have to do that!"

"I think she's still worried we can't fend for ourselves. But I think we've done fairly well, almost like we've gained a whole new perspective on what it means to be free."

"That's what Mother was just mentioning. Freedom." I say, setting down my cup in exchange for a piece of gingerbread and a napkin. My eyes dart to my parents.

"Oh, really?" Father asks.

"Yes, really." Mother says.

"Care to share?"

"No."

"Why?"

"Because I'm not very happy with Martha." Mother's brow furrows, but it is the pout on her lower lip that makes my father bite his own in an attempt to hold back his enjoyment.

"Why, because she's feeding us?" he asks, reaching for his pipe and tobacco pouch on the table next to his chair.

"Because she doesn't believe I can do this on my own!"

"And how does the shoe feel on the other foot?" Father pauses as he opens the pouch and pours some of the contents in the palm of his hand.

"What's that supposed to mean?"

Silence.

"Jacob, what does that mean?"

"Pipe to fill, much concentration." Father tips the pipe into his palm as he turns the bowl in his hand to fill it with loose tobacco. When he completes this, he puts a pinch of tobacco at the top and tests the stem for air, drawing from the stem placed between his lips.

I look to Mother, adding my definition to the conversation. "It means Mother, that neither you nor Father thought I would become a teacher and find my way as an independent woman."

"Who still lives under her parents' roof and is engaged to be married," Father clarifies as he pulls a small flame from the fire, lighting his pipe and sitting back.

"Well, that is because I am still courting."

They both turn to me with alarmed stares.

"What do you mean we didn't believe in—" Mother begins.

But Father is leaning forward once more. "Courting! You found another beau?"

I sigh, rolling my eyes. "No Father, what I mean is I'm courting freedom, and therefore, it is perfectly acceptable to still live under your roof while I establish this new and fulfilling relationship."

Father takes his pipe from his lips, the twinkle fading from his eyes as he tries to catch up to my logic. "So, you're not marrying Thaddeus?"

"I am, but at the same time, I realize that my role in society is not as confining as I once thought it to be. Is that what you meant, Mother?"

"In a sense." She sits back with her cup in hand. "I mean, we've all had big changes in our lives. My children are grown and my nest near empty. Your father has gone from managing land to farming it with his own hands."

"And let's not forget the Blackwells have a new life to live—as promised," I add with a warm smile.

We all look at each other, each lost in remembering the accomplishments of the last year, our memories flickering like fireflies frolicking in a night field. The crackle of the fire and the low moan of the wind blow through the cracks around the sills, and the house quiets around us as the ghosts of our loved ones sit with us, anticipating what is in store for us in the next year.

Perhaps ...

My hand glides across the cushion of the sofa in search of his ghostly touch, longing to feel his calloused warmth entwine around my fingers. I smile to myself, seeing his smile in my mind's eye, and his deep blue hues regard me with that playful grin.

"What do you think we'll be doing next year at this time? I personally hope we will all be together again."

"Absolutely," Mother adds. "This war can't possibly last another year."

Father sighs, abandoning his smoke before he stands. Mother and I look over to him, as he rubs his stomach. "Perhaps, perhaps not. But what I do know is I better not let Martha's stew go to waste. You two want some?"